DARK RAVEN SOCIETY

Celebrating the first publication of

DARK RAVEN CHRONICLES

BOOK 1: RAVEN'S WAND

My thanks for your Support

Steve Hutton

DARK RAVEN CHRONICLES

Book I : Raven's Wand

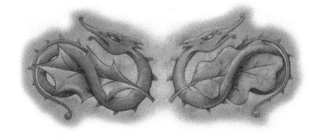

by

Steven Hutton

Books Illustrated Ltd

Raven's Wand

Published in Great Britain

by Books Illustrated Ltd

Books
Illustrated

This edition published 2016

1 3 5 7 9 10 8 6 4 2

Text and illustrations copyright © Steve Hutton

ISBN: 978 0 9934 6214 6

All rights reserved. No part of this publication may be
reproduced, stored in a retrieval system, or transmitted in
any form or by any means, electronic, mechanical, photocopying,
recording or otherwise, without the prior permission of
the publishers.

Set in 11/14 pt Century Schoolbook by Books Illustrated Ltd

www.**booksillustrated**.com

Printed and bound in Great Britain by CPI, Melksham

'For mum, and all those who value greenery greater than gold -
yours is the heart and soul of a witch.'

TABLE OF CONTENTS

Delicate Threads

The great spider known as the Timekeeper sat entombed inside his ancient hourglass ceaselessly weaving life and death across the Earth, threading and snipping with a surgeon's care. Each thread was a life and when its time was over he would cut it and weave it again according to a new pattern.

It was 1886 and Britain was gripped by a great revolution of coal and steel overseen by a queen-empress who controlled half the globe, but to eyes that had seen the birth and death of stars this was just a day in the life of the world. The hourglass was his prison and purpose and the sand inside poured through it infinitely slowly, measuring the life of the universe. Before all the sand was spent he must ensure souls met or missed one another precisely as the Patternmaker decreed.

He raised himself up, heeding the Patternmaker's commands, then he bowed humbly and set about weaving. He selected seemingly random threads: an old witch, a gifted child, a tormented man, and monsters of Ruin. With all the right threads gathered he began to weave, unaware of the incredible consequences that would follow.

CHAPTER ONE

Seventeen Shillings

Solvgarad, Eastern Europe

Today was Davey Warner's eighteenth birthday and finally his age exceeded his salary. Seventeen shillings was a good salary for a squire, but since joining the Illuminata's ranks a year ago he had become a superstitious young man and the number seventeen gave him the shivers. His first knight had been killed on April 17th, his first battle injury required seventeen stitches, and his first flogging was seventeen lashes. Yes, it was fair to say seventeen was an unlucky number. Many of the Illuminata Knighthood's squires were superstitious, but with good reason perhaps. Theirs was the only military order in the world created to fight witches.

In the last year he had ridden alongside his knight, or sometimes under his huge metal feet, on five occasions. Granted, the enemies had only been rival knights competing for the Illuminata's crown, but the bullets and cannons were just as deadly. Today was different, however. Today he was riding to face a coven of witches for the first time. He told himself all would be well because he was no longer seventeen, but that didn't stop his hands from trembling.

"Warner, saddle not stirrups. You make too big a target," someone commanded.

He sank back into his saddle and looked about to see Captain Ross. "Aye, sir."

"One day you'll get your fool head blown off and I won't be around to tell you about it," Ross grunted.

The twenty-strong party continued towards the ragged limestone pinnacles known as the Vesturor, meaning the 'Giant's Palm'. He disliked the name because that's just what it looked like: a giant hand waiting to clench around them.

"We'll stop here." Ross decided, already dismounting.

The rest of the company followed and tethered their horses where they could, which wasn't hard because this dank corner of Romania bristled with pines, while the endless forest seemed shrouded in perpetual twilight.

"That's it then, sir. The coven?" Warner slid his rifle from his shoulder.

"In there, yes." Ross retrieved a short telescope and inspected the rocky fortress. "Intelligence has it there are fifty of the snakes living in there."

"Good place to hide. It looks like a maze, sir."

He snapped the telescope closed. "Maze is just what it is. And deadly too."

"With a coven at the heart of it." Warner imagined them like a fat spider brooding at the web's centre.

Ross turned to the rest. "From here on bayonets fixed, eyes quick and lips tight."

They all signalled their understanding and so began their witch hunt.

There were two ways into the Vesturor, one east and one west. Ross's company were taking the western path with the intention of penetrating the coven and driving the witch scum eastwards at bayonet point. When the rabble exited the Vesturor's eastern wall they would find a little surprise in the form of the Knighthood's finest company, ready there to greet them; forty Knights piloting their towering kraken steam-suits, and two hundred infantry and squires, led by Knight Superior Krast himself. The witches of Solvgarad were going to be stabbed, crushed or shot. Any method suited Ross. He still got paid and there would be fifty less 'Jiks' in the world. A very tidy result.

Warner noticed it first. "Are those paintings?" he whispered.

Ross had been too focused on the forest to notice, but now he saw what Warner meant. There were dragons painted all over the sheer cliffs. "Aye, dragons."

"Why dragons, sir?"

"Huh, you are green, aren't you. The Jiks worship a pair of them, Hethra and Halla or suchlike."

"You mean like the one cast out of Eden?"

"Is there any other kind?"

Warner swallowed a lump. "You mean they worship the Dev –,"

"Shh!" he hissed. "Don't speak that word here of all places. Now, eyes front and mouth shut."

Warner did just that and as they crept forwards through the bracken his rifle began to feel heavier and his throat drier. The impressive rock formations were shaped like great blades thrust up out of the earth, but they concealed countless passages and corridors. A natural trap, he thought darkly.

Ross stopped and knelt in the bracken, quickly appraised the cliffs and selected the one where the earth was beaten and the rocks shiny with passing hands. "That's it. That's the way in." In the next instant he was up and running. Warner and the rest fell in behind, following their captain to the tune of thumping boots and rapid breathing. At the Vesturor's entrance they stopped and Ross pressed a finger to his lips. From here on their mission was stealth. After a quick inspection of his rifle and revolver Ross slipped between the towering rocks and out of sight. Warner came next and one by one the whole company vanished inside the formidable coven of Solvgarad until not a man was left.

Unseen by all, a raven sat watching intently from the branches high above. As the last man slipped through the serrated rocks he cawed once, launched himself into the air and was off. He had an important message to deliver.

Inside was just as he'd feared. Warner found the going dark and narrow, with only enough room for them to advance single file. The soil was compacted by passing feet – witches' feet he told himself – while the vertical rocks reminded him of giants' tombstones. He touched the silver cross around his neck. "Deliver us from evil," he murmured.

"Shh!" Ross jabbed his rifle backwards and butted him in the belly. "Keep it down."

"Sorry captain." Penned in between the opposing walls, Warner could hear his frightened heart echo back to him and his breathing sounded taught and metallic. He tried to keep his eyes front even though all he could see was the back of his captain's head, but the wall paintings repeatedly drew his gaze.

"Worship us," the dragons seemed to tempt him. *"Worship at the altar of the aeons, before man had even dreamed of god."* Dragons or devils they might be, but Warner couldn't dispute their eerie beauty. The beasts flowed across the cliffs, reaching up from this murky world to where the sunlight hurt his eyes. There were dragons everywhere, but he saw only two types: both had horns like twisted tree boughs but one had scales of oak, the other of holly. Hethra and Halla, he thought, wondering who was who.

"Yes, I am Hethra, the dreaming dragon of oak. My twin sister is Halla. We were here before man and without us man would cease to be."

Warner shook his head clear, wondering whose thoughts were rattling around up there.

Ross looked around. "Don't go weak on me private."

"Sorry, captain," he gulped.

Red and green dragon's eyes stared down at him and Warner didn't care for their quiet accusations. *"Have you come to kill us, Davey Warner?"*

"Witch scum," he muttered and blew a drop of sweat from his nose. He was cleansing the world of wickedness, he reminded himself. "Only Jik scum." The rifle in his hands felt hotter by the minute and he wondered if Satan's imps were stoking the fires for the souls who would go there this day.

"But whose souls?" the dragons teased.

Eighteen. He thought stoically. *Seventeen's gone, and all my bad luck's been used up. Seventeen's gone.*

Without knowing he marched right into the captain who spluttered angrily, "Damn it Warner! You trying to get us caught?"

The column halted and Ross raised his revolver level, and jabbed a finger to where the rocks swept around a blind bend. His message was clear: the coven was through there. Just as he advanced a raven called from out of sight. Warner thought nothing of it and instead followed his brave captain into the heart of Solvgarad coven.

The smell was so unexpected that it took him a moment to place it. Someone was cooking food, he was sure of it. For a few seconds all Warner could see was the captain's back, and then the rocks peeled away from each other and opened into a natural amphitheatre. They were inside the coven.

As Warner moved from behind his captain and into the large clearing he caught sight of a cooking fire with a large pot strung across it. The smell was coming from there. *We've caught 'em having a meal!* The ordinariness of it all startled him, but if he expected stewing limbs he was in for a disappointment. The broth smelled like plain old vegetable and it somehow offended him to find that it smelled good. "Captain?"

"Fan out." Ross swept his revolver across the clearing, anxious for something to shoot at.

Warner saw a grassy glade surrounded by small huts. There was even washing drying on a line and he frowned when he saw the small tunics and shirts. There were children here too. The little garments unsettled him more than if they had been flayed skins. In the grass he saw what were unmistakably skittles and a wooden ball. Close by there were rows of cabbages and other crops. It reminded him of his grandmother's garden back home. The glade was wide and airy, there were even wild flowers growing in the tall grass, and the surrounding walls were again decorated with dragons.

"Smith, Howell." Ross directed two men to check a large wooden hut.

"Where's everyone gone?" Warner drew close.

"Dunno." Ross turned slowly, searching, but not seeing a soul.

"Ambush?" he suggested fearfully.

"You've a lot to learn, lad," Ross gave him a cynical smile. "Witches run, they don't fight."

"Maybe they got wind of us and just left," he hoped.

Smith and Howell emerged from the hut and waved their arms to signal a negative. "Nobody home," Ross muttered.

"They must've gone days ago."

"And left a pan on the boil? Pull the other one." Ross directed his revolver to the cliff tops, but there was nobody there either.

The rest of the men were now searching the encampment with less caution. They jabbed bayonets into sacks of flour and tipped over baskets of apples. Some ripped down the decorative lanterns hanging from huts and branches, while others kicked open doors and pointed rifles inside. Nothing. The witches of Solvgarad had vanished and if not for the bubbling pot Warner could have easily believed they had indeed gone days ago. "So what do we do, captain?"

"Do? We push through, that's what we do. They might be just ahead of us making a run for it." Ross savoured that notion. He longed to see the Jiks herded through the Vesturor and into the Knighthood's waiting arms. Knight Superior Krast would make mincemeat out of them. "Come on! It's a witch hunt!" he grinned. The company scrambled to obey just as a raven sailed overhead croaking as it went, and thunder rumbled from the east, sounding very close. Ross froze motionless but with his soldier's instincts jangling.

"Thunder's coming?" Warner puzzled.

Ross listened to it roll around the valley. "That's no thunder." He frowned as more thunder boomed and this time they all saw a mushroom of black smoke billow up about a mile distant. He knew the sound of an explosion when he heard one. "Sweet Jesus," he uttered.

"Captain?" Warner quailed.

"RUN!" He burst into a sprint, heading eastwards towards the sound of battle. Even as he ran he saw two more clouds race up into the sky and even detected sparks of hot metal. The witches of Solvgarad had not fled, it seemed.

Witches don't fight! This thought battered Ross as he dodged and weaved through the Vesturor's maze. He knew now that they wouldn't find a straggle of wretches fleeing their coven, but the alternative was too horrible to think about. Never in the Illuminata's history had a coven taken the fight to them, yet as he charged ahead, ripping his uniform on jutting ledges, the sky darkened with more smoke and the thunder became constant. His imagination added screaming men and horses to the mix and when he eventually flew between the last pinnacles what he saw was impossible yet inevitable.

Kraken steam-suits were the Knighthood's chief weapon. They stood over seventy feet high and weighed over one hundred and twenty tons. The knight piloting the machine from within the helmet could wade through the fiercest battle without a scratch. In the past they had marched into covens and literally crushed their homes and their will with a manoeuvre dubbed 'shock & awe'. It was a formidable tactic, but today Ross was the one being shocked and awed. "Dear God, no!"

Warner again ran into the back of him, but there was no chastising rifle to jab him in the ribs. "Captain?" He looked across the clearing beyond. This is where the witches should have run screaming and sobbing into a force of over forty krakens, but what he saw instead numbed his wits.

It happened so fast, but he recognised the kraken as belonging to Sir Julian Field. The giant machine had a helmet sculpted like a snarling lion. Regimental banners as large as ship sails fluttered above it and the silver armour gleamed. The machine pivoted at the waist in a bid to turn and face an attacker, grinding metal and venting hot steam as it struggled. Warner didn't see the assailant even pass. Their speed was incredible. One moment Field's kraken looked implacable and the next there was a brilliant flash and the helmet erupted molten steel and a cascade of sparks. "What was that!" he screamed.

Ross grabbed his collar and thrust him forwards. "WITCHES! NOW FIGHT!" He charged onwards, now blasting randomly at the sky with his revolver.

If Warner believed his bad luck had been spent he was in for a monumental disappointment. "What do I do?" he yelled.

"Shoot 'em down!" Ross roared. Already his revolver was empty and he was frantically reloading.

Warner raised his rifle and finally saw what he meant. *Witches!* He should have fired, or quailed with fear even, but he was wonderstruck. The sky was full of them and they raced back and forth on those sinister flying staffs he'd been warned about. They made tiny targets and drove suicidal charges at the giant krakens and when they passed metal exploded and fireballs blossomed.

Warner fired without aiming, reloaded and fired again. Only after six shots did he realise he was screaming. Around him he heard horses and men cry out in panic. Hooves rumbled past on all sides, riders dodged airborne attacks and krakens shook the earth as they danced a deadly tempo. They were too large to tackle such mobile fighters, Warner saw that at once. The knights must retreat into the forest or they would all be destroyed. He saw Sir Robert Hodge, his own knight. The huge machine was draped with burning banners, obscuring the pilot's vision and waving its ponderous metal arms in a bid to swipe witches from the air. Davey Warner's training finally engaged. "Sir! I'm coming!" he felt a rush of nobility and ran to his aid.

Before him was a churned field of pandemonium. Horses threw their squires and trampled infantry. Clouds of smoke as thick as London fog rolled across them carrying the bitter tang of sulphur and deadening the sounds of battle. They cleared again just as quickly and then Warner heard a noise, unique in the Illuminata's history – a kraken falling by the hand of a witch.

It was a terrible and glorious sight. The machine's helmet and unfortunate knight had been destroyed, and the decapitated giant lurched a step and then crashed to the ground. Banners trailed out behind it and the furnace stacks bellowed tortuously. The impact was brutal and the earth seemed to bounce under his feet and Warner stumbled and fell. As he did the open sky filled his vision and he saw witches streak overhead, both men and women, and impossibly even children. The sky darkened as a horse leapt over him and then a fierce wind engulfed him accompanied by a tremendous roar. The kraken's furnace had exploded. Molten shards rained down and the heat blast rushed over him. Warner screamed and flung his arms around his head, while nearby a terrified horse bucked and whinnied and its rider howled in protest.

Warner rolled over, climbed up and staggered on with cinders smouldering in his hair. Countless rifles were aimed skywards and a hailstorm of bullets peppered the air, but the witches had passed. "Sir!" He drove toward his knight. Hodge's kraken staggered and crashed into an adjacent one with a bull-fashioned helmet and scarlet banners. Warner saw sparks shower down and bullets ricochet off the armour. "Sir, I'm coming!" What he intended to do when he got there was anybody's guess.

A series of explosions briefly drowned out the chaos and Warner saw the knights were trying to regroup under a protective artillery barrage. He glimpsed Knight Superior Krast and his kraken's fluttering swan and crown banners, as well as Hathwell, his mounted squire. Falling shells ripped up curtains of earth, but the witches continued to make their devastating charges. In the noise and confusion he could hear them screaming their war cries as they shot overhead. Some were singing, while others were howling like wolves. One or two were hit and tumbled to the ground, falling as human wreckage.

Warner pressed on. He dodged fallen soldiers, burning wreckage and riderless horses, and finally stood before Hodge's kraken. "Sir, behind you!" His voice was tiny and useless and Hodge never even saw what hit him. A witch flew by and lashed out with something. Warner screamed and covered his eyes against the brilliant light. Thunder echoed around the valley, real thunder this time and when his eyes cleared and he looked up he saw the kraken's head had gone, leaving just a vent spewing smoke and flames. "SIR!"

The machine swooned and began to fall gracefully. Warner watched in disbelief as it grew larger and larger. He backed away, lost his footing, stumbled and landed hard. The dead kraken powered down towards him spitting gouts of boiling water. Warner thrashed with his feet, trying to drive backwards, but the mud was treacherous and slippery. He looked upwards and saw the heraldic symbols painted on the battered chest plate bearing down on him. There, amid the proud lions and eagles he saw a painted number. "SEVENTEEN!" he screamed. An instant later he was pounded into the mud of Solvgarad and the kraken exploded.

CHAPTER TWO

A Witch's Duty

Valonia lay in a hammock strung between the branches of her small tree house, but her sleep was far from peaceful. The thatched oak leaves above cast a soothing light that belied the terrors unfolding in her head. She found herself in the grip of a familiar nightmare. In her dream she was young again and not as skilled in magic as she was now at almost eighty. The dream never changed and not a shred of it was imagined. It was a memory that refused to die or know its place. It was the first time she'd ever confronted a crib-robber, a creature of Ruination. She'd never encountered one since and she thanked Hethra and Halla for that mercy.

Coven-mother Valonia Gulfoss was no faint-heart. She had survived two purges, fought the Illuminata and founded Wildwood-coven decades ago, but she groaned fearfully as her dream deepened. The hammock creaked in response, while her hand clutched at nothing and her eyes rolled under their blanketing lids, seeing only the past. In daily life she was commanding and sure, and so the sight of the tormented woman strewn in the hammock would have rightly shocked her witches. Her hair spilled over the sides like rivers of silver and her face, normally shrewd yet benevolent, was an anguished grimace. "Skald!" she barked, but didn't wake.

A strange creature, ape-like but winged, with a hooked beak and no bigger than an owl, turned from his resting place at the top of Valonia's staff. His name was Skald and he was a thunder-sprite. He hopped down the staff without taking his eyes off her, distressed by her suffering. He stopped, torn between what he wanted to do and what was best for her. Although he'd seen her like this many times it still pained him.

Her hands rolled into fists. They were ravaged by time but in her dream they were young and strong. In her dream she really did hold a wand, a wand of black ash fully eighteen inches long that she still owned, a wand named hrafn-dimmu or 'dark-raven'. In her dream she waited for the crib-robber to take the bait while in the real world Skald held his breath, knowing the worst of her nightmare was now unfolding.

The thread of lantern light along the bottom of the door dimmed and was finally swallowed by darkness. Now the mind of Ruination whispered to her. Valonia saw a lighthouse in the dark with no light, unseeing eyes licked by bluebottle tongues, dancing bears shackled with chains. They all spoke of despair and degeneration.

A rasping sound followed. The crib-robber was exploring the gap around the door looking for a place to enter. It was maddened by the scent of the newborn in the cot. Valonia looked down to where infant Marla lay sleeping. Although hidden by the darkness, the child's wholesome scent was a torment for the creature outside.

Valonia muttered the hiding spell to mask her aura and the other less magical signs of her presence such as the stink of sweat and her thundering heart. The scratching outside the door ceased and her stomach tumbled. Had it detected her, she thought? This horrible notion settled upon her like drifting cobwebs, but just then the crib-robber began its scratching again with renewed urgency. Although she couldn't see them, she heard the whisper of groping arms, as thin as bootlace worms, flutter across the floorboards.

The spell of concealment was masking her. It wouldn't protect baby Marla, but that was the whole point. Marla's scent was the bait. It was reckless and callous to use the infant so, but this creature had already taken three newborn in as many days, and she couldn't think of any other way to stop it. It was not called 'crib-robber' for nothing. She raised her atheme-knife and tightened her grip on her wand. Marla moaned and wriggled in her innocent sleep. In response, the scratching noise became more ardent.

Light from the hallway showed once more and she knew it was in the room with her. She stared in disgusted fascination at the shadow groping its way towards Marla and raised the knife ready to strike. When the knife reached its maximum height she halted, poised and ready. Silence spun around her. The squirming shadow was inches from her feet and the delicate tapping she could hear were its filament arms dancing across her boots, tasting and searching as they went. The moment was seconds away, then suddenly a scream filled the room. There was a moment's bewilderment before she realised it was Marla who had awoken. The masquerade was broken and the room exploded like an over-wound spring.

The crib-robber lunged with awful speed and in that same instant it was no longer a shadow. Valonia's wand exploded into light revealing the creature in all its terrible beauty. It shrieked at the brilliant light and she saw, with revulsion, its tentacles caught freeze-frame reaching through the cot's rude bars. As the atheme sliced through the air she heard another scream join Marla's and she realised it was her own. The atheme plunged through the monster's flesh and rammed into the floorboards beneath with a resounding crack. Agonised tentacles whipped around her lower leg and bit like a snare. She dropped to the floor and thrust her wand through its ring of barbed teeth and deep into its gullet. It thrashed furiously, but the wand was already at work undoing the spells that maintained it.

Marla's cries continued and then another scream rang out, but one so wrong that it cut clean through Valonia's fury and turned her guts to water. The scream came from the crib-robber. It sounded to be laughing even as it choked on her wand and its body began to dissolve and seep away back to Ruination. "Witch!" it screamed. She leaned on the atheme to keep the creature pinned but she was horrified to realise that it knew who, and what, she was. She looked away so that it couldn't read her further, but too late. "Witch," it cried again. "Your demise shall be first-dawn." For a creature that was beaten she was chilled by the triumph in its voice.

"Let the future be unknown and haunt this place no more!" She poured her remaining will into the undoing spell. For a second she was blinded by hrafn-dimmu's light and deafened by Marla's screams. Finally the light dimmed and the creature's howls drained away, leaving only a dark stain on the floor to mark its passing. She slumped into a heap at the foot of the crib, feeling boneless and weak. Behind Marla's cries she could hear a tremendous pounding, but she wasn't sure if it was the baby's mother running along the corridor outside or her own galloping heart.

Like all who suffer recurring dreams she knew this one had reached its end and any moment Skald would call her name. And as reliable as a guiding star, he did so. "Valonia!" he shouted, and she quickly passed from the womb of dreams into wakefulness. Her eyes fluttered open. "Valonia?" he called again, but gentler this time. He dropped to the floor, jumped up into her hammock and landed squarely on her chest, making the old witch grunt indignantly and the hammock sway.

"Why don't you ever wake me before the worst part, Skald. You think I like reliving that night over and over?" she asked groggily as she rubbed at her brow. Her question was as recurring as the dream. She didn't look at him but rather to the thatched leaves above.

"Dreams that don't go away have something to tell you. When you understand their meaning they stop coming," he said sagely,

"I think it was I who told you that," she replied crisply.

"This 'first-dawn' that's haunted you so long. Let it go."

"It'll keep coming until I know what the crib-robber meant." She spoke as though repeating the terms of a contract.

"Are you so desperate to know your own death? You've reached a good age without knowing the dream's meaning. Why's it so important now?"

"Now I'm old and close to the end anyhow, you mean?"

Her sarcasm bounced off him and he just shrugged. "Something like that."

Skald, like most of his kind, was often rude and reckless, but thunder-sprites were the finest ally a witch could have. Like all sprites he was more primate than man and broad wings sprouted from his back. He had pointed ears and a hooked beak, making him look like a stern eagle, and he was covered in steely blue feathers. "You'll be late with the daily spell work," he said, changing the subject.

She frowned in a mix of annoyance and affection, but when she still refused to shift he gave his wings a sharp crack, signalling her to be up. For added effect he ruffled his feathers and a haze of fine ice crystals spun around him like smoke before fading.

"The daily spells can wait a few moments. The world isn't going to fall apart just yet." She struggled upright. "Besides, it's barely dawn, not even five yet." He regarded her quizzically. Pride stopped him asking how she knew that without a single timepiece amongst the room's clutter. She smiled at the expression on his chiselled face. "A quarter before five, I'd say."

"So you say." He sniffed indignantly and flapped away to the tip of her staff and perched there.

Like all witches she'd cut her staff from a lightning-tree as a child, although that was back home in her native Iceland where trees were hard to come by. The instant a tree was struck by lightning a thunder-sprite was born, which on that occasion had been Skald. The gnarled staff wasn't just his perch, it was also his home and he could vanish into it at will. Without him it would be just a staff, for without Skald it wouldn't fly.

In years gone by witches disguised their staffs by attaching twigs, making them appear as ordinary brooms and so the myth of 'flying broomsticks' was born. Her staff carried no such adornments. She thought them vulgar and reckoned a staff flew faster without them. Her staff was heavy, business-like and carved with angular Runes. She yawned and clambered out of the swinging hammock. "A hammock's a young woman's bed," Skald said as tactful as an anvil, and after almost eighty years she was beginning to agree.

She made for the shutters, fit snug in an arch of living oak, and she could see from the glow between the planks that it was already a lovely day. She pushed one open a hand's width and the glorious sight of the gardens below was enough to dispel the last of the dream. She basked in the beauty of Wildwood-coven, pushing her hair into a workable ponytail as she did. Rope ladders and walkways threaded their way through the surrounding trees, linking a village of dwellings similar to her own, while below them nestled the esteemed gardens and orchards. It was at the centre of these that her own tree stood.

A hungry robin fluttered onto her shoulder looking for offerings, but found nothing snack-worthy. She could almost sense the bird's indignation, and a shy chaffinch waited amid the branches gazing up at her with wanting eyes. "Is a witch's duty never done?" she grumbled, already feeling guilty. This time Skald was diplomatic enough to keep quiet and just preened his lustrous feathers.

She went to her rocking chair where her dress lay in a wrinkled heap. At some time during the night Hercules had clambered up and made a nest of it. She could just see the old hare's nose jutting out from under the faded material. She had a special meeting scheduled this morning and the dress she'd wanted to wear was now his den. Not having the heart to move him, she instead went to rummage through her chest for another. "Oh, Herc'," she grumbled. "Why today of all days?"

"Are you nervous?" Skald asked, catching her off guard.

She stopped, aware of the morning ebbing away. "No, why do you ask?" But both of them knew she was.

He looked thoughtful. "I hope for both our sakes the search is over today."

Her face softened. "When Kolfinnia comes, please, remain in your staff. I don't want her feeling that she's under scrutiny, or being tested."

"But you are testing her, that's the whole point."

She sighed heavily. "Yes, I suppose I still am."

"Then I hope she passes this final test, for Wildwood's sake."

"And for Hethra and Halla," she said with gravity and reached out and caressed one of the thick branches. Far away she felt the rhythmic pulse of the dreaming serpent-twins. No witch had ever seen them or knew their whereabouts, but in her dreams she always saw them crowned with twisted horns like great branches and bristling with scales of either oak or holly. Hethra the serpent of oak had eyes that burned vivid acorn green while his sister's burned blood red. *Time's wasting, Valonia,* she thought and turned back to the chest and her sparse collection of old clothes. *First-dawn. If there really is a Timekeeper, then how much of my own thread remains?*

May has the most beautiful face of any month and nowhere boasted springtime's best than Wildwood-coven, on the banks of the Appelier River along the lonely Cumberland coast where mountains meet the sea. The surrounding woodland rang with birdsong in summer, flamed orange in autumn, and burst with delicate flowers in spring. The witches lived in and amongst the trees. Aerial walkways, rope ladders, balconies and huts adorned their limbs, while the bunkhouses, vegetable gardens, field kitchens and store quarters clustered around their trunks. At the heart of this splendour was Valonia's tower; a humble wooden dwelling high in the branches of an ancient oak sometimes called Hethra's tree, and accessed by a spiral of steps that wound precariously around its great girth.

Valonia dedicated Wildwood to women, as others established male or mixed covens, and structured it around the seasons: four houses of thirteen witches. Moon-Frost for winter, Snow-Thaw for spring, Flower-Forth for summer and Seed-Fall for autumn, each overseen by a senior witch known as a Ward. Valonia was Ward of Moon-Frost and the twelve witches under her guidance. The other Wards, Esta, Hilda and Lana were not just senior witches but her close friends. Wildwood might not have been the grandest coven in Britain, but it was the largest and many witches studied magic here before braving a solitary life in service of the serpent-twins, or founding their own covens.

A young woman named Kolfinnia Algra made her way towards Valonia's tower. Wildwood was her beloved home, but in September she would turn eighteen and likely have to establish her own coven as her witch's duty. "Kolfinnia's coven," she muttered fearfully. Not liking the thought, she pushed it away and picked up her stride. But these chilling doubts stalked her as she walked along an avenue of hollies called Halla's path.

"Are you nervous?" Gale asked, echoing Skald's question.

She turned to Gale, her own thunder-sprite, riding the tip of the lighting-staff she carried. "I'd be a fool if I weren't, but today she'll make her mind up. I know it." She never slowed, and her long dark hair swished against her back with each stride.

"If you say so."

"No, it is!" she bristled. "Today Valonia will make her decision."

"Well, I hope so. She's been pressing you hard for weeks, and it's taken its toll. You don't smile much anymore, you know that?"

"I do!" She protested. But he was right. Valonia had given her plenty of mundane duties lately, such as washing spell bottles or copying out pages of herb lore. Each time she summoned her she hoped the issue of Wardship would arise. So far, though, all she'd received was one menial task after another. She shouldered them humbly, but her heart sank another notch with each disappointment. No wonder she didn't feel like smiling. "Giving me more duties means she's building up to something," she reasoned. *And I hope to God-oak it's Wardship,* she added to herself.

"Oh, she's building up to something, I agree."

Yes, hardening me up for when I leave. The thought reared up before she could swat it away.

"It's alright to be afraid," he continued softly.

She stopped dead, gripped her staff and just stared at the ground. "Gale, there are folks out there who'd betray me for a shilling." She looked up at him, frightened by her own words. "A shilling!" Now she looked past him, to the holly trees, and thought of the world beyond. She hated and feared it in equal measure. "I could be imprisoned or hung for just *owning* a wand."

"Then don't show folks your wand," he shrugged.

She stifled a begrudging smile, and set off again.

"And plenty of witches go off 'out there' and do fine," he continued. "You might even find you like it."

She blinked back her surprise: she hadn't even considered that. "Now that's the scariest of all."

"But whatever happens, remember – you'll always have me," he added.

She smiled faintly as way of thanks. "Anyway," she argued, fighting the tightness in her chest, "Hilda might be leaving. Maybe Valonia wants me to take her place?"

"That's the rumour, yes."

"You think she'll stay then?" She was very fond of Hilda Saxon: her Ward and mentor.

"I couldn't say."

She bit her lip. "I hope so. I couldn't fill her shoes anyway," she admitted.

"Nonsense!" His eyes glinted with conviction. "You're a fine witch and if Valonia throws you out, she throws us out together."

For the second time she stopped mid-stride. "Thanks." She wanted say more, but knew it would only embarrass him, and instead set off again, feeling better . . . but only a little.

She'd done her best to look smart this morning. She'd straightened her pointed witch's hat. Her ritual tattoos were re-inked with vegetable dye, and now a dragon flowed majestically along each forearm. Her finest holed-stone hung around her throat and she'd chosen her best dress. All Flower-Forth witches wore lilac, and her knee-length dress was smart but practical. But while it was the best she had it was also faded, patched and tatty. Jaunts through undergrowth looking for spell-fodder had taken their toll. Maybe she would press beetroot again this year and re-dye it. *Do it before September, a cruel little voice said, before you're out on your own, and if anything's going to stain your dress, it'll be blood not 'beet . . .*

She reached the end of Halla's path, passing a small cluster of graves marked with wicker pentacles. Here were sleeping souls who'd lived and died at Wildwood. *The lucky ones,* she thought. Others weren't so lucky. Valonia could count all too many friends who'd simply vanished. Perhaps they'd died by rope and blade under 'correctional-blessing', or suffered the living nightmare of experimentation in Illuminata labour camps.

Kolfinnia hurried on, wanting to leave these morbid thoughts behind, and she arrived at the perfect antidote. Before her was a maze of vegetable gardens at the centre of which stood the great tree with Valonia's tower nestling in its branches, and although in a hurry, she stopped.

Thirty yards away a young woman and a girl were kneeling before a row of pea plants, as if praying. Kolfinnia recognised the older one right away, and she knew what was coming next. She'd seen it countless times, but always the spectacle humbled her and made her skin tingle. And she didn't have to wait long. Without warning, the entire row of plants spontaneously shot up and burst into flower. Fresh tendrils and leaves sprouted from nowhere. Pink and white blossoms suddenly swept through the crop, like a snowstorm, rustling and whispering as they went, and then they were just swirling petals, rolling across the gardens in colourful clouds. Neither woman nor girl looked up, even as the petals engulfed them and dispersed.

"God-oak she's good, it always gives me a shiver," Gale whispered.

"Me too," Kolfinnia agreed, and when sure the miracle was over, she advanced. Before she even reached the pair there wasn't a single flower left to be seen; just drifts of petals, and stems now sagging with ripe peapods. This was magic in its purest form.

The young woman stood and stretched away the effort, then turned, saw her, and smiled. "Morning Kol, morning Gale."

"Flo," Kolfinnia smiled back.

Flora Greyswan was her closest friend and Wildwood's most gifted garden worker. She wore the same season colours, but there the similarity ended. She was a year younger, her hair was fair and she was slightly taller, but the most telling difference was her eye-patch. It happened long ago and she never spoke about it, but she'd been lucky. Most witches taken for correctional-blessing were never seen again. Rosalind, Flora's mother, certainly never was. "You think today she'll make her mind up?" Flora enquired.

Kolfinnia sighed, "By Halla's claws I hope so! I can't take much more of this."

"Neither can I. It'd be good to see a proper smile on your face for once."

"Like I said," Gale grunted.

Kolfinnia just rolled her eyes at the pair of them.

"But I don't think she's up yet," Flora went on, gesturing to the tower.

She eyed the tower with trepidation. "She told me to be here bright and early."

"Don't tell me you're going to wake her?" Flora teased, splitting open a pod and nibbling the peas. "I hope you've got your lightning-staff ready, she's not at her best first thing."

The young girl stood watching their exchange. She was wearing a grey work apron over her blue tunic and Kolfinnia noticed that her wand-sheath almost reached down to the ground.

"You know, she was up late last night with the Wards." Flora revealed, and mouthed 'bracken wine' so the young girl, named Lilac, wouldn't hear.

Kolfinnia looked from her friend to the tree and back again. "Flo, if I didn't know better I'd swear you were enjoying this."

"Well you do know better, and I'm not."

The young girl simply stared at them like a puzzled owl.

"Well, no use hanging around. The morning's getting old." Kolfinnia straightened her hat and wand-sheath then started for the tower.

"Blessings go with you!" Flora called after her. "And come back with a smile this time!"

She rose her hat in salute without looking back, feeling she was walking towards the executioner's block.

The tree was huge. It gripped the earth in a knotted tangle of roots like a giant fist and a spiral ran up around its girth to the tower above. The lower branches dripped with strips of cloth tied as offerings over the years.

Kolfinnia paused at the bottom. "Here goes nothing," she muttered before banging three times on the step with her staff. Gale swayed with each strike as he clung on. They waited, but after what felt like minutes there was still only silence.

"Hmmm, she's not responding," Gale remarked.

"I can see that," she replied through gritted teeth.

"You wish me to rest in the staff?"

"For now, please." She cast him a sheepish glance.

"Then let me just wish you good luck." He melted away into the staff without another word.

She looked down at the steps. It was still early and the staves that usually held offerings stood bare. An irritated robin flitted around looking for absent tit-bits. Far off she could hear witches beginning their morning duties. Wildwood was coming to life and Valonia was usually first to rise. She stole a glance back at Flora, but she seemed immersed in garden matters. Then, knowing there was no way of avoiding it, she rapped again, louder this time, but her only reply was a startled blackbird flapping through the undergrowth. She was beginning to feel foolish. "Right, there's only one thing I can do." She took a deep breath – and her first step.

Flora heard her knock a second time and looked up to see her climbing the spiral uninvited and vanish into the crown of leaves. "Brave girl," she murmured absently.

"Who's brave? Me?"

Flora looked around at her young helper. "It's not important. Now, Lilac, magic or not – these peas won't harvest themselves you know." She stooped, collected a bucket, pressed it into the girl's arms and set her to work.

Kolfinnia stroked the bark as she ascended, feeling miniature mountains and valleys skim past her fingertips. Strips of cloth brushed her hat and a flock of chaffinches flitted alongside as she climbed, pausing every now again to regard her with their tiny apple-pip eyes.

When Kolfinnia and her bird escort reached the top, the door was still shut and the tower remained silent. The only sounds up here were the whispering leaves. The tower's door was salvaged from a shipwrecked steam cruiser and fittingly numbered '13'. She rightly assumed that had been the cabin number, but she didn't want to think of what had befallen its last occupants. Valonia once said that sea serpents preyed upon vessels around her homeland.

She could see Flora through a break in the canopy. She had shielded her eyes against the rising sun to watch her progress. Kolfinnia offered her a tentative wave and Flora raised a hand in return.

She thumbed her lightning-staff, and as she stood uncertainly she idly began to read it, sensing memories from its parent tree. She saw the sights and sounds it'd witnessed, such as badger cubs playing and highwaymen laying in wait.

"Kolfinnia!" Gale berated her from within. *"Don't put it off!"*

She heard him through her touch on the staff. She was stalling and even he knew it. "I know," she sighed and held out a fist that was almost steady and knocked on the door, ready to face her duty. A bear-like growl came from inside and suddenly the door was flung open and Valonia filled the doorway.

"Kolfinnia, don't just stand and stare. Come in. I've a big task for you today." She rolled her r's and her s's carried a soft whistle, a heritage of her homeland.

Kolfinnia left her staff by the door, and as always, when she let go of it she couldn't feel Gale any more, and she felt bereft. *Here goes – is Wildwood to be my home forever or not?* she thought, imagining those peaceful little graves, and stepped over the threshold and into Valonia's tower.

CHAPTER THREE

Way-beware

"Hear no evil, see no evil, speak no evil," Baxter repeated again, still holding the surgeon's knife.

Wilde struggled in the chair. He had strapped many witches into it down the years but he never for a moment thought those stout leather straps would be lashed around his wrists and ankles. He wasn't a witch; he was a member of this very organisation. "Please, sir," he pleaded, "I never said a word."

Baxter looked towards the back of the old railway carriage, at a man standing in the shadows, hiding from the gaslights. Wilde tried to turn but the iron clamp around his head held him fast. It didn't matter though because he knew full well who was directing Baxter's every move. The man in the shadows cupped a gold pocket-watch in his hand and delivered a silent nod. Baxter's eyebrows twitched in response and he brought the blade closer to Wilde's face. "You were heard talking about your duties here," he said regretfully.

"Never sir! I never said a word, I swear!" Maybe he had, though, he thought in a panic. Maybe he'd let something slip to his wife Mary, but just an innocent remark – and she was hardly a threat, hardly a witch spy. Had they been watching him all along?

"The project you were working on is of the utmost significance to the Illuminata Knighthood and the empire. Did you or did you not speak of it?" Baxter leaned closer.

Wilde's heart gave a fearful thud and his face crumpled. "Yes," he uttered in a tiny voice.

Baxter looked at the out-of-sight man again, and then twitched his eyebrows in acknowledgement of an unseen order before turning back to Wilde. "Then I ask again. Hear no evil, see no evil, speak no evil?"

"Please, sir," Wilde moaned.

"Hear no evil, see no evil, speak no evil." All members of the Knighthood knew the cost of breaking the oath, no matter how small the transgression. Baxter was uncomfortable about doing this to one of their own, but project First-dawn had turned the world on its head and they couldn't risk rumours. From outside the carriage came the clatter of a passing steam train followed by a shrill whistle.

"Hear no evil," Wilde whispered. Tears leaked from between his eyelids, but he didn't open them.

"Very well," Baxter agreed regretfully before taking hold of Wilde's left ear and raising the knife.

The silent man had seen enough. He'd blessed plenty of witches down the years and certainly wasn't squeamish, but it was different when it came to one of their own. Times were unprecedented. First-dawn could re-write the world. He slipped his pocket-watch back into his waistcoat and started towards the carriage door, passing under one of the gas burners as he went. The light briefly glinted across a mess of strange golden scars on his face and hands, then it was gone. Knight Superior Samuel Krast stepped back out into the daylight and closed the door just as Wilde began to scream.

"Sit, sit." Valonia waved impatiently at one of the few chairs.

Kolfinnia seated herself, removed her hat and laid it in her lap. "Forgive me. I hailed you, but you didn't answer," she apologised weakly.

Valonia seemed not to notice. She was busy rummaging in her hammock and swatted her words away with a distracted 'yes, yes'. She could have been addressing Hercules, who Kolfinnia noted took up the rocking chair by the window. He slid a golden eye open, immediately lost interest and went back to sleep.

Kolfinnia loved the tower. 'Tower' was a grand word for a one-room tree house, but it was cosy inside. The canopy was woven into a rainproof thatch and willow panels filled the irregular gaps between branches. She loved how organic it all was. Thanks to the shelter having been woven around the tree, there was barely a straight line in the room. Living beams of oak curled around her, some of them lined with books that leaned at crazy angles. One of the books was wrapped in black velvet and she knew it must be the Almanac of Ruinous Forms, something only senior witches were permitted to study. She also noticed lots of spare blankets tucked between branches. It must get cold up here in winter, she thought, but supposed Valonia forbid fire out of respect to the tree, although a few candle stumps seemed to dispute this. She eyed Valonia's lightning-staff leaning against a branch. Being from Iceland made it very rare indeed, she'd heard that the place was virtually treeless. She rightly assumed Skald was inside although she had no idea that he was listening.

A squirrel darted along a branch, across the floor and out through the opposite window, making her smile, while potion bottles tinkled as the great tree shifted in the breeze. Even with the shutters closed a good deal of light filtered down through the canopy, bathing the room with spring light. She drank it all in while Valonia continued her search, huffing impatiently.

The old woman ransacked a wooden desk, shaking the mirror, and pestle and mortar on its top as she rifled the drawers. But it was all pantomime; she knew what she was looking for and precisely where to find it. Kolfinnia's throat felt dry, and she was nervously toying with her wand-sheath when Valonia's sudden cry made her jump.

"A-ha!" She took a black parcel from a bowl in the trunk that resembled a shrine and Kolfinnia's heart leapt: black was the colour of Wardship. As she retrieved the package, Kolfinnia also caught a glimpse of Valonia's infamous cloak within, reputedly sewn from the garments of witches taken for correctional-blessing. Each square of fabric was the last remnant of one of Valonia's friends and she felt a lurch that had nothing to do with the settling tree.

The old witch flopped into a chair and set the package on her knees where her experienced hands hovered over it protectively. "This is for you, Kolfinnia," she said with gravity, indicating the package tied with black ribbon.

This is really it! She's going to make me a Ward! Kolfinnia restrained her joy. After all, it wasn't honour she longed for, but security. Valonia studied her intently before she deftly sprung the ribbon. Kolfinnia caught her breath and leaned closer, anxious to see the contents. "What is it, coven-mother?" She didn't want to appear too self assured, and so she played along. But at the sight of the drab canvas within she realised it was likely nothing to do with Wardship. She swallowed her disappointments and sat deflated but tight-lipped.

"Hercules came home yesterday covered with grab-hooks." The old woman said sadly.

Kolfinnia just blinked, turned to look at the old hare, and smiled as

sweetly as she could. It was imperative she look attentive, although the
act was harder than she'd anticipated. She wanted to sob her heart out,
and scream and rant, but she remembered her duty. "They're awful
things," she agreed, remembering having two on her thigh last year.
The ticks had swollen to the size of peas and left scars where they'd
sucked her blood. "How many?" she added.

"Fourteen, Kolfinnia, fourteen!"

She almost said, 'Thirteen might have been luckier,' but thought it too
flippant and mumbled a feeble, "Berries-be-red. So many!"

"Indeed," Valonia nodded. "So I've come up with a solution that'll deter
grab-hooks and pin-tips too." Pin-tips were the tiny biting flies that
made summer miserable, and a way to deter them without harming
them would improve life no end. "And so this is my solution." She took
the canvas bag from its velvet sleeve, unhooked the toggle and began
to unroll it. Inside were slim pockets and tucked into each was a small
wooden figure. She drew one out and Kolfinnia shivered a little, there
was something disturbing about the malformed doll and the way its legs
were shaped into a single long spike, like a dagger, and wasn't there the
faintest sound of pitiful sobbing? Valonia noticed her unease. "So then,
they work well enough!" she smiled craftily. "You don't like them. They
disturb you?"

"Yes." She couldn't take her eyes off the doll. "It makes me feel uneasy,
like I want to run away from it."

"Strong magic here, Kolfinnia. Way-beware." Valonia held the doll up
to the light.

"Way-beware?"

"A spell we used at home in Iceland when I was a girl. Sometimes
trolls would come and try to steal our winter grain. These dolls were a
solution my coven-mother invented. Way-bewares she called them. We'd
put them around the coven. They form a protective circle and sing a
spell that warns unwanted people and creatures away."

Some of this sounded familiar. Wildwood had its own way of keeping
intruders out: a ring of scarecrows concealing charms marked the coven
frontier. The charms didn't harm people, but they made the area seem
unappealing to passers-by and as such they were rarely bothered. "Do
they hurt people?"

"No, no, no," Valonia shook her head. "They only make people want to
turn away, even though they may not know why, and even though that
might've been the very direction they wanted to go. But go they do, and
most importantly they go unharmed." She seemed pleased, and again
scrutinised her as if looking for something.

"And these dolls are for pin-tips and grab-hooks?" Kolfinnia smiled, grasping their purpose.

"Indeed! Very sharp." She clapped her hands in satisfaction. "Scarecrows for our unwelcome little visitors who take blood and give only an itch in return. Now we've never used way-bewares here before and their magic is strong, and so this is an honour I chose for you." She regarded her fondly and Kolfinnia could do nothing but smile back as she was handed down another mundane, dirty task.

"Thank you, coven-mother." She felt a rush of sadness that soon even this joyless aspect of coven life would be gone. "It's a great honour."

"I want you to walk the inner coven and drive one into the ground every three-hundred paces." She rose from her chair. "Take someone with you, someone with a good memory who'll be able to help you collect them when autumn comes. The girl from Seed-Fall with the remarkable memory, Rowan, I think, yes Rowan Barefoot."

Collect them in autumn before my birthing day? Kolfinnia thought sourly. My last ever task at Wildwood.

"Oh, and Kolfinnia, keep them in the black wrapping, then you won't feel ill when carrying them." She thrust the package at her and made for the door, opening it and waiting for her to leave.

"Thank you." Kolfinnia was a little taken aback by the meeting's brusque end. She walked demurely to the door and across the threshold, back from her unsuccessful venture into Wardship and into uncertainty.

"Oh, and kindly ask Flora to bring me a kettle of hot water, would you?" Valonia finished. With that she ushered the slightly bewildered Kolfinnia out onto the balcony, closing the door behind her.

Kolfinnia just stood there for a moment clutching the package. Stupid girl, and stupid fanciful daydreams! How'll you survive out there if dreaming's the best you can do? she silently berated her hopes. She exhaled in a juddering stream and wiped a tear away from her eye, snatched up her lightning-staff and began the downward spiral, feeling September looming closer with every step.

Valonia stood with her back to the door listening to her fading footsteps, looking pleased but drained. She'd hurt the young woman again and that didn't make her feel good, but she had to be sure and overall the meeting had gone well. Skald immediately appeared at her side. "You look satisfied."

"Aye." She let out a pent up breath. "She's the one, Skald. I always knew it. My little wolf-mother." She even managed a smile. If Kolfinnia had thought the meeting was tense she had no idea of the gravity Valonia had placed upon their five minutes together. Valonia's own witching gift was particularly rare: she could read auras that were invisible to the earthbound eye, but she kept it secret, however,

finding people changed if they knew they were being observed. If she
wished, she could read an individual in the brilliant display of colours
that played about their crown, but it was like peeping at a diary and
to be used only when necessary. When Kolfinnia arrived she could
see brilliant embers drifting around her like dragon hatchlings and
understood she was filled with hopes, and not, she was pleased to
see, for any vain political reasons. She wanted to study Kolfinnia's
reaction to the way-bewares and how she accepted her duties. She'd
been testing her quietly for weeks now and she'd not been disappointed.
"I'll announce Kolfinnia's Wardship in September at her eighteenth
birthing-day." She smiled to herself.

Skald flexed his wings. "So, you've found our new Flower-Forth Ward."

Valonia nodded and looked long at her wrinkled hands. "And one day
our new coven-mother," she said at last.

"What!" Tiny flashes of static flickered across his wings. "Kolfinnia's a
fine witch, I grant you, but there are others more seasoned."

She raised a hand to stop him. "First-dawn's coming, Skald. I don't
know what it is, but I feel a great upheaval approaches. The crib-robber
prophesied all those years ago that this first-dawn would be my demise.
I daren't risk leaving Wildwood without a successor, someone with their
life ahead of them and a strong sense of duty."

"It was a lie! The filthy thing lied to punish you because you'd beaten
it!" He hated the way she had let its last words haunt her for almost
sixty years. "I wish you'd let me stay with you that night," he snarled.
"I'd have finished that bastard thing before it even opened its mouth."

"And if you'd done so," she reminded him, "the crib-robber would have
been killed, not merely returned to Ruination. Remember that death is
always a last resort."

"And let me remind you we've killed a foe or two down the years," he
challenged.

"To survive! No more!" she retorted.

"It lied to you," he muttered sulkily and looked away, furious with her
and afraid for her.

"I suspect not." She went to him and reached out a soothing hand.

At first he was sullen, but soon yielded and turned to face her. "You
think first-dawn means doom for all Britain's witches or you alone?" He
hated talking about this.

"I think of it more often. The universe speaks to us in coincidence, and
I hear the words 'first' and 'dawn' in separate conversations and I think
of it again. I feel haunted by it, Skald. But whether this is doom for all
or just me, I can't say." She stroked his feathered brow tenderly. "Only
the Timekeeper knows that," she added wistfully, wishing the fabled

spider was real and that she could ask him once and for all.

Kolfinnia composed herself as she drew level with Flora.

"I'm sorry," Gale's thoughts pulsed through the lightning-staff.

"It's nothing," she lied quietly. "I half expected to be disappointed." A moment later she was at Flora's side.

"Well?" Flora noticed her distinct lack of a smile, and scrutinised the bundle in her arms, while nearby, Lilac continued harvesting peas.

"Coven-mother wants a kettle of hot water, if you please, and as for me, well . . . " she faltered and looked down uncertainly at the package. "I'll tell you later. I've an errand to do, nothing newsworthy, though." Her words carried a weight she hadn't intended.

"I'm sorry." Flora read everything from her face. "Listen," she perked up, "why don't we go looking for mermaids this evening?"

"Mermaids!" Lilac suddenly looked up wide-eyed.

"Never mind. This isn't pip-staff business," Flora added from the corner of her mouth, then flashed Kolfinnia a roguish smile. 'Looking for mermaids' was code for a campfire, and if they could manage it a bottle of something strong. "Well, will you?"

Kolfinnia tipped her hat in acceptance. "Oak-be-dammed, why not!" she growled, before turning and setting off in search of Rowan Barefoot, her companion for the day ahead.

Six and a half year old Rowan had arrived at Wildwood under a year ago, having been raised by an uncle after fever claimed her mother. The girl's strange talents disturbed him, as did the burden of raising her. And so he'd put aside his mistrust of witches and secretly taken her to a local villager, who in turn delivered her to a trusted contact, and then finally the girl was collected like baggage and taken to Wildwood. All but Rowan seemed to agree it was the safest place for her, and she became one of the thirteen Seed-Fall witches under the benign Wardship of Esta Salt.

Kolfinnia hardly knew her, but everyone remembered Rowan's incredible trick from the last solstice feast. She had recited the name of every leaf on Hethra's tree and the spectacle had gone on for hours.

It seemed that remembering was Rowan's gift. Not only could she remember everything she'd ever encountered, but even events she'd never witnessed and information she'd never read. This was so unexplainable that she made even the most well-meaning witch feel uneasy, and as far as Kolfinnia knew she didn't have any close friends.

She found her at the stream cleansing cauldrons in the flowing water. The brim of her pointed hat shaded her face, while her cream dress was darned and patched and over the top of it she wore a long russet waistcoat common to the Seed-Fall witches. "Rowan," Kolfinnia called pleasantly, "Rowan Barefoot?" But when the girl didn't respond Kolfinnia rolled her eyes and huffed. Rowan was indeed barefoot, and from behind all she could see of her were a pair of filthy feet and the tip of her hat as she knelt over the stream. "Rowan?" She drew level and gently prodded her heel with her boot.

The girl didn't flinch or jump in the slightest. She merely reeled in the dripping cauldron, heaved it on to the grassy bank, and turned around wearing an expectant look. "Yes?" Her voice was gentle like the stream.

Kolfinnia thrust her staff into the ground and planted her hands on her hips. "Didn't you hear me calling you?" She almost added 'dung head!' Her mood was delicate to say the least.

"I did hear you, but I was busy." Her hazel eyes brimmed with hurt and she had the manner of a timid finch that holds back at the bird table while its fellows gorge themselves.

"Busy doing what?"

"I was counting the pebbles on the stream bed."

It's going to be a bloody long day! Kolfinnia groaned to herself, but smiled her best smile. "I'm Kolfinnia Algra. Coven-mother sent me to find you. There's a job needs doing and she thinks you and I would make a good pair-up." She tried to make it sound thrilling.

The mention of Valonia was like a charm. Rowan scrambled up, looking alert. She was small for her age, and her shoulder length hair was the colour of chestnuts. She smoothed her tunic, tightened her belt, straightened her pointed hat, then stood nervously fiddling with the oak leaf pendant around her slender neck. "Coven-mother wants me?"

"Yes, do you remember naming all the leaves on Hethra's tree?"

Her face lit up. "Oh, yes! I remember, first comes Dapple, then Rust, then –,"

"Enough!" she interrupted.

Rowan bit her lip.

"Your skills are remarkable," Kolfinnia added to soothe the creases of hurt on Rowan's brow. "That's why Wildwood needs you. I have to place spell-dolls and I'd like you to come so you can remember where they are when it's time to collect them again in the autumn." She held out the parcel for Rowan to see. Autumn, when you leave here, Kolfinnia, she thought again and felt a rush of anxiety. "So pack some lunch and a canteen and meet me by Halla's path as soon as you're ready, yes?"

The girl nodded earnestly before turning and dashing away.

Kolfinnia watched her go, and her mind turned again to that small collection of graves. It never struck her as odd, that all she wished for right then was for an old Kolfinnia to be buried there one day. "I should be so lucky," she whispered hoarsely, then shook an angry tear away and got started.

It was mid-morning before they began, starting by the evergreen avenue of Halla's path and passing other witches busy about their duties. The path would lead them through the great pines that surrounded Wildwood and there they would turn east and begin in earnest.

"Why have you brought two staffs? I've got one of my own, look." Rowan waved her dainty hazel staff.

"One's for walking, the other's for something else," she replied mysteriously. Her lightning-staff hung over her shoulder, this would be a heavy walk and she didn't want to risk breaking it, carrying instead an ordinary walking staff. The breaking of a lightning-staff, by accident or intent, signalled the end of the union between witch and sprite, then the sprite was free to return to the thunder-heights above. Kolfinnia couldn't image life without Gale and she treated her own staff with the utmost care.

Rowan was too young to have one of her own. "That's your lightly staff!" she gasped.

"Lightning-staff," she corrected.

"Are we going to fly?"

"Never you mind," she smiled wanly.

Rowan said no more, but several times Kolfinnia caught her eyeing the staff as though it were a dangerous snake and might lunge at her.

The going was tough and as they pushed through thickets of dead bracken it crackled in protest. The stems were brittle and sharp and hid an army of rocks ideally placed for them to crack their toes against, something Kolfinnia made a miserable habit of while Rowan, true to her name, made the whole journey barefoot. It wasn't long before the sun coaxed out the troublesome pin-tips, and Kolfinnia bid Rowan stop as soon as she felt them bite her bare legs, which were now latticed with scratches. "Rowan, pass me the first way-beware."

She obediently untied the package and Kolfinnia instantly felt the doll's song crawling in her ears like gnats. A flock of long-tailed tits fluttered past and detoured with alarmed chattering. She supposed it was because all the dolls were gathered together and she hoped their effect wouldn't be so potent once they'd been spread out.

"Is that the dolls?" Rowan meant the eerie crying, just out of earshot.

"Hmm. But don't worry, it won't be so bad once we've spread them thinner." The song was upsetting, like listening to an animal in a trap.

"But it'll still scare off the biting things?"

"That's the idea, yes. Just the biting things, not the pretty fluffy things."

Rowan didn't smile at her humour and her face remained solemn.

She drove the first doll into the gap between the rocks while Rowan held the bracken aside so she could see. Before they moved on, Rowan committed the scene to memory before letting the grasses spring back and their strange little doll was quickly swallowed up.

When noon came, with a third of the dolls placed, they ate their provisions by the Appelier River. Rowan's meagre snack of fruit and oatcakes was over in a moment and she tipped her satchel inside out in the hope of finding more.

"Didn't you bring enough?" Kolfinnia asked with sisterly concern. In truth she was glad of Rowan's company as it took her mind off things.

"I brought enough, I'm sure I did, but I'm still hungry." She looked crest-fallen.

Kolfinnia laid aside her own wedge of bread and stood up, beckoning her to a small sapling by the water's edge. It was wiry and toothy little buds ran along its branches. "A clever witch learns to ask the serpent-twins to provide lunch, look." She eased Rowan to her side where she knelt by the frail looking shrub. "Watch, and later I'll show you how." She cupped a branch between her hands and leaned close enough to kiss it, then closed her eyes and whispered something.

Rowan couldn't catch the words but felt her eyes prickle with tears, the good kind that come when all's fine with the world, and saw the buds open, blossom, swell and fruit within seconds. "Hazelnuts!" she gaped, "Kolfinnia, how?"

She smiled fully at last, delighted by the girl's expression. "Flora showed me. She can make whole gardens bloom if she wants to, but the most important part is remembering to be grateful to Hethra and Halla." Still smiling, she plucked the hazelnuts and dropped them into Rowan's tunic pocket. "I can't make a nutcracker appear so you'll have to eat them when we get back. In the meantime, share my bread."

For a second Rowan looked bewildered then smiled shyly. "You promise to show me how?"

"How to make the spell or how to crack nuts?" she teased, but Rowan just looked baffled.

"But how?" Rowan asked again.

She thought for a moment. "You can make the real world change and become something else. Like I changed buds into hazelnuts." She tore a chunk off her bread for Rowan. "And if you ask correctly and ask with a good heart, whatever you want can be changed."

"And if you ask with a bad heart?" Rowan anticipated.

"Then nothing will happen," she reassured her. It was a half-truth because this wasn't the time or place to speak of dark Illuminata-magic.

"Is that what witches mean when they say 'Will commands the world'?" She deliberated over each word.

"Quite so." She approved.

"I didn't know what it meant before, but I think I do now!"

"I think you'll make a fine little witch."

Rowan beamed and patted her pocket, where there were suddenly hazelnuts five months early.

It was almost six hours before Rowan slipped the last way-beware from the now limp canvas roll. The terrain had stayed stubbornly unhelpful throughout and the weather had grown hotter, drawing ever more pin-tips from the undergrowth, but Kolfinnia was pleased to note that the flies seemed to be keeping a distance.

They stopped for a rest at clay-town, a jumble of ruined brick-kilns that supported a luxuriant forest of ferns and a small colony of feral cats in their shady chimneys. One of the ferals was curled up in a brick recess where an iron door hung from its hinges. He watched them intently before rising and slinking away. All around them was the cleansing scent of pine-sap and the droning chant of dragonflies, and just beyond, both witches could feel the way-bewares' song. Kolfinnia took stock of their work. She'd earned plenty of cuts across her knees and calves and an extra tear in her battered dress, but there seemed fewer pin-tips and neither of them had found any grab-hooks after a thorough search of one another's skin and clothing. What's more, spending energy on hard work dulled her worries.

"We're done now, aren't we, Kolty?" Rowan rubbed at her hot cheeks.

She frowned. Kolty? Only Flora called her 'Kolty', and even then only rarely. How did Rowan know that? The girl removed her hat and brushed chestnut hair from her brow, and that was Kolfinnia's first clear view of the mysterious child. "First we have to test the dolls before we go home." She decided.

Rowan just blinked up at her expectantly.

"How many pine needles around the seventh doll?" She asked suddenly.

"One-hundred and seventeen." Her reply was instant and brisk, as though she thought Kolfinnia witless for not knowing such a simple fact.

"All right," she agreed, "and at the twentieth doll, how many crumble caps growing on that beech stump?"

"Almost sixty-three." Rowan again looked apologetic, as if this was something everyone knew

"What does 'almost' mean?"

"A slug was eating the sixty-fourth one. There was only half left!"

Kolfinnia couldn't help but laugh. "Remarkable! I think our army of dolls is safe with you as their general." Without thinking she stroked Rowan's cheek like a big sister. "Now fasten your hat because we're flying home," she added casually.

"Flying?" Rowan felt a touch of fear. "But I'm not ten!" She tugged on Kolfinnia's arm. "It's forbidden, I'm still a pip-staff!" She even looked around the deserted wood, fearing she'd be found out.

In the months that followed Kolfinnia remembered, sometimes with terrible sadness, sometimes with overwhelming fury, that that was the moment she decided she liked Rowan. She smiled secretly, "I won't be telling coven-mother. Will you?"

"No!" She pressed a finger to her lips, locking their secret away.

"Very well then." Satisfied, she slid her lightning-staff from her shoulder. In truth Kolfinnia suddenly yearned to fly. "I don't have to tell you what this is, do I?"

"Your lightning-staff." Rowan reached out a tentative finger to one of the loops tied around the staff, commonly used like stirrups or reins. "Lightning-staffs are alive, aren't they?"

"Oh yes." She held the staff horizontal at waist level then delivered a delicate tap from her forefinger. The staff quivered and thin veins of lightning flickered through the grain, and for an instant it shimmered like sunlight on water. Rowan took a half step backwards. "Witches cut their first lightning-staff at the age of ten and the sprite only succumbs to a partnership if they can beat them at riddles or feats of daring." Kolfinnia recited what all witches knew. "That's the part that's alive, the thunder-sprite, and one day you'll strike a partnership with a sprite yourself."

Rowan's eyes filled her face, as if she was being told her very future.

"Ever flown before?" she asked, and a timid head-shake was Rowan's reply. Kolfinnia felt Gale's heat as he uncurled from sleep and throbbed through the wood. Then she slowly withdrew her hands, leaving the staff floating with nothing but thin air for support. Just as Rowan took in this wonder she was confronted with another. Gale materialized and perched proudly on the staff, making her gasp.

"Allow me to introduce you," Kolfinnia announced. "Rowan, meet Gales-Howl-Over-Stormy-Waters, but he's named Gale for short." All sprites were named for their parent storms' achievements, while their witch names were always much shorter. "Gale, this is Rowan Barefoot, general of the way-beware army." Kolfinnia added formally and tipped a little bow in the girl's direction.

"My pleasure, general." He dipped his head in salute, embarrassed but playing along for Kolfinnia's sake.

Rowan giggled, not sure what to say.

"You'd better say hello before you climb aboard." Kolfinnia invited.

"Gale." She reached out to the proud creature on the staff, and as her fingers touched his glossy flight feathers the staff trembled for a moment like a horse ready to charge.

He appraised her openly. "Hmm? You look small for ten." He squinted suspiciously and sniffed loudly. "You smell like a pip-staff to me."

She looked to Kolfinnia for help.

"She can fly with my blessing." Kolfinnia lay protective hands on the girl's shoulders.

"Is this because you had a bad morning? You're defying her?" he enquired and Kolfinnia gave him a look that Rowan didn't understand. "Very well then, you're the one she'll will be angry with." He turned towards Rowan. "As long as you don't get scared. I don't carry screaming whelps." Without another word he melted back into the staff.

"Time to fly." Kolfinnia mounted in one fluid movement and perched sideways on, while slipping her feet into the fabric loops like stirrups. The staff yielded minutely as it shifted under her weight. She felt Gale crackling in readiness and reached out her arms, inviting Rowan to fill them. This was breaking a strict rule, but today she relished it. "Ready to go?"

"Can he carry two?" Rowan looked concerned.

"Carry two? Don't let him hear you say that! When he was born he split an ash into nothing but kindling. He'll shoulder us both, I promise." She splayed her fingers and waggled them, waiting.

To her delight Rowan flung herself into her arms with a cry and then wriggled around against her chest. She hooked her hands around the older girl's arms and braced her bare feet against the staff, which now hummed like a generator.

"Home to Wildwood, please, Gale." Kolfinnia asked simply.

He set off slowly before picking up speed, determined to show his paces, and sweeping over the bluebells to the sound of Rowan and Kolfinnia's laughter, and then they were gone and the silence of the wood returned.

The circle of way-bewares was complete. The first sang to the second who passed the song to the next until it travelled the circle again, completing a chorus of warning. As Rowan's laughter faded and the hush of the wood returned, living things busied themselves with spring. The way-bewares sang, and without knowing why unwanted insects found the air hostile and flew elsewhere in search of blood.

But by autumn very different intruders would come seeking witches' blood and the way-bewares would cry their song of warning for Wildwood-coven itself.

CHAPTER FOUR

The Devil at Home

Despite her worries Kolfinnia found life the same pleasing blend
of routine and surprise. There were spells to be recited without fail
to maintain Hethra and Halla's harmonious sleep. As for surprises,
while working the rain-calling spell unlucky Esme Plumb set her
garden broom a-fire. This was the same girl who'd once incubated a
rescued bird's egg only to find that it was a stone. For Kolfinnia, each
completed job was like another chapter finished, which always left her
clammy with worry. While she did her best to relish the routine tasks,
Valonia continued to make them as testing as possible. Since first
meeting Rowan, Valonia often paired them up for grubby jobs, such as
harvesting spell ingredients like nettles or bird-droppings. Yesterday
she and Rowan had found themselves weaving hemp ropes, which left
her fingers blistered while Rowan had loved every minute of it, leaving
her wishing she had the girl's innocence, not to mention nimble fingers.

Duty wasn't the only reason they came together. They soon found
friendship, and just yesterday they had accompanied Esta Salt's witches
down to the sea to learn the art of wish-calling, which sounded magical
but was a spectacular flop. Everyone had drawn pictures in the sand of
personal things they wanted to change and watched the sea creep up
the shore to erase them. Unfortunately they had miscalculated the tide.
It was all very grand until the waves began to retreat and in the end
they had to finish erasing their drawings with fronds of seaweed. Then
came the ceremonial bonfire, but when a flock of gulls landed on it and

refused to leave, it went unlit and the gulls cackled in triumph. Despite all of this everyone including Esta saw the funny side and she remarked that the rite had gone so badly that unlucky Esme Plumb ought to have been in charge.

That same night was clear and Kolfinnia had named the stars for Rowan. The brightest of them was Vega, the witch-star, from where the first witches had come carrying the serpent-twins when the Earth was still lifeless. Rowan was so taken by the myth that she later wove a star pendant for Kolfinnia from birch twigs, and named it Vega. The result was lopsided and crude, but Kolfinnia was touched and in return she braided her hair. As she did she told her of fairies and why they were so abundant yet so invisible. "They shepherd souls to Evermore," she had disclosed, and went on to name dozens of fairy species. That's how things went through the early spring: routine and surprise. Kolfinnia found that she loved Wildwood more with each passing day, but that also made September look even darker.

May might be glorious for witches in their hidden covens, but for Londoners it brought a spate of problems such as festering sewers and smelly rivers. The city heaved with people trying to make a living, either honestly or otherwise. Coster-mongers sold fruit, vegetables, hot eels, pickled whelks, lemonade and a whole other array of goods on the open streets while children darted between them, some sweeping gutters to earn a penny, others helping themselves to purses and wallets.

While most witches had only ever seen London in etchings, there was one place in the capital that they knew and feared. Just as mothers told unruly children that the Devil would take them if they misbehaved, witches told tales of the Order of the Knights Illuminata and how they spirited away their kin, never to be seen again. And these were not just fairy tales. Their purpose was the subjugation and control of magic, and the means to that end were often fraught and bloody.

The Illuminata's headquarters was a severe red brick building with bristling iron railings. It sat squarely on the Albert embankment south of the Thames, overlooking the Houses of Parliament and the great murky river itself. It was known as Goldhawk Row and a heavy brass plaque bearing their crest of a unicorn and a dragon chained to a thunderbolt, was set by the gate. Tellingly the name was etched in letters usually reserved for gravestones.

The Illuminata had begun life as a military order centuries before. Afraid that disciples of esoteric law would erode their power, the early

church established the Knights and many of the earliest recruits were
actually witches either tortured or bribed into betraying their fellows.
If there was such a thing as black magic the Knighthood Illuminata
would be its coven. As the centuries passed their aims twisted in on
themselves and now they secretly explored the merits of witchcraft
to see if it could be exploited, although they still openly persecuted
practitioners of magic.

Many bloodlines feuded for control of the Order, but at any one time
only one man controlled it. Samuel Krast was the Illuminata's current
Knight Superior. Today he was chairing a meeting so sensitive that
Goldhawk Row wouldn't do. It might be susceptible to spies – rival
Illuminata families and witches alike. Only Hobbs Ash was suitable for
today's gathering.

Krast surveyed the scene from the signalman's box that served as his
office. It gave him a commanding view across the disused railway yard
of Hobbs Ash, although this wasn't its real name. Officially marked on
the map as 'Holts Arch', it earned the nickname from the rail-workers
who imagined the acres of blight as an ideal abode for Old Hobb
himself. The site occupied an isolated loop of the Thames, overlooking
the Battersea Reach on its southwestern flank and defended by the
Chelsea Creek on the other. Krast liked the place. It felt separate from
London and privacy was essential to his work.

Hobbs' was once destined to go from coal yard to passenger station,
until the Knighthood had taken a fancy to the site and stepped in and
bought the whole area . . . whether the rail company approved or not.
Abandoned tracks, overgrown and rusty, criss-crossed the site, although
a few were shiny and operational, while the station, although never
completely finished, was a grand affair of iron and glass. However, its
rails had been entombed under asphalt and the station that'd never
seen a single passenger now acted as a hanger for other steam-powered
engines – kraken war machines.

The Illuminata's towering coal-fired armoured suits, known as
krakens, enjoyed an illustrious and bloody history. Aside from
housing these krakens, station buildings had been modified into
barracks, detention blocks, stables and a private coal power station.
Interrogations and 'blessings' were conducted here and the whole area
was defended by a fortified embankment and armed patrols. Old Hobb
might have felt at home here after all . . .

Krast took a pocket watch from his tweed waistcoat and marked the
passing of noon with an impatient sniff then snapped the lid closed.
He hated it when people showed disrespect for time and place. Just
then a pillar of steam shimmered off to the north along one of the few

operational lines. This one reached all the way back to Parliament like a silver highway, maintaining a discreet link between the Illuminata and the government. "At last," he sighed.

"They're here, sir?" Bertrand Hathwell, Krast's former squire, stepped up to his superior's side. He was a short, heavy-set man in his fifties who always looked as though he carried a great burden. His dark hair was combed back and the silver at his temples made him look more like a noble knight rather than a faithful squire. The weather was unseasonably warm and he felt his heavy suit suffocating him. He hated visits from dignitaries because it entailed wearing his most uncomfortable clothes. To make matters worse his bad knee felt like it was on fire today. There was a metal plate there where bone ought to be thanks to an errant mortar shell many years before.

"Welcome our guests will you Hathwell," Krast commanded smoothly without taking his eyes from the approaching train.

"Very good sir." He paced away, trying not to limp.

Krast retrieved his watch again, but this time he didn't spring the lid. Instead, he smoothed a thumb across the worn gold, engraved with a unicorn and a dragon chained to a thunderbolt. "Titus," he murmured, not hearing himself speak.

The clatter of pistons drew closer until the train finally rumbled past making the window panes rattle like drowsy wasps. They'd kept him waiting Krast thought; it seemed only fair that he repay the favour. He logged the train's arrival, but not its passengers. Paperwork could sometimes record too much. Then he pocketed his watch again and slid a sheath of files from the table.

He reached for the door handle and stopped. There was a small mirror by the window. Pale eyes stared back at him from a discoloured face. His lean face and hairless scalp were mottled with blotches the colour of tarnished gold. They even glinted with a metallic lustre and gave him the appearance of an ancient statue with living eyes.

Hathwell didn't quite have the nerve to ask what had caused this, even after years of service as his squire, but he rightly suspected a witch's curse. Krast knew of course. It was still there, locked away in the vaults of his mind but no force on Earth would make him recall that day again. "I followed my orders Titus," he said to the empty room and the vault in his mind rocked once as if something inside wanted to escape.

The din of the steam train died away. He opened the door and descended the wooden stairs carrying the sheath of folders tucked under his arm. They were all marked *Ministerial attention only: First-Dawn*.

Kolfinnia was peeling potatoes under the shade of an ancient mulberry bush when Flora came to relieve her. "Hope you kept the skins," she reminded her.

"Every last one." Kolfinnia nodded towards a bucket brimming with peelings. "Even Rooter won't get through that lot." Rooter was the fearsome wild boar who'd adopted Wildwood years ago and often raided the gardens, although at present he was nowhere to be seen.

Flora inspected the mound of scraps. "Oh, he'll love that lot!"

"You pamper him too much, he's getting fat," scowled Kolfinnia.

She just smiled the remark away. "Anyhow, time's up, it's my turn. Are there many left?" She looked to see what was left in the basket.

"Just the small ones that roll away from the knife so you end up cutting yourself," she said with false cheer.

"I'm sorry."

"It's not your fault." She rubbed at the nettle stings on her leg and looked accusingly at Valonia's tower.

"She has a plan, she always has a plan." Flora pushed her hair away from her face, which was strikingly beautiful, but as always she left it hanging like a curtain to conceal her ruined left eye.

"I suppose."

"Besides," she added, "you've made a new friend out of all this. Little Rowan."

"Rowan? Yes, I'm very fond of her." This sounded like news to Kolfinnia herself and she smiled.

"See, it's not all bad."

"Just another friend to miss when I get shoved out." She immediately wished she hadn't said it. It sounded snivelling.

"Come on." She clasped her shoulder. "You don't want to look too ruffled."

"Another duty?"

"She's asked for you again," she said apologetically. "Put on a good show. The hard work's leading somewhere, I know it."

She picked up her lightning-staff from next to the wheelbarrow and planted her pointed hat firmly on her head. "How do I look?"

"Like you could mud wrestle a bear, or least ways, like you've just tried. Did you leave any dirt on the spuds or is it all on you?" She brushed a crumb of soil from her nose.

"Well, if she gives me a dirty job I'm halfway there aren't I? Let's hope coven-mother's ready shall we?"

Rowan had orders to wait in the orchards for Kolfinnia, but while waiting she was pressed into service by Ada Crabbe, one of the senior gardeners, given a broom and told to sweep. Ada was a gnarled old witch as thorny as brambles. The breeze picked up and Rowan felt a shower of last year's leaves drift down, scratching and tapping at her hat. "Get 'em swept up lass!" Ada barked.

Rowan began sweeping, all the while glancing around, hoping Kolfinnia would show. "Can't I make plants grow instead?" she whined.

"Can yer 'call' plants?" Ada scowled.

"Erm, well," she flustered.

"Aye. Thought not. Come 'ere then." She dragged the girl to a bed of marrows and stood her before them. They were only young plants but many bore small fruits. "Call 'em," she ordered.

"Erm, I," she stammered.

"Then watch," Ada sighed, and swept her aside. "Them's young marrows." She pointed with a gnarled finger. "Posh folks call 'em cor-jets. But it'll be a marrow in a tick, just see." She fished for her wand, while Rowan obediently observed. "Now then." She held up her wand and waved it. "You watchin'?"

Rowan nodded earnestly.

"This is 'ow we 'call'. This is 'ow we stay fed, and most importantly – stay *free*." She directed the wand at one of the small fruits. Her face grew serious and her lower lip quivered. Suddenly she stabbed her wand forward. "Grow up yer little sod!" she shouted. Her word was her will, and her will changed the world. In response the slender fruit rapidly swelled in size.

Rowan heard leaves rustle and gravel crunch as it shoved them aside and achieved maturity in moments. "Mrs Crabbe!" she gaped. Grinning, she turned to find the old woman staring intently at her over the top of her battered spectacles, which had one blackened lens, but there wasn't a trace of frivolity on her face.

"That's why they hate us lass." She sounded stony but proud now.

"Hate us?"

"Aye, cos a witch who learns to call need never toil in a mill, factory or mine for pennies, and can never be made a slave of. You understand?" Her seasoned hands rested firmly on Rowan's shoulder. "Never!"

Rowan forgot her delight and instead felt something deeper, although she didn't recognise it as the thrill of freedom. "I understand Mrs Crabbe."

Ada grunted and slapped her shoulder. "Free an' fed! Now shift it lass!" She swept her arm impatiently and turned back to her gardens.

Rowan, smiling again, ran back to her sweeping. *Free and fed*, she told herself, and vowed to remember it.

When she arrived at the tower, Kolfinnia wasn't at all surprised to see Rowan sat on the bottom step. Clearly she already knew they'd be off again because her satchel bulged with food. Kolfinnia saw that the girl had tried to fix her own hair just as she'd shown her, but the plaits were floppy and ragged.

"Kol! You should see what Mrs Crabbe just did, she made a marrow right in front of me, so we can stay 'free and fed'!"

"Well we know what's for evening meal then don't we?" she said not unkindly. "I believe coven-mother has another duty for us?"

"I know!" She jumped up.

Her good nature was infectious, so much so that Kolfinnia begrudgingly found herself looking forward to their day together. "There's always jobs to be done Rowan. Sometimes I think we're Wildwood's caretakers."

"Why are you so filthy?" she noticed at last.

"Potatoes." She replied simply, looking down at her battered dress, which was now more brown now than lilac. "Oh, come here," she couldn't help herself, and reached out and loosened Rowan's scruffy plaits. "I'll help you with them when we get back."

Rowan removed her hat and ruffled her hair free. "Promise?"

"On Vega I promise."

Rowan noticed the small amulet she'd made hanging around Kolfinnia's neck. "You kept it."

"Of course! And I promise to do your hair again later."

" . . . And we all know Kolfinnia always keeps her promises." At the sound of the voice they both turned to see Valonia descending her tower. She passed out of sight as she rounded the great trunk and appeared again at the bottom. She was wearing her wand, hrafn-dimmu, buckled around her waist.

She's been wearing it more and more lately, Kolfinnia thought with a hint of anxiety. *What is it she senses?*

"Morning to the both of you." Valonia greeted them, although it was past noon by now. They bowed respectfully and it was then that Kolfinnia noticed a large crow perched on Valonia's shoulder. "Morning also to Jerrow here." She raised an affectionate hand to the large bird. "He'll be helping you today."

He was an unusual looking crow with one pink and one amber eye, both of which stared unblinking at them. "He looks familiar, coven-mother. I'm sure I've seen him around Wildwood." Kolfinnia regarded the impressive bird.

"There's your sharp eyes again, Kolfinnia."

Kolfinnia reddened slightly, it seemed that no amount of rotten jobs could quell her love for the old woman.

"Although he does not venture into the heart of Wildwood often. Jerrow is captain of the crow patrol, part of our most vital defence." Valonia stroked his beak lovingly. "He came this morning to report several scarecrows have toppled under heavy rains."

Kolfinnia knew what was coming next while Rowan looked like a puppy eager to fetch a stick.

"And so," Valonia went on, "I want you two to follow Jerrow out to the scarecrows, right them again, and restore any broken cloaking spells." She held out a small sack and Kolfinnia could hear bottles tinkling within.

"These are for restoring the cloaking spells?" Kolfinnia asked, taking the sack and slinging it over her shoulder.

"Quite so." Valonia appraised them both. "This is a very important task I trust you with. Collect what tools you'll need, and Jerrow will guide you. Wildwood thanks you both." She was about to leave when she turned back to them. "It'll be quicker if you both fly. I think Rowan liked it last time." She turned with a satisfied smile and made her way back up the spiral. The young witches exchanged stunned looks, before both smiled guiltily.

Jerrow launched himself from Valonia's shoulder and was airborne in a rush of feathers. He scythed low across the gardens and away.

Kolfinnia reached down, took Rowan's hand and squeezed gently. "Let's get going, little sister."

"Fed and free." She squeezed back, and smiled up at her in reply.

"Gentlemen, the Illuminata welcomes you." Krast kept his voice neutral, something he always did when he couldn't find the patience to be pleasant. He set the files on the desk at the head of the carriage and bowed discreetly to the small gathering. With him in the state carriage were four senior cabinet ministers. Four identical top-hats, looking like funnels on a steamship, sat in a neat line on a table at the rear under a painting of the queen-empress. Home secretary Stanton, defence minister Lord Partridge, science minister Barrington, and Wallace Maccrae the minister for religious affairs.

They sat in deep chairs either side of a large mahogany table. In front of each, was a small desktop microscope. All were brand new and the brass casings gleamed. The men regarded them with mild suspicion, fearing they'd be called upon to do some actual work. A rectangular object the disconcerting size of a child's coffin lay at the table's centre, concealed under heavy black velvet. Krast was pleased to see their nervous eyes continually drawn to it. "Knight Superior," they muttered in unison.

"Hathwell, if you would," Krast ordered, and Hathwell took the stack of files and began distributing them. At once Partridge began to finger the string binding. Krast thought his name was an ironic pun: he looked more like a bird of prey with his hooked nose and hunter's eyes. "Lord Partridge." He struggled to control his irritation. "The file is not to be opened, just yet." Partridge swapped irksome glances with his fellows, who sympathised with his indignity, and tossed the file back onto the table. Krast smiled flatly then pressed his hands together in front of his chest as if about to pray. "Gentlemen, I understand this meeting was scheduled for next month, but my results can't wait."

Partridge sighed, "I note from the file we're forbidden to open that our summoning relates to the first-dawn experiments?"

"Indeed. The cyclotron has been operational for some months now," Krast confirmed.

"Took long enough to build it," Stanton clasped his hands over his ample stomach. Murmurs of agreement floated around the carriage.

"Your additional funding was most generous, home secretary." Sometimes his job called for a little acting, and his gratitude was as real as his liking for these men. "As you all know," he began, "the Illuminata has experimented with knowledge confiscated from defeated covens and through it we have made many discoveries, which have benefited the empire enormously."

They nodded lethargically. It was no secret to them that the Illuminata, founded to persecute witches, had been stealing their secrets for centuries. There was little difference, other than morals, between a witch and an Illuminata Deviser: men who twisted witchcraft into weapons or curses.

"Your funding made the cyclotron possible." Krast complimented hollowly. Again, the ministers nodded dismissively. The first-dawn cyclotron was housed underneath Hobbs Ash. But so far they'd poured buckets of money down that hole and seen nothing worthy come out of it. "Our intention was to isolate the smallest particles of creation. It was hoped that by studying them, we'd better comprehend some of the more complex magical theories."

"We know all this," Maccrae interrupted.

"You have the findings for us today?" Stanton hushed his subordinate with a wave of his hand.

Krast frowned. "In short, yes. The findings that resulted in your summoning here today were an unexpected side-discovery, one we literally stumbled upon. But I must stress, what we found will both excite and disturb you." He gestured to the middle of the table where the rectangular box sat under its black shroud and an uneasy hush settled. "First-dawn succeeded in isolating the smallest particles in God's creation. We named these particles 'minutus'. But what we didn't expect to find is the reason I've called you here today." He turned to his squire. "Bertrand, if you'd be so good."

Hathwell began circling the table, fixing glass slides under each microscope with nervous hands.

"One key esoteric doctrine has eluded us," Krast continued, "but I think, no longer. We found that while studying minutus, something peculiar would happen. Something dare I say 'magical'." They all stared at him expectantly. "The minutus *changed* while being observed."

"Changed?" Stanton sat up. "How?"

"They changed their nature, as if in response to the observer's will."

"Speak plainly man!" Maccrae complained.

"Changing from an iron minutus for instance, into a lead minutus."

"Nonsense!"

Krast smiled coldly, and then annunciated his following words with great deliberation, "Matter changed by will alone."

"So," Maccrae blustered, "you changed one thing into another. Bakers turn flour into bread. Have you used the cyclotron to bake bread?" he sneered.

Krast marvelled at the man's stupidity. "Not bread," he corrected. "Gold."

Their stunned hush was quickly followed by muted gasps and a comical pantomime of swivelling heads as each man checked his neighbour to see if they'd heard correctly. "These instruments," Barrington gestured to the microscopes. "They prove your claim?"

"Please, see for yourselves," Krast invited.

They exchanged wary looks before slowly leaning over the microscopes. Krast watched impassively and after what seemed an age Barrington sat back, with his Adam's apple bobbing nervously in his throat like a stricken diver. "Dear Lord, is that what I think it is?"

"It is."

"You mean to tell me this creature was once flesh and blood, and has been *changed*, as you put it?"

Krast nodded stiffly.

"Or a clever forgery," Maccrae interrupted.

"They were all once flesh and blood, I assure you. And now they have been transmuted into gold." He had them: all he had to do was tighten the noose. "Now, shall we discuss the potential of this 'nonsense'?"

CHAPTER FIVE

A Golden Dilemma

Along the way, Rowan stopped to check her satchel and provisions again, and in catching up to Kolfinnia she automatically slipped her hand into hers. Kolfinnia gladly accepted, but she stole a worried glance at the girl, imagining a grown-up Rowan 'out there' one day too, and she shivered.

"Kol?" she enquired with a frown.

"It's nothing. Come on, Jerrow's waiting." They bid polite welcomes to the other witches they met. Captain Jerrow sat at the end of the path perched on a stump surrounded by fluffy dandelion heads. He cawed once and although Kolfinnia couldn't commune with animals as well as some, she detected impatience in his call. Once they'd caught up, he flew ahead, but never too far, bidding them follow through the tall pines. Rowan had a small spade over her shoulder while Kolfinnia carried the spell ingredients and a jar of hemlock oil to soothe insect bites, for they were going beyond the protection of the way-bewares, and of course she took her lightning-staff.

"He's grumpy, isn't he?" Rowan said from behind her cupped hand, meaning Jerrow.

"That's for sure."

"Maybe he's worried about his family?"

"What makes you think he's got young?"

"He does, he has seven chicks and they live in one of the scarecrows that's fallen down and he's worried if we don't fix it up quickly then something will come along and gobble up his babies." She sounded excited by the whole drama.

Kolfinnia was stunned. "Rowan, how can you know that? I mean, there's no way you can know that."

"But I do. I'm not lying!"

She looked hurt and Kolfinnia thought again about her mysterious talents and how little she really knew her. Ignoring Jerrow's irate calls, she cupped Rowan's shoulders and asked again, "How do you know?"

Rowan was silent.

"How? Tell me!" she pressed.

"I'm not lying!" Her lower lip began to tremble.

"I know you're not. I'm sorry, I just wondered." Shocked by how quickly Rowan saw accusation in her words, she hugged her, wondering what sort of life she'd lived before coming here. "I know you're not lying, Rowan." She held her at arm's length. "Friends?"

"Friends." Rowan offered her a weak smile that looked way too old for that of a child.

"Caaaaw!"

Jerrow startled them both from their misunderstanding. He'd landed close by and his eyes blazed, but this time Kolfinnia read a father's concern there and she had no doubt Rowan was correct. She pulled her lightning-staff from her shoulder as Jerrow flapped ahead, and in one swift move she'd awoken Gale from sleep and mounted. "It's quite a way to the scarecrows. We'd better fly, and this time we're not breaking any rules." She hoped the promise of a flight would cheer Rowan up, but she didn't smile nor fling herself at Kolfinnia this time, rather she clambered up and sat against her.

"I'm sorry." Rowan wiped her eyes.

"There's nothing to be sorry for." She wrapped her arms around her, to comfort her and steady them both. With that they set off. Crow and witches tore through the maze of fallen trunks and mossy hollows heading for the coven frontier and the scarecrow circle. Above them the overcast May sky was now the colour of slate and the first raindrops fell to earth.

Stanton scrutinised the creature under the microscope, vainly searching for any hint of forgery. The golden creature was faultless, from the tiny hairs sprouting from its exoskeleton to the individual globes on its compound eye. A flea, a perfect flea made of gold. If this was a hoax then the goldsmith at least should receive a Knighthood.

"Unfortunately the cost is high," Krast paced slowly around the room as he spoke and they were so captivated that they twisted to follow him as if bound with invisible thread, golden thread perhaps, he thought, and smiled to himself. "Transmutation requires substantial will from the deviser. Commanding just a single particle to transmute specifically is Herculean, so imagine the task of changing the countless billions in these tiny insects."

"And you think disciples of witchcraft can do this easily?" Stanton asked.

"I have seen it with my own eyes, home secretary." He gave Hathwell a meaningful look.

"Explain?"

"In battle, long ago. A coven chose to stand and fight. Hardly sporting I agree, but they fought never-the-less, and they died. But there were some amongst them who were adept at such as this."

"What happened?"

He looked at the floor. "Steel krakens became lead in the wink of an eye and fell under their own weight."

There were worried gasps at this. Krast and Hathwell exchanged weighty looks. Both of them remembered that day twenty years ago very well indeed. Solvgarad was the closest they had ever come to total defeat. The battle was a stain on their honour.

"So the coven brutes can manage with ease what your devisers cannot?" Maccrae gloated.

"Only at present," Krast retorted. For some reason he couldn't explain, witches, or at least some of them, were able to change matter with will alone. Their devisers, however, struggled to transform just a few particles. Clearly witches knew a truth they failed to grasp. He found it deeply frustrating, and their experiments so far had proved grim to say the least. They had tried to amplify the deviser's will by mechanical means, but their entire metal energy was spent in one great blast. This proved sufficient to do the job, but left them shrunken and dead. Suffice to say nobody wanted to take part in further testing, so they had turned to alternative methods.

"And the devisers who 'willed' these creatures to transmute, why did they fail?" Partridge demanded.

"They did not fail, they were harmed," Krast insisted.

"Harmed?"

"Yes, and so we developed a system where-by the deviser could work without paying the spiritual debt, so to speak," he replied, skimming over the worst details.

"But someone had to pay," Barrington said uneasily.

"That debt was settled by volunteers. Each insect you see here extracted an enormous toll on their former owners." Everyone felt an uncomfortable twinge at the word 'former'.

"And who were they?" Stanton chipped in.

"Fallen women. To know more might be inconvenient." He danced lightly over this last word.

"And what became of them?" Maccrae dabbed sweat from his brow.

"Perhaps you could ask them yourselves." He rolled his eyes deliberately towards the casket. "They are with us right now."

All heads turned to the casket as if it were some terrible magnet. "Dear Lord!" Partridge grimaced. "What? You mean to say all four of them are inside that thing?" It was far too small for that, clearly something had chewed them up and spat them out, namely the machinery Krast had eluded to.

"Fret not," Krast smiled. "The casket is airtight, and the remains are virtually desiccated. There's no risk of contamination."

"Four!" Stanton sipped his water. "But merely unfortunates you say?"

"Very unfortunate," Barrington muttered.

"I needed four specimens today." He smoothly involved them in the plot. "Ironic that each transformed a worthless parasite into something profound."

"Why on Earth would anyone partake of such?" Maccrae ventured.

"Their participation was not entirely voluntary." Krast elaborated. Did he have to spell it out, he wondered?

"Did they suffer?"

"Not at all. The process is very swift. Besides, they had a lifetime of poverty and debasement to look forward to, that surely constitutes true suffering."

He nodded vigorously, glad to have an excuse no matter how flimsy.

"So what do you want from us?" Stanton sat back in his chair, his tone now business-like.

"We have a dilemma." Krast smoothed a hand across his scalp. "What you've seen presents evidence for the heretical theory of alchemy, but there is one major drawback: first-dawn proves a cornerstone of witch-lore correct."

"I see your point," Stanton conceded. "Haven't covens always preached that thought controls matter? That it can be changed with will alone?"

"Indeed, and haven't we the Order founded to fight them, proved them correct this very day?"

The enormity of the problem loomed over them. How do you exploit an incredible discovery that you have spent centuries denying, not to mention persecuting supporters of? "If we use it, we acknowledge that the doctrine of witch-lore is correct," Maccrae thought aloud.

"And then?" Krast encouraged.

"Then we risk admitting our faith is based on deceits," Stanton finished.

You can have your gold, or you can have your God, but not both, Krast thought.

"We can't have that," Partridge growled. "The Empress would never allow it."

"If proof of alchemy leaked out there'd be a resurgence of sympathy for covens and their deities, the so called serpent-twins." Krast continued pacing, making not a sound on the plush carpet. "Before we can seize this discovery we need to turn the masses against all acts of magic no matter how petty. Once support for the old ways is crushed we can claim transmutation is a scientific law that covens had hoarded for centuries, and we've liberated it." He reached the head of the table. "Make example of anyone who shows sympathy for witchcraft."

"You're suggesting a new purge?" Stanton rumbled. "This won't be popular."

"A hard road, but afterwards all the potential of first-dawn shall be yours."

"The covens are of little note these days. Hardly anyone takes their beliefs seriously anymore. There hasn't been an insurgency in over seventy years." Partridge didn't like the idea of rocking the boat.

"We'd have covens springing up in Westminster if this discovery became known." Krast warned. "People by the thousand would be turning coppers into gold. If you were poor, wouldn't you do the same?" He looked down at his expensive shoes and pointed out what they had so obviously missed. "Besides, to power first-dawn we need more subjects, and convicted witches would suffice wonderfully. Each would be worth a thousand commoners."

The carriage remained silent but he could sense his words eroding their will. Then he added a new card to the deck. "In light of the minutus discovery, I'm now willing to entertain the idea that other witch doctrines might have a grain of truth about them. Such as the myth that there exists a great relic they revere, a power source that could fuel endless transmutations."

They all blinked at him.

"Gilded fleas from diseased whores?" he sneered. "Rather mountains of gold, tea, silk, gunpowder, rubber, cotton and rivers of oil."

"And what would this power source be?" Stanton asked casually, while under the table his hands trembled.

Krast turned to the window and regarded the wasteland that was Hobbs Ash. "You may open your files now gentlemen." He stared off into the distance where a forest of belching chimneys stained the sky.

Behind him four pairs of hands fumbled with string bindings and each man drew out a single piece of paper upon which there was a lithoprint. It showed a sphere cut in cross section. Inside were two serpent-like creatures curled tenderly around one another. Their expressions were serene and regal, their scales were shaped like the leaves of oak and holly and their horns were like branches. Hethra and Halla.

Perhaps only witches truly understand the interconnected nature of creation. Krast would have scoffed at the idea that words spoken in a carriage in London might be enough to distort the natural order of the world. But in a distant place unknown, the twins perceived his plot as faint echoes within a dream. They rolled anxiously in their sleep, sending esoteric shockwaves across the globe. For one instant, migrating birds forgot their route, bees couldn't locate their hives, ocean currents stilled and whale song fell silent. But dark dreams didn't just afflict the twins: as they suffered restless sleep, so too the mind of Ruination dreamed the strange and disturbing. Its dreams emanated outward towards Earth where they would become flesh and blood. This is how monsters are born, and few are as terrible as barghests.

The fallen scarecrows lay at the very edge of the coven where the larches thinned out. Recent storms had unsettled their footings. Four of them lay in the heather like wounded soldiers, while a parade of upright scarecrows stretched away into the distance. All of them harboured jostling crows on their outstretched limbs.

Jerrow landed on a fallen scarecrow and cawed over and over. Not far behind Kolfinnia and Rowan came racing through the trees. They glided to a halt next to Jerrow who hopped and flapped in something like a victory dance. Kolfinnia could easily see why. Crawling around in the scarecrow's belly was a nest full of helpless young. Rowan dropped to the ground and was already swinging the spade from her shoulder. "This one's Jerrow's," she said, using her eyes and not that unusual skill of hers.

Kolfinnia anchored her staff in the spongy turf and thanked Gale for his efforts. He materialised, shook himself and squatted on the staff's end. "Don't mention it," he yawned, "I was just getting warmed up." He'd turned a walk of several hours in to a flight of moments.

Kolfinnia reached for her own spade when suddenly she felt faint, the world turned monochrome and a blinding pain shot through her left temple. "Hethra's tail!" she groaned and pressed a palm to her forehead, but the stabbing pain had gone as fast as it had come.

"Kol?" Rowan looked worried.

"It's nothing. Let's be about our business." She shook the pain away and looked to the sky, which had darkened without warning, and she felt a deep sense of foreboding. *Just a passing twinge*, she told herself without conviction.

Before anything else both of them donned their cloaks. Conditions were eerily chill and from the look of things it would soon be wet as well. Gale meanwhile clearly thought his work was done because he remained crouched preening at the top of the staff, indifferent to their work. A cold wind swept through the wood behind them, over the heathery plain and onwards towards the rugged hills beyond. The trees swished in response and summer felt so very far away. Out here they were a long way from the heart of Wildwood and at the very limit of its magic. The frontier was a place of ragged scarecrows and fearsome cackling birds, and beyond it was a world of suspicion and danger. *And that's where you'll be heading in September, and I'll wager you'll be imprisoned or swinging from a gallows by October.*

"Shut up," Kolfinnia growled and pushed the voice away. Why did she go on tormenting herself like this? Instead she put her mind to the task at hand. She could just see the tip of Jerrow's tail as he burrowed into the toppled nest, attending his young, and she wasn't at all surprised to see there were seven of them. Pacing circles around them was Petra, Jerrow's lifelong mate. *Rowan does it again*, she thought then looked to where Rowan was hacking at the turf. "Don't wear yourself out. There's plenty of work to go around." Thinking she could make better time with the larger tool, she knelt and exchanged her trowel for Rowan's spade. "Here, I'll take the bigger one. You use this." The pair began hacking out a new hole as quickly as they could. A feeling of wrongness seemed to have just oozed out of the ground and Kolfinnia felt unsettled. "You managing all right?"

"Mmm." She thought Rowan was still upset over their misunderstanding, but when she finally looked up she saw that the girl wasn't just upset, she was scared. "Let's get finished quick. I don't like it here," she whispered, then lowered her head and stabbed furiously at the ground.

"Then I'll get going on one of the other ones and we'll finish quicker." She was about to stand when Rowan dropped her spade and clutched her dress.

"No!" She shook her head furiously. "Don't, we have to stay together, we'll work together. I didn't mean to be rude to you before. Just don't leave, please!"

Her self-blame touched Kolfinnia's heart. "Nobody's going to leave you." She tried to sound relaxed, but instincts told her something was wrong here, something far worse than toppled scarecrows. She didn't know how deep Rowan's skills ran, she wasn't even sure just what kind of skills the girl had, but she hoped that whatever had unnerved her was just the feeling of being at the magical frontier and nothing else. *What if she senses something you can't? A sheriff's patrol 'out there', looking to burn a witch or two?* She didn't know if the thought was hers or not, but it gave her a shiver and suddenly she had the horrible sensation of being watched. It was so tangible that she wanted to scrub at the back of her neck where she felt hostile eyes crawl across her skin like grab-hooks. Just then thunder rolled far away, sounding like an argument in a distant room, but when it faded she heard something far more disturbing.

A low growling noise made the air freeze in her lungs. She spun around alert for danger, and without thinking she'd drawn her wand. The army of crows had fallen silent, leaving the world filled only by that horrible growling. And when she saw who was making it, fear goose-fleshed her whole body. It was Gale. He'd arched into a gruesome shape like a frightened cat. His wings flared out stiffly and his head was twisted to one side. He was facing east where an anvil of black cloud spewed miles into the sky. "Gale?" she whispered, hardly knowing him. "Gale?"

Rowan clutched the trowel to her chest. "Why's he doing that?"

"Gale!" She stepped towards him. He neither sounded nor looked anything like her beloved sprite. "Gale, what's wrong? Stop that at once!" The growling ripped through her like a saw.

"Not my storm!" he growled, staring eastwards at the looming black cloud. "Not my storm!"

"Gale, sto –,"

Suddenly, something pressed against Kolfinnia's hip and clung like a limpet. "He sees them!" Rowan cried, "He sees them coming!"

"Gale, what do you see?" Kolfinnia grabbed her staff, only to find with horrified amazement that it was as cold as iron in January. "Gale!" she screamed. "Stop this and answer me!"

"Gale sees them!" Rowan howled. "They're coming because those men want to hunt Hethra and Halla! And the twins' fear has let them through. We have to go, please Kol we have to go before the barghests of Ruin come!"

Thunder roared and the world darkened as the storm raced their way and Kolfinnia knew that if she didn't take action something terrible would find them. She stopped thinking and just reacted.

She snatched Gale from the staff, expecting him to hiss and scratch, but he just stopped growling and fell into her arms, limp and dazed. Still clutching him, she hauled Rowan to her side and threw her cloak over them, and in the darkness of their little huddle began a basic witch's chant. "Oak and Holly bless and protect us, Oak and Holly bless and protect us, Oak and Holly bless and protect us."

Over and over, the words poured from her mouth and then Rowan's trembling voice joined in while Gale lay stunned in the crook of her arm. On and on she repeated the spell, forcing the storm to leave them in peace, trying to push it away. Each word was a brick, building a wall to keep out whatever horror approached, but terrible images seeped between those bricks like messages from another realm.

She saw lifeless butterflies pinned in boxes, shameful rooms sealed and forgotten, gasping fish in shrinking pools and an ocean of tears deep enough to drown all hope. She knew without doubt that Ruination was with them. "Oak and Holly bless and protect us," she chanted on and on. Outside their huddle, Ruination swept over them, looking for a weak point to enter this world.

You long for a grave at Wildwood with your name upon it? Then why live further Kolfinnia Algra? Give in now and embrace oblivion. Let the worms slither through your hollow bones, swim in your putrefying eyes and choke the once great canals of your silent heart . . . Time kills everything. Why resist?

The words might have sprung from her mind, or another mind all together. But their most terrible aspect was their allure. *Fight it Kolfinnia, fight it!* she urged herself.

Embrace oblivion, worship futility, a mind insisted, but was it hers?

"Oak and Holly bless and protect us," she continued desperately. She expected the world to fill with torrential rain and savage thunder and she cringed briefly when thunder did roll again, but now it sounded further away. "Don't stop the spell Rowan," she whispered.

She peeled back her cloak as Rowan continued to chant, scattering tiny rain droplets, and saw a wholly different world. It was just the frontier again, bleak and lonely perhaps, but the atmosphere of doom had gone. One by one the crows began their calls again, shouting to one another as though nothing had happened, but Kolfinnia was awed by the sight of the monstrous storm that boiled eastwards. Lightning flickered in eerie silence at its black heart. The storm, or whatever it was, had changed direction. "Rowan, the spell sent the storm away."

Rowan twisted her head to look and flinched when she caught sight of the blackness. It looked like the shadow of some enormous bull that had charged them and missed by a whisker. "It's gone?" She sniffed and brushed wet hair from her face.

"Gone, now help me. I think Gale's injured, we may have to walk home and there are still the scarecrows to put right."

Something inside Rowan seemed to connect and she sprang up and made for the spade. "Soonest begun is soonest done," she sang nervously, like a little spell of her own.

Gale began to move sluggishly in Kolfinnia's arms and his stunned expression melted away. "Kol?" He croaked and she immediately hugged him before setting him back at the tip of the lightning-staff, where he clung weakly. "That wasn't one of my storms." He sounded apologetic. "It wasn't natural," he gasped.

"I was so worried, I didn't recognise you."

He barked a small laugh. "Fuss me later. Let's get done here and report back. I've never felt anything like that before."

There came another distant peal of thunder and all three looked eastwards to where a dark column of rain funnelled downwards like a tightening screw.

"That's where the storm went." Rowan clutched the oak leaf pendant around her neck.

Kolfinnia shivered to think that it might have broken right on top of them.

"Get going," Gale ordered. "I'm fine."

"I've never seen you like that before."

"I'm fine, I said. Now get going!"

She nodded and went to join Rowan who was already hard at work digging. Blades of grass threaded her hair and her tunic was muddied. "We get done and we get back. While you dig I'll repair the broken spells, does that sound good to you?"

"Yes. I really like the bit about getting back."

Kolfinnia assembled the spells and concentrated as best she could, but her hands shook and her eyes often strayed eastwards to where the last of the storm was devouring itself. "When Gale's had chance to rest I'll ask him to take us home at top speed." She leaned forward, "He's taken quite a liking to you."

"Has he?" Rowan blushed behind the muddy streaks and Kolfinnia felt a blissful moment of normality. Jerrow landed and hopped towards them, and helped by tying knots in the new spell bags with his nimble beak.

"Soonest begun is soonest done." Rowan continued to hum her little rhyme and one by one the new posts were dug and set, but when Rowan wasn't looking her way Kolfinnia cast wondering and even admiring glances at her.

'Those men hunt Hethra and Halla.' That's what she'd said. How could she even wildly guess at something like that? Just what kind of special little witch are you? Kolfinnia had never needed to speak to Valonia as badly as she did just then.

Gale assured them he was fighting fit and he carried them away to the clamour of squabbling crows.

"We're going the wrong way!" Rowan called over her shoulder.

"Just a short side trip, I promise," she shouted back.

Rowan looked alarmed. "I thought we were going straight back?"

"Just a couple of miles to where we saw that storm break, then home."

"But why?"

"Duty!" Kolfinnia grimaced as they dodged a bristling pine trunk. "We take a look then report back." It wasn't easy talking and flying at the same time.

"But I don't want to!"

"We've no choice!" she barked, and to her shame the girl cowered and fell silent.

They slalomed around mossy tree stumps, thrust through the ground like fangs, and streaked between trunks cleaved by forgotten storms. Rowan marvelled at the blurred ground tearing past only feet below. The girls whipped through crowns of wet grass, which splashed droplets across them in a sparkling shower, and as they raced through the pines sunlight pierced the leaden skies, making summery islands on the forest floor. Sunlight never had felt so welcome and Rowan was just beginning to enjoy the ride when she saw it.

Several hundred yards to their left in one of those sunlit oases was a column of glittering colours moving and swirling like a tornado. The mysterious object leaned and lurched as it spiralled up from the forest floor in a funnel almost as high as the trees. "Kol! Look at that. You see it?" Rowan cried.

"Of course. Hold on!" she called and turned them towards it.

Rowan expected them to accelerate but instead Kolfinnia slowed, then came to a complete halt where she dropped expertly to her feet, pulling Rowan with her. "What are we stopping here fo –," Rowan didn't finish. Instead, Kolfinnia barred her mouth with her fingers.

"Shhhh!" she hissed, "not a sound."

Rowan felt that feeling of dread catch them up, as though it had a lightning-staff of its own. Kolfinnia led her gently by the wrist and brought them both through the undergrowth to crouch behind a twisted old pine. She leaned out to get a better look. "What is it?" Rowan whispered.

"Not sure," she replied distractedly, "but I know what I feel and I feel something of Ruin, something bad. Can you?"

"Kol, can't we just go home? It's scary."

"Not yet. What happens here affects all of Wildwood. We can't go back and say we ran off." She looked down at Rowan knowing that her sense of duty might cost them dearly. *Please don't let her cry again.* It was a mean-spirited thought and she regretted it instantly. "Now stay here, I'm going to –,"

"Look! Kol, I can see your breath like it's winter!" Rowan was staring at her in shock, as though she'd cursed.

Kolfinnia blew into the air, creating a misty vapour. The temperature was dropping and now she felt the tiny hairs along her arm rise up. She risked another look and saw the funnel's apex had touched down in a tangle of foxgloves. She could see something injured but alive crawling through them in pointless circles.

"Something's hurt there," Rowan peeped from under the crook of Kolfinnia's arm. The strange thing in the foxgloves was no bigger than a goose, but from this distance all they could make out was that it had dark fur. "Butterflies!" Rowan gasped suddenly.

"Butterflies?" Kolfinnia frowned, then saw what she meant. The strange shifting tower comprised thousands of butterflies. Species far and wide had gathered and were circling above the wounded creature in the foxgloves.

"Lots of butterflies!" Rowan, lost in the spectacle, made to run to them until Kolfinnia pulled her back, making her squeak in annoyance. "Kol, stop, don't!"

"QUIET!" Kolfinnia's voice boomed in her head, but she hadn't even opened her mouth.

Rowan's wonderstruck expression melted. "How did you speak without speaking?" she whispered fearfully.

"I'll explain later. Just be still," she said more softly. "It's not the butterflies I'm wary of. Can't you feel that same sense of wrongness as at the scarecrows?"

"A bit, yes."

"You spoke of barghests back there, Rowan."

"I don't remember," she said truthfully. "Anyway, I don't even know what they are." She hoped that simply not knowing what a barghest was meant that they wouldn't meet any.

Just as Kolfinnia was about to say, *"And let's hope you never know"*, she saw one.

A black hound as large as a horse skulked into the clearing from the darkness under a fallen tree and began stalking towards the foxgloves, where something precious was desperately trying to hide. The barghest was smoky and insubstantial and its clawed feet drifted inches above the ground without actually touching down. It looked like a living ink smudge and flowed with sickly ease through the undergrowth. It was so completely black that Kolfinnia felt a hole had opened in the universe and through it began to pour horrible dreams: an unanswered cry for help, the lone egg in the clutch left to go cold, musicians with crippled hands. There was no doubt, it was a creature of Ruination, a barghest, and it had no rightful place on Earth. *You were right again Rowan*, she thought with sinking dread. *You're always right.*

It was colder now and although they were too far away to see, the grass beneath the barghest withered and froze dead in a rime of hoarfrost.

"I want to go home!" Rowan whimpered.

"Oak and holly! No, it can't be!" Kolfinnia moaned, but it was inevitable. 'Barghests' she had said – plural.

From the west came two more, silent as winter stars, and now the pack began to circle the butterflies, creeping and gliding through the trees, tightening their loops until confident the kill was theirs. Unaware that her hand was moving Kolfinnia gripped the Vega amulet Rowan had made her. "They're protecting it," she understood. "The butterflies are trying to protect whatever's lying on the ground." She spoke as if Rowan wasn't even there and in an instant her temper grew wrathful. "We can't allow this!" she snarled and before she even knew it she'd drawn her wand.

"Kolfinnia!" Rowan pleaded, but she saw a darkness in her that she'd never seen before, and for a moment she was afraid of her.

"Stay here! I'll come back when it's done." She flattened Rowan into the bracken with a strong hand and snatched up her staff.

"Do I smell a fight?" Gale growled from within.

"You do. Three barghests against the two of us."

Rowan only caught one half of their conversation and she was about to beg her to stay when the older girl broke cover and bolted. She ran the first ten yards and then mounted her staff, screaming in defiance with her wand held like a sword.

"Kol!" Rowan saw her only friend plunge into a fight against the unknown and did the only thing she could think of. She drew her own wand, screamed her own unpractised war cry and charged after her.

Kolfinnia charged with no plan other than the rage of injustice. She hurtled into the largest barghest, the pack leader they'd seen first, dropping from her staff and screaming. She fell upon it like a sparrow charging a bear, wielding her lightning-staff, aiming for the creature's head. What the other two were doing she had no idea or even cared. Her senses had been dashed from her head by anger. Gale answered her cry, spitting lighting that flamed along the staff, but the barghest was faster than either could have guessed and it swirled away easily like fog before reforming a yard to her left and lunging at her.

"Left side!" Gale roared.

She twisted around, but not fast enough. Its jaws clamped around her wrist and she felt the burn of frostbite and watched her arm and wand sink into the creature's mouth like a pool of ink. Horrible images flooded her mind again. Sharpened hooks, open graves and broken promises and she thought she'd choke with the grief and horror. Instead she shrieked and stabbed her staff downwards through its head in a brutal blow, giving Gale just the chance he needed. He unleashed his fury and the barghest flashed neon blue, illuminating alien organs and bizarre bones. *"Let go, you bastard!"* he raged.

It jerked in agony, released her wrist and streaked away through the trees. She steadied herself, but her arm dripped foul ooze and felt numb. She turned and saw the creature's pack mates bounding across the glade towards her silhouetted against a curtain of swarming butterflies. "Hethra and Halla defend my purpose and I deny your hunt!" she screamed and held the trembling wand at arm's length and raised her staff high.

"You're weakening. We should take our chance and go!" Gale rumbled.

"No, they'll catch us, we have to make a stand here!" In readiness she called a channelling spell that might just magnify the sunlight enough to burn the creatures away. It was her last option, but she held little hope for it.

The barghests halted. Kolfinnia felt the whole world teeter on a pivot as they quivered with indecision. They had seen their alpha injured. Now would they charge or run? In the next instant she had her answer. They flattened their horned ears to their faceless heads and she knew attack was imminent. "Lord Oak, no!" she despaired. They burst into a terrifying charge and despite her defiant words she knew she wasn't strong enough to repel them. *I'm sorry Rowan, sorry I ever brought you here*, she thought and prepared herself for whatever might come next.

What came next was Rowan Barefoot screaming through the bracken, crashing to her side in a shower of leaves and soil, her small wand and short spade raised with a child's heartfelt belief that they might somehow defend them. But she needed neither. "KATHKAR! GARACH! ULVERVALK!" She screamed the barghest's names in hoarse succession and the two charging hounds and their skulking leader instantly vanished as if swept away by a hurricane, leaving only dark haloes in the frigid air.

Kolfinnia spun around and a shower of frost crystals snowed down from her dress. "You *named* them!" She was incredulous.

"Where did they go?" Rowan stood panting clouds of freezing breath. "You named them!"

"I don't remember, I don't care, I just want to go home!" she stammered.

"Kol we have to be gone!" Gale insisted, but she seemed not to hear him, she was staggered by Rowan's feat.

"But Rowan, you *named* them! How's that possible?" How indeed? Creatures of Ruination guarded their names so jealously that over time even they forgot them, but this was mysterious little Rowan. They were alive, that was all that mattered for now.

"Your arm, Kol. The horrid thing bit your arm!" She ignored her question, dropped the spade and gingerly touched her wounded wrist. Her sleeve was ragged and the flesh there was grey and frostbitten, but the skin was unbroken.

"I'll be fine, Rowan," she said with more certainty than she felt and gently pulled her close. "You saved all of us."

Rowan nuzzled her teary face against her muddy dress. "I thought you were going to die."

"We would have if not for you." She'd never been more sincere.

A butterfly landed on the brim of Rowan's hat. First a peacock, followed by a small copper, then an orange-tip, then a host of them flocked around them like living jewels, and the flutter of their wings seemed to sweep away the lingering poisons left in the barghests' wake. Other guardians had come too. Kolfinnia heard the buzz of innumerable bees as butterflies caressed her face and breezed through her tangled hair. "They're departing, Rowan. I think they sense the danger's passed." She tactfully pried herself free of Rowan's bear hug.

"So why did they come, what were they looking after?" She dried her face.

She straightened Rowan's crumpled hat and smiled. "Let's go see who we risked our lives to help, shall we?" They walked through the butterflies to the secret hiding in the foxgloves, but before they got there they were in for another surprise.

Rowan saw it first. "Kol, what's that?" she drew close, afraid once more.

Kolfinnia halted. "In all my days," she uttered.

Lingering by the foxgloves was a winged creature as large as a thrush, but with arms and legs.

"A fairy." Kolfinnia stopped still, "A real fairy." A moment later it saw them and simply vanished.

"Where did it go?" Rowan's mouth was as wide as her eyes.

Kolfinnia barely heard her. Fairies never appeared to strangers. This was worse than she first thought. "We'll worry about that later. Now come on, help me pull them aside." She crouched by the foxgloves and got to work, and although she didn't wince or complain, Rowan saw how she guarded her injured arm. Something had burrowed deep, driven by dread, and when they dragged the broken stalks apart both of them heard a deep rumbling buzz. Rowan gasped and took a step back.

"Kol?" she called warily. "Is that a fairy again?"

"I doubt it, don't fret," she gently parted the woody stems and peered inside. "Oh! Rowan!" she gasped, and pain was chased from her face by wonder. "It can't be!"

"What! What is it?"

"Oh, but Hethra's horns! Rowan it really is! No wonder the fairy was here."

Rowan stood with her hands clasped to her chest, her mouth agape. "Can't be what? What is it?"

Before reaching into the hollow she uttered a brief spell, promising they meant no harm. "Blessed be, Regal Lady. We ask you to accompany us, your servants, in good faith." Then she cast Rowan a worried glance before crawling into the thicket. Awkwardly, but tenderly, she slid her arms under their charge and shuffled backwards into the sunlight and drifting butterflies. When she emerged Rowan saw that she was cradling a bumblebee of gigantic size, as big as a full-grown swan. "This is Lilain," Kolfinnia said reverentially, "the hive-empress."

Rowan was still young in witch-lore and didn't grasp the enormity of their discovery, but she was quick to act and she pulled her cloak free and went to wrap Lilain in it. For such a large creature the hive-empress was remarkably light, but weak. Her legs worked feeble circles and every so often her stubby wings rattled a drowsy buzz. "Poor thing's soaking wet." Rowan was appalled.

"The storm brought her down." Kolfinnia looked to the sky through a web of branches as if seeking an answer.

"Did the storm bring the dog monsters as well?" Rowan asked while tying the cords on her cloak into a carrier for Lilain.

"I don't know, but what I do know is that we have to speak with Valonia." She wasn't even aware that she'd dropped Valonia's title. She was wounded and exhausted, but worst of all she was offended. How had Lilain been forced to earth and fallen prey to barghests? She would have felt the same shock at seeing Valonia naked and deranged. Something had reached up and shaken the foundations of her world.

"Something's very wrong here," Gale cautioned her.

"I know," Kolfinnia agreed, "I know.

CHAPTER SIX

Wildwood's Regal Guest

Valonia heard distant thunder and turned to the window. The sky was an innocent blue but for some strange reason the name 'first-dawn' fluttered through her mind and she felt a tremor, as though something huge but remote had flinched.

"Valonia?" The voice was mellow and soothing. She turned to Lana, sat on the floor beside her.

"Nothing, Lana," she shook her head briefly. "I just didn't feel that it was thunder weather, that's all." Her gaze lingered on the window a moment longer. *A storm's happening somewhere*, she thought uneasily and absently scratched Hercules's ear. The old hare lay in her lap utterly content.

"It's almost June, the weather warms," Lana replied as way of explanation.

"I suppose," she agreed uneasily. Valonia was sitting with her Wards, her most trusted witches and closest friends. All four sat on pillows occupying their appropriate compass point. Valonia sat at the north as was fitting for Moon-Frost. It wasn't a rule, it was just something they all felt comfortable with.

Next to her was Lana Zuri, the junior-most of them at a youthful fifty-one. As Snow-Thaw's Ward she wore green for spring and sat to the east. Her dress was a multitude of greens, but this wasn't deliberate, it was just that over the years it had been patched so often. Where her dress wasn't patched it was decorated with bright geometric shapes. She wore her hair in long dreadlocks that age had barely begun to grey and her cheeks were decorated with witch tattoos. The symbols sat against her dark skin and seemed to radiate wisdom. She blew a mist of smoke from the pipe before passing it to Swanhilda on her right. "Don't worry about the two of them, they'll be fine," Lana assured her as the scent of sage-brush began to fill the tree-house.

"You've been pushing Kolfinnia hard." Swanhilda, or Hilda as most knew her, graciously took the pipe from Lana.

Valonia smiled. "You think she's not up to it?"

"Oh I know she's up to it, I just don't know if she knows it yet." She took a delicate draw on the pipe, which was so typical of the elegant Hilda Saxon, Ward of Flower-Forth. For a woman in her mid-fifties Hilda was strikingly handsome. She was tall, and her dark hair fell almost to her ankles. Her skill with needle and thread was superb and her dress and even her canvas boots were richly embroidered with flowers. Hilda regarded the pipe thoughtfully. "I'm so pleased they found one another. Rowan gave me cause for concern." She passed the pipe to Esta, the fourth and last of their group.

"I'll second that, *and* she's one of mine," Esta agreed. "Rowan's come to life. I had real worries about that lass." Esta Salt, Ward of Seed-Fall, sat to the west, the direction of autumn. She accepted the pipe with a polite nod. "Thank's Hilly," she said in her rounded northern dialect. Esta had a shrewd but kindly face and at sprightly sixty-eight was second senior-most after Valonia. She was a diminutive woman and wore a long tatty coat the colour of autumn leaves, beneath which she wore a robe covered in darned patches like scars. Esta favoured short trousers, and her lower legs were bare come summer or winter. Her hair was cropped short, but a grey plait threaded with oak leaves hung down her back. All four wore wand-sheaths, and charms around their necks or about their clothing.

"It wasn't planned," Valonia conceded. "I just needed someone with a good memory and Rowan seemed perfect."

"Coincidence," Esta winked.

"Ah! The language of the universe." Valonia smiled and took the pipe from Esta. Hercules stirred and slithered from her lap before scratching his ear with an arthritic leg. "So Lana, what news from the gathering?" She pressed a thumb into the pipe, firming down the sage-brush that smouldered there.

Lana considered. "Well, you'll be glad to know that rumours of a wraith haunting Gisburn Forest proved false, thank Oak. And we helped Rook-Bill coven trace the cause of that river contamination, as you asked."

Valonia murmured approvingly. Journeys beyond Wildwood to gather news and ingredients were casually known as 'gatherings'. Midwifery was another reason to go. It allowed them to locate newborn with strong witch-skills and fostered good relations with the poor, many of whom still clung to the old ways. And a successful delivery sometimes brought tokens of gratitude. Lana and her small party of novices had just returned from such a trip. "And your witches?" Valonia enquired.

"They kept a low profile and a level head."

"Any trouble with the authorities?"

At this she looked grave. "By sheer bad luck we arrived in Tippington as a man was being executed outside the court house."

"God-oak!" Hilda hissed.

"Don't know who the poor wretch was," she went on, "but I got the others away before they sensed his death-agonies. Later that night we had a conclave about what we'd seen: to expel the bad energies."

"Rightly so," Valonia agreed sadly, gazing down at her hands, which lay between her crossed legs. The others knew she was choosing her words and waited respectfully. She drew a long breath. "And this portent I asked you to look out for, did you see any trace of it?"

"I kept a keen eye," Lana reported. "But none of the witches I met could tell me anything of this 'first-dawn'. It was just as mysterious to them as it is you." The pipe returned her way and she clasped it between strong teeth and took a long puff before continuing. "But I learned something worrisome. I met a lone witch who'd recently passed through London and even ventured to Goldhawk Row."

"Oak and holly," Esta muttered fearfully.

"He loitered nearby, posing as a beggar." She smiled in admiration as she spoke. "Constables moved him on, but before they did he overheard talk concerning Hobbs Ash."

"Our old friends are up to something," Valonia concluded.

"I'm sure of it," Lana agreed. "I thought they just housed war machines at Hobbs, but my intuition tells me it's now the venue for far more sinister happenings."

As Valonia considered, she heard more distant thunder. "Strange thunder and bad news in one day," she brooded.

"Do you think first-dawn is connected with Hobbs?" Hilda asked.

"Even if it is, Hobbs is so well defended it'd take some serious digging to find out." Valonia rubbed her chin, readying to ask something she had been considering for months, since first-dawn had started to haunt her waking hours. "I want to ask your permission for a dangerous undertaking." Three staunch faces stared back, ready to do their duty. "I need answers about first-dawn, what it might be and who's behind it, and I can't see any other way of getting them." She gave her head a decisive shake as if to be totally certain of her next words. "I wish to seek the Hand-of-Fate."

The women froze, and the canopy above stilled.

Esta cleared her throat and elected to answer for all of them. "I think I speak for everyone when I say that you've our blessing and we'll accompany you to find it." She reached out, clasped Valonia's hand and gave it a firm squeeze. "They say the Hand knows all. We'll find our answers, Val." *If we're brave enough and if we return alive*, she thought.

"Thank you," Valonia sighed. "Thanks be to all of you. I'll make the preparations and we'll set out after the next new moon, agreed?"

"Agreed," they echoed in unison.

She closed her eyes and let out a long breath and with it went a great deal of tension. "Now!" she beamed, as if they'd not spoken of the creature witches feared most. "Lana, what other news from outside? And make it good news this time."

They talked for some time. Gossip and laughter floated around them like smoke from the circling pipe. There was fresh tea and fruit bread, and Lana thrilled them by providing sugar-ginger. The talk turned from coven matters to chatter between friends and Valonia felt better than she had all month.

"How much did you pay for the ginger?" Esta looked up from her third cup of tea.

"It was a gift for delivering a baby boy in Shilwell," Lana replied.

"A witch boy?" Valonia raised her eyebrows.

"The little 'un doesn't have any natural witch talents, but who knows in time? Anyhow, he had all the right bits in all the right places so everyone was happy." The others chuckled. "They also gave me a shilling, but I've spent it, I'm afraid."

"A whole shilling on yourself. Where's your sense of charity?" Valonia joked. "So what did the shilling get spent on?"

"Bloomers, of course," Lana smiled. "When Rooter's run off with your last pair they get to be something of a luxury."

Esta managed to look impressed and disgusted at the same time, "Rooter's taken to stealing bloomers?"

"Not by choice. He pulled down my washing line and got them wrapped around his snout. When I went out to grab them he galloped off into the woods, and they were my best pair."

Valonia shook with laughter. "They'll be eaten now for sure!"

"Aye, either that or he'll be wearing 'em!" Esta cackled.

Lana and Hilda, the more refined, exchanged exasperated looks while Esta and Valonia swapped ribald jokes about pigs and bloomers. All in all it was business as usual in the tower.

Valonia delighted in laughter because it was precious, but like all precious things it could be vulnerable. It was Skald that heard it first and his shout killed the room's joyous mood. "Valonia! Someone approaches!" he warned, and the footsteps on the spiral outside finally registered in her ears.

Damn to getting old! she cursed, feeling that she'd been caught off-guard. The thunder and the tremor she'd felt: something was wrong. Even before they could scramble up there was a hammering at the door.

"Coven-mother, are you in? Coven-mother." Then louder, "Valonia!" It was Kolfinnia and she sounded desperate.

Valonia almost tore the door from its frame and a battered Kolfinnia stumbled through, still clutching her lightning-staff, followed by Rowan who carried a bundled cloak. "Help me!" Valonia ordered, and Kolfinnia found herself instantly surrounded and eased gently to the floor where she sat slumped against Hilda.

Rowan pressed through them and slid an arm protectively around her friend. Both of them were filthy and exhausted. "It's her arm!" Rowan sobbed. "She's been bitten!"

"It's not so bad, I swear," Kolfinnia lied, but her arm was swollen and black from wrist to elbow.

"Rowan, make room," Valonia snapped. *That storm*, she thought guiltily. *That storm had a hand in this and I should've gone out after them.*

"She needs medicine right now." Lana was already up and hurrying away and Kolfinnia heard the spiral creaking as she charged down it to fetch her kit.

"Esta, the door." Valonia jabbed her head towards the open door; she wanted the drama contained in here for now. Then she cupped Kolfinnia's face in her warm hands. "Lana's gone for medicines. You're safe now my girl. Tell us all that's happened."

"We went to the frontier as you asked," Kolfinnia swallowed, hardly able to believe she and Rowan had set off so carefree, hand in hand. "There was a storm, but not a natural one. We went to see," she took a deep breath, "and found a pack of barghests."

Gale silently appeared from the staff still clutched vice-like in Kolfinnia's hands, and sat by her side. Valonia could barely credit what she was hearing and she glowered at Gale, almost accusingly, but he acknowledged her account with a solemn nod.

"A pack!" Esta echoed and lay a comforting hand on Rowan's shoulder.

"That's not all we found," Rowan gently lifted the bundle for them to see.

The door clattered and Hilda shuffled over to make room for Lana.

"We also found Her Highness, and a fairy was guarding her!" Rowan began to peel back the cloak.

Valonia was in no mood for childish stories, but as Rowan pulled the ragged cloak open, they all saw the miracle nestling inside and total hush fell upon the tower. Without a word Valonia and her Wards knelt in a rustle of dresses and bowed, while at their centre sat two muddy girls cradling an empress.

May had passed and June was proving to be hot. Barnabas Cobb mopped his brow while examining the small bottle. He gave it a gentle shake and watched the tiny spell-doll inside spin with the swirling fluid. Flecks of dried herbs whirled like snowflakes.

All workhouses were obliged to employ at least one medical officer, and doctor Barnabas Cobb was the only such officer at Marylebone workhouse. One doctor, three hundred inmates and an almost empty medicine cabinet. "Add two drops of this tincture to water, or tea, everyday." He showed the potion to the elderly man who sneered at the mention of tea.

"Sir," he rumbled through his wiry, tobacco-stained beard. George Gorple had been a butcher until his addiction to gambling and drink had wrecked his livelihood.

Cobb pitied people like him, but he tried to keep a professional distance. His wife Eliza, on the other hand, was touched by their plight and insisted her husband, who was frequently short of medicines, use her potions instead. And when she insisted he knew it was wiser to agree. She was a good woman but a stubborn wife.

At first he'd used Eliza's potions to pacify her but he soon saw that they clearly worked. Although he had complete faith in orthodox medicine, nothing worked nearly as well as her homemade remedies, no matter how bad they tasted. He scoffed at the idea that she dabbled with what some might call 'witchcraft'. The notion of Eliza being a witch was offensive gibberish. He, like many others, still thought witchcraft was the realm of 'broomsticks and bats', and having never seen Eliza ride a broomstick it was therefore impossible for her to be a witch. She was just a charitable woman with a knack for traditional remedies: it was as simple as that. But just in case, they never spoke openly about it. He'd heard of people still being tried for witchcraft. With that thought in mind he chose his words carefully. "Be sure not to mention this to the taskmaster." He shook the bottle gently to make his point. "If he sees your hands are better you'll have more rocks to break, eh?"

Gorple managed a surly nod, but didn't smile back, then he took the bottle, reaching out with a pincer-like hand. He suffered from iron-knot, a disease that ravaged the joints and now his hands were clawed and swollen. As soon as he took the bottle he glanced towards the door, as if he was waiting for something.

"Gorple? Was that all? I have other patients to see." He looked to where Gorple stared intently at the doorway. *Maybe the man's wits are as useless as his hands?* he thought. The glass was cloudy with grime but Cobb could see someone lurking outside. "Mr Gor –," he began, but the old man cut him off.

"It's done, it's done!" He yelled, and a bead of saliva jetted from his mouth and glistened on his scruffy beard.

The door was instantly thrown open and a tall man wearing a bowler and a dark overcoat marched in flanked by two constables. At once the room felt very small and Cobb shrank back into his chair. The tall man in the bowler took a notebook from his overcoat and read from it. "Barnabas Joseph Cobb?"

"Can I help you gentlemen?" he asked frostily. He noted that Gorple was edging his way to the door. "Identify yourselves!" he demanded.

"I am senior correctional Baxter. Are you, or are you not, Barnabas Joseph Cobb?" the tall man demanded without looking up from his notes.

"Yes," he said cautiously, "I am he, medical officer to Marylebone workhouse."

Gorple and Baxter exchanged a decisive nod which Cobb didn't like one bit. They looked like farmers agreeing on the price of a cow. Gorple passed the illegal remedy to Baxter who held it in gloved hands, regarding it with distaste, then stared at the doctor with something like contempt.

Cobb was growing ever more anxious. "Excuse me gentlemen, but I must insist that –," But for the second time in as many minutes he was silenced.

"Barnabas Joseph Cobb." Baxter snapped his notebook closed. "The Illuminata arrests you for supplying potions contrary to the 1842 Control of Curses Act." The instant he finished the constables stepped forward and hauled him out of his seat, rough enough to send his spectacles clattering to the floor.

"This is a jest, surely?" Cobb protested, but when neither relinquished their grip he began to struggle. "This is utter madness! Unhand me this instant. I am the medical officer of this establishment and I demand you unhand me!" He felt his feet leave the floor, and saw the doorway loom closer as he was bundled towards it. "Let go of me!" he roared. "I've never heard of this Curses Act, put me down!" His mind turned cartwheels, but no answers followed. *Did Eliza know all about this? If so, why'd she never told him? Just who in God's name were the Illuminata?*

Gorple stood looking down at his feet. The last he saw of Cobb were the man's shoes thrashing across the dirty floor. The doctor's angry shouts became pleadings, then sobbing, then faded and finally vanished altogether.

"The Illuminata thanks you for your assistance." Baxter held out a shilling and dropped it into Gorple's expectant palm.

"Thanks be to you, too, kind sir," he mumbled greasily.

"I'm afraid I'll be needing this for evidence." He gave the bottle a shake. "I'm sure you wouldn't be so foolish as to use such a potion. It could be quite serious for you."

"Naw," he rasped, misunderstanding the threat. "I dunt trust witch brews and such like."

"Indeed," Baxter agreed pleasantly before making the bottle vanish into his overcoat. Then he tipped a finger to his bowler in farewell and marched from the room.

It was dark inside the hood and all she could smell was sweat and rotten canvas. They'd secured the bag around her neck, making it painful to swallow, and stuffed her ears up with cotton wool and wax. The only sound she could hear now was the river of blood in her own skull.

Eliza Cobb felt that she'd been tied to this chair for hours and she had the cramps so bad that she didn't think she could move even if she was untied. They'd come for her this morning, breaking down her door and hauling her away hooded and bound. She was cold. They'd taken her clothes and left her with nothing but a dirty gown that didn't even reach her knees. She gritted her teeth, determined not to sob; they wouldn't get that satisfaction from her. Someone was in the room with her. She could hear snatches of conversation rumble beyond the cotton wool and tiny vibrations tremble through the chair as they paced back and forth. There came the distinct thud of a door being opened and closed but it sounded like an event on the other side of the world. A new voice silenced the others. This one was barely audible. *Whatever's going to happen it's going to happen now.* She tried to gather her wits before they scattered like clouds before a hurricane. *Stay calm, Eliza. Remember, you're a witch*, she told herself.

The thumping grew closer and suddenly rough hands grabbed her head, the binding around her neck loosened and the canvas hood was drawn up like a curtain, scraping her nose and chin as it went. She screwed her eyes shut against a sudden blaze of light. The wadding was pulled from her ears and noises rushed in making the world a large place once more and then, clenching her jaw, she looked up to face her captors.

Before anything else she saw a tall man standing in front of her, regarding her intently. The room looked like the inside of a railway carriage, but the seats were missing, the windows were boarded and lanterns cast a yellow light and gave off a faint hint of sulphur. Despite her fear, Eliza was fascinated by the man's face. It was lean and stained by a topographic map of gold patches resembling continents on a globe. Pale eyes stared out from strangely darkened sockets. He was well dressed in an olive-black suit. *I know how you got those scars*, she thought incredulously, and instantly felt a fierce satisfaction. At some point in this man's past a witch had attacked him. She couldn't find it in her heart to pity a man that was likely going to kill her and so she naturally felt glad that he'd been scarred.

If Eliza had lived the coven life and not practised alone she might have seen the marks on Krast's face for what they really were. But she didn't, and all she knew for sure was that they were the vestige of an encounter with one very angry witch. Something in his expression faltered for a second and she recognised that he hated her and all her kind. She also saw why. It was there in his aura.

"Eliza Mary Cobb." His tone was frigid. "The Illuminata formally charges you with the brewing and passing of potions, practising witchcraft and possession and worship of pagan idols." Now that Westminster had the scent of gold, the hunt for Hethra and Halla was underway and Krast was increasing interrogations such as this. He scrutinised her for a reaction but she gave him none. "Correctionals searched your home this morning and gathered evidence to support these charges."

They must have found my altar, she thought with a sinking realisation. She kept a small piece of driftwood decorated with shells and candles as her humble altar. Central to it was a tiny watercolour of Hethra and Halla that she'd painted herself.

"The sentence for this crime, Mrs Cobb, is execution." He looked mildly regretful at this. "Although," he added cautiously, "we might be able to help one another. Your husband, Barnabas," he elaborated, in case she'd somehow forgotten her own husband's name, "is also charged with the same offence. He has confessed to passing potions, but claims no part in worshipping pagan idols."

Barney! she thought with horror. *They've arrested him as well? He'll blame me for dragging him into all of this. He thought it was so harmless!*

Krast saw her torment and pursed his lips. "Your husband's sentence has been reduced to penal servitude. He convinced us that he had no part in worshipping the idols in your home, the so called Hethra and Halla." Their sacred names sounded insignificant coming from him.

How could he? she thought, and then more soberly, *What choice did he have? Poor Barney!* He didn't know about her small altar under the stairs. She writhed in her restraints and tried to contain the hatred she felt for this man. It was un-witch like, but it was a stupendous struggle. Instead, she straightened defiantly and glared back at him.

"Really, Mrs Cobb," he sighed. "I'm trying to assist you. Your sentence can be reduced like your husband's, if you assist us."

She took a shuddering breath and almost said something.

He shook his head disdainfully, then stepped aside revealing a table behind him and its contents. One was cylindrical, about eighteen inches tall and draped in black velvet. The other was her own small watercolour of Hethra and Halla and her heart ached, pained by how distant the twins seemed then. She swallowed her tears and bit her lip hard. *Let them do their worst*, she thought. *So be it if they kill me. I'll travel the Evermore-spiral and begin a new life.* Krast was talking but she wasn't listening.

"These are your choices," he pointed to the small painting of the twins. "Tell us the whereabouts of the relic witches call the 'serpent-twins', and of Britain's hidden covens, and your sentence can be reduced." He paused to let this sink in. "Or we must take the harder path and retrieve our information, using this." He unfurled a long arm and gestured to the object lurking under the black material. "Your choice, Mrs Cobb. Help yourself, or hurt yourself."

She heard liquid sloshing and gurgling underneath the black drape. There was a tank of some kind under there.

Krast tilted his head sympathetically. "It's alive and hungry, Mrs Cobb."

Tremors of fear now set her shivering, but still she said nothing.

"Then you leave me no choice." He tried to look dismayed, but he sounded satisfied. "I respect your decision, but know that this will be . . ." he considered, "Messy," he finished. He looked beyond Eliza to someone standing at her rear. "Sedate her and prepare the chromosite," he ordered blandly, then breezed past on his way to the door and she caught the scent of bitter iron as he did.

The smell of rusted Iron, she thought. The hallmark of a witch attack.

Whoever you were I'm sorry you didn't finish the job and I can't do it for you. How many of her kind had he 'blessed' down the years? Something inside the tank thrashed again. *Alive and hungry.* She looked with foreboding at the black shape squatting on the table, wondering what was inside it.

Kolfinnia was bound for another meeting with Valonia, and again her dragon tattoos were refreshed and she wore her finest. May had passed and June was upon them.

When they'd arrived back at Wildwood with Lilain that day, the empress was taken to hastily erected quarters and treated for her wounds, while Lana had tended Kolfinnia's arm. *'If you hadn't been holding your wand when you were bitten you'd have lost the whole arm, for sure,'* she had told her, and so Kolfinnia had worn her wand everyday since and even slept with it.

News of their extraordinary guest had filtered through to every coven in the northwest and beyond, and now witches arrived daily hoping for a glimpse of, or better still an audience with, Lilain. The hive-empress had been given quarters in the gardens and Flora was thrilled at having her in residence, not merely for the honour but for the endless stream of bees that came to pay their respects, and she held great hopes for a bumper crop of seeds in the months to come. In grateful thanks she brought Lilain daily cocktails of nectar blended from her finest blooms and during her visits she often found she wanted to stroke Lilain's rich yellow and black fur, but one just didn't pet an empress no matter how fluffy she might look.

Valonia had been very clear with Kolfinnia, Rowan and even Gale: that they were to say as little as possible about the barghests. *'Three is very bad, Kolfinnia, unique,'* she prophesied darkly. After that she would say no more until she was ready, which left Kolfinnia wondering the worst.

"It's not fair," Rowan sulked. "We can't tell anybody how we really rescued Lilain." She'd said this at least five or six times a day for the last two weeks.

"Not yet, no, but rescue her we did and everyone's talking about how you saved the day." This was Kolfinnia's stock reply to her constant gripe.

She brightened and started to skip as they walked along. "Tell me again what they say."

Kolfinnia watched her, feeling slightly saddened by her joy. *How will the girl take my leaving?* she thought, and for a terrible moment she almost wished they weren't friends.

"Kol?" Rowan badgered.

"Yes, well," she recovered. "They all say that you're a mighty witch who banished a barghest with its name, a feat no other can claim," she said solemnly.

She tugged Kolfinnia's dress and from behind a shielding hand she whispered, "But it was *three*, though, wasn't it!"

She grinned. Rowan was blooming. *And about time too*, she thought, and then yet again her mind turned to her own constant gripe: *But how did you know their names, Rowan, how?* It was something Rowan just couldn't answer or even see the significance of. She just did, and that was all.

They reached the edge of the gardens. Valonia had requested her presence this afternoon and although the dreary jobs had stopped the instant they'd rescued Lilain, her future was still very uncertain. "I have to go now Rowan, why not help Ada pick blackcurrants? Free and fed, remember?"

Her smile melted. "I'd rather come with you."

"Sorry, coven-mother's expecting just me. I have to go."

Rowan regarded her sadly. "I know you have to go."

She swayed minutely, before forcing an innocent smile. "Just and hour or two. I'll see you at even-meal. Yes?" She casually stroked the girl's hair from her eyes.

"Kol?" the girl asked hesitantly.

"Hmm?" She squatted level with her, fearful of her impending words.

"How did you make that voice in my head when the barghests came?"

She relaxed. "Crowning, Rowan. Witches call it crowning."

"Can you show me?"

"Certainly, but it's best when used close up, and it takes patience and effort," she instructed.

"Really?" Rowan asked silently.

She ought to have expected such a thing, but once again mysterious little Rowan caught her off guard and Kolfinnia's gaping mouth quickly spread in a grin. "What other secrets are you keeping from me?" she teased, making Rowan laugh behind her hands. "But don't forget the most magical way to talk is also the best." Kolfinnia looked serious now.

Rowan awaited her wisdom. "Yes?"

"You open your mouth, waggle you tongue and words come out." She stood and gave her a last hug. "I'd better get going."

"Good luck," she whispered and squeezed her hand.

Valonia and her Wards were sitting in the privacy of the tower awaiting Kolfinnia. Valonia passed around the customary pipe and an old plate with straggly roots draped over it. Esta took a piece and regarded it with some admiration.

"Where did you get liquorice from this far north?" She nibbled at the delicacy.

"Many witches are most insistent on seeing Lilain and so, well you know. . ." she trailed off and passed the pipe to Hilda.

"You swapped liquorice for a meeting with the empress," Lana concluded.

"We should charge a proper admission," Hilda joked, blowing out a stream of smoke and passing the pipe along. "A shilling a time." This was racy talk for Hilda Saxon.

Valonia took a puff from the pipe that had now completed the circle and considered a moment. "Next year we'll put a big river-cobble in a crib and tell everyone it's a sovereign to see Hethra and Halla's egg."

There was a stunned silence then they all burst into laughter. Esta slapped her knee, and Lana gave a throaty chuckle, while Hilda stifled a smirk behind her fingers. "Really!" she protested, "it's not right to carry on so." But the glint in her eye said otherwise. Valonia felt in need of light-hearted talk. When Kolfinnia arrived the talk would turn to darker matters.

Outside the tower, Kolfinnia found herself staring at the number 13 on Valonia's door and heard hearty laughter from inside. She knocked politely with her good hand. Valonia opened the door cautiously. "Welcome, please come and sit with the others."

Others? Kolfinnia had assumed this was a private meeting.

"No, bring it. You'll need it," she insisted when Kolfinnia went to prop her lightning-staff against the doorway. Valonia ushered her inside and once again Kolfinnia entered the heart of Wildwood, which smelled of ginger and spices. Sitting cross-legged in a light haze of pipe smoke, inside a circle drawn with salt, were Lana, Esta and Hilda. They all smiled as she entered and greeted her respectfully by pressing fingertips to their forehead, the mystic third eye.

"How's your arm today?" Lana enquired.

"Much better now, thank you, Ward Zuri." The barghest's bite was well mended, although she still felt a tingling in her flesh.

Lana shuffled over and patted one of the spare cushions and Kolfinnia was deeply moved. Here she was with Wildwood's senior witches and she was being invited to join their circle. They were accepting her as an equal and she understood that this wasn't going to be the meeting she'd anticipated.

Valonia joined them and took a cushion of her own and sat down with a grunt and crunch of hay. "Well Kolfinnia, are you going to join us or not?"

"Erm, of course," she floundered. "Thank you, coven-mother." She placed her lightning-staff on the floor outside the circle. It fit neatly into the missing portion of the pentagon formed by everyone else's lightning-staffs.

Gale was thrilled to be with his own, and in that most special of shapes the sprites could flow through one staff to the next and the next, charging in circles, enjoying the electrifying rush and strengthening the protective barrier around their witches. Kolfinnia knew straight away that dark talk was coming. "Make sure you go home in the right staff," she hissed to Gale, not wanting to be shown up today of all days.

She stepped over the salt, careful not to touch it, and lowered herself down between Lana and Valonia. Remembering her manners, she was about to bid them a formal greeting but Lana rest a hand on her knee.

"Inside the circle we're all equal, so first names only."

"With blessings," she swallowed back an unexpected lump, then bowed and named the circle of witches. "Lana, Hilda, Esta," then finally, on a level of intimacy she'd never expected, she named her coven-mother, "Valonia."

"I'm sure you realise why we asked you to keep details of Lilain's discovery a secret and we apologise that we haven't been able to speak openly before now, what with all the guests coming and going. We want to know all about the storm, Kolfinnia. Tell us again, everything that happened at the frontier." Valonia sat back expectantly.

She began with the strange feeling of dread at the scarecrows. As she unravelled her tale they listened attentively and decorated her account with approving 'mmms' and 'ahhs', but nobody spoke while she held court inside the circle. When she explained how Gale had driven the barghests away the throbbing lightning-staffs seemed to rush higher in pitch then fall again to a deep humming. Clearly all the sprites loved that part of the tale. She rounded off with their flight from the frontier carrying Lilain and again paid tribute to Gale who had all but flown by himself, and she loved him for it.

When she finished there was a long pause. Outside there came the distant thud of spade work in the gardens, the flutter of small birds in the branches and the occasional murmur of day-to-day talk rising from below like embers from a fire.

"Barghests," Valonia considered and chewed on a strand of liquorice. "Barghests are creatures of Ruination. What do you know of Ruination, Kolfinnia?"

She took a deep breath. "That it is a realm with its own rules albeit chaotic."

"Straight from the book. I told you she was good!" Valonia smiled and the others laughed warmly. Kolfinnia felt that she'd been the subject of talk before arriving, praiseworthy talk, and she blushed. "What you may not know is that Ruination is not a place at all, but rather a mind," Valonia finished.

"A mind?"

"Yes, just as Hethra and Halla's dream manifests as the physical world, Ruination is a cosmic mind whose conscious thoughts emanate as 'time' into our universe. Without time nothing would grow, fail or decay."

Kolfinnia was already feeling out of her depth.

"You see, Kolfinnia, the minds of Earth and Ruin are very close. They touch like twins in a womb." She held up clenched fists and rasped them against each other in demonstration. "Ruination gifts us with death without which there would be no renewal, and we gift Ruination with life and the power of animation."

"So we *need* Ruination?"

"Both need one another," Lana interceded, "like a spider needs its web but doesn't want to be caught in it."

"And because it's an idea rather than a place it's all around us," Valonia continued. "Hethra and Halla's dream expresses as order, such as in the symmetry of a flower, while Ruination expresses in the random and the chaotic, the blotches on a rotten apple or the way a disease spreads through the body."

"So time is a necessary emanation from Ruin. It brings death and change, and Ruin is a mind, not a place?" Kolfinnia repeated slowly, trying to understand it.

"While other emanations are very unwelcome."

"Like barghests?"

Valonia stroked her chin. "The subconscious controls the dream world, and when Ruin dreams, my lass, it dreams of monsters."

"Like barghests." This time it wasn't a question.

She nodded. "Ruination's nightmares can manifest as living entities, that we see as monsters of Ruin. Most, like barghests, don't last long, days or weeks. Others, the more intelligent, realise there's no way back to the mind that dreamed them and they try to survive here."

"Intelligent living dreams?" She thought this conversation was getting stranger and stranger.

"Mmm," Valonia nodded, "clever enough to know they can only survive if they hide, but everything they occupy decays prematurely and so they must constantly keep moving. When a tree falls it might be because a

Ruinous creature was hiding in it, likewise a river that dries up, a rock face that slides away or snow that tumbles as an avalanche."

Kolfinnia let out a long sigh as Valonia took a moment to re-light her pipe.

"But back to our problem. Three barghests at once is unheard of. Something disturbed the sleeping mind of Ruin as surely as a kick in the pants. Tell me, Kolfinnia, what do you know of Lilain?"

She thought back to her teachings. "That she brings prosperity to her hives across the world, she never touches earth, her realm is cloud and wind."

"Quite so," Valonia looked sorrowful, and Kolfinnia remembered her shock at seeing Lilain powerless. "No wonder you spotted that fairy. It'll have been drawn to help her."

"It was gone before I knew it," she lamented.

"Pity you didn't see one under happier circumstances," Hilda sympathised.

"One thing's certain," Esta said dryly. "It's going to be a rotten year for honey."

Lana smiled briefly then became serious. "We think the barghests appearing, coupled with Rowan's dramatic prophecy, proves that Hethra and Halla are in danger."

"Danger?" Kolfinnia flinched.

"We don't know what this danger is yet, but it's almost certain the Illuminata are behind it and if it isn't stopped things are going to get very bad," she finished.

"To say the least," Valonia added. "Remember I said that Earth and Ruin are close?"

Kolfinnia nodded.

"Well, in its most basic sense. Whatever the Illuminata are tinkering with it has already disturbed Hethra and Halla's dreams, which in turn caused Lilain to lose her way, and also why Ruination sent us three unwelcome visitors. The natural order is in peril."

"So Rowan was right. They're really out to find the twins? But no witch knows their whereabouts?" Kolfinnia touched the small amulet around her neck.

"Hethra and Halla sleep within the terra-soula. It moves deep inside the world, under oceans and mountains, following vast rivers of magma," Valonia explained. "It slowly circles the earth and rarely comes close to the surface, except where currents bring it up from the deepest roots of rock."

"So surely it must be impossible to reach?" Kolfinnia hoped.

"Maybe if it's deep enough," she reflected.

"Even that won't stop determined people from searching," Hilda insisted. "I've heard that men have built looking glasses that can count grains of dust on the moon. Believe me, if the Illuminata have found something that can be turned to profit they'll stop at nothing to seize it."

Valonia sighed wearily. "So far the effects are sporadic, which suggests they're just dabbling, but while they do we can assume that more creatures like the barghests will manifest."

"They'll return?" Kolfinnia despaired.

"Until they're stopped, we'll see more like them, yes. And so I think it prudent for senior witches to have a little more insight into what may be lurking out there."

The word 'lurking' conjured images of places where creatures with no love of the sun would hide during daylight, and Kolfinnia shivered.

"Let's get started then," Valonia cracked her knuckles loudly. "Fog-hounds, or barghests, you already know since you've had the pleasure of meeting them."

"Erm, forgive me," Kolfinnia interrupted as politely as she could. "You said *senior* witches. How does this concern me?" She was feeling as though she'd missed part of the conversation.

Valonia rolled her eyes but couldn't disguise her delight. "Because bad news wasn't the only reasons we asked you here today!" The others smiled too, like they knew a wonderful secret. "Now then," she wore a mischievous expression. "How'd you feel about becoming Flower-Forth's new Ward?"

"Ward! You mean it?" She could have hugged them all, thunder-sprites included.

"Hilda's compelled to return to her former coven," Valonia said simply. "So Flower-Forth needs a new Ward and you've been in our thoughts for some time. You'll of course begin as a junior until fully trained, that's if you wish to accept?" She arched her eyebrows.

"With absolute pleasure!" She nodded fervently and felt her cheeks burn.

"I was hoping to return this autumn," Hilda explained. "My old coven-mother has been ill for some time and if the coven's to survive they'll need an experienced hand at the helm." She glanced at her friends of long years and Kolfinnia lowered her eyes when looks of sorrow and love, not strictly meant for her, passed around them.

"Good!" Valonia exclaimed. "It's decided then. Blessed be one and all," she concluded, and the elder witches began to rise.

Only when across the salt circle did they go from witches to old women again, rubbing stiffened joints and shaking creases from their garments, picking up staffs and hats, chatting and laughing.

I'm one of them! Kolfinnia thought. *This is my home.* She was jubilant and still only half certain she'd heard correctly: she would live out her days here. With that thought she stifled a huge grin of relief behind her bandaged hand and quickly brushed a tear from her eye. She left the tower feeling empowered and walked as if in a dream with all her fears banished.

Only one matter remained for the Wards to discuss, but it was perhaps the most important of all. Valonia watched Kolfinnia through the willow panels and saw that the young woman had a new spring in her step. She smiled in satisfaction and then she dealt with the last, most urgent, matter. "Rowan banished the barghests with their own names," she said without taking her eyes from Kolfinnia who strolled away happily through the gardens.

"Now, that scares me more than barghests," Esta said in a low voice. "That girl understands summat of the universe that we don't."

"Her skills are like none I've ever seen or heard of." Hilda shook her head.

"I've heard a theory that all living things create a universal-mind," Esta continued, toying with a loose thread on her coat as she spoke. "All awareness and knowledge pooled into one great consciousness some call God."

The word 'God' hung in the air like an axe ready to fall.

"She knows things that are impossible to explain. Could it be simple mind reading?" Lana ventured.

From outside came a curlew's lonely cry.

Valonia's eyes narrowed, Kolfinnia was now out of sight. "If one can read the mind of God, then yes."

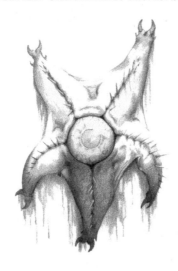

CHAPTER SEVEN

The Accusing Eye

Krast exited the interrogation carriage, passing correctional Baxter as he did.

"Sir," Baxter acknowledged.

Krast ignored him. Last year Baxter had bungled an interrogation. Krast thought him incompetent, and the incident also awakened uncomfortable echoes of his own past. The Cobb woman had seen something, he was certain; seen something about him that left him feeling vulnerable and it gnawed at him. The vault in his mind rocked as something cried to be let out and he shuddered. He took a breath, held it for a few seconds then let it whistle through his clenched teeth. "Stay dead," he commanded and the vault fell silent again.

Eliza heard the door open and close again behind her, but the imposing man with the strange scars didn't return. For a brief moment she caught the sweet smell of fresh air outside and although it was corrupted by chimney smoke and sewage her heart was gladdened. *Outdoors where Hethra and Halla rule*, she thought sadly and tears pricked her eyes.

They'd forced a foul drink on her and now she felt groggy. Purposeful footsteps advanced and stopped at her side. The voice that accompanied the footsteps fired off a string of orders and apothecaries began hurrying around the cramped carriage. One moment it was empty, the next, masked and gowned men filed from their stations like disciplined ants. "Mrs Cobb," the assured voice began. "I am senior correctional

Baxter and I shall be conducting the interrogation today." He made it sound like a privilege.

She held onto the lingering sweetness of outdoors. *Where Hethra and Halla rule.*

"You will not be required to speak," he instructed. "The chromosite will retrieve all the information we require."

There was a flurry of white as technicians began turning valves on sodium-arc lamps. The carriage went from dim to brilliant and the sulphurous odour became pungent. Suddenly something like a metal cage swung across her face and clamped tight, restraining her head and it took all of her will to smother the scream that boiled in her chest. *No! You'll not get that satisfaction from me.* A faceless man came to her with razor and soap and quickly shaved her crown, making it feel cold and sore. She hardly noticed as her greying curls fell into her lap. Where Hethra and Halla rule, she repeated, but she'd never felt so far from greenery and goodness.

"Bring the chromosite." Baxter sounded animated. She heard the sound of sloshing liquid again and thanked Oak that at least she couldn't see the horror.

Alive and hungry, Mrs. Cobb.

Baxter's mechanical voice came again. "You will be shown a series of lantern images. The chromosite will draw images from the depths of your mind that answer our questions. You will have no control over this process, and you will not speak during questioning."

The irony of *not* talking during an interrogation struck her as sublimely funny. These men would soon learn that no living witch knew the whereabouts of the serpent-twins. They could question her forever and never find their answer, neither had she any intention of leaving this world meekly. She was a witch and she had a surprise for Him, the man who carried the scars on his face.

A projector began to clatter and hum, and a square of light appeared on the screen at the front of the carriage. It trembled as adjustments were made to the lens. Occasionally, finger-shaped shadows played across it like snakes. A splash of cold liquid on her shoulder told her it was near, and in the next instant something cold and wriggling gripped the bare crown of her head. It was the chromosite.

Hungry and alive.

The scream that had festered in her throat all day rushed up like burning magma. She clamped her teeth hard and the scream broke silently against them like a wave. She groaned with the effort and stabbed her nails into her palms, as more fluid dribbled down her neck and brow.

"Chromosite introduced, sir," someone declared.

The creature was like nothing in natural creation. It resembled a pallid starfish with a single blind eye at its centre and it was placed against her shaven head. Hungrily, it suckled the bare skin and began to invade her thoughts. She stiffened and moaned in revulsion, struggling against her restraints as the chromosite tightened its grip. Something warm, her blood or the creature's secretions, trickled down her brow and face as it bit harder, and raped its way into her memories. In retaliation, she summoned the only thought she wanted this thing to steal. It was the only weapon in her arsenal and she would spend her last breath making sure she burned it right into its prying eye.

Like Valonia, Eliza had a particularly rare gift. This picture was for Him and she'd seen it hiding in His aura. It was the face of a woman partially concealed, as if He'd tried to seal her away. It was the face of the witch who had scarred Him, and for her to linger so many years in His aura proved she was deeply significant to Him.

She wouldn't leave this chair, she knew that, but in the end all the chromosite would show Him was the face of his nemesis: her final devastating insult. *Dear Barney*, she thought one last time, then she hid all her memories behind the unknown woman's face where they would be safe, and readied herself.

The lights were dimmed, and the projector brightened as the carriage grew dark. A picture slide clattered into position showing the same lithograph Krast had swayed the ministers with weeks before; Halla, the holly serpent of winter and her brother Hethra, the oak serpent of summer, dreaming inside the terra-soula.

Baxter crooned directly into her ear, "You will show us the resting place of this object, the so called 'serpent-twins', and what its true nature is." He repeated the question over and over, trying to wrestle the image from her subconscious while on the screen the slide was swiftly replaced by another, identical to the last.

Eliza felt the sedative smothering her, but she curled her hands into fists and fought. *This is for Him.*
She pictured the woman she'd seen in his aura, and thrust it at the chromosite with all her might.

So far Krast was pleased. Prime Minister Stokes had sent a courier the very same day to give first-dawn the seal of approval. The ministers must have raced back to Westminster tripping over their own tongues, but he knew there was a tough road ahead. Witches would fight to protect the relic known as the terra-soula. He didn't believe in dragons, or elves or unicorns. He believed the term 'serpent-twins' was akin to the same colourful name bestowed upon first-dawn. He also believed that the covens knew what the object truly was and if it fell into his lap right now he doubted very much that it would contain baby serpents. He thought Stokes didn't go far enough, however. Men and money were all well and good, but he thought Stokes a lightweight. What about dedication to a cause greater than mere money? What he needed was for Britain to turn against witches and vilify them. He wanted everyone to see them for the progress-hating vermin they were. As he walked through the growing army of labourers at Hobbs Ash he began to formulate a simple plan.

Wherever he walked men toiled harder. Lathered horses lumbered from the docks dragging steel girders, and boys as young as ten struggled with buckets full of rivets. Hobbs had found a new lease of life and it stank of manure, sweat, and hot iron. Foundry hammers rang on steel, saws ripped through timber and there was the ever-present panting of steam engines bringing fresh supplies. Workers were busy constructing new war machines to spearhead the offensive. It was busy but ordered and best of all fear of empty bellies kept everyone in line. Workers built machines not knowing their true purpose, and if they began to ask bothersome questions they were shipped back to the city to contemplate starvation from their squalid homes.

He reached the signal-box and found Hathwell sitting at the typewriter wearing a troubled expression. As always he wore a black waistcoat over his white shirt. He stood to attention when Krast entered. "Sir," he said and looked ahead at nothing.

"At ease," he said wearily. "You and I are no longer army fellows."

"Very good, sir." Hathwell sank back into his chair. The two had served together; with Hathwell as his squire riding through the chaos of battle, ready to serve his lord. Squires were expected to be proficient in emergency repairs and basic medicine. Hathwell's squire days ended when his knee had been shattered and replaced with steel. Now he was Krast's secretary and it'd been a long time since they'd marched together.

"A man knew his enemy back then, a man knew where he stood on the field of war." Krast idly drew a finger along the dusty window sill.

"Indeed," Hathwell agreed. The two were so familiar that 'sir' was sometimes forgotten.

"Orders were given and a good man would follow them," he lamented.

Hathwell sat with his fingers hovering over the typewriter keys and looked away, back to the past, and inevitably to Solvgarad. Glory and honour weren't his lasting impressions. "Something on your mind, sir?"

Krast stared through the cracked window at his own little empire.

"Not like now."

"Sir?"

"No sense of direction. Hard to distinguish friend from foe these days."

"That's politicians for you I suppose."

Krast licked his lips. "The ministers, what did you think of them?" He made the question sound unimportant.

Hathwell couldn't see his face but he knew his old knight well. He was like a stalking tiger trying to conceal himself in the long grass. "Erm, in all honesty I didn't formulate an opinion."

"Bertrand, every man has an opinion, even if that opinion's never uttered. It's the only real freedom we have."

"I suppose they're used to getting what they want, sir," he replied cautiously.

"Hmm."

He couldn't tell if Krast was agreeing.

"And what opinion did you formulate about Wallace Maccrae, our minister for religious affairs? You recall the chap. He had a rounded gut and skin like unbaked dough."

"Yes, I remember. He seemed unconvinced."

"He's an obstacle," Krast added forcefully. "He's keen to avoid risks but still wants the best returns. I'll wager it was his meddling that diluted the Prime Minister's support."

"Why Maccrae?"

"Because he speaks for the church and they certainly don't want people discovering that the world view they've been offered since birth is a contrived fiction."

"But even so, funding's generous sir." Hathwell tapped the pile of remittance notes on his desk.

"Funds are first rate but what of the *will?*"

"Sir?"

"Will." He worded it slowly. "Stoke's support lacks will. He'd be content to let covens alone if they allowed him to exploit their knowledge."

"Isn't confiscating their secrets the primary aim, sir?"

"Not to me." Krast hardened. "Stokes has forgotten that the project is to exploit witch-lore and dissolve the covens. He's casually forgotten the latter because he believes, like most, that witches are a harmless if outmoded tradition." Something about the Cobb witch had put him a foul mood, but he couldn't say what.

"But the task-force is proof Westminster means business, isn't it?" He thought of the war machines outside. He certainly wouldn't like to be on the receiving end of them.

"I think not," Krast brooded.

Something's certainly put you in a bad mood. Hathwell thought.

"Only belief, not steel, will finish witches for good. Consider how unpopular they'd be if . . ." he pretended to think. "Someone prominent was harmed by them."

"I dare say they'd be very unpopular, sir."

"I suppose." He shrugged indifferently, as if the idea was silly and turned to he window again. For a while silence dominated and outside Hathwell could hear the hollow boom of steel plates, but he was aware of a half formed idea hanging in the air like a poison cloud. Suddenly Krast turned, wearing a smile. "Now, faithful squire, I have a task for you. How about some time away from Hobbs?" He sat down and propped his legs up on his desk.

"Where did you have in mind, sir?"

"The esoteric library at Goldhawk Row. I'd like you to compile anything we have on these venerated snakes: Hethra and Halla." He leaned back and laced his finger over his rich waistcoat. "Crude names, for crude beasts I'm sure."

And get me out of the way too? he suspected. "I'll get onto it first thing in the morning, sir."

"Capital, Hathwell, capital," he said contentedly.

Later that afternoon, Krast stood lost in thought watching workers swarm across their latest war machines, and while krakens had at least some measure of finesse, these things were ugly and brute looking. They were enormous black spheres armed with locomotive spikes over three yards long – mobile prisons to house captive witches. His gold pocket watch had unerringly found its way back into his hand where he stroked it possessively. Suddenly he twitched. Something had set his nerves buzzing. There it was again – the clamour of an alarm bell, and he instantly recognised it as the interrogation alarm. His eyes flew wide then narrowed with anger. "Baxter!" he snarled and flung open his office door. He charged down the steps and ran the two-hundred yards to the interrogation carriage. He had mistakenly left Baxter to supervise the Cobb interrogation and from the sound of the klaxon something had gone wrong.

"She's all but dead, Mr Baxter." A worried apothecary thumbed back one of Eliza's eyelids to reveal nothing but white.

"Damn her!" Baxter hissed. "Time!" he snapped.

"Fifty-six, twenty-three," came a taut reply. "There's no pulse either."

Let her pass the hour mark, he thought with rising panic. An hour was the minimum time required for an interrogation. *After that she can die all she likes.* If he could get her past the hour mark, Krast wouldn't have cause to reprimand him. "For God's sake save the chromosite, forget the prisoner!" He shoved a technician aside, who was trying vainly for Eliza's pulse. "Remove the chromosite, you oaf, and get it under the ice blanket! And silence that bloody alarm!"

Just then the door swung slowly open, like the jaws of a mantrap, and Krast entered flanked by two guardsmen.

Eliza was finished. The effort had crushed her but it was worth it. She'd left a message for Him, a picture buried deep inside the creature. Evermore was calling, the pathway from this life to the next, and that floating feeling wasn't due to any sedative. She no longer felt the chromosite's kiss or even the rough hands trying to elicit some response from her dying body. The voices, the fear and even the room faded and before her she could see a magnificent spiral of stone steps lit by the countless luminescent souls that flowed along it. She felt a draught of cool air as sweet as spring and there, where the stairs rounded the turn of the spiral, floated a dragon covered from snout to tail with scales like holly leaves. She sighed in reverence and lifted effortlessly from the restraints, shaking them off like raindrops, compelled to follow. The dragon turned silently and led her upwards, and Eliza left her broken body behind in the hell of Hobbs Ash and rose to follow.

The carriage fell silent, while the projector continued to hum happily to itself. "Lights!" Krast ordered. The lighting was restored and the image on the screen faded, as did Baxter's hope. "Time."

A technician inspected his pocket watch. "Fifty-eight, eleven, sir."

Baxter glared accusingly in his direction.

The projector was silenced and the tension grew palpable. Krast stalked closer and looked down at Eliza and then to Baxter who knelt with his hands still clasped about her head, as though he had been trying to shake a response from her.

Krast examined Eliza's shaved crown where the chromosite had fed. In anticipation of what he was thinking a technician brought the creature pooled upon a specimen tray. Krast pinched the corner of the ice blanket and lifted it. The creature pulsed sluggishly and its single blind eye stared upwards like a fat glistening pearl. He reached out and tilted Eliza's head from where it lay slumped against her chest. She was dead, that much was clear. He pricked the tension with a deliberate cough. "November 19th, last year." He withdrew his hand, letting her head wilt slowly back down.

"I don't follow you, sir?" Baxter frowned.

"That was the last occasion a subject expired before the hour mark, an interrogation conducted by you, correctional Baxter. At the time you assured me it would never happen again, and yet . . ." He pinned him with the unfinished question.

Baxter felt his scalp ooze sweat. "She somehow hastened her own demise." He glared at the dead witch. "She was pronounced fit for interrogation, some kind of self-induced expiration, no doubt about it." His tone quickly went from defiant to defensive.

Krast flicked his eyes towards the guardsmen who immediately stepped up beside Baxter and seized his arms.

"Now wait!" He looked like a spindly marionette between the two large men. "Just wait! The medical officer pronounced her fit. She relinquished her life of her own free will! I swear it!" Apothecaries shuffled away from him, distancing themselves from his failure, and then events at Marylebone workhouse were replayed with exquisite irony. "Knight Superior!" He thrashed and scrambled but the guardsmen simply hauled him off the floor. He vanished through the doorway with a final scream: "Samuel!" Then the door slammed shut and senior correctional Baxter effectively vanished from the world.

Krast turned to the man holding the specimen tray. "Take it to the dissection carriage." He nodded mutely and left, balancing the tray with its gristly cargo, and Krast looked down at her again. What secrets has she taken with her and why had her stare troubled him so, he wondered?

"Josephine," a voice called and he had to stop himself turning to look. That voice was dead and ghosts weren't real. "One less witch in the world," he concluded coldly, and then turned to leave.

Outwardly the dissection lab resembled every other at Hobbs Ash; a railway carriage shunted under cover, stripped of its finery and refitted. The windows were boarded and the carriage was empty except for a single steel trolley lined with lethal looking instruments. Central to this array was the dead chromosite, and a single electric light hung over the trolley suspended by sagging wires.

Krast closed the door behind him and fastened the bolt. He'd begun to shake, just a tiny tremor in his palms. For the very first time they'd questioned a witch on the location of the fabled serpent-twins, something he'd have dismissed as chasing fairytales just a month ago, and he marvelled that the creature lying on the trolley might show him a miracle. He quickly donned his white coat and gloves. "So no living witch knows their whereabouts?" he gloated, confident he'd soon prove that wrong. "Thank you, Mrs Cobb." He selected a scalpel, and with practised skill quickly had the chromosite's milky retina quivering on the specimen tray. He pushed his eyepiece up to his right eye and held it there with a frown and a squint, then slowly leaned over and inspected the gelatinous mass.

'Josephine' the voice came again, and that vault in his mind didn't just rock, it exploded.

What he saw punched the breath from his lungs and he jerked violently, toppling the stool with the back of his knees and sending the eyepiece across the room where it clattered into a corner. His head skimmed the light and sent it spinning, throwing a spotlight in crazy loops around the carriage. Inside the disembodied eye, swam the face he kept locked in that most secret place. He pointed an accusing finger at the eye. "How can you be in there? YOU!" he stammered.

The light see-sawed back and forth over the trolley, glinting across the moist eyeball, making it look to be winking. He curled his hands into fists and he held them out like a man ready to brawl and took a wary step back into the shadows. Sweat chilled him as he stepped away from the hot examination lamp, and his rubber gloves made anguished creaking sounds as he wrung his hands. He had a child's fear the chromosite would rear up and make him look into its dead eye. "You're not there!" he shouted, then scuttled past it and into the furthest corner to hide in the shadows, but the brilliantly lit table was like a beacon and he couldn't take his eyes off it. "Why have you come back?"

The eye didn't reply.

"Josephine." The name fell from his mouth after years of entombment and he had a sudden and vivid memory of himself screaming, his skin burned where she'd struck him down with magic. The light above the trolley continued to sway, but so gently now that he couldn't be sure if it was the light moving or himself. He remembered how she'd wept uncontrollably. Was she tormented by having hurt him, or not having killed him? It was this unanswered question that made him who he was. "I loved you." The words had no heart and he wasn't even aware he'd said them.

The eye still said nothing and in a sudden rage he ran headlong at the trolley and swept the tray and its contents across the carriage. There was a bright clatter of spilled tools followed by a moist, weighty thud. The eye smacked against the wall and then slid slowly downwards, leaving a glistening trail before it finally pooled on to the floor from where it regarded him pitifully. She was in there watching him from beyond the grave and it was unbearable. He stripped the lab coat from his back in a fury, and whipped the wretched eye over and over, screaming until his anger boiled dry and the walls were spattered red. "You cannot be there!" He screamed until he was hoarse, then threw the stained lab coat over it, and there he left it. The ruined coat bulged where the eye stared up at nothing but soiled cotton, and then he collapsed, exhausted, and stared out from behind his fingers and began to cry softly. "Josephine," he whispered her forbidden name. He'd come looking for the serpent-twins, but all he'd uncovered was the grave he had spent his life trying to forget.

Chapter Eight

Sunday Flowers

The entire upper floor of Goldhawk Row housed the greatest collection of esoteric writings anywhere in the world, and Hathwell felt that the dreary place had become his prison. It had been over a fortnight since Krast had appointed him this task and his every waking hour was spent there. How he hated the place. He felt entombed by books. Krast had allocated him a staff; a clerk of barely seventeen called Thomas Moffat and a copyist called Tobias Skulle who looked as old and grim as the texts he was assigned to copy. Skulle wore absurdly strong spectacles that made him look like a frog, and only spoke when he had to.

Books were forbidden to leave this library, and so when he found something relevant amongst the endless shelves he'd pass the document to Tom who'd run it to Skulle for the old man to type up. Hathwell would hear the distant clatter of a typewriter and another page was added to his report. All copies he requested were double checked and approved for removal by the chief librarian, a dour man by the name of Cedric Holloway, blessed with a twisted nose and a slaughter-man's charm. He was lean and bitter looking, and his black hair lay slick and lifeless against his cone shaped skull. He skulked in his small office at the library's entrance, which always smelled of sour milk, and he and Hathwell had taken an instant dislike to one another. Holloway had barked with contempt when Hathwell had asked where the reading rooms were. "Reading rooms are for gents who take *The Times*.

Witchcraft is our speciality here," he had scolded him. The librarian was like a gaoler who seemed to abhor the idea of reading, preferring instead to keep books under lock and key. Indeed, there wasn't even an indexing system and Hathwell had to select books at random.

While most libraries were places of enlightenment, the Illuminata's library, in stark contrast to its name, was perpetually dark. It was built into the eaves and roasted in the June heat because the windows had been tarred over and boarded up with bookshelves, which were impossibly tall and soared away into the gloom. The walkways between them were severely tight, which was fine for Holloway's spindly frame but not Hathwell. He had to shuffle sideways through the narrowest sections, scraping along the books' leathery spines as he did. Sometimes he might hear a cough or the shuffle somewhere in the library, but seldom saw anyone other than his staff.

Whoever had designed the library had a liking for cruel mazes, Hathwell thought. The slivers of space between the towering shelves chopped left and right at will, and some turned into claustrophobic dead-ends where the air was so still and the dust so even that he wondered if anyone had been down them in years.

He'd taken to carrying a small footstool, upon which he could sit and read confessions, spells, curses, myths, court reports, trials and other unsavoury documents that revealed much about the institution he'd served almost his whole life. He read them for hours until his neck was sore, his knee ached and his back throbbed, hoping to find what Krast needed.

"They can discover minutus, but can't build a decent library," he grumbled to himself. "It's as if they don't want anyone to use this blasted place." He was sitting hunched over a heavy volume called *Witchcraft and Potions of a Fiendish and Diabolical Nature in Honour of the Terrible Dragon Twins*, an Illuminata manual on the evils of witchcraft written in an archaic text that made for hard reading. The words 'dragon-twins' had caught his eye but the book was next to useless. Without exception, everything he'd read over the last two weeks was Illuminata comment and speculation and he was beginning to wonder if there were any documents here penned by actual witches. "They never write anything down about themselves?" he puzzled.

"Sir?" Tom's voice came from behind.

"Damn it, Moffat! What've I told you about creeping up behind me?" He couldn't turn in the cramped space and having Tom's disembodied voice ring out of the black was unnerving to say the least.

"Beggin' your pardon, sir."

"Dispense with the formalities, 'Mr Hathwell' will do," he said over his shoulder.

"As you please, Mr Hathwell," he said cheerily, "I've brought these two volumes back. Mr Skulle has finished typing up the sections you wanted."

"See to it please." He heard the rasp of books as Tom replaced the volumes on the shelf.

"It gives me the creeps workin' here." The lad's subdued tone made him look up.

"Well, it's not light reading I'll give you that."

"Hard to credit it all though, eh?" Tom gazed around at the arcane volumes.

"Credit what?"

He leaned closer and whispered. "That witches can do all of this horrible stuff." He jabbed a thumb at the shelves where the books seemed to be listening.

Hathwell was a man who went through life following routine, and where possible, taking the path of least resistance. Tom's innocent question prodded him towards one of those grey areas that until now he wasn't aware he'd been avoiding: Was it all true? Absurdly, he'd never once asked himself that. He'd simply assumed that there was a truth of sorts behind the myth and left it at that. But sitting here day after day, reading reams of Illuminata records, he couldn't tally what he'd read here with what he'd seen on the battlefield as Krast's squire.

"Mr Hathwell?" Tom broke his chain of thought.

"What? Oh, yes, well, it's representative." His answer was deliberately vague because he couldn't lie. He couldn't say the Illuminata's texts were correct any more than he could say that the crimes witches found themselves accused of were false.

"So they do, then?"

"Do what?"

"You know, go into graveyards, dig up bodies and old bones to make spells with?" Despite his reservations Tom loved a good horror story.

"Can't say I've ever seen it myself."

"But you've fought 'em, haven't you? Right by the Knight Superior's side!"

"Until my knee was blasted to smithereens and replaced with steel, yes I did."

"But you must've killed loads of witches?"

"Mostly we fought enemy knights or infantry." Hathwell was growing uncomfortable with his questions.

"But witches too I'll wager?" He'd forgotten both 'sir' and 'Mr' in his excitement.

"On rare occasions."

"Well?" Tom leaned over his shoulder.

"Well, what?"

"Did you find covens full of bones and stolen babies, and see," he looked around nervously, "see naked rites and such?" Tom had images of nubile young ladies prancing in the moonlight. What young lad didn't?

"Stolen babies? Naked rites?" Hathwell was bewildered, not to mention disgusted. "Master Moffat, I don't know what you've been told or what you've read, but never in my years as a squire did I ever see any such thing. Now enough of this clap-trap."

"Sorry sir," he said sulkily. "Just having fought 'em, I thought you'd have a better idea than a load of old books."

Tom had a point, he thought. "If you must know I fought witches only twice." He twisted around as best he could and caught a glimpse of Tom's expectant face.

"Really?" He sounded disappointed.

"Oh, we destroyed plenty of covens and Knight Superior took many away for blessing. Most fled at the sight of us. That's why krakens were the weapon of choice, so big and powerful the enemy flees rather than fights. But not always. Twice they stood their ground and then we met witches in battle."

"What was it like?" Tom asked soberly.

Hathwell stared off into the darkness and saw through the years to that day at Solvgarad.

He landed heavily. His horse bucked and almost trampled him in terror as it galloped away from the falling kraken. He looked up to see the towering machine ablaze and its banners falling in a shower of embers. The furnace exploded and he heard men scream. The kraken dropped to its knees, making the ground shake, then swooned forwards trailing smoke and fire, and still the witches came at them, screaming like demons.

"Mr Hathwell?" Tom prompted again.

Knights and squires often referred to witches as 'Jiks', scum and filth, degenerates bent on evil, but the witches Hathwell had faced on those two occasions, most memorably in Solvgarad, fought with a valour he'd never seen. In the end they had been defeated, of course, and been executed, but he never forgot how they met their end. There was no begging or pleading; they possessed a dignity that'd left a mark on his soul as livid as the scars on Krast's face, and he wondered more often as he grew older if he'd meet his own end with the same stoicism. "They fought well," he said quietly. He felt Tom's puzzled gaze on his back but knew there was nothing more he could say.

When it was almost five o'clock Hathwell called it a day. "Finishing time, Master Moffat," he said wearily.

"Right you are." Tom hastily began thumping books back away in a hurry to be off.

Hathwell returned a particularly old volume back to the shelf, one he hadn't had time to inspect, and as he did a few loose sheets sailed down from it and whispered against the floor. "Bloody hell!" He bent and coaxed them up with his fingertips, intending to replace them, but it was clear they belonged to another book altogether. They were much smaller, for one thing, and far older. He would have shoved them back and forgotten them but for one thing: the uppermost page bore a simple watercolour of the serpent-twins inside a globe or such like. "Now there's a coincidence," he said in mild surprise.

He checked his pocket watch and saw it was three minutes before five. He would look the pages over, but not today. Without thinking he tucked them into his slim briefcase, scooped up his footstool and rubbed at his numb backside, glad that nobody was around to see.

It was three minutes after five when he reached the library reception. Skulle sat behind his cumbersome typewriter. There were no more documents to copy but he wouldn't rise until ordered. "Finishing time, Mr Skulle," Hathwell said, taking his overcoat from the stand and draping it over his arm, hiding his briefcase.

"Not for all," he replied gloomily.

He frowned and looked down at the typed pages on Skulle's desk. There were two piles. One looked depressingly thin for a full day's work, while the other looked more promising. He reached out, thinking it was his own research, and slid the cover towards him for a better look.

"Begging your pardon, sir, but those are for Mr Holloway." Skulle's voice was as harsh as his typewriter.

"You've been copying for him besides me? What's he compiling?" He studied the cover paper, casually ignoring his disapproving stare and slightly irritated that Holloway had pilfered Skulle's time. "The nature of curses," he muttered, reading from the topmost paper. "What's he want with this?"

"That'd be the Knight Superior's business," Holloway answered coldly. He turned to see the librarian framed in the office doorway.

"Knight Superior," Holloway said smugly, "has requested that I research a matter on his behalf." He marched over and swept the bundle up.

"On curses?"

"That's the Knight Superior's business," he warned again.

Much to Hathwell's relief Tom appeared just then. "Time for home, Mr Hathwell?" The lad looked tired.

"Aye then, be off, Master Moffat."

The youth trotted off and a silence settled between the three of them. Holloway and Skulle continued to stare at him, and although he was technically senior it was clear they didn't approve of him hanging around.

"Well, as I say, Mr. Skulle, time to be away." He looked at his watch and he felt his evening meal calling.

Holloway interjected. "Mr. Skulle shall be aiding my own research for a few hours this evening." The two shared a peculiar glance.

Hathwell seethed, but he knew retreat was the best option. "Then make good use of the extra money Mr Skulle. I'll bid both of you gentlemen a good evening." Suddenly he craved sunlight, even if it was London's smoke-blackened variety. He left with the documents hidden in his briefcase and with their eyes burning against his back. He struggled to maintain a modest pace as he walked to the staircase and when he reached the corner he was tempted to look back, but he knew he would see them staring after him like guard dogs. Instead, he let out a worried sigh and headed down the stairs, wondering what his old knight was up to.

Since leaving Valonia's tower as a junior Ward two weeks ago Kolfinnia had felt each day was a rebirth. The very first thing she'd done was to share her news with Gale, Flora and Rowan. She traded a beautiful holed-stone for a bottle of turnip wine and shared it with Flora by the sea that night. They'd invited Rowan and even allowed her a taste. The girl had puckered her face then pronounced it lovely and asked for more, but making children drunk wasn't a good way to start her Wardship and so she insisted that Rowan's first mouthful was also her last. They had lit a fire and stayed up long after dark, then crept back to Wildwood late hoping to go unnoticed. And so they did, aided by Rowan who assured them that everyone was sleeping. Kolfinnia marvelled again, this time through a haze of turnip wine, at Rowan's mysterious skills.

During her weeks of recovery Lilain was appointed a different steward each day, which involved greeting visitors who'd made the long journey to see her, and introducing them. Kolfinnia saw witches come and go like never before, coven-mothers and coven-fathers, young and old. They all arrived in drab cloaks, but while at Wildwood they displayed their finest robes, dresses, tunics and gowns. There were dozens of coven uniforms she recognised and dozens she didn't. It was a heady time of socialising and news gathering. Wildwood felt like an endless festival and the excitement touched everyone.

When her day as steward arrived she dressed in her finest and wore her hair in the most eye-catching style. As she reported to Valonia's tower where Lilain's visitors would be waiting, she consulted the list again. Awaiting her there would be two guests from Regal-Fox coven, which was many miles away in Surrey.

"I see you haven't let Wardship go to your head." Flora joined her unexpectedly, matching her stride and eyeing her decorative hair.

"I'm stewarding today," she replied breezily.

"I was going to ask you to help gather bladder wrack for the gardens. You could braid some into your hair. It'd go nice with the daisies."

"I'd likely come home covered in kelp flies and gull droppings, but thanks for the invite."

"I see your faithful escort's still in attendance." She pointed to a lone honeybee circling Kolfinnia's head.

"Valonia says it'll wear off after a while." Since rescuing Lilain, both she and Rowan found themselves the attention of bees. One or two of them were always hovering close by, as if protecting them. "It's like having a guardian angel," Kolfinnia confessed.

"You wouldn't be saying that if you'd rescued the wasp-empress instead. I hear she has a rotten temper. So, Regal-Fox, eh?" she mused, changing the subject. "They're supposed to be a bit full of themselves. It's said to be the grandest coven in Britain, something to do with Saxon treasure. I don't know the full tale, it's a bit of a mystery. Nobody likes to admit that they're rich, do they?"

"I've heard the same but it's my task to keep them happy today so don't put me off before I've even met them." They were drawing closer to the tower and Kolfinnia dropped to a mutter so they wouldn't be overheard. "I've not really thanked you."

"For what?"

"For wishing me well and not being, well, you know . . ."

"Jealous? You deserve Wardship, and it's good to see you've finally lost that long face of yours! Besides, I have the gardens and as long as I keep putting food on tables Wildwood will always be home."

Kolfinnia meet her gaze, "I'm so glad about that."

"So am I," she said earnestly.

Valonia was waiting for them and standing beside her were two cloaked figures. She smiled politely and stepped forward to present their guests. Flora stepped to her friend's side, but a half-pace behind; it was Kolfinnia's day, after all, and she really ought to be busy with her gardens.

"I give you Kolfinnia Algra, Ward in waiting." Valonia spoke grandly and Kolfinnia felt a tingle at being called 'Ward in waiting'. The guests were cloaked and hooded in wayfarer grey. "Kolfinnia is steward today," Valonia continued, "she'll attend your needs as well as presenting you to Lilain. Anything you need is merely to be asked for." Then she bowed stiffly and excused herself. In truth she had little fondness for formality.

"You must be Sunday Flowers." Kolfinnia addressed the tallest of the pair, reading her name from the day's guest list.

"Correct," the young woman answered in a velvety voice and lowered her hood, almost ceremonially. Immediately Kolfinnia saw that she was magnificent. She was perhaps a couple of years older than herself and her perfect face looked to be sculpted from marble. In fact, there wasn't a blemish anywhere on her fair skin. She openly appraised Kolfinnia with critical eyes of dazzling blue, found her appearance adequate and smiled flatly. Her companion was a boy of perhaps fifteen. He lowered his hood and stepped forward and Sunday presented him as though he was little more than a pet. "I give you my attendant: Farona Firecrest," she waved a limp hand at him and spoke as though she really did want to see him given away.

"Farona," Kolfinnia said in her grandest tone and dipped him a little bow. It was only a small gesture but one she hadn't afforded Sunday.

Farona was tall and slender, with a crest of spiky red hair, just like his namesake bird. Under his drab robes he wore his coven colours; white trimmed with orange and black, which reminded Kolfinnia of a fox. He returned her bow with a genuine, but puzzled smile.

"And it's my pleasure to give you Flora Greyswan, Wildwood's most gifted garden worker." Kolfinnia turned to her friend and Flora stepped forward, amused to be included.

At sight of Flora, Sunday's eyes narrowed and darkened, then like a passing cloud her poise returned. Flora had a beauty of her own and Sunday didn't tolerate competition. As Flora turned to greet them, Sunday caught sight of her ugly eye-patch, and Kolfinnia saw something shocking: a tiny but triumphant smile surfaced on her smooth lips.

Flora didn't notice the insult. "Witches of Regal-Fox, I trust you enjoy your stay and eat well of my gardens." Her greeting was stiff but sincere.

"Thank you," Farona smiled shyly at her.

Meanwhile, Sunday saw her chance. "Coven gardener-girls, spending their days in the dirt, where would we be without them?"

Flora struggled for words, stunned by her sudden attack.

"Your kind perform a valuable service on behalf of witchcraft, Flora," Sunday pressed, smiling cruelly, while Farona looked away. It appeared he knew her all too well.

Your kind? Flora saw mockery in the compliment like a wasp in a bloom and clenched her fists and stiffened.

"We'd all be hungry without them," Kolfinnia countered quickly, trying to defuse a situation that had blown up out of nowhere.

"I'm sure you're right," she smiled absently, savouring Flora's red face. The servant knew her place, and she was satisfied. "I myself hold rank of summer solstice queen," she announced loudly, as she loosened her cloak and let it drop to the earth. In that moment it was like the clouds parting to reveal the sun in all its majesty. She wore a long, yet revealing, snow-white dress that flattered her stunning figure, and a necklace of amber sun-stars and gold circlets around her upper arms. Her sexual radiance was electrifying, almost to the point of being overpowering, and already a crowd was gathering. Kolfinnia stifled a gasp and at her side she sensed Flora's dismay and even envy.

Sunday sensed it too, and she smiled faintly. Everything was as it should be. "Farona, could you please," she waved at the cloak in the dust. It wasn't a question. The youth immediately collected it and draped it over his arm. "I fear the journey has ruffled my appearance for Lilain," she purred, smoothing her dress, drawing everyone's attention to her exquisite form. She let her preening hands draw their eyes ever downwards, teasing all the way, until at last she pressed them together before her groin, making a perfect V between her legs, knowing its subconscious effect on all: especially the men. "*One does not meet an empress dressed like a gardener-girl, does one?*" she laughed brightly and tossed her hair, a cascade of gold that reached below her waist. Kolfinnia and Flora stood tight-lipped and tense, feeling like mere girls, as she basked in the crowd's appreciation. "Kolfinnia, please lead on, I'm so looking forward to my meeting with Lilain." She spoke as though Lilain was the honoured one.

Kolfinnia watched her performance with horror, and even a hint of envy. "I trust I'll see you later, Flo?" she said, feeling her friend's hurt.

"Mmm," Flora mumbled, just staring at the ground.

Kolfinnia led their guests away but cast a worried look over her shoulder at Flora, who stood alone and impassive.

After a while Flora set about her gardens. In the cover of the towering corn she stabbed at the earth with her trowel. Her targets weren't stones or weeds, but Sunday's words, yet the more she jabbed the more mocking they sounded. One does not meet an empress dressed like a gardener-girl, does one?

She had endured cruel words before, but never here in the one place she felt safe. Turning the earth over was like uprooting old memories, "One-Eye! Half-Face! Cyclops!" She jabbed harder and small stones flicked through the air and pelted the corn. Sobs rose from her gut and before she could stop them she was crying. Kneeling in the dirt, she curled her arms about her head. "Monster. Ugly. Stupid." She cried softly and rubbed at her wounded eye as if trying to erase it. She'd lived with the hateful thing since she was four. "I hate you," she whispered: to the men who'd scarred her, to herself for being upset, and to Sunday for making her want the impossible.

She flinched as something prodded her hip, and looked around feeling embarrassed. Rooter the boar was standing by her side. She swallowed in relief and dried her face, then risked a look around, hoping nobody had seen her. She smiled sadly at Rooter and scratched his bristly snout. "Beauty and the beast," she sighed. "Which one do you want to be?"

He grunted in reply and head-butted her hand. He hadn't raided the gardens for some time, and it was time for her to uphold her end of the bargain.

"I've kept some tender cabbage hearts just for you. Don't tell anyone," she scratched his ear, collected her hat and led him to his reward.

The remains of Eliza Cobb and the chromosite were incinerated and dumped in the Thames. They had disappeared from the world and it ought to have ended there, but her parting gift had infected Krast.

More and more lone witches were apprehended and interrogated, but he was no longer content with just finding an answer to the Hethra and Halla myth. As he walked the deserted platforms at Hobbs Ash a voice came at him from nowhere. *What if she hadn't tried to kill you, Samuel? There'd be no excuse for what you did.*

He stopped and listened. He even glanced back over his shoulder. Was that the Cobb witch talking to him or his guilt? This had happened more and more in the two weeks since he'd examined 'that' chromosite. Old memories sat up and shouted with voices he'd once known, but he couldn't be sure if they were real or not. "Fatigue," he muttered, then hurried from the deserted platform. He'd not been sleeping well and to make matters worse he was on his way to another unscheduled visit from the odious Wallace Maccrae.

"You're late." Maccrae tapped his pocket watch.

"Minister." Krast threw him a small nod as he entered the state carriage. Maccrae had made himself comfortable, pouring a sherry and taking the chair at the head of the table. "And before you even ask, Mr Maccrae: no, we haven't yet located these witch idols." He was growing tired of his almost daily visits and he went to fetch a sherry of his own.

The minister raised his eyebrows as though he'd expected as much. "So far a great deal of money has found its way to you, and the people who make this possible want to know when they can expect a return for their investment." His furred jowls twitched a smile.

"As well I know, they send you here daily to remind me." He swept his jacket free and hooked it over the coat stand. "Do you think I take my duties to the empire lightly?"

Maccrae stroked the silver cap of his walking cane. "Some say the empire would benefit from a change in the Illuminata's hierarchy."

"She wanted rid of you too," a voice called from far away, except he wasn't sure if it was Eliza or the gurgling Thames where her ashes rested. "What?" Krast demanded, forgetting he wasn't alone.

"I said you need to be more ardent," Maccrae explained, believing he'd addressed him.

Krast stood motionless for a second while reality and his inner world merged then separated. He felt faint and he'd hardly heard Maccrae speak.

"Krast! Are you even listening to me?" He barked.

"Mr Maccrae!" His face flushed behind his scars. He downed his sherry in one gulp and calmed himself before going on. "Until all the covens are located we do nothing. The balance of power will simply shift. They can spring up like weeds. We need to take them all at once."

"And how long might that take? You need to speed things up!" Maccrae brooded.

"At last we agree." He crossed to the desk, took a file from its polished top and tossed it over. It glided across the table and stopped directly in front of the large man. "If you really want to speed things up have this bill made law."

"What is it?" He squinted at the cover page.

"Seizure of Occult Assets Act."

"That was repealed over a century ago!" he frowned. "You want me to propose renewing it. Why?"

"Speed things up, you said, and as minister for religious affairs who better to champion a bill that confiscates coven lands and assets for the church, who in turn increase their wealth and thus are better equipped to help the needy?"

"I'll have to speak with the cabinet, of course," he grunted.

"Of course. And remind them: it is for the good of the empire." Krast glowed at how convincingly pious he could sound when he had to.

"I shall give the matter my full attention." Maccrae sounded more dutiful.

He was so easy to manipulate that Krast almost pitied him. He would make the perfect martyr. "Care to join me in another sherry?" he beamed, suddenly feeling better.

Maccrae sat back and held out his glass. "Perhaps I've misjudged you, Knight Superior," he smiled.

Krast poured him a drink and smiled back. "Think nothing of it. I'm a forgiving man, Mr Maccrae."

Early evening brought a respite from the heat. Around the gardens visiting witches came and went, which Flora had found exciting until Sunday's arrival. "Emmie," she turned to her small helper.

"Mistress?" The young girl looked up from picking red currants.

"You've worked hard enough today. I think you should run along for supper now."

Emily Meadows always called her by her formal title 'Mistress', no matter how often she asked her not to. Today of all days she didn't want to be reminded of her station as a 'gardener-girl'. "Thank you!" Emily grinned and slapped dust from her dress. She was Wildwood's own solstice queen and you couldn't find anyone more different to Sunday. She was barely seven and totally unschooled in malice.

Long may it be so, thought Flora. She watched Emily retrieve her satchel from the sacking shed and wander away. Then, quite defiantly, she swept her hair into a ponytail, revealing her wounded face. Anger made her feel perversely proud of her eye-patch, and suddenly she wanted to fly with Torrent-Sweeps-Away-Bridges. Energised by the idea, she hurriedly packed away, took up her lightning-staff and pressed it to her cheek. "Torrent?"

"Would it be anyone else?" her sprite replied laconically and she smiled despite her bad day.

"I want to fly somewhere, anywhere, and fly fast."

"Ah . . . been one of those days, eh?"

"I'll tell you about it when we're aloft."

"Then let's get you aloft so I can hear about this bad day of yours." He began building his electrical charge and her smile spread into a grin.

Valonia read each poster with disgust, and some with mild amusement.

"For palmistry?" She asked Hilda, waving the bill contemptuously.

"That's now a punishable occult crime?" She tossed it back onto the pile with the others.

She and Hilda were reviewing, mostly with horror, the latest collection of propaganda bills that visiting witches had collected. Many offered a shilling reward for people informing on a witch and in large cities there were plenty of people who'd do far worse than sell a man or woman for a shilling.

"A shilling for a life!" Valonia spat.

"They're all alike," Hilda sighed. "Causing children to squint, or cows to suffer sore udders."

"They might as well add 'squinting cows'. They're getting desperate." She didn't know whether to laugh or cry, but the most disturbing bill announced that babies delivered by practitioners of magic suffered disfigurement or disability. Anyone found to have allowed such a person to attend a pregnant woman must pay the sheriff's court a comfort tax of five pounds. Fines not paid within a year would be levied against all inhabitants of the accused's parish. "Us and the old ways are going to get a bad name." Valonia pressed a hand to her brow, feeling a headache lurking there.

"The tide turns against us," Hilda admitted.

"It'll turn back. That's what tides do," Valonia assured her. "Just one week until the new-moon. Then we'll seek the Hand-of-Fate when it's at its weakest and we'll get our answers. We'll know for sure what this first-dawn is and how to fight it." Her mood grew defiant.

Hilda came and sat by her side. "I've got something that'll cheer you up." She held up a sack and gave it a shake.

Valonia's brow wrinkled in question. "Do tell?"

"Mandrakes!"

"Oooh!" She rubbed her hands. Mandrakes were the rarest ingredients a witch could hope for. "Who brought them?"

"Never mind, let's just say we can take our pick, but only two at most."

"I wish Lilain would visit every year," she chuckled.

They appraised each root in turn noting its colour, firmness and overall form. "This one looks peculiar," Hilda said. She held it up and smiled suggestively. It was well formed, a little too well formed. A stout root thrust out from its groins.

"Oak-be-green! Hilly, put it away. There's plenty of girls here don't know a man from a mandrake. That'll scare 'em half to death. Best choose one that's a little less excitable," she finished with a husky laugh.

When they'd completed their selection Valonia rose and paced to her window.

"Restless?" Hilda asked.

She sighed and watched Flora in the gardens below packing away her tools for the night while Emily Meadows skipped away through the crowds without a care in the world. She feared for all of them and her heart clenched to think all of this could be taken away. Flora troubled her in particular. She'd watched her all afternoon and noticed how colourless and still her aura was. Clearly something had upset the young woman. She watched her leave the gardens in a hurry. "Hilly?" She asked from nowhere.

"Hmm?" She looked up from re-packing the mandrakes.

"Start the evening spells without me, would you? I've a walk that needs taking, a talk that need talking."

Hilda smiled. "Someone needs lifting?"

"Aye, and one of our best." She clutched her lightning-staff and set out after Flora.

CHAPTER NINE

Lonely Sands

As far as Flora was concerned you could keep spectacular mountains and mighty forests because the sea was her goddess and she always came here to let it wash away her hurts. The endless plain of Appelier Bay was riddled with treacherous quicksands and when the tide came in it swept across the bay faster than a person could run. It was dangerous and wild but a playground for a witch on a staff. She scored a perfect groove in the wet sand with her bare toes as it raced past, and even that small signature was gone as Torrent lifted higher. She screamed out her frustrations as they tore across the miles of empty shore. A flock of oystercatchers piped in outrage as she buzzed past. "Sorry!" called.

"Bloody noisy damned birds!" Torrent huffed. *"So this Sunday, she made you jealous? Made you want to look like all the rest?"*

"Yes," she admitted. Out here you could confess your fears and they felt tiny. The wind snatched away her reply, but Torrent heard it loud and clear. It was almost mid-summer and the sun was still high for early evening, but a chill wind blew across the bay. Her clothes and hair whipped at her face but she loved the sense of wilderness.

"Was she blonde?" he asked from nowhere.

"Of course!"

"And was she beautiful?"

"Like the sun!"

"Huh! The trouble causers always are!"

"You're slowing," she teased him.

"So what does she have that you don't but an extra eye?" She wouldn't have taken such blunt talk from anyone else, but it sounded sweet coming from him. She avoided his question and banked the staff seawards, willing him to build speed again, but he seemed more in the mood to talk than fly. *"Many new witches around the coven these last weeks,"* he said offhandedly and she knew he was preparing one of his little sermons. *"Girls, boys, women . . . and young men,"* he added suggestively.

"Just up to that wreck and then inland, if you please." She half ignored him, and steered towards a small boat sunken in the sands.

"And do you know what?"

"Tell me."

"A good number of those young men took an interest in you. One eye or not."

"Perhaps they did," she agreed casually, but her stomach fluttered pleasantly. While holding the staff they could read one another easily and he barked a satisfied laugh. Her mouth tightened around a begrudging smile. "Thank you, Torrent, your point's taken." She slowed and the rushing in her ears finally dropped, but her throat felt sore from their shouted conversation. She wiped wind-tears away and raised herself up to get a better view of the upturned boat. "Tide carried it a long way in," she observed.

"Boats float and seas pound," he said idly. *"We'll turn home now?"*

Something about the boat pulled her closer. She slowed until they were going no faster than a shore crab. A pair of scavenging gulls flapped up, startled by their approach, their beaks red with carrion. She wondered what might be lying in the boat for them to eat and she suddenly felt cold. They were fifty yards from the dark shape now and she wondered how she could have ever thought that it was a boat. It shimmered in a way no boat could, not like wood, but skin. *Shark's skin*, she thought.

Just then it twitched.

"It's alive!" she jerked back in surprise.

"It's no boat then."

"Take us closer."

"What for?" he exclaimed.

"Because it might be hurt."

He wanted to remind her that if it was something like a barghest then they'd be the ones getting hurt, but he obliged and they drifted closer. The black shape flexed again, this time slowly raising a huge tail that flopped back to the sand with a crack and a spray of rainbow mist. It slithered out of its foetal position, uncurling with horrible grace and easily doubling its size. Its tail gouged a deep fan in the sand and then two large hands slapped down against the beach as it pushed itself upright and turned to regard them.

"Kelp-harpy!" Flora cried and immediately backed away. She felt her toes sink into something wet, and without looking down she lifted her feet from what she knew was quicksand and gripped the staff even tighter.

It stared at them intently. Its oily eyes were black and bottomless and its skull was covered with long hair that pulsed like jellyfish stingers. It rolled back its blunt head and yawned wide to reveal rows of needle teeth, all angled backwards into its fleshy throat. It looked to be calling or screaming, but no sound emerged.

"It's hurt, Tor!"

"A good thing too."

"It's not exactly a barghest," she snapped, annoyed by his indifference.

"It's not a mermaid princess either."

He was right. Kelp-harpies were vicious, deep water cousins of mermaids. They were intelligent and cruel but what one was doing so far from the crushing depths was a mystery. Both of them could clearly see that it was severely wounded. A great ragged hole had been bitten out of its flank, just below its chest. It was struggling to breath and its gills fanned sluggishly.

"We can't just leave it. It needs help."

"All we can do is put the wretched thing out of its suffering. Oak knows it's probably caused enough suffering in its lifetime."

"That's cruel!"

"It's a cruel beast. Leave it for the gulls I say."

"Torrent!"

"You've heard the tales. They roam in packs hunting down whales, dolphins and sharks. They even eat their own young! Leave it to rot I say."

"Maybe we can talk to it." She wasn't ready to give up just yet. "Take us closer, but keep out of striking distance."

"By Halla's crimson eyes, girl! What are you thinking?"

"Because of the barghest and Lilain, because the world's changing and this may be part of it," she hissed at him.

She made a convincing, if unappealing, argument and begrudgingly he continued forwards. *"Bloody duty,"* he grumbled. They swept wide to avoid its fearsome tail, and as they sailed gently around, the kelp-harpy turned its head to follow, moving with clockwork jerks, tracking them intently. Flora saw its hooked hands clench at the sands warily. It had no more liking for the situation than they did. *"Pegalia, remember,"* he prompted.

Pegalia was the common witch language. Flora's command of it was faltering but understandable, or so she hoped. "Understood," she whispered, then addressed the kelp-harpy. "You're wounded, we can offer you aid."

It coughed a series of gristly croaks that sounded eerily like laughter. "No help." The slushy sounds boiled up from its gullet carrying a rotten stink with them.

"Right, you've done your bit and it's declined. Now let's leave it to its own misery."

"Not yet!"

The harpy yawned again and reared up like a cobra, letting its long arms dangle in front of its chest. Flora saw that the wound was far worse than she'd expected and she marvelled that the creature was still living. "How did this happen?" She couldn't take her eyes from the hideous injury.

The creature turned and regarded the sea hungrily. "Ruin," it gasped.

"A creature from Ruination attacked you?"

It shuddered with laughter, perhaps laughing at the savagery, or her pity. She couldn't tell.

"What kind of creature could inflict a wound like that?" Torrent asked, but she didn't want to ponder that right now.

"I can return with help on your oath that you'll not attack." She wondered if there was anything in creation that could mend the gaping hole in its flank.

The kelp-harpy slowly lowered itself back onto the sands and dipped its head. Its mass of hair flopped down to conceal its face, and Flora was relieved to be away from that unblinking stare. It remained that way for some time and she wondered if its posture was meant to signal agreement or had it surrendered to death. "Help," it hissed at last without looking up.

"On your oath?"

"Oath," it groaned, and she saw its hooked hands rake the sand once more.

"Very well." She breathed a tiny sigh and relaxed a fraction.

Then it struck, lunging forward in a shower of water, muzzle agape.

"Torrent!" She screamed, meaning to turn, but slipped backwards from her staff. She expected a harsh impact, but the ground sagged under her like a mattress and she realised with horror that she'd hit quicksand.

The kelp-harpy pulled back with predatory swiftness and halted just yards from where she lay.

"Flora!" Torrent roared, torn between saving her or striking the creature.

"Torrent!" She clawed wildly from where she was sprawled in the mire and found a grip on the staff, but only one hand, while her other arm was already sinking. He growled and hissed as he kept the staff steady, but as she tried to push herself up her trapped arm just sank further and the strain on her grip increased. Foolishly, she tried to push with her feet, but the sand just swallowed them down too, which in turn slowly peeled her fingers further away from the staff. "Torrent!" she begged. The mud dragged her one way and Torrent the other, and she felt like a wire pulled between two magnets. "Torrent!" It came out as a pathetic sob.

The kelp-harpy began circling, dragging its heavy body around them and blackening the sand with its blood. It hissed and tested the sand with claw-swipes, calculating a way to reach her. Flora desperately tried to keep it in sight, but as it passed behind her it vanished from view. She wrenched her shoulders trying to turn but now it was just a slithering sound somewhere to her rear. "What do we do?" She pleaded.

"First get you out," he growled. *"It won't risk getting trapped itself. Get you up and out then use speed to get away."*

Suddenly she felt something slice through the air to her left, her blind side, and she screamed.

"It's taking swings," he shouted.

"I can't see!" she cried, furious that it was cheating somehow. She tried to turn but the mud was like a straitjacket. The sun was lower now and she could just see its shadow hovering to her left, at the very edge of her vision. It was keeping to her blind side, where she wore that wretched eye-patch. *It's so cunning,* she thought in dismay.

"I could have told you that!" he shot back, reading her thoughts.

She tried to haul herself up again, but it was like fighting cement.

"Heave!" he urged.

She strained but only managed a few inches before sinking back. "I don't know if I can," she sobbed.

"If you die here it'll be Sunday's doing," he said coldly.

He was right. A beautiful witch had sent her out here to cry like a child. If she died would that beautiful witch even know or care? She stopped struggling and framed herself. "Can you fly alone?" she whispered.

"What! And leave you here?"

"Just long enough to bring help."

"You'll go under before I even get back to Wildwood."

"We'll have to risk it."

She heard the creature's rippling laughter, somewhere behind her. It sounded like boiling fat.

"What if she attacks while I'm gone?" he growled. *"What then, eh?"*

"It won't risk it. Please, go for help. Tell Valonia what happened. She has to know about it before the thunder-heights call you." But if she died before he got back and he returned to the thunder-heights, nobody would ever know what'd become of a poor witch named Flora Greyswan.

"No, there's a better way. If you dare let go of the staff for a second I can finish her off."

He might, but he was quickly depleting his strength just keeping her from sinking. Could he manage to kill it and keep her from sinking afterwards, she thought? "You'd not have enough strength left to keep me up!" It was a terrible dilemma.

"Let me try!"

"No, do as –," Just at that moment the shadow moved.

"It's coming!"

Something sharp glanced across her back and she screamed. The harpy lashed out again and she felt a rush of wind as its tail missed her by a hair's width. "NO!" she raged. Her right arm was paralysed by mud and somewhere under the ooze her wand was still buckled to her hip. It might as well have been on the moon for all the use it was to her.

The kelp-harpy dragged itself around to her front and regarded her, cocking its head this way and that as it calculated a way to reach its meal. Its instincts were so strong that even mortally wounded it couldn't stop itself grabbing one last feast, and Flora was little more than prettily packaged meat.

Her grip was failing. *I'll die here,* she thought calmly. *I'll die here, and all because I was jealous of Sunday Flowers: to be desirable instead of scarred and ugly. Maybe this is my punishment? Maybe I deserve this?* The kelp-harpy was less than twenty feet away, watching her from the edge of the quicksand. "You broke your oath!" she spat.

It yawned, looking unconcerned, and then coughed up a spray of blood and a long grey tongue lashed out and seized her arm like a whip, splattering her face with rank saliva. Flora screamed, then it heaved, almost tearing her arm from its socket as it dragged her towards its gaping jaws. As the mud yielded she tugged frantically at her trapped arm trying to free it. A second later she wrenched it free and flayed at her hip, groping for her wand-sheath, and when her fingers found it her heart leapt. But it was empty. She clawed at it in disbelief, but her wand was lost in the mud. Now she knew with certainty that she'd be eaten alive. "Torrent!" she cried hopelessly.

Then from nowhere lightning struck.

A brilliant flash momentarily blinded her and a shrill scream filled the air. The pressure on her arm vanished as its tongue snaked away. She blinked her vision clear and saw the creature swoon backwards, trailing smoke from its mouth and eyes.

"*SKALD!*" Torrent cheered.

"Valonia?" Flora gasped. Her coven-mother stood on the firm sand, holding her staff like a halberd. The kelp-harpy finally crashed to the ground, making the quicksand ripple in the shockwave. "Valonia!" Flora cried in joy.

Valonia mounted her staff and crossed the deadly ground to where she lay, and hovered there and drew her wand, hrafn-dimmu. "Take hold," she commanded.

Flora released her staff and snatched the wand in one swift move. As soon as she let go, Torrent sailed the staff to safe ground and emerged looking exhausted and pale.

Valonia uttered a command, sending a hot pulse racing down her wand like a current. The drowning mud rippled as if struck and Flora felt its crushing grip fail. She immediately reached up, grasped Valonia's lightning-staff and was hauled up. The sands gurgled one last time as she finally left their embrace, trailing huge clots of mud, and then she was unceremoniously dragged to safety. Valonia knelt and threw her arms around her regardless of the filth.

"I'd have died here," she cried against her shoulder. Torrent hopped to her side and clutched her hand tenderly, while Skald glowered at them all as though he couldn't see what all the fuss was about. "I'd have died and nobody would've known," she sobbed, feeling the first tremors of shock.

"Oh, we'd have known, when the plates and dinner tables ran bare. After all, solstice queens are two-a-penny, but what would we do without our gardener-girls?" Valonia winked.

Flora hugged her fiercely, plastering the old witch with mud while Skald and Torrent sat close by like sentinels watching the tide, which had now begun to turn. Soon it would race across the bay and the kelp-harpy's remains would be washed out to sea, into the black depths where creatures from the mind of Ruination had appeared once more.

It had been an eventful day for witches and knights, and that evening Hathwell had a revelation of his own, albeit a less dramatic one. He lived alone but was seldom lonely, and that evening after his meal he took a closer look at the fragmentary pages he'd slipped out of the library that day.

He soon saw that they were written, not by Illuminata historians, but by a separate source. It transpired that they were translations of an earlier Latin text written by a 12th century Irish monk named Mannix who had sailed across the Irish sea to Wales in a small boat but been wrecked on the rocks. Mannix described how he had been saved from the sea and hostile locals by a small band of people living outside the tribal system. They lived a comfortable if simple lifestyle in a hidden location and had the skills to live self sufficiently, not to mention mend his broken bones.

Mannix recovered and stayed with them through the winter and the following spring, learning their customs. Although he never used the words 'witch' or 'coven' Hathwell recognised right away who his rescuers were because he wrote of their deities, twin serpents that lived in 'the soul of the world', as he put it. What had become of the rest of Mannix's account was a mystery. Hathwell wished he could have read it, but even the small fragment he did read kept him awake into the small hours. Would demon worshippers really show such kindness to a stranger?

He lay in his bed and listened to London's night symphony outside: hooves on cobbles, lonely footsteps and the occasional drunken shout far off. He kept trying to reconcile the Illuminata accounts against the Mannix account, but his mind just couldn't bend that far. One account must be true, the other false.

He rolled over, chasing sleep, and wondered why an obscure account from a monk who'd been dead for centuries seemed to carry more weight than all the books in that blasted library put together.

Later that evening when her painful steward duty was over, Kolfinnia changed into less formal dress. The guests from Regal-Fox were spending the night with Lana's witches and due to leave the next morning. Hopefully she'd have no cause to see Sunday again.

She spent the early evening with Rowan, sat by the small stream close to the Flower-Forth camp and anxiously awaited Flora who she'd not seen since their clash with Sunday. "Farona told me that Regal-Fox is named after the barrow of a Saxon king in the heart of their coven. Foxes built a den inside, right amongst the king's treasure." She recounted her day, although she was careful to leave out their confrontation with Sunday. Now her place at Wildwood was assured, she felt even more protective of the girl.

"What do fairies do?" Rowan asked from nowhere.

She considered. "They make sure souls get to Evermore safely. Everything in creation has its own soul and own special fairy to guide it."

"All?"

"Hmm, yes, all things."

"Is that why we saw one when we found Lilain? It had come to take her away?"

A good question, she thought with a shiver. Maybe Lilain was so close to death the fairy had come in readiness. "Maybe," she said tactfully.

Rowan seemed to dismiss the idea. "That's Vega," she pointed to the brightest star. "The witch-star," she added sleepily. The darkness wasn't yet complete and only the very brightest stars showed.

"Trust you to remember, and the small star to the left is Therion, Vega's own thunder-sprite." A vixen screeched a lone call somewhere in the woods, and to take her mind off her worries she told Rowan the story of Vega again. "The very first witches came from Vega carrying with them the terra-soula containing the serpent-twins Oak and Holly, and they buried their precious cargo here so the twins could dream and that life could flourish." As she spoke she adjusted Rowan's cloak.

"The twins first came from Vega." Rowan melted against her friend and closed her eyes.

"So the story goes, yes." She rested her cheek against Rowan's hair. She thought the girl had dozed off when she spoke again in her half-sleep.

"Clovis cares for his own serpent-twins far away on Vega."

Kolfinnia frowned. "Who's Clovis?"

"A great warrior-witch," she sighed before sinking into sleep.

"Clovis?" Kolfinnia uttered and felt that it wasn't a friend she held in her arms, but a great mystery disguised as a child.

She watched the heavens for a long time with only the sound of Rowan's breathing for company. One by one stars emerged as night deepened, but she couldn't relax. Her thoughts kept turning to Flora and she heard the hurry of approaching feet long before she saw their owner. "Flora?" She called, but instead Esta and Hilda came out of the darkness.

"Kolfinnia, I thought we'd find you here." Hilda held up her wand and the gentle light from its tip made her look ghostly.

Esta scooped Rowan out of her embrace. "It's away to bed with you, little Rowan." She blew a puff of air and grimaced, "Not so bloody little!" She carried Rowan away to bed, which fortunately for Esta wasn't too far.

"Hilda, I've been waiting for Flo all evening. Have you seen her?"

"Indeed I have. There's been an incident and she was involved. No, no!" She shook her head firmly upon seeing her worried face. "She's fine. Shaken perhaps, but not hurt. I want you to come along. Everyone's waiting for you, even Gale." Hilda kept her voice hushed. She didn't want the news to spread. She paced away, and Kolfinnia, not to mention a good many moths, followed her illuminated wand as it bobbed through the dark.

"Who summoned Gale? How long have you been looking for me? Hilda! Can't you tell me what's happened?" The faster she walked the more questions poured out of her.

"All will be revealed. Flora's tale is for Wards alone." She put a cautionary finger to her lips and despite everything, again Kolfinnia glowed at being addressed as 'Ward'.

Her apprehensions made the spiral around the tree feel to go on without end and she bounded up each step thinking only of reaching the top, and until she did no amount of reassurance could convince her that Flora was safe and well.

"Flora's well, don't fuss!" Hilda said repeatedly.

I bet Sunday was involved! she thought venomously. When they reached the balcony Hilda ushered her inside and there was Flora sitting in an old armchair. She looked up as the door swung open and immediately stood. The blanket across her lap fell to the floor and Kolfinnia saw that she was wearing a dress of Moon-Frost blue, an ill fitting dress that had silver clasps down the open neck. Flora hauled up the hem of the baggy garment, rushed to her friend and embraced her so fiercely that Kolfinnia was even more worried. "Flo," she whispered against her ear, "what's happened? You're all right aren't you?" She held her at arm's length looking for some awful injury.

"It's fine," she smiled, "I'm fine, really. Thanks to Valonia."

Both of them turned and Kolfinnia saw that the tower was full, crammed even. Valonia and her Wards stood watching their reunion, while thunder-sprites nestled in the branches above, watching the proceedings. Amongst them she saw Skald and Torrent and her heart warmed when she saw Gale's familiar face.

"Please, be seated," Valonia eased her towards one of the cushions on the floor where the others were already making themselves comfortable. Flora sat beside her and without thinking the two clasped hands.

"You're sure that you're all right?" Kolfinnia asked again.

"Fine," she squeezed her hand.

"Blue suits you," She admired the borrowed dress.

"My best one too," Valonia scowled. "So don't go rescuing any more kelp-harpies in it."

Kolfinnia gaped. "You did what?"

"Coven-mother wants you to hear the tale because it might well have something to do with the barghests," Flora explained.

She caught the plural and looked around the Wards.

"We've taken Flora into our confidence and soon you'll hear why," Valonia said as she set about lighting her pipe. "Flora, would you please . . . ?"

Flora began but made no mention that it was Sunday's words that had sent her off to Appelier Bay in the first place. Kolfinnia listened with admiration and fear, and she couldn't say how or why, but Flora appeared different and it wasn't just the borrowed dress. She listened to the escalating drama fearing it would have a terrible ending and Flora would simply vanish before her eyes, and when Flora told them the kelp-harpy had spoken of Ruination, Kolfinnia remembered, against her wishes, that the threat to Hethra and Halla was very real. She'd begun to hope it was something imagined and that life could go on as it ever had. "And after I'd scrubbed off the mud and changed into clean clothes, Ward Saxon went to find you," Flora finished.

She turned back to Kolfinnia, and that's when it struck her. Her freshly washed hair was neatly combed back to reveal both her exquisite face and her eye-patch and with her new look came an air of strength she hadn't seen in her before.

"Kolty?" Flora asked.

"Sorry," she shook the revelation away, "I'm just bewildered." Everything she cherished now stood in peril. She looked around at the witches and sprites in the tower. "This is just awful!"

"Awful that I lived or awful about the harpy?" Flora joked.

Kolfinnia attempted a smile. "Then it's all true. 'They hunt the serpent-twins', Rowan said. I somehow believed that it'd just go away. I *wanted* it to go away."

"We all did, Kolfinnia, we all did," Valonia agreed sadly.

"Was it a barghest that attacked the kelp-harpy?"

"We can only guess at what maimed it, and Lord Oak knows there are more creatures in Ruination than any sane witch could guess at. The twins' peril deepens, and so more creatures emanate from the dreaming mind of Ruin." She took a deep breath and prepared to tell her the worst part of her news. "In response we have accelerated our plans. We can't wait."

The other Wards looked stonily at the floor.

"We set out at first light tomorrow to seek the Hand-of-Fate," Valonia made a point of catching her eye, "all five of us."

Speechless, all Kolfinnia could manage was a slight nod. The Hand-of-Fate was a creature considered so dangerous that she was yet to hear of a witch reckless enough to seek it and lucky enough to survive. Flora looked down at the floor, afraid and dejected.

"Understand, Kolfinnia," Hilda said sensing her shock, "it's the only way we can discover the Illuminata's plans. When the Hand speaks it's never wrong and it never lies."

"This'll be your initiation," Valonia added gruffly. "But rest assured that I shall be the one to summon the Hand and I shall be the one to question it. You are not to go near it, you understand?"

Kolfinnia looked to Flora. Her face was a mask of dejection and she couldn't help but second-guess Valonia. "Now that you've taken Flo into your confidence, couldn't she accompany us?"

Flora straightened, looking hopeful, while uneasy glances passed around the others. Valonia stared at her blankly and Kolfinnia thought she'd annoyed the old woman. Valonia drew thoughtfully on her pipe before answering. "Five are needed to summon the Hand: four to guard the compass points and one to hold it and question it. I shall be the one. I am sorry but Flora cannot come with us."

She saw Flora wilt.

"Besides," she continued, gentler now, "Flora keeps Wildwood fed. She's perhaps our most important witch, despite what arrogant, half-dressed solstice queens might think." She afforded Flora a warm but somewhat cunning smile.

The pipe continued on its way, missing both young women, passing from Valonia to Esta.

"Best not. It'll blacken your teeth." Esta winked.

Lana tapped the pipe stem against her lower lip thoughtfully before speaking. "We'll be away for a whole day. The Junior Wards will take the helm while we're gone and you, Flora, we'd like you to take charge of Valonia's duties."

Flora gasped audibly.

"This is a great honour, Flora, but be warned, it'll be a trial by fire," Lana continued. "There are plenty of visitors waiting to see Lilain and they know how to grumble if they're kept waiting." Her tone was so rhythmic, the hour so late, and the pipe smoke so fragrant that Kolfinnia was starting to feel drowsy.

"With honour, Ward Zuri," Flora accepted graciously.

"Cheer up, Flo! It means you get to keep all the gifts they bring with 'em!" Esta barked her husky laugh.

"And besides," Valonia added, "the party from Regal-Fox leaves tomorrow. As acting coven-mother, they'll be obliged to show you the same courtesy they'd show me. Miss Flowers will have to say a formal goodbye. Do you know how that's done?"

Flora shook her head.

Valonia looked pleased. "She'll have to bow and kiss your hand," she said with wicked relish.

There was a satisfied silence, then Torrent barked a single laugh which sparked a flurry of laughter amongst them all.

"Make sure it's good and filthy!" Esta prodded her in the ribs. "Lots of compost work tomorrow!"

When the laughter died away Valonia folded her arms, looking pleased with the result. "Well, it's an indecent hour and we face a painfully early start. Time to retire." This prompted murmurs of agreement and everyone began to rise and make their goodnight blessings.

Sprites vanished into staffs and Wards carried them down the darkened spiral, which was lit only by glowing wands. Kolfinnia and Flora were last to leave, and as they did Flora stopped in the threshold and turned back. She still didn't really know how to thank Valonia. She had saved her life and all because she kept a close eye on her witches. "Thank you, coven-mother. For everything."

"Blessed be," Valonia returned, and then never being one for formality she added, "Oh, and Flora, be so kind as to give my dress a pressing if you find the time tomorrow, would you?"

She smirked and stepped out onto the balcony, and then it was Kolfinnia's turn to glance back. Valonia stood alone, and the sombre look on her face made her fear the approaching dawn. "Goodnight, Valonia," she murmured.

"Sleep sound," she wished her.

She stepped out into the night and closed the door behind her.

The sound of footsteps faded, the branches rustled gently and the tower fell silent again. Valonia extinguished all the candles, except for one. That one she left burning and sat down in front of it. As she peered into the tiny flame a moth purred past her ear and an owl hooted softy somewhere above. There was one last spell to enact before she clambered into her hammock, where she knew already that sleep would be thin and troubled. She muttered a few words into the flame, which flickered in response. Skald crawled down from the branches to join her and they began chanting the spell together, because they were both equally guilty. They finished the spell of sorrow for having taken a life. They asked the kelp-harpy's soul for forgiveness and afterwards, as Valonia climbed wearily into her hammock, she wondered if the Hand-of-Fate felt guilt for all the witches it had killed down the centuries and whether it would say a prayer for their souls if it should best them tomorrow.

CHAPTER TEN

The Hand-of-Fate

Dawn rolled across the landscape, erasing the night and revealing a misty and unseasonably cool Wildwood. The grass gleamed with a galaxy of dewdrops scored here and there by badger tracks, and the moist air rang to the clamour of rooks that had the world all to themselves.

Kolfinnia pulled her cloak tighter around her shoulders and wondered if the cold was just a hiccup in the weather or some dour omen connected with the Hand. She wore a plain and practical dress as grey as the sky, knowing that they'd be leaving the safety of the coven, and she carried a small pack of supplies and of course her lightning-staff.

"Did you sleep at all?" Gale asked.

"Hardly."

"You'll sleep well enough tonight, I suppose," he assured her.

"Lets hope it's not the eternal kind of sleep." She instantly wished she hadn't said it.

"Come on!" He rallied her. "We stopped three barghests. We'll be home for lunch." His bravado was genuine, but she didn't like to remind him that Rowan had finished the barghests and she wasn't coming with them.

Her sleep had been erratic. She'd woken several times thinking that she'd slept for hours only to see that the moon had barely shifted, and the next thing she knew Flora was waking her and from the look of it she'd slept no better than her.

"Kol, it's time to go," she'd told her regretfully and Kolfinnia had never seen her friend looking so forlorn. They shared a silent embrace and in the end she had to ease herself out of Flora's reluctant arms. Flora was distraught and with good cause. Her friend was setting out to confront a creature synonymous with death and there was no other at Wildwood she could tell, not even Rowan.

Kolfinnia tramped through the wet grass and within minutes the dew soaked her boots and the cold licked her feet. She passed lines of laundry left out overnight and wondered who'd be getting a tongue lashing for forgetting to collect it. She even envied the witches who'd spend the morning wringing and scrubbing. She would have traded anything to stay here and let the Hand-of-Fate remain where it was, somewhere underground.

A few small tents threaded the verges along the path to the tower. Inside, sleeping soundly no doubt, were folks come to see Lilain. In a few hours Wildwood would wear its carnival atmosphere again and nobody but Flora would know how dark the world had grown.

She entered the gardens and felt a surge of relief when she saw Lana and Esta ahead, and hurried to catch them. They turned at the sound of her footfalls, smiled and bowed in greeting. Both were dressed like Kolfinnia: in plain wayfarer grey, and wore their cloaks so that their wand-sheaths wouldn't show. Both women carried lightning-staffs, and Lana had a curiously large sack strung around her shoulders and as she walked, her long coat dragged over the ground, collecting a forest of twigs and grass.

"Morning, lass!" Esta surprised her with an embrace, her second that morning. "We were wondering if you'd run away in the night. We wouldn't blame you. Did you sleep well?"

Kolfinnia shook her head.

"You sleep at all?" Esta frowned.

Kolfinnia shrugged.

"That makes three of us, then," Lana didn't look up as she tied her coat buttons. "So cold today," she said, almost to herself.

"There's a good chance," came Valonia's voice, "that it'll be colder still where we're bound for." She joined their huddle followed finally by Hilda. Without exception they all wore wayfarer grey, carried lightning-staffs and atheme-knives. Their real purpose was symbolic but today Kolfinnia thought that each blade might have to earn its keep.

"And that'd be where exactly?" Esta prompted. "That tiny bit of the plan you forgot to tell the rest of us, Val."

"Up, into the high fells. The Hand, as you'll know, always appears from underground. There's a disused lead mine called Troller's Ghyll.

I reckon the opening is plenty big enough for the creature to crawl through." She looked away as she spoke, squinting as though trying to penetrate the miles and see that awful sounding place.

It occurred to Kolfinnia, unexpectedly and with some alarm, that she knew virtually nothing about this creature. She wasn't even sure what it would look like and for an instant she felt like a fraud amongst the wise.

"Kolfinnia?" Valonia shook her from her thoughts. "You're ready for this?"

All eyes regarded her. She couldn't let them down. "Can it be any worse than facing three barghests?" She borrowed Gale's bravado, even though her guts writhed like a sack of worms.

"Ahh!" Esta drawled. "Watch this one, Val. She's after your tower: our new barghest slaying coven-mother!"

Valonia chuckled, wondering if Esta knew that's just what she hoped for.

"So, how far to this Troller's Ghyll?" Hilda turned them back to the business of the day.

"Seven miles, give or take," Valonia pointed northwards. "We'll have to walk, let the sprites save their strength."

For fighting, Kolfinnia thought.

Lana slung her staff over her shoulder where it hung like a rifle. Esta did likewise while the others held theirs like walking staffs.

"You have the kindling?" Valonia gestured to the bag hanging by Lana's side.

"Aye." She gave it a firm pat in way of an answer.

"Very well then, let's be away. Soonest begun is soonest done." She raised her staff to signal them forwards and Kolfinnia suddenly thought of Rowan singing that same little rhyme.

Rowan, she thought. Esta had taken the girl back to bed last night and she'd not had chance to say goodbye, which made her feel very sad.

The party started out with Valonia spearheading and Kolfinnia bringing up the rear. She stopped briefly at the edge of the gardens before they ventured into the wood beyond, the wood where she and Rowan had first cemented their friendship, and she promised that when, if, she came back she'd find Rowan at once. "I promise," she said quietly. Then she turned away from her home and followed the others, up towards the high fells where the wind moaned through abandoned mine shafts that led downwards into the earth, like open throats, to where the Hand-of-Fate awaited.

"What do you know of it, Kolfinnia?"

She was busy replacing her boots when Hilda broached the big question. They'd just forded a stream, having crossed barefoot. She understood that 'it' meant the Hand and that Hilda was reluctant to name it.

"In all honesty, very little," she fumbled with her laces, feeling ignorant.

"Huh! That's probably for the best." Esta plucked river debris from between her gnarled toes.

"May I, Valonia?" Hilda asked.

"If she wishes it." Valonia was wringing water from the hem of her cloak: the ford had been deeper than they'd realised.

They continued, and Hilda told her what she knew, or just what she thought prudent, about the Hand-of-Fate. "The Hand represents blind luck or chance. It can answer any question and is always correct. It is a creature of the dark places under the earth. The honeycomb of tunnels that span the world are its home and so when summoned it always appears from underground. That's why we must travel to the fells and find a shaft large enough for it to emerge from."

"It lives close by, then?" The thought of this creature under her feet was very disturbing.

"Yes and no. In a way it is everywhere. I've heard tales of it appearing at either ends of the Earth on the same night. How it covers such distances is a mystery. I don't think you need worry about having it as a permanent neighbour."

"How is it summoned?"

"You see Lana's shoulder bag?" She gestured with her staff.

"Yes?"

"Firewood."

"Why would we bring firewood?" Kolfinnia frowned.

"Because we're heading to the fells, there's little wood up there and it's needed for the summoning ceremony."

"And why do we guard the compass points while she questions the creature?"

Hilda looked uncomfortable at this, and Valonia, having overheard her question turned back. "Tell her, Hilly. She might as well know it all."

Hilda cleared her throat. "Kolfinnia," she began, then moistened her lips and tried again. "Kolfinnia, the Hand will not be alone. It will have a host of familiars and we guard the compass points to stop them from disrupting the ceremony."

"So we walk and let the sprites save their strength?"

"Quite so." She patted her arm affectionately.

She wanted to ask Hilda what kind of host accompanied the Hand, but sensed that knowing would only make matters worse. *Sometimes*, she thought, *ignorance is bliss.*

After an hour's walk they crossed the scarecrow circle. The others passed the mouldering scarecrow without a second glance, although Valonia stopped briefly to pet the crow nesting in its belly. As she passed, Kolfinnia ran fingers over the scarecrow's ragged garments and quietly bid Wildwood farewell.

The high fells were dominated by limestone and the witches picked their way through piles of jagged scree and over limestone pavement where fingers of hart's tongue reached up from crevasses like hands testing prison bars. She began to see nothing but desolation. The trees thinned, the rocks pressed through the malnourished soil like bare bones, and she thought of the creature they hunted, scuttling under their feet through a labyrinth of tunnels. The wind grew bolder, the overcast sky began to weep, and veils of mist rolled in from nowhere as they climbed ever higher. Without map or distinguishable landmarks, Valonia led them through one limestone scar after another, each one the same battlefield of shattered rock.

The ground was covered with tussock grass and progress grew slow. They reached a plateau where dry-stone walls were the only evidence that people had ever come this way, but the walls were collapsed and engulfed by moss and grass. It was still only mid-morning but the early start and heavy terrain had fired a serious hunger in Kolfinnia's belly. Valonia led them to a hollow out of the wind's reach and there they huddled together for comfort and warmth and ate their provisions.

"Damned coldest June I can recall," Esta grumbled as she unwrapped her bread. "You're looking pale, lass. This'll sort you." She passed a bottle of sweet nettle tea.

Kolfinnia swigged from it and felt a little revived. "It's just the cold, Esta." She wiped a little of the drink from her lower lip. "I'm fine." She felt she'd been saying that a lot recently when in actual fact she felt nothing like it. She felt a long way from fine because she regarded anywhere outside Wildwood as populated by folks who believed that witches and gallows were made for one another.

"It's fine *not* to be fine, you know." Valonia interrupted. "We all feel it and if you're a sensible witch, you will too."

"I feel it," she confessed gladly. "I feel vulnerable." The wind chasing across the top of their hollow sounded mindless and Kolfinnia longed for home, but what was the use of a home that was doomed? She felt like a snail hiding in its shell from the approaching hammer. "Valonia, is the Hand a creature of Ruin?" She asked as she passed the canteen back.

"That's a good question, and the best I can say is I don't think so," she brushed a stray lock of grey hair away from her face. "It's something altogether different. One tale says it's the hand of the Patternmaker himself and that after he'd created humanity he was so disgusted with his creation that he severed his offending hand and cast it down to Earth. The Hand seeks revenge on his former master by telling those crazy enough to try what the future holds, and so disturbing the webs of fate."

Kolfinnia was intrigued. "So this Hand is really the hand of what, of God?"

"Ha! No, girl!" she scoffed. "It's a colourful tale, I'll grant you that, but it's a tale and nothing more."

"The part about 'those crazy enough' is true though." Esta circled a finger around their huddle.

Kolfinnia chewed her bread and considered all of this. "Pardon my ignorance, Valonia, but this Hand, I take it that it looks like, well, er . . . a hand?"

"It's not called the Hand for nothing Ward Algra," she smiled.

"Like my own?" She held up her own hand, fingers splayed.

"A touch bigger, perhaps."

"How much bigger?"

"I said it needs a big opening to crawl through, and a mine shaft will suffice. That ought to give you an idea of its size."

"Oh," she said simply and picked patches of crust from her bread and nibbled them while she tried to ignore the tremors in her gut. "Valonia, what would happen if the Illuminata prevailed? If the twins of oak and holly were . . . well, if they were found?"

She noticed the others had stopped eating.

"There'd be no more green Earth, that's what would happen!" Valonia threw her hands up and then slapped them down on her knees.

"Truthfully?"

"If *they* got their hands on the twins, their dream of life would become a living nightmare. I don't need to explain what would happen then."

"Still want to be a Ward?" Lana smiled crookedly.

"More than ever."

"That's my girl." Esta chuckled as she lit her pipe.

"So far I've encountered barghests," Kolfinnia asked. "And I've read of others, but what else might come from Ruination? What are they and how do you send them back?"

"You certainly pick the right places for tales of terror, lass." Esta looked mildly impressed.

Valonia took a gulp from Esta's bottle then rubbed her hands against the cold. "Very well, where to begin?" she considered. "The dead-walk, now there's a horror for you. Nobody knows if it's plant or beast, and I only saw one once as a girl. It'd invaded a healthy wood and was corrupting the trees there, making more of its own kind. It took the whole coven to kill it, and it left a good number of us injured." She drew a long breath and added, "And I can still hear its dying screams to this day."

Kolfinnia was appalled but fascinated. "It's some kind of tree?" she asked.

"It's a creature of infiltration, one of the very few Ruinous creatures that can survive in our realm, as well as the only one that can reproduce here. It's a parasite creature that only looks like a tree. It needs a host to spread its seed, which is like a grab-hook, and falls from its parent when it senses an animal below. Then it makes its way to the host's ear, crawling over skin and through fur to get there."

Kolfinnia sensed where this tale was heading and felt her own skin crawl.

"Once inside the host's brain it matures, the victim feels nothing. When stronger, the seed takes control of its host." Valonia tapped a finger to her temple to illustrate her point. "It commands the host to walk for days on end without food or sleep until the body is utterly spent. The host quickly passes away having both spread the seed and provided it flesh upon which to grow. And so there's always a skull, be it human, bird or some other animal, at the dead-walk's rotten heart."

"And crib-robbers?" Kolfinnia went on.

"Crib-robbers," Valonia repeated slowly.

"First-dawn is your demise."

Valonia looked up, convinced the voice had been real. She opened her mouth but faltered and looked down at her old hands. "Crib-robbers are one of the few creatures that can pass between Ruin and Earth at will, and have a taste for infants," she said simply. "A 'robber is little more than a mouth with a stomach. It's completely flattened like a disc of oven-bottom bread." She held her hand up flat, palm down. "That lets it slide under doors and suchlike. It seems no gap is too tight for a determined robber and the rest," she sighed heavily, "the rest is inevitable. It swallows infants whole, spirits them away but for what purpose I wouldn't wish to guess at."

"That's horrible," Kolfinnia uttered.

"If you're to be Ward, Kolfinnia, you must know of this particular creature."

"I understand."

"I don't think you do, not yet," she said softly. "Crib-robbers sometimes *follow* witches in hope of snatching the infants we deliver. A witch acting as midwife must know the spells that send them back to Ruin."

"I'm ready to learn such spells."

"You'll have to learn how to deliver bawling babies first," she laughed, defusing the tension.

"How much further to the Ghyll?" Hilda asked.

"Not far," Valonia said quietly, "one mile perhaps."

One mile, Kolfinnia thought and looked down at the ground between her feet, which no longer felt solid; somewhere beneath were endless tunnels occupied by a gigantic hand. *One mile to Troller's Ghyll.*

Sunday felt grubby. She had found Wildwood's accommodation barely adequate. Farona might have loved spending the night in a glorified treehouse but she found its rustic charms far too basic.

She sat under the shade of a white canvas pavilion. Two witches from Chalk-Stag coven brought it with them, but Sunday had soon charmed it from them. Where the two fools who'd carried it all this way had gone to find alternative shelter she neither knew nor cared.

Wildwood had shed the mist and turned into a June heatwave, a world away from the high fells. Sunday sat regally within her new pavilion and enjoyed the sensation of Farona arranging her hair into a luxurious plait festooned with swan feathers that radiated from her head like a halo. As soon as they'd farewelled Valonia they'd be leaving.

"May I admire your handiwork, dearest?" She lifted an expectant palm and Farona dutifully offered her a looking glass. Sunday liked mirrors: she always saw something there that pleased her. She studied her reflection and the headdress of dazzling swan feathers. "Farona, you're an artist, truly you are," she reached up and stroked his cheek, letting her fingers slide sensuously from his chin. She knew he had a deep attraction for her and she'd never missed the chance to exploit it.

"My thanks, Miss Flowers." He didn't like her gesture but at the same time he loved it. Sometimes it made him feel like her pet and at other times it made him feel grown up. He was fifteen, a confusing time, and he didn't like the way he sometimes felt trapped between childhood and manhood. He admired her discreetly, with a mixture of resentment and longing as she admired herself in the mirror again.

Sunday concealed a smile and pretended not to notice his interest. "Your efforts are a great credit to Hethra and Halla," she turned suddenly to the bemused youth. "It's important that workers of magic be proud of their heritage."

"Yes, miss," he agreed politely, looking away in a hurry.

"A witch, just like magic itself, is a regal soul. Always remember that." Her expression darkened. "Now, I think it time to venture to the tower. I'm sure Valonia will be waiting for us by now." She stood, smoothed her white dress and buckled her golden wand-sheath about her slender waist. Then she gestured to the pavilion's canvas doors and he obliged by parting them. "Farona, run along and inform Valonia of our impending departure."

"Yes miss," he obeyed, still holding the canvas aside for her.

Sunday believed in making a good impression in the name of Regal-Fox and witchcraft in general. She ardently believed magic should be proud. Witches had lived in fear of the Illuminata, and to some extent their own skills, for too long. The covens ought to rise up and declare themselves. Politics aside, she was confident that she'd made a great impression and hoped witches would leave with tales of Regal-Fox's splendour and its radiant solstice queen. She sighed contentedly, collected her elegant white lightning-staff and stepped out into the sunlight to bask in the attention of her admirers. Farona guiltily savoured her heavenly scent as she passed, before sighing heavily and turning and being about his errand.

Flora had spent an hour rummaging through Valonia's belongings, which felt very wrong but she was desperate and had no choice. Plus, the day was waning and there were duties she hadn't yet dispensed with. "He must be here somewhere, he must!" she moaned.

"He could've fallen out of the tree," Torrent added unhelpfully.

She suddenly felt sick with dread. Could Hercules have hobbled away and fallen out of the tower? "Lord Oak!" she breathed. This was turning into a hellish day.

Suddenly there was a gentle knock at the door. Flora froze and swapped guilty glances with Torrent. She cleared her throat, pulled creases from the front of her dress and smoothed back her ponytail.

When she opened the door she recognised the tall lad's pleasant face and his crest of red hair, but couldn't place the name. There was a brief moment of puzzlement, when neither had expected the other, before Flora found her voice. "Good morning." She forced herself to sound calm while she seriously hoped Hercules wasn't lying in a mangled heap at the foot of the tree. "It's Farona isn't it, Farona Firecrest?" She'd placed him now: Sunday's attendant.

"Yes, miss." It was the girl he'd met briefly yesterday in the gardens, and suddenly he forgot about Sunday's message and his tongue wouldn't work properly. "Erm," he started, "I came looking for the coven-mother."

"And you've found her. Valonia and her Wards are away on important business. I'm acting coven-mother today."

He swallowed his surprise. "You're very young for a coven-mother." He regretted his clumsy flattery as soon as it dropped from his mouth. *As well as very pretty*, he thought and his cheeks flushed.

She smiled. "Young or old Wildwood's all mine today. I take it Miss Flowers is ready to depart?" He nodded and she sensed her hour had come. "Then please inform her that I'll attend her in the gardens forthwith." She didn't know what more to say and hoped that she'd sounded dignified enough.

"Very good, miss." The nervous lad started away, when Flora stopped him.

"Farona, you didn't happen to see a hare in the gardens, did you?"

"A hare, no I don't think so," he considered. "Why, was it important, miss?"

"Oh, not really. Sometimes they nibble at the corn. Thank you," she laughed nervously, slammed door and slumped against it. "I can't do this!"

"Good luck! I've found him. He was asleep in the hammock!" Torrent cheered.

Flora heaved a gasp of relief. "Hurry back, Valonia, please," she prayed. "Hurry back safe."

"Ah, Farona," Sunday found him returning from the tower. "Will the coven-mother meet us soon? I'm keen to be away. The charms of 'roughing it' last only so long."

"Coven-mother will meet us at the tower as soon as you're ready, miss." He didn't reveal who the coven-mother would be today. She'd make him pay for it later, but he reckoned it'd be worth it to see her face.

"Excellent!" She shooed him ahead with a clap and lifted the hem of her dress to avoid soiling it, and if that should reveal more of her long legs than was modest, well there was no harm in that, she thought.

Farona carried their baggage and led her through the coven towards the gardens. All along the way Sunday collected appreciative glances like a trophy hunter gathering rare butterflies. She walked with deliberate graceful steps and held her head high enough for the swan feathers to catch the breeze. Around her she sensed the buzz of envy and desire, all of it directed at her, and the sense of power was intoxicating.

Once they reached the tower, Farona halted. Sunday had devised a fitting presentation, in which her escort would announce her then step aside to reveal her waiting demurely to kiss Valonia's hand. She'd insisted that they rehearse it this morning in the privacy of their pavilion and knew it would look wonderful.

Sunday kept her eyes fixed on the path at her feet. She heard the spiral stairs creak and footsteps grow closer and louder. She snatched sly glances left and right. Sure enough a crowd was gathering, and she felt a contented glow. The sound of feet on wooden steps became the crunch of gravel and then halted just yards away. Farona's voice came next.

"Mistress Flowers, I give you Wildwood's coven-mother."

"Coven-mother," Sunday sang, dipping a gracious curtsey, then she straightened and looked up.

There before her was Flora.

She blinked once in disbelief, and her knuckles whitened around her staff. Behind her beautiful mask counter-measures were already whirling. She would not stoop to kiss the hand of a half-blind garden girl, even if the serpent-twins themselves depended upon it.

"Mistress Flowers," Flora was genuinely pleased to see her. "It is my honour as acting coven-mother to wish you a safe journey and bid you visit Wildwood again without delay." Then with exquisite slowness, she held out her hand to be kissed. She wanted all of Wildwood to see this.

Farona felt he was standing on thin ice, while at the same time did his best not to smirk. He stared ahead at nothing and waited for the storm to break. But Sunday recovered with artful speed.

"Coven-mother," she oozed sarcastically, "I have decided, in light of Wildwood's wonderful hospitality, to remain another day and humbly ask you to grant us an audience tomorrow, to farewell our party with all good blessing."

When Valonia's returned, Flora understood and grudgingly admitted that she was a fast thinker. "Then your party shall eat well of my gardens," she said sweetly with her expectant hand still thrust out for all to see.

There were many spectators now, and many puzzled glances. A gesture was required. Sunday stepped forward, took Flora's fingertips and gave her hand a single shake. "Coven-mother."

"I look forward to seeing you again tomorrow, Mistress Flowers," Flora said prettily.

"And I look forward to Valonia's swift return," Sunday warned. Then she stepped back and gathered herself, and Flora saw that this was not a witch to make an enemy of. "Farona." She called him like a dog and after a last glance at Flora he fell in behind her as she swept through the gardens back to her pavilion, but the smile she wore was as lifeless as a pinned butterfly.

They approached Troller's Ghyll through a narrow gorge where the rocks were green with corruption. Sheep bones littered their way and greasy wool rose from yellowed ribs like steam. The tapping of their staffs on the rocks echoed back to them, sounding cold and grating.

"This place is awful," Hilda whispered.

"The Ghyll is at the far end, not fifty yards." Valonia made it sound like an accusation.

They picked their way through the rocks and at last came to Troller's Ghyll, a great horseshoe-shaped depression. The mine opening looked like an ugly bruise and a mountain of slag spewed out from it. The place had the odour of sheep urine and dung, and a few gnarled hawthorns looked down from the grassy cliffs like spectators. Their bark was smoothed and oiled where generations of sheep had rubbed against them. One or two saplings struggled towards the sky, but they were diseased and bitter looking. As they stepped from the gorge into the sunken clearing they disturbed a flock of crows who flew off and cursed them with their jagged calls. These weren't crows like captain Jerrow; they had no more liking for witches than they did for men.

Without slowing, Valonia headed towards the mine and the group closed ranks, each woman feeling that the very landscape itself was watching. "Esta, Lana, build the fire there." She pointed to a cluster of rocks where a fire wouldn't harm the grass. "Hilly, instruct Kolfinnia on the rest, will you?"

The rest of what? Kolfinnia thought.

Hilda sat her down amid the rocks. Without thinking they'd all begun to speak in hushed tones. "Take one of these." She opened her satchel and passed her an irregular piece of mirror glass with the edges ground smooth. "We shall each have one."

Kolfinnia nodded but said nothing. She could hear the faint crackle of burning wood as Esta and Lana got the fire lit.

"Valonia will call the Hand. It will come from there," she indicated the mine. "When it comes Valonia must use her atheme to subdue it."

"How?" Kolfinnia began.

"By finding the first letter of her name on the creature's skin."

Kolfinnia was more confused than ever.

"Never mind, that's Valonia's worry," she said impatiently. "We'll have our own business to deal with. Each of us will face outwards to guard the compass points and stop the Hand's familiars from reaching Valonia. They'll try and take the spell bottle from her. Do you understand?"

"Yes."

"You take the south. Protect Valonia and the spell bottle at all costs.

Keep the mirror facing outwards, not towards yourself, outwards, do you understand?" she stressed.

"How do the mirrors work?"

She grimaced, unsure what to say. "They'll hold the familiars back for a while. As long as they see their reflections they'll be afraid to advance."

Kolfinnia looked at the piece of mirror glass and curiosity overcame her fears. "But why?"

"Because their reflection reminds them of what they once were. When they come you'll see what they are and what becomes of witches who summon the Hand and fail." The older woman looked terribly grave.

"Hilda?"

"I'm fine," she pretended. "Keep your mirror on them. Eventually they'll outflank us and then it's time for lightning-staffs."

Kolfinnia could smell smoke now, but the fire's meagre light multiplied her fears rather than dousing them. It was like a signal announcing their presence when all her instincts told her to hide.

Esta came to their side and knelt down. "Val's ready to start the summoning and asks that we take our places on the compass." For the first time Kolfinnia could remember, Esta didn't have a witty remark to spare. She simply curled her mouth in an attempt to smile and patted her on her back. "Blessed be, lass," she said roughly.

Valonia stood alone by the fire, holding a tiny spell bottle in her hand. One by one her Wards made their way to the points of the compass, forming a square around their coven-mother, with their backs facing inwards.

Kolfinnia looked southwards across the wild grass and rubble, seeing only the dank gorge. In her right hand she held her lightning-staff; in the other, the mirror. *"Are you ready for this Gale?"* she asked.

"Aye," he replied quietly, saving his strength.

Her whole body tingled and she thought the mirror might snap in her grip. *'This is what becomes of witches who summon the Hand and fail,'* Hilda's words came back to her.

Valonia saw that the fire was sufficiently hot. Angry embers pulsed at its heart. *It's now.* She rolled back her sleeve, and holding the spell bottle in her fist she slowly eased that fist into the smoke, into the flame and finally into the embers.

In the quiet depths under the earth a six-fingered hand as large as an ox twitched and unfurled in response to her challenge.

Valonia hissed in agony. The spell bottle preserved her from damage but the pain remained undimmed. "A hand for the Hand," she groaned, labouring against the agonies. "A hand for the Hand." The summoning had begun.

Kolfinnia heard her agonised groans. "I see nothing!" she cried, expecting an army of familiars to spring up immediately.

"Eyes front, be patient!" Lana commanded.

Her eyes darted back and forth but she saw nothing other than rocks and mouldering bones.

The Hand-of-Fate charged towards its challenger with impossible speed. The scent of magic was strong and within moments it had homed in on Valonia's call and the racing hoofbeats of her heart.

Valonia's chest heaved and she knew she must pull her fist from the fire soon: the pain was crushing her. "Face me!" she screamed. Then, when she was sure the agony would tear her open, she saw it.

A swarm of tiny black creatures heralded its arrival. They drifted up from the mine entrance like a warning smoke. Then the first pallid fingers appeared, each as thick as a tree trunk. Great ragged nails scraped against rock and more black specks swarmed around their master like plague flies. The Hand-of-Fate finally crawled into the daylight.

They all heard Valonia's gasp of horror and knew there was no turning back.

"Eyes front!" Lana shouted.

Kolfinnia fought the craving to turn.

"They'll come now for sure," Esta called.

It paused at the mouth of the shaft and raised itself up, scenting the air like a snake. Valonia snatched her own hand from the fire, still clutching the spell bottle. The pain vanished at once, and she was able to see it clearly now. It was massive, with two thumbs; one on either side of its span of fingers, representing both left and right. It was corpse pale and its skin writhed with countless letters and symbols like tattoos, but they were alive and they swarmed and fought one another, moving over its flesh in waves, rippling over knuckles and tendons and sometimes spiralling through the air like dark snowflakes before returning to their keeper. Now she stepped forward to confront it.

It dropped and crawled down the slope, shoving rocks aside and dragging its calloused wrist-stump behind it like a tail.

Valonia had moments to scrutinise the symbols on its skin. She must press her sword tip to the first letter of her name to gain command over it, or else they were all lost before they'd begun.

V for Valonia. She desperately sought that one letter amongst the writhing symbols. Every letter of every language devised by humans was represented there.

It was only feet away and it reared up on its fingers like a crab and lunged, and there she saw it, on the knuckle of the index finger, in amongst a babble of living letters – a bold 'V'. She screamed and lunged.

Kolfinnia turned, drawn to help her, when Hilda shouted to them all. "The host have come!"

She whirled back, Valonia's plight temporarily eclipsed. "Where?" The gorge was grey and empty. "Where? I see nothing!" The spectre of panic loomed close.

"The grass girl, look to the grass!" Esta yelled.

She looked down and finally saw what became of witches who failed to subdue the Hand-of-Fate, and she screamed.

An army of severed human hands was speeding towards them, crawling through the grass like spiders, coming from all sides. She saw, with dumb wonder, hands of young and old, black and white, men and women who all now served the great Hand. "Lord Oak save us!"

"The mirror!" Gale cried.

She held up her trembling mirror and thrust it out. The tide of severed hands slowed, clenched and halted.

Valonia's atheme buried itself in the Hand's tough hide with a wet thud and pinned the V dead centre. It froze then clenched into a great fist, its dagger-like nails gouged trenches in the ground and suddenly it stilled.

It was physically subdued, but now she must pit her will against it, and trust her Wards could hold its familiars or they too would join its ranks as crawling hands. She drove her will through her atheme and the Hand's ageless consciousness crashed down on her own like a leaden weight. She almost dropped to her knees; its strength was dreadful and she knew that she couldn't resist for long. "The Illuminata," she gasped, "tell me their plans."

VALONIA Its will was cold and timeless and it rumbled up from the ground like an earthquake, sending shock waves through her mind. JOIN THE RETINUE OF THE FATED HAND

"NO!" She pressed harder, with both steel and will. "Show me their schemes!"

Incredibly, the letters on its skin realigned and spelled out a message. THEY BUILD WAR MACHINES TO CRUSH YOU

"Why now?" she groaned.

BECAUSE OF FIRST-DAWN

She recoiled as if struck. The Hand twitched as her concentration lapsed, but she recovered and pressed back harder, driving her atheme deeper and the V wriggled like a trapped snake. "What is first-dawn?" She sensed a great piece of a cosmic puzzle was about to become known.

A MACHINE TO TRANSFORM MATTER The letters swirled again.
Alchemy! she thought. "And why do they hunt the twins?" It flinched and wrestled against her will. But soon it would have her, she knew. "TELL ME!" she commanded, and sweat poured from her brow.

Kolfinnia swung her mirror left and right, but the approaching foe was spread too wide, when she repulsed some the mirror was facing away from the others and so on. Yard by yard the ghastly horde were creeping closer. "Hilda!" she moaned.

"I know," she shouted back, facing the same dilemma. "Be ready with your staff."

Kolfinnia's staff throbbed so hard that it was like gripping a wasp's nest. *"Gale?"*

"Ready," he snarled.

"Tell me! Why do they hunt the twins!" Valonia bellowed.

THEIR ESSENCE WILL FUEL FIRST-DAWN FOR KRAST

She had no time to ask who this 'Krast' was. She cut to the most important question. "How do they intend to find them?"

INTERROGATION

"But no witch knows where they lay sleeping!" she cried triumphantly, convinced the Illuminata's plans were already sunk.

ONE DOES

She gaped. "Who?" she whispered, and the universe held its breath.

Yard by yard the host pincered towards them on all sides. They poured from between rocks and clambered over one another. They were so close that Kolfinnia could see many still wore rings or bracelets. She swung the mirror left and right, holding them back with their shameful reflection, but as they crept closer the cordon tightened. A cruel law dictated that for each one she stopped others were free to advance and those freed of their refection now lunged at her.

A large hand adorned with rings sprang from the grass towards her throat and suddenly an electrical discharge cracked, smoke hazed the air and the withered thing fell dead to the ground. She held her staff before her and turned quickly to see the others doing the same. The mirrors could no longer help them and she dropped hers into the grass and briefly glimpsed her own terrified face reflected there, just as a swarm of clutching hands pounced up to tear at her. She screamed and lashed out, Gale bellowed and she fought for her life.

Valonia heard Kolfinnia scream, closely followed by Esta, Lana and

Hilda's war cries. There was a sudden barrage of hefty cracks as sprites started striking their enemies down, but she must know this last answer. As soon as she had it she'd break the spell-bottle and banish the Hand and its foul host. "Tell me!" she roared. "Who knows?"

ROWAN OF WILDWOOD

"Rowan?" She sagged in disbelief and her knife tip strayed an inch. And the monster, sensing her slip, lunged.

She screamed and expertly swung her staff from her back and thrust it upwards into the open palm about to crush her, but as she did the delicate spell-bottle tumbled from her hand and rolled away. Skald bellowed and there was a blinding flash. The creature jerked and toppled, but as soon as it crashed to the ground it rolled over ready to spring again.

She threw herself flat, landing with a terrible jolt, and reached for the bottle. But as her fingers brushed against it something seized her legs with brutal force and she was dragged over the stony ground. The Hand-of-Fate had its prize and it began to haul her towards the open mine, where it would take her into the darkness and initiate her.

Kolfinnia was dragged to the ground, kicking and screaming. Charred hands lay in a smoking pile, but countless more wrenched and tore at her. She tried to cry out, but felt cold fingers push at her lips and force an entry to her mouth. She gritted her teeth against them, flailing blindly with her staff. Another gripped her neck and fingers closed around her throat; hands yanked at her hair and clothes. She heard the others screaming and fighting. Gale's voice tried to fight its way through the drowning terror, but she couldn't hear him any longer. She screwed her eyes against fingers trying to gouge and blind. She clawed at them but still they came, entombing her, determined to drag her into the very earth.

"VALONIA!" Skald screamed as her fingers slipped away from her lightning-staff.

"The bottle, Skald. Break it, break it!" Her head crashed against a boulder as she was dragged along and for a moment the world turned grey with the pain. "Skaaaallll . . . " she slurred, half dazed.

He turned saw that the host had broken the cordon and were now rushing to snatch the spell-bottle. The Wards themselves were little more than writhing mounds, like blooms smothered in flies. If he didn't do something they would all die here.

He lifted into the air on his broad wings and plunged downwards into a nest of tangled fists, all of them fighting to claim the spell-bottle.

He crashed right into them and his clawed feet came down on the thin glass with crushing force and the spell-bottle exploded into glittering fragments.

The enormous Hand suddenly twitched and splayed its fingers in an agonised spasm, tumbling Valonia to the ground. She winced and crawled away, half expecting the beast to strike again, but instead she saw it slithering back towards the mine looking sluggish and mindless. It had failed to capture the summoning spell and it must flee. It struggled up the slope, hauled itself up to the lip of the shaft and tumbled inside with a rattle of stones. A few stray symbols buzzed after it and then it vanished from sight.

Valonia coughed, spat and clambered up. Her long hair plastered her face and she could feel blood trickle from a scalp wound. She looked around and saw the fire had burned itself out and the host had vanished. Kolfinnia and the others lay battered and groaning, but the only hands she counted now were the blackened and lifeless ones littering the grass. "Wards?" she gasped and staggered over to Esta.

"Give me a mo'," Esta coughed hoarsely.

Lana wearily raised her staff, signalling that she was more or less intact.

Hilda sat up, streaked with mud, her clothes in tatters and her usually neat hair a forest of tangles. She nodded mutely to Valonia. Nobody spoke, the only sounds were laboured breathing, coughing and someone crying softly. It was Kolfinnia.

Valonia hobbled to where she was kneeling in the grass, and the young woman looked up. Her face was bruised and her nose was bleeding, her hair wild and her clothes torn. "You did well, Ward Algra," she croaked.

"It's just a child's," she grieved.

A pitifully small hand lay in the grass: the same one that had tried to prise her jaws open and choke her.

Valonia helped her up and gently wiped the tears from her face. "We're done here," she said.

Kolfinnia nodded and then, acting on some unknown compulsion, she pulled a handkerchief from her pocket and placed it gently over the child's severed hand. Valonia regarded it for a moment and suddenly thought of Rowan. *Rowan of Wildwood knows*, she thought.

The crows that had cursed them earlier had returned and now lined the ridge above. Valonia knew as soon as they left they would make short work of the defeated host, which were now just carrion. In a few days there'd be nothing left of the battle but yellowing bones on the empty, high fells.

CHAPTER ELEVEN

The Librarian's Task

Goldhawk Row possessed many doors. Some were for men to be seen using and others weren't. The door used by librarian Holloway was of this latter kind.

Stone stairs lit by weak electric lights drew him downwards and the further he went the stronger the river's smell became. The steps ended abruptly in a puddle. He gingerly stepped over it and into a short section of tunnel that no longer descended but ran level with the Thames. The corridor was just high enough for him to walk without stooping. The lantern light glided over the ceiling, illuminating delicate stalactites sprouting from between the masonry, while underfoot was gritty and his footfalls had an eerie tinkling echo.

He paused, looked back over his shoulder and saw only a string of lights disappearing into the gloom. He was a suspicious man and even in the cramped tunnel suspected that he might not be wholly alone. He continued forward until he saw the vague shape of an archway ahead. "Knight Superior, sir!" he called warily.

The silence continued unbroken, then a lozenge of light began to glow, increasing in brightness until Holloway could see the chamber beyond. This was the master's gallery, he knew. Krast stepped into the light like a shadow puppet. "Mr Holloway." His voice rolled down the corridor and echoed from the walls.

"Aye, sir," he breathed.

Krast disappeared from sight and Holloway advanced, snatching another look behind before he did. As soon as he stepped into the master's gallery he squinted against the illumination.

The master's gallery was a grand hexagonal chamber laid with alcoves, each of which housed a statue of some past dignitary. The floor comprised tiered stone steps and at their centre was the speaker's pit from where former Knight Superiors would address the men watching from behind the hollow statues in the alcoves. The statue's watching eyes were inky black and all of them stared down at the flooded speaker's pit. Its surface was pockmarked by debris swept in by the river. Krast was standing opposite and in the glare of the lights the bronze markings across his face and hands made him look as though he was slowly transforming into a statue like the ones around him.

"Sir." Holloway lay his lantern down.

"Testament to better days," Krast sighed deeply. "I first heard my mentor speak from here many years ago." He gazed at the well of filthy water.

"Men like you'll make glory come again sir, I'm sure of it," Holloway simpered.

Krast fingered a line of scum running around the walls, a flood-line from the last time the Thames had invaded this chamber. "Some restoration work is needed first, I fear." He sounded melancholy.

The past weeks had not been kind to him. A great many lone witches and sympathisers had been rounded up at a shilling a piece, and all of them put to the chromosites, and after each interrogation he experienced a wave of nausea at what might be waiting for him. This was something he'd never known before. The Cobb witch had possessed a skill he'd never encountered. He had no idea how she'd plucked Josephine's face from his mind, but now each time he sliced open a chromosite he trembled so much that he insisted on working alone. The dread would escalate until he forced himself to look, and as always found nothing there. But in that vulnerable moment he felt Josephine's memory like a tightening noose, and so far it had all been for very little. The campaign map collected more red pins as more covens were uncovered, but Hethra and Halla remained more myth than fact. He was ready to concede that the artefact might take many years to locate and all the while Maccrae and his ilk continued to hound him. He found the hunt for the twins diminished now. The Cobb witch had steered his crusade from enlightenment to vengeance and he subconsciously believed that the more witches he punished, the sooner that vault in his mind would be locked again.

"Were you pleased with the information I retrieved, sir?" Holloway asked.

"Indeed, and with it I've finalised a solution to our problem. The curse is being purified by the devisers." Krast thumbed his pocket watch.

"I must say, sir, how honoured I am that you chose me. I'd have thought Mr 'athwell, being so closely bound to you sir, would've been first choice."

Krast smiled. "He's an idealist."

"He did take a peep at the documents I was collecting for you, sir."

"I trust you didn't tell him our purpose?"

"Lord no, sir!" he almost choked, "just a quick look is all he got. We've been very discreet."

"Bertrand was a fine squire but he's a straightforward man. An honest man, in fact, but the task ahead needs someone who understands that what is right is not always honest."

"It takes a certain man for a job like this," he agreed.

"Quite so." Krast slipped his watch back into his waistcoat. "And if you'll be that 'certain man', then you'll find everything you need there." He pointed to a small parcel no bigger than a matchbox at the foot of the archway where Holloway stood.

The librarian looked down and sniffed. "So small!" he marvelled, understanding its effect would be anything but.

"It must not to be opened until it's within touching distance. The creature has tasted his essence and will feed from him alone."

Holloway looked impressed. "Where, if you'll permit my asking, sir, did you acquire the minister's essence?"

Krast twitched a small smile. "He joined me in a sherry and left traces on the glass."

Holloway leered at his slick work.

"Remember, deliver the creature within striking distance, if done too soon or too far away it'll die, as will much work and planning."

"Trust me, sir, and my congratulations. The good folk of Britannia have much to thank you for." He reached down, scooped up the packet and dropped it into his jacket.

"Let me remind you the timing is crucial. He makes his first reading of the revised seizures bill in two days. Exactly two weeks after, the bill enters its second reading. The creature's life-span and digestive process have been precisely devised to peak in time for the second reading."

"I'll see it's delivered tomorrow sir, without fail." Holloway assured him.

"Then I'll bid you good night."

"And you too, sir." He collected his lantern, turned the flame up higher and stepped back into the dank corridor and back towards the daylight.

Krast watched his lantern bob away into the darkness and listened to his fading footsteps. The master's gallery was silent but for the sound of dripping water and the rush of the gas flame. He listened for Eliza's voice, then looked down at the murky pool in the speaker's pit, half expecting to see Josephine's face but saw and heard nothing other than his own monochrome reflection.

After surviving the Hand' Kolfinnia thought she would be jubilant, but the return journey was slow and everyone seemed sullen and withdrawn. As they descended into gentler territory she hoped their mood might lighten, but instead the heat drew out the flies and the exhausted witches became their sole interest.

"I'll be happier once we pass the way-bewares," Esta said irritably.

The circle of dolls was still some way off and none of them had much appetite for chatter. They found a small stream and tidied their appearance before they returned. Blood and bruises were certain to stir up plenty of gossip. After that they moved along in quiet reflection, mulling over what Valonia had told them.

The Illuminata are on the brink of achieving alchemy and are readying for war against us, to erase the covens once and for all and to pave the way for unearthing the twins.'

They'd survived one danger only to be confronted by another more insidious and far-reaching one.

"What can we do, Valonia?" Kolfinnia had asked, feeling helpless.

"That's best discussed over tea and a pipe." She hadn't mentioned Rowan's significance. That was something else best discussed back at Wildwood. Rowan's special gift made Valonia's journey a heavy-hearted one and she wondered if she could ever look at the girl in the same way again.

"Kolty!" It was Flora who was first to greet them.

It was only mid-afternoon but Kolfinnia felt she'd been away for a year. Flora rushed at her and gave her a crushing hug even more emotional than the one she'd farewelled her with. Valonia and her Wards left them to their reunion.

"I knew you were fine. Rowan said so." Flora looked in disbelief at her ragged dress.

"Rowan? What did she say?"

"She came and asked me where you were. She seemed very upset when I told her you were all away on special duties, but I didn't say what."

"What did she say to that?"

"She looked terribly wounded then she said 'the Hand went empty-handed'. As soon as she said it I knew that you were all safe, but I swear I never breathed a word of your business, witch's honour."

"Where's Rowan now, do you know?"

"At the Seed-Fall camp, last I heard."

"I'll go speak to her, then clean up properly and try to catch some sleep. Valonia has called a special meeting tonight. She wants you to come as well."

"Me?" Flora looked surprised.

"Finding that kelp-harpy has involved you in something that shows no sign of getting better," she admitted.

Flora leaned closer and touched her arm. "What did it say, the Hand, I mean?"

She looked haunted and suddenly Flora regretted asking. "Valonia will tell us all tonight," she said, then abruptly changed the subject. "How did *her* farewell go?"

"Her?"

"Our 'solstice-seductress', the one who's determined to outshine Lilain herself," she sneered.

"Oh, Sunday! I got a cold little handshake," Flora grinned. "She couldn't do it."

"No! In front of everyone?" The harmless gossip felt good.

"Oh, she's slippery that one," Flora cautioned. "She declared aloud they'd be honoured to stay, so now she's leaving tomorrow when she can kiss Valonia's hand instead."

"I'd like to see her shake another kind of hand entirely."

Flora looked long at her friend and thought that she'd grown since dawn. "I'm so glad you're home."

"That makes two of us," she confessed and went to find Rowan.

Valonia found her tower just as she'd left it, and she was somewhat surprised that Wildwood had survived her absence. She'd been a part of it for so long that she'd forgotten how well they could cope without her, which pleased and rattled her a little. She invited her friends inside and instructed Lana to draw a salt-circle on the floor while she prepared some rose-hip tea. A moment later they took their places inside the protective barrier. All of them carried an assortment of cuts and bruises and looked drained and spent. Everyone gulped down their tea: there was no lady-like sipping this afternoon.

"Flora and Kolfinnia will join us for our meeting tonight after even-spells," Valonia began, "but out of respect for your courage I wanted to tell you what the Hand said, so you can ponder it before this evening."

Lana, Esta and Hilda all looked ready to find their bunks but they sat upright and listened.

"The Hand confirmed what we've feared for some time, since Lilain came to us, in fact. The Illuminata are seeking Lord Hethra and Lady Halla as some dire plan to power matter transformation experiments."

"Alchemy! It still drives them mad," Esta groaned.

"I still insist that they can't be captured. No witch knows where they lie," Lana argued wearily.

"Even if they never find them, their intentions alone are enough to disrupt their sleep." Valonia wanted to make this very clear. "I'd hoped that would be the very worst we could expect, but it turns out that fate has been both cruel and kind to us today."

"We're all tired. Please be direct," Hilda said impatiently, rubbing at her bruised face. "What did you learn from that . . . thing."

"Something so fantastic I can hardly credit it."

"Well!" Esta said. "Share it, then."

"What we've always thought is wrong. There is one witch who knows where the twins lie." Valonia watched her news sink in. There was a brief silence and then they all began to speak at once, asking impossible questions.

"Do the Illuminata know this?" Lana demanded.

"Why's this witch never come forward?" Hilda rattled her teacup down, looking outraged.

One by one, more angry and confused questions ricocheted around the room.

"You're all asking the wrong questions," Valonia shook her head and closed her eyes. She was starting to wish she'd let them sleep first. She held up her hand for quiet and they saw an ugly blister in the centre of her palm, despite the spell's protection, and they remembered how she'd faced the worst dangers for the information she was trying to share. They swapped a few shameful glances and the room grew quiet.

"Forgive us," Lana murmured.

"Aye, sorry," Esta said. "Been a tough day."

"And what should we ask?" Hilda added gently.

"You should ask *who* this unique witch might be." She tempted them with a little smile. "And I'll be glad to tell you."

It was Esta that guessed it. Her brow went from a tangle of confused wrinkles to wide-eyed astonishment as the insight hit home. The hand holding her cup slumped into her lap, and just as well for her that she'd already drained her tea. "Rowan!" she whispered, mouth agape. "The lass knows!"

Kolfinnia returned to her camp using the aerial walkways and avoiding the footpaths. She didn't want to pass visitors with a ripped dress and bloodied face, and the last person she wanted to see was Sunday.

Drooping branches caressed her face as she walked along the swaying gantries. It was usually a feeling she cherished, but today it made her think of clutching hands and she hurried, wanting to be back at camp and get out of her ruined dress. She reached a narrow circular gallery around a beech tree and chose a rope ladder leading down. She could see the turf-roofed huts of the Flower-Forth camp right below. She slung her staff and climbed down.

Luckily she had the camp to herself, and she quickly took advantage of the rare privacy. She drew water from the stream and hurriedly stripped down to her smock, then bundled the violated dress into a sack, wasting no time in getting it off her back and out of her sight. She stripped naked and used a rag to scrub herself down, desperate to wash away the blood, dirt and lingering touch of the familiars. She combed her hair vigorously, pulling out every scrap of debris and wincing with the effort. When she was clean she hastily pulled on a fresh dress and then set about scrubbing her lightning-staff, worried that it might have absorbed foul energies, and worried for Gale because he'd been very quiet. "Gale?" She whispered.

"Hmm?" Too weak to talk aloud, he spoke as a gentle breeze in her head.

"I didn't thank you as I ought to have."

"Just need rest," he mumbled. *"Just rest, that's all the thanks I need."*

She kissed the staff then wrapped it in cloth scented with yew oil and slid it under her bunk. "Thank you," she said again to the sleeping thunder-sprite and then set off to find Rowan.

It took some time to locate her. She asked around and finally little Rilla Baldragon told her that she'd spent the morning gathering fallen feathers with her, and she'd left Rowan sorting them by Three-swords.

Kolfinnia thanked the young girl and made her way to Three-Swords, a cluster of small standing stones. It was a ten-minute walk along a shady path beyond the broad-leaf trees to the first giant pines. Three-swords was secluded enough for witches to use as a retreat when they needed solitude. If Rowan was still there then Kolfinnia guessed she had something important on her mind and found herself wondering if she'd upset her in some way. She could be very sensitive, very deep.

Sure enough, when she caught a glimpse of Three-swords through the larches she saw Rowan sitting against one of the stones with her knees draw up to her chest and her chin resting on her folded arms. A small sack rested by her side and one or two downy feathers drifted from it like snowflakes.

She didn't try to hide her approach, preferring her footsteps to break the ice because she had the uneasy feeling that Rowan was angry at her, but the girl didn't look up. "Rowan, I've looked all over for you."

"You didn't come," she mumbled, so quietly that Kolfinnia had to ask her to repeat herself. "I said, you didn't come," she said flatly without looking up.

"Going today wasn't my idea." She stood before her feeling awkward.

"You could've told me, told me you were off and said a proper goodbye. I fell asleep last night and when I woke you'd all gone to . . . " she bit her lip, unable to finish.

Kolfinnia knew this was delicate. "Flora was injured yesterday evening and that's why she didn't meet us. And Valonia needed me to leave early on a special errand." She knelt and lay a hand on her arm, but Rowan inched away. "It was very late when we finished talking and very early when we set out. There wasn't time to find you, and I didn't want you to worry." The girl just sat there and the silence felt as thick as treacle, and Kolfinnia wished she'd say something.

"It would've taken you," she whispered, still staring at the grass, "taken you and you'd become just a crawling hand like all the others."

She didn't even stop to wonder how Rowan knew this. For someone with her unique skills, true friendship couldn't tolerate secrets. "You told Flora earlier that 'the Hand went empty-handed'," she said softly.

"I don't even know what that is!" She turned her stricken face to Kolfinnia. "I just knew it wanted to take you all under the earth and keep you forever, and you didn't tell me or say goodbye!"

She was stung by her words. "Rowan, if I'd believed for a moment that you'd know what I was doing then I'd have said farewell properly." It was the best answer she could offer.

Her eyes swam with accusation and her lower lip trembled. "I don't want to see a scary hand with six fingers, I don't want to know anything. I want to be like Rilla and the other witches." She jumped to her feet and dried her palms on her dress.

Kolfinnia wondered how much of their awful battle she'd glimpsed and began to see that distress made her skills more potent. She stepped towards her. Rowan started away, but she reached out and turned her back.

"I apologise and I'll never leave you again without saying goodbye first. And I'm sorry that being upset makes your knowing stronger and clearer. I didn't realise."

The girl regarded her coldly.

"I don't want you to be angry," she wrapped her arms around her. "I'll never go away again without saying goodbye first."

Rowan yielded slightly. "You'll say goodbye next time you have to leave?" She spoke softly against the crook of her neck.

The word 'goodbye' sent a shiver through her, and Kolfinnia had to finish the thought off. "Just so I can say 'hello' again later," she said, and wondered what fate had in store for the witches of Wildwood.

London was enjoying a heatwave, but Wallace Maccrae insisted on appearing in public as a respectable gentleman should and so on his Sunday afternoon stroll around Hyde Park he looked oddly out of place in his heavy suit. His companion was his long-suffering wife Marie, who walked by his side holding a parasol and with her slender arm hooked through his. He wielded his ubiquitous walking cane and ambled along, while Marie for the most part concealed her sour face behind her parasol.

"Isn't this pleasant, dear?"

"Charming," she said coldly.

"I'm giving the protector's bill its first reading tomorrow," he said through a fixed smile. "It's garnered much interest, so play the dutiful wife, just this once." Krast had dreamed up the name 'protector's bill' feeling it struck the right chord. It sounded strong but just.

"They think you're his puppet." She slipped an insult through her fake smile.

"You and they can think what you like, and this isn't the place to discuss matters best left to men of wisdom."

"If this bill falls on stony ground it'll end your career." She was perversely enjoying that prospect even though it meant ruin for them both.

"There isn't a man in Westminster who doesn't want the protector's bill to become law," he insisted.

"There isn't a man in Westminster who won't profit from it, you mean."

"And what, but my profit, is keeping you in the manner to which you're accustomed?"

"But why now, haven't you always said covens were merely gangs of rogues exploiting old superstitions? An insignificant minority, you called them. Why gamble your career?"

He thought of first-dawn's incredible potential. "Politics isn't suited to the female mind, please don't tax yourself in this heat." He raised his cane in greeting to a man strolling past.

"Where's the good in being married to a man who sets about ruining his own career?" she complained.

"My dear!" he said sarcastically, "I thought you married me for love."

She hid her thunderous expression behind her parasol and looked away.

Up ahead a small group of children were running down an avenue of beech trees, chasing a white mastiff. Behind them followed an older girl vainly trying to round up the children, who were trying to round up the dog.

The mastiff headed straight for Wallace and Marie and bounded around them in circles, wagging its stout tail and panting furiously. His first instinct was to strike it, but he remembered that they were in public and so he forced a smile for the approaching children, who all appeared well-dressed. The dog sniffed his shoes and he shuffled back in distaste. The children quickly followed: two boys and two girls, who rushed around trying to restrain the excited animal. "Ceaser!" they shouted, snatching at the wriggling lead.

The eldest girl finally caught them up and Maccrae saw that she was almost a young woman. "Begging your pardon, sir," she apologised, "he slipped away from us. I do hope you're not too angry." Her cheeks were flushed and she panted almost as much as the dog. She was very pretty, Maccrae saw, and being a man with an appreciative eye, he softened.

"Nonsense, my dear, I was just saying to my good wife what a charming animal you have."

Marie dug her fingers into his meaty forearm. He ignored her and made idle conversation with the young woman, knowing how Marie hated it.

The girl, or young woman – Maccrae couldn't decide – retrieved the lead from one of the boys. "I'll take that thank you, Edgar," she said firmly. "You've caused quite enough trouble for one day."

While she kept Maccrae's attention, the boy called Edgar slipped to his rear and looked to where a gaunt man with a twisted nose sat alone on a bench hiding his face in a book. At that moment Big-Ben signalled noon and the man looked up, caught the lad's eye and nodded once.

The boy, who used the name Edgar today and would be someone else tomorrow, took a small box from his jacket and opened it just inches from Maccrae's broad back. The man sitting on the bench almost forgot to breath and sat mesmerised, waiting to see what would emerge. "Don't mess this up, lad," he whispered.

There was a silvery flash from the small box and something small and pale, like a moth, fluttered up and spiralled around Maccrae's shoulders. Just as the last chimes of Big-Ben faded the moth creature passed into Maccrae's shadow and instantly vanished. He reached up absently and flicked at his neck where he'd felt a brief tickle.

"Right on the nail!" Satisfied, Holloway snapped his book closed and stood up, ignoring the minister, the dog and the children. It was time to make himself scarce.

Krast also heard the chimes of Big-Ben. He was sitting in his study at Goldhawk Row awaiting just this moment. When the chimes began he drew out his pocket watch to check. "Perfect," he said, expecting no less, and took another sip of tea while his treasured watch started ticking away the hours of Maccrae's life.

Valonia lay in her hammock with Hercules happily ensconced on her chest. She rubbed his furred crown and turned the day's events over in her head.

Flora was holding the position of coven-mother a little longer so that she could find some rest but she couldn't sleep. She gazed up at the shifting leaves and tasted the warm air, guessing that it was a little before four in the afternoon. After even-spells were said and the meal finished and cleared away, Valonia would finally reveal to Kolfinnia what the Hand had told her concerning Rowan. At some point she'd have to tell Rowan herself, but tell her what? That she was some kind of supreme witch? They were all deeply afraid for her, and afraid *of* her. "Ahhh. . . . Hercules," she sighed, "what's to be done?"

He never answered back and that was fine; she had enough suggestions and ideas whirling around her head right now. Skald would know what to say, but he was resting. All of the sprites had been sorely tested today. She reached out and stroked a finger down her lightning-staff where it was propped by her hammock. She'd never been more proud of him. He'd saved them all and a few hours peace was the least she could give him.

She heard a creak on the stairs and groaned inwardly. Someone had disobeyed Flora and come calling on business. She coaxed Hercules to one side, scrambled out of her hammock and smoothed her long hair. Just as she'd finished making herself presentable there was a knock at her door. "Come," she ordered.

The door swung open and she saw a young man standing there, peering in at her. "Excuse me, Mother Gulfoss. I've a visitor asking for your time." He looked around nervously.

She couldn't quite place him, so many new faces around Wildwood recently, but his spiky red hair was familiar.

"Thank you," a cool voice beyond the doorway said. "That'll do, Farona. Please await me at our pavilion." Even before she entered the tower Valonia knew who it was and her heart sank. Sunday waved Farona away and stepped nimbly over the threshold. She bowed gracefully and Valonia saw she was wearing the same dress she'd dazzled the coven with that morning. Valonia wasn't a prude but she was a little perturbed by the amount of bare skin on display. "Forgive my intrusion coven-mother."

"Ah, Miss Flowers, yes?" She folded her arms and suddenly felt very tired.

"It was my wish to come and explain in person that we of Regal-Fox have chosen to remain another night, with your blessing of course."

"That's very thoughtful, Miss Flowers, but there really is no need. Flora has already instructed me thus. And an extra night with your party can only be a blessing for us." She was ready to see her out and crawl back into her hammock with her pipe.

"Ah yes, Miss Flora." Sunday wore a strange little smile. "May I congratulate you on such a wise and insightful choice for acting coven-mother."

Something in Sunday's tone prickled her. She stole a glance at her aura, but it was clear. If Sunday was lying she was an expert.

"In fact," she clasped her hands under her chin and brought her two index fingers together to make a steeple, "some might say a bold, perhaps even *daring* choice."

Valonia tensed. "Flora always works for the well-being of the coven. I see nothing daring in that Miss Flowers."

"Coven-father Berwick will be most impressed by all I have seen here. You may be sure that I shall waste no time in relaying every detail when I return," she flattered and threatened in equal measure.

Alfred Berwick was one of thirteen witches who sat on the council of Britain, which had the power to order a coven disbanded if not serving the best interests of Hethra and Halla. Valonia had been asked to join the council many years ago, but her love of Wildwood was too strong and she let the chance go. Berwick had taken a dislike to her after that, and she wondered how much influence this beguiling young woman had over him. After the nightmare of Troller's Ghyll, Sunday and Berwick were no more than kittens, but ones with claws, she conceded. "I wish your party a safe journey tomorrow, Miss Flowers, and hope that I can farewell you myself."

Sunday scowled. "Hope? I trust no further errands will deprive Wildwood of your sage guidance?"

"Who knows what tomorrow might bring?" she said with maddening calm. *Let her have a restless night wondering*, she thought with satisfaction. "Now, can I be of further assistance?"

"Your devotion to witchcraft is assistance enough." Sunday bowed farewell and then swept from the tower in a swish of white fabric and swan feathers.

Kolfinnia slept and inevitably she dreamed of grasping hands. In her dream she heard a loud crash and she was jolted from her sleep.

Emily Meadows regarded her sheepishly from where she was picking up apples from the floor. "Sorry Ward Algra. I didn't mean to wake you."

Kolfinnia rubbed her brow. "It's all right Emily," she sighed and craned her neck, feeling tendons creak and flex. "Do you know the hour?"

"Evening meal is just starting. We're eating outdoor 'cos it's so nice!" she smiled.

Kolfinnia reckoned she'd slept for maybe three hours. She crawled from her bunk and sat on the edge of the mattress.

"I have to take these," Emily indicated the apple bowl. "May I go, Ward Algra?"

"Yes Emily, don't keep them waiting," she replied and the girl skipped away.

She was no longer just plain Kolfinnia anymore, even though she shared this cabin with Emily amongst others. It was the downside of Wardship: she felt a little distance from her friends, but she hoped it would pass in time. She stood, and new aches trembled through her limbs. She pulled her nightdress up to inspect a swollen and blackened knee, and then down to find a livid bruise from her shoulder to her breast. She didn't recall suffering any of these injuries, but battle had a way of numbing pain and tricking the mind. She dressed quickly, buckled her wand-sheath about her waist and combed her hair. Evening meal was waiting, and Hand-of-Fate or not she would be expected to join the coven in saying sleeping-spells for the twins. She reached under her bunk and stroked the rough sackcloth and wondered how long it might take Gale to recover. In the years since she'd cut her staff she'd never had to call upon him in battle, but now in the space of just a few weeks he'd fought alongside her twice. "Bless you, Gale," she whispered, and then she followed her growling stomach to where a good meal waited.

The early evening was beautiful. It was just over a week to the solstice and the sun rode high. Usually, solstice preparations were all consuming, but Lilain's presence had overshadowed them, somewhat, although Emily Meadows didn't seem to mind. Tradition dictated that as the Wildwood's own summer solstice queen she had to ride around

Valonia's tower four times without putting a single toe on the ground. Each time she passed the rising sun (which on the solstice was an achingly early hour) she would scatter painted leaves beginning with lilac for Flower-Forth and so on until each season had been represented. Wildwood didn't have a horse and so they always improvised. Rooter would be bribed with a meal as he was each year, and he'd carry Emily around the tree while she held the sun standard. Last year, though, Rooter, having completed two circuits of the tree, lost interest and charged off into the gardens looking for cabbages, leaving Emily a sobbing wreck in the dust. This year they planned to carry her in a decorated litter, which was safer and couldn't be distracted. Evening meal was a spirited and communal affair and during the summer all of Wildwood ate outdoors in a square of greenery south of the gardens where there was the music of a fast-flowing stream. Long tables were hauled out and an eclectic assortment of chairs lined up. Kolfinnia took a stool next to Flora.

"Well done to Kolfinnia!" someone shouted, and for a horrible moment she thought they meant the Hand. "No pin-tips to spoil the meal!"

She looked around and saw Daisy Nettles toasting her and understood what she meant. "Thank the way-bewares, not me!" She waved back.

"You feeling refreshed?" Flora said from her side.

"A little."

"You look a little better. You looked awful when you got back." She passed a dish of fragrant onion bread down the line. All of Flower-Forth sat together and Valonia sat with her Moon-Frost companions.

Kolfinnia looked over and caught the old woman's eye and smiled. "I do feel better." She tore a piece of bread and devoured it.

Flora leaned closer. "You're quite the talk of Wildwood, had you realised?"

"Me?" She half caught the remark, too busy looking for Rowan.

"Everyone's been asking me where you've been today. Not surprising really when Valonia leaves and takes all of her Wards with her – tongues are bound to wag."

Kolfinnia looked up and saw Emily opposite. "I hope you didn't bruise too many apples," she joked. Emily shook her head solemnly and she began to see what Flora meant. Under the smiles and chatter there was a current of apprehension. Valonia had taken her Wards and they'd all returned battered and bruised and nobody knew why. She was still looking for Rowan when she heard someone calling 'Ward' and it took a second or two to realise that someone was addressing her. "Sorry?" Kolfinnia turned.

"I must have said 'Ward' three times." Morag Heron picked at her corn and smiled. She was a fearsome-looking witch Kolfinnia's age, whose ears were pierced with rings and she wore her hair dyed and bunched into tribal plaits. "Can't we just go back to calling you Finny?"

"Sorry, not while coven-mother's about. I'm still getting used to it myself."

"So where did you go today?"

"I can't say . . . yet."

"Oh! Come on, what's the big secret Finny? Where did you all go?"

Kolfinnia set her mug down hard. "I can't tell you Morag. Don't make me pull rank."

She leaned back, as if struck, and went back to her meal without another word.

Ashamed, Kolfinnia drained her mug, while a blue-tit hopped amongst the crockery looking for crumbs. She flicked a glance Morag's way and saw her curious, even affronted, gaze. What could she say? Beside her, Emily plucked an apple from the bowl and again she saw that wretched child's hand.

JOIN THE RETINUE OF THE FATED HAND

"I'll tell you where we went today," she said at last.

Morag watched and waited.

" . . . Nowhere as nice as this," she said with feeling.

Chapter Twelve

Rowan of Wildwood

One by one they arrived at the tower that night. The air was hot and the tower fragrant with the smell of the growing tree.

"Hethra's putting on a few inches," Esta laughed as she patted the tree's trunk.

"Aren't we all," Valonia said dryly. "Eight-hundred and seventy-four, and still growing."

"The tree or your belly?" Esta sniggered.

"Ya, ya," she slipped into Icelandic and smiled at the well-worn joke.

There was a soft knock and Lana entered closely followed by Hilda. The four seated themselves on the floor leaving three cushions vacant in the circle of seven, which centred around a cloth with a collection of mysterious objects hidden beneath.

"I know Flora and Kolfinnia are coming," Hilda pointed to the seventh cushion where Valonia had laid her wand, "but who's our seventh?"

"One of our tasks, if not our greatest task, is to decide if we invite this seventh witch to join us and tell them all that's happened these last few weeks. It's not a decision I'd take alone."

"Rowan, you mean?" Esta guessed.

"And the . . . er," Lana pointed to the objects under the linen.

"Ah!" Valonia adopted a serious tone. "Very strong magic to be taken in." She lifted a corner and underneath they all saw an incredible assortment of cakes.

"Magic I'll study most earnestly!" Esta rubbed her hands.

"What's the occasion?" Hilda enquired.

Valonia sat up straight. "We start our meeting as friends and matters of this morning will not be spoken of until these plates are clean. This is my thanks to you all."

"And not until Flora and Kolfinnia arrive!" Hilda tugged Esta's hand away.

She shrugged, looked at her hand and wiggled her fingers. "The Hand-of-Cake." She grinned, and their chuckles welled up into full-blown laughter.

When Flora and Kolfinnia arrived they began their meeting 'as friends' as Valonia had put it, eating, laughing and drinking. But as each plate was cleared they felt the hard talk grow closer until finally they could avoid it no longer. It was Flora who asked the question they needed to get them going. "What really happened today?"

The pipe had been lit and they sat in a haze of sage smoke.

"We survived!" Valonia laughed gruffly. "Thanks be to Skald."

"Thanks be," they all agreed.

Valonia recounted the tale for Flora, and everyone chipped in. They swapped accounts tentatively at first as they relived the horror, and then with more enthusiasm as the talk drew the poison from their souls. It was Flora again who inadvertently moved them along.

"And the seventh place," she pointed to the empty cushion. "Who else was to come?"

Valonia cleared her throat, "And so, Flora, you've brought us full circle, to the most important matter of all. Dare I say, a 'cosmic' quandary we must find a solution to."

"Tonight, if possible," Lana added.

"Flora, Kolfinnia." Valonia spoke their names, securing their full attention. "There's one last thing the Hand told me, and now I tell you and it concerns our missing guest who knows nothing of these matters."

The two young witches sat patiently and waited to hear the rest.

As darkness fell the balance of power in the wood subtly shifted. Small animals burrowed deep into their dens and predators readied claws, wings and fangs for the night.

A fox trotted nimbly through the coven. Over the years he'd learned that this was one place where humans did not set traps. To him, the humans here were no threat. He raised his muzzle and detected a multitude of scents and something else, a human scent different from the others who lived here. This one wasn't as harmless as the others. She, for he could detect her gender, was more like the night owls, stoats or martens.

The fox watched from the long grass as a tall slender figure clothed in grey walked alone through the darkness. He watched her cross to the great tree, where candlelight flickered in the windows of a tree-top dwelling. He saw that she moved like a hunter and carried a long stick wrapped in black. The fox yawned: loosing interest in the figure, and feeling drawn by the night he slunk away into the black.

Sunday moved stealthily through the gardens. Her elaborate hairstyle and spotless dress had been replaced by a simple plait and a hooded grey cloak. She carried her lightning-staff, which, because she kept it painted white, was now wrapped in black velvet.

Her instincts told her that Valonia was concealing something, and like the rest of the coven she was curious as to why she would leave a common gardener-girl in charge. Berwick would be most interested in this information and with it perhaps she could climb even higher. 'Coven-mother Flowers of the Council of Britain' had an intoxicating ring to it, she thought. "Strike." She gave the staff a gentle shake.

"Here, Miss Flowers," her thunder-sprite said quietly.

"As we planned, just close enough to hear."

"This is for the betterment of our coven, miss?" he asked uneasily.

"That and nothing more," she said impatiently. Strike could be timid and overly conscientious and sometimes she felt ashamed of him, seeing these things as weak. "Now carry me," she commanded. The staff hovered level with her knees and she sat neatly upon it and pulled her hood up over her head. "Upward," she hastened him.

Strike lifted her silently into the air and circled slowly around the tree gaining height until he brought them level with the tower. She could hear voices inside and saw candlelight flickering through the windows. She perched on her staff and waited and listened. It was Valonia she heard first.

"There's one last thing the Hand-of-Fate told me, and now I tell you and it concerns our missing guest who knows nothing of these matters," she scratched her head as she thought. "For some time we've been intrigued by Rowan's talents. She knows things and it's impossible to say *how* she knows them."

"Sorry," Kolfinnia was confused. "Do you mean that this place is saved for Rowan?"

"I do indeed."

"But what does she have to do with all this?"

"If you'd stop interrupting I was getting to that part!"

"Sorry," she apologised.

"Rowan's important because the Hand named her as the only witch who knows where the twins lay buried," she explained, as though this were the most natural thing in the world.

Flora and Kolfinnia stared around, suspicious of a prank but saw only serious faces. "It can't be true!" Kolfinnia insisted.

"The Hand has spoken," Hilda reminded her, "and it explains so much."

She was starting to see that she'd been left out somewhere along the line. Valonia anticipated her next question and spoke first, "Don't be angry, Kolfinnia. I didn't tell you earlier because I knew you'd rush off to find Rowan as soon as we got back and I didn't want you –,"

"Telling her?" she finished accusingly.

"No!"

"Why, then?"

"Because I didn't want Rowan plucking that particular bit of information from your head, that's why."

"Sorry," she mumbled. "So she's unaware that she could locate the twins if asked?"

"I'm certain of it, and just as well for us."

"Poor little lass," Esta murmured.

"We must decide if she is safer living in ignorance for now or should we tell her everything tonight," Valonia spelled it out.

"Tell her what, though?" Hilda spread her hands. "That she can know the mind of the universal being countless cultures call God? And that through that mind she can know everything that has happened or is happening anywhere?" She shook her head. "She's not even seven." Her words received cautious nods.

Valonia considered. "Kolfinnia, you know her better than anyone. Would you call her a friend?"

"Yes," she replied without hesitation. "We've become very close, and she's taken a shine to Flora and Gale. It's taken her so long to make friends that telling her would only make her feel separate again."

"Hmm." She considered. "Then I'm inclined to agree with Hilly. We postpone telling her, but pay particular attention to anything she says, no matter how strange or trivial it is."

"She's said plenty of strange things that have made me wonder," Kolfinnia confessed.

Esta shuffled on her cushion. "Such as?"

"Oh, so much! She named the barghests, she knew captain Jerrow had young in a fallen scarecrow and she said that Hethra and Halla were being hunted."

"Huh! That much is true," Esta grieved.

"And she spoke of a great witch she called 'Clovis'," she added.

This was news to all of them.

Valonia leaned closer, fascinated. "Go on," she urged.

She thought back. "I didn't think much of it at the time. We were waiting for Flora, sat telling stories, and I told her of Vega." She cupped her mouth as she thought back. "She said that Clovis was a great witch who came from Vega and he looked after serpent-twins of his own there." It was as close as she could remember.

"Well, I never!" Valonia shook her head.

"You believe her, that there are witches in the heavens?" Flora looked sceptical.

"Have we any reason to doubt her?" The implications were incredible.

They'd been sitting for a long time and the darkness outside was total. A wood mouse scurried across the floor and looked surprised to see people up at this late hour. He turned and darted into the clutter of books.

"Can she command this talent, Kolfinnia?" Hilda asked.

"It appears to come and go, but it's stronger when she's upset. She knew that we'd been looking for the Hand today." There was a long silence.

"She kept the barghest secret. I'm sure she'll keep this one as well," Valonia assured them.

"A gift like that in the wrong hands . . ." Esta suggested, then wished she hadn't.

Valonia stretched. "I propose a motion. Keep Rowan close and as safe as can be. The less she knows the better for now. Lord Oak forbid that she ever falls into the hands of the Illuminata, but fortune's on our side. To them she'd just be another witch-whelp."

"Why would they come again now?" Flora took another sip of tea.

"They're maddened by the prospect of finally cracking alchemical law." Valonia shook her head and smiled. "They misunderstand utterly."

"Misunderstand it or not, they're coming, aren't they?" Hilda looked forlorn.

"Hilly, the Illuminata have been coming for us since I was a girl. They will always come for us, but a well-ordered coven has plans ready."

"Ah, the dandelion plan you mean," Hilda smiled.

Kolfinnia looked to Flora who, she was pleased to see, was equally confused.

"Dandelion?" Flora sniggered. "Forgive me, that doesn't sound like a battle plan to me?"

"Aye, but ask any gardener which plant never gives up and what'll they say?" Esta tipped her a shrewd wink.

Flora took a moment and then smiled in understanding, "The dandelion."

"We break the coven if we have to and disperse just like dandelion seeds." Valonia saw the look of horror on Kolfinnia's face. "I said if we have to, and we'll spring up elsewhere."

"Like dandelions!" Flora finished.

Valonia clicked her fingers. "Quite right, my lass!"

"But we need to warn other covens as well," said Kolfinnia.

"I've also given this some thought. Lilain will be well enough to leave soon. I'll speak with her and ask her swarm to carry word to the furthest covens of Britain."

"That's brilliant!" Kolfinnia beamed.

"Old I may be, but not in here." She tapped a finger to her temple and smiled craftily.

"And don't forget Wildwood is a hub for travellers at the moment. They can carry the warning too," Flora added.

Kolfinnia felt a weight drop from her shoulders that she hadn't even realised was there. A fight lay ahead but perhaps it wasn't the hopeless one she'd feared.

Sunday made ready to slip away. She'd heard things that set her pulse racing. There was a girl in this backwater coven who had the whole universe at her feet and didn't even know it. "Away, Strike!" she hissed and they melted into the night just as the door to Valonia's tower creaked open and the first of her friends began to leave for their beds.

Elizabeth carried the coal hod up the stairs to the drawing room. She was particularly careful not to blacken the red carpet, but it was hard going. The hod was heavy and she had to lift her dress to keep from tripping as she struggled upstairs. It was unusual enough to light a fire in June but this was the second load she'd carried upstairs this evening and she wondered if Mr Maccrae had caught a fever. She reached the landing and made her way along the dark corridor to the drawing room. There she straightened her white cap, knocked once and entered without waiting. The room was stifling; the heat from all that coal was trapped by heavy velvet drapes and none of the windows were open, not even by a crack. But despite the almost forge-like heat Maccrae still felt a chill.

"Put it by the hearth, Elizabeth. I shall call when you're needed," Marie instructed the young woman, who curtseyed in reply and hurried away.

Maccrae had a blanket over his legs and sat as close to the fire as he could, but he still felt a chill. "Damn if I didn't catch some malady," he grumbled as he firmed the blanket around his legs.

"A consequence of mixing with the wrong kind of company." Marie thought of the young lady, her siblings and her excitable dog.

"Your meaning?" he growled.

"That while taking the air it might profit you to keep a distance from strangers. Who knows what ailments they might be carrying?"

She worded it so cleverly that he couldn't be sure if she'd just rebuked him. "Huh!" He grunted, and left it at that.

"I'm sure you'll be well enough to attend tomorrow's reading of the protector's bill." She made the statement sound more like a question.

"Well or not, I've got to be there," he said sullenly. "If it misses this reading it'll be months before I can propose it again."

"If you're under the weather tell Westminster to go to Goldhawk Row and speak with the bill's authors." She held her sewing up to the window. The light in the room was of London's gloomy evening variety.

"It's getting dark in here," he changed the topic and pulled the blanket tighter.

Without a word, she put her work aside, fetched the matches and lit the lamp. The shadows in the room retreated into the corners where they seemed to lurk in displeasure.

"Damn this!" he said in agitation, threw the blanket aside and knelt by the crackling fire. He pushed his hands so close she thought he was reaching for the red-hot coals.

"I'm certain you'll feel revived in the morning, and if not we'll send for doctor Abbot." She sat and continued her sewing.

"You most certainly will not," he wrung his hands before the flames. "Don't need a doctor and don't make a fuss."

Her eye was drawn to his shadow: it stretched out across the carpet behind him casting an elongated profile that flickered in time with the fire's pulse. "What if they come for you?" she asked as she teased at a stitch.

"Who?" He took the poker and roused the fire even more.

She considered. "Witches," she said at last.

"Here? In London, the heart of the empire?" he scoffed, but she heard the doubt in his voice.

"You're playing a dangerous game, Wallace."

"Politics is not a game. It is for the betterment of the empire."

"Save that honeyed talk for Westminster. It's just you and me tonight."

He looked long into the fire before replying. "I've given it some thought," he admitted.

"Are their promises worth it?" she asked softly.

He seemed mesmerised by the fire and didn't answer.

She swallowed and bit at her lip. "There was a time when you and I were very much in lo –,"

"Ahem!" He cleared his throat loudly to signal that this conversation was to go no further, then he stood and rubbed his limbs. In the fire's glow he looked older than his fifty-eight years and nothing like the young man she'd married. "Damn this chill," he repeated.

She stared blankly into his trailing shadow, listening to the ticking clock emphasise the gulf between them. Outside she heard a horse and carriage rattle past, and the great clock of Westminster signal the hour, telling her that the evening was drawing in. She watched the pattern of flowers on the carpet undulate in her husband's shadow, first muted and then glowing hellish orange as the fire danced in the hearth. A fleck of something silvery caught her eye and for an instant she thought she saw a tiny moth fluttering in the depths of his shadow, and then it was gone and she shook her head and gave it no further regard. Marie packed away her sewing and headed for the door. "I'm retiring, Wallace," she told him.

He didn't turn. Instead he raised a hand and waved it limply in a goodnight gesture. She slipped out through the door, closed it softly behind her and made for her own bedroom.

Monday, June 13th dawned much like its predecessor, full of sunlight and promise. Maccrae had declared that he felt fighting fit despite his pallor, but his servants noticed how his teacup trembled in his grip. His driver had offered him a helping hand when he struggled to climb the carriage steps that morning, but the helping hand had been gruffly refused.

The protector's bill was read at 11am, and by thirty-five minutes past the hour it'd already been seconded and scheduled for its next and final reading two week hence. Maccrae's bill received enthusiastic support and was on the road to becoming law. He then cancelled the remainder of his appointments to go home early. Since leaving home on this fine June morning until returning in the early afternoon he'd only removed his overcoat once as a formality inside Westminster. A persistent chill stalked him and he found it only abated once he was back by the fire. He felt 'wrong', his limbs ached and they were slow to respond as if they were getting heavier. His skin tingled, feeling overly sensitive to even the slightest knock and his eyes throbbed in their sockets. He spent the afternoon by the fireside attended by his wife and the household staff. None of them ever thought to look at his shadow – they had no earthly reason to do so – but if they had they might have seen something like a tiny moth hiding in the depths there, where it continued to feed.

"And how did our minister look to you, Hathwell?" Krast inspected
the pressure gauge on another tank. They were in the chromosite
shed where the creatures were bred and there were hundreds of the
cylinders.

"Like a man recovering from an illness. Or suffering one."

"Mmm, well," he sighed. "Politics can be taxing." He noted the
pressure. Too low and the embryo would be malformed, too high and
it would die. "I'm confident the protector's bill will become law, and
despite what I think of the man it was admirable of him to propose it in
the first place."

Did he? Hathwell wondered. He had found plenty to trouble him
since reading the account of Mannix, the Irish monk. He knew he
couldn't show it to Krast, firstly because he wouldn't put any faith in
it; secondly, something told him it would get 'lost' for good this time
and with it something honest would vanish from the world. "Sir, about
minister Maccrae," he fumbled. "I was wondering if his illness was
something contrived by someone meaning him harm?"

Krast stared at him suspiciously and Hathwell imagined fearsome
machinery ticking away behind his pale eyes. Just when he expected
a backlash Krast exploded with laughter. "Bertrand!" He slapped a
friendly hand on his shoulder. "My dear Bertrand! All these years I've
had you wrong, I had you marked as a straightforward man but you
speak like a politician!" He gave his shoulder one last squeeze, and still
laughing, returned to his clipboard.

"I'm sorry for asking, sir. It sounds so foolish." But the old soldier in
him was far from convinced.

"Think nothing of it, although I share your concerns," he tapped
his clipboard thoughtfully. "It occurred to me that Maccrae's noble
intentions might make him a target for vengeance."

"Vengeance?"

"From witches, of course. Poisonous wretches, the lot of them. I
fear his passion for this undertaking was so great that he ignored
my warnings. But look who I'm telling. You know as well as I do how
dangerous witches are."

Until recently he wouldn't have argued, but after endless research in
the Goldhawk library he'd begun to re-evaluate his fighting days. The
knights had trampled covens and rounded witches up for correctional-
blessing, but it had taken a lowly clerk like Tom to make him see the
obvious: they'd hardly ever *fought* witches. What kind of enemy was it
that shunned violence? What kind of enemy gave refuge to shipwrecked
strangers and healed their wounds? "So it's possible Maccrae's illness is

some kind of vengeful spell?"

Krast shook his head. "Witches are adept at such underhanded cunning, but I'm sure it's nothing more than a cold."

"I suppose so."

"Trust me, at worst the man's got a touch of influenza, and callous though it sounds I for one couldn't be happier. At least he won't be making any further visits to Hobbs for the foreseeable future."

"If you're sure, sir."

"He'll be right as rain in no time and breathing down our necks again." He inspected another tank, and from inside Hathwell could hear something groping against the cylinder.

"Have you had chance to look at the documents I've been compiling?" Hathwell asked casually.

"Not yet," he lied smoothly.

When Krast said no more he felt compelled to go on. "The object we're hunting seems to regulate the world in some way."

"Many cults assign awesome powers to their relics and protect them with curses and mumbo-jumbo. They're nonsense." Krast regarded him for what seemed a long time before speaking again. "The Illuminata will soon march again and I'll be in need of a faithful squire. Will you be that man or will I have to find another?" He sensed unrest in his old squire, and because he was fond of him the very last thing he wanted was to send him for correctional-blessing.

Hathwell snapped a salute even before he'd had time to think. "My loyalty is to you alone," he insisted, but the words that came out of his mouth didn't quite match the feeling in his heart.

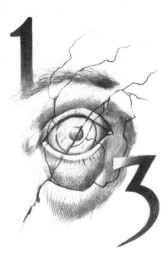

CHAPTER THIRTEEN

Heart of Stone

Sunday's party left Wildwood the following day. It was one of the coldest, wettest June days anyone could recall, which suited Valonia because Sunday was obliged to wear more modest garments instead of parading around looking like Venus herself.

"Don't take this as a lesson in witchcraft, rather it's a lesson in politics." Valonia had invited Flora along to witness Sunday's farewell.

"And the difference being?" Flora asked.

"Politics is transient, witchcraft is forever." They trod the spiral steps down from her tower with care because they could be slippery in the wet. *And it doesn't come much wetter than this*, Valonia thought, and pondered whether or not the change in climate was caused by the serpent-twins' distress.

Sunday was awaiting them at the bottom, and Farona was holding a parasol over her head, leaving himself unprotected from the shower. When Sunday saw Flora she bristled. The old woman had set this up, she could sense it. Since arriving she'd been made to feel that solstice queens ranked lower than garden-girls. She wore a painted smile and hid her frustration. Farona, on the other hand, couldn't think of a better way to start his journey home than one last look at Flora. He'd likely never see her again, so he did his best to drink in her image without making it too obvious.

"Miss Flowers, I believe that you know Flora," Valonia began with an introduction that wasn't needed. "And a good morning to Farona too."

She could barely hear her own voice over the rain drumming down on her hat.

The youth looked flattered that she remembered him, while Sunday noted with peculiar satisfaction that she'd been excluded from her good morning greeting. *All the more to tell coven-father Berwick*, she thought. She could imagine his dismay when she reported all of the slights she'd suffered since arriving, not to mention the astonishing news she'd heard last night. "Coven-mother Valonia, may I thank you for your generosity and hospitality. Lilain could not have chosen a better coven for her recovery." She stepped forward, took Valonia's hand, bowed gracefully and brushed the briefest of kisses against her aged skin, and it was done.

Sunday sensed Flora watching intently, but now she was far more concerned with Rowan Barefoot. She'd taken the trouble of looking for the girl at daybreak, thinking it might be useful later. Her efforts had paid off and she'd spied Rowan from a distance, carrying buckets of water. Sunday thought she looked rather humble, perhaps even witless and certainly not the majestic little goddess she'd been expecting. *So this is the witch who knows all that's ever been?* She thought it fitting that Wildwood's supreme witch looked scruffy and dull and she felt angry at fate for choosing a common girl to bear such a priceless gift. She had always believed that covens should follow Regal-Fox's example and hold magic to be dignified. Witches were separate to Britain's ignorant masses, and if not for their efforts Hethra and Halla would have sickened long ago. The world had no idea just how important they were, and instead of respecting them they forced them to live in crude hideaways like Wildwood. She curtseyed and turned to leave but Valonia grasped her hand and leaned closer for a quiet word. "Coven-mother?" She suddenly felt wary, convinced the old woman knew of her spying.

Valonia clasped her elegant hands between her own. "Miss Flowers, there is news abound that the Illuminata are again plotting. I'd ask you pass this news to each and every witch you meet." She squeezed her hands firmly and Sunday relaxed.

"I understand, coven-mother. What witch doesn't remember the Knights Illuminata?"

"You're not old enough to remember them, at least." Valonia dressed her small complement with a smile.

She breathed a delicate laugh. "I shall pass on your news." Sunday felt a brief spark of kinship with the old woman. She might disagree with the way Valonia ran her coven, but they were both witches and in her eyes that set them apart.

"Pass my best to Alfred," Valonia finished and let her hands slip from her own.

"Coven-father Berwick will be touched by your greeting." She made to leave and for an instant Valonia briefly saw a witch who feared for the future rather than an arrogant solstice queen.

She could go far if she put her mind to it, Valonia thought as she watched them leave, not realising that Sunday had that very intention.

After they'd departed Valonia held a brief meeting with Kolfinnia and her Wards, although this time out in the gardens for all to see. She was aware that many were wondering why she spent so much time engaged in private conclaves or off on secretive business, and that wasn't good for morale.

She strolled through the gardens pretending to inspect the vegetables, pointing and smiling at this and that, but keeping her voice low. The rain was a welcome ally. Not many witches walked Wildwood this morning and the drumming on their umbrellas was loud enough to mask their conversation. "Esta, I'd ask you to take two trusted witches and what little coinage we have and use it to buy three sturdy boats, not like the small rowers we've already got. They must be sea worthy. We'll keep them stocked with fresh water and supplies and moored on the Appelier, well hidden."

Esta bowed her agreement. "If this weather continues I'll be able to row them straight to the tower."

They moved on in a huddle.

"Lana, ask captain Jerrow to widen the patrols. I want nightly reports back from him." She stepped around a wheelbarrow half-full of rainwater. "And how'd you feel about a short reconnaissance trip, Lana? Nothing too far, just out to Leadchester and back to gather news?"

"The new moon is two days away. It'd be a good time for night flying," she said.

The group ambled slowly on, squelching along the muddy paths, inspecting tomatoes beaded with rain and swooning sunflowers bent double. Two of Valonia's witches passed by and she made a point of telling them to buckle their wand-sheaths. She enforced standard rules as though routine, and not invasion, were the most important thing in the world.

"And what about me?" Hilda prompted when they were alone again.

"I've a delicate job for you, Hilly. Brief the junior Wards on Ruinous creatures, a refresher course on what they are and how to defeat them. But keep it discreet. I don't want the coven in a panic."

"That just leaves me," Kolfinnia reminded her.

"You're coming with me, my lass." Valonia strolled ahead with her hands clasped behind her back, regardless of the rain.

"Where to?"

"We're going to have a chat with an empress."

They made their way to Lilain's refuge, a willow pagoda surrounded by a little fence. "Let's hope Lilain will help us," Valonia sounded anxious.

"Why wouldn't she?"

"She's the hive-empress. She's flown the skies since her kind came into being aeons ago. What she cares about witches and their woes is anybody's guess."

"I'd just assumed that as a magical creature she'd be certain to assist us?" Kolfinnia was taken aback.

"I'm hoping she will, but it can't be taken for granted. She'll be around long after us. We're just ants on an oak to Lilain."

Lilain's refuge was surrounded by birches. Kolfinnia noticed how they looked strangely dark and swollen and then she realised with wonderment that there were thousands of bees clustered on each tree, just gathered as if waiting for something. "They know she's almost ready to leave," she said sadly.

"It's their help I'm after. I'll do the talking, Kolfinnia. I'd like for you to wait out here, make sure nobody comes calling while I speak to Lilain. I've things to say that won't sit well in passing ears."

"Yes of course. Good luck."

"Take heart, Ward Algra," she winked and then tapped on the shelter's small round door.

"Announce yourself!" a voice called from inside.

"Don't be a clod Annie. Let me in, it's soaking out here!"

There was the sound of shuffling and then the door was pushed open and Annie Barden's cheerful face peeped out. "Coven-mother, welcome!"

Annie was one of those witches you just couldn't help but like. She wore her hair dyed and tribal looking, while on her cheeks she wore painted symbols. She had a profound knack in communicating with all creatures and it had been a natural choice to make her Lilain's attendant.

Valonia removed her dripping hat and eased herself through the opening with as much dignity as she could, into Lilain's cosy dwelling. "Annie, how's our guest today?"

"She's keen to be away, coven-mother, tomorrow if possible." Annie sat on a small stool beside Lilain's crib, which was covered with a canopy of fine white lace.

"Annie, I need to speak to Lilain about something important. As her translator you'll hear me say things that are shocking and must be kept

172

secret. Can you do that?"

"Anything said between Lilain and her guests is privileged, coven-mother." Annie looked solemn, and over the last few weeks she'd certainly heard plenty.

"Thank you." Valonia pulled up a small stool. "Now then, shall we begin?"

Annie drew back the curtain and Lilain stirred in her hay-lined crib. Her yellow and black fur looked glossy and her wings were no longer tatty and wrinkled but sharp and gleaming. She rattled them briefly and turned her inscrutable eyes on Valonia. Annie reached into the crib and laid a hand gently on Lilain's luxurious fur to make a mind bond with the empress.

"Annie, please tell Lilain that we'll be sorry to see her leave, but in doing so she might do the witches of Britain a great service," Valonia began.

Empress and coven-mother began their informal meeting. Annie learned of their battle with the Hand-of-Fate and its dire warning, though Valonia rightly kept the marvel of Rowan Barefoot a secret, and Annie retold all of this for Lilain.

Annie had learned a lot about the empress: she was ancient and her thoughts were alien to humankind. Lilain had witnessed a time when mighty lizards dominated the land, before they were swept away by fire. She'd seen vast continent-sized sheets of ice scour the planet, and the cataclysm of magnetic north and south flipping places in an instant. In Lilain's epic life the scurrying humans that swarmed over the earth seemed to have come overnight, but while she had little understanding and regard for humanity, she understood that her rescuers were dedicated to the serpent-twins. It was for that reason that she agreed to instruct her host of bees to carry a warning to the other covens. Annie wrinkled her brow, concentrated and relayed Lilain's final message to Valonia. "She agrees, coven-mother."

Valonia sighed in relief and bowed gratefully. She had just recruited countless millions of helpers to their cause.

"Is this true?" she asked meekly as Valonia made ready to leave.

Valonia looked at her sadly. "It is true, and to be kept quiet for the time being."

Annie looked even more lost.

"But come and see me when the burden's too great and we can discuss it, perhaps over a bottle even."

Annie just smiled.

"Have faith, young witch. Forewarned is forearmed," she wagged a determined finger at her, hoping she sounded more confident than she felt. Then she stepped out into the rain as Annie prepared Lilain's final dose of healing herbs.

As it transpired, Lilain left Wildwood that very same afternoon and it was Annie that ran to find Valonia and tell her. Being of such ancient origins, Lilain didn't have a grasp of formality or occasion; those were human things. She simply felt the need to leave and with her wounds healed she could. It was efficient insect logic.

Valonia sent word that everyone was to gather in the gardens within the hour and so Lilain made ready to depart with little notice, little fanfare and no time for an elaborate farewell. The weather at least began to brighten, the rains passed and the mood of melancholy around the coven lifted slightly.

"Do you think your meeting with her this morning has had anything to do with her decision?" Kolfinnia asked.

"The time was close anyway, but who knows? She may have remained until the solstice if I hadn't spoken with her," Valonia said regretfully.

"At least word is beginning to spread." She tried to sound cheerful, but the idea of Lilain leaving made her feel sad. Her presence had been a talisman and she only now realised that while the empress had been with them she'd naïvely believed that the coven couldn't be assailed.

Valonia laid a hand on her shoulder, "Lilain has never touched earth in all the ages she's flown the skies. What happened here was a miracle and one that we'll never see again."

"That's a good way to look at loss," Kolfinnia smiled.

"Count yourself blessed to have met her. Now, if you'll excuse me I have ten minutes to think of a farewell speech fit for an empress."

Annie was accorded the honour of carrying Lilain to the top of the tower where she would lift her to the wind and set her to flight. She walked the spiral with the utmost care, cradling Lilain and followed by Valonia and a veil of protective bees. When they reached the balcony she leaned over the railings so that the gathered crowd might get their final glimpse of the empress, and a round of applause went up.

"I hope she doesn't drop her," Rowan said quite innocently, still clapping.

"Rowan!" Kolfinnia tried not to laugh. "Don't say such things."

They were surrounded by both guests and familiar faces and some were conspicuous by their absence. Esta and Lana were off somewhere and hadn't heard the news. She knew it'd be an awful blow to them when they returned and found the empress gone. Hilda was there. She greeted Kolfinnia with a brief kiss and kept snatching secretive glances at Rowan. Other witches had run from their daily chores and stood wiping dirty hands on aprons or clutching spades, brooms, peeling knives and scrubbing boards.

"She wouldn't have made it if not for us." Rowan's happiness was selfless. That was one of the things Kolfinnia loved most about her.

A huge swarm of bees had gathered like a fleet ready to escort their flagship and they swirled in a dark cloud high above the tree. Not surprisingly, one or two butterflies fluttered amongst them and Kolfinnia's mind was drawn back to when she'd hauled a battered Lilain out from a tangle of broken foxgloves. She tried to detect bee-fairies amongst the swarm, certain they must be there, although blessedly drawn by ceremony not death. She struggled to see, but it's said only the strongest witches can see fairies and Kolfinnia's fleeting glimpse weeks ago appeared to be her first and last.

After Valonia's farewell speech Annie lifted Lilain to the wind and everyone watched anxiously.

"This is it!" Hilda's hand flew to her mouth.

As Lilain's soft fur whispered against her hands for the last time Annie felt both loss and joy. Lilain's wings beat so fast that they were just wispy smudges at her back and they swept her to freedom. The gathered witches cheered and threw a storm of hats skywards in celebration. Lilain's mellow buzzing was the only farewell and thanks they needed, and they watched her spiral up into the overcast sky followed by a dark comet tail of bees until she vanished from sight.

Kolfinnia felt something clutch her hand. It was Rowan and she was crying. Hilda stood not far away dabbing a handkerchief to her eyes. Witches looked around, slightly lost and sad, and then bent to find their hats. Before long the crowd began to dwindle as they returned to peeling, scrubbing, mixing and spell making.

"Don't be sad," Hilda said cheerfully, but it didn't appear that she was taking her own advice.

"Lilain will be fine," Kolfinnia said solidly.

"She's gone to tell the covens something important," Rowan guessed.

Hilda and Kolfinnia exchanged ominous glances and then looked up to the skies, which were now grey and empty.

Over the next two weeks, between the first and second readings of the protector's bill, Wallace Maccrae kept his public appointments to a minimum and rarely left home. Instead, he sat by the fire and tried to make headway with dreary paperwork that demanded his attention whether he was ill or not.

Sometimes, when the weather was warm enough, he sat by the open window where he'd watch the world pass by and noted bitterly that even the lowliest street urchins seemed to enjoy better health than him.

The strange chill ebbed and flowed but never left him, and instead clung to him like an icy shroud. There were other changes also: he found that the sound of the ticking clock in the drawing room had become like needles against his ears and so he'd ordered Elizabeth to remove it. Shaving was also an agony. The razor juddered over his stubble as though it was gravel, not hair, and the lethargy in his heavy limbs had sunk deeper, right to the marrow so that just rising from his bed demanded supreme effort.

Maccrae's ghoulish companion, that tiny moth-like creature, continued to nibble away at his essence, hidden deep in his shadow safe from all but the sharpest eyes. While the damage it had caused so far was bad enough, it had hardly begun. Its metabolic rate was fixed to peak this afternoon. At the thirteenth minute past one o'clock it would consume what remained of Maccrae's essence in an instant.

Although he had no idea, his limbs were set to grow significantly heavier. It never occurred to him that when he complained of feeling as 'heavy as stone' he was alarmingly accurate. As the creature ate, more of his body was converted from animal into mineral. He was slowly petrifying and the transformation would shift into ghastly overdrive this afternoon.

The drawing room door opened and Marie entered. She stood with her hands clasped neatly at her waist and regarded her suffering husband with the cool detachment of one frequently rejected. "Your driver's here, Wallace," she said emptily

"Which one?" he grunted.

"Simonstone, I think."

He snorted, sounding pained. "Fool drives too fast and hurls the carriage around. Where's Chambers? I prefer Chambers." He peeled the blanket from his lap and pushed himself out of the chair as though it was a great magnet dragging him down. She twitched, ready to go to him, then restrained herself. "Can do it," he growled, and rose shakily to his feet. "Tell Simonstone I'll be down presently."

She shook her head. "Cancel this, Wallace. The bill can wait."

"Can't wait." He suddenly thought of the first-dawn machine and how it'd drained those four unknown women, and he began to wonder if the project cursed all those it touched. He waved his hand at her. "My cane and hat."

She took them from the sideboard, carried them over and saw how his skin looked like marble. It was smooth and featureless as if the pores had closed over and become a shell rather than a skin. His eyes were still pale and dangerous, though, no change there. He adjusted his stiff collar and smoothed his manicured moustache. "What hold do they have over you?" she implored him.

"None. My duty is to Westminster."

"Which in turn is owned by the Knights Illuminata. Wallace, they're killing you." She had no idea how accurate she was.

"Then I shall at least find some peace from your inane chatter." He snatched his hat and cane from her hands, flashed her a spiteful smile and hobbled to the door.

"You have a heart of stone, Wallace," she said to his back.

He halted and she watched his shoulders rise and fall. The room was baking hot, but the draft that rolled in through the open door brought no respite; rather it seemed to beckon him away to his fate. He didn't turn back. He fixed his top hat to his head where it sat askew making him look like a boy dressed as a man. Then he left, pulling his overcoat tighter around him. Marie stood alone by the fire, wringing her hands as the clock chimed noon.

Westminster palace was steeped in tradition and history and the grandest of its chambers was the speaker's hall at the heart of the Gothic building. It was a long hall with rows of tiered seats on either side from where government faced their opposition and forged new laws in heated debates that could sometimes run on into the night.

Presiding over the hall was the speaker's platform, a rostrum from where members of the house read new legislation. The protector's bill had set the house alight and the initiates who knew first-dawn was the inspiration had whipped their fellows into line. Hathwell was too well-known to appear at the house at such a sensitive time, and so Krast had dispatched two devisers to act as his eyes.

Maccrae shuffled into the chamber as the speaker appealed for calm, and Krast's men placed themselves in the gilded ante-chamber just behind the speakers rostrum. Men hurried to their seats, attendants ushered senior officials to their benches and the speakers' hammer beat insistently amid calls for order. In the racket and clamour nobody but Krast's staff noticed the great clock strike one. Maccrae made his way to the rostrum with his head high and his eye fixed on his goal. Sweat soaked his shirt back and his legs moved like leaden pendulums. The speaker called for order again and at last a sense of discipline began to descend. Chatter gave way to the rustle of papers, stifled coughing and the creak of leather as men took their seats.

Maccrae was helped discreetly up the rostrum steps. He lifted his lifeless legs from one step to the next, watching his own shiny shoes rise and fall without feeling connected to them, and grimaced through a face that felt as lifeless as cement. As he mounted the last step the speaker moved aside and Maccrae laid the pages of his speech on the rostrum. He fumbled for his glasses, found them and slid them into place. A few strands of his hair crumbled down against his shoulders like ash. He stared out across a sea of faces and as he turned to regard the house he heard tendons grind in his neck like millstones.

Perhaps Marie is right, he thought. It was time to see a doctor. He resolved that he'd do so when he returned home this afternoon. He coughed once and then began to read.

At the stroke of one Krast left his chair and went to the window where Westminster palace dominated the skyline across the Thames. He stared at his pocket watch where the second hand sliced away at the last moments of Maccrae's life.

Sunlight cut through the grey clouds and burnished the inky river, and he thought again of the Cobb witch, Eliza. Although the current had swept her away to oblivion, her parting gift remained and for the first time in years he'd become self conscious of his scars, feeling that they screamed his crimes aloud. It was now four minutes past the hour and Krast looked across the water to Westminster and imagined the drama unfolding within.

All things considered, Maccrae began well.

"Honourable members of the house." He propped himself upright with two meaty fists and struggled for air. "For generations, subversive elements within our society have undermined the moral foundations of Britannia, preaching godless acts of magic and questioning man's divine place at the centre of creation," he paused, chasing breath. "I speak," he swayed momentarily, "I speak, of course, of Britannia's outmoded pagan factions."

He paused as appreciative murmurs rippled through the house and when he began again his mouth felt drowsy and drunk.

"Morethanagenerationago," he slurred as he tried to forge words with a tongue that lagged behind his thoughts. He coughed loudly, stalling to collect himself. "More than a generation ago," he resumed, but still smacked of a drunkard trying to pass as sober, "This house abolished a law that is now essential in curbing these diabolical excesses." He swayed and there was an audible gasp from the members sat in the first few rows.

Maccrae pushed onwards regurgitating his words rather than speaking them. He swallowed and it felt like a stone was lodged in his throat. "To eradicate this menace, I propose this house passes the newly authorised protector's act." He made to raise a finger to emphasise his words but no matter how hard he tugged at his fist it wouldn't budge from the rostrum. It just sat there looking sullen.

Dear God! he thought. *What's this? Some kind of seizure?* He stared down at his disobedient hand, aware of the confused looks aimed his way. Move! he willed it.

He grunted in effort and finally his hand grated over the polished wood and lifted a few inches into the air. Worried faces gazed up at him and he tried to ease them with an apologetic smile, but he found that his lips flexed like aged rubber and the best he could manage was a deathly grimace.

Dear Lord! He tried to think of what he should do. Cancel? Continue? Call for a physician? His thoughts moved slower than cooling tar, and a spark of panic began to glow in the furthest most part of his mind. *Am I dying?* he thought with horror.

"Minister?" The speaker hissed for the third time, "Are you able to continue?"

He tried to turn to the concerned voice, but his legs weren't taking orders and they stood as immobile as marble columns.

"Minister Maccrae?" The speaker stepped up to the large man and cupped his elbow, but when he saw his face he could barely conceal his shock.

Maccrae's skin was crazed by hairline cracks like an aged oil painting and it was the colour of slate. Maccrae didn't see any of this. In fact, he didn't see the speaker's face at all: a milky veil had descended and if not for his rigid jaw he would have screamed. He wanted doctor Abbot, he wanted to get the hell off this rostrum and go home, and after all these years he found that he wanted Marie. He tried to tell all of this to the speaker, but he couldn't articulate more than a stifled cry. "Helllppp. . . . ." he grated.

Krast's men noted the thirteenth minute past one approaching and they stepped away, satisfied that everything was on course, and made themselves inconspicuous.

As the minute hand left twelve and nudged against the thirteen, the creature hidden in Maccrae's shadow was suddenly racked by tortuous spasms and it responded in the only way it knew how, by devouring its host's life essence. It gulped him down in savage chunks. Maccrae's very soul was eaten alive and he tried to scream.

He reached out to the speaker, but only in thought. His body failed to respond, rather it jerked and he lurched to one side. The speaker forgot his compassionate Christian duty and leapt back with a scream.

Maccrae's mouth yawned open and he tried to cry out, but his tongue cracked and dropped to the rostrum with a resounding thud. The petrified tongue bounced away and hit a man sitting in the first row, glancing off his shiny pate.

"For God's sake, what's wrong with him?" someone shouted.

Maccrae began rocking back and forth like a spinning-top losing momentum and making wet churning noises in his throat. The house erupted into a storm of shouts and men clambered away from the horror, or towards it for a better view. His face was unrecognisable now: it was grey and crystalline and he gurgled like shingle on a stormy beach.

"Call the constable at arms!" the speaker screamed, but nobody heard him.

The house sounded as though it was full of animals who'd realised their final destination was the abattoir, and in the depths of Maccrae's shadow the moth writhed with the agony of starvation, and tiny though it was, it clawed and shredded his essence like tissue paper.

His left knee shattered spilling a hail of rubble, leaving an empty trouser leg dangling like snake skin. He teetered for a second on his remaining leg with his tongue-less mouth hung wide, and the jagged stump inside waggled as he tried to cry out.

Then he fell, like a great mill chimney, crashing through the rostrum in a racket of splintering wood and a choir of screams as men fled in panic. The pages of his speech scattered and he plunged into the lower benches. The floor heaved with the impact and benches flew upwards and cart-wheeled through the air. As Maccrae hit the floor he literally shattered, spraying up a fountain of gravel and one or two grotesquely recognisable body-parts. A stone ear plopped into a man's lap; contorted fingers spun in all directions; an eyeball, featureless and smooth, hummed past like a child's marble. Teeth skittered across the polished floor and a large, wedge-shaped stone rattled away, spinning like a top before it rumbled to a halt. Maccrae's petrified heart lay amongst the crumpled pages of his speech. It twitched one last time and then fell still.

Silence settled and men peered from behind shattered benches or cowered in doorways, and one by one the country's leaders began to creep back into the great hall like frightened children. A circle of astonished faces gathered around the fall-out that had once been Wallace Maccrae, moaning, gasping and muttering. The constable at arms finally arrived, flanked by two ceremonial guardsmen, and pushed his way to the front. They stared down at the crater of rubble, splintered wood and Maccrae's empty clothes, but none of them had the faintest idea of what to do. Little by little the men found their voices again and the stunned murmurs quickly grew into outraged accusations, and inevitably they all seized upon the same conclusion: this was the work of dark magic.

A tiny moth-like creature fluttered weakly amongst Maccrae's fossilised remains, dying of hunger. Eventually its gossamer wings stilled and it crumbled to a fine dust and became one with the late minister, yet not a soul there noticed.

At precisely fourteen minutes past the hour Krast clicked his watch closed and breathed a sigh of contentment. Outwardly, Westminster looked strong and proud, but he knew the scene inside would paint a very different picture. He also knew that tomorrow the press would scream 'Assassination', and like a line of dominoes events would fall irresistibly into place. Very soon witches wouldn't have a single ally left on these shores.

"Josephine." A voice wafted through the room and he looked around, but the room was as empty as he knew it would be.

CHAPTER FOURTEEN

Kraken's Hunger

London was faster to react than even Krast anticipated. The press printed lurid articles accompanied by generous use of the word 'Assassination'. By dusk the following day there'd been forty-two separate incidents of petty retribution within the capital.

A Romany fortune-teller had been assailed by a mob in Pentonville. A man, mistakenly identified as a witch for merely peddling pots that vaguely looked like cauldrons, had his wares destroyed and his barrow set alight. A theatre on Oxford Street had to cancel a performance featuring a mind reader on tour from America. Children delighted in chasing black cats through the streets and bombarding them with stones, while a synagogue in Walworth was pelted with stones because someone mistook the Star of David for a pentacle.

Krast found all of this highly amusing. The public's gullibility never ceased to amaze him. The protector's bill earned wholehearted support and Maccrae was afforded a grand funeral, but what was left for his mourners to bury was anybody's guess. Within three days of his death, even before his burial, fanciful illustrations of his demise began to appear in the penny-press, those gratuitous publications crammed with stories of murder and intrigue. All of it helped Krast's cause.

Such reports spread through the entire empire over the next few weeks and the further it spread the more twisted the tale grew. What happened to Maccrae was used as an excuse to take long-held grudges a step further. People were being accused of using forbidden arts for the pettiest of slights: publicans for watering down their ale, doctors whose patients didn't recover, farmers for enjoying a bumper crop while their neighbours didn't. It became fact that witches were in league with the French, Russians, Dutch or any foreign power that envied Britannia's crown. Small gangs driven by the promise of reward roamed the wilds determined to root out the hidden covens they'd been told of, and in some instances remote cottages were burned and their occupants beaten. During these weeks of turmoil the witches of Wildwood made secretive sorties into the surrounding districts gathering news, and none of it was good.

"The iron yards on the Heyway and Mersey have increased production, as have the coal pits around Leadchester," Hilda reported what she'd learned.

The now familiar gathering of five sat in Valonia's tower listening to her news with despair. Valonia couldn't and wouldn't keep the threat a secret any longer and everyone knew that a state of invasion was looming.

"Iron and steel are being shipped south, my guess is to weapon foundries. Perhaps this Hobbs Ash place," Hilda finished.

Esta shook her head in disbelief, "I still say we're being too pessimistic! We've built good relations with the working folk of Britain, and the army recruits from them mercilessly. Many still respect the old ways. Surely it wouldn't be so easy for this government to convince 'em to take up arms against us?"

"If only that were so, Esta. How did your pages feel, Hilly?" Valonia spoke of the young witches she'd taken with her.

"They were often hushed and afraid of something, as though we were being followed."

"And any portents?"

"Just one, camped in the forest near Rothwaite," she warned. "We saw a great black owl. It circled us three times before vanishing. I've no doubt it was a haggen-thrall, drawn by some approaching calamity."

Valonia sat silently, digesting this news.

"Valonia?" Kolfinnia asked gently.

The old woman wore her bravest face. "We have the advantage of being forewarned."

"Thankfully Lilain agreed to spread our warning," Kolfinnia sighed.

"Who'd have thought that meeting barghests would've been a lucky stroke, eh?" Esta said without humour.

"Rowan's our greatest concern. How is she, Kolfinnia?" Valonia asked.

"Fine. She asks about the feeling of apprehension in the coven. I know she worries about it a lot. I try to keep her mind occupied, and so we spend a lot of time together," she smiled, "which is a duty I enjoy."

"Has she mentioned the Hand or what it said?"

"No, only that one time."

Valonia nodded. "It's safe to say she doesn't realise the depths of her talents?"

"I'd say so," she agreed, "but for how long I don't know. She mentioned this 'Clovis' again."

"What did she say?" Lana asked cautiously.

Everyone waited for her answer.

"That Clovis and Wildwood have the same problem – persecution. And she wishes that he could come here to help us. By all accounts he's a formidable coven-father." Kolfinnia saw their eyes widen and she told them the rest. "I only learned this last night. Rowan said that his coven faces a similar threat to us." She was very unhappy, feeling that she was spying on her friend.

Valonia looked up to where Skald sat amongst the branches, and both of them knew. "The Illuminata will be collecting intelligence, to build a map of Britain's covens. I see no other option."

Esta rubbed her tired eyes. "Must we?" But she knew the answer.

"We abandon Wildwood and find a safer place, a place that hasn't already been betrayed to them." Valonia ordered calmly.

"Can't we stand and fight?" Hilda asked.

"The older ones with little to lose might, but we have Rowan to think about. She's our main concern and we must protect her at all costs," Valonia was adamant.

"And Hethra and Halla?" Lana asked.

"We're no good to them dead," Esta said bluntly.

Valonia considered something that had been on her mind for some time. "Escaping and keeping Rowan safe is only part of the problem. We still have to stop this first-dawn. It's the reason the twins suffer."

"There hasn't been a Ruinous incursion since something attacked the kelp-harpy," Lana tried to sound optimistic.

"Perhaps that's just because this wretched first-dawn thing hasn't been operational, but they'll tinker with it and when they do the twins will suffer," Valonia postulated.

"This device they have," Kolfinnia asked, "it makes matter change?"

"Indeed, and there's only one kind of matter they're interested in, regardless of the damage it causes."

"They'd run such risks for wealth?" She thought the concept suicidal.

"Gold has a strange effect on folk," Valonia said wearily. "Since time began someone somewhere has been looking for a way to turn the worthless into the priceless."

Kolfinnia's understanding of the process was turning buds into hazelnuts, far more useful in her eyes. You could at least eat hazelnuts. "Alchemy," she said aloud.

"Not as you and I understand the word, no," Valonia clarified. "Their view is upside down. They believe gold is alchemy's ultimate aim when in truth it's the transforming of the soul."

"Their machine does away with the spiritual insights that come from learning true alchemy," Hilda explained.

"Aye," Esta chipped in. "You may as well invent a daft machine that goes to church and does all your praying for you, but still expect to be allowed through the gates of heaven one day. It's bloody nonsense!"

"A hard road ahead," Kolfinnia spoke softly.

"A hard road indeed." Valonia looked at them all. "We move the coven first, then bring first-dawn to a halt. It'll be my duty to select witches to spy out the Illuminata's operation and sabotage it." She felt that she was confessing to murder. She would certainly be sending them into grave danger.

The atmosphere in the tower was subdued. Not only were they preparing for war, but they were leaving Wildwood. That wouldn't happen just yet, but it was coming and Kolfinnia suddenly felt that this wasn't her true home any longer. She heard a rustle in the leaves above and saw Skald vanish into the canopy, maybe to hide his own upset. She looked to Valonia whose face was hard and unyielding, Lana rubbed a tear from her eye, Esta looked down at her hands while Hilda chewed at her thumbnail. She couldn't stand the air of defeat any longer. "So, who's going on a night-patrol this evening?" she changed the subject.

Valonia looked startled as though she'd forgotten that they were all sitting there. "Night-flight? Ah yes, well, how about you and Flora?"

"Really, you'd let us both go?" She suddenly perked up.

"Be back for dawn," Valonia insisted.

"Thornlee's thirty miles north. None of us have scouted up there yet," Lana suggested.

"Thornlee it is, then. Bring back what news you can," Valonia agreed.

"And bring back a nice lad for Flora. The lass looks sour." Esta earned a few tired smiles.

"And fly with care. Villagers might not catch sight of you but there's other things about at night that could," Lana fussed.

Kolfinnia thought of the haggen-thrall Hilda had mentioned. "We'll be vigilant."

"I call this meeting ended," Valonia said abruptly and rapped her knuckles on the floor in conclusion.

They left in silence, and the hot July weather seemed at odds with the threat of war. Solstice had come and gone and even though it was still summer, Kolfinnia felt the nights growing in strength as the balance between light and dark shifting. She'd believed that she'd avoided the autumn darkness, but one way or another it seemed determined to have its way. As she went to be about her duties, she wondered if she'd ever see Wildwood in its autumn glory again, or by October would her home be just a collection of mouldering huts and overgrown gardens?

London was a city besieged by paranoia. Threat lurked on every street corner and every small aliment became a curse, because if senior ministers weren't safe from assassination then who was? Thanks to the tide of feeling against them, the Illuminata had plenty of trials to conduct. Typically the accused was read the charges and given time to state their innocence or admit their guilt, but their allotted time depended on a spinning coin.

'You have until God sees fit to stop this coin to state your innocence or plead your guilt,' was the common line. If the coin spun too long the accused was suspected of using unnatural arts to prolong it. If it stopped quickly they had even less time to splutter their worthless defence. This was how a lone witch of no importance named Godfrey Hallam, and many more like him, were charged under the new protector's act.

Found guilty, he now lay dazed and lethargic in a narrow metal box, his frail chest punctured by tubes and pipes. Krast gazed down at the elderly man with a peculiar, alien pity. *How many times do I have to tell them not to over medicate!* He shook his head. To be sure Hallam wasn't totally unconscious, he reached down and pinched his nose and squeezed hard. The old man immediately stiffened and gulped for air. "Adequate," Krast nodded, then turned to where his kraken stood in the centre of the hanger, supported by a sprawling wooden scaffold. It was the very one that had seen service at Solvgarad. Hobbs Ash housed the entire armoury of over a hundred krakens and the former station made the perfect hangar.

Krast's kraken was named Purity. It was a living relic of his military career. Its hulking shoulders were decorated with medals as large as a man, and dripped with richly embroidered banners celebrating his achievements. The broad chest-plate was etched with a dragon and a unicorn chained to a thunderbolt. Its helmet was smothered in gold leaf and sculpted to look like a serene angel with flowing locks and a firm jaw, but today that helmet hung fifty yards distant in a cradle of chains and pulleys. Purity's arms ended with crushing gauntlets run by boiling steam, and the whole thing was encrusted with rivets and finished in dazzling white enamel edged with gold. Its furnace was cold today and if the experiment worked there'd be no need to power krakens with coal again.

The furnace door stood open and a tangle of pipes cascaded from it and snaked their way across the hanger to an iron cradle resembling a sarcophagus. It was here that Hallam was restrained. Some of the pipes plugged directly into the cradle while others wormed their way under his skin.

The modifications were dangerously experimental and intended to exploit bio-kinesis, converting spirit into energy. The experiment had begun two decades earlier when devisers had given machines the most simple consciousness and imprinted upon them the same kind of hunger Maccrae's assassin had experienced: machines that fed on life. Krast had begun by using pigs in his experiments, but the results from the unfortunate animals were poor, yielding barely a spark. He hadn't been too disappointed, though. He concluded that it was the test subject that really mattered, a subject blessed with innate spiritual skills for instance, someone who 'believed', such as a witch. The whole project had been abandoned, but now with fresh support from Westminster Krast had seen fit to resurrect it as a precursor to the technology needed to feed the serpent-twins to first-dawn.

His commanders were unhappy at the idea of launching an offensive in experimental krakens, but Krast was compelled by a force beyond his control: Josephine. She refused his help. She *made* him take the action he did. He was *not* the guilty party. This twisted logic enabled him to pardon himself and build a new wall around her memory, and a key part of it was punishing the prisoners. "Progress, Hathwell?" he asked.

"Almost there, sir."

"And our witch?"

"His heart's holding up. He's old but strong." He kept his eyes down and scrutinised his clipboard without really seeing it. He felt nauseous, being a man used to combat, not torture.

"Does this bring back memories?" Krast gazed up at Purity.

"Many, sir,"

"I'm sure you haven't lost your squiring skills."

"I don't think I could get on a horse again, let alone fit my old uniform."

"Fear not. We'll find you a noble stallion for our next battle charge." Krast's laughter sounded like a struggling engine.

Had those days been so noble? Hathwell thought, or was it just his memory playing tricks?

Krast checked his watch. "Have the pilot board and seal this witch in the cradle." He made for the control platform where devisers were making final adjustments.

A steam-whistle echoed through the cavernous hangar and after a brusque salute the pilot climbed the wooden gantry to the kraken cockpit, which bristled with dials and levers. He buckled himself in and lowered the safety goggles. If this were a battle situation he'd sit protected by Purity's helmet, but today the giant was headless. He raised a gloved hand to the control desk to confirm his readiness and devisers all turned for Krast's command.

At his signal a horn blasted three times and the lid of the cradle slid into position, entombing the old man. The rush of conductive liquid followed as it coursed through the pipe work and flooded the chamber where Hallam lay bound and helpless.

The tests were rudimentary: the pilot received instructions through a speaker-tube known as a communicare, and moved Purity accordingly.

Left arm raise. One pace back. Pivot thirty degrees. Extend arm and contract claw. Raise boiler pressure by two bars.

Amplified by the huge building, the noise was deafening and Hathwell had a sudden memory of a terrible field in Solvgarad.

He dragged himself up from the mud. His horse was nowhere to been seen. The first column of knights had been turned to scrap metal and just through the smoke he caught a glimpse of Krast's swan and crown banner. The ground lurched as another kraken was downed and he heard witches howl in triumph. The smoke cleared and he saw a lad running towards him, a lad of only twelve or so. He was a witch.

Hathwell fumbled for his revolver even as the lad drew his wand. The smoke thickened again and the young witch vanished from view. Cannons roared in his ears and he saw a huge white kraken lumber through the smoke. Krast was leading a counter-strike, trying to salvage victory from defeat. Someone screamed a war cry and without thinking he fired his revolver. The muzzle flashed three times and he heard a scream of pain.

Hathwell blinked, the past vanished and Solvgarad was just a memory again. Purity continued to wheel and pivot, thrust and swing, and the wonder of it was seeing all of this without a single puff of smoke. The exhaust chimneys were clean and silent, the furnace cold and black. The pilot was operating the suit purely from Hallam's life force.

"Incredible," Krast clapped excitedly. "Incredible!" He held his hand up impatiently, and at once the huge machine dropped into a sullen kind of slouch. As the echo of grating iron diminished and rolled away down the vast hanger, all heads again turned to Krast. "Open the cradle," he boomed as he marched towards it followed by a phalanx of devisers. "I want to see him."

Once the pressure had equalized and the chamber pumped dry, devisers worked the locks around the lid and began to lever it open. A crowd of apprehensive men gathered around, craning and peering, wanting to see, but also afraid to see. There was a gurgling sound as the seal was breached and foetid air rushed from its innards. Krast walked into the ring of spectators and right up to the cradle. "Let me see him." He grasped the cradle's rim and peered over and he saw . . .

Godfrey Hallam died a hard death, and as he did Halla the serpent of Holly flinched and coiled tighter around her brother. Her nightmare grew more intense, and monstrous living dreams from the sleeping mind of Ruin gathered behind the veil, a breath away from Hobbs Ash, waiting for the chance to pass through.

. . . he saw a pool of liquid, ragged clothes and limp pipes that he first mistook for intestines, but Hallam had vanished utterly. Krast turned to his gleaming kraken. Purity had eaten everything, from his skin and bone to his hair and teeth, and the idea gave him a peculiar thrill.

"He's been devoured," Krast heard a horrified whisper from behind, strangely echoing his own thoughts.

"No," he declared firmly. He couldn't afford to let them think something as revolting as that, even though it was essentially true. "The machine *blessed* him, but rather too strenuously," he conceded with a modest smile. He stepped away from the cradle and addressed the devisers. "Re-calibrate the consumption rate. Give Purity more time to chew the fat, as it were." He smiled coldly.

Hathwell remained at the rear with no desire to see, feeling he had enough demons to wrestle.

Far away from knights, assassins, gold and war, further away than Hethra and Halla and even Vega the witch-star, Clovis fled along Evermore, the eternal-spiral, running ever upwards with his pursuers close behind. "Just pick any door and open it. We can't run forever!" Tempest, the thunder-sprite clinging to his shoulder, shouted angrily.

"No, not yet," he insisted. "We have to find the right door, the one I dreamed of and saw in the dark mirror. It can't be far now."

Clovis Augmentrum was a coven-father, or had been until betrayal had sent him fleeing from the burning ruins of his coven and the bodies of his slain brothers. Clovis and his sprite Tempest were perhaps the last survivors of a great coven that only yesterday numbered seventy-eight warrior witches.

He charged onwards, scanning the endless array of doors in seconds. His ornate armour clashed with each footfall and his scabbard hammered painfully against his thigh as he ran. He was tiring and from the sound of it their pursuers were growing closer. He pricked his ears and caught their distant footfalls gaining on them.

He clutched a large glass jar in one hand as Tempest scrabbled for grip on his shoulder. Both of them tried to ignore the fleet of souls that sailed alongside, but the souls it seemed had no interest in them. As they bounded along the stairs a little stone figure inside the liquid filled jar bobbed and swayed. This was Janus, the god of doorways, the key that had allowed them to enter Evermore and both of them prayed he'd allow them to escape it. The spiral was outside creation and had no beginning and no end. The stairs wheeled on forever and the walls were lined with an infinite number of doors. The presence of the living here was impossible. Nevertheless, here they were inside the backbone of eternity, the ladder between life, death and rebirth. But to be trapped here meant damnation and Janus wasn't always to be trusted; he might have led them here as a trick.

The variety of doors was staggering. Neither of them had seen two the same. Some were ornate and tens of feet in height while others were mouse-sized and made of matchwood. Spectral souls joined the spiral through these doors where their former lives had ended, guided here by fairies of endless species, and streamed upwards seeking new doors to begin new lives. Clovis briefly wondered if the doors were fashioned to reflect the lives on the other side of them, which made him wonder about the door he was looking for: who or what was on the other side of it?

"Slow down, we're passing hundreds without a second glance!" Tempest shouted.

"I'll know it!" he panted.

"What kind of door is it?"

"Wooden, not tall. I'd have to stoop to use it." He bounded along the steps feeling his heart burning from the chase. "The handle's golden, decorative." The sweep of the spiral was starting to make him feel dizzy. "There's a word on the door, but it's small. Keep a sharp eye."

"What's the word?" Tempest yelled.

"A place, I think, or a name," he gasped.

"What word, though?"

"ROWAN!" he bellowed and his fearsome teeth gleamed and his hunter's eyes burned golden. He said no more and instead they charged onwards through eternity seeking this most special door.

CHAPTER FIFTEEN

Summer Sleeps, Darkness Wakes

Valonia announced that she intended to relocate the coven in the autumn and it had a profound effect on everyone. After much soul-searching, two of Wildwood's witches decided to leave, thinking life as a lone practitioner a safer bet, and although Valonia sent them off with blessings she was deeply shocked by their decision. In this way the magical number dropped to fifty and seasons Snow-Thaw and Seed-Fall lost a witch each. Lana in particular felt terrible, seeing it as her failure to keep her witches loyal, but Valonia assured her these were unprecedented times and it was no reflection on her Wardship.

Valonia's Wards flew regular sorties throughout the summer. Hilda delayed her departure until after Wildwood had moved, which meant Kolfinnia remained junior Ward, but she was wholly glad of that. The idea of Hilda leaving on top of everything else was almost too much for her to bear. Wherever they flew, Valonia's witches always seemed to return with worse news than before.

While Wildwood was making preparations other covens sought to lay low, hoping the tide of propaganda would blow over. But Valonia knew the Illuminata had barely begun their campaign. Jeremiah Deere was one of the few witches to travel to Wildwood late that summer. He knew Valonia of old and one stifling day in August they walked the coven together. Sunlight sliced glowing shafts through the trees and it was easy to forget that war loomed. "It's a huge undertaking." He spoke of her intention to move.

"Don't try talk me out of it."

"No other coven's taking this threat so seriously." For a man in his late seventies, Jeremiah walked at a brisk pace.

"Not many other witches have had the honour of meeting the Hand-of-Fate."

"Ah, yes, the Hand," he smiled as if not quite believing her tale. "I've heard that Lilain's host have carried warnings to covens far and wide."

"You sound disapproving."

He pursed his lips. "It pays to be vigilant, but it also pays to be prudent. You've created quite a stir."

"Then I'm glad," she retorted. "It might spare a few witches from those unnatural interrogation creatures."

"Or it might dissolve the coven hierarchy and send more witches off to practice alone." He hooked his thumbs into his belt and looked thoughtful.

"And what of Ivy-Maiden? Wouldn't you want your own coven to be ready when the enemy comes?"

"*If* they come, Valonia, not *when.*"

He sounded pompous, she thought. "Take my warning or don't take it, but as for Wildwood, the preparations are already underway. Perhaps we've been here too long anyway." She touched her wand, hrafn-dimmu, for luck.

"Safer? Valonia this is one of the most secret covens I know. Where are you thinking of going that could be more isolated? St Kilda?" An annoying smile surfaced on his lips.

"I've already dispatched hrafn-dimmu several times to seek out a new location," she retorted.

"And? Has the wand found a new site?"

His tone was airy, suggesting that he didn't take this seriously, and Valonia stopped walking and regarded him. Three times now she had cast her wand into the sea where it had spent the night submerged, seeking out the lines of earth magic that would lead it to a new coven, and three times it had been washed ashore the next day having found nothing. "Jeremiah, you are one of the finest witches I know, but if you continue to take that tone with me I'll knock you flat on your back." She folded her arms and tipped her chin.

Deere spread his hands and shook his head, smiling. "Valonia the valiant," he chuckled. "Move if you really must but I for one will need more evidence than whispering bees before I break my coven."

She sighed. "Then I wish you luck and blessing, Jeremiah."

Sometimes, she thought bitterly, *sometimes we do the Illuminata's work for them.*

The summer was getting old. September had dawned and Hobbs
Ash burst with war machines and fighting men. Betrayed covens
were marked with pins, and Krast's map now bristled with them. The
smallest ones would be taken by infantry, the largest would face the
wrath of the krakens. But as predicted, Prime Minister Stokes ordered
him to deploy only half the task force, fearing too hard a strike would
be seen as brutal and expensive. Krast had other ideas, however. He
would send out all the krakens, but not the likes of Purity, as his grim
experiments were still in their infancy. Soon Britain's covens would
be decimated. The political climate was ideal and public opinion was
won, except for the furthest rural districts, which clung to their old
traditions. Maybe a witch could still find a friend in such places, but
only maybe.

In the same gigantic hanger where he had fed Hallam to his metal
monster, Krast now addressed his knights. He climbed the stairs to
the top of the scaffold that surrounded Purity and once at the top there
was a wild cheer from the gathered knights, squires, infantry and
devisers. Over three thousand men applauded their Knight Superior
with complete devotion. They brayed their war chants, and blistering
applause rang through the station.

Krast smiled and raised a hand for calm and slowly the station
drained of noise until it held only anticipation. He took a moment
and stared upwards, framing his thoughts and using the silence to
emphasise his air of command. Through the glass roof he could see
hovering airships ready to airlift the hardware of battle up and away.
Today he was sending them off to war.

"Knights of the Illuminata," he began. "Almost three months ago a
great man was struck down before our very eyes by disciples of evil."
His voice rolled all the way to the rear to where the gleaming krakens
stood like waiting Titans. "And once again the empire's oldest and
staunchest defenders are called upon to ensure that freedom remains
a fundamental right for all. The freedoms you enjoy this day were
bought by the blood of your fathers. The world's greatest empire is your
heritage because of their sacrifice. Now Britain asks you to protect that
legacy, to ensure this land does not sink into darkness. Let lesser men
fight for riches. You are knights and when you march to battle two days
hence you fight for the greatest reward possible, the gift of justice."

Wild applause rang through the hanger before he raised a hand for
calm.

"As you march to war, know every step of your great krakens takes

Britannia into the glorious light of illumination. Knights of the Illuminata, Britain salutes you!"

A thunderous cheer went up and Krast sighed in satisfaction. Soon the only witches left in Britain would either be hiding under stones or strapped to the interrogation chair, and then the hunt for Hethra and Halla would begin in earnest. The plan was to announce that during this offensive they had recovered secrets jealously hoarded for centuries. The Illuminata would 'liberate' these secrets, chief of which was the theory behind first-dawn. Maccrae would be a martyr, the covens would be wiped out, Europe's rival Illuminata families would look to Britain's new science in awe. Everything was turning out so very well, he thought. If only the Cobb witch was here to see it.

As part of Valonia's preparations she ordered all magical traces be removed, which included the circle of way-bewares. The dolls had protected them all summer, but today summer was over in Valonia's eyes, for it was the equinox, and from today darkness would have the upper hand. "Take the utmost care of Rowan." She had no need to remind her, but she had to say the words aloud.

"She's like a sister to me." Kolfinnia touched the Vega amulet at her neck.

"Don't dawdle. Just collect the dolls and be back by dusk at the latest." Valonia showed an uncharacteristic nervousness.

"We'll be fine and fast, I promise."

"I know," she sighed, and patted her arm tenderly. "Just come back safe."

Kolfinnia smiled and turned to leave when Valonia stopped her.

"Oh, and Kolfinnia," Valonia regarded her from under the brim of her hat.

"Yes?" she turned back.

"Wildwood wishes you a happy birthing-day." The old woman smiled at her.

She grinned, bowed politely and made off to find Rowan, not knowing that was the last time she would ever see Valonia.

Rowan sat on a tree stump under the chestnut trees eating her breakfast. Nearby, Kolfinnia could hear someone chopping wood. It seemed pointless now they were leaving, but routine was a good way to beat sorrow. "Nice way to spend your birthing-day," Rowan pulled a face at the wet weather.

"Silly as it sounds I'd almost forgotten. Since becoming a Ward I haven't worried about this day."

"Did you worry a lot?"

"No, not really," she pretended.

"Well, today you're a proper grown-up," Rowan sounded impressed.

"Only when you get there do you realise how good childhood is, and then it's too late." She smiled as Rowan frowned, trying to make sense of this. "Now come on, finish your breakfast. We'd better set off, like it or not." She looked out at the rain from the snug shelter under the chestnut trees where the ground was still dusty and dry.

Autumn had come in an instant, it seemed, and summer was just a list of faded stories. The rain, which had seemed so refreshing when it began earlier, was now just a depressing downpour and Kolfinnia couldn't muster anything pleasant to say about fighting her way through dripping bracken, retracing all the way-bewares.

"Are you worried I won't be able to find them again?" Rowan asked, gathering the wrong impression from her face.

"I'm worried we'll get wet, that's what."

Rowan hurriedly finished the last of her oatcake. "Ready now!" she sang brightly as she stood up, tumbling crumbs from her lap.

As soon as Kolfinnia was clear of the sheltering chestnuts the rain drummed down on her hat. She adjusted her cloak and, using her walking staff for anchorage, she started out over the sodden grass. Behind, she could hear Rowan's splashing bare feet. They began at the avenue of holly, where the changeless leaves were glossy with rain and the earthen path still bore the scratches of a recent sweeping. There were no other footprints but their own.

"It's a horrid day," Rowan chirped, trotting along while tucking her wand-sheath deep into the folds of her cloak.

"Think of tonight's meal," Kolfinnia called, "sat next to a warm stove, and Valonia's got a surprise for us." She could just see Rowan's eyes sparkle under her hat.

"What is it?" she asked eagerly.

Kolfinnia laughed. "You mean you don't 'know'? That makes a change!"

"Kol!"

"Don't say I told you, but she's arranged a hot bath for when we get back, in return for collecting the way-bewares."

"A real bath!" Rowan cried. "With bubbles?"

"That depends on what you eat for lunch," she said and then laughed at her confused face.

They left Halla's path and the comfort of Wildwood behind. From now until they returned they would have only trees and rain for company.

The larch trees were furred with needles the colour of peaches and all around them was the distant applause of falling rain. Pools of water sat in the hollows, fringed by ferns and sailed by rafts of curled leaves. Underfoot was greasy with mud and the tree stumps wore gloves of velvety moss. It was so wet that Gale sat on Kolfinnia's shoulder and took refuge under the brim of her hat, while her lightning-staff hung around her shoulders. "How far to the first way-beware?" Kolfinnia asked.

"This way. There's a big rock by your left foot. It's slippy, take care."

Sure enough, as she said the words, Kolfinnia's toe snagged against the rock in the undergrowth and she clattered her staff against another one. "Blast it!"

"I told you!" Rowan smiled. "There's a rotten branch in that heather. Watch your footing."

Gale was impressed. "Is that how you manage to wander around without shoes, because you know where every sharp stone is hiding?"

The small girl skipped through rain, bracken, stones and branches without a care. "I don't know, I just do," came her stock reply.

Kolfinnia and Gale shared an exasperated look and stumbled on. Cold water ran down her boots, and the hem of her dress slapped at her knees like a wet tongue. "That bath better be hot, and I want real soap, not that slimy stuff Aphra makes from daffodil bulbs. That stinks," she grumbled.

"Funny, isn't it, that Aphra makes soap for everyone but doesn't use it herself," Rowan said innocently.

"Can you blame her? Even Rooter won't touch the stuff."

It was hard to say why, but Wildwood felt more precious and vulnerable today. Kolfinnia supposed it was just the melancholy of moving on and nothing more.

"I'm in the bath first!" Rowan called.

"Only if you leave your feet dangling over the edge." She indicated Rowan's filthy feet, but despite the chatter and smiles she felt strangely tense.

"You feel it too?" Gale asked.

"Feel what?" She said quietly so Rowan wouldn't hear.

"That Wildwood is 'falling' somehow."

Stunned by his insight, she halted. "Nothing to worry Rowan with," she whispered and he said no more.

The rains had transformed the woods. Miniature waterfalls sprang from nowhere and rushed by like foamy serpents, and tumbling along in them were twigs and leaves like golden scales. Between the pine trunks

Kolfinnia could see a misty panorama of mountains threaded with silvery braids, and the streaming mist along their flanks looked like the breath of Earth itself. She felt overwhelmed by the beauty and was all the more sad for having to leave it.

"Will you let me ride with Gale by myself?" Rowan asked from nowhere.

"Certainly not! Riding with me is one thing, but alone? You're still a pip-staff. It wouldn't be wise." Rowan seemed to disregard the matter with a shrug and Kolfinnia hoped it wouldn't crop up again.

When they found the first of the way-bewares, Rowan knelt in the grasses that had grown since May, parted them and beamed with pride. Buried deep was one of their dolls. The witches owed them greatly for a pest free summer. "He's still singing," Rowan said.

"They should've stopped by now," Kolfinnia suddenly felt wary.

"The song sounds different somehow, doesn't it?" she remarked lightly. "Anyway, it's time he stopped singing and went to bed for a rest." She drew the doll from the earth and wiped the dirt from its single spiked leg. "Bedtime, little way-beware."

"How do you know the doll's a 'he'?" Kolfinnia realised she had done it again, used one of her now famous 'how do you know' questions. She expected one of Rowan's famous 'because I do' replies but instead the girl shocked and delighted her.

"Easy, look under there," Rowan said, flicking the dolls' ragged dress.

"Rowan Barefoot!" Kolfinnia blushed, and for a brief moment she wasn't sure who was the oldest between them.

Rowan brayed a donkey laugh and wriggled away from Kolfinnia's amused looks, suddenly embarrassed. "One down."

"Thirty two to go," Kolfinnia finished and they walked on, happy in one another's company.

Some miles from where Kolfinnia and Rowan were collecting the dolls, Captain Jerrow raced through the air like an arrow. Behind him at the frontier the scarecrow circle was a wreck of broken poles. Wildwood's first line of defence had been breached and Petra, his mate, lay pierced by a crossbow bolt.

He had to reach Valonia with warning while his army of crows fought a rearguard action against a force of trained gyrfalcons. The Illuminata had caught them unawares, using raptors to first attack the crow patrol. As the two bird forces clashed in a deadly flurry of black feathers versus white, knights, squires and infantry made ready for their assault.

Jerrow swooped low between the trees while above him a pair of gyrfalcons screamed and tumbled downwards in attack. If it was the last thing he would ever do, he would reach Valonia. He would do it for Petra.

After a two-mile hike they arrived at the southern bank of the Appelier River, upstream from Wildwood. The rain had been falling constantly all morning, swelling the river's coffers, and now it looked lazy and well-fed. Tall pines, peppered with grey lichen, stood a ghostly watch in the mist on the opposite bank.

"Next one's here." Rowan pointed at a clump of grass, but her smile faded when she caught the look on her friend's face.

Kolfinnia was staring at the opposite bank.

"Kol?"

"Listen. The dolls have started singing again." She held a finger to her lips.

Sure enough, even through the black velvet both of them could hear the way-bewares crying in unison.

"Why are they singing like that? It sounds like," Rowan didn't like to say it, "it sounds like they're screaming."

"Something's wrong, like that moment before the barghests came." She laid a protective hand on Rowan's shoulder, but continued to stare across the river.

"That was horrid. It's not that again, is it?" Rowan pressed against her, but Kolfinnia didn't seem to hear her question.

Rowan didn't care for the expression on her face one bit. She swallowed back a lump. The barghest story was fun because they were safely behind her, but thinking of them coming again was enough to raise goose-flesh. She let go of Kolfinnia's hand, fell to her knees and began to scramble around in the grass. The sooner the way-bewares were collected the sooner it was bath and cake time; that made a lot of sense to Rowan. "Kol! Here it is, almost the last one!"

But Kolfinnia seemed almost hypnotised by the gloomy pines across the river. Rowan clutched her hand and pushed the muddy doll between her fingers, but she stood motionless as though hypnotised.

"Kol! What is it? Please come back," Rowan sobbed. She hadn't seen her like this before.

Suddenly she gripped Rowan's hand, and in a flash dropped to the ground pulling her close. The young girl instantly became limp and lay trembling against her. "I saw something move in the fog, out there across the river," Kolfinnia whispered.

Rowan turned slowly to look. She saw nothing but the ashen skeletons of trees in the mist and the river shimmering under the rainfall. "Was it a fog-hound? Is that why the dolls are screaming?"

"No, bigger than a barghest. Easily as big as the trees, but all I saw was just a shadow." She eased an arm around Rowan's shoulder.

Suddenly it was clear to Rowan. "The dolls are singing to warn us!"

"How do you –," Kolfinnia started, but Rowan suddenly clamped her wrist and gripped tightly.

"There! I saw it too. It's bigger than the trees!" She curled tighter, keeping as small as possible like a hunted vole.

Before Kolfinnia could even answer they both heard the hideous sound of live wood being torn and twisted. A large pine opposite swayed gracefully, then lurched and crashed down into the river throwing up a thunderous tide of water. Both of them clutched at one another and instinctively tried to burrow further into the wet grass.

A gigantic figure stepped from the fog spewing black smoke from exhausts around its shoulders and barged the trees aside with great metal claws. It was draped with a flowing tunic emblazoned with heraldic beasts, and huge medals clanged against the armour as it lumbered forwards. It had a snarling face like a sea serpent and feathered plumes towered over its head. Rowan had never seen one before and she screamed and grabbed at Kolfinnia. "What is it?" she howled in terror.

Kolfinnia was dumbstruck. The Knights Illuminata had come to bless the witches of Wildwood.

Without conscious thought she reached for her staff and instantly Gale stood hissing and bristling. "Do we fight? They'll easily outnumber us." He made it sound like a good thing.

Before replying she called out in warning, but already knowing the distance was too great for crowning. "VALONIA!" Her call was desperate but nobody would hear her. There was no other choice. She turned to Gale. "I'll hold them back as long as I can. You take Rowan to Valonia."

Rowan was staggered. "No! Kol, we –," she began.

Kolfinnia pulled her close and hugged her tight in a silent farewell. "Take Gale and raise the alarm. Go!" Another falling tree screamed as if to emphasize her urgency. She pushed her staff at Rowan's chest and the young girl had no choice but to grasp it. As she did, a jolt ran through her arms making her feel taught and electrified.

"I'll take good care of her," Gale promised.

"Thank you." Kolfinnia's fingers dropped from the staff and she looked upon her beloved Gale one last time.

"But Kol," Rowan sobbed.

"Warn them!" She commanded.

Stunned, Rowan looked down at the staff understanding she would fly alone after all. Fate was so very cruel. "I'll come back and help you." Her promise was genuine, but heartbreakingly naïve.

"Do that." Kolfinnia reached out and stroked her hair, knowing Valonia would allow no such thing. Gale melted into the staff, and then copying what she'd seen Kolfinnia do many times, Rowan mounted. "Don't tell Valonia I let you fly alone," she smiled bravely.

Then before Rowan could even utter farewell or good luck, Gale tore away, racing back to Wildwood leaving Kolfinnia to stand alone at the river. *"Hold tight!"* he ordered.

Cold rain pelted her face and drowned her tears as she flew at incredible speed. Today she was no longer a pip-staff and Kolfinnia was no longer a child and both felt terrible.

Kolfinnia caught a last glimpse of them weaving through the trees before they vanished into the gloom, then she turned back to the river where fallen trunks lay and the churning waters were darkened with silt, needles and twigs.

As she watched in horror, one emotion above all thundered in her heart: anger. Consumed by the same rage that had empowered her against the barghests, she drew her wand and broke cover, running headlong to the river still wearing the satchel full of screaming way-bewares.

The advancing knights tore a pathway through the trees leaving trails of oily black smoke in the fog. Their furnace plates sizzled and steamed in the rain, and the air around them ached with the clash of metal and crack of splintering wood. Birds flapped frantically away and the machines were surrounded by a storm of leaves. They'd already begun to wade into the river where shattered trunks bobbed around their steel legs, booming against the armour before rolling away with the current. More trees crashed down, either uprooted or guillotined by brute claws. A hail of rifle fire cracked around the valley and Kolfinnia heard the vicious thud of bullets ripping through the undergrowth around her. She could see squires riding frightened horses through the mists, and they in turn had spotted the day's first witch.

She raised her wand, but she only knew magic intended to honour Hethra and Halla, not halt an advancing army. She had to win Rowan enough time, and while she'd probably be cut down the thought of dying seemed trivial. Aside from her anger, her only other ally was the river itself and she did the only thing she could think of: she recruited it to her cause. "Help me now," she pleaded and lay on the muddy bank in the cover of the rocks.

She cupped a handful of water, heedless of the bullets, and gulped it down. Aided by affinity, almost immediately she could detect the river's consciousness and most importantly, its secrets. The river's memories flashed through her mind along with images of cobbles along the river-bed, and she knew what to do. "Thank you," she breathed. She crawled for cover amongst the undergrowth, then drew her wand and began the spell. "Rage in your bones, tumble these stones, make underfoot sway, give them no way."

The rhyme strengthened the will, and the will would alter the world. She closed her eyes to deny the approaching horrors and repeated it over and over. With the Appelier's waters in her veins, she closed out everything and poured herself into the spell.

As her words became will, the river began to flow with purpose, throwing all its strength into turning the cobbles resting on the river-bed. As more debris swirled along the river's foundations the cobbles began to rattle against one another, then one by one they were wrenched free of their muddy sockets and began to roll under the force of the rushing waters.

The knights in the river found the rolling cobbles as unsteady as shifting sand. Sir Mortimer Pryor was one such knight. The kraken's cumbersome legs strained against the flow and the treacherous cobbles, which now rolled like an army of scurrying beetles. Pryor sat inside the protective helmet of his suit, heaving on levers that wouldn't respond. "Move, you blasted thing!" He wrenched his shoulder as he wrestled the sluggish controls. They were veterans of long campaigns and bloody battles. They'd reduced towns to rubble and marched across battlefields carpeted with enemy dead. They certainly hadn't set out this morning expecting a rag-bag gathering of old women to give them any trouble. The chimneys on Pryor's kraken coughed thick clouds of smoke and the furnace laboured at full capacity as he fought against the unexpected torrent. "Move!" He snarled but he had the sickly feeling of lurching sideways and knew collapse was inevitable. "Bloody hell!" he screamed.

Kolfinnia repeated the spell and her wand felt to burn in her grip. The river churned with marching cobbles and the earth beneath her trembled. Angry bullets whistled past, some barely missing her, and at least the fog and rain made marksmanship harder.

Suddenly the world was filled with a huge roar, breaking her concentration, and she opened her eyes just in time to witness one of the krakens lurch drunkenly and crash sideways into one of its companions, bringing both down into the river in a towering wall of muddy water. The furnace billowed steam and was quenched with a furious hiss and the thunder of their fall echoed around the valley, drowning out the gunfire.

"YES!" she screamed with savage joy. The Appelier's water burned in her gut like strong spirit and she took satisfaction in knowing the knights wouldn't leave this day without some wounds of their own. She disregarded the harm she might have inflicted upon the pilots; her concern was to save Rowan. With the river still in a torrent she fell back into the woods, revived by her success and intending to keep the spell going for as long as she could.

She ran for deeper cover, to a rocky hollow under the roots of an overhanging pine, and slung her satchel inside. The bag hit the earth with a thud and out tumbled the way-bewares. Then as she slid into the hollow, grazing her bare legs, she heard another chorus of twisting metal and shouts of alarm. The river had taken a third knight but she dare not peer out to enjoy the spectacle. Inside her shelter, hot with sweat and effort, Kolfinnia drew her knees to her chest and sat upon her sodden cloak. She began to word the spell again, rocking back and forth as she did, flexing her aching fingers around the wand and urging the river to bring its wrath to bear against the invaders.

Hysterical shouts and screams across the river reached a peak and infantry let loose round after round, convinced that they faced a host of savage witches. The gunfire was random and panicked. A round cracked against her hiding place, spraying her with splinters of rock. She flinched but her chanting never faltered.

"Rage in your bones, tumble these stones, make underfoot sway, give them no way."

Not far away there came a hollow thud that sent tremors through the earth, followed by a second. Artillery began to pulverize Wildwood, and soil and shredded plants showered high into the air. It appeared that they were going to flatten everything just to flush out one stubborn witch, while the 'brave' knights now held back.

She flinched at each screaming shell and felt her grip on the river-spell grow thinner and thinner until it faded altogether. "No, no, not yet!" She clutched the wand harder trying to rekindle her failing strength, but the spell's momentum was spent. The burning in her gut faded. She looked down at her hands, now white from her deathly grip, and knew she didn't have the strength to continue. "Still, I got three of them," she consoled herself. "I got three, and bought Rowan some time, bought them all some time." She stroked her hawthorn wand, seeking warm memories of spring one last time, as the sound of machines grew closer. "So this is adulthood? The darkness found me after all," she said to no one, and instead of turning and running as she should, she dropped her head down to her chest and tears began to fall.

There was a shrill scream, then a mortar shell crashed down just yards away. The ground heaved and the blast roared through her head, leaving only piercing bells in her ears. She screamed and threw her arms about her head, not hearing the tree slide from its overhang, or roots being torn from sockets, as the huge mass toppled over. Seconds later the earth shuddered and the light vanished as the falling tree engulfed her. She screamed and scrambled wildly, pushing herself as far into the hollow as she could. Branches ploughed into the sodden ground, shattering as they did, then even consciousness was taken from her as something cracked against her head. She crashed into the mud and lay bloodied and still, surrounded by the scattered way-bewares, and knew nothing, not the piercing bells, not the guns, not even the way-bewares singing their mournful song.

Without Kolfinnia's guiding will the river fell into a dreamy forgetfulness and the rolling cobbles slowed as the waters eased. The first knights to successfully cross clambered up the banking in a hiss of pistons and rumbling metal while dirty streams poured from their armour. Behind them the first squires and infantry followed, even as bracken and grass continued to float down from the barrage.

Immediately, krakens began butchering a swathe through the wood using their slashing claws, carving a highway straight to the heart of Wildwood, while close behind, squires whipped their horses onwards and nervous infantry crept through the shattered trees seeking survivors. Knight Superior had been very specific: he wanted living captives and the more the better. The soldiers were convinced that a considerable force had held them off and the wrecked krakens, bleeding oil into the river, seemed to prove this. They thrust bayonets between fallen branches expecting to find plenty of casualties.

There was one fallen pine, however, that the soldiers and knights unconsciously avoided. An eerie miasma surrounded it, and they gave it wide berth, unaware that inside the cage of broken branches was the lone witch who'd thwarted them. Kolfinnia lay lifeless and crumpled in a protective circle of magical dolls that sang as they never had before.

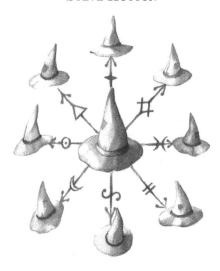

CHAPTER SIXTEEN

Valonia's Nine

Rowan tore through the outer fringe of the coven like an arrow towards Valonia's tower. Then, when the great tree was in her sights she dropped to the ground, trampling over the tomatoes and kale that had no further purpose for the doomed coven. Flora looked up. "Rowan! In God-oak's name!"

Rowan ignored her. "Valonia!" she screamed, knowing formalities were as useless as the ruined vegetables now. "Valonia!" Alarmed witches began running towards her stricken voice.

Valonia was sat in her tower staring into her black mirror when she heard Rowan's call. She jumped up and the mirror clattered to the floor and smashed. It was a terrible omen.

"Valonia!" the scream came again.

As she scrambled up, something black darted through the open shutters and flopped to the floor. Captain Jerrow lay sprawled on the floor. He cawed once and gasped in exhaustion. She scooped him into her arms. He was bloodied and his flight feathers were torn but he was otherwise intact. She barely needed crow language to see that he brought the worst of all possible news.

He croaked a warning and a second later she was in action. Still holding Jerrow, she grabbed a fire-seed from a bowl on the desk, threw open the door, stormed onto the balcony and hurled it into the air. It had come from the volcanic fissures of her homeland and inside lived children of Surtur the fire god, and this was Wildwood's alarm call.

The fledgling fire spirit broke from the basalt shell and raced skywards in a spiral of flames, screaming and spitting as he went. For a moment Wildwood was tinted hellish red by his passing then he vanished into the sky in search of a volcano to call his own home. "WILDWOOD!" Valonia bellowed. All the witches turned to her call and saw a sign they prayed would never come, and the scream of the fire-seed was like broken glass against flesh. Below the tower was an ever-widening circle of witches and Rowan knelt at its centre. Even from the height of her tower, when she met the girl's wide-eyed stare Valonia knew that Kolfinnia was either dead or captured.

More confused and frightened witches began to pour into the gardens: Freya Albright, Daisy Nettles, Morag Heron, Annie Barden, Jenny Heartsease . . . Valonia put a name to each face in a split second and in her heart she'd already began the ritual of separation, knowing that she'd never see them gathered together again. Just then Esta, Lana and Hilda came thundering up the tree.

"Rowan says she left Kol fighting knights at the north river," Esta gasped.

"Jerrow brings warning from the south," Valonia declared, "they're out to crush us from both sides." Without even stopping to gauge their reactions, she bent to the old crow in her arms and whispered to him. "Thank you for your years of service, captain."

He cawed in grief, not hearing her.

"Petra is dead?" She grasped his meaning, and the depths of his hurt. Crows paired for life and in the distant past she'd once had a partner of her own. He flapped in her arms, anxious to return to his beleaguered crows, and she launched him into the air. He climbed high before soaring over the gardens and disappeared from sight.

Valonia turned to her friends and Lana stepped forward and held her lightning-staff out. "You'll need this, and it looks like we'll need ours."

"Bastard knights have beaten us to it! Could this day be any more cursed?" Valonia pressed a hand to her brow, desperately thinking of counter measures. "The rest of the coven will need time to escape." She regarded them gravely. They all knew what this meant. "We'll mount a defence and hold them long enough for the boats to make it past the mouth of the Appelier and out to the sea. This isn't about fighting, it's about winning time."

"You can count on us," Esta answered.

Valonia snatched her staff from Lana and led them down the stairs reeling off her orders. "Junior Wards are to take the children down to the river. Are the boats ready, Lana?"

"Just as they have been for the last month," she confirmed.

"Esta, tell the captains they have one minute to gather what they can, then off to the boats, and tell Annie Barden to collect Hercules. He can't stay here."

"Aye, right away," Esta agreed.

"Hilly, tell Flora to summon a river fog to hide the boats. She'll have no problem calling a mist."

"Yes," Hilda said simply.

Valonia touched down from the spiral and her Wards split away and darted off in different directions. She stabbed her lightning-staff into the ground. "Warm it up, Skald!" she snarled.

He made no reply but the staff began to hum.

Valonia barged through a throng of frightened witches to where Rowan lay crumpled and filthy, still clutching Kolfinnia's lightning-staff. "Witches of Wildwood!" she shouted and the chatter hushed. "Follow the junior Wards to the boats without delay. Cloaks, rations, wands and staffs only. Leave all else. Wildwood is under assault and our plans have changed. Now move!" She finished with a frantic series of hand-claps and they dispersed as the earth trembled minutely to the first distant rumbles of armour and falling trees. Flora tried to push her way through, fearing for Kolfinnia, but Hilda took her aside and relayed Valonia's orders. Then Flora was swept away by the crowd, all of them heading for the river, and in a few moments the gardens were all but empty. Left alone at last, Valonia knelt and cupped Rowan's face between her sage hands. "Now, girl, speak to me."

"Kol's at the river," she sniffed, "trying to stop them, and she's all by herself."

Pride flickered in her heart. She had chosen her new Ward well, but fate was cruel and Kolfinnia's Wardship, not to mention her life, might end abruptly. She laid a calming hand on Rowan's shoulder. "She's a friend to be proud of, and although I can't tell you all, what she did she did for you. Now don't throw her gift away. Follow everyone to the boats."

Rowan clutched the staff to her chest. "No, she's alive and I promised her I'd go back."

"You've already done Wildwood a service beyond your duties. Now head for the boats, Rowan, that's a coven command." The looming fight had roused her wrath. "The Wards and I will rescue Kolfinnia, not you."

Rowan backed away and shook her head, spraying droplets from her wet hair.

"An order Rowan!" Valonia barked and pointed towards the river.

"No!" She backed over the trampled vegetables. "I know she's alive!" And before Valonia could say a word she turned and sprinted away. "I'm sorry!" she cried without looking back.

"Rowan!" Valonia snatched at thin air, stumbled over the vegetables then crashed to her knees. She saw the girl clumsily mount and head back towards the river. "Rowan!" she screamed, clambered up and ran, but she wasn't carrying her own staff and had no hope of catching her without it. "ROWAN!" She watched in horror as Rowan, bearing the secret of Hethra and Halla, flew in the direction of their enemies.

Just then Esta was at her side. "Everyone's packing on the boats."

"Esta!" She jabbed her finger in Rowan's direction, speechless with fear and fury. "Quick, give me your staff. Rowan's gone back to the river!"

"What!" She whirled around. "No, I'll go. She's a witch o' mine, a Seeder. I'm after her." She hauled her own staff from her shoulder, mounted and shot through the gardens shredding withered corn leaves and toppling runner beans as she passed.

"Esta!" Valonia cried. "Be careful!"

Esta didn't look back but raised a hand in salute and vanished into the woods at tremendous speed. Valonia felt claws scrabble at her shoulder and she looked around to see Skald sitting there, his face set like granite. "Esta'll bring her back. Now concentrate on keeping those bastard knights from getting to the boats." He spoke as though this was his coven and she was just a pip-staff.

"If this should be our last –,"

"Don't!" he cut her off. "Don't say it."

Lana came running from the direction of the moored boats, where the bulk of the witches had gone. "Boats are ready." She looked around, "Esta came this way. Where's she gone?"

"After Rowan. The girl took off back to Kolfinnia," she said gravely, expecting a rebuke for letting her slip away so easily.

Lana's eye's widened and she too looked to the north, where Rowan, Kolfinnia and now Esta stood separate from the rest of them. "We four are broken," she whispered and Valonia felt a chill. This day was turning very bad.

"Esta'll bring them home. Our task is to stop the knights. Kolfinnia paid dear to give us warning. Now we'll return the favour."

"Kolfinnia," Lana hung her head. "She might be –,"

"No, she's alive. Rowan says so and I believe her."

"And if Rowan's taken?" Skald said the unthinkable.

"If Rowan's taken then one of us must ensure we're also captured to protect her, rescue her even." Valonia was trying to think of all possible outcomes and none of them looked good. "Pray to Hethra all three return."

"Dreaming dragons bless them," Lana added.

"Before the Illuminata can!" someone shouted. Both women whirled around at the sound of Hilda's voice.

"Are the boats off?" Valonia asked.

"Flora's called a mist so thick you could slice it for bread," she almost smiled.

"Some good news at last."

"And more good news. I have volunteers for our cause!" Hilda jerked her head to the rear.

A straggle of witches came hurrying behind her led by Ada Crabbe, the crotchety old gardener. She was carrying a roll of sackcloth and she threw it on the ground at Valonia's feet. It landed with a heavy thud and Ada stood with her hands upon her knees. "Val," she gasped. "We've elected to stay an' fight with yer." She waved a hand at the tattered gang of elderly witches.

Behind Ada stood Sally Crook, Mary Fife, Agnes Finch and Sarah Flood. They were older, and by rights ought to have been aboard the escaping boats. Valonia's brow creased: she'd been adamant that only the Wards should stay.

"You can't send them away," Hilda whispered from close by.

"We've no young 'uns. Not much to lose," Ada said coolly, guessing her reservations.

"Very well," Valonia said quietly, knowing her acceptance had probably condemned even more of her witches to death.

"There's more." Ada pulled one corner of the sackcloth aside to reveal its contents. "Parting gifts on the understanding that they be returned when we're done with 'em," she said in a strange mix of humour and regret. Inside were six lightning-staffs. Valonia could hear the angry sprites buzzing inside, already primed for the coming battle. "One extra for each of us. Some of thems that's in the boats agreed to loan 'em. Now we've two staffs apiece, one for flight and a second for fight." She spoke without ever taking her pipe from between her teeth, but she had one last surprise. She drew two ornate bows and a quiver full of arrows from the bundle and passed one to Sally Crook. "Me 'n Sal are better at shooting than flying these days, hips too stiff forrit. But when them arrows are spent we'll follow after yous."

Valonia examined one of the arrows. Its tip was a spike of fire hardened wood, carved from the wand of a former witch. They would pack a considerable punch if used right. "This was Connie's." She recognised the vibration emanating from the arrow's tip.

"Aye, fine lass she was," Ada said fondly.

"Nine witches, a score of wand-arrows and fifteen thunder-sprites."

Valonia looked around the circle where their number was ominously only eight, but it would be bad luck not to include Esta. "I almost pity them."

Hilda smiled faintly and then looked northwards. "They'll be here soon."

"They'd have been here without warning if not for Rowan and Kolfinnia," Lana pinned back her dreadlocks, looking renewed by the extra help.

"Then after we grind the knights into the dust accompany me to the river. There are three friends that need us." Valonia gave them reason to survive as well as fight. "Agreed?"

"Aye!" they all called and thumped their staffs on the ground.

Smoke columns streaked the sky both north and south.

"I count at least twenty," Lana noted calmly while buckling her wand-sheath.

"They must really be soiling their britches to send a force so big," Valonia commented.

They all lashed their cloaks tight, secured satchels and hats, then took a second staff and asked the name of the sprite inside. When the hasty preparations were finished they stood lost in thought, kissed by gentle rain and bound by silence. Now that the moment was at hand, fear seemed to melt and there came a peace and clarity perversely at odds with the approaching battle. Valonia took her last look at her tower and at Wildwood, her home of five decades. Many of the younger trees she'd planted herself with the very tools that Flora had inherited. Spades, hoes and rakes lay where good food would now go back to the earth uneaten; apple staves would stand naked like winter trees because there was nobody left to make offerings. Without the witches Wildwood was a clearing and no more.

"I hope Rooter got away," Hilda said distractedly.

"I'll wager he's still got Lana's bloomers," Valonia chuckled. The Wards laughed, but the newcomers just looked puzzled. "I'll tell you about Rooter's little fetish when this is done," she winked.

"Really?" Sarah Flood looked shocked. "He doesn't, you know, wear them, does he?"

Valonia cracked with laughter and soon everyone joined in.

"Oak n' 'olly! I needed that!" Ada cried, wiping a tear from her eye.

"Sorry," Sarah looked embarrassed. "No offence meant."

"None taken. I must look a pig in bloomers anyway," Lana smiled before turning back to the columns of smoke, and which were now accompanied by the rumble of pounding metal.

"I wish Esta was here," Valonia muttered.

"She'll be back," Skald said quietly.

"We should stand here as four." She had a sense of foreboding about Esta's absence; this wasn't going to be a day for witches. *The inner circle is broken*, she thought, but said nothing, not even to Skald.

Valonia and her defenders stood in a rough circle facing outwards in defiance of the approaching knights. The sound of tearing wood erupted all around them and the trees circling the gardens began to sway and break. Above them the air was fogged with smoke and the stench of oil was like the perfume of death, making the thunder-sprites hiss in fury. "The knights think big machines are enough to send folks screaming in fear, but size makes them vulnerable. Strike at the head where the pilot sits, but beware the squires and infantry – they'll carry rifles and be harder to see," Valonia called over the roar of approaching engines.

"Stop them getting to the boats!" Lana stressed.

"Transmutation!" Hilda called over the din. "They've always wanted to turn lead to gold. See if they like steel turning to lead!"

"Aye, let's!" Ada spat on the ground.

Valonia struggled for meaningful words, but in the end she just let her heart speak. "It has been my privilege to share a lifetime with you all." She spoke clearly and deliberately, and then uttered something quietly and tenderly in Icelandic to Skald, something for his ears only.

A barrage of steam-horns hammered the air as the knights sounded their battle charge and for a few seconds even the constant thundering of their feet was drowned out. Valonia felt her teeth shake, her eardrums surge and the ground tremble. Trees fell like matches as krakens slashed their way through them, presenting a wall of snarling helmets, and her heart blazed with anger.

Then a new horror approached. A huge black sphere bristling with deadly spikes rolled through the wreckage, pulverizing stout tree trunks like weeds and crushing the witches' bunkhouses. Flanked by towering krakens and adorned with banners, one of Krast's new prison machines, named Fortitude, arrived to claim living captives for the chromosites.

Ada and Sally took up their blessed arrows and stood ready, one facing north, the other south to where the knights were advancing on both fronts. Valonia's defenders unleashed a defiant scream as they broke into a run. The witches of Wildwood mounted their staffs – some of them for the last time in this life – and flew straight into the heart of their foes.

"I'm coming Kol, I'm coming," Rowan sobbed through gritted teeth.

Through the trees ahead she could see the lumbering krakens and the bright but random flash of rifle fire as spooked infantry shot at imagined witches.

"*Squires dead ahead!*" Gale warned.

"Then faster!"

"*Your plan, little witch?*"

"Just go through them," she said with simple faith.

"*Just go through them! That's the sort of plan I like!*" He surged and she instinctively curled tighter, screwing her eyes into slits against the driving rain, becoming a bullet of her own.

Her one hope was to punch a hole with speed and surprise through the closing net and be past them before they even had time to blink. She watched the krakens grow larger, like lumbering prehistoric beasts, and she could see their armour was plastered with leaves and dripped tears of rain. The first infantry skimmed by to her left; she didn't pay them a second's notice. Then uprooted trees flashed by and she saw the woodland now suffered gaping holes where trees had once stood. She flew through a kraken's sooty exhaust and out again with her mouth bitter with sulphur, while shredded leaves and grit pelted her face.

"Almost through. Hold on, Kol!" she cried.

"*We're seen!*" Gale roared.

To their rear, soldiers took pot-shots and bullets chanced the air in a bid to bring them down.

"Faster and higher!" she screamed, still convinced daring would win through.

The woods opened out into tall pines, almost bare of branches and with virtually no ground cover. Now they were exposed and vulnerable. She saw cavalry two-hundred yards ahead, and they clearly saw her. She had no cover and no way to outflank them.

One hundred yards now.

Despite Gale's speed they had time enough to sweep rifles from their shoulders and take considered aim. Everything seemed to happen so slowly, everything except bad luck, that is.

"*Rowan!*" Gale shouted. "*Look out!*"

Fifty yards.

"NO!" she screamed, thinking the word itself would get them through.

"*Hold on!*"

Yards from the enemy line Gale took control. He banked steeply upwards, seeking cover in the higher branches. Rowan screamed as he suddenly changed direction and felt her guts roll over with the inertia, but today was not theirs.

There came a confident crack and a second later Rowan was swatted from her staff like a fly. The net smothered her and she crashed down through a tangle of branches, screaming and struggling, and was snagged there. The lightning-staff careered into a tree at full speed, snapped in two and both halves spun away like blades.

Free from the wood that had been his home for many years, Gale was drawn back to his ancestral home above. The call of the thunder-heights was too strong and whether he liked it or not, the affairs of men and witches were no longer his. "No!" he scrabbled at the air. Ice crystals streamed from him and showered down upon Rowan's upturned face.

"Gale!" She tried desperately to reach through the net.

He fought against all natural laws, but it was no use: he was beaten. The lightning-staff was broken and his link to this realm was gone. He howled in anguish as he rushed upwards towards his kin, leaving the troubled world far behind. "Kolfinnia," his cry grew fainter.

Rowan kicked and screamed, trying to tear her way out. "Gale! No, please!" she shrieked, but a mournful echo was her only reply.

"Kollllll. . . . ." Then he was gone.

"Cut this brat down, brand her and take her to the Fortitude," a gruff voice came. "First catch of the day."

"Aye, sir, right away."

Rowan struggled to see what was happening.

Someone slashed at the cords holding her up and she thudded to the ground with a yelp and writhed like a snared rabbit. She looked up and saw a hard-faced man looming over her with a rifle. "She's nowt but a young lass," he sounded disappointed.

"Lass or not, she's Jik scum and she'll stew yer guts in a flash." A second face loomed over her, the owner of that gruff voice. He was bearded and flabby. "Now get her to the Fortitude." He prodded Rowan hard with his boot. "Gerrup!" he shouted, making her cringe. "I said ger –,"

She heard a crack as loud as rifle fire and saw the sergeant topple away with his eyes blank, his jaw slack and smoke trailing from his ears.

"What the bloody hell!" The younger soldier turned, but a fraction too late.

Esta whirled around, her long plait snaking out behind her, and slashed at him with her staff and he too fell dead in a flash of brilliant white. A third trooper dropped his rifle and fled. A fourth dodged behind a tree, took aim and raced off a series of wild shots. Esta dropped down next to Rowan, moving with a strength that belied her years as bullets whipped overhead. "Stay calm, lass," she whispered as she began cutting the net.

"Esta! Gale's gone. I broke the staff and Kol's at the river." Rowan tried to relay everything at once.

"Aye, so I believe." She dragged Rowan from the ruined net while trying to ignore the bullets still thumping down around them. Lying next to them were two smoking bodies. Esta tried to ignore them also. "You're off back to Valonia."

"But –,"

"But nowt!" she barked. "You've no idea how important you are! It'll be up to us to fetch Kolfinnia, not you." Now she addressed Midnight, her sprite. "He's got us pinned. Can you make a pass and finish the bugger?" Another round of gunfire proved her point.

The thunder-sprite appeared from his staff and took a look around. "I'm away." He streaked off, looped around the tree and Esta saw a tell-tale flash. Midnight raced back and was by her side even before the soldier toppled. He fell, trailing smoke, and hit the ground with a thud while his rifle clattered against the tree. It was done.

"Neat work, lad. Right, we're off. Rowan, get on." She hauled the girl up and pushed her towards the staff. Midnight vanished into it and it began to hum, ready for flight.

There was a chorus of shouts to their rear and a full company of troops charged from cover, right towards them. Almost at the same time Esta heard a rattle of gunfire and felt something like a hammer blow. Her leg gave way and she fell and it took her a few seconds to realise that she'd been shot. "Midnight!" she cried. "Take her, just take her!" She pulled her wand free and clutched at her bleeding leg and the staff began to move. Rowan felt the wood hum, but it sounded wrong. Esta's sprite was torn between duty and loyalty. "Just take her!" she screamed again, and stood as best she could to face the approaching soldiers. She brandished her wand and screamed a war cry. Several dropped to their knees seeking cover, but others rushed onwards without slowing.

"Esta!" Rowan screamed, but Midnight had made his choice and began to accelerate, intending to run the gauntlet back to Valonia.

Esta drew her atheme and the soldiers, seeing at least three smoking corpses, decided that this was a witch too dangerous to be taken alive and opened fire in one murderous volley. She was hit many times and slumped down to her knees. "Send her safe," she gasped, clutching at her bleeding chest. A trooper ran forward and she unleashed a channelling spell. There was a brilliant flash and he was momentarily blinded and fell to the ground, seeing nothing but a haze and screaming in pain. "Come on, yer bastards!" she snarled. She knew the second she stopped breathing, Midnight, just like Gale, would no longer be bound to this realm. She must resist Evermore's call as long as she could.

Each breath she took sped Rowan closer to rescue. The next soldier to come at her wasn't so fortunate. Things were as desperate as they could get and she took drastic action. "DOWN!" Her next spell was more like a curse. With it she stopped his heart and didn't care if it started again or not. His eyes rolled white and he slumped into the bracken.

Her spells sent them diving for cover behind fallen trees from where they opened fire again. Esta, already bleeding from numerous wounds, was hit by a second volley. Her arm fell limp and her wand rolled from her grasp, and her chest felt like it was wrapped in iron. "Not yet!" she groaned.

As she died, Midnight weakened, and the staff slowed and its course became erratic and jerky. They'd travelled less than a quarter of a mile.

"Midnight! Go on, go on!" Rowan urged, terrified and confused. The staff ground to a halt and she slid into the wet grass. Less than two-hundred yards to her left a towering kraken slashed a path through the trees. A company of soldiers swarmed around its feet and some of them broke away and headed in her direction.

The staff finally dropped like a stone and Midnight appeared, bent double as if racked by pain. His feathers were dull and matted. "Esta," he groaned, clutching his head. "She's dying!"

Esta heard the clamour of battle grow fainter and her body jerked as she was hit for a third time, but she hardly felt it. All she could see was the sky above, and now she realised that she was lying on her back. Tracer bullets skimmed overheard leaving bright little trails. But beyond them, swirling in the clouds and untainted by the misery of battle, she saw a mighty dragon of twisted branches and oaken scales. His eyes burned like the aurora, his tail spanned the firmament and his wings reached across galaxies. Her senses had dwindled, and nothing of the outside world was real other than the majesty of the dragon above.

"*Estala Janice Salt, will you walk the Evermore-spiral with me?*" Hethra called her.

His voice was the sound of every leaf falling and the roar of the autumn tide. She dragged an arm across her heaving chest to the oak leaf pendant around her neck and clasped it in bloodied fingers. There was nothing more she could do for Rowan or Wildwood and her heart was broken by bullets and grief. "Aye, I'll do that, my Lord," she whispered with a regretful smile, and then Esta Salt left her broken body and this troubled realm behind.

Midnight wailed in grief, "Esta's dead! Rowan, run!" Then he began to lift away from her just as Gale had.

"No, come back!" She leapt up, trying to snatch him out of the air. Tiny ice crystals drifted down upon her upturned face and mingled with her tears, but Midnight, just like Gale, accelerated upwards until he was just a glowing speck darting towards the grey skies.

Rowan turned and staggered on, blinded by tears, grief and confusion. Wildwood was an unrecognisable maelstrom of screaming metal, gunfire and tearing wood. She ran because it was all she could think of and she didn't even know in which direction she was running. But she didn't run far. Strong hands grabbed her cloak and jerked her backwards so forcefully that she landed flat on her back and the wind was knocked from her lungs. Still gasping for breath, she was hauled upright and came face to face with another grim-looking soldier. "Got yer!" He gripped her tight, and this time there was no Esta Salt to save the day.

"Here!" Clovis shouted triumphantly. The door was small and insignificant but otherwise just as he'd described it. It was wooden with an ornate brass handle and lock, and the word 'ROWAN' was carved upon it in delicate letters.

He retrieved the sacred jar from the folds of his cloak. It was octagonal with no apparent lid, being cast of a single block of thick glass, and swimming in the greenish fluid was the small figure of Janus.

The little god was carved of some dark stone or suchlike and his form was crudely configured. He had rudimentary arms and legs and a chubby body, and his face was plump and disconcertingly smug. He resembled something that a child might make and always looked like he knew a secret. Clovis set the jar down carefully before the door and inside it the stone god turned lazy loops in the liquid, which still swirled and churned.

"Make him open the door. They're not far behind us now." Tempest stared back down the dark curve of the spiral.

"Patience. You know as well as I that Janus must be asked, not used," he said curtly.

Clovis knew that he wasn't good at asking for help. He also knew that Janus could be fickle and cruel. If he did this without the right degree of acquiescence Janus would string him along and he'd end up screaming his demands to the trickster god. Janus had allowed them to enter

Evermore and escape their doomed temple, but he revelled in being begged by those in need of him.

"Clovis, they're almost on us." Tempest tried to remain calm.

Clovis knelt before Janus while souls flowed between lives, oblivious to their troubles. "Janus, once again we need your help. We have reached the Rowan door as commanded but it remains locked," Clovis concentrated.

"I did not send you to this door." Janus spun merrily inside the jar.

He clenched his fists, holding his anger there, and felt bile rise up as he dredged humiliating words from his gut. "Who sent us is not a priority right now, but escape is. I humbly beg that you command this door to allow our passage, mighty Janus." He bowed his head to conceal his contempt.

"But there are so many other pretty doors I may wish to open. Why should I travel to places of your choosing?" Janus mused in a slippery voice.

The rumble of their approaching pursuers broke Clovis's delicate patience like iron on glass. "God you may be, Janus, but if we die here then you'll face an eternity with nothing to do but admire our bones and count the stones around you. How long do you think that will keep you amused?"

Janus giggled, "Eternity is nothing for a god, Clovis. Even this staircase must crumble in the end, then I shall be free!"

"The hunters are only one twist in the spiral below us," Tempest whispered.

The shambling on the stairs below sounded nothing like the footfalls of his own kind, which were deft and confident. This was somehow clumsy and mechanical and Clovis knew what it was. "Amalga!" he said in disgust and turned back to Janus and thrust his face close against the glass jar. "Even a god might go mad waiting an eternity, and even if the walls of this spiral one day crumble to dust what will be left of the universe outside for you to enjoy, little god?" Janus ceased his taunting dance. *So much for tactful flattery*, he thought.

The amalga lumbered into view, thumping up each stair with unfeeling will and scattering terrified fairies before them.

The witch-hunters had not risked following them for fear of losing their quarry. If Clovis escaped with Janus, his pursuers would have been trapped, hence they'd sent disposable warriors fuelled by magic.

The first was a mass of broken artefacts moulded in crude humanoid form. Clovis recognized shards of broken wood and slivers of stained-glass from their ruined temple. Behind the first was a second, far more sinister figure. Their pursuers must have raided the sacred catacombs below the temple. This creature was a mountain of teeth and bones mockingly sculpted into a figure and given 'life' by a tiny spell-bottle buried deep inside it. "From our own scared dead!" Clovis was aghast.

Behind these were at least two more, but the shadows masked whatever they were and perhaps that was a mercy.

"If you won't open this door, Janus, then I bid you farewell." Clovis did his best to sound regretful. "Enjoy counting souls as they pass to places you'll never see." Then he turned and drew his sword.

"Clovis," Janus purred. "I am grieved at your lack of trust in me." There came a muffled click, and a thread of daylight burned brilliantly around the rim of the ROWAN door which now miraculously stood ajar. His bluff had worked, this time at least.

"Tempest!" In one move he scooped up Janus and kicked the door open, and before he could even gauge where it would lead them he plunged through. A fraction of a second later, just as the amalga lunged for them, the ROWAN door slammed shut with a finality that resounded through eternity.

CHAPTER SEVENTEEN

Steel and Storm

They were airborne now and Valonia led Agnes and Mary northwards towards six krakens that had broken through the trees and into the gardens. She waved an arm, indicating that they should tackle the first while she flew towards their company commander, an armoured giant painted gaudy red and framed by ghostly wings of exhaust smoke. Its helmet was fashioned like a snarling leopard and dozens of leopard skins hung from its hulking shoulders where huge medals rocked and clanged against one another, while banners swirled above its head. One hand was a brute claw and the other held a crushing sword ten yards longs and four inches thick. Valonia never thought she'd live to see such an obscenity violate her coven and rage boiled in her veins. "That red one!" she shouted to Skald.

"I see it!"

As she rushed towards it she saw its clawed feet dig huge clods of earth from the gardens and she couldn't contain her anger any longer. She pulled Skald vertical, weaving deftly between the kraken's scissoring legs before looping around its back, passing through foul exhaust plumes and within feet of its ceremonial banners. "Wildwood!" She screamed and lashed out with her borrowed staff.

The sprite within was named Glass, after a lightning-bolt that had fused sand into silica during one tumultuous strike. He used that incredible heat now and a searing bolt arced from the tip of the staff and whip-cracked against the helmet, incinerating the banners and turning steel molten. There was a tremendous explosion that rumbled around the forest.

"Direct hit!" Skald cried triumphantly.

"A fine piece of work!" Valonia praised him, but Glass didn't waste time answering. Instead, he began building his charge again.

Valonia raced away in a tight curve, bringing the red kraken into her sights again, and this time she couldn't believe her eyes. It no longer marched across her coven in contemptuous strides; instead, it was a towering torch. Blazing leopard skins, banners and plumes were dripping like molten wax, and the snarling helmet was now just a mess of twisted metal. Steam boiled from its furnace and severed pressure hoses lashed frantically, spraying water like blood. The headless machine swayed undecided before it sank sideways and crashed into a second knight to its left. Veteran colonel Valhorst, the commander of the Wings-of-Mars and pilot of the dreaded Crimson Reaper was brought down by a single old woman.

Valonia glanced two brilliant flashes in rapid succession from the corner of her eye. She risked a quick glance and saw that Agnes and Mary had found targets of their own. One kraken had the face of an eagle and she saw its eyes blaze orange as the explosion flared outwards from the cockpit, buckling steel and making the eagle look a bloated chicken. "Ha!" she cheered.

The Crimson Reaper, meanwhile, staggered against its companion like a drunkard. The pilot of the second, with a helmet fashioned like a bull, did his best to steer away from the fireball that had once been his commander. "Valhorst is down!" he screamed over and over into his communicare. But he was abruptly cut off as the now decapitated Reaper dragged his own kraken down. He saw the horizon first tilt then flip vertical, and he crashed against the cockpit's hull spraying blood from his ruined nose. He screamed and vainly flung his arms over his head as tons of burning wreckage buried his machine under a mass of pulverised steel. A wall of earth belched upwards from the impact, but Valonia barely gave it a second glance. Instead, she began another pass at the knights as more of them began to crash through the trees amid a frenzy of rifle fire.

To the south, Lana, Hilda and Sarah faced a similar wall of krakens that ripped through the tree cover in unison. As they flew closer the witches saw with horror the black strip of churned ground leading away to the horizon, to where Jerrow and his crows had first encountered them. All of the krakens were smeared with leaves and some had branches wedged between their armoured joints.

"I'll lead!" Hilda cried. She pushed forwards and Lana and Sarah formed up behind as they climbed level with the treetops. They raced in front of the advancing giants and Hilda saw one ugly helmet after another streak past and smelled grease and hot metal.

Infantry tried to bring them down, and their endless bullets chimed and pinged as they ricocheted off the krakens, chipping paint and thumping into their fluttering banners. They were shooting without discipline, and squires galloped around barking orders trying to direct their fire.

Hilda focused on her timing. She waited until she was at the very end of the rank before she wheeled her staff. A torrent of energy forked through the helmet's visor and everything within was incinerated in a moment, including Sir Joshua Holmes who barely had time to register his astonishment let alone cry out. His kraken fell, trailing its banners which continued to flutter happily, unaware that they were finished. Hilda heard two explosions behind her as the others made successful strikes.

Behind her, three headless krakens lolled and pitched into their fellows, turning the ordered rank into a confused tangle, like giants drunkenly trying to out-dance one another. So far, six krakens were destroyed, and with each second that passed the witches prayed that the boats were further downriver and that Esta and the others were closer to home.

"There!" Ada shouted to Sally. They were the last two witches on the ground: all the others were either airborne or paddling safely away.

"Where?" Sally glanced around.

"That black globe thing, the one with the spikes like an 'edgehog." Ada pointed to the fearsome looking machine that had first rumbled into the coven, but had now retreated into the tree cover where knights flanked it protectively.

"They're keeping it well defended." Sally was already putting an arrow to her bow.

"Aye," Ada agreed. "Take a shot, Sal?"

"I'm already there." She took aim at one of the krakens. "Last spell of Jannie Dewhurst," she murmured. Sally held her breath and released. The arrow whisked past her cheek as it shot towards its target. A second later they were rewarded with an orange flash as the kraken's furnace plate was smashed from its hinges. The heavy door spun through the air, cleaving a tree clean in half and then amputating a second kraken's arm at the elbow. The great forearm, still holding its massive sword, thundered to the earth scattering a host of terrified infantry, while the suit with the gaping furnace lost pressure and buckled at the knees, dropping with colossal force like a beaten prizefighter. The Fortitude jerked and smoke poured from its chimneys as it made a furious bid to retreat from the falling kraken.

"Nice work," Ada commented.

"Ada, to the north!" Sally shouted.

She spun around and saw Jerrow and his crows flapping wildly around a kraken's visor as it tried to negotiate the ground underfoot, which now bristled with wreckage. Its arms waved ponderously, trying to bat the troublesome birds away, but Jerrow had Petra's name in his heart and he wouldn't retreat. "Kathy Faithful!" Ada called the name of her chosen arrow and aimed.

Sally's hit on the furnace plate was impressive, but Ada had something more spectacular in mind, and once confident of her mark she released. "Ha!" she shouted as the arrow left her bow.

Seconds later its right knee exploded. It lurched over with pipes dangling from the severed joint like veins, and leaving its amputated leg standing like a lost boot. It hit the earth in a spray of soil, with its bright banners rippling in its wake.

"Very clever," Sally complimented, sounding like a woman playing a game of croquet rather than engaged in battle, "but I reckon Jenny Hogg'll have something to say about that." Jerrow and his crows moved to a second kraken.

Ada saw at least two birds splutter feathers and spin to the ground. "Two of Jerrow's lads gone down," she said regretfully. "Make 'em pay forrit."

Sally selected a kraken resembling a gulping fish. She strung an arrow, but before she drew it she whispered a spell into its grain.

"Hey! That's cheatin'," Ada complained.

"A lesson in transmutation. They've been after it long enough," she replied through a crooked mouth as she squinted and took aim.

The bow made a deep thumping sound as it catapulted the arrow towards its target, and both witches looked on and counted their heartbeats in anticipation. There was a delicate blue flash against the kraken's wrist where it held a brutally long sword, and although they were too far away to see, the sword began to darken as the spell spread.

At first nothing happened, but men soon looked up in horrified fascination as the looming sword turned from steel to lead. Its mass went on growing heavier until joints groaned in complaint. Rivets popped from between buckling steel, and steam hoses stretched like warm toffee and ruptured as the stupendous weight ripped the kraken's arm from its socket. Men ran, cursed and cried out. Some even opened fire into the gardens, hitting nothing but corn or scarecrows.

"Fall back!" The squire screamed and waved them away just as the kraken's leg began to inch up from the ground under the lead's irresistible pull. The squire gave up trying to direct the infantry and instead ploughed through them in a bid to escape as the huge machine slumped in a death dive. The kraken thundered into the earth and sent up a cloud of splintered wood as it demolished a row of camp huts. Its helmet ruptured and the bulging eyes actually jumped from their steel frame and rolled out across the gardens.

"Aye, very clever," Ada conceded. "Yer could say his eyes were all over the place, eh?" she cackled.

Sally smiled broadly and then both strung their bows and took aim again.

Wildwood's defenders dodged claws, gigantic swords and bullets and continued to strike at krakens, reducing them to chimneys spewing fire from their ragged necks. Knights saw their fellows toppled by enemies flying so fast that they were gone before they even had chance to react, and it dawned on them that they were just brightly decorated, lumbering targets. Cockpits grew hot with sweat and fear, and communications flashed between knights and their commanders, each more frantic than the last.

Before long the knights made a tactical withdrawal. Krakens jostled and barged one another, many streaming burning banners and pock-marked by fire from their own infantry, and retreated into the remaining tree cover while soldiers advanced fearfully towards Valonia's tower. They edged forward wide-eyed, passing shattered krakens they'd once considered invincible: many attended by squires trying to rescue their Lords.

With infantry advancing and the knights taking cover, being airborne was no longer a tactical advantage and Valonia decided that they'd make their last stand at the tower and force them to advance at a snail's pace, earning as much time as she could. She gestured towards the tower and, understanding her command, Agnes and Mary followed. She snatched a rearward glance to make sure they understood, and in that horrible instant she saw Agnes, a friend of more than twenty years, reel backwards. There was a puff of crimson mist where the bullet struck her and she tumbled into the chaos below and out of sight. "Aggie!" she screamed and Skald responded, making to turn back even before she'd commanded him, but suddenly Mary was flying at her side and tugging on her arm.

"No, we can't do anything for her. Back, Valonia! Back to the others!" Her face was stained by soot and sweat and two bullets holes were drilled through her hat.

Valonia shook the tears from her vision, snatched one last glance to her back to where Agnes had fallen, and made towards the tower ahead of the creeping carpet of troops. She desperately hoped they would find Esta awaiting them, and as they approached the tower she saw a huddle of figures clustered around the tree's trunk and her heart leapt. "Please be Rowan," she begged.

"I don't smell Gale's scent, or Midnight's," Skald said ominously.

Valonia and Mary finally landed and ran to the others who were taking cover at the edge of the ruined orchards. Lana knelt clutching her forearm where a bullet had rendered it useless. She was ashen and her eyes were glassy. "Lana!" Valonia was at her side instantly.

"Nothing to worry about, bullet passed right through," she hissed through the pain.

"Where's Aggie?" Ada looked around for her friend.

Valonia just looked at her, but said nothing.

Ada took her meaning and loosened her last arrow with a scream. "Bastards!" she cried, but her shot was unfocused and it thumped harmlessly into the earth not far away. She realised her blunder and cried out in frustration. "Bastards!" she spluttered again.

"And Sarah?" Valonia looked around the small group.

Hilda shook her head and Valonia felt the air turn cold. "Five of us left," she muttered.

"Six," Lana gasped.

"Not with that arm," Valonia shook her head and her wild hair was a thunder cloud of grey. "And remember if Rowan's taken we must follow, not throw our lives away."

"They ought to have come back by now." Hilda looked northwards.

Now the krakens had retreated into the trees, a strange lull had settled and distantly they could hear soldiers barking their orders.

"Valonia, we should get flying and hit them again!" Sally insisted.

"This isn't just about buying time, Sal. There's something about Rowan I've not told you, something crucial." She looked around guiltily.

Ada took her pipe from between her teeth. "You pick a fine time to tell us yer secrets. Out with it then."

"This better be a secret worth the fight." Sally looked hurt.

"It's Rowan's secret and if they get her it'll become theirs and witches over the Earth might as well just give up. And for your own safety I can't tell you." She hated the way they were splitting into two factions: those that knew Rowan's gift and those that didn't.

"We trust you, Val," Ada said wearily. "We allus 'ave."

"Me too," Sally and Mary agreed at last. The situation was bad, but they weren't going to make it worse by arguing.

"Esta should've come back by now," Hilda said quietly.

"They must have been captured," Valonia straightened, preparing for the worst. "If so, then we must follow, to protect Rowan."

A look of realisation crept over Ada's face and she was staggered. "You mean allow ourselves to be taken?"

Valonia nodded. "Me, Hilly and Lana will stay, that's our responsibility. But the rest of you leave now while you still can."

Mary risked standing up for a brief look about and saw that the infantry were still some distance away. They could easily make it to the river and freedom.

Valonia saw their turmoil and couldn't stand it. "Go," she said. "That's my command."

For a moment the three just stood there looking torn.

"Go and catch the others," Valonia urged. "They'll need senior witches now, and tell them about how Agnes and Sarah gave their lives."

Mary and Sally began slow, reluctant nods while Ada refused to shift.

"Return these," Valonia held out the borrowed staffs. Then incredibly, Hilda and Lana also offered their own staffs, the ones they'd had since being ten years-old.

"Keep them safe for when we meet again, and if not you'll know if we should die." Hilda felt a terrible sadness as she let go, and Lana looked away to hide her tears.

"And you?" Mary asked warily, seeing how Valonia still clutched her own staff.

"Skald has a job to do. Now be away."

Mary and Sally gathered the staffs and turned west, where their chance to escape grew ever slimmer. "Ada!" Sally hissed. "Come on, let's move."

Ada hung her head as she thought. "Am too old to run off. You go, the pair of yous. I'll be fine." She jabbed a thumb at Valonia, "Someone needs to take care of 'em." Then she handed over her own lightning-staff. "Take him. I don't want him stayin' ere," she choked.

The clatter of approaching troops was growing louder.

"I hope to see you again soon," Mary said sadly.

"And we you," Valonia replied. There was a shout from somewhere close by. "Best be away," she said gently.

They turned and ran. Valonia saw them both steal glances behind before they disappeared into a thicket of apple trees and then they were gone.

"Blessed be," she said to herself. "Now, Skald, I've a task for you," she added.

"Name it," he agreed.

She muttered her last command to him, and then took the staff with him hidden inside and thrust it into the ground amongst the crops where it looked like just another post. Then she knelt and hastily buried something at its base. When her hand dropped from the staff for the last time she lost her mental link with him and felt suddenly naked and alone. "Goodbye, brave poet," she whispered. "Remember Mörkdalur."

The sound of voices grew louder until finally a dozen soldiers broke through the undergrowth. One cried out, startled and terrified, and Valonia thought they'd be shot right there and part of her welcomed it.

"Hold your fire! Hold! They're captives," the sergeant commanded. He grasped rifle barrels and shoved them downwards.

Valonia saw scared faces and smelled hate all around her like a poisonous cloud. Ada, Hilda and Lana gathered around her protectively, then she swallowed back her anger and gave the hardest command of her life. "We surrender," she said and raised her hands, but her gaze strayed to her lightning-staff, hidden amongst the runner beans. *Good luck, Skald*, she thought.

Kolfinnia couldn't remember what had happened, but she was certain it was something terrible, and so she clung to her amnesia like a life belt.

She was sprawled on the ground between fallen branches and her limbs were so stiff and cold that she didn't know what was flesh and what was wood. Her sodden clothes were pasted to her body, and when she tried to lift her head pain flashed down her back. She flexed her fingers tentatively and somewhere out there in the dark numb fingers moved, although she couldn't see them. She steeled herself and flexed all her limbs at once, expecting to feel broken bones scream out, but miraculously she felt only aches and stiffness. As sensation crept into her muscles again her heart pumped not just blood through her veins, but scattered memories. *Here comes the storm*, she thought. *Something terrible.*

Knights. Artillery. Way-bewares. Rowan.

"Rowan!" She gasped.

There was no gap between the now and then. For her, the barrage happened only seconds since and as if to prove it her ears still rang. She lifted herself up onto her elbows and her body cried out in complaint, but she was determined to return to Wildwood, believing in a disjointed way that she could still do something to save her coven.

Wildwood's already dead and so is Rowan. You thought you'd escaped the September darkness, but it came to you instead! The whispering voice was hers and it was more chilling than a pack of barghests.

"No!" She started to drag herself upwards through the thicket of branches.

At the sound of her voice her wand began to emit a cold green light. It lay close by and cast its spectral light across a heap of way-beware dolls, and upon seeing them her memory flooded back.

The dolls were deathly silent now. They'd spent whatever magic Valonia had imbued them with to keep her from being discovered, and a tear of gratitude ran down her cheek. She reached through the branches and plucked her wand from the dirt. Then without knowing why, she clutched one of the way-bewares too, and slid it into the folds of her wet dress. She reached up to where the pain was worst and patted her scalp gently. Sure enough, her exploring fingers found a considerable lump and came away sticky with blood, which looked black in the glow of the wand-light.

Black.

Black as barghests, black as Lilain's royal fur, black as the cauldrons Rowan had been cleansing the day they met.

"Rowan," she whispered again. She had to find Rowan.

She heaved herself out of the fallen pine. Neither Gale nor Rowan had returned and she prayed that both had reached Valonia safely. She stood under a bald moon of terrible brightness and gaped at a highway of shattered stumps that stretched away right to the heart of Wildwood. "Lord Oak, no!" There was nothing left but destruction. She began to walk, then to run through the devastation, ignoring the pain, the cold and her sodden clothes. Some time in the unspoken hours before dawn, when hope was always at its most frail, she arrived at what had once been her home.

She passed storehouses and camp huts crushed by iron feet. Spilled grain and fruit had been dashed from carefully tended larders, and the sacks of flour had been spitefully slit open and disgorged. The heaps of flour looked ghostly under the moonlight.

Her heart leapt at the sight of garments lying in the mud. At first glance they looked like crumpled bodies: a green Snow-Thaw scarf, a russet Seed-Fall waistcoat and a tattered Flower-Forth dress. "Maybe they got away?" She repeated it like a mantra; the more she said it the more likely it became. "Will controls matter," she reassured herself, but that notion looked pitiful in the face of this destruction.

She stumbled over broken walkways and splintered planks, and severed rope bridges dangled from trees like cobwebs. Then smelling soot and oil she slowed her pace, dropping into a crouch as she did. The angular silhouette against the moon was unmistakable. A kraken had been felled and she felt a wave of feral satisfaction. It seemed that her sense of empathy had also died with Wildwood.

She found at least three toppled krakens. Their banners lay limp, and dying embers pulsed in an open furnace like malevolent eyes. She hurried through the machine's metal innards, keeping her course towards Valonia's tower. She scrambled under giant pistons twisted by explosions and cogs as large as cartwheels. Machine parts dusted the ground like volcanic ash and all around was the acrid stink of ozone from the lightning.

The sprites have been busy. She thought of Gale and her heart ached. Feeling fresh tears she pushed on, weaving under giant limbs scorched by lightning and wincing at her every footfall, fearing she'd be heard. Tramping over a fallen Illuminata banner, she delighted in grinding it into the mud. Only when she found a broken hoe did she realise that she was in the gardens. They were an unrecognisable battlefield.

"Flora." She knelt and touched the hoe but didn't pick it up, convinced momentarily that her friend's cold hand would still be clutching it. She raised her wand to cast more light. There were broken gardening tools scattered around, but mercifully no Flora. She wasn't far from the tower now, but although this skyline had been her companion from childhood tonight it looked somehow alien.

Hethra's tree and Valonia's tower were gone.

She saw only unsympathetic stars where it had once stood and the strength in her legs poured away like sand. "Valonia!" she moaned and stumbled on into the black knowing only horror waited there.

When she saw how the tree had been killed she clamped a hand over her mouth. The trunk ended in a savage wound that cut it in two, and its fallen branches lay in a circle around its severed neck. A few crooked steps leading nowhere ascended the trunk before halting abruptly in a pincushion of splintered wood. She'd never seen anything so symbolic of futility.

Now she was beaten. Her body might have survived, but her soul may as well ascend those pointless steps and drift away into the black. She crawled over the roots, level with the naked stump that had been slashed and hacked by mechanical claws. "I'm so sorry, my lord," she uttered.

Tears showered down gently as she shook her head in disbelief and she reached out her trembling hands, needing to know what had happened, even if the knowing would be like a slow knife to her heart. She lay her palms on the severed trunk and felt for the tree's last memories.

Incredibly the great tree still lived. It winced at her touch and she was momentarily startled and repulsed: this was akin to seeing blinking eyes in a decapitated head. "My Lord." Her tears rained upon the grotesque stump, but she had to see. She delved deeper, past the tree's pain and shock, and saw, as if from a distance, Rowan and captain Jerrow arrive almost simultaneously. Witches gathered in the gardens, running to their posts in readiness for a disaster they had prayed would never come. Rowan was given orders by Valonia, but then fearfully backed away. Kolfinnia focused harder, pressing her palms to the stump, prying and straining. She saw Rowan hop astride her staff and tear away back in the direction she'd come. "She came back for me." She felt humbled by the girl's unbreakable faith in her.

There was a blurred kind of gap where she lost the tree's awareness and when the vision returned she saw how Valonia had elected to mount a defence. She pressed harder but the tree was failing and its last memories were seeping into the earth.

"Please!" she urged, and the great tree, named for Hethra the oak-serpent of summer, answered her call and summoned its final strength from century-deep roots.

She watched with pride as her friends took the battle to the knights and gasped in horror as their enemies finally surrounded them. The images began to grow faint and she tried to press for a clearer view, but the tree and all its centuries of living history quaked beneath her fingertips. "No! Please, what of Valonia, what of Rowan?"

Her answer was a confused avalanche of the tree's disjointed memories: a sapling's joy at putting forth new leaves centuries before, weathering spectacular storms, and of the bears and wolves that used to call Britain their home. Memories flashed from past to present and back again as the tree's strength flickered, faltered and then without another word it died, leaving her alone with only frozen memories locked in silent wood.

She slumped down and began to cry freely.

"Stifle your cries. Soldiers might still be lurking," someone said.

She let out a little yelp and whirled around at the sound of the voice. "Gale!" she cried, but this was another sprite entirely.

Skald sat perched at the top of his lightning-staff where Valonia had left it hidden. He glowed with an inner radiance and she wondered if she was seeing a spirit or a sprite.

"Skald?" She took a cautious step forwards, wishing it was Gale.

"I'm glad to see you survived," he observed.

She looked around at the devastation, thinking he was only there because her mind was so bent and battered. "Skald, are you real?" She took another step and reached out her fingers until they brushed his feathered chest and she snatched her hand away. "Is this a trick?" she demanded, absurdly expecting Valonia to leap out of hiding any moment and surprise her.

He shook his head once.

"Skald, what happened?"

He took a long breath and bowed his head. "Valonia, Hilda, Lana and Ada were taken, by their own volition."

"Why?" she gasped. "Why would they do such a thing?"

"Rowan set off back for you, Esta went after her and neither returned."

This news hit her like a hammer. "They took Rowan?" Just saying it made her feel sick.

He gave a slow nod. "Almost certain."

"And Esta?" Just then an owl called and Kolfinnia thought of the haggen-thrall that Hilda had seen and wondered who the premonition of death was for. Oak knew there were plenty to choose from now. "What became of Esta?" she repeated.

"Only Rowan knows that," he said quietly.

"They took her," she uttered again, trying to make the truth fit somewhere in her reluctant mind.

Although it had happened hours ago her first impulse was to look around for Rowan. It was ridiculous but she was powerless. "Skald, what do we do?" His stony composure was starting to unnerve her. She stood before him with her arms spread, awaiting an answer.

He ruffled his feathers and stretched his wings. In the moonlight, and awash with the peculiar inner light, he looked like a spirit returned at Samhain. "Valonia had one last command." His tone continued flat and measured and she finally realised that he was struggling to master his own grief. "She thought very highly of you, wanted you as one of her Wards but more besides. She wanted you coven-mother when she was gone."

She blinked and backed away a step, scared of the responsibility his words conveyed.

"And now she has gone, but she has left you two gifts," he continued.

The more he spoke the more fearful she grew as he heaped greater expectations on her.

"One is hrafn-dimmu, her wand. She has buried it where this staff stands." He looked down at the earth to make her understand. "The wand still needs to be cast, to find a new coven before it can call to the survivors of the old one."

She accepted with a humble nod. "And the other thing she left?"

He cocked his head and gave her a strange smile. "Why, me, of course."

"You!"

"I fear Gale has returned to the thunder-heights."

Her hands flew to her mouth. "No!"

"I'm sorry," he confirmed.

She didn't believe there were any more tears in her, but here they came. "Don't say he's gone, please don't say that." But he could have, she knew. While lying unconscious her beloved Gale had left, and she hadn't even been permitted to say farewell. Could this night be any more cruel?

Skald avoided a direct answer. "I need a witch, you need a sprite and a new coven needs a coven-mother."

Each revelation dropped on her like a stone, and suddenly the cold, fatigue and fear all came crashing in and she dropped her head to her chest and began to cry again. She hated her own pathetic sobs and felt utterly wretched.

Something soft landed on her shoulder with a flutter, and she looked up and came eye to eye with Skald. He no longer looked stern and she saw a torment equal to her own in his eyes. "Ward Algra," he began and then corrected himself. "Coven-mother Algra, I promise to carry you. And if you'll have me, then I make a new pact with you, to be your sprite and you to be my witch."

"Is that even permitted?" She'd never heard the like.

"'If need of witches be so great'," he quoted mysteriously.

She palmed hot tears from her face and fought to control herself. Her answer would be binding until the day one of them died. The gravity of his offer was enormous and not to be taken lightly. He would forsake Valonia even though she still lived. This had been her last command to him and in it lay her only hope that together they would find a way to rally Britain's surviving witches and thwart the Illuminata before they stumbled on Rowan's secret. She didn't even have to consider it. "Skald, I am your witch," she said, and with that their fates were bound.

CHAPTER EIGHTEEN

To London

For the hundredth time Rowan strained to see through the tiny glass pane in the door. She was too small to reach up, but once in a while a masked face would loom up, peer inside and melt away again.

She pulled at the manacles fixing her wrists and ankles, but they gave her little room to turn or even stretch. Waiting was the worst, along with the confusion of not knowing. Back at Wildwood she just seemed to know things and never questioned how, but in here her mind was a muddled knot.

She was certain of only a few things: one was that Kolfinnia was still alive out there and that gave her hope. The other was that they were moving. Her tiny cell rocked and there was a distant rumbling, like a locomotive engine, but most importantly right now she knew Valonia was somewhere nearby. She pulled at the restraints, but this time not trying to escape. She'd learned hours ago that wasn't going to work. Instead she pushed out the horrible thoughts and tried to let her knowing return. If she couldn't see out of the window she would clear her thoughts and *know* what was out there instead.

She breathed in stuffy air and screwed her eyes shut and fleeting pictures filled her mind. She saw the machine was shaped like a great hollow ball. The curved walls were lined with metal hatches. Inside some of them were captives, but almost all were empty and Rowan knew their captors would be punished for not filling them all. In fact, she knew their captors were as apprehensive as she was. In a twisted way this comforted her. She was a child and still believed that anyone capable of feeling fear must have some capacity for sympathy.

She wanted to see more but just that short effort left her feeling dizzy, as if the machine was alive and didn't want her to know things. "Mother Gulfoss," she called in a low voice knowing she was close by, perhaps even in the next chamber. "Valonia!" she tried again. Then, remembering words were useless, she spoke without them instead. *"Valonia!"* She pushed the thought out like a kite, feeling it tug and pull as it drifted to its intended source.

In her own chamber Valonia was as alert and charged as she'd ever been. Someone had called her, she was sure of it. Even over the repetitive clash of metal and roar of the furnace she had heard someone call her name. It was a child's voice. There was something about this machine that dampened magic, but not utterly. "Rowan, was that you?" she whispered but there was only silence. She'd almost given up hope when the voice came again.

"Valonia!"

Impossible as it seemed someone was trying to reach her. *"Rowan, is that you?"* She called through her crowning.

"Valonia, I knew you'd hear me!"

She was overjoyed. *"First names now is it, little Rowan?"* she called back and incredibly Rowan sobbed a small laugh. *"Rowan, I have to know, what happened to Esta and Kolfinnia?"* She braced herself and it was a long time before Rowan answered.

"I tried to find Kol but Gale crashed, broke and flew away and then they caught me, but Esta came and then. . . then she was shot and, and she died and it's my fault. If I'd not gone back for Kol . . . but I promised."

Valonia tried to curl into a protective ball, but the chains held her fast, although they couldn't hold back her tears. They spilled onto her dress, painting dark spots on the tattered blue fabric. She heaved a shuddering breath and was dimly aware of Rowan's voice dancing around her head trying to be heard. She wanted to answer the girl, but couldn't control her grief.

"Valonia, don't hate me!" Rowan pleaded, thinking silence was condemnation.

"I don't," was all she could manage.

Rowan waited, wishing this nightmare would end but knowing it had just begun.

"You did better than a little Valonia would have done," she gasped at last, wiping the tears from her face. *"Kolfinnia's right to be proud of you, and Gale only did what he must. Sprites can't help but leave*

when a staff is broken, don't be angry at him." She thought of Skald and wondered if he would find Kolfinnia as she hoped. She couldn't bring herself to talk of Esta right now and so she directed their conversation away. *"Many escaped down the river, thanks to you, Jerrow and Kolfinnia."*

"How many are here?"

"Not as many as they wanted," Valonia said with pride.

"I can sense fear."

"We're all afraid," Valonia said.

"No, them, the men who caught us."

"They've just cause to be afraid, and for what their masters will do when the news of their defeat leaks out."

"What did you do to them?"

"We gave them a lesson in witchcraft they'll remember for a long time." She heard Rowan breathe a tiny laugh.

There was a long silence before Rowan spoke again. *"Are they going to hurt us?"*

She could almost feel the girl's racing heart. *"Hush now. I've survived two purges and I'll soon survive a third and you with me."*

"I'm sorry for Esta." Rowan added again.

"Her death wasn't your doing. She's left for a better place where witches don't have to live in fear." Valonia actually found her own words stirring.

"Where are they taking us, Valonia?"

"Probably London. But we'll think up an escape, fear not." She wasn't sure of her own words but it felt good saying them. *"You should sleep, Rowan."*

"No, I can't sleep, not now. I miss Kolfinnia. I promised I'd come back and that's why Esta died. It's all my fault." She was becoming upset again, *"I'd do anything to see them again."*

"Then dream of them," she said, and through their crowning she ushered Rowan a gentle sleep-spell. The exhausted girl deserved some rest. Pushing the spell was harder than she'd anticipated as there was something in the walls that dulled magic, but with a last shove she managed. *"Rowan, can you still hear me?"*

"I miss . . ." she murmured, but didn't finish.

Valonia strained and detected the girl's peaceful breathing. She had indeed fallen asleep. *"So the walls aren't entirely magic-proof. Rest for a while, Rowan. Wildwood owes you that much at least."* After a deep breath she set her mind to finding an escape, and that was a task for which she would need help. *"Hilda, can you hear me?"*

"I'm here, Valonia," she answered from the next cell.

Valonia smiled defiantly. The fight wasn't over yet.

Kolfinnia had been watching geese trail across the sky for hours and when she finally looked away her neck was sore. Watching them, she found herself wishing that she could follow and fly away to a safer place.

She left Wildwood in the small hours, understanding she would never see the place again, and flown with Skald down the coast. Here she had performed the rights of separation for Britain's fallen witches just as the sun was rising on the first morning after the darkest night of her life.

She looked down again at Valonia's tattered patchwork cloak. She'd salvaged it from the ruined tower at Skald's prompting along with some odds and ends: a knife, pots and plates, and a fire-seed of the kind Valonia had used to warn Wildwood. Now she sat in the lee of a rocky outcrop with no fire and down to her last hunk of bread waiting for Valonia's raven-wand to call to them. She had found it buried just where Skald said it would be.

Earlier she had carried Valonia's wand out to the furthest point, where the cliffs teamed with birds, and cast it into the boiling surf. After that she had found shelter, changed into drier clothes, eaten without relish or desire and slipped into a merciful sleep, spending the day curled around the lightning-staff and shielded from the elements by Valonia's heavy cloak. She ought to have felt guilty at using the relic for such, but she felt very little.

Around mid afternoon Skald had woken her. She had been dreaming of Gale and in her dream he had come back to her. She could feel the prick of his talons and the caress of his soft feathers, and for a few blissful moments they were whole again. But when she awoke to see Skald's stern face reality drowned her beautiful dream. She had been watching the passing geese since then.

She was homeless and heartbroken. Valonia's wand had been cast for one reason: it would find the secret lines of magic that encircled the globe, and like a compass tuned to the mystic rather than magnetic the wand would lead them to a location where a new coven could be founded. Valonia had attempted it three times, but had been frustrated on each attempt. The wand-casting tradition was intended to be spiritual and renewing, but in light of everything Kolfinnia found it an empty ritual. She gazed blankly at her dragon tattoos, Hethra and Halla, and wondered angrily why witches must risk all to look after their gods, while followers of the Cross, and others, had a god that looked after them. *Magic didn't save us*, she thought bitterly and immediately felt like a betrayer. "Has the wand called yet, Skald?" It felt like she'd asked this question a hundred times.

"Look at the geese, look! See their flight." He was perched on a rock gazing upwards.

"I've been watching the geese for hours."

"No!" he snapped. "You've been *daydreaming* for ages. Shake out of it and look for signs, look now!"

She looked up and saw he was right. Countless geese still streamed away southwards in perfect V formations but all of them skirted an empty area of sky, choosing to detour rather than fly through it, and there was a faint tinge of the winter-lights there, the kind often seen in the far north. Intrigued, she stood up. "What's going on? Is Valonia's wand making that signal up there?"

"It's hrafn-dimmu's sign. I've seen this before." The wand had finally called and he was thrilled. He only wished Valonia was here to see it.

"The wand's right below, in the sea?" She gazed in awe as the winter-lights grew more vivid.

"Yes, and the geese avoid its signal."

"It'd interfere with their migration?"

"You learn fast, coven-mother!"

"Hrafn-dimmu is calling at last!" She suddenly had a purpose again. "Then we set off at once."

She grabbed her satchel and fastened her clothes as tightly as possible, for it was going to be a long cold ride across open water. She found her hands trembled with anticipation. Despite everything she was still a witch with duties and now those duties had fired her again. She scolded herself for her lack of faith and began to wrap strips of cloth around her hands, improvising gloves, almost afraid to take her eyes off the sky.

She rummaged through her salvaged goods. She pulled a green Snow-Thaw scarf around her face, lashed a Seed-Fall waistcoat about her middle and swirled a Moon-Frost cloak around her shoulders, pulled it tight then belted it leaving her arms free. Lastly, she fasted her hat under her chin hard enough to make her wince. In the end she looked like a scarecrow but she felt honoured to be wearing every colour of Wildwood. She slung her satchel and Valonia's cloak, rolled and bound, around her shoulders and held out the lightning-staff.

Skald landed on it and perched there regarding her.

"You promised to carry me, Skald," she said from behind her scarf. "Will you honour that promise now?"

"Now, tomorrow and every day after," he pledged.

She looked sky-wards again. The winter-lights had deepened and started to spread south making a river of light, and she knew that was the direction they would take. She took a deep breath and spoke her first command as coven-mother. "We'll follow raven's wand, rally survivors, and rescue our friends."

"Lots of work ahead," he growled, and vanished into the staff.

She took a last look at the distant hills, which were now ruby red in the setting sun. "I'm coming, Rowan," she promised, and the hills softened behind her tears.

She turned away then and broke into a run trailing rags from her assorted clothes, staff at the ready. The cliff loomed closer and the dusky sea looked to stretch on forever, but she didn't slow, instead she launched herself over and into thin air. Skald roared and she screamed the name of her coven. "Wildwood!" The name rang around the cliffs and rolled out to sea.

Startled kittiwakes darted away as she tore downwards, gathering speed until she smoothed into a level course across the scarlet waves heading to where Valonia's wand shone brilliantly, ready to follow the irresistible forces that called it. When they were close enough to see its light, hrafn-dimmu darted away like a silvery fish, skimming through the sea and leaving a galaxy of bubbles in its wake, leading them towards renewal.

The winter-lights rippled like a billowing pennant across the sky. They spanned the heavens reaching from the north all the way to the far southwest, hundreds of miles distant, touching down on a sea-stack along a lonely stretch of coast, yet perhaps the real miracle was that only a witch could see them.

On a nearby hill stood the Swords of Britain, a ring of eleven stones watching over the Atlantic. A mile of perfect sand lay in the rocky bay below like a golden sickle while behind it grassy dunes gave way to heathery hills. That hulking sea-stack, which seemed a magnet for the beautiful lights, stood watch at the bay's southern end, looking out to the horizon as if waiting for something that might never arrive.

The eleven stones were set in a circle, but puzzlingly none of them were aligned with the stars. Each stone was carved with the symbol of a downward pointing sword with vines growing up the blade. The carvings were old and time had softened their edges.

Locals believed they were the tips of a great crown buried under the earth that had once belonged to a trollen king. Superstitions lingered and none of the nearby farmers let their animals graze here, and so the stones stood in a thicket of birch and heather. A few patches of velvety grass showed where rabbits, oblivious to fables, had grazed safe from snares and other such cruel devises. Witches once worshipped here, even before Britain had even emerged from under the ice, but it had been many centuries since witches had honoured the dreaming dragons here and certainly the stones had never been visited by the likes of Clovis and Tempest.

Clovis looked down at the hole by his feet. He'd been meaning to bury the bones from the amalga since yesterday when they'd arrived here so dramatically. Its fingers had been severed when the ROWAN door slammed shut, and a small heap of bones had followed them through. Now free of the spell that had animated them, the bones were merely those of his ancestors again and so Clovis had buried them along with a short blessing. "You're a long way from home, ancestors." He regarded the patch of fresh earth.

When they had plunged through the open door they had found themselves in the centre of this circle, but disturbingly there was no trace of a door on this side, only heather and rock. Clovis said nothing to Tempest, but he worried whether or not Janus could open this portal again, provided he could even persuade him. Yesterday's bluff had worked, but would it work again, he thought? He cast a glance towards his pack, where the trickster god lay sleeping.

"I wish I knew where this was." Tempest stared up at the winter-lights, mesmerised.

"I wish I knew when this was," Clovis speculated. They might have spent seconds or aeons on the spiral; time didn't exist there. "Escaping Vega might have happened centuries ago," he warned. *And if so, is there any point in trying to go back there?* he added to himself gloomily.

"It looks like the Siorine sky-river," Tempest continued to stare at the lights, thinking of home.

"A little," he agreed sadly. He got to his feet and his armour clattered softly. He was reluctant to take it off until he knew more about this place and what kind of creatures lived here.

So far they had only seen small animals that hopped on all fours and fled into burrows when alarmed. Clovis was a predator by nature but like all witches he'd taken an oath not to eat flesh, and so he was content to go hungry for now knowing he could summon fruits and other edibles later.

"You think the lights are connected with this ROWAN?" Tempest asked.

He stroked his chin thoughtfully, where his lustrous mane was woven into two long plaits. "I think we'll have our answer soon." He raised a clawed finger to the winter-lights, which touched down on the sea-stack making it look like a huge candle. His instincts told him that something or someone was coming.

"Why would you be led to this ROWAN by a dream?" Tempest asked.

Clovis blew a puzzled sigh. "A very good question. Tiber asked me the same thing before . . . " He trailed off, thinking of his close friend and that final fight with the traitors. "Maybe this ROWAN can help us?" He changed the subject from grief to guessing, which was his least favourite pastime, but it was better than mourning Tiber. "Or it's a place we must travel to in order to find help? Either way at least Janus is still safe. They didn't capture him."

"There's a great mystery at work here," Tempest conceded. "One far greater than just Janus, or even treachery on Vega."

"Indeed." He unfolded his stout arms and pointed to the sea-stack. "Not least of which is that."

"The rock pillar?"

"Hmm, or rather the power underneath it." The ominous stack was now just a black tower as dusk deepened and the winter-lights continued to stream from its crown. *Something living under it*, he thought, but not knowing what, and not knowing that a witch named Kolfinnia and a sprite named Skald were following those very lights.

CHAPTER NINETEEN

Raven's Wand Crosses the Sea

As the sun passed away westwards the sea lost its radiance and became oily and fathomless. Darkness bloomed from the east, first turning the sky violet before autumn blackness finally settled across the heavens, and still Kolfinnia flew onwards under the winter-lights following the ragged western coast of Britain.

The wind roared and thrashed in her clothes. It invaded each seam and buttonhole and despite her efforts it blew right through them and chilled her, while at the same time her mask was stifling and moist. She endured shivering fits, her teeth chattered, her shoulders groaned and her thighs and buttocks had long since gone numb. Lightning-staffs were flown fast and brief as a rule, but she'd lost count of the hours she'd been flying.

Occasionally, she wiped her face against her shoulder, rubbing away the salt-spray from her eyes, but as soon as she did it began to form again. Her hands were bundled with so many rags that she could barely feel Skald and so she flew with a profound sense of isolation and dare not loosen her grip. If she plunged into the waves not only would an impact at this speed result in injury but it would leave her dangerously cold and waterlogged and even Skald might struggle with the extra weight.

The glowing shaft of hrafn-dimmu raced ahead of them, occasionally vanishing as it plunged into the trough of some monstrous wave, but despite the dark she followed its path easily. It shone like an iridescent swordfish leaving a trail of tiny bubbles that glimmered briefly before dissolving into the gloom. Raven's wand had become her beacon in this black world of wind and water, and its hopeful light did more than just guide her; it hinted at the realm beneath, sometimes reflecting off silvery creatures as they piloted the depths. At first she thought these brief glimpses were random, but as the miles drew out the retinue of mysterious swimmers continued to hold their course and the wand's light continually played across their flanks.

"Skald?" she cried. At once the staff's note rose in pitch and static flashed between her hands. The faint spark was almost blinding after the prolonged blackness.

"I see them." The craggy voice in her head sounded breathless and worn but she was thrilled to have his company.

"They're following the wand?"

"Just as the wand follows the lines of magic. Now let me be. I can't speak more." He melted away from her, deep into the staff, throwing himself into the chase.

At his brusqueness she felt a pang and longed for Gale's own 'gentle roughness'.

Skald felt it too and knew to be more tender. *"All sprites watch from the thunder-heights, and Gale will too. Fly well and make him proud,"* he added.

"Bless you," she murmured gratefully and the Runes flashed once in response, and then they were no more than after-images on her retina.

As she flew onwards, skimming the wave tops, she began to imagine the immense blackness around her akin to a mysterious city where creatures unseen by human eyes lived out their whole lives in secret. This was a Britain of the night, with wholly different inhabitants and none of them human bar her. *The night is the last wild place*, she thought, and as she shuffled into a more comfortable position one of the inhabitants of this last wilderness startled her.

It erupted in a spray of frigid water only feet away. Something fast and sleek leapt from the waves and arced gracefully through the air before plunging back into the sea with a confident splash. With her heart still racing there came a second crash to her left and although she couldn't see what it was she sensed some large creature momentarily sailing at her side before plunging below the waves again. She had thought little of magic since fleeing the ruins of Wildwood, and even felt that magic was puny and insignificant compared to the iron and steel of the Illuminata. 'Magic hadn't saved us,' she'd cursed, but now those words came back to shame her as something grand and magical unfolded.

The moon slid from behind the clouds like a spotlight and the armada of sea creatures was finally revealed to her astonishment.

The sea heaved like the skin of an immense dragon and turned to polished iron under the moon. For miles around its waters teamed with leaping dolphins and porpoise. Hundreds of them raced alongside her, hurtling up from the deep and into the night air before plunging back again, all of them following hrafn-dimmu which shone like a burning spear tip.

"Oak be blessed," she breathed in awe. Glad tears pricked her eyes and an important lesson she'd forgotten in the heat of battle wrapped its soft arms around her: celebrating life was true magic.

Just as this thought arose, a calamity of geese calls startled her and she realised that her escort wasn't just ocean-bound. Disciplined formations of geese cruised along under hrafn-dimmu's spell. Although darkness hid most of the company, she guessed from the racket that hundreds of them were flying above and beside her. Their longing calls urged her onwards and she felt revived and privileged. "How much further, Skald?" she shouted over the clamour of geese and tearing wind.

"Not even hrafn-dimmu knows that!" He sounded more like his old self. *"Call back to them!"*

"Call, you mean like a goose?"

"You think to cluck like a hen? Of course like a goose!"

She wasn't sure if he was serious or enjoying a private joke. "Are they here to help?"

"They're not here by chance. Now call back, else they get offended and pass away. Geese are lucky!"

"Very well," she agreed uneasily. The idea of calling to them made her feel self-conscious, but who was to know out here in the dead of night, she told herself. With that in mind she took a deep breath, threw back her head and bellowed a series of crude and comical honks, which made her think of Rowan and how she'd brayed with laughter when joking about what way-bewares might keep under their skirts. It had happened only yesterday but it felt like a memory from a former life.

The geese called back in ones and twos, and then hundreds added to the chorus until it sounded like a living storm. She bellowed again, regardless of convention, and their raucous reply surrounded her and she felt part of something bigger, part of a family once more. How she missed Wildwood. And with that feeling of loss came fresh pain and her calls turned to howls. She lowered her head to her chest, out of the wind, and choked back the tears. "Skald?" she sniffed.

"I miss them too," he said abruptly, guarding his grief even from her.

The moonlight revealed a maze of dark islands that Valonia's wand skilfully negotiated. Kolfinnia had travelled further from home than ever before and what little she could see of the mainland showed a rugged coast indented and dashed with islets and coves. Occasionally she'd spy tiny lights in the dark where townships nestled on the coast.

Kolfinnia and her host followed the speeding wand all that night under the brilliance of the winter-lights. The clouds moved in ragged waves, sometimes plunging everything into darkness. When this happened the world was defined only by the glowing wand and thousands of calling geese. The huge birds flanked her protectively as hrafn-dimmu continued to follow the secret lines of magic, and perhaps it enjoyed the companionship because now it travelled at a speed that the escort could comfortably match.

They passed the miles in anxious silence and growing anticipation. Sometimes the geese calls would rise to a deafening chorus and then melt away again, leaving only the ghostly rasp of beating wings. And when the wind rose in strength and the moon was cloaked, then she could hardly believe they were there at all.

She stifled a yawn and blinked weariness from her eyes, and maybe she only imagined it, but she was convinced that the ranks of geese around her robbed the wind of its ferocity. Her hands felt as lifeless as clay and she wondered how much longer she could endure, but little by little she sensed a tingling warmth in her fingers and palms and she lowered her face out of the wind. "Skald, is that you?" A few stray geese calls answered the sound of her voice. She was about to ask again when he startled her.

"Your hands must be cold?"

She looked to her fists, which were little more than ragged bundles, and was touched by his gesture. As well as the rigours of flight he'd found enough strength to warm her fingers. "Thank you," she said humbly.

They continued to fly in formation and just as dawn broke hrafn-dimmu headed inland. She snatched down her mask and gulped clean air. "We're almost there."

"Then the real work begins." He appeared to know more about what was going to happen than she did.

In reply came more birdcalls, but the geese were dispersing now and in the stolen light of dawn Kolfinnia could just see milky waves crashing against a lonely coast, and standing sentinel-like away from the shore was an irregular looking tower. Valonia's wand veered away from the open sea and directly towards it. *Why's it heading towards the tower?* she wondered, knowing she was compelled by tradition to establish a coven where the wand landed. For a ridiculous moment she imagined having to set up camp at the top of it.

She made minute adjustments to their flight as she tracked it through the waters. Along the coast she could see the tell tale smudge of white breakers. The night was at last withdrawing its blindfold. The wand streaked towards the ominous tower and as they drew closer she dropped lower, gripped by a new found sense of caution. She flew just above the waves and felt droplets splash against her face as she sought cover from the imagined eyes watching from the tower's dark windows. "I don't like the look of the tower, Skald. We shouldn't be in full view like this." She actually wished it was dark again.

"Trolls."

"What?"

"Back in Iceland we had many trolls. They turn to stone if caught in sunlight."

He seemed to disregard her worries, but she thought it sounded absurd. Could the tower really be the remains of a petrified troll?

It looked like a sword thrust up from the depths, but something about its stonework was wrong because the walls were irregular and crooked. There were small white flags fluttering up the whole length of it and she was about to shout as much to Skald when she was overcome by a distinct feeling of foolishness. The 'tower' was a huge sea-stack and the white flags were sea birds: no wonder Skald hadn't shown any caution. She flew towards its hulking base where lacy sheets of foam briefly obscured Valonia's wand. *Did this stack draw hrafn-dimmu?* she wondered uneasily.

To Kolfinnia and Skald the tower was inert, but hrafn-dimmu saw the world differently. When Valonia had cut it long ago it had been equally lifeless and only through years in her service had it absorbed enough of her will to become self-aware. To its 'eyes' the tower was a brilliant beacon, as fearful as a raging volcano. The energy of will, fate and creation flared from its crown and soared upwards into the heavens. Since leaving the north the wand had followed one of these threads, and while it had been faint at first it had quickly deepened and widened into an undeniable highway that converged here with millions more. If equipped with complex emotions and told that neither Kolfinnia nor Skald could see this magical river hrafn-dimmu would have been astounded. It was a simple, even innocent being, and it was curious to know where all those pathways erupting from the tower led to, but it also had a duty and so it held its course aiming to make landfall on the broad sandy bay.

The wand darted away from the sea-stack and into calmer waters. A hundred yards behind and from her vantage point Kolfinnia spotted its tell-tale light once more. "Skald, I can see it! It's not taking us to the tower after all, but past it." Even before the words had left her mouth she was turning, sensing the closing moments of their journey.

"One last push then." He stepped up his speed.

Wherever this place was, it was going to be their new home. They swept past the stack less than fifty feet from its slimy, weathered flanks.

Then it happened.

They unwittingly sailed right into the unseen force that had drawn hrafn-dimmu. Immediately she was gripped by something enormous and infinite, like a sliver of wire channelling a massive current. Skald felt it too, like an earthquake in his heart. Then he felt Kolfinnia's hands clench the staff with murderous strength before suddenly sliding away. Something unknown had stunned her senseless. He reeled in the shockwaves emanating from the tower, and his flight became erratic, and lacking her steadying hand the staff veered sharply upwards. Meanwhile hrafn-dimmu sailed onwards unaware they were in trouble.

"Mother!" Kolfinnia groaned drunkenly. "Mother, the wood speaks. It is alive!"

"Hold on!" Skald roared.

"Mother?" she called again, sounding heartbroken, "Mother, it's alive, it's evil. Don't touch it!"

"I'm not your bloody mother!" he yelled, then realised her mind was no longer her own. Something from the tower was inside her. *"Kolfinnia, do you hear me?"*

She slumped against the staff and barely hung on, but her weight slid backwards and forced them into a vertical flight parallel with the tower. Skald screamed garbled instructions, but she couldn't hear him. She was lost in an incredibly vivid memory. It had reached out from the tower and seized her mind.

She was a child and it was the day she'd first practised magic, and the memory was awful.

"Pull up, Kolfinnia! Pull the staff up!" Skald screamed, but there was no room inside her mind. Something else had taken hold there, something so strong it blotted out all else. He fought desperately to descend but inch by inch her hands slipped as her body slid backwards. In seconds he would reach the pivot point and flip, then he would lose her to the waves far below, the staff would break against the stack and Skald would return to the thunder-heights leaving Kolfinnia – and Valonia's last hopes – to die alone. "No!" he howled. "Not like this!" To come all this way only to be killed by magic was unthinkable. *"Bastard rock. Fly, Skald, fly!"* he roared nonsense and watched helplessly as the stack loomed closer, like a giant file ready to shred them.

Salvation came from nowhere. A strong hand suddenly gripped the staff, jerked it down and away from the stack, and they shot forwards and out of its influence. "I have you." The stranger spoke Pegalia. He sounded bestial but intelligent.

Kolfinnia was still clinging on, but she was barely conscious, and although Skald repeatedly reached out to her it was like looking for candle smoke in a gale.

"We're heading for the beach," the stranger commanded.

Skald's first impulse was to challenge this newcomer despite having saved them, but for Kolfinnia's sake he was more concerned with keeping his flight steady. They were heading to the shore where Valonia's wand lay peacefully on the beach.

"Once she's across the waves we're out of danger," the stranger continued.

"To the beach," Skald complied, although outraged that this stranger should lay a hand upon Valonia's staff.

This stranger's hand wasn't as any that had piloted Skald before. He sensed rough pads against the wood and sharp claws. Their rescuer was flying alongside on a staff of his own, but what kind of creature this was he could only guess at. Despite being concealed by a hood and the gloom of dawn, Skald could discern that his face was stern, his eyes glinted amber and he was clearly not human. Skald felt very protective of his new witch and if this rider intended to harm her then he would have a fight on his hands. Again he reached out to Kolfinnia. He needed her to be that fearsome witch again, the one that'd stood against barghests and knights, but when he tasted her mind he felt only a child's confused horror. *What's happening in your head, Kolfinnia?* The beach was drawing closer and a showdown was only moments away. *Skald's ready, Valonia. I won't let her come to harm*, he promised, wishing she was there.

Kolfinnia was young again, so young in fact that she didn't even know her own age and certainly had no sense of numbers and years. This 'little' Kolfinnia could barely walk without swaying, but she liked the cobbles in the yard. They were smooth and warm under her bare feet. This was a Kolfinnia of long ago who wasn't yet two years old.

She was standing in the spring sunshine outside the only place other than Wildwood she'd ever called home. It was a square of small neat cottages overlooking a courtyard where vacant sockets of missing cobbles sprouted grass and the whitewashed walls shimmered in the heat. Halfway along the row to the east was a gateway facing the sea

and a shingle beach. A rough packhorse track led north to the ruins of
Dunstanburgh castle and south to the village of Craster. A stone trough
sat in the middle of the square and three herring gulls perched around
its rim, keeping a keen eye on Little Kolfinnia.

Coven-mother Kolfinnia watched all of this from a distance like a
phantom. She moved closer to her infant self without walking and when
she held her hand before her face she could see no trace of it, only the
rough walls and shuttered windows of the surrounding cottages. She
was reliving this memory through her adult eyes and she saw all those
details that were meaningless to an infant. She saw that each cottage
had different holes cut in the window shutters, diamonds, hearts or
crescent moons. The shutters on her own home carried a five-pointed
star and she smiled at the memory, but was this truly a memory or
was it now? She couldn't decide if this was a vision of her past or was
she was actually there seeing events unfold like a visitor from her own
future. The tower had overwhelmed them the instant they had flown
into its influence and although she knew her real-self and Skald were
somewhere out there it felt flimsy and unimportant.

The door to her cottage was open and Kolfinnia could hear her
mother singing softly as she worked making bread or darning clothes.
Her mother would most likely be alone: her father was a Norwegian
deckhand who worked on a cargo vessel and he would spend many
weeks at sea. Little Kolfinnia hardly knew him.

Little Kolfinnia stumbled over the cobbles in her cream smock with
her child's eyes seeing wonder in the mundane. Something had caught
her attention and Kolfinnia watched her infant self totter towards a
small wood store below the kitchen window. She had never seen herself
so young and she smiled. Photographs and portraits were only for the
very rich and so she marvelled at what an ungainly child she'd been
and how her hair had been a curly mop. Her smile turned to a grimace
as a wave of nausea swept through her and she knew something
dire was unfolding back where her real-self was. Their flight was in
peril and they were going to crash, she was sure of it. "Skald?" she
whispered, unsure if he even detected her.

"Kolfinniaaaaa!" he wailed, sounding worlds away.

She watched Little Kolfinnia venture towards the store where
kindling was piled for their stove. A butterfly basked on the sloping tin
roof, gently pumping its wings. Smiling, Little Kolfinnia reached for
the beautiful insect, which fluttered away even before she could register
its escape. It trembled to a rest again, this time on the kindling below.
She reached out again and the instant she did coven-mother Kolfinnia
felt an icy wave wash over her. This was not, as she'd first thought, a

nostalgic daydream, but the reliving of a horrible memory. "No, don't!" she called out to her little self, but the small hand continued to reach for the butterfly.

It had happened long ago, and because she'd been so young she'd never been certain of what had happened, but now the unknown energy streaming from the tower was replaying her darkest moment and she realised that an old secret would become known.

"Skald!" This time she cried out with real urgency, wanting to leave this vision that had started so benign. A gull shrieked in reply and the feeling of falling was so overwhelming now that she felt sick. To make matters worse she knew that Little Kolfinnia would scream in horror the moment her fingers touched that innocuous piece of kindling. "No! Don't Kolfy, please don't!" She tried to reach into the memory and undo something she'd done years before, but she was merely a shadow here.

Little Kolfinnia reached for the butterfly again, but it flitted away and all she grasped instead was a stick of kindling. Instantly her eyes flew wide and she began to scream as though burnt, startling the gulls into flight.

"Kolfy?" There came a lovely but stricken voice from the open doorway and in a flash there was her mother, Cara, trailing needle and thread and the tattered nightdress she'd been repairing. She hurried to Little Kolfinnia and snatched the screaming child from the cobbles and up into her arms. "Kolfy? What is it, what's wrong?" she cried, but Little Kolfinnia continued to scream.

Kolfinnia was pained by the look on her mother's face and wanted so badly to reach out to her, but all she could do was watch and endure.

Cara ran trembling hands along her daughter's legs and arms looking for cuts, fractures, stings, anything to explain why her daughter was screaming. "Kolfy? Kolfy?" She shook her shoulders, but Little Kolfinnia couldn't stop and her wide eyes saw nothing. "Kolfinnia!" Cara screamed, and at last she did the only thing she could think of and struck the mask of horror from Little Kolfinnia's face with a reluctant slap.

It was the only time she ever raised a hand to her daughter and it haunted her for the rest of her days. Little Kolfinnia at last dropped the piece of kindling, which Cara hadn't even noticed in her panic. Whatever demon she had seen was instantly banished and she saw her mother at last, and confused hurt swam in her eyes. Cara engulfed her in a fierce hug and both of them sobbed while the circling gulls cried in mock sympathy.

Kolfinnia knelt beside them unseen. "She was sewing that day," she whispered between the tears and finally understood what the foul thing in the wood store really was.

The piece of kindling that had so terrified her as a child lay at her feet, and through her adult eyes she thought it looked sly and cunning, only pretending to be a harmless piece of wood.

The tree this kindling had come from had once served as gallows for convicted witches and Little Kolfinnia, oblivious to her skills, had no choice but to see the hanging women, taste their final moments, hear the shouts of torment and suffer the illusion of choking. The tree had seen it all, preserved it and been corrupted by it. Only someone with the right skill could unlock the language of the grain. Little Kolfinnia had unknowingly performed her first act of witchcraft.

"Kolfy, it's gone now, it's all right." Cara rocked the weeping child and cried softly against her dark curls. "It's gone now, it's gone now," she repeated gently, and glanced around the empty courtyard, which was now gloomy and sunless. She seemed to be watching out for something. One of the gulls had returned to the trough. It met her gaze and screamed a harsh cry and Cara carried her daughter indoors. She had secretly hoped Kolfinnia would not inherit her skills, but when the gulls cried in unison she thought it sounded like they knew better. She kicked the door closed with her heel and as if the slamming door was a signal, the memory began to crumble just as Kolfinnia and Skald were led away from the stack by their unknown rescuer.

The illusion melted away and Skald's mind rushed in to meet her own. *"Kolfinnia! Thank Hethra's scales! I thought you were gone!"*

"Skald?" she groaned.

"Be still, Kolfy," he said to her alone. *"We've a new problem. We're clear of that blasted tower, but now a kindra has come. Be thrifty with your trust, remain still and guard yourself,"* he warned.

She smiled weakly at being called Kolfy, but the word kindra was like an alarm, meaning an unknown worker of magic, neither Ruinous nor aligned to the serpent-twins. The kindra could be an agent of the Illuminata for all they knew. She glanced down and saw shallow waves flashing past below. She also realised with acute embarrassment that she clung to the staff like a seasick sailor. It was a miracle she'd held on, but the price for that was looking terribly undignified.

"The wand has landed and we'll touch down in a moment. Be ready," Skald prepared her.

"Try and take us over Valonia's wand," she pushed her thought towards him, hoping he would catch it and not the kindra.

She risked a quick glance at their rescuer. He sat with his back to her, hidden by a hooded cloak and flying on a strange lightning-staff as he guided them with a furred hand that looked like a paw. *He's not even human!* she thought with shock.

Sand glistened underneath them and she knew they were landward, and ahead of them just to the right lay Valonia's wand. As luck had it, they startled a flock of oystercatchers, and as the stranger glanced towards the noisy birds Kolfinnia dropped the role of helpless victim.

Hrafn-dimmu streaked past below, and fast as a snake she reached down and snatched it up leaving claw marks in the sand. In the same instant Skald bucked wildly, ripping the staff out of the stranger's grasp and veering away. *"Yaaaaaa!"* he screamed triumphantly and raced away down the shore.

After a burst of speed she looked back, holding hrafn-dimmu at the ready, expecting the kindra to be bearing down on them. Instead, she saw him sprawled on the sand and his lightning-staff cart-wheeling away. "Skald," she shouted. "Go back!"

"Back? Are you mad?" He was still angry at being led.

"No, he's not chasing. We were wrong!" She hauled the staff around, leaning into a curve that would take them back and Skald, bound by his allegiance, could do nothing.

"Bloody stupid. You'd go back and help a fallen bastard knight too, eh?"

"He tried to help us and Evermore knows we need all the help we can get."

"Help? What if he made the tower do what it did?"

She hadn't thought of that. Still, they headed back to the stranger who was up on his feet and growing larger as they approached. Their rescuer was hooded, and other than her earlier glimpse she had no idea what kind of creature he was. He had the chance to finish us and didn't, she rationalised.

They were almost level now. He stood by a mess of scars on the sand where he had tumbled down and if injured in the fall he certainly didn't show it. Flinty eyes sparkled deep in the shadows of his hood and he clutched a lightning-staff that wasn't wood but shone like metal. Kolfinnia saw his hands were covered with luxurious grey fur and tipped with short claws. *God-oak! I was right – he's not human!* she realised with fearful wonder.

Clovis watched them approach and wondered if this proud looking woman was ROWAN, or perhaps it was the sprite in her staff.

"Is this ROWAN?" Tempest whispered.

Clovis flexed his fingers around the staff. "We'll soon see," he muttered.

Skald slowed to a dignified pace and finally halted twenty feet away. Kolfinnia slid from her staff and pulled her hat from her head. As she touched down she swayed on her feet, only now remembering that she'd been flying for over twelve hours.

The stranger watched her intently.

She swept the staff upright, holding it like a spear while Skald gathered his strength should it come to a fight. She bowed formally and announced herself in Pegalia. "My name is Kolfinnia Algra of Wildwood-coven."

The stranger never moved and Skald throbbed inside his staff like a brewing storm.

"I forgot to make my grateful thanks known before I so rudely left you, forgive me." She bowed again, then straightened and the tilt of her chin told him this was all the introduction he was going to get.

The stranger thrust his staff into the sand. At first she read it as a challenge and her fingers tightened around hrafn-dimmu. He brushed the sand from his cloak then he raised his hands and slowly pushed back his hood to reveal his face.

"Good God-oak!" She stifled a gasp of admiration and even Skald was hushed. Their rescuer would have felt at home amongst the feral cats back at Wildwood. He had thick fur the colour of steel, a spray of whiskers, sharp ears, although the left one was ragged from some past fight, but most tellingly he had the same hunter's eyes. A luxurious mane of fur ran under his powerful neck while the fur on his chin was braided into two plaits, and just showing from his upper lip she saw the tips of sharp canines. He sniffed and his blunt nose twitched as he read her scent. He was a Therion, an impossibly – even miraculously – rare soul these days.

"Then Clovis Augmentrum greets you, Kolfinnia Algra," he replied in Pegalia and his voice rumbled like the incoming waves.

At the mention of his name she suddenly saw Rowan's face and it took her a few moments to grasp what her ears were telling her. Before she could say anything he took advantage of the silence.

"And the hero who lives in your staff, he flies very well, well enough to save your life. Will you not announce him too?" He cocked his head.

Her jaw tightened. "He's called Skald and he'll appear only if he wishes to," she said primly. *There goes the element of surprise*, she thought.

"As does Tempest." Clovis gestured to his staff in the sand.

Then as if on cue, Skald erupted with a shout and spiralled upwards before landing neatly on the staff's tip and regarding Clovis with cold blues eyes. He flapped his wings once, making sure they beat a resounding crack. "I am Skald," he declared and now it was Clovis's turn to be impressed.

"Then greetings to you, Skald." He dipped his head.

"I don't recognise your coven. Am I to understand that you're a witch?" Kolfinnia pressed, annoyed with herself for giving so much away. He'd not mentioned anything about his own title.

"I was," he said quietly. "But for now let me simply say welcome." He swept a broad hand along the length of the beach as though it was his kingdom and it was they, not him, who were light-years from home.

"Welcome where?" she asked cautiously.

"The lights I saw last night . . . that was a wand-casting spell, was it not?"

"It was."

Clovis flashed a crooked smile. "Then welcome to your new home, of course," he purred.

CHAPTER TWENTY

Clovis

The state carriage at Hobbs Ash was crowded again, this time not with ministers but with commanders, and many had cuts and bruises. They sat in tense silence around the same table graced by the likes of Wallace Maccrae back when the weather had been fair and the prospects for first-dawn were rosy. Now the weather was poor, the first flush of orange had tinted London's parks, and still first-dawn waited for its hour of glory.

The door opened and Hathwell entered along with rain and noise from outside. He looked beyond the open door and snapped a brisk salute and instantly the commanders stood to attention. The doorway darkened and Krast swept into the carriage wearing a long overcoat and bowler hat. "Be seated." He swung his coat from his shoulders and threw it into a vacant chair along with his hat. "Now," he demanded, "I'm told of several defeats." He cut right to the news that'd kept him awake most of the night. "Valhorst? What became of Valhorst and the Wings-of-Mars?" He pointed to the vacant chair where Valhorst ought to have been sitting. "Rushton, you tell me." He snapped his fingers at a middle-aged man with frosty grey hair and a flat nose.

Commander Rushton took a deep breath, steeled himself and stepped up into the firing line. "Valhorst was killed in action, sir," he stated in his rolling Scot's accent.

"So I gather," Krast said icily. "But how?"

"His company were sent to attack the Appelier River coven in

Cumberland also known as Wildwood. Britain's largest coven," he added hastily, as if this explained their humiliating defeat.

"I bloody know!" Krast fumed. "I orchestrated the entire operation. I know *where* Valhorst's company went. I'm asking you how a rag-bag hovel of old women and girls could defeat a regiment of knights!"

"His force met with an unexpected counter-attack, sir."

"Enough!" His fist came down on the table like a thunderclap and the carriage fell deathly silent. "The Wings-of-Mars are disgraced. Their colours and family arms shall be put up for sale amongst the bloodlines."

This was severe punishment indeed, but then again Krast was deeply vexed. Wildwood's witches had mounted a triumphant defence and many had escaped along the river under cover of an unnatural fog. Clearly something was different there, something intangible. They shared the same beliefs as any other coven yet they employed their spells with a flare and imagination he'd seen only once. He swore never to live through another day like Solvgarad, yet here he was twenty years later faced with a similar humiliation. He looked up at Hathwell, loitering at the back of the carriage, and he knew they were both thinking of that same day long ago. He pulled up a chair and lowered himself down. "How is it that this Wildwood did what no other coven could? How many did we lose?"

Rushton's lips quivered. "The company's still a day away, along with their captives, but preliminary reports suggest at least ten krakens destroyed and as many knights killed in action."

"And their squires?"

"They can be replaced, sir," he placated, forgetting that Hathwell was in the room.

"And how many captives did we earn in this 'heroic' venture?"

Rushton ran a hand over his silvery hair where an angry scalp wound nestled. "Less than half a dozen," he gulped.

There were a few unsettled murmurs.

"They're still a day away, you say?" Krast clarified.

"They'll be here by nightfall."

"Inform me as soon as they arrive."

"I'm told that they captured the head witch, sir, a woman," he added.

"No doubt," Krast needled him. "The coven is, according to intelligence, wholly female, which makes our failure there all the more catastrophic. This coven-chief, was her wand captured also?"

"We've not been able to ascertain that yet." He shook his head.

"Unfortunate. You know what happens when a coven is broken? Traditionally the senior witch's wand is used to establish a new location."

"It's just one wand and it would need a witch to find it and use it. It's immaterial."

"It's a loose end," Krast brooded. "And one loose end can undo the whole tapestry. I ought to have led the operation myself. As soon as she arrives I want to see her, regardless of the hour."

"Yes, sir."

"And how did your own operation go?"

Rushton looked pleased at last. "Regal-Fox was a resounding success. We suffered no losses, and only six of the twenty criminals managed to evade us."

"It was rumoured to be a wealthy den of vipers." Krast studied him closely, wondering if he'd taken plunder.

He diverted the topic elsewhere. "A rumour, sir, nothing more. But I'm pleased to report that the coven-father, Alfred Berwick, was captured although we believe that his second, the so called 'solstice queen', made good her escape."

Krast nodded as he digested this. "Gentlemen, this afternoon I must tell ministers that the heroic Wallace Maccrae has been avenged. Rest assured that they'll hear nothing of what we've spoken of here."

They muttered their obedience.

"Remain in barracks," he continued, "ready to reconvene for further debriefing." They all nodded, looking relived that they'd avoided his wrath, but not knowing *how*. All in all he'd been lenient.

Without any formal close to the meeting he simply got up and left. He was on his way to tell ministers an embellished tale of events. They in turn would tell the newspapers who would add a little sparkle of their own. People would tell their neighbours, and by tomorrow evening all of London would know of the landslide victory against Maccrae's killers. The additional news about the spoils of war and the staggering secrets of matter transformation was more sensitive and would follow later. He'd already decided to use the wealthy Regal-Fox coven as a backdrop to his pantomime. The Saxon king's barrow was the perfect kernel to weave their alchemy story around.

If Krast had been lenient it was because essentially the plan was still on track, but rather his plan, not Westminster's. He had more than enough witches to feed to the chromosites. At last count almost twelve hundred prisoners were on their way to Hobbs. But he found himself anticipating the arrival of the Wildwood witches in particular. So far intelligence had no information on the coven-mother, not even her name, but his instincts told him that here was an equal and an opposite. He had grown complacent as one solid victory followed another. Wildwood's triumph had energized him. "Hathwell, walk with me," he muttered as he passed.

Hathwell closed the door and stepped out into the blustery autumn day with his knight.

"A missing wand from the first coven to best us in a lifetime," Krast contemplated as he marched along, buttoning his coat.

"Aren't you troubled a new coven will form, sir?" Hathwell dodged a cart that rattled past loaded with barrels.

"Of course, but if one does I'll attend to it myself. Does your uniform still fit?"

He stopped mid-stride. "You're serious, sir?"

Krast frowned as though he didn't know how not to be serious. "I can see you're troubled." His tone was sharp.

Hathwell looked into the older man's face. More than once Krast had left him to die on the battlefield. He had followed him through bullets, trailing like a faithful dog, and he would probably do so again if told, but he just couldn't tell his knight of his doubts about the cause. The Mannix document had been his wake-up call.

"You're afraid, Bertrand?" He groped for an explanation.

"Perhaps, sir," he lied.

"Don't take Rushton's words to heart." He seemed oblivious to everything but his troubled squire, which struck Hathwell as strangely tender. Comments about squires being an underclass came with the job. "Knights ought to be noble, and thus respectful to their squires, who in turn should be faithful." He pulled on his gloves and balled his hands into fists, making the leather creak, certain he had thrust to the cause of Hathwell's unease.

"You always have been, sir." The words were weak and his heart felt like a stone.

"I'd be negligent of my duties if I hadn't been. Besides, who else would keep Purity in battle-worthy order?"

"Thank you, sir."

"Speaking of which, I'd like the old girl to have a proper service, you know, right down to the last rivet."

"I'll get on to it right away."

"You never know when knights will march again. Next time I'd like for us to be in the ranks as well." He obliged him with a thin smile and clasped his arm like an equal.

The machine had been rocking gently for hours, but now the swaying sensation suddenly ceased. *We've stopped moving*, Valonia thought.

Being sealed away from growing things left her disorientated and the metal walls dulled her sense of time. The rush of steam and the sound of pistons surged as the airship carrying the Fortitude touched down at Hobbs Ash. There was a massive jolt. The whole structure shook and she rocked forwards, clicking her teeth together as she was thrown against the wall. Pistons and valves settled with a long sighing sound and the only noise she could hear was the Fortitude's idling furnace somewhere under her feet.

We've arrived, she realised, and her thought was so potent that someone heard her.

"Where?" came an alarmed voice. It was Rowan.

Startled, she looked around again. Rowan was better at this than she realised. She placed a hand where Rowan sat only inches away on the other side. *"Probably London. Rowan, listen. I've spoken to the others. We're trying to work out a way of escape, but we need you to help us."*

"Anything," she agreed, and in her own cell Rowan pressed her hands against the cold wall, reaching for Valonia.

"Getting you away from here is top priority." She hoped Rowan wouldn't ask why.

"I understand." She innocently assumed that she meant getting them all away, not just her.

"Help us. Pretend you know nothing of witchcraft." Valonia pressed her cheek to the wall. *"Can you do that?"*

"Yes."

"Promise me!"

"I promise," she agreed, trusting her totally.

Valonia heard footsteps clang past her cell as men hurried about their duties. *"Good lass, now stay quiet."* She rubbed at her wrists where the restraints had chaffed her. The machine dampened her skills and even her short conversation with Rowan had left her with a headache. She sat crossed-legged on the floor, took a deep breath and tried to focus. Once still, she conjured the faces of her companions in her mind's eye and then nudged at their auras. It was a less strenuous way of making contact. She felt her mind 'bump' against Ada, Hilda and Lana's and smiled as they nudged back at her. They didn't exchange words, but she knew they were all as ready as they could be for what might happen next.

Frightened children, men and women were shoved, ordered, catalogued and pressed into the detention carriages as dusk turned to night. Adults cried and children whimpered. Some looked defiant while others just looked beaten, but all of them looked like a rag-bag collection of Jik scum to Krast and he watched all of this happen with a detached coolness.

All had arrived in machines just like the Fortitude, transported by airships. All of their belongings, wands and charms had been confiscated and they stood in the clothes they arrived in, and would likely die in them also.

It was late, almost midnight, and the wind continued to drive swirling clouds of drizzle. But Hobbs Ash glowed under countless gas lamps, allowing the work to continue unabated. Across the acres of blight Krast could see the faint glow of forges hard at work and hear the distant rumble of trains. But none of these things were important to him right then because the Fortitude had finally arrived.

Scores of mechanics and guards bustled around it. Some of them were pumping out the waste systems, others were opening a pit under the machine's belly where spent coke from its furnace would be dumped. The Fortitude's hull was pitted and scarred from battle and its locomotives spikes were bent by some incredible force. An embossed steel plate midway up its hull showed Mars the war god flanked by angel's wings, bringing the gift of bloodshed. Krast was moved to see that it was split in half and the name 'Fortitude' was partially melted.

He fidgeted as the labourers secured the machine, but the crew pushing the steps towards the entry hatch looked to be moving at a snail's pace. This moment had been on his mind all day, even overshadowing his meeting at parliament earlier. His hand went to his scarred face again, and his fingers traced those discoloured blotches. "Move the damned thing," he cursed under his breath.

A crack appeared in the machine's belly, followed by another, and then a perfect rectangle of light shone from the access hatch. He thumbed a dewdrop from the tip of his cold nose and then, unable to contain himself any longer, he broke into a brisk walk, feeling his feet urging him forward. Men saluted as he steamed past them but they may as well have been invisible.

"Will you do to this woman what you did to Josephine?" The Cobb witch seemed to speak from the mist around him.

If he answered, he would be acknowledging a ghost. He was Knight Superior and ghost stories were for children. He reached the gantry steps, gripped the metal railing with a gloved hand and started up the stairs followed by apprehensive glances from the technical crews.

"Maybe Josephine realised begging wasn't going to work, so she took more drastic action to stop you from killing – ,"

"Silence!" he snarled. Krast stopped and listened, while his pulse raced at double speed. "Be silent," he said quietly, not to any imagined voice this time but to himself. "Be still." He closed his eyes and took a steady breath, unknowingly mirroring Valonia's own preparations.

The drizzle was moist against his face, cooling his strange scars, which now felt inflamed by his past, and for a moment he stood silently and welcomed the night air. He remembered how Baxter had implied the Cobb witch was responsible for her own demise. Was it possible Josephine had done the same, thus leaving him with a lifelong burden of guilt? Looked at from that perspective, who was the cruel one? "I tried to correct her ways," he muttered. "To bless her." He listened, but the awful Cobb woman remained silent and he dared to believe that she perhaps agreed with him.

Around him, men went about their work and tried not to notice their supreme commander frozen on the gantry steps, mumbling to himself.

Reassured, Krast continued upwards into the rectangle of light where machinery hummed and the air stank of hot wiring and grimy oil, into the Fortitude's innards to meet Wildwood's coven-mother. A metal staircase ran steeply upwards into the Fortitude and machinery rumbled womb-like all around him. He calmed himself by counting the steps, ". . . Eighteen, nineteen, twenty."

The shaft ended at a second, smaller hatch. He pulled on a chain and he heard a steam whistle pipe its shrill note somewhere beyond, summoning Moore, the duty-warden. Seconds later a broad, bearded face appeared behind the glass and the man's eyes widened when he saw his chief commander. The warden seized the wheel and heaved it into motion, spinning it with purpose. The door shrieked open and Warden Moore flattened himself against the wall and proffered Krast a rapid salute. "Knight Superior, sir," he said without pause, running the words into one.

"Duty-warden," he replied without interest.

"I hadn't thought you'd begin your inspection so soon. The pilots have yet to disembark." He tried to make it sound like Krast was doing them an honour and not being a bloody nuisance.

"I'm not here to inspect the crews," he stated, too preoccupied to notice the man's relief. "The captives, it's the captives I want to inspect."

Moore exhaled. "Right this way, sir." He started away down the corridor that was only just wide enough to accommodate his girth, and with a treasure trove of keys jangling at his hip. Krast followed, stooping every few yards to duck under the electric lighting, which looked sickly and yellow. "There's precious few of 'em, sir," Moore shouted over his shoulder.

If it had been his responsibility to capture witches in the first place and not just imprison them, Krast knew that he'd have chosen his words with more tact. "Which cell is the senior witch in?" he asked, trying to peer over Moore's shoulder as they walked.

"Number one. Last one on this row, sir."

"Name?"

"None, sir. Hasn't said a word since she was brought on board."

Krast felt a tingle of worry. "Then who declared her to be the coven's head?"

"I wasn't there when she surrendered, sir, so I can't say. But you can tell. Oh yes, you can always sniff out the queen-vixen in the den." He chuckled a grubby laugh that Krast didn't care for.

They followed the corridor as it curved its way through the machine, finally arriving at the first cells on this level. Krast snatched a look through each little window and saw that cells twelve through to six were empty.

As the numerals on the doors counted down his anticipation began to rise. When they came to the door marked V he took an exploratory peek to see a fearsome old woman sitting, arms folded, staring up at him. Her tatty dress was russet brown and she wore small spectacles with one lens blacked out, and he passed her without further interest. Cell IV held a black woman who sat hunched over her wounded arm. She didn't even look up, but he noted that her richly decorated dress was a multitude of green shades and guessed she was one of the more senior witches. The woman in cell III was evidently ready for him. She stood erect, staring out through the murky glass with clear blue eyes. Her clothes were fine quality, if tattered from battle, and everything she wore was a shade of summer heather. He was momentarily taken back by her beauty, then like a stone sinking into a well his brief admiration vanished.

He passed the next cell without interest, a child in the same dowdy colours as the first old witch. She sat crumpled in a corner. Just another brat to sell for labour when he was finished, he thought.

"Here's your number-one lady sir!" The warden shuffled back to allow Krast a glimpse of the Fortitude's prize prisoner.

Krast gazed at the door's single 'I', somehow imaging that it represented his nemesis: proud, singular and alone. He didn't look through the window; he wanted to meet her face to face. "Open it," he demanded.

Moore fumbled for the right key and rattled it in the lock. At their own windows, Ada, Lana, and Hilda peered out, aching for a glimpse, but seeing only Krast's shadow play against the opposite wall like an elongated puppet. Rowan, who was too short to see, tried seeing with her mind instead. Moore slid the door aside and even before the clash of bearings had faded Krast stepped into the doorway to face her.

He saw nothing but a blank metal wall. His eyes darted too and fro and then finally downwards to where a proud looking woman sat cross-legged on the floor in a pale blue dress and surrounded by long steely-grey hair, and he felt a pin-prick of foolishness for not having noticed her immediately. Her eyes were calm and her posture was controlled. He didn't see her inner turmoil and Valonia made sure to control her amazement. Her attention was immediately drawn to the ragged patches of golden flesh around his face and she forgot to breathe.

She'd heard of witches being branded with fool's-gold, but it was extremely rare and she'd never seen it first hand, and the very last place she would've thought to find it was on the face of the Illuminata's Knight Superior. His golden scars immediately told her that not only was the man before her a witch, but that he was a witch who'd betrayed his own. The wonder of it, she saw, was that he didn't even know it himself.

Hilda felt Valonia's amazement as a pressure wave; Rowan looked up and clasped her hands as if in prayer; Lana momentarily forgot the pain in her wounded arm; Ada chewed on her thumb, wishing it was her pipe, and all of them knew that something incredible was happening in cell I.

Valonia continued to stare in amazement and without even realising she was already studying his aura. It crawled around his head like a wounded animal, and floating within the banded colours she could see bricks concealing something.

Krast saw something in her stare that troubled him. He took a sly step backwards and folded his arms defensively. Although she sat on the floor and he towered over her, his height made him feel vulnerable rather than commanding. "I am told that you are chief of Wildwood-coven. You are their senior witch?" he asked stonily.

"I'm certainly most senior in age." Her voice was steady and cool. She wasn't even aware of her own words. Instead she grappled with the revelation that this man was of witch-blood and he'd been marked for life by another witch for betraying his own kind. It was considered the worst punishment a witch could inflict. The question she raced to solve now was who had done this and why.

Krast was uncomfortable, to say the least. There was something about her that made him feel that his past had crawled out of his pores and screamed his guilt for all to hear. *Don't be a fool*, he scolded himself. *Just some witch trickery.* "I am Knight Superior Krast," he announced, hoping she'd respond with her own title and name.

She wasn't at all surprised to hear the name match what the Hand-of-

Fate had told her. "Krast, senior most of the Knights Illuminata," she registered his rank dismissively.

"I am certainly senior most in rank, yes," he said, echoing her words.

"And the man who ordered my home destroyed and my friends murdered."

"And I understand you led your witches against my knights and killed a good number of beloved fathers and sons," he replied with a cold smile, and she thought of the kelp-harpy's serrated grin and dead eyes.

She found his piety sickening, and she saw his aura crackle as he spoke, but she also saw something hiding behind it, something he was trying very hard to bury: the image of a woman's face. "Had they come in peace they'd have left in peace instead of pieces," she declared flatly.

"Peace has its price, and to preserve it we must take steps to protect it," he lectured.

"Really? I thought you'd come to murder us because of first-dawn."

His eyebrows arched in shock, and his aura rippled angrily and through it she caught a better impression of the woman's face. She was amazed to see a family resemblance to this man, a sister or mother, perhaps?

Was that her? she wondered. *The one who'd marked him?*

He saw something troubling in her, and began to feel even more exposed. *She's up to something.* He was about to demand her name when she spoke first, and what she said was devastating.

"You have your mother's eyes," she peered up at him.

For a second he didn't even breath or blink, and when his mind finally grasped what he'd just heard, the world swayed beneath his feet and his head spun. He felt as transparent as glass and had the horrible urge to run and hide.

Moore saw his shock and put a steadying hand to his elbow. "Steady there, sir," he boomed.

"Don't touch me!" he hissed, snatching his arm away.

Moore backed off and Krast stood alone, staring down at Valonia. He tried to argue back but his mouth was dry, his legs quaked and he felt sick.

Valonia saw that she was playing a very dangerous game, but she judged it her best chance of keeping this monster from taking an interest in Rowan, and perhaps it was a little retribution for Esta and the others.

"We'll continue later," he said finally, sounding like a drunk pretending to be sober. "Lock her up," he waved Moore aside and staggered away down the corridor.

A little way down from the standing stones stood the tumbled ruins of a mine where lead and tin were once extracted. The site was built on a slope, and the only access was via the old railway that took a sharp bend around a keel-shaped hillside before following the valley and running away into the distance more or less straight. This 'keel' gave the mine some seclusion from the approaching valley, and as soon as she'd seen it Kolfinnia realised that it would make a good defensive position.

The derelict mine buildings centred on an overgrown courtyard. There was an engine shed where ore was once shipped out along the railway track, which had long since been eaten by sea-air and a jungle of weeds. Next to that a packhorse track led away in the same direction, passing a small area of woodland as it headed inland. Also around the courtyard stood a row of worker's cottages, and to their west was the pump-house, housing the massive machinery that once kept the mines free of flooding. It was a tall, sturdy building with a flat roof that looked like a castle tower, and one or two brave kittiwakes had nested on its ledges. Behind the pump-house were outhouses, lavatories and a ruined barn with a slumped roof like a broken back. To the south stood a quaint little chapel in a small churchyard protected by a dry-stone wall. That too was derelict and a few headstones encrusted with lichens reared up from the tall grass.

Kolfinnia and Clovis sat in the dip of a grassy hollow between the chapel and the pump-house sharing a hot drink of dandelion coffee laced with plenty of sugar. She badly needed rest and a meal, but for now a drink and bread would have to suffice. Her lightning-staff was propped by her side and Skald sat at the top keeping an eye on Tempest, who sat by Clovis in an identical pose. She kept wanting to ask this strange witch where they were, but she guessed he'd have even less idea than her, and she didn't want to look foolish. "We'll have to share, I'm afraid. I only have one mug." She rattled her spoon around the tin cup, still speaking her rough Pegalia, and offered Clovis first drink.

"My thanks." As he took it she briefly felt the touch of his furred hands and wondered how long it had been since humans had seen his kind, probably centuries she guessed. Certainly she'd never seen a Therion before and it was hard work not to stare: he was magnificent.

He took a sip and raised his brow approvingly. "Dandelion, you say?"

She nodded. "It means lion's-tooth. The plant has tooth-shaped leaves, and a lion is a fierce creature." She was going to say 'like you' but thought it too personal.

He took another sip and sat in silence for a while.

"So, your coven was destroyed?" he said from nowhere.

She wondered if being tactless was his speciality. "And yours?" she asked, quickly tossing the question back. He'd said little of his background and something told her not to mention Rowan just yet.

"Gone," he said, so vehemently that she thought their brief conversation was over. "Betrayed," he added softly while looking into the fire. "Unlike you I've no need to cast my wand. There'll be no survivors able to find me here, no coven to forge."

She caught his meaning. "You're a coven-father?"

"Was," he said for the second time that morning. He passed back the mug and the touch of his sleek fur was like a balm to her cold skin. She found that she couldn't take her eyes off him.

"Thank you." She took a gulp and tried to think of more to say while again working hard not to stare.

Under his dark cloak she could see that silvery armour protected his torso and shoulders. It was elegant, close-fitting and trimmed with what looked like gold. Underneath that he was wearing a mail shirt which looked light but tough. Around his waist was buckled a stout belt, but oddly his scabbard was empty. She wanted to ask what had become of his sword but bit her tongue. His knee-length boots and tunic were embroidered with stars and studded with bronze-looking badges and symbols she couldn't decipher. As for Tempest, he was almost identical to Skald, but when the light caught his feathers just right they had the sheen of emerald, not sapphire like Skald's.

"What's the name of your coven, Clovis?"

"Vega," he said proudly.

'Clovis looks after his own serpent-twins on Vega,' Rowan's comments came back to her. "So you're not from the outer isles then?" she asked, suspecting he was from isles very much more 'outer' than she first realised.

"Not the outer isles."

"And your coven, Vega, it's named after who, or what?" she probed.

"It's named after my home, my realm."

She wasn't any clearer, so she chose to take a leaf out of his book and be direct. "Do you mean to say that you travelled here from across the star-sea?"

"Did I not make that clear?" He threw a weary glance at Tempest, as if to say, 'The woman's a simpleton!'

She was annoyed, and a little amused, to see Skald try not to smirk. "You do not believe me?" he asked.

She considered. "I have a friend, a special friend. Would you believe me if I told you she'd spoken of you?" She watched carefully, to check his reaction and also admire him while she could.

He nodded casually as if he heard this kind of thing every day. "Tell me," he asked as he prodded the fire, "would your friend be called Rowan?"

She just stared at him dumbfounded. On one hand she had no reason to trust him, none at all, but on the other she had every reason. She swallowed her doubts, took the plunge and went with her heart. "Rowan's my friend." She wrestled with her emotions and stared at him over the rim of the mug. "She's only a girl."

"And where's she now?"

"Most likely captured by our enemies."

"I'm sorry to hear that," he said with genuine concern, and for a while he sat looking pensive. "What would you say if I told you that your friend might have led me here?" he asked quietly.

She frowned. It seemed each time he spoke it was just another riddle to chew over. "I've seen and heard of many strange things," she thought of the Hand-of-Fate, "and I don't dismiss the idea, but how is such a thing possible, and why?"

"I'm not sure myself, but I escaped my enemies carrying a great relic." His gaze shifted to the bag where Janus was hidden. "I came here through a door, a door I had dreamed of, the letters on it read 'ROWAN'." He looked at her for answers, but she had nothing to offer him other than a baffled look. He sighed in disappointment.

"I've no idea how or why you two were joined across such vast distances," she said at last, "but Rowan's not just an ordinary witch. She has a talent, and if our enemies found it they could use it to cause terrible damage."

"I know the problem." He glanced meaningfully towards Janus again.

She looked down at hrafn-dimmu in her lap and wondered if she ought to just tell him everything. "Valonia, my coven-mother gave me a last command, to establish a new coven giving survivors a safe place to come, and maybe think of a way to rescue Rowan." She felt Skald's approving eyes on her as she spoke.

Clovis propped an elbow on his knee. "This special talent of Rowan's, that I note you wish to keep to yourself – you want it and her back again?"

"More than anything!"

Is this the reason I'm here? he wondered, and stared off out to sea.

"Clovis?" She saw thoughts tumbling through his head, and for a crazy moment she imagined he was formulating a rescue plan.

"Why not get another coven to help instead of going to all the trouble of forming a new one?"

"Because," her voice almost cracked, "because I don't think there are any covens left."

"As happened to me," he leaned forward, "and perhaps others too."

"You think this tragedy goes beyond these isles?"

"Would I be here if it didn't?" he asked himself, forgetting she was there.

The notion that covens across the milky-river had suffered the same calamity was horrible. "Then I've work to do." She felt the seconds rushing past, she must set the wand to dream right away and rally the survivors. *If there are any*, she thought despairingly.

"So I see," he pointed to hrafn-dimmu and flashed her a smile full of fearsome teeth.

"I've delayed too long. Each minute lost is a minute longer they've got Rowan. This is my duty and I must attend to it." She put the mug down and stood up.

"I understand. Have you considered the safest place to leave the wand to dream?" He might be a long way from home but they shared the same rituals.

"That's what I'm off to ascertain," she replied sharply.

"Then may I offer you my advice in this matter, as coven-father to coven-mother?"

"You know of a safe place for the wand to dream?" she challenged. "I thought you'd only just got here, not what I'd call 'local' knowledge."

"It's so obvious, you don't need to be local," he laughed and rose to his feet, and while he might have been an inch shorter than her, he exuded a tangible sense of power.

"Well, are you going to share this with me, as coven-father to coven-mother?" He made her feel as though she was lagging behind. She heard Skald ruffle his wings just as Tempest did the same. The two sprites were engaged in their own silent stand off.

He turned and took a few steps away from their fire, up the grassy slope, and gestured for her to follow.

"Watch me, Skald," she whispered and he winked in reply. She followed him up the bank and stood overlooking the bay. Clovis raised an arm and directed her sight over the rolling dunes, out across the surf and towards the strange tower standing patiently by the rocky cliffs.

"There," he said pointing, "at the very summit."

The tower looked to beckon her back for a second try, and Kolfinnia's heart jumped.

CHAPTER TWENTY-ONE

Spider of Glass

Kolfinnia looked again at the tower. "Surely you're not serious? It almost killed us!"

"A great power radiates from it. That's how I knew you were in trouble when you passed so close." Clovis tried to calm her.

"Yes, a great power that almost killed us."

"You're not listening," he said softly. "Putting the wand up there would make its call ten times more potent. Trust me. I've been fascinated by that tower since we got here."

"And just how did you get here, Clovis, if you don't mind my asking?" She had endured enough secrecy.

"It's a complex story." There was a long silence and he made no effort to fill it.

"A story you don't seem inclined to share," she accused.

"Like Rowan's secret?"

She just glared at him.

"I had help," he conceded and looked to his pack with Janus hidden inside. "Let's just leave it at that for now." She turned to leave, clearly annoyed, when he caught her by the arm. "What happened? What did you experience as you passed through the tower's will?"

"I blacked out." She said and shook her arm free.

"Was that all?"

"It was a memory from childhood."

"It must've been strong to make you lose yourself like that?"

"It was like being there, but seen as an adult."

"Being where?" he pushed.

She saw an opportunity. "I'll tell you later, on the promise that you'll tell me how you came here."

"Very well," he twitched his head in agreement.

She looked at the tower again and bit her lip. "You really think that's the best place?"

"Without doubt."

"It's dangerous."

"Then let me escort you."

That sounded somewhat chivalrous and a smile tempted her lips. "How's it possible to get close if there's so much power flowing through it?"

"The birds have found a way," he pointed to the gulls swirling around the tower. "It might be a case of just asking permission or getting the right spell."

"I can't make a spell against a power I don't understand yet," she retorted. She felt inadequate next to him, which made her irritable.

"Maybe you just need to go slower. You hit the tower's barrier too fast this morning." He smiled pleasantly, which annoyed her even more.

"You had the advantage of knowing the tower was alive somehow. We just ran right into it like a brick wall," she regarded him sulkily. "Anyway, what do you mean by permission? Permission from what?"

"From whatever's living under it," he said coolly.

"Under it?"

"Something dwells under the stack, I'm certain."

She gave him a hard look, thinking of the Hand.

"I'll travel with you to the barrier," he reassured her, "to the tower's magical boundary, after which you are free to go on alone and set the wand to dream."

She looked at Skald and wanted to ask him how she was doing as a new coven-mother, but the decision was hers alone and time was wasting. "Very well," she agreed reluctantly.

"Excellent. Then later there's something you can help me with." He patted his empty scabbard and she suddenly felt manipulated into a deal she didn't fully understand.

Before anything else she performed the sleeping-spell for Hethra and Halla, the kind she had performed three times a day her whole life, the spell that kept their sleep peaceful. She used dune grass to weave a small pentacle in their honour. The act of making the charm consolidated her love and the spell was done.

"Will you be all right this time?" Skald was concerned.

"If I can't pass the tower's boundary then we'll set the wand to dream elsewhere." She tried to look confident but he saw the way her hands trembled while she wove.

"What do you think's under there?"

"Something that likes water," she joked, not wanting to think about it.

"If the birds can get close then it can't be anything evil," he rationalised.

"At the first sign of trouble we turn back."

"Kolfinnia, are you ready?" Clovis was standing on the rim of the grassy hollow.

"This is dangerous in daylight," she cautioned. "I don't really want to be seen."

"It's quiet enough," he remarked. "Now, are you ready?" His whiskers twitched impatiently.

"Skald, if you would," she asked.

Skald vanished in a blink. The Runes glistened like quicksilver then darkened. She tucked hrafn-dimmu into her clothes and fastened her cloak, then took her staff and walked up the banking. As soon as she reached the top she smelt good sea air and heard waves crash and gulls cry. "After you, coven-father." She swept an arm over the beach, inviting him to lead, curious to see how well he could fly.

He flattened his ears and bowed formally, then before she could even mount her staff he launched into flight.

Undaunted, she sprinted over the dunes and mounted in a shower of sand. Before her feet even found the stirrups Skald had reached galloping speed. She squinted against the wind and shook her head in dismay: here they were heading for a dangerous force and the men had decided to make a race of it. Ahead, Clovis flew like a torpedo, but Skald was doing a fine job of closing the gap. "It's no race!" she shouted.

Skald careered across the beach and out over the water and she felt the staff grow cold as he accelerated. He was already going faster than Gale had ever gone and she realised that she still knew almost nothing of him. Hard on the heels of that thought she felt a sudden pang of loss and just then she'd have given anything to see Flora.

The staff began to slow.

"Skald?"

"Not wise to charge into danger. Let that fool try his luck."

She wondered if that was his real reason, and reminded herself to tame her thoughts when she was flying with him. Clovis had turned westwards around the stack, keeping a wary distance but getting close enough to startle the sea birds. She could just see them swirling like dandelion seeds in the wind. "He's reached the boundary."

"I hope you know what to do next."

She didn't. She simply hoped that an idea would present itself, and preferably before she reached Clovis who hovered just above the waves on the tower's western side. She dropped low and paid the price for her stealthy approach by being buffeted and sprayed.

"What do you think of him?" Skald asked.

"I'm not sure yet."

"You trust him?"

"Only so far," she answered quietly.

Clovis regarded her thoughtfully as she drew close, then he looked up as though he was scanning the invisible wall around the tower. "From this point on you'll have to devise a spell or ask permission."

"Very well." She edged forwards, feeling vulnerable and continually glancing back to shore, convinced eyes were watching.

They inched slowly ahead and she felt the air thickening around her and knew this was the tower's boundary. She gripped Rowan's amulet and clutched it tight. As they pushed deeper into its shadow she saw foamy breakers dissolve over its black rock and gulls nesting on the ledges, and she understood that Skald was right: whatever lay under the tower wasn't evil. The air continued to thicken and she felt like she was walking into a strong wind. She looked behind and saw Clovis watching with fascination, and then from nowhere she heard her mother calling again.

"Kolfy?"

Suddenly she heard a child crying.

"It's coming Skald," she said fearfully. But this time she was ready. It was a memory and no more, and if she didn't master her fear the tower would defeat her again.

'Hang the evil hag!' 'Split her guts and fill her with stones!' 'Burn the witch whore!' The tainted wood screamed again, but unlike Little Kolfinnia, coven-mother Kolfinnia grasped every word. The air in her throat dried up and she felt a clamp tighten around her neck.

This is how it must feel to be hung, she thought with horror. "Just a memory," she insisted, holding Rowan's amulet tight. "Just the past, no more."

"Kolfinnia?" Skald called.

"I'm fine," she breathed.

"Kolfy!" It was her mother again.

It occurred to her vaguely that if the tower was the fountain of memory why should she let horrible ones molest her when she had wonderful ones as well? That was the revelation she needed and the floodgates opened. Wonderfully vivid memories tumbled through her: Valonia building a tree-house and she and Flora playing in it. Riding Rooter around the gardens, watching him devour cabbages not knowing he shouldn't and being scolded by Ada for encouraging him. Cutting her lightning-staff and meeting Gale.

They came faster and faster, but this time they didn't blot out the present; rather they were divine companions. At last she passed into clear air again, exhaling like a diver up from the depths, and she slumped over her staff. "That's it," she gasped, "we're through!" Controlling her memories was key to penetrating the tower's will, she realised. She looked back at Clovis and waved.

"Up now," Skald insisted, and lifted away from the sea, ascending the tower in a spiral.

As they climbed, the tower appeared as a spindle on her left that rolled ponderously, while the sea and the coast spun like a merry-go-round. She caught a glimpse of Clovis and raised her arm. If he signalled back she didn't see because just then Skald brought them back to the tower's southern side and Clovis vanished out of sight. The tower shrank in height as they climbed and before long there was only blue sky above and they were level with its summit. It was flat, grassy and littered with slabs of rock, bird and fish bones, broken egg-shells and the occasional crab claw. She wondered if anyone had ever come here, and at the centre of the tower's summit there was a surprise. There was a small shaft opening directly downwards, like a chimney.

She gauged their landing carefully, avoiding the strange hole, and touched down gently amid pink thrift that'd never felt passing feet. The wind was stronger up here, but now that the sun had begun to shine she had to admit that the view was spectacular. To her right the beach looked like a scimitar of polished bronze, while the sea was crystal blue and the rocks looked desert red. She pulled hrafn-dimmu from her clothes, laid her staff down and got to work. Skald appeared and watched, and she could feel the wand's anticipation and excitement as well as his critical gaze.

"I know what to do, Skald," she assured him, and began piling rock slabs into a crude shelter.

"So I see. But make sure it's stout against storms."

She built a rough circle of stones and then found two flags big enough to make a lid, which she heaved into position. Once she was happy with her shelter she reached for hrafn-dimmu and brought it to her lips where she uttered the dreaming-spell before kissing it gently. The wand was still pulpy and damp from its long journey and it tasted of salt. She finished the spell, aware of Skald looking over her shoulder. A lone fulmar whistled past, curious to see what was going on, and just as the last words of the spell left her mouth hrafn-dimmu suddenly felt light and insubstantial and Skald's eyes widened. In all the years he'd known Valonia her wand had been alive like a bird that always sings, even if you grew so used to the song that you didn't hear it. Now, though, its constant song faded and he felt a terrible loneliness.

"Skald, are you all right?"

He nodded. It seemed that Kolfinnia couldn't hear the song drift away, and that made him feel even more alone.

She wrapped the wand in Valonia's patchwork cloak and then reverentially lowered the bundle into the shelter and plugged the gaps with grass and turf. "Do you want to say anything before I seal it?"

He considered a moment. "Come home," he said quietly.

She smiled in agreement, then pulled the rocks over the roof to complete the little chamber, kissed her fingertips and pressed them to the lid. "Dream, dark raven. Call the survivors." A tear ran down her cheek and she was glad that Clovis hadn't come with her.

The wind swirled her dark hair around her face and when she brushed it aside she saw Skald sitting on the flat stones adding a few silent words of his own. She thought of Valonia, and of Rowan and of Flora and her family that had been scattered, captured or killed. "Let's be off," she said suddenly. Being up here was like being a statue on a pedestal.

Skald flapped on to the staff and then, as if on cue, they both turned to the strange hole in the middle of the summit, and she knew one of them would eventually ask. "I wonder where it goes?"

She instantly wished he hadn't asked. "Down to whatever power calls this place home," she concluded ominously. Without knowing why she stepped closer and peered down. Lichens and grass had colonised the first yards of rock but after that the darkness strangled growing things. As she leaned further over she thought she heard voices rising like smoke from below, it was faint at first but the harder she listened the more she discerned them. It seemed that an endless number of lives were rising up through the stack and streaming outwards. "Do you hear that?" She waved a tentative hand over the opening but felt nothing. "That's the power that threw us off course." Skald knew what she was about to say even before she said it, and when the words sailed from her mouth he felt the well-oiled cogs of fate click into position. "Shall we go see?"

"Valonia always said you were too bold," he smiled.

She was sure of one thing: there was something at work here bigger than witches, knights, magic and perhaps even Hethra and Halla themselves. They had to go.

Skald vanished, and she held the staff out over the hole, as if to drop it like a plumb-line. Trusting him, she reached over with her right foot and stepped into one of the fabric stirrups. It creaked as it took her weight, then she lifted her other foot out over the black and into the other stirrup. Now there was nothing under her feet but a mystery.

She looked down and into a void that had never been penetrated. The stream of voices funnelling upwards surrounded her and she could easily believe it was the voices, not the wind, that tugged at her hair and clothes. She drew her old wand from its sheath and held it tighter than ever. The darkness below made it suddenly feel a hundred times its worth. She called an aura spell and it began to shine. "Ready?"

"Slow and careful," he replied and started to sink downwards.

She saw the distant hills vanish, then the beach, then she saw blades of grass wave before her eyes then soil, then rock and then the sky was just a receding blue scrap above her as they sank further into the shaft.

The descent took much longer than the height of the tower would suggest. The shaft was slightly crooked, but overall it ran straight down, narrowing then opening then narrowing again. She gripped her staff for dear life as Skald nosed his way down the cramped passage, and eventually the keyhole of sky above finally vanished.

"Skald, the sky's gone," she said fearfully.

He didn't reply, but instead concentrated on navigating the tunnel.

She used the wand's light to avoid the jutting rocks and keep her face and elbows from being scraped. The deeper they dropped, the colder it grew and the more insistent the voices from below. She felt them streaming past her like fog, telling her their secrets as they passed out into the world, and not for the first time she wondered if coming down here was a good idea. *Hrafn-dimmu wouldn't have come here if the place was dedicated to Ruin*, she told herself.

Eventually she could feel the pounding waves outside as pressure in her ears and a deep rumbling in the rock. They'd arrived at sea level and the tower's very roots, and logic told her that everything from here on down would be flooded. "That's it, Skald. We've reached the bottom, we can't go further." The staff halted and she felt relieved and disappointed at the same time.

"Wait!" he called.

"What is it?" She ought to hear the slurp of sea-water in the flooded shaft, but it was silent except for the strange whispering voices.

"There's more!" he said incredulously.

"There can't be more. This is sea-level!"

"Tell me that when we get wet."

He continued down into the stack, below sea level and into a dry and silent passageway. Kolfinnia risked waving her wand towards her feet, hoping to see something below, something that might explain how this tunnel was defying the laws of nature. "This should be underwater!"

"So I see."

"How far does it go?"

"How should I know?"

The voices were stronger, like a gathering of thousands all talking at once. Some of them started to sound eerily familiar and she began to fear that a cavern of ghosts awaited them below, awaited them with open arms and were determined to make them stay. "Skald, maybe we should go back," she whispered.

He stopped again. "Do you want me to go on or return?"

A simple yes or no answer, one that might change her life.

"We go on." Her voice was lost amid the whispers. Ghosts, she wondered. Mother?

The Runes on the lightning-staff flashed. "Don't dwell on such things," he warned.

They continued to sink and the shaft retreated away from the wand's faint light. Suddenly there was nothing but blackness all around and Kolfinnia felt she was adrift amid the stars. For a moment she experienced a rush of panic, thinking that they'd never find the opening in the roof again and be entombed here forever. Perhaps the voices she heard were people who'd come this way and never left.

"The tunnel's widening into a cavern," Skald sensed her worry.

"Keep the staff plumb," she said warily. "If we don't hit the floor in another minute then we go directly back upwar –," The staff cracked against something hard. She lurched to one side expecting the sickening sensation of falling into emptiness, but a second later she landed on a stony surface and heard her staff clatter down beside her echoing right through the cavern. They'd certainly not arrived in secret. Kolfinnia crawled up. "Skald, are you there?"

He appeared, framed by that same spectral glow she'd seen at Wildwood, and that at least drove the darkness back a little. She swept her wand left to right, while she groped for her lightning-staff with her other hand.

"Are you hurt?" he asked.

"No, I'm all right." She retrieved her staff and got to her feet.

She heard the flutter of wings and Skald was clinging to the staff and peering about, clearly as confused as she was. "Well, we're at the bottom."

"Bottom of what, though?" The blackness was alive with voices, all interacting with one another in an incredibly complex pattern. "Skald, we're under the sea." She couldn't fully grasp how impossible this was. Some unknown force was keeping all those crushing tons of water out of the cavern and in that instant she knew that Clovis had been right: something alive and eternal existed down here, and they were so small and transient that it might not even recognise them as being alive. "But now what?"

"We go on," Skald said simply.

She caught the shimmer of something polished and smooth directly ahead, but it could have been yards or miles away in the confusing darkness. "Something's there," she murmured.

Before they moved off, she piled a small mound of stones to mark where they had descended, so they could locate the opening again. After a deep breath she started towards the strange object in the blackness, carefully picking a path through the rocks. The air was ancient and cold and she could see her breath.

She could hear running water ahead and she felt even more confused. If they were under sea-level then where could water run to? The reflections ahead grew stronger and a shape loomed into view.

"It looks like . . ." she knew the word but couldn't say it because it was impossible. "It can't be, but it looks like an . . . hourglass?" She waited for Skald to tell her how stupid she was being, but he didn't.

As they approached it grew larger, rearing up over them now, and the shape was no longer vague. It wasn't just hourglass shaped; it was a real hourglass. Wand-light spilled across its curved surface, thinning and fattening as it flowed over the contours. The sound of rushing water was louder now and her wand revealed a river flowing past the hourglass's base.

"Skald, it really is an hourglass," she whispered, believing that she must be losing her mind.

The hourglass was the source of the voices, and above it stalactites hung down like fearsome jaws, showering it with droplets, and at her feet, separating her from the miraculous object was a narrow but deep-looking river which vanished into the blackness.

She turned to check Skald's expression and saw his angular profile tipped backwards, taking in the impossible sight, and for the first time since leaving Wildwood he thought of something other than Valonia.

The glass was huge, and it looked impossibly old. Its surface was pitted and distorted by tiny cracks but through it she could see layers of sand that looked as if they had been left undisturbed since time began. She raised her wand higher and its light rolled over the hourglass's narrow waist, where she could see grains of sand frozen in mid-air as they fell

impossibly slowly. Higher still she saw the trails of woven silk behind
the glass, and dozens of childhood stories began to fall into place.

The hourglass, the frozen sand hardly moving, the delicately woven
threads. Every rhyme, myth and fable she'd ever heard about this object
had become real before her eyes. The voices she heard were the fates of
millions being woven and broadcast into the universe.

"God-Oak, no, it can't be!" she exclaimed, now feeling terror and
rapture.

Skald saw it first, a movement in the upper glass.

"Oh, but it is!" he said slowly and raised a pointing finger.

She stared up at the unmistakable shape of a huge spider behind the
glass. The wand-light glinted in eight globe eyes like distant stars, and
she saw herself reflected there in the spider's bottomless stare and the
last piece of the puzzle fell into place.

Impossible though it was, this was the great Timekeeper.

Valonia awoke with a jerk and sat bolt upright. She couldn't quite
remember the dream and as she listened to her thudding heart she
wondered if it'd been the crib-robber dream again, but it didn't feel the
same. She eased herself up and gathered her thoughts. She wasn't clear
of the hour but it felt like dawn or just before. She'd spent the last few
hours since meeting Krast wrapped in a coarse blanket and trying to
sleep. "The dream, remember the dream." She cupped her head in her
hands. Trying to recall it was like trying to catch snowflakes without
them melting. She stretched her legs and her feet rattled the tin cup
and plate left over from last night.

After Krast had gone, warden Moore had thrown her the blanket and
food, and while she'd chewed her bread and sipped the metallic tasting
water she thought endlessly about the Knight Superior who was also
a traitor-witch. She'd hoped to deflect his attention from Rowan, but
now she found another good reason to know more about him. Krast
had likewise fixed upon her, which suited her plans, but she didn't
understand his motives. Now, though, she had to clear all of that clutter
away and try to retrieve the threads of her dream, which was fading
fast. "Relax, Valonia," she contained herself.

She caught leftover shreds: an ocean with a tower rising out of it, and
a great power radiating from its crown. Right at the tower's summit,
something had been buried and it was this that she struggled to see.
The final shreds were vanishing like ice on hot coals, and just when
she thought that there were no secrets left she glimpsed it: a shaft of
wood balanced on the summit like a compass needle. She threw back

her head in wide-eyed realization. "Hrafn-dimmu!" she whispered triumphantly.

That simple fact started an avalanche of certainties. Kolfinnia had survived, she had found Skald, cast the wand and miraculously only days after Wildwood's destruction, her youngest Ward had begun to gather the survivors. "Well done, Kolfinnia! Very well done, my little wolf-mother!" She punched the air in victory. A second later she heard the rattle of keys in the lock and the door was swung open, whereupon she played the role of a broken old witch for Moore.

"It's dawn, you piss-stinkin' old Jik. Fifteen minutes yard time followed by breakfast. That's an order, now on yer feet. But don't leave the cell 'til I says yer can." He held a wooden cudgel and from the way he tapped it against his leg she guessed he wouldn't need much reason to use it. "Understand?"

She nodded her compliance. He grunted and then moved onto the next cell. A half dozen armed guards dutifully trooped after him, one of whom waited outside her cell watching her suspiciously. Valonia heard keys tumble in locks and other doors open, followed by the same gruff command, but despite this she felt exalted. Kolfinnia had started to forge a new coven, and Hethra and Halla were still protected by witches, for now at least.

"Are you sure?" Lana asked hopefully.

"No doubt," Valonia said quietly. "Kolfinnia's set the wand to dream."

They'd been driven down the Fortitude's gantry and out into their new home: an acre of compacted coal debris. Krast thought they might be a destabilising influence and so isolated them from the other prisoners. Valonia looked through the wire mesh where sentries were posted every fifty yards, and she counted a total of five floating prison hulks moored on the Thames. She thought of the men, women and children crammed inside them for the crime of caring for the Earth. They were gathered in a huddle with Rowan at their centre, shuffling slowly around the Fortitude in the name of exercise. Valonia noted the machine's battle-scars and thought back to how her dear friends had paid with their lives.

"Kol's alright!" Rowan grinned.

"Best keep that between us." Guardsmen hovered close by and Valonia spoke in a hush. "But you might all get a taste of the dream over the next few nights," she encouraged. "It'd be much stronger if not for this blasted prison machine."

"It's blockin' it some 'ow," Ada said moodily.

"Others will sense it, and if they can they'll make their way to

Kolfinnia." Hilda smiled.

"Protection for Hethra and Halla." Valonia sounded satisfied.

Moore stepped up to the fence and blew a whistle three times. "Five minutes," he shouted, sounding bored, "then yer in." He jabbed a thumb at the Fortitude.

None of them responded, but Valonia had plenty of questions to ask. "Did any of you get a good look at him?"

"Who?" asked Hilda, "The man who came last night?"

"My door was kept shut an' just as well, I'd 'ave spat in the bugger's eye." Ada reached for her wand, and for the hundredth time remembered that it had been confiscated.

"I didn't." Lana held her wounded arm tenderly. The only medical attention she'd received was from a callous surgeon who'd scrubbed the wound with carbolic and declared it free of shrapnel. "I'm afraid I was in too much pain to notice."

Valonia gave her a sympathetic look and passed something to her in a tiny bag. "Here, crow-root for the pain."

She took it with a grateful smile.

"The glass was too murky for me to see much," Hilda added.

Rowan said nothing, but just looked out between the wall of witches and wished with all her heart that she was at home with Kolfinnia.

"Well I did," Valonia stared at her feet as they shuffled along, trying to keep their conversation private. "He opened my cell and announced himself as Krast, the same name the Hand-of-Fate warned me of."

"You went lookin' for the 'And-o-Fate?" Ada was aghast.

"It wasn't a picnic, Ada."

"Aye, well nobody tells me nowt." She sounded upset. First Rowan's secret and now this.

"Do you wish we'd taken you along?"

"I'd rather be hoein' cabbages," she grunted and Valonia smiled.

"There's something else, something incredible," Valonia revealed. "Our captor, the so-called Knight Superior, he took the fool's-gold."

The huddle suddenly stopped in shock, while Rowan carried on a pace without them before noticing and hurrying back.

"You're serious?" Hilda looked disgusted but fascinated.

"Yes," she sighed.

Rowan didn't have a clue what they were talking about, but their expressions troubled her.

"You mean to say that Britain's covens were destroyed by one of our own?" Hilda thought the idea obscene.

"He has little idea of his heritage, I think," Valonia guessed.

"Can it be used against him?" Lana asked.

"It'd prove a useful distraction," she nodded surreptitiously in Rowan's direction. "Keep his attention where it would serve us best."

"Anything else you can tell us about him?" Hilda took Rowan's hand in hers.

Valonia looked down at the girl, whose helpless expression made her heart sad and wrathful at the same time. She wondered what the girl might be able to tell them about Krast, but tempting her to use her skills here of all places was reckless. "I saw a woman's face in his aura. If not for that blasted machine," she glared up at the Fortitude, "I'd have got a better reading."

Hilda shook her head. "Fool's-gold," she marvelled again.

The witches huddled closer, ready to go back inside, but now they had a purpose and the beginnings of a plan.

Hathwell heard feet thudding up the stairs to the signal-box and knew that it was Krast. He straightened from his typewriter, but his troublesome knee sent a twinge into his hip. "Bloody thing," he groaned, and rubbed at the steel plate under his skin.

Krast entered to find him hunched over, working a hand at his leg trying to rub away the pain. He tried to stand to attention but Krast excused him. "At ease."

Hathwell slumped back into his chair. "You look tired, sir," he managed at last.

"Processing captives takes an age," he lied and removed his coat. Krast came and sat next to the small paraffin heater, which did a fine job of heating the place but made the air unpleasant. Valonia's five words had kept him up all night. *'You have your mother's eyes.'* "I'm taking charge of the Wildwood witches and keeping them isolated."

"Makes sense, sir," Hathwell admitted. "They caused the most damage after all."

You have no idea, he thought. "I've passed on the duty of processing the other prisoners to the senior correctionals, so I can concentrate on them – I think we can learn much from them."

"What are they like?" He had a grudging admiration for them.

"I made a brief inspection last night."

"And?"

"One child, four women. I only gave them a glance, but I shared pleasantries with their alleged coven-mother."

"Alleged, sir?"

"She was a tight-lipped old crone. Never even told me her name, let alone her title." He put a confident spin on his meeting with Valonia.

"And what did you think of her?" He hobbled out from behind his desk, pulled up a chair and sat down next to Krast and the paraffin heater. They looked like two old signal men sharing a quiet moment between passing trains. Krast cupped his chin as he considered and Hathwell saw his long index finger idly trace the contours of a golden scar across his cheek. He knew better than to interrupt him, and instead gazed through the dusty windows to the world of Hobbs Ash. His thoughts turned yet again to something that had troubled him all summer. *'How do you turn a man to stone?'* he wondered for the thousandth time. The answer was simple – it would take someone who knew magic, but not necessarily a witch.

"Perceptive." Krast's reply shook him from his thoughts.

"Sorry, sir?"

"The Wildwood witch, she's perceptive." He sat back in his chair, crossed his legs and cupped his knee between his hands. His pose was confident, but his heart wasn't. He needed time to prepare before he faced her again. Hathwell saw his mental cogs turning and knew a request of some kind was imminent.

"When are you going to question her?"

"She doesn't trust me, but you might have better luck. There's much I wish to know about her." *About my past,* he thought.

"Me, sir?"

"Yes. You have a common touch."

Hathwell recalled Rushton's class comments. He'd thought Krast had shown touching loyalty for defending him, but Krast was like a chameleon that changed his opinions to suit his mood.

"Go see them, her in particular. Get to know them and report back to me. Even the smallest detail could be useful leverage."

"Why not the chromosites?"

"Because it's a war of wills," he stated mysteriously.

Hathwell was confused. Krast's method for gathering information was to drag witches kicking and screaming to the chromosites. The wretches on the prison hulks would go there in less than a week once all the processing was done. Getting to know individual names was very un-Krast like. "You think it'll help find these serpent-twins?" he asked uncertainly.

"Perhaps, but I'm anxious to learn how they knew we were coming and how they defeated one of our greatest companies."

He makes a good point. But Hathwell suspected there was more.

"Pay them a visit. Pretend you're on an errand of some sort, but just get them talking." He waved a hand at his squire, wanting him out of the office.

"And once I've found out all I can?" he asked as he got to his feet.

"Then I'll step in. Start with the coven-mother, get her name."

"She interests you doesn't she, sir?"

He looked up and Hathwell imagined he'd disturbed an angry tiger. "Haven't I just explained why that is so?" His tone was sharp.

"I only thought there was a chance to better understand . . ." he trailed off and gestured to his own face to indicate Krast's scars.

Krast blinked and his jaw clenched. He leapt to his feet as fast as a whip, sending the chair screeching over the wooden floor. "How dare you!" he shouted. "You forget your place!"

Hathwell jumped to attention and his knee screamed in protest. He instinctively stared ahead at nothing, keeping his body rigid and his arms by his side.

"What would you know of curses? What would you know of –,"

From nowhere he saw her again, just after she'd hurled him across the interrogation room with her last spell. He wanted her to hate him, but what he saw undid him: she still loved him.

The image faded and all he saw was Hathwell's flushed face and frightened eyes. "You're not my equal," he said icily. "Now get out."

Hathwell jerked a salute and marched out of the office, not even stopping to collect his hat or coat, and not even sure where he was heading other than away from Krast's fury.

Krast stood motionless for a long time after Hathwell left.

"She tried to kill me." He spoke like an actor rehearsing his lines.

"Did she?" Eliza sighed from close by.

He jerked, and his eyes rolled this way and that looking for someone who couldn't have been there. "Of course!"

He listened for a reply, a contradiction, laughter, anything from Eliza's drowned ashes in the Thames, but the only sound was the rush of the paraffin heater.

"Didn't you hear me?"

There was no answer and that was somehow the most condemning of all. He shuffled to the window, breathing rapidly and shoulders hunched. He ran a hand across his brow, it came away sticky with sweat, and he stared across to the sheds where chromosites were bred and behind that he could see the Fortitude's spiked dome. *Did she see all of that, the Wildwood witch?* The uncertainty was tearing him apart.

He believed there were two ways to silence Eliza Cobb and lock Josephine away forever: one was to kill the Wildwood witch and take satisfaction from her prolonged death. The other path was more dangerous, and although he didn't know it, it was the better part of him that urged him to take it, to confront his past and ask for her help. He pulled his coat from its hook with numb fingers and headed for the door not knowing where he was going, or which path he would take.

CHAPTER TWENTY-TWO

The Timekeeper

"We should go back," Skald urged. "Things like this aren't to be tampered with."

She couldn't agree more. Why this mythic creature had chosen this place to weave fate from was none of their business. "We'll never come back, never tell anyone, not even Clovis." She took a step backwards while still gazing at the incredible sight, but as the thought of leaving passed through her mind, the spider's legs slowed and it turned around to confront them. "He's seen us!" she gasped.

Her first instinct was to douse her wand and hide in the blackness, but she stood rooted to the ground. The Timekeeper sat motionless and studied them and Kolfinnia felt as if everything in creation had stopped to inspect them, and them alone. Should she apologise, introduce herself or make a run for it? She had no idea and Skald was no help, he was just as speechless.

The Timekeeper raised his two front legs and through the glass she saw that he held a single thread. He pulled gently on the thread and stretched it. All at once she felt breathless and faint and she knew the spider's meaning. That thread was the life of Kolfinnia Catherine Algra and the Timekeeper held it now for the very simple reason that she was standing here before him. He had known she was there from the start. He had woven her coming here into existence.

"You are Kolfinnia and Skald." The voice by-passed her ears and rushed through her soul like a river.

"Yes," she swallowed, "I am." Should she say 'your highness', 'my lord' or 'sir'? How did you address fate itself? *He's stopped weaving!* she thought giddily. *How can that be?*

She wondered if the universe had ground to a halt outside, just so the Timekeeper could spend a few moments with her. Kolfinnia saw the single thread in his grip vibrate, buzzing with her thoughts, but whether he wove her thoughts or the thread simply responded to them was too deep to ponder.

"This thread is you?" The Timekeeper was fascinated.

At first she thought it was a statement, then it dawned on her that it was a question. "Yes, I believe it must be," she said helplessly. Was it possible that he'd never met any of the beings he wove life and death for, she wondered? She couldn't take her eyes from the silvery thread, knowing that the slightest pressure would snap it and if that happened her life would end in an instant. The thread in the Timekeeper's grip vibrated again and he deduced her worries.

"Fear not, the breaking of this thread is not today."

She felt sick with the enormity of it. If not today then when? Could she learn when she was destined to die just by asking?

"That is not for me to decide," he said, answering her unspoken thoughts.

Skald looked around, frightened. "What's he talking about, for Oak's sake?" He was listening to one half of a very profound conversation.

"Skald, he knows what we think and he knew we were here. How could he not? It's all there in the threads he's weaving." She pointed with a trembling hand.

Under the first pair of legs he raised a second pair into view and they too clasped a glittering thread.

"You mean that's me?" Skald spluttered.

"Those threads are us!" She couldn't believe she was talking to a being that dictated what she would say next.

"No," the Timekeeper said, knowing her thought. He crouched down, dropping their threads amid billions of others. *"No, not at all, Kolfinnia and Skald. My purpose is to weave fate, not plan it."*

She could ask him anything, know anything, just like Rowan. The idea terrified her but there was something she *was* compelled to ask. "Rowan and Valonia . . ." she could have added a dozen more names. "Their threads are unbroken?" Her question bubbled up in his mind even before she voiced it.

He drew two threads from thin air and she plugged her mouth with her fist, trying not to cry out. The lives of the two people she loved most hung within reach behind the glass. She wanted to snatch them away and guard them forever.

"What will happen to them?" Skald asked fearlessly.

"The Patternmaker decides, not I," he replied, somewhat sadly.

She thought about the Hand-of-Fate's origins. *'The Patternmaker, so disgusted with his creation, severed his offending hand and cast it away.'* Was it just a story? That was one question she didn't want an answer to. "How can creation continue if you stop weaving?" she blurted clumsily.

"Time exists in your world, not mine."

She guessed that his world consisted of the hourglass and no more and time inside it was not linear.

He returned Rowan and Valonia's threads to a forest of others, which lay so thick against the glass they looked like snow.

"This morning, I passed this tower and had a memory of my past, my mother. How was that possible?"

"This chamber is the fountain of past and present. You passed through your own history, that is all." He casually collected hundreds of threads and with one clean slash he severed the lot, making Kolfinnia jump.

"What happened?" she cried.

"An earthquake, far away."

"Why would the Patternmaker demand that?"

"The Patternmaker's mind is hard to comprehend, but his instructions are always clear."

"But each of those threads is a person!" she argued.

"Like you?"

"Yes." Her answer made her feel inconsequential.

Skald cleared his throat. "What of the thread we know as Esta Salt?"

He paused, placing the name. *"That thread was broken."*

Kolfinnia felt the wind punched from her gut and she turned to look at Skald with horror.

"So, Esta died rescuing Rowan," his head flopped to his chest and his feathers dulled. "The inner circle was broken before we even began."

"Skald, we have to go," she begged, "Clovis will be waiting. We should never have come here." There were a million questions she wanted to ask this creature, but she felt that each one she asked was interfering with creation. However, she couldn't resist one last question, and she chose it with great care. "Rowan, what makes her thread so special?"

The Timekeeper considered before answering. *"The girl's thread crosses that of the Patternmaker. She can see his mind as clearly as I see you, although she does not fully realise it."*

Both of them reeled at this.

The Patternmaker has a thread of his own? Who or what commands that thread? Kolfinnia thought, but the idea was too enormous. "No, don't tell me!" she stammered, afraid the great spider would perceive her thought and his answer would boil her mind away.

"Let's go, it's wrong to be here." Skald landed on her shoulder and dug his claws in to make his point.

"Last thing," Kolfinnia asked. "I've left a precious object at the tower's summit. Will you promise to leave it in peace?"

"That is the Patternmaker's concern, not mine."

"Very well," she said weakly, as if she had any say in what beings like the Patternmaker chose to do.

She started away through the rocks, edging backwards, afraid to take her eyes off the hourglass. Little by little her wand-light trickled away from the Timekeeper and his glass prison, letting the shadows return and shroud him in darkness again.

He watched the wand-light until it became just a faint spark in the blackness, a firefly alone in the night, then even that was gone and his perfect isolation was restored.

He cut and snipped with a surgeon's care at the Patternmaker's behest, but with each thread he broke he now thought of the brave young woman who'd ventured to his cavern. And for the first time since the very beginning he pondered the 'why' of his task.

Kolfinnia made a home in one of the deserted cottages. Tacked to the crumbling wall outside was an enamelled plaque. It was baked by years of salt-air and only a few words were legible, *'Tin & Lead Mine'*. Tin, ruled by Jupiter and governing luck, and Lead, ruled by Saturn and symbolic of defence and protection. She hoped it was a good omen. Her mattress was a pile of sacking and dry grass, and her cloak was her blanket. She'd not slept properly for what felt like an age, and as soon as she lay down she fell into an exhausted sleep. Skald lay in his staff beside her and the pair slept heavily, paying for almost two days of fight and flight. She dreamed of her lost friends, of Gale and of mythical spiders and swimming wands and terrible machines, and when she didn't dream at all she knew nothing, and that was good.

When she awoke, the mid-afternoon sun was still high but the shadows had a suggestion of autumn about them. She went to wash, brush her hair and change into her last clean clothes and then, leaving Skald to sleep on, she went in search of Clovis.

She searched everywhere, but she didn't call out his name. During her search she inspected the buildings with an appraising eye, venturing inside the pump-house and even going up onto the flat roof from where the view was spectacular. *This will be my own tower*, she thought to herself.

Eventually she found him in the engine shed at the head of the disused railway. The building was still surrounded by mounds of pulverised rock, many of which had shaggy crowns of weeds growing out of them. He was busy stacking driftwood and a small campfire crackled where he was cooking something. His keen ears heard her approach and he turned and dipped her a little bow. "You slept well?"

"Well enough, thank you." She still felt groggy and her sleep had been deep rather than refreshing.

"I took the liberty of retrieving a few items from your pack." He took up the tin cup from where it'd been keeping warm next to the fire. "Lion's Tooth," he said carefully, passing it over.

"Dandelion," she corrected with a smile.

"Ah, yes of course." He bid her sit by the fire, and though the sun was pleasant enough the fire's warmth was also welcome.

She sipped her drink and felt it steal down into her tired bones. "This is good, Clovis," she complemented.

"I've a little soup here, made from the herbs around and about. I've saved some for you. It's hot and nourishing so don't complain about the taste."

She took the small cook-pot and helped herself. The soup was everything he said but at least it eased her rumbling belly.

"When you're able I'll take a rest of my own, that's if you'll keep vigil."

She looked startled and then shamefaced. "I'm sorry, it didn't occur to me you hadn't slept. Why didn't you say something?"

He shrugged. "Of the two of us, you looked the worse for wear."

"I still owe you that favour." She indicated his empty scabbard resting against the engine shed, along with a few other strange items that she was burning to ask him about.

"When you're done," he said affably.

"Where's Tempest?"

"Sleeping. I left him in the cave."

"Cave?" It was hard work communicating in Pegalia. "Oh, you mean the cottage?"

"Cottage," he tried the word and she gave him an encouraging smile. He'd set up his bunk in the same cottage as her, but downstairs.

"You know, they look so alike."

"Who, the sprites?" He threw another stick onto the fire.

"Yes, they could be brothers."

He held his hands out, palms up. Kolfinnia saw rough pads, fur and claws. "They're of the same elemental forces. It seems natural for them to be similar." For a moment he looked sad. "It's good to know even far from home some things can stay the same."

She was touched by his sorrow and warmed to him a little. She thought that there were worse witches to be stranded with. "Right, then," she drained her mug. "What's this thing you need my help with?"

He grinned and his eyes brightened.

She left Skald to rest and followed Clovis to the stone circle on the hill. He immediately went to one of the huge stones and pulled away armfuls of heather to reveal something carefully hidden.

"Here it is," he said, standing aside proudly, and she went to see his secret.

A magnificent sword gleamed in the heather. It looked newly forged and the metal was a delicate blue, like sapphire-tinted silver.

"Your sword, it's beautiful," she said, clearly impressed. "But why chance leaving it here? Anyone could've taken it."

"Unlikely," he said ruefully. "That is the dilemma. Pick it up and see for yourself." He stepped back, inviting her to try.

She gave him a sceptical look, then leaned over, grasped the hilt and tugged. Nothing happened. It didn't even move by a whisker. The sword remained resolutely anchored to the ground, in fact it looked almost embedded in it.

"See?"

"Is it some magic at work?" She stroked the blade, admiring the skilful work.

"Magic not at work. The sword's special and spells are needed to keep it light enough to handle."

"I don't follow you. The sword is magic, you say?"

"No, the sword is logic, but magic lets it defy science." He faltered as he tried to explain in a foreign language. He scratched at one of his pointed ears and then he knelt by his swords and gestured for her to do the same. "The metal is steel," he said, drawing a sharp claw down the blade and making a thin whistling sound. "But inside is one single grain of gravantium-stellaria."

"And that would be?"

"It is what the heaviest stars are made from. It makes the sword weigh more than these stones around us, and gives it unstoppable power, but to counter the alloy so that the owner can lift it requires a spell."

"So you've forgotten the spell that makes the sword light enough to use?"

"Far from it!" He sounded offended. "I've repeated it endlessly. The moment I arrived my sword fell to the ground overcome by its own weight." He stroked his furred chin, "The spell doesn't work in this realm."

"I see," she finally understood. "So you need to translate your spell to appease the twins of this world, make them understand it."

"Then I'll be able to lift it!" He sounded hungry to have the weapon back.

"I can ask Hethra and Halla, the serpent-twins, to recognise your sword spell, but it'll be up to them, not me, to decide." She tried to prepare him for limited success.

"I appreciate your trying, coven-mother Algra."

She laughed. "Kolfinnia is fine, but in return I believe you owe me a tale of your coming here?"

"Then we've a late night ahead of us," he said dryly.

"This may take a while, and privacy is best."

"Indeed." He took her meaning and strode away though the heather. She heard it whip and brush against his boots until he was out of earshot and then she shifted back to the fabulous sword and readied herself with a long breath.

"Let's make a start then," she said uncertainly.

Clovis sat with Tempest a little way past the stones where they could keep and eye on the mine that had become their unofficial home.

"She was a very long time up on that sea-stack," Tempest reminded him.

"Whatever happened up there is her business. She'll share it if she needs to." He was too tired to speculate.

"She set the wand to dream, that much is certain," Tempest flexed a taloned foot and yawned.

"You sound very sure?" He was busy tapping sage into his pipe, making ready to light it.

"I should be. I dreamed of it myself while I rested this afternoon."

The pipe stem stopped just inches from his mouth. "Already? My word, if it's at work so soon then the dream'll be having followers here by tomorrow." It was meant as a jest, but seemed like a distinct possibility.

"Is she fit to command, though?"

"She's young and inexperienced, but she's also resourceful and best of all stubborn." He smiled as he remembered his own youth.

"Do you think she'll help us?"

Clovis found vengeance a good reason to go home, but not the best reason. "Maybe, but there's still this 'Rowan' to consider. Why I dreamed of a door named after her still baffles me." He looked back at the stones where Kolfinnia was presumably still working on the sword. "Tonight I'll tell her all I can, and in return I'll ask her what else she found, other than bird droppings, on the tower this morning.

If she's forthcoming I'll tell her why Janus was the cause of our coven's downfall." He sounded satisfied with his decision.

"I'll say one thing, they both fly well," Tempest complimented.

He hummed his agreement and took a long draw from the pipe. The two sat admiring the sea and before long they were talking of old friends they'd left behind.

"Clovis!" a voice called in triumph.

Both of them jumped and turned to see Kolfinnia marching in their direction cradling a gleaming sword in her arms and wearing a victorious smile that made her look all the more beautiful.

"By all the Gods!" Clovis dropped his pipe and leapt to his feet.

"You really did it!" Tempest cried.

She laughed at their amazed faces and for a moment felt like a carefree young woman again.

"I thought it was lost," Clovis shook his head in disbelief. "I tried everything." He reached out to caress the blade.

"Then it pleases me to return this to you with Hethra and Halla's blessing," she bowed and proffered the sword for him to claim.

He wrapped a powerful hand around the hilt and lifted it cleanly, lovingly turning it this way and that, letting sunlight play across the blade. "My thanks, coven-mother," he said gently, holding the sword as though it was an old friend.

"It was simple," she said modestly, but the looks of respect she got made her cheeks burn.

"Simple? I couldn't have done it." He slid the sword into its scabbard and the steel sighed against the velvet lining in what sounded like relief. "A sword like this can decide the outcome of a battle."

"I don't think you'll need it for fighting here." She gestured to empty hills, but he gave her an unsettling look.

"Those who came to destroy you, this 'Illuminata', they won't take kindly to a new coven being founded. If they hear of it they'll come and when they do," he touched his sword hilt, "I'll pay back your kindness, and their cruelty."

Later that day, Kolfinnia and Skald made a short exploration of the beach and found the skeletal remains of a small boat in the sands looking like a gutted fish. It was just a rotted frame, but the name on the bow was still legible; it read 'Kittiwake' and she knew they had the name for their new coven.

By evening she and Clovis had made the cottage tidy and weatherproof. She salvaged a couple of chairs and a broken table from one of the other buildings, hastily repaired them and used a spray of twigs to sweep the cottage clean. She mentioned her idea of making the pump-house their 'tower' and official headquarters and Clovis warmed to the idea.

When they'd finished making the place as comfortable as they could, Kolfinnia stepped out to admire the stars, and the first one she looked for was Vega. "We're coming to get you, Rowan," she promised, holding her special amulet. "And we'll bring an army with us."

The sea-stack was just a dark sword against the sunset's afterglow and she imagined the power streaming up from the Timekeeper's cavern and out into the universe, carrying hrafn-dimmu's message with it, telling the surviving witches to come.

Clovis came to the open doorway. "Food's ready," he announced then turned away, following his hunger.

"Clovis, just a moment." She beckoned him back and pointed upwards to Vega, the witch-star. "There, you can't miss them, Vega and Therion."

He looked up at his home. The sun that had warmed him since birth was just a pin-prick in the blackness. He said nothing for a long time, then finally he spoke just two words. "One day," he murmured.

They talked long into the night. She told Clovis about Rowan's miraculous talents, of the Hand-of-Fate and finally even about the Timekeeper. He listened in respectful silence thinking how in her short life she had faced gods and monsters and he felt humbled.

In return, she learned of Clovis's order of warrior-witches, charged with protecting the serpent-twins of Vega as well as acting as some kind of magical peace-keepers, and how the treachery of a witch named Acola had resulted in his coven being slain in a bloody confrontation with an organisation chillingly similar to the Illuminata known as the Unitari.

Then he revealed his coven's greatest secret, Janus, who could transport living beings through Evermore proving that death was not the end of life. He explained how he escaped with Janus and seen the miracle of souls leaving old lives and finding new ones with his own eyes. He told of seeking a door marked 'Rowan', but neither of them could explain how or why there should be such a door in the first place.

It was her first night in the newly founded Kittiwake-coven and she and Clovis blessed it with their stories and secrets.

Hathwell found the Wildwood captives wandering the yard during their last fifteen minutes of yard time. Soon they'd be locked up for the night and be served porridge and barley-crackers. The more he thought of it, the more he was convinced that prison rations were designed to break morale through boredom, and his confrontation with Krast had left him angrier than he could remember.

He arrived at the perimeter fence to find Moore's second in command at the helm. He was a stout-looking oaf with balloon features that all appeared to melt into one forgettable face and went by the name of Dobbins. Hathwell thought the name was more than fitting. "Secretary Hathwell, here under orders from Knight Superior to question the prisoners."

"As you have it," Dobbins replied without interest. "There's all but five minutes of yard time left, though."

"Then extend it until I'm done," he said brusquely. "I'd rather be out here with them than inside that." He pointed to the Fortitude and started away, not giving him a chance to agree or disagree, but he heard a tired 'as you have it' from behind.

Dobbins didn't care. If Hathwell wanted to take his chances with the witches outside of the Fortitude's protection, that was his affair. He'd heard all sorts of horrible tales, mostly from warden Moore, about witches.

'Watch yerself Dobbers, they know many a foul spell. Evil hags can make a man's 'gentleman' shrivel to the size of a walnut with just one word, I swears it,' Moore had delighted in telling him just last night. Dobbins had no intention of going through life with a walnut-sized gentleman and so he let Hathwell go on alone.

Hathwell passed through the gate, and then there was nothing between him and the witches but thin air. They stopped their aimlessly shuffling and turned to watch and he saw a girl huddled in the centre of their group. The evening was setting in, the sun had fled behind the clouds and the shadows had all bled into one gloomy mass. He heard his feet crunch over the coal slag and felt the wind's chill, then remembered that he'd left in such haste that he'd forgotten his hat and coat. "Noble knight," he growled under his breath. Now his latest duty was to spy on old women and children. *Well, I don't have to make a good job of it, do I?* he thought angrily.

He walked right up to the group, trying to ignore his complaining knee, and saw the girl slide slowly behind the oldest witch, a commanding looking woman in a pale blue dress, and the others all closed in around her. He saw the girl peep out at him from behind her and he remembered Krast's words, 'prisoners of war'. They might have toppled a company of knights, but they didn't look war-like.

Next to the oldest witch and the girl, he saw another old woman. She wore a russet coloured dress and spectacles with one blackened lens and a scowl as bitter as sloes. Two tall and striking women stood on the flanks. Both might have been about Hathwell's age and both had an undeniable beauty. The taller of the pair had fair skin and a ponytail of dark hair that almost touched the ground, and her clothes were the colour of summer heather. Her companion was dark-skinned, her hair fell below her waist in thick dreadlocks and she wore a green dress and long overcoat. Her wounded left forearm was wrapped in a grubby bandage.

As Hathwell approached, the oldest woman pushed the girl to her rear and the four adults stepped forwards like cavalry ready to charge. He stopped just a few paces short and held out his hands before letting his arms flop to his side. "I am First Secretary, Bertrand Hathwell." He tried to sound friendly.

They all looked at one another and swapped cynical smiles, except for the oldest witch: she never took her eyes off him, or more precisely, she never took her eyes from *around* him. He noticed that she appeared to be looking at something around his head. He needed some hook to get the chat going and so he took a shot at the woman in the green dress and long overcoat. "Amongst other things, I've come to make sure your wound is mending."

Lana appraised him and found him a harmless fool. "I can take care of myself."

"I'm trained in medicine," he tried again, speaking of his days as a squire.

"Then perhaps you ought to have a look at that knee of yours," the oldest witch said. Hathwell looked her way and noted that she rolled her r's slightly, and he guessed she hadn't been born in Britain.

"It's beyond medicine, I'm afraid, madam." Had he been limping badly enough for her to notice, he thought?

"Well, war will do that," she said coolly. "You should try skull-cap and valerian, it's good for such things, but I believe these days you'd be tried for witchcraft if you were found gathering those ingredients."

He didn't know what to say about her oblique reference to the protector's act and so he changed direction.
"If you agree to talk with me then we can remain outside. You won't have to go back to your cells just yet." Part of him wanted to win their trust just to annoy Krast.

Rowan tugged on Valonia's dress. "I don't want to go back. I feel sick in there."

Valonia gently patted the little hand clutching her dress. "I know what you mean little pip-staff." She looked around at her friends, "Fancy an evening out, ladies?"

"It's a lovely night," Lana said caustically and looked up to a ceiling of dirty clouds.

"A walk'd do me good. There's nowt to sit on in that cell but a teeny box. I feel like a gnome on a soddin' toadstool," Ada complained and Hathwell stifled a smile.

Hilda just stood and stared at him with mild contempt. She saw that he was flustered, and why. The thought of one of their enemies finding her attractive made her flesh crawl. "I'll take the air," she said graciously, "if our chaperon promises to behave like a gentleman."

They began a slow circuit of the perimeter fence, with Hathwell between them and the battered Fortitude. He didn't delude himself into thinking they chose his company willingly; the longer they walked with him, the less time they spent inside.

He did most of the talking, filling the silence with tales of his childhood, life in London or the foreign lands he'd seen. They said little, they never mentioned their names and he never insulted them by asking, but he still deduced much about them from the way they moved. They kept the child protected at all times. She walked hand in hand with the oldest witch, the one in blue. That a child was here at all, let alone be classed as a prisoner of war, made him feel ashamed, and so he chattered on, aware that he'd played his own small part in their capture.

"And I once caught sight of a mermaid in Denmark." He made small talk as best he could.

The girl peeped out from behind her protector. "Mermaid?" Rowan smiled.

It was the first time she'd looked at him properly, let alone spoken to him, and when he smiled down at her she darted away behind the old woman just as fast as she'd appeared.

"Forgive my friend," Valonia squeezed Rowan's hand hard, hoping the girl would bite her tongue. "Fairy tales fill her head, she's likely to say all manner of silly things!"

Well done Valonia, Lana thought.

Hathwell lost count of the number of circuits they completed, but now the arc-sodium lights were being lit and the perimeter guard were changing shift. Warden Moore returned to relieve Dobbins and he was clearly angry that Hathwell had messed up his schedule. He stood by the gantry steps, blew furiously on his whistle and waved his cudgel. He wanted the prisoners in, fed and locked up.

"We'd best be gone," Hathwell said reluctantly. Just before they came within earshot of Moore, Hathwell ventured the question that'd troubled him all summer. He took a step to Valonia's side so he could be discreet. "Madam," he started awkwardly, "forgive my asking, but what kind of magic would turn a man to stone? How would a witch do such a thing?"

At first she looked confused, then horrified. Then she saw that his clumsy question wasn't a part of his spy assignment, but rather something deeper that might even work to their advantage, and she softened. "Mr Hathwell, a witch wouldn't," she said with utter conviction, then continued onwards, clutching the girl's hand. Just as he was digesting this she turned back to him. "Oh, and Mr Hathwell, remember, skull-cap and valerian," she winked and then turned away, back to her cell.

Krast had been watching them for over an hour from the cover of the chromosite shed. He had come here without a plan and ended up skulking in the gloom and spying on his squire, who was spying for him. From inside the shed came the comforting gurgle of chromosite tanks and he wondered what Hathwell had talked about for so long.

He drew his old pocket watch and stroked the golden case. She knew something about him that he didn't even know himself, maybe something about Josephine, but to ask her outright took a courage of the kind that he wasn't sure he had, and he hated himself for it. "Titus," he sighed. He smoothed his golden watch with one hand and one of his golden scars with the other, and wondered again which path he would take.

CHAPTER TWENTY-THREE

Queen of Kittiwake

As soon as Kolfinnia had lain the wand to sleep, hrafn-dimmu's dreaming soul left its shelter and crossed the width and breadth of Britain spreading the call. Witches that escaped the Illuminata's onslaught would go to sleep one night sheltering in a hedge or barn, and awake the next day with an incredible urge to travel southwest. A great number did, but others shied away from the call, and inevitably some long-held friendships were broken.

They came from far and wide, travelling in secret, carrying pots, pans, wands and spell-bottles or in some cases nothing but the clothes they stood in. Many had lost loved ones and wanted answers or in some cases vengeance. Even the prisoners at Hobbs experienced the dream and watched the skies longingly from the confines of their prison hulks, wishing they could fly away.

For the first three days Kolfinnia could hardly sleep. She was up at all hours taking short patrols, hoping for signs of survivors, but in particular witches from Wildwood. The thought of Flora arriving was both her hope and her despair. She knew the Wildwood boats had escaped but where had they gone? Had they been intercepted or lost in stormy weather? Not knowing was an agony.

They kept busy getting Kittiwake-coven ready. She made a sortie and discovered that the nearest hamlet was over fifteen miles away: a distance that would afford Kittiwake some privacy. They placed spell bundles to deter unwanted guests, and collected driftwood as a fuel supply. She planted seeds retrieved from Wildwood's trampled gardens and Clovis dug beds to grow them in. They made provisions their top priority because neither of them knew how many witches were on their way. Clovis gathered seaweed to enrich the new gardens, while Kolfinnia blessed the seeds and brought them on just as Flora had shown her, and even though she wasn't as skilled she still managed to produce crops for drying and storing. She worked on getting the pump-house fit for their tower, first purging any unwanted energies then decorating it with anything she could find, including shells and driftwood, pebbles and feathers. It was rare for thunder-sprites to go far from their staffs, but Skald and Tempest flew alone far inland and returned with news of passing strangers or good places to forage. After all this preparation the only things missing were witches, but then on the fourth day after hrafn-dimmu was set to dream, the first survivors arrived at the newly founded Kittiwake-coven.

It was just after dawn. Kolfinnia was carrying a bucket of water back to the cottage when she saw them coming around the keel along the old packhorse trail: an old man leading a boy about Rowan's age. Without knowing how she knew they were witches.

She put her leaking bucket down in the grass, then wiped her hands and straightened. When he saw her, the boy looked fearful and the old man tugged at his hand urging him to follow. Both of them looked bedraggled and in need of rest. The old man carried a staff that may or may not have been his lightning-staff and had a bundle over his shoulder. It was all he owned besides the bewildered child clasping his hand.

Kolfinnia approached and saw he had a beard that might have once been distinguished, but was now scruffy. He wore wayfarer grey, and his long white hair was bald on top and tied in a pony tail, while the boy was delicate looking. She thought a stiff breeze would blow him over.

The man regarded her. "I had a dream," he said vaguely.

"I know." She smiled.

He looked relieved, "Laurie had it too." He patted the boy's shoulder. "We were told to come here."

"Then welcome," she said.

He looked around, as if he wasn't sure how he'd ended up here. "Where is this place?"

"Kittiwake," she said, "the last coven in Britain."

"Rowan, how are you feeling?" Valonia pressed a testing hand to the girl's brow. "You look feverish."

"I'll be fine."

"Hmm, that's not what I asked you. Tell me how you feel."

They were taking the second of their short yard breaks that day. Ada had come to call them 'ramblin' round the conker' because they had beaten a circuit around the Fortitude.

"I feel tired and scared." She looked dreadfully unhappy and her hair and her eyes were dull. "When I'm inside that cell I don't know things anymore."

"We all share the same burdens," she squeezed her cold hand.

"I wish Mr Hathwell was here," she said looking at her feet as they walked.

"Well I don't," Hilda said with distaste.

Hathwell came often and always ordered yard time to be extended. He did most of the talking and they listened, mostly in silence. Valonia liked the way he didn't give a damn about the angry glares he got from the guards. When they were locked up, the guards could play cards and drink tea, but when Hathwell came they had to stay on duty outside and they resented him for it. Hathwell hadn't come this morning during their first yard break and he hadn't come this afternoon either, and she was surprised to find that she missed him. So far nothing had happened to them since they'd arrived and that made her very uneasy. It also troubled her greatly that Krast was nowhere to be seen, but at least Hathwell's visits were a diversion.

"And don't get too used to this place or Mr Hathwell. We're not staying." Hilda was in a bad mood.

"Will Kolfinnia come for us, do you think?" Rowan asked hopefully.

They all exchanged furtive glances, and as usual it was Valonia who spoke for them. "Why would Kolfinnia come?" she asked innocently.

"To rescue us, all of us, even the witches on the prison ships out there on the river," she pointed beyond the fence towards the Thames.

"I thought they were just cargo ships," Valonia pretended.

"No, they're prisons full of witches, but there are still some free witches out there, and they're going to join Kolfinnia and Clovis, they're going to come and . . ."

"Clovis?" she interrupted.

"He's a warrior coven-father. He came from Vega running from an army just like we did. He and Kol are going to train an army of witches and come here to Hobbs Ash and take us all away!" She couldn't contain her mounting excitement.

Valonia didn't know what to say, she looked around at her stunned companions. If Kolfinnia came here, even with an army they'd be cut to pieces, but she refused to crush Rowan's small hope. "Then we best be fighting fit to help them when they get here, eh?"

Rowan grinned and looked more like her old self.

"Why didn't you tell me this before?"

She scowled at the ugly machine. "It's that thing. I don't know anything when I'm in there. That's why I like coming out, that's why I like it when Mr Hathwell comes, because we get to stay outside."

Hilda looked a little guilty. "I'm sorry, Rowan. Then I hope he comes this evening, for your sake."

Rowan looked past her to the perimeter gate and a broad smile spread across her face. "It's Mr Hathwell!"

"Remember, be careful what you say around him," Valonia warned, not liking the girl's fondness for him.

"Ha!" Ada barked. "Look at 'em!" She pointed a gnarled finger. Moore and the perimeter guards had all converged on the gate and were making a racket as Hathwell barged through.

"You've no authority to come here whenever the bloody whim takes yer!" Moore was clearly angry that yard time was going to get longer.

Hathwell spun on his heels and marched back towards him. "Knight Superior's orders," he snarled just inches from his face. "Do you have a problem with that, duty-warden?"

The large man shuffled uncertainly, and his men clustered around smelling the beginnings of a fight. "You're nothin' without Mr Krast, and we all knows it," Moore growled under his breath, and a few of his men muttered in agreement.

Hathwell was struck by a horrible realisation. *The Illuminata's made of men like this.* He sighed and Moore, taking that as a retreat, puffed out his chest, but Hathwell had no intention of retreating. He thought of the witches he'd seen executed in Solvgarad and recognised each of them as worth ten of this man.

"These Jik sluts are ours, and we do what we wants with 'em. Now be off!" Moore threatened.

It all happened so fast. He couldn't contain his anger any longer and although Moore stood four inches taller than him, he grabbed his lapels, hauled him forwards and smashed his forehead into his face. He saw a red mist erupt from Moore's broken nose. The large man buckled and dropped to the floor. Hathwell took the chance to finish him because if he didn't Moore would get up and easily thrash him. He brought his metal knee up into the underside of his chin and a firm crack rang out over the yard. Moore groaned and crashed sideways into the dust, where he lay with his eyes blinking rapidly and his mouth agape. Hathwell rounded on the idiotic guards with a roar, "Back to your posts, or it'll be correctional-blessing for all of you!"

Even Valonia, who'd said a prayer for a monster like the kelp-harpy, had to admit there was some satisfaction in seeing Moore lying in the dirt. Rowan's eyes were wide with admiration, but the old woman didn't like the way she looked at Hathwell, who was now marching over to them. "Remember, Rowan, he's not here to help us, but his master. Take care what you say around him."

She smiled to show she understood, and Valonia earnestly hoped she did.

When Hathwell reached them he was breathing heavily and inside he was boiling with anger, and not because of Moore, but because of Krast. "Madam," he offered Valonia quick bow, "I'm authorised to extend yard time for your companions, but not you."

"Really?" she asked, looking amused. She'd already guessed why he'd come. "You think I've had enough exercise for one day, Mr Hathwell? I'm not as frail as I look, you know."

He reddened and looked down at his feet. "Knight Superior has requested you join him for a private talk."

Behind him, Moore was being helped to his feet, and the rest of his rabble had formed a disciplined rank as someone important entered the compound. Valonia saw Krast stalking towards the prison machine with long purposeful strides, but he never even glanced in their direction.

"I'm sorry," Hathwell said, "but Knight Superior has asked I escort you back to your cell."

Valonia felt Hilda and the others close in. "It's alright," she assured them, "you go ahead and take the air." She fixed Hathwell with a hard stare. "Moore won't be happy, Mr Hathwell. Will my friends be safe out here?"

"I'll return to the yard and walk with them. Rest assured, nothing will harm them." He sounded like the perfect gentleman.

Until the day you're ordered to drag us to the chromosites, eh, Mr Hathwell? she thought coldly, although today she couldn't help but find his chivalry appealing. She gently passed Rowan's hand to Hilda. "Take care of her for me. It looks like I've to advise the Knight Superior on a private matter."

"Advise the bugger to choke in his sleep," Ada blurted.

He didn't say anything, but Valonia saw Hathwell's aura glow in amusement, and she thought again that this might be a man they could make an ally of. With that in mind she threaded her own arm through his. "Lead the way, Mr Hathwell," she said.

"Aye, madam."

"Call me Valonia, dear." She turned and winked at the others and flashed Rowan a parting smile.

The girl sank further into the folds of Hilda's dress and returned a feeble wave, but she didn't smile back.

Witch and squire walked arm in arm like a mother and her doting son, to meet the Illuminata's supreme commander.

They stopped a few paces shy of her cell where the open doorway threw a feeble yellow light out into the narrow corridor. "Knight Superior awaits you." He almost called her by name, but he didn't want Krast overhearing. It would feel like a betrayal and he felt bad enough as it was.

"Thank you," she said politely, as though he'd escorted her home after a night at the theatre, and stepped into the doorway.

Krast looked up from where he was sitting on a small metal stool. His elongate frame filled a good half of the cramped cell, and he smoothed his golden pocket watch with his right hand. He said nothing to Valonia, but looked past her to Hathwell. "Moore holds grudges. Make sure you don't wind up on the wrong end of a knife one dark night."

He couldn't tell if this was a friendly piece of advice or a veiled threat. "Thank you, sir," he said blandly and promised himself he'd carry his army bayonet from now on, just in case.

Krast turned to Valonia and dismissed his squire without looking at him. "Now leave us."

Hathwell made a half salute and then did as instructed.

His fingers stopped stroking the pocket-watch and curled around it into a fist. He looked out into the corridor, not sure how to begin. Valonia's aura reading was muffled by the Fortitude, but she knew without a doubt that he hadn't come here on official business.

"Be seated," he gestured to a stool opposite.

She edged past him and sat down. The cell was cramped and she was closer to him then she cared for. She folded her hands neatly in her lap and waited for him to speak.

"My apologies for leaving so abruptly the other night." He didn't sound like the same man who'd come to gloat four nights ago.

"You must be a busy man, I'm sure you have many witches to torture," she accused.

"Regrettably, information-gathering can be a trying business." He ignored her insult and gazed at his watch.

"And is this going to be one of those times, Mr Krast?"

His eyes flicked around restlessly as he made a strenuous effort not to look at her. "I hope not Ms . . ?"

"I am Valonia," she said at last.

He nodded, rocking gently as he did, digesting her name and considering what to say next. "I am looking for answers and would rather they came from you and not a chromosite," he said with effort.

"The torture creatures you breed?"

He scowled. "I wish for you and I to talk."

"And if I do not wish the same?"

She saw his jaw clench.

"Then we must talk in the company of the interrogation carriage," he concluded.

"And what would you have us talk of, Mr Krast?"

Now he'd reached the hardest part. He'd spent four days planning this and he'd never come further than this point, the bald question of what he really wanted from this woman. He wasn't sure himself and perhaps that was it, he wanted her to tell him what questions he should be asking. "What do you know of this?" He raised a hand and drew it down in front of his face.

Now she was closer she could see the scarred flesh on his face was as smooth as metal. There were no veins or wrinkles of any kind. "The marks you bear?"

He nodded slowly.

She felt like the tiger had walked up to her with a thorn in its paw and in taking it out she'd be putting herself only inches from its mouth. "Mr Krast, those marks tell the world very little, but they tell me, a witch, a great deal."

He looked at her properly for the first time. The weak electric light glistened across his scars and the face in his aura burned brighter for a moment, offering her a better look. There was a family resemblance, she thought, the same narrow face and small mouth. They looked petite on this woman while Krast wore them with hardness. "Tell you what, exactly," he regarded her with fascination, "Valonia?"

"They tell me that somebody hurt you," she chose her words with extreme care. She didn't want to indulge him, but neither did she want to provoke him. She had Rowan's safety to think of. Krast's personal demons were not her concern. "That you encountered a witch," she added tactfully.

He laughed softly and it sounded rather boyish, which surprised her. "I'm encountering one now, but that doesn't explain this," he held a hand under his chin, drawing attention to his face.

Her heart was racing. He was on the cusp of asking a question crucial to who he was, but if she answered too quickly her advantage was gone.

"What . . ." he faltered, swallowed, and readied himself to try a second time. "What happened?" He couldn't add the words: 'to me'.

She could see that he half believed he'd been the target of a spell intended to kill. What else he believed was so confused and tangled that she didn't have a hope of solving it in just the brief glimpse she'd seen. Krast was obviously a man with a tormented past. "You've spent your life convinced that this witch tried to kill you," she said quietly.

He said nothing, but sat rooted to his seat and listened.

She saw his pale eyes widen and wondered if this was wise. Would he have any further use for them once he had what he wanted? Then it would only be a matter of time before Rowan was questioned with a chromosite. When that happened Hethra and Halla were as good as lost. "What I see here," she copied his hand movement, drawing her own hand over her face, "is not what you think it to be, Mr Krast."

He slowly began to sit up straight, pulling away from her a little.

"If you tell me the 'how', Mr Krast, perhaps I can enlighten you as to the 'what'." She wanted get him to do the talking. Each day she delayed him bought Kolfinnia another day to strengthen her coven.

He toyed with his lip as he considered this. She tried hard to explore the images in his aura, but the metal walls seemed to radiate interference.

"You've given me much to think about, I shall consider this." He wasn't ready.

He stood up slowly, looking to grow from the stool rather than rise from it, and his rounded skull almost brushing the cell's metal roof. He smoothed his hands purposefully down the front of his dark suit.

Valonia tried to catch whatever scraps she could from his aura, but the colours were mingled and the shapes fragmented. "What's your reason, Mr Krast? Why do you hate witches so much?"

His aura flickered like a broken light.

"So many questions, Valonia," he said amiably, then frowned as if he was listening to a voice only he could hear. "I look forward to our next meeting."

He stepped out into the corridor and she heard his feet clang over the metal floor and thought of the kraken's pounding feet trampling her home.

Kolfinnia's first arrivals were from Red-Shawl coven in Devon. Of a total of fifteen, Walter and his grandson Laurie were the only survivors. They'd been tending reed beds when they'd heard the assault. Walter confessed that he'd grabbed his grandson and fled, leaving everyone else behind. At first they had no plan, taking their chances and travelling mostly by night, then the dream had come and he was powerless to follow it.

Walter was ashamed of running out on his coven, but Kolfinnia couldn't blame him. She gave them the neighbouring cottage where they found floor space to lay their blankets. She reminded Walter and his grandson that Kittiwake would only be a true coven if they all did their share of work. There were gardens to prepare, spells to make, firewood to gather and new shelters to be erected and they threw themselves into the work with gusto. She expected a stream of survivors, and Walter and Laurie were hopefully only the tip of the iceberg.

"What do you think?" She asked Clovis. Now their conversations were held in equal parts English and Pegalia. Clovis was a fast learner.

"There'll be many more like him, people just looking for refuge. If I were you I'd think twice about rescuing Rowan."

She couldn't believe her ears. "Are you serious, after all I've told you? Have you considered the damage they could do with her skills? It's nothing short of what your enemies could achieve with Janus!"

He held up his hands to stop her. "If Valonia and her Wards are half of what you've told me then I think she's safe enough with them."

He pointed to where Walter sat astride the cottage roof repairing slates. The day was warm for late September and he'd taken his shirt off while he worked. He was thin and his ribs showed like a toast rack. "Kolfinnia, look at the man," he said softly.

She looked. Walter threw her a wave and she felt a selfish pang that it wasn't Flora. Where were they, the Wildwood witches? It was a thought that dogged her every waking moment.

"Walter's skin and bones," he continued. "He might be a devoted witch, but could you see him holding a lightning-staff in battle?"

She leaned against the cottage wall, knowing she had a bitter pill to swallow. She couldn't turn refugees into warriors. Clovis was right. "I want her back," she whispered tearfully.

"And you will, but Kittiwake is your first duty, just as Rowan is Valonia's first duty."

She looked at him, searching for answers.

"Give them a home first," he advised. "Win their love and then they'll follow you anywhere."

"There's no time!" she despaired.

"Then make Kittiwake as strong as possible. Leave someone you trust in charge and lead a small group to rescue her." He tapped a claw against his sword hilt, "I for one will accompany you."

"Thank you." She was deeply moved by his offer. Then without thinking she embraced him and if he could have blushed he would have.

Walter began a trickle that became a flow. Kolfinnia found herself greeting new arrivals at all hours and the first thing she asked for was news of Wildwood. Each time Walter told her that someone was approaching she hoped it would be Wildwood, but she was always disappointed. Perversely, the more survivors that arrived the more alone she felt, and they all came with similarly tragic stories of fleeing or missing loved ones. Some of the new arrivals roughed it, sleeping outside in makeshift shelters. Others bunked in the engine-shed, hanging up blankets or whatever to make screens and provide a little privacy.

Kolfinnia charged Walter with keeping an eye on rations. As more witches arrived the supply was constantly being re-appraised, but Walter was good with numbers and juggling lists. There was just enough to go around and most of the arrivals were skilled enough to call food from the gardens, but Kittiwake remained a whisker away from poverty. And although nobody said anything, Kolfinnia suspected that some found this a poor reward for following a dream they believed had promised so much.

It had to happen eventually. Kolfinnia's first confrontation over her authority came with Walter of all people, and a rather ugly one it was too.

"All I'm saying is the spell-bottles need to be further out, make the coven area bigger." He took exception to the way she'd placed the concealing charms, insisting that they spread them wider.

"Walter, for the tenth time, that'll weaken the bonds between each charm. It won't provide an adequate protection."

"Was that the way you did it at Wildwood?" He said this every time she gave an order. Since arriving he'd recovered some of his self-esteem and Kolfinnia decided she preferred him when he was a little more humble.

"It worked there well enough," she said cautiously.

"Until the knights came along."

She heard a few onlookers mutter their agreements.

"You know as well as I do that spells alone won't stop krakens. The charms protect the coven from casual passers, and they stay where they are and we fly sorties to protect our boundary. Keen eyes are better than charms alone." She struggled to master her anger, trying hard to be like Valonia.

"Plenty of sharp eyes here," he smirked, and cast a glance at the gathering crowd.

"Meaning what?"

"Nothing, coven-mother," he said graciously and even bowed.

It looked mocking, she thought. "My order stands, Walter, and in the meantime," she turned to the crowd, "if anyone has a complaint about the way Kittiwake is run, I'll be in the tower." She stormed away, hoping they wouldn't see how upset she was.

Kittiwake's ranks had swollen to forty-nine, and two dogs. There were enough of them now to make a simple command structure. Some patrolled the surrounding countryside, others worked the gardens and collected ingredients for spells and medicines, and of course everyone took part in saying sleep-spells for Hethra and Halla.

What they thought of Clovis was anyone's guess. Nobody dare ask the fearsome warrior where he was from, but Clovis reminded them all of that mythic time when humans and other races shared the Earth. Little Laurie took a real shine to him. He followed him around, asking to see his sword, nagging him to teach him how to fight, but most demeaning of all he often wanted to stroke his mane.

'Tempest will be getting jealous!' Kolfinnia had joked.

'It's like being pursued by amalga again!' he'd complained, but secretly loved the attention.

Clovis had a quiet chat with Kolfinnia one night. They now shared their cottage with a dozen others and it was getting so crowded that she considered sleeping in the tower. They took a late stroll along the beach to find some privacy. The moon was bright and the sea-stack was just a black shape against the horizon. He found that he loved the sea. His original home had been landlocked and he'd never seen the ocean before now and it had quickly cast a spell on him.

"I think it best for now that we don't say anything of Vega." He didn't want to have to explain to everyone about Janus.

"I agree. There was a time when humans and Therions lived side by side."

"Therions?" He didn't grasp the English term.

"Races not like men," she explained politely. "There used to be whole nations of them, or so I'm told, fabulous beings just like you."

"Fabulous?" he purred approvingly.

She looked away, embarrassed. "Walter keeps asking where you're from. I hope you don't mind but I remembered what Valonia said of her homeland, I said you were from there."

"And where would that be exactly?" He liked the chance to play-act.

"A place called 'Iceland'."

"A nice place?"

"It's surrounded by the sea and covered in fiery mountains and rivers of ice, and there are countless waterfalls, and lakes." She remembered Valonia's love for her home.

"You make me homesick for a land I've never visited." He was beginning to take to this world.

They walked in silence for a while.

"Clovis, when will they come?" she asked eventually.

He stopped. "Wildwood? I wish I could tell you."

"I've been thinking, I could visit him again," she glanced sheepishly towards the sea-stack. "He could tell us where they were."

He looked out to the miraculous tower. "You know you won't, and I for one would not enter that chamber, even for the chance to go home. Some questions are best left unanswered." They continued again and when he took a deep breath she knew he was about to say something important. "The time's coming when you should decide what to do about Rowan."

"I know, but I can't see any of them volunteering to rescue a girl they don't know. And as yet I can't think of anyone I'd want to leave in charge." She felt silly now, thinking of how she'd initially hoped to raise an army. It was reckless and romantic and it would have resulted in many deaths.

"You'll have to put them in a fighting mood sooner or later. Before long the Illuminata will come. Tell them that, Kolfinnia, and tell them unless they want to run forever they should learn some fighting skills and spells."

She shivered. The idea of harming spells was anathema to witchcraft. "They won't do it, Clovis. Witches aren't warriors."

"I am," he stopped, "and your Wildwood companions were."

"Understand that was something we were forced to do. Nobody took any joy from killing those knights."

"How many did you kill?"

She flinched. "I'm not sure," she said crossly. "The point is I didn't train or want to do it."

"And a fine job you made of it from what you told me."

"I wasn't boasting!"

A light glowed at the top of her staff and she looked up to see Skald appear, interested in their debate.

"I'd have been outraged if you had," he said gently. "Make them understand that spells of defence aren't something evil. On Vega we say 'people find what they look for'. It means we have the choice. If the Illuminata come – do you want them to find witches who'll surrender without a whimper, or fight to the death? It is your choice."

"I agree with Clovis," Skald interrupted, "and once they've learned a few fighting spells, a rescue mission won't sound so hopeless."

She had learned over the last two weeks to take criticism without offence. It was tough but vital, and this was one of those times. She

306

regarded Skald. "Would Valonia agree?"

"You saw how she defended Wildwood."

She thought on this as they walked along listening to the rhythmic surf. "Well, if Kittiwake's to ready its defences, I think you already have your first recruit, Clovis."

He tilted his head in question.

"Little Laurie," she smirked.

Kolfinnia established routines as soon as she could. Getting the coven self sufficient was paramount, but after a couple of weeks she wanted to implement the kind of routines common at Wildwood. But some of the others didn't like it. It was again Walter who spoke against her. They butted heads over her request to put aside offerings for the birds. They were standing in the gardens, and again there were plenty of spectators to see their disagreement.

"Birds can fend for themselves!" He made her suggestion sound trite, but she was coven-mother and had to stand her ground.

"If we give a little back to Hethra and Halla, then they'll pass their blessing onto us. What you put out comes around."

"So you want me to tell the folks working hard to grow food to scatter it for the birds?" He had an annoying habit of always sounding assured.

"We're only talking of a handful of produce. It's an offering, Walter, a gesture. I'm not suggesting folks go hungry."

"Still," he smoothed his beard, which was now manicured and neat. "It's a charming idea, Kolfinnia, but it's not practical." He made an annoying 'tut' sound.

She stung at not being addressed as coven-mother. "Walter, this is the way Kittiwake will be run. It was founded by my own coven-mother's wand and I was the one who cast it." She spoke loud enough for everyone to hear. "I'd remind all here that traditions are to be respected. My wand, my coven, my rules."

"A coven works for the well of all, not its mother or father alone," he lectured.

She was very angry now, and all eyes were on her. "Did you have your own coven's well-being at heart when you deserted your fellows?" She couldn't stop the cruel words, neither could she stop the satisfaction they brought.

His expression hardened and he gave her a spiteful look. She felt ashamed for attacking him where he was weakest, but she remembered the knights, the gunfire and battle. She'd stood firm then and she stood firm now. "These are my orders, Walter, and they will be respected." She didn't wait for an answer, but turned and marched away.

"Bloody Walter," she seethed as she strode along, head down, not wanting to look at any of Kittiwake's witches. *My witches*, she reminded herself bitterly.

"Kolfinnia," Clovis jogged after her. She heard his soft footfalls and his armour rattle. "There are more witches come, they're in the courtyard."

"Wildwood?" She asked hopefully.

"I only saw them from a distance, but they arrived riding on a creature's back."

"Creature?" She suddenly thought of a dragon.

"Four legs, long tail, big ears."

Her shoulders sagged. "A horse, Clovis. It's called a horse."

"I'd greet them, but I have to prepare for this morning's defence class."

"I'll go," she said reluctantly.

She wanted to speak to Skald about Walter, but welcoming new witches was priority, she just hoped that these newcomers would be wise and willing. She couldn't stomach any more trouble causers.

She hurried between the pump-house and the mine, where she could hear hammers at work inside as people made bunk quarters for new arrivals. She skipped over the rusty rails and between redundant wagons still loaded with ore, and rounded the corner and into the cobbled yard. There before her was a lithe figure with a flash of red hair. He was tending a white horse, and when he turned her way she recognised him.

"Farona?" she said to no one. It was him, and that could mean only one thing. She smiled at him, even as icy fingers squeezed her heart. Farona blinked, not trusting his eyes, then a huge grin spread over his face. She approached with a fixed smile. "No, don't let her be here. Please, oak and holly, don't let her be here!" she pleaded quietly.

Another figure, taller and more elegant and again clothed in grey, stepped aside from the horse and Kolfinnia saw her pale skin, and her hair shine like ripe wheat. Dazzling blue eyes turned in her direction and perfect lips turned up into a beautiful but insincere smile. "No!" she groaned, but it was her. Kittiwake had a new queen. It was Sunday.

She walked over with a practised smile and a heavy heart. Sunday looked up, but her face remained as fixed as a portrait. "Sunday, Farona, I'm overjoyed to see you alive and well." Kolfinnia had a vivid deja-vu of an almost identical meeting just a few months before when the world was a happier place.

Sunday didn't seem at all surprised to see her. "I'm sorry we're not meeting again under happier circumstances, Kolfinnia." She looked tired, but as radiant as ever.

At last we agree on something, she thought. Sunday swept her long coat open and started brushing horsehair from her grey trousers, which were muddy and creased. While she did her best to preen her drab clothes, Kolfinnia took the chance to give her attendant a more personal welcome. She hugged him hard, genuinely pleased to see him. "Farona, I'm glad you made it."

He hugged her back fiercely. "It's been a nightmare," he whispered into her ear. She didn't know if he meant running away or enduring Sunday's company. "How many have made it?"

"At last count over fifty, including yourselves."

"It's a lot for a single coven, I suppose," he said, but in truth that was a very small number. "Has, erm, has Miss Flora come with you?"

Her expression killed his hope, and Sunday finally looked up from adjusting her clothes. "Well?" she prompted. "Who came from Wildwood?"

Kolfinnia steeled herself. "Most of them escaped and Flora was amongst them, but so far none have arrived."

"You were separated from them?" she asked.

Kolfinnia sighed and nodded.

"So you're Wildwood's sole survivor?"

"For now."

"And what of your young friend," Sunday said delicately, meaning Rowan.

For a moment Kolfinnia didn't speak and they all read the worst from her silence.

"She was killed?" Sunday asked, appalled, but when Kolfinnia shook her head her frown deepened further.

"Five I know of were taken by the Illuminata," Kolfinnia managed.

"No! You mean Rowan?"

She mistook Sunday's horror as concern. "Yes," she managed.

"And what of the others?"

"Valonia and her companions stayed by choice to buy us time to escape. When they learned Rowan had been captured they went to rescue her, but they were taken prisoner. Rowan's Ward, Esta, was killed trying to save her." Her angry words with Walter seemed insignificant now.

"Dear Oak," Farona muttered in despair.

"But what of you?" Kolfinnia moved on quickly.

Sunday's expression darkened, "The day they came we were just setting out to pay our respects to Crow-Shilling's coven-father. He'd died unexpectedly."

"If we'd have left an hour later we'd have run into them," Farona said angrily, as though he regretted missing the fight.

Sunday had learned what she wanted and now fatigue was catching up. She wiped the last of the horsehair and dirt from her hands, then she smiled casually. "Now, is it possible to meet the one whose wand brought us here?"

"You just have. I cast Valonia's wand." She readied herself for a stinging comment, but Sunday just made a tiny sound of surprise and then tipped her a small bow. As soon as she did Farona replayed her gesture. She felt a little embarrassed but knew she had to say something grand. "Kittiwake-coven is blessed by your presence." Her greeting was short but she was surprised to find that she actually meant it.

"Kittiwake?" Sunday raised an eyebrow, "A beautiful name."

"I hope you think the same after you've seen the place."

"It'll suffice, I'm sure, and I'll be glad to be back around workers of magic. The rest of the world is barbaric." Sunday found she didn't care how rough Kittiwake might be. After sleeping under trees and in draughty barns, all she wanted now was a good rest.

"There's a churchyard that way, Farona. It'll do as a paddock." Kolfinnia pointed.

"Right away, miss." He led the mare away to where she could find some well earned grazing.

"This way please," she invited and they made their way over the cobbled yard.

Sunday's eyes were everywhere, evaluating everything, and Kolfinnia expected a hail of sarcastic remarks to hit her like well aimed rocks any moment, but the solstice queen remained strangely silent and Kolfinnia wondered why, never guessing that Rowan occupied her thoughts.

She deliberately led them through the gardens. They were coming along nicely and she was proud of them.

They were defended from the winds by an embankment of mine waste, overgrown with nettles and sea holly. Several witches looked up from their work to watch them pass. Sunday thought they had a lost look about them, and she fumed that workers of magic were living as refugees when it was their efforts that protected the serpent-twins. Kolfinnia felt nervous as she always did when new arrivals came. Even though they might be exhausted, she couldn't help but wonder whether they were appraising her efforts with a critical eye.

The gardens were their priority and each new arrival was allocated a patch of ground. One witch called Clarissa Kale was almost as adept as Flora. She'd brought a dozen apple pips with her and now they had a dozen fruit trees. It was those kinds of witches she needed, not the likes of arrogant Walter.

"Impressive gardens," Sunday complimented.

"This was all derelict when we arrived. It's been our priority. With Hethra and Halla's blessing, we'll have fruits and vegetables right through the winter," she said proudly.

"So who is this 'we'?" Sunday asked.

"This coven was founded by two witches. I'm just one of them. I'll introduce you to the coven-father as soon as I get chance." She wondered how she was going to explain Clovis, while Sunday was already wondering if the coven-father was young and handsome. "And here he is," she announced grandly, "Clovis Augmentrum, our coven-father. And while his English improves daily, it might be best to introduce you in Pegalia."

Clovis was on his way to his first session of weapons practice and many had signed up to learn some fighting skills. It troubled Kolfinnia that a lot of them had vengeance in mind, but for now she held her peace.

As they drew closer she could see that he'd polished his armour and was carrying his staff and sword. Tempest sat on his shoulder, bathing his armour with a peculiar emerald light and the effect was stunning. Clovis looked magnificent, reminding Kolfinnia of a noble lion. His face was a mask of determination and his ears were pricked forwards looking like horns. His ragged left ear only added to his appearance. He'd combed his mane until it was silky and luxurious and plaited his beard. His great whiskers flared from his muzzle like a fabulous moustache. When he saw Kolfinnia he smiled, and his impressive teeth came into view and his golden eyes sparkled.

"You look to be in a good mood," she observed, aware of Sunday's stunned silence. It was petty, but she couldn't help but be proud of him. Any coven with a witch like this was a coven to be reckoned with.

"It's been too long since I used a sword," he beamed.

"Clovis, I'd like you to meet out latest arrivals." She swept an arm towards Sunday's party, where Farona was just catching them.

"Sunday Flowers, and Farona Firecrest, of Regal-Fox coven." She made the introductions, and watched her new guests carefully.

Farona was speechless while Sunday no longer looked tired. She stepped forward and bent to kiss his hand. "Coven-father Clovis," she gushed.

Clovis swapped a puzzled look with Kolfinnia who just smiled knowingly. If he'd not been blessed with thick fur she'd have seen him blush. "Miss Flowers," he said awkwardly. "And Master Farona." Their names sounded endearingly clumsy on his tongue.

"Coven-father." Sunday still clasped his hand, and stared him directly in the eye while she gently massaged his fingers. "I've long wanted to meet a witch who agrees that magic is a cause worth fighting for," she said, in fluent Pegalia. Kolfinnia didn't like the seductive tone of her voice: if she couldn't exploit a physical attraction, she'd win his heart.

"A worthy cause, to be sure." He could sense some animosity between her and Kolfinnia, and so he chose his words carefully. "But fighting is always a last resort."

"I sense there's much we could learn from one another, coven-father," she let her fingers glide over his fur, down to his clawed fingertips where she finally let go.

"We can all learn from each other," he said, feeling uncomfortable. Farona just grinned broadly, liking him already and no wonder, for he made people feel safe. Sunday smiled prettily and looked the picture of innocence. "Now, if you'll excuse us, Tempest and I have witches to train." Clovis marched off to the courtyard, where young and old were gathering to take their first lesson.

Sunday watched him leave. "Magnificent," she breathed softly.

Clovis looked back and found the disconcerting young woman still watching him. He was a predator and he recognised she was equally predatory. He just hoped her loyalty was to magic and not herself.

CHAPTER TWENTY-FOUR

The Revelation of Samuel Krast

As autumn deepened the nights grew in strength. Miles around Hobbs Ash there was nothing but brick and iron. Even the Thames was devoid of life, except for the occasional child scouring the mud, looking to earn a penny from what trinkets they could salvage.

Valonia looked out through fence posts and sharpened wire and wondered again how people could live so separate from growing things. There wasn't a shred of green at Hobbs. Even the ground was a blackened mess, scalped and pounded flat. She was starting to lose track of the days, something that would have been unthinkable at home, but here nothing changed apart from the rust that crept slowly down the Fortitude's hull. "Oh, Skald," she sighed, wishing again for something that couldn't be.

"Valonia?" Rowan came to her side, draped in her blanket, shielding from the rain. She pressed against the old witch, who folded her arms around her. "Why are they doing this to us?" the girl asked.

"I wish I knew."

She hadn't seen Krast for over a week. His fascination with them kept them from being taken to the chromosites. At that thought she spared a glance to the prisons hulks and wondered what torments their occupants suffered.

Lana, Hilda and Ada all stood under the Fortitude out of the rain.

"You'll get wet out here. Why not join the others?" She didn't want Rowan catching her melancholy.

She shook her head, "I want to stay with you."

"It's almost time to go back in."

"No it's not. Mr Hathwell's on his way again."

Valonia looked around but she didn't see him, only Moore scowling at them from the gate. His nose was still misshapen and bruised.

"When he comes," Rowan's arms tightened around her, "he wants you to go inside and talk with the tall man."

Valonia's heart jumped: Krast was coming. But she shielded her worries. "You like Mr Hathwell, don't you?"

She looked up. "He brought his own medicines and looked at Lana's arm."

"I know. He's been kinder than most." But she knew that despite his sympathies Hathwell was never just going to open the gate and let them all run off, not even Hilda, for whom he held quite an attraction. It was all there in his aura. *Still, she thought, one day he might find his courage.* She just hoped they were all still alive if he did.

"He doesn't like the tall man, really. He's afraid of him," Rowan said from nowhere.

"Huh! With good reason!"

"Krast is angry all the time," Rowan sounded sad.

Valonia held her breath. Dare she ask? "Do you know why he's angry all the time?" she ventured, knowing she might only have minutes to find out.

"It's because he thinks she tried to kill him. Or wants to think that, because it makes him feel less bad about what he did to her. But making the lie real is so hard and he's spent his life lying, not living." Valonia listened, rapt, while Rowan's gaze strayed to the gate and the sadness on her face was replaced by a shy smile. "It's Mr Hathwell," her smile quickly melted, "and he's with him."

She saw Hathwell approaching while Krast went to the Fortitude's gantry. In response Lana and the others moved out of its shelter, as though he sent a poisonous vapour before him.

"I've some business to attend to, Rowan. Wait with Hilly, please. And thank you, what you've told me was most useful."

Rowan looked up at her, pleased to have been a help, and without a word she slipped her hand free and went to stand with Hilda. Hathwell marched towards them through a rash of small puddles, looking gloomy and with Moore's wrathful stare burning against his back.

"He's still not happy with you," Valonia warned.

"I'm ready." He thought of the bayonet under his coat. "Besides, men like that aren't happy unless they're making others unhappy," he noted sourly.

"You talk like a witch," she said playfully. "Have you come to make me happy or unhappy today, Mr Hathwell?" She saw his aura dance in agitated shafts; it was clear he was far from happy himself.

"Knight Superior requests your presence."

She looked past his shoulder and saw Krast vanish into the machine's underbelly. He looked like a hermit crab scuttling into an abandoned shell. "Very well then," she sighed.

Valonia was escorted back to her cell while Hathwell remained with the others. After his fight with Moore he was loathed to leave them unattended, although something told him that they could probably handle themselves. He watched her leave, then took his usual stroll with them whether they wanted him to or not. He talked, they listened, and Krast lurked inside the Fortitude where he would have Valonia all to himself.

She found her cell just as it had been on his first visit: two small stools, one in each corner, with barely enough room for their knees not to touch.

As before, he was already sitting poised and thoughtful. She shuffled into her corner, careful not to touch him, and sat down with her hands on her knees. His head was inclined towards the wall where she had kept herself amused over the weeks by scratching knot-work patterns on the metal with a sliver of slate. He admired the intricate patterns and followed the loops and knots with an appraising eye. "Like life, all patterns are connected somehow," he said distantly.

"The pattern reminds us that all things return to their origins," she elaborated, even though she thought wisdom was wasted on this man.

His head rocked in a vague agreement. "It is of origins that I come to see you about, Valonia," he sighed, and the breath in his nose sounded like scales on parchment. "You said that if I was to tell you the How you could enlighten me as to the What."

"I remember."

He swallowed loudly. "Then I'll start by telling you of the How." He raised his hands, backs to Valonia to indicate the strange golden scars.

He looks calm, she thought. *He thinks the past can be easily locked away again with a few simple answers.*
She knew otherwise however. She knew that once demons escaped their boxes it took unimaginable strength to kill them.

"The How," he pondered in a small voice.

She saw him looking back down the years, perhaps to a time when he was quite a different man. His lips were pressed tight as he concentrated, but after a few moments they slowly parted and hung limp. He unlocked that forbidden box in his mind, fully this time, and when he looked inside he saw nothing but the past, not even Valonia.

As he slipped away from her, his aura faded to almost nothing and his stare penetrated the years one by one until he saw every detail of that day almost forty years ago, and when he spoke he sounded young again. He was the man before the Knight Superior: he was Samuel.

"Samuel!" His father ordered, and he jumped to obey.

Titus Krast was an imposing man.

"Sir." Samuel, a young man with a sensitive face and a head of thick black curls, stood to attention outside the interrogation room door. He understood his father's command, but his heart galloped ahead as if trying to run from it. "I don't know if I can, sir." He'd called his father 'sir' his whole life and it was nothing to do with them both being in the Illuminata's ranks.

Knight Commander Titus Krast looked down at his son with shame. Samuel saw the disgust on his face and knew, without even being aware of it, that he'd go through life surrounded by that contempt. Titus clamped his son's arm with a huge hand, more used to hauling on the controls of a kraken than showing affection. In his other hand he produced a golden pocket-watch. The metal was as yellow as butter and engraved with a dragon and a unicorn chained to a thunderbolt. "What I demand of you is more than just initiation. Family honour is at stake," his eyes rolled meaningfully towards the interrogation room.

"I understand, sir. I just don't know if I can," he pleaded as he backed up against the tunnel wall.

They were in the master's gallery where Krast and Holloway would square the Maccrae business in forty years time.

"If you don't, she'll be executed and her soul will be damned," Titus gave him a firm shake. "Before you can claim this," he dangled the pocket-watch, "she must be blessed and freed of her delusions, no matter the cost."

"Please." Tears streamed down his face.

Ashamed that this boy was his son, Titus lashed out and slapped him. "Does your family name mean nothing to you?" he roared, no longer sounding like his father but a beast caught in a trap.

Josephine was that trap. The woman he'd married was proven to be a witch and unless she either begged repentance or died under correctional-blessing, the Krast bloodline would be stricken from the Illuminata forever. It never occurred to Samuel that his father was forcing him to pay for his mistakes. Sobbing, Samuel raised a reluctant hand and curled his fingers around the watch suspended from his father's fist. When he pulled it free of his grip, Titus exhaled.

"Commendable fellow," he sounded satisfied and patted his son's shoulder firmly. "Commendable fellow, Samuel. Now go, set her free."

He slid sideways along the wall and out of his father's shadow towards the interrogation room with the watch swinging from his fist as though it was no more than a fairground trinket.

The interrogation room was a stone octagonal chamber illuminated by gas burners that radiated harsh light as bitter as lemons. Josephine Krast sat strapped into the blessing chair at the room's centre, and a trolley lined with blessing tools lurked close by like a vulture. She was a fined-boned woman, striking if not traditionally beautiful, with pale eyes and the same dark curls as her son. She'd led the life of an ambassador's daughter in India. But now she sat in a filthy smock, strapped into a wooden chair that had soaked up the last torments of many witches. She regarded him with disbelief. "Titus sent you?" She was stunned that her husband had passed on this duty to their son.

He dried his eyes. "Mother," he said weakly. He wanted to say so much, but then realised that the watch dangling from his hand probably spoke volumes and he quickly fumbled it into his pocket. His mother had never wanted him to join the Illuminata. "Father says this will be simple if you just denounce witchcraft," he mumbled.

"And if I don't?" she managed.

He clasped his hands to his chest pleadingly, "Then the Knights Illuminata will try you as a witch-spy and execute you. There's nothing he can do to save you. You have to do this yourself."

She looked beyond the iron door and could almost see Titus standing in the tunnel outside. Could he hear her, she wondered? She hoped he could. "I shall strive to be truthful," she said loudly. Titus could have spirited her away, denounced the Illuminata, divorced or exiled her even. Any of those would have been better than this, but he wouldn't endure the shame; he'd rather see her die in the blessing chair.

The 'truth' was the reason this blessing was being held in secret, and conducted by a Krast upon a Krast. There were no other correctionals present.

"I'm proud to say your father knowingly married me, a witch, *before* he rose through the ranks of this foul organisation," she shouted towards the door.

Samuel looked scared. News such as this would ruin their name, and Titus had done so much to raise them from obscurity. He scuttled across the empty room towards her, his eyes looking all over for prying devices. "Shhh!" he begged. "It's dangerous to say such things!" He crouched at her feet and looked up into the face of the woman who'd brought him into the world. "Denounce witchcraft and accept blessing."

It was so simple to him, but he was young and he didn't see the ancient conflict between witches and their dark counterparts. "Just say the word," he shuffled closer.

"And he's sent you to do this?" she said scornfully.

"Just denounce witchcraft and I can sign the confession."

Titus has taken him from me, she thought in dismay, not recognising the young man at her feet despite their shared eyes and thick hair. "What has he done to you, Samuel?" Her words melted into tears.

He felt a flash of anger. This was a dilemma contrived by the Devil himself and God knew he was doing his best. "I'm trying to help you leave this room, but you must help me."

She ignored him and began to cry freely. Her husband had twisted their son into a vision of himself. She'd lost both of them.

"Please stop!" He climbed to his feet and sympathy gave way to exasperation and finally anger. "Mother! I demand you stop this and see reason."

He sounded so much like his father, rigid and logical, but she continued to wail and he felt the first tremor of panic. If she chose the hard way he wasn't sure he could do it, yet his father waited outside and he couldn't leave until the deed was done. He was being torn apart.

"Samuel," she pleaded, "what has he done to you?"

In fear, he snatched up one of the blessing tools from the trolley, trying to show her the consequences rather than with any thought of using it. He clutched a luminare, a steel shaft tipped with a crystal lens used to examine the eye. It quivered in time with his trembling hand. "This can be avoided," he took a step forwards, hoping the luminare would to make her see sense.

She shrank back into the chair and he was stunned by the fear on her face: fear of him. Did she really believe he was capable of this? In truth, he didn't know himself.

Her eyes were red with tears, her mouth clung onto a scream, and blood pounded at her temples. He moved closer, aware that his body was doing things that his heart would never be ready for. He saw the luminare move towards her right eye, and for an instant he believed he was strong enough to do this after all. As he closed in on her, her mouth finally burst open and her scream echoed around the room. "Samuel! No!"

At the sound of her scream, the real Samuel fled to the furthest corner of his mind, leaving his numb body still bearing down on her, determined to begin the blessing. Her head flapped side to side to avoid the device and he saw one of his hands reach out and clasp her head firmly.

As his fingers clamped around her chin, two things happened: one was that Samuel realised he could do this if he stayed hidden from his conscience, and the other was that Josephine realised that her son was going to obey his father.

She wanted to scream, but instead, enraged by betrayal, an involuntary flood of raw power exploded out of her. "NO!" she screamed again, almost breaking the restraints as she convulsed.

He was hit by the blast and thrown backwards. The luminare clattered away and the crystal lens shattered. He crashed against the wall, the wind was punched from his lungs and he felt his face and hands burn.

Her head slumped to her chest and she saw Samuel and the room at a drunken angle. He was cowering on the floor with his face behind his hands. She thought the screaming was hers, but it was her son's, and now despairing at what she'd done she wished for the end to come.

Behind his agonised cries, she heard the sound of metal scrape on metal. The door was opening, and there was only one person who would walk through it. A hulking shadow loomed over her, blotting out the gaslight: it was Titus, bellowing in rage. She could feel his hot breath on her face and spittle fleck her cheeks, but his words, and the room with all its shame and fear, began to dissolve and she knew her time to walk Evermore had come.

Samuel looked up from behind his hands and saw his mother slumped in the chair with Titus hunched over her like a ghoul, his shirt pasted to his back by sweat, shouting into her face. He crawled to his feet and noticed through the tears that his hands looked different. Was it dirt from the floor, he wondered? He rubbed them against his shirt, absurdly fixed on this tiny problem while his world collapsed around him, but rubbing at the marks had no effect whatsoever. Patches of his skin glittered like newly minted sovereigns. He scrubbed at them in panic, desperate to return to normal, but the part of him that had hidden and permitted betrayal realised that these marks would never fade and nothing would be normal again.

From then on, the only way to live was to live the lie. All witches had to be guilty to make Josephine guilty. If not, the lie would fall apart and this twisted philosophy sank deeper and deeper into his bones until at last it became him utterly.

Titus Krast ordered the master's gallery sealed shut. The tunnels under Goldhawk were left for the river and the rats, and the memory of Josephine Krast was walled away, until a witch named Eliza Cobb found her again forty years later.

Knight Superior Krast looked down at his hands. Age had puckered his skin, but the scars, with that hint of newly minted gold, remained. As he finished he half expected the world to shatter right there and then, but all he heard was Valonia's steady breathing.

"And that is the How." He spoke to the wall, finding it easier to look at.

She watched his eyes grow sharp again as he poured back into his body like water into an empty vessel. She recognised it as a witch technique, but she doubted very much if Krast knew he was also a witch.

The wall lost its fascination for him and he turned to face her squarely. After months of torment beginning with Eliza Cobb, the old Krast reasserted himself. He was Knight Superior of the Illuminata, and she was a worthless old woman that he could have killed in a hundred different ways. "I believe that answers to What are now in order," he insisted.

Countless ways of telling him he was a traitor-witch raced through her mind, but she knew she wouldn't lie. "What happened to you was not what you believe. This," she indicated his scars by raising her hands; backs to him, just as he'd done, "was not her attempt to kill you."

He sat fascinated and slave to her every word. Shock and denial would come later, but for now he was all hers.

"She marked you, so that other witches would recognise you for what you are."

"And what am I?" He sounded like a drowsy serpent charmed by a tune, but one that wouldn't last much longer.

She had reached the molten core of who he was, and any time she'd bought over the last few weeks was probably at an end. "You are a witch, Mr Krast, a witch who betrayed his own."

Outside the Fortitude, Hathwell circled with Lana and Ada while Hilda deliberately lagged behind with Rowan. Ada was doing a fine job of keeping Hathwell busy, battering him with endless facts about gardens in a way that only she could. Lana trailed at her side wearing an amused expression and almost felt sorry for Hathwell, who visibly stooped under Ada's assault.

"Mr Hathwell looks tired of listening," Rowan whispered to Hilda.

Hilda looked down at the girl. "Oh Rowan, your button's come loose again," she squatted level with her and fiddled with a button that was already fastened. She glanced quickly in Hathwell's direction. "Rowan," she whispered, "Valonia's come up with a plan to escape here but we need your help."

"Go home, to Kolfinnia you mean?"

"If you'll help us?"

She nodded so hard Hilda thought her head might roll off her shoulders.

"Valonia says she's detected tunnels underneath us, and that the rock they pass through is faulted. Do you know what that means?"

Rowan frowned. "That there's a join in the rock?"

"Good girl. Now Valonia says the fault is lined with a seam of iron. If we can awaken the iron we might be able to ask it to move." She continued to fasten buttons that weren't undone. "If that happens the earth'll shake and open, and there's a chance we can climb down into the tunnels, or escape in all the chaos."

"Really? And the witches in the ships, can we take them?"

"I'm afraid not, they'll have to be patient for when we come back, or maybe if the fault opens wide enough they can escape by themselves in the confusion. But as I say, we need your help," she had moved onto combing her hair.

"How?"

"You seem good at knowing things. Can you tell us for sure there are tunnels and a fault with lots of iron under our feet?" She looked around at the fence. Guards were patrolling just beyond the wire but they seemed bored.

"Yes, there are tunnels under us. They were used to take witches for . . ." She suddenly looked afraid.

"Hush!" She didn't want the girl to see what had happened down there. "Just knowing the tunnels are there is enough. Now can you say if the faulted rock has a band of iron in it?"

"Yes, lots of it. It's rich in magnetite and haematite." She named the minerals without knowing what they were.

"Good girl," Hilda smiled, and couldn't help from asking another question. "Just between us, does Mr Hathwell like us?"

Rowan smiled, feeling to be back on happier ground. "Oh, yes."

"Now, think. I don't just mean us, I mean all witches."

"He's starting to. He doesn't like what he has to do."

Then he shouldn't do it, she thought angrily.

Rowan leaned forward, resting a hand on her shoulder and whispered into her ear, making it tickle. "He *really* likes you!"

Her cheeks flushed, and then smiling, she took Rowan's hand and guided her after the others.

Samuel struggled like a comet trapped in the gravitational pull of a huge planet. He wanted to escape the man called Knight Superior Krast, but the force of all that self-hate was too much. The Samuel of old reached up for Valonia's answer through years of denial. It made perfect sense: he was a witch born to a witch, and he'd committed a terrible betrayal but redemption was there if he had the courage to seize it.

She saw the enormous conflict in his eyes and willed him to win, to break the crushing pull of gravity. Krast quivered in rage, he made moaning sounds deep in his throat and rolled his hands into fists and red blotches bloomed on his cheeks.

Lord Hethra, let him win! she pleaded silently.

He alone had to embrace the strongest of all spells if he wanted to be free. The strongest yet simplest spell in the universe: *'Forgive me.'*

Samuel tried to escape the hiding place he'd curled up in forty years ago. He clawed at the delusions Krast had buried him under but to him they appeared as a mountain with no summit in sight and the task appeared hopeless. "Let me out!" he screamed and clawed up the first few yards of rock only to slide back again and again. "Let me live!" If he could reach the summit he could cry out for forgiveness. He tried repeatedly, but the mountain was colossal and in the end perhaps Titus was right: he wasn't strong enough. He slid back down and lay there broken and defeated, leaving Krast unchallenged.

She watched in dread, knowing this would either save or damn Britain's witches, but the crushing embrace of planet Krast was too strong and Samuel was engulfed.

The Knight Superior took a huge gasp and then straightened. His tremors quietened and his breathing became smooth and regular. His face melted into a bland expression and when Valonia looked into his eyes she instantly knew she'd lost. Samuel was dead.

He swallowed and stretched as if waking from a dream and what a dream it had been. She had told him he was a witch, born to a witch, but that couldn't be. He was Knight Superior and his two personalities met like fire and water and in the aftermath only one side of him could remain. He chose Krast the knight over Samuel the witch and felt strangely liberated. He stood slowly. "I should thank you," he said shakily. "You helped me discover myself again." He felt exhausted but finally at peace.

"No, you've found a way to bury the past again, and live the lie. That's as far from discovery as you can get." She struggled to hold on to her anger.

"It's no lie," he said with total conviction.

She was devastated. After this he'd have no further use for any of them other than interrogation. She glared at him racing to think up another gambit.

"Guard!" he called and outside the cell came the sound of marching feet. "Despite what you might think of me Valonia, I am not a monster. I do not wish any of you to suffer, and so in gratitude I shall conduct your blessing myself." He stepped past the guard and into the corridor.

"Krast!" She jumped up and lunged for the cell door, but she was shoved back by the guard. "Samuel, come back!" she screamed.

Krast continued down the corridor without looking back, oblivious to her shouts and insults, and by the time he reached the gantry he was whistling a merry tune.

CHAPTER TWENTY-FIVE

Gardener-girl

Normally by the first week of October witches would be preparing for Samhain, the end of the old year and the end of summer. Yet Kittiwake's gardens not only continued to bloom, they continued to multiply.

The coven had grown into a shanty town of a hundred and three souls, where bedraggled tents and shelters jostled for space. Clovis and Kolfinnia found a brief respite from all this activity on the beach where they went most days to find time for themselves.

"One-hundred and three. This isn't a coven, it's an army." Clovis still wore his armour from that morning's weapons practice.

"A couple more and we'll be twice the size of Wildwood." Kolfinnia welcomed each survivor, but with each one came new problems and still no news of Wildwood. It was now a month since she'd seen Flora and many others dear to her.

"It's odd, isn't it, that the more witches who come the more worried you look," he observed her tight mouth, and creased brow.

"I just want to make this their home, make it the best I can. There's plenty to worry about." Rations were her greatest concern, then sanitation and a hundred other matters.

"It's a joint effort. It's up to them to make it a home as well." As always his advice sounded solid.

For a while they walked in silence. Skald rode her shoulder and Tempest did likewise with Clovis. The two sprites didn't have an agenda; they were bonded by kinship and she wished Kittiwake's witches would follow their example. "How are the cloaking spells holding up?" This was another prime worry for her.

"Well, we haven't been discovered yet," his muzzle twitched in a smile. "How is Walter, by the way?"

Skald snorted contemptuously at the name.

"Sulking." She didn't care if Walter left or not.

"He wouldn't listen then?"

"No," she admitted. He'd been trying to recruit others to join him and form a splinter coven. She'd had a private meeting with him in a last attempt to restore harmony, but it hadn't gone well. "If he wants to leave then he can. It's Laurie I feel sorry for."

"This isn't the time to be divided," Skald said gruffly. "They should leave and make their own covens only when Kittiwake's well established. These are dangerous times."

"I wish Walter could see that." She raised a hand and stroked his wing. "He said some awful things."

"Oh?" Clovis rumbled.

"Such as I'm inexperienced and you're too war-like." She wanted him to be equally upset, but he just laughed.

"Maybe he's got a point, but there'll come a time that they'll be glad of war-like Clovis, and be glad hrafn-dimmu was cast by you and no other."

He never seemed to let any problem get under his skin and she kept wanting to ask how old he was. His wisdom seemed ageless yet his vigour was so youthful, but the question was rude. "Do you ever feel like running away?" she smiled at the impossibility of it. "Just taking Janus, opening a doorway and leaving this place?"

He looked serious. "Janus sleeps for years at a time and opens doorways only when he wishes. He's not known as the 'trickster god' for nothing."

"How did Janus come to you?" she asked carefully.

"A coven relic, he was there long before me," he said guardedly.

"Janus might leave you stranded, just for his entertainment," Tempest added.

"I wish I could leave Walter stranded," she muttered. "He's been telling witches it'd be better for them to worship alone, abandon covens all together."

"Bloody fool!" Skald growled.

"A few are starting to agree with him, though."

"Let 'em leave," Skald said bluntly. "If it comes to a fight, I only want the willing by my side."

"The Illuminata might not come for some time, perhaps long enough for witches to leave here in goodwill and start their own covens." She tried to sound optimistic.

"We seem to be stuck in an impossible situation," Clovis kicked at an empty shell on the sand. "Building a coven and preparing for war at the same time."

"How are the defence tutorials going?"

"Smoothly. They're all eager and they've a score to settle."

"I've told you before, don't play on their hatred. Our purpose is to honour Hethra and Halla, not fight knights, or worse, take vengeance." She told him this frequently.

"And as I've said to you –,"

" – If witches are defenceless, there'll be none left to honour anybody," she quoted his oft said reply, but he just shrugged. She couldn't deny he made a strong case, but when she watched witches as young as twelve learn to thrust and strike she felt uneasy.

"Don't be too concerned," he gave his mane a gentle shake. "We've only got ten genuine lightning-staffs."

"They'll not down many knights with plain old walking sticks, unless they drag them from their krakens and beat them over the head." She thought it might even come to that.

"We'll find a way," he assured her. "And in the meantime the lessons keep them focused, keeps their morale where it should be. Let them believe, Kolfy."

She rolled her eyes at his pet name. They walked on enjoying the breeze and the waves, and inevitably her thoughts turned inwards to which would come first, battle or a rescue attempt.

"It might be a good idea for us to patrol the wood," Skald said from nowhere.

"A short flight then back," Tempest agreed and took off, with Skald trailing after him.

Kolfinnia's hair ruffled as he swept past and delicate feathers fell from his wings. "Don't be long!" she shouted, like a concerned parent.

"They don't like it when we're sad," Clovis observed.

"Neither do I." She reached out and took his hand. It was like walking with a bear, she thought, and smiled.

They walked together for a while, and she wrestled with an idea that had bothered her for some time. "Clovis, I have to know what's happened to them. I want to see the Timekeeper again."

He stopped unexpectedly while she took another step forward, stretching their joined hands. She looked down at the sand waiting for him to speak, and although she didn't require his approval she wanted it. He turned for a second to regard the sea-stack. It was misted by spray and surrounded by its constant retinue of gulls. He dropped her hand and took her by the shoulders. "If I'd found that tunnel and if I'd known what lay at the end of it, I would've turned and run."

"You?" she smiled faintly. "I thought you weren't afraid of anything."

"It's bad to go down there."

"The Timekeeper is beyond good or bad. He just 'is'." She defended him.

"That's not what I mean. It's not the creature I speak of and you know it. Don't go there again, for my sake. Something tells me that to do so would disturb something vast." He sympathised, but he knew sympathy wasn't enough. "Wait, that's all I ask. There are other ways to discover the truth, less dangerous ways."

"Very well then, I'll wait." She looked again at the sea-stack and felt the pull of duty. It was time to get back, but she had one last question. "What do you think of Sunday?"

He considered this for a moment. "She's a strong witch."

"But?"

"But she throws tight coils."

She tilted her head. "And what does that mean?"

He struggled with the language barrier. "That she can talk people into doing things they know aren't good for them."

She took his hand, which was more like a lion's paw, and held it between her own. "Can she throw a coil around you?" she asked disarmingly.

"Fear not – I like my ladies with longer whiskers."

She smiled uncertainly, not knowing if he was serious or not. "Keep an eye on her, that's all I ask. She's very taken with you."

He looked surprised. "Me?"

"She believes magic should be regal, like herself. You, Clovis, appear to match her idea of what a 'real' coven-father should be." She pushed her windswept hair from her face. "Now, shall we fly home?"

He held his staff up and waved it. "Empty, remember?"

"Ah, yes, then I suppose we'll be walking."

They set off together, back to their duties, but she spared one last look at the tower, where all her answers were buried.

As the afternoon drew into evening Kolfinnia decided to check hrafn-dimmu's shelter. Storms had rolled in twice last month, shaking the cottages and lashing the shore, and though the wand still dreamed she needed to see it again for her peace of mind.

"It's the Timekeeper, isn't it?" Skald sat watching as she prepared to fly out to the stack.

"I just want to make sure hrafn-dimmu's protected." Her excuse held some truth, and that was better than none, she told herself.

"Remember the barrier."

"I know. We won't be long, then right back here."

Turnip stew was the evening meal. Back at Wildwood turnip stew always took some eating, but here at Kittiwake where hunger always lurked around the corner she wolfed down anything hot. "Who's on cook duty, do you know?" she asked as she tied a scarf around her neck. She shared the small room with two other witches now and she'd erected a curtain around her bunk for privacy.

"Sunday Flowers," Skald sounded amused.

"Sunday? Cooking!" she blurted.

"She volunteered for the duty. She's going to great trouble to make allies," he warned.

"I wish she'd not come here," she muttered.

Skald jumped off her bunk and crawled up her lightning-staff until he was level with her. "She's a fine cook by all accounts," he teased.

"If you like your food sickly sweet and spiced with venom, then yes." Since arriving, Sunday had kept a low profile. Even so, she'd turned more than a few heads. It was fair to say there were many at Kittiwake who already adored her. "Do you think she wants to take Kittiwake as her own?" This idea had plagued her for some time.

"I can't say," he shook his head.

The Timekeeper could tell you, she thought.

"Kolfinnia?" he cautioned, "what are you thinking?"

"Nothing," she lied. "Come on, daylight won't last for ever."

She skipped down the narrow stairs and out through the front door. She crossed the courtyard with her head down, passing witches carrying firewood, water buckets and laundry. All of them greeted her with a respectful 'coven-mother'. Children ran up and touched her wand-sheath. It was a game they played and Kolfinnia remembered how she'd done the same to Valonia. She enjoyed the sound of children's feet scampering across the courtyard and their laughter lifted her spirits, but it also made her think of Rowan. Some of the witches she passed touched their hearts, others touched their temple, some bowed or raised their hats, but however they greeted coven-mother Algra she always returned their greeting by name. She'd gone to great trouble to learn their names, and if possible their original covens, small acts of kindness like that helped oil Kittiwake's cogs. All the same, she envied Skald hiding in his staff and wished she could do the same, and as she walked requests fell like autumn leaves.

'Is it possible to have another blanket? My only needle's broken, where can I find another? We're low on eye-bright for the binding spell, do we have any more?'

Just stepping out of the door demanded leadership and tact, and it took her the best part of twenty minutes to cross the courtyard. "Oaken Roots! Was it the same for Valonia?" she asked from the corner of her mouth.

"Why do you think she hid in her tower so much?" Skald revealed.

She scrambled up the grassy dunes and drank in the glorious sight of the sea. "It's so beautiful, Skald," she murmured.

"Daylight's wasting," he reminded her.

Dune grass whistled past at tremendous speed. She flew over the beach, drawing a line in the sand with her toe as it rushed by, just as she used to do on Appelier Bay with Flora, but now there was just her. She lifted higher, out towards the tower and the dreaming hrafn-dimmu, leaving her sorrows behind.

The journey was swift and smooth, but three-hundred yards out she was astounded to see a figure standing on the tower's summit. "There's someone up there!" she cried, and it could only be another witch. *How dare they!* she thought in outrage.

Skald accelerated. Whoever they were they had a bird's-eye view of their approach, which made Kolfinnia feel even angrier, and when she arrived at the strange barrier she expected a similar ordeal to last time. She was so agitated, however, that she didn't even realise she'd passed through until she was on the other side. It seemed that whatever she had achieved last time was permanent, but there was no time for satisfaction: hrafn-dimmu might be in danger. She saw the glint of golden hair and realised that it was Sunday.

"I told you!" Skald shouted. *"She solved the barrier. Clovis said she was strong."*

As well as slippery, Kolfinnia thought.

She dropped down neatly onto its grassy top. Finding Sunday here was like having her search through her most private possessions, and to make matters worse she looked unrepentant.

"Coven-mother," she said as if overjoyed to see her, and bowed briefly. She was wearing the grey wayfarer clothes she'd first arrived in, but now they'd been washed and pressed, and draped on her slender frame they looked altogether elegant.

"Sunday," she replied curtly, scanning every inch of the summit for signs of mischief. Topmost amongst her concerns was hrafn-dimmu, but at first glances its shelter looked undisturbed. Next, her eyes were drawn to the shaft that led to the answers she was seeking, and perhaps the true reason she'd come here.

"The view from up here is magnificent." Sunday held her white lightning-staff level with her hips, and Kolfinnia saw something challenging in her posture.

Without stopping to reply, she bent to inspect hrafn-dimmu's casket, while she wrestled to contain her anger. Her own lightning-staff throbbed, and she knew Skald would like nothing more than to send Sunday hurtling into the waves. "What are you doing up here, Sunday?" she asked at last.

"I wasn't aware the tower was off limits?" she smiled prettily.

"Shouldn't you be on cook duty this evening?" Without realising, she mimicked Sunday's stance and the two looked like they were about to duel.

"Walter gladly took my duty," she smiled. "He's such a dear, isn't he?"

She felt a shiver of anger. "I chose this tower to leave the wand in peace." She tipped her head towards the shelter, which looked more vulnerable with Sunday standing nearby than with all the surrounding sea.

"My apologies, coven-mother. I had no idea."

"Yes, really, Sunday. I chose this location specifically because it's remote." She emphasised her last word, to underline the sense of trespass.

She nodded earnestly. "A wise location. All of us wish the wand to remain guarded and safe. It's a lifeline for Britain's witches."

"Then why did you come here?" she demanded.

Sunday gave her a sideways glance. "I assure you I had no idea that you'd put Valonia's wand here. If I had then I wouldn't have come. This place is sacred."

Kolfinnia had the absurd feeling that now it was Sunday berating her for violating the tower. There was a long silence broken only by the wind, and the whoosh of passing fulmars. "So why did you come?" she pressed, hating the way she used silence as an ally.

Sunday made a point of looking around her and especially at the shaft. "I was drawn here," she stated. "A great power radiates from this tower. I've sensed it since I arrived."

Great power? Kolfinnia thought. *No wonder you were drawn here, Sunday. It's what you love most, isn't it?*

"But I suppose you already know about this tower's energy?" Her tone was disapproving, implying that Kolfinnia kept secrets.

"You're right," she admitted. "A fabulous power resides here and the first time I came it almost killed Skald and I, but thankfully Clovis rescued us."

"Clovis," she sighed longingly. "If only every coven had a witch such as he, the Illuminata wouldn't dare raise a finger against us."

Leave him alone Sunday, he's not yours! she thought darkly.

"And may I ask, does coven-father Clovis know about this tower's energy?"

"He accepted my word in good faith when I told him what I found at the end of that tunnel." She pointed towards the hole that looked like an open throat.

Sunday turned slowly and regarded it anew. "The source of the power lies down there? I thought as much. And you went to see it, you say?" Her eyes narrowed. "What did you find?"

"Tell the crafty vixen!" Skald insisted. *"Maybe the Timekeeper'll take a liking to her and never let her out."*

"Tell her? Are you mad?" she thought back.

"She knows now. She'll go without your permission anyway. Tell her and it might put her off."

"It's rude to whisper, coven-mother," Sunday taunted, guessing her conversation.

Kolfinnia stiffened. She didn't fear Sunday but sparring with her was like trying to catch an eel with greasy hands. "Skald and I were deciding whether we should tell you."

"How gracious."

"Of course, you could discover it for yourself," she continued, ignoring her sarcasm. "It's not my place to stop you, but I'd urge you not to go down there. The consequences might be catastrophic."

"Please," she shook her head, "I'm sure there's nothing down there that warrants such melodrama."

"Then leave this place be. Do what's best for Kittiwake and not your own agenda."

"My agenda, as you put it, is how to best serve Hethra and Halla, as yours should be," she said frostily.

Kolfinnia took a pace forwards, sensing they were close to a fight. "Don't lecture me on duty. Serving Kittiwake is the best way to serve the serpent-twins."

Sunday went and stood at the edge of the tower, looking out to sea. The wind lifted her hair in a cloud of gold and she was silent for a while. Kolfinnia dared hoped she'd given in, but when she turned back, she saw she was as implacable as ever. "You and your kind would have witches living in holes in the ground and hiding forever more, but we should be honoured for keeping the world from falling apart!"

"The twins face a bigger threat than you know, and rebuilding Britain's covens is the best way to protect them."

Sunday gave her head a disdainful little shake. "Tell me Kolfinnia, have you ever thought about the spells we say that keep the twins' sleep restful, the spells witches have said three times a day, everyday, for thousands of years?"

She began to feel cautious. "Without them, the twins' dreams would be restless, and Earth would be in turmoil."

"Just as I've always believed," she agreed, "but have you ever considered that the sleeping spells are less than selfless, that it is we humans than benefit most from keeping the twins lethargic, in a perpetual stupor?"

Lethargic? Perpetual stupor? Kolfinnia had never heard anything like this before, and from the growling sounds inside her staff, neither had Skald. "You're suggesting witches actually harm the twins!"

Sunday said nothing, again, using silence as a weapon.

"I won't listen to any more of this, Sunday," she flustered. "It's obscene."

"Kolfinnia," she took her arm, "have you ever thought what would happen if we were to liberate Hethra and Halla, if we should awaken them?"

"Are you mad! That would kill them!" she whispered in horror.

"No, not kill them, set them free!"

"And what would happen then?" she pulled her arm free, wondering if Sunday had lost her mind.

"The twins' dream of life would no longer be controlled for humanity's benefit. Earth would rise up and humanity would learn some much needed humility."

Kolfinnia groped for words to express her horror, but she was speechless

"Don't tell me you've never wanted to see humankind taken down a peg or two? Learn to respect Hethra and Halla's realm, even if they must learn by force?" Sunday was breathing rapidly and her eyes sparkled dangerously.

The terrible truth was that a tiny part of Kolfinnia agreed. "You can't know for sure that's what would happen," she countered. "Using the twins for your own purpose? You talk like the Illuminata!"

"You'd rather *they* found the serpent-twins?"

"I'd rather they stayed under the earth, away from vain witches and cruel knights, and it does my heart good to remind you that no living witch knows their resting place."

"But what if one witch did know, what then?" Sunday stared at her expectantly.

Kolfinnia suddenly felt cold.

"Does she know?" Skald whispered.

Sunday saw her error. She visibly relaxed and breathed a delicate laugh. "But as you say, 'no witch knows' so our argument does little to unite us, does it?" she smiled wearily, "I'm not your enemy, Kolfinnia. Indeed, if you're looking for recruits to help rescue your friends then I'll gladly come."

Kolfinnia looked down at the grass, unsure what to say. Sunday was an enigma: she could be generous and spiteful in the same breath.

"Now," Sunday turned back to the shaft, "crawling down there is going to ruin my hair, so will you spare me the indignity and just tell me the tower's secret, or should I ask coven-father Clovis?" She played with the neck of her dress.

Sorry Sunday, he likes his ladies with longer whiskers, Kolfinnia thought, and smiled. Skald was right: if they refused, she'd just go anyway. "Sunday," she looked her in the eye, "fate is woven down there inside an eternal hourglass." She waited for her cryptic message to sink in.

Sunday naturally suspected that she was being toyed with. "You're lies are too ridiculous to be even half credible!"

"It was *he* who told me Valonia still lives, *he* who told me Rowan is a prisoner! He told me so much, Sunday," she finished with a mysterious smile. *Wonder now you harlot what the Timekeeper might have told me about you!* she thought with satisfaction.

"You mean to say that down there resides the great Timekee –,"

"I do," she stopped her.

Sunday looked to the hole and back to Kolfinnia. "The truth?" she whispered.

"The truth."

For the first time Sunday looked humbled. "Then I concede you're right," she murmured and glanced back at the beckoning hole. "Some things are best left undisturbed." If she wanted to, she could descend that tunnel, but she wasn't sure her courage matched her curiosity. She would never admit it, but she was in awe of Kolfinnia. "I'll leave you to your privacy coven-mother." She awoke Strike in a second and was making ready to fly back.

"Sunday, wait," she took a step forward. "You're right, we're not enemies. It's likely the Illuminata will come again and we'll all be fighting for the same cause, regardless."

"Fear not. My first duty will always be to Hethra and Halla," she promised, meaning every word of it.

"Then Kittiwake-coven thanks you."

"Blessed be," she said without smiling, then mounted her staff gracefully. "Away, Strike," she commanded and swept away towards the shore.

"Do you trust her?"

She turned to Skald, who was now balanced on her staff.

"I believe she thinks she has the serpent-twin's best interests at heart."

He smiled at her evasive answer. "That part I don't doubt, even though she has a strange way of showing it. Awakening them indeed!" he snorted.

"It was touching of her to offer to help rescue Rowan."

"Suspicious, more like. I wonder if she knows?"

"Is that possible?"

"Wasn't she at Wildwood when we learned about Rowan's talents?" he asked. "And what's more, she pledged allegiance to Hethra and Halla alone."

"What's wrong with that?"

His eyes were turning fiery in the sunset. "Isn't it tradition for a witch to pledge allegiance to their coven instead of the twins directly, or am I just splitting hairs?" He cocked his head in question.

She looked across the sunset waves, but Sunday was no longer visible, and she wondered just what lengths she would go to in order to serve the twins.

When they returned, Kolfinnia found more bad news: Walter had left with Laurie and persuaded nine others to go along. "He can't have!" she exclaimed.

"I'm afraid it's so," Clovis regarded her sorrowfully. Next to him was Betty, a short, middle-aged woman who'd supported Walter's frequent criticisms, that is until he and his followers had taken off and not invited her to go with them.

"Tell me again, what was the last thing he said to you?" Kolfinnia demanded.

"He just said he was off out collectin' firewood and such." Betty scrubbed a dirty handkerchief over her reddened eyes.

Kolfinnia gathered that Betty had been rather sweet on Walter, but he clearly now didn't return those feelings and she was only starting to see that. "When did they leave?"

Betty honked loudly into her handkerchief. "They set off at midday, were meant to be 'ome by mid afternoon. But now look, it's almost dark!"

"How do you know they've left and aren't lost or in trouble?"

She shot them a sheepish glance. "We was all meant to go tomorrow, me included, but he didn't wanna take me in the end, did 'e?" Her last words came out as a squeak, then she started blubbering again.

"You planned to go with them?" Her tone made Betty flinch and Clovis twitched a frown telling her to go easy on the woman. She was stranded in a coven she'd openly criticised and she didn't have any allies left.

"Yes," Betty confessed, staring down at her feet. When she looked up, the wretched expression on her face softened Kolfinnia. After all, she'd been strung along and left behind.

"Very well, Betty, thank you for your honesty."

"I'm sorry, coven-mother," she sniffed, unable to look her in the eye.

"Now, would you be so good as to help with kitchen duty? I believe they'll be short of helpers tonight."

"Am so sorry, my lady," she clasped her hand and kissed it and then slouched away.

Kolfinnia remembered that Walter had swapped his duty with Sunday. Had Sunday's meeting with her on the tower been planned to buy time for him and his rebels to run away? She wouldn't put anything past her, but one thing was for sure, the solstice queen hadn't gone with them. "Walter," she snarled when Betty was out of earshot.

"Let's hope he's taken the trouble causers with him and we can get on with building a coven." No matter what, Clovis always found something to be glad about.

"It's not just that. He never said anything, as though I'm some kind of tyrant!" She felt as wounded as Betty.

Clovis, Skald and Tempest all stared at her blankly as though she was fretting about birds migrating or the tide coming in. Walter's leaving just 'was' and that was that.

Kolfinnia took her evening meal with the rest of the coven and there was a hushed atmosphere. Her authority had been judged and found wanting and those who'd judged her had left to make a life of their own. As she ate she felt curious, even pitiful eyes on her, and found herself wondering if Valonia had really chosen wisely after all.

Although she didn't see Sunday again that night she felt the woman's presence dog her all evening and well into the night when she lay in her bunk trying to sleep, but instead she couldn't stop thinking of Sunday's parting remark earlier.

'My first duty will always be to Hethra and Halla.'

What was wrong with those words? She knew there was something buried there that could tumble them all into chaos, but she couldn't quite dig it out and it gnawed at her.

That night she gave her bunk to a child who'd been taken ill, and instead slept in the tower. She'd done the best to make the pump-house like Valonia's tower, believing if she copied her great coven-mother she'd enjoy her same success, but it all seemed so futile now. In the early hours when Kolfinnia should have been sleeping, she lay awake thinking unpleasant thoughts and there came a soft knock at the door.

"I'm asleep Clovis. Go away."

"How do you know it's me?" his muffled voice came.

"Because I was stupid enough to tell you I'd be here tonight, now let me be," she rolled over and pulled the blanket over her head.

"There's someone here to see you. She's just arrived."

"Tell her to bed down somewhere and I'll see her in the morning," she shouted from under her blanket. She was weary of being coven-mother, weary of witches like Sunday and Walter, and the last thing she wanted at this unholy hour was to meet yet another witch. She groaned inwardly when she heard the latch clatter and the door creak. Lantern light poured through and Clovis looked in.

"She's been on the road for many days," he said.

She peeped out from under her blanket and flashed him an angry look. "So has horse manure! She's not a special case."

"But she's come with others. They're tired and hungry. I think they'd like a meal." He relayed this like it was good news.

"We're all bloody tired and hungry," she yelled.

There was a considered silence and then a new voice spoke from just behind Clovis, out in the dark passageway.

"If you're hungry, I have some hazelnuts."

She knew the voice immediately and it was like listening to a river of silver. She threw back the blanket and leapt from the bunk, scattering straw all across the floor. "Is it?" She daren't hope.

Clovis held up his lantern, stood aside and shoved the door wide open. A beautiful young woman wearing an eye-patch was standing next to him. She looked tired and ragged and she held a cluster of hazelnuts in her cupped hands as Kolfinnia had with Rowan so long ago. Clovis smiled, left the lantern hanging on a hook and slipped away, knowing this wasn't for his eyes.

"Flora?" she stammered, afraid to move in case she awoke and the vision vanished. She wanted to say her name again but she couldn't speak and the next thing she knew she was crying.

Hazelnuts rained down and rolled away unnoticed as Flora ran and embraced her so fiercely that she knew this wasn't a dream. Neither said a word. They stood in silence and let their perfect embrace talk for them.

Sunday flew across miles of dark countryside, dressed in black and with her distinctive white lightning-staff wrapped in black cloth. She had tried to make them see that witches should be proud, but Kittiwake was like every other coven: they all wanted to live a secretive and shameful life. Well no more, she thought. She carried a note, intending to deliver it to the church at Trebbington some fifty miles away.

Once Kittiwake realised its location was known and the knights were coming the witches would flee, leaving her free to take a select band of loyal followers and save Rowan, and she would put the girl's great secret to a worthy purpose. This was her one chance to set the twins free, and she wouldn't let anything stand in her way, not even other witches. "Faster, Strike!" she ordered her tired thunder-sprite, and raced on through the darkness carrying her note.

CHAPTER TWENTY-SIX

Ada, Ash, and Ruin

Despite being lost in foul weather and their boats wrecked, Flora
and twenty-three others from Wildwood had come at last. Kolfinnia
felt light-headed and light-hearted with joy. There was Annie Barden
who cradled Hercules, and Sally Crook and Mary Fife who'd fought
with Valonia's defenders, to name but a few, and despite the late hour
and the cold starry sky, or perhaps because of it, they lit a fire in the
courtyard. A meal of potato and barley soup was prepared and they sat
around the roaring fire while sprites perched on staffs, gathered like a
family again with their new coven-mother at its heart.

Kolfinnia made a welcome speech and paid tribute to those who'd
fought to the end, but never left the soil of Wildwood. Then she told her
own news, of confronting knights at the river and sending Rowan back
with warning. When she recounted what had become of Valonia and the
others her voice cracked and there was a deathly silence. She told them
of hrafn-dimmu's voyage through the sea and of meeting Clovis, but
she prudently kept the Timekeeper and Rowan's gift a secret for now.
Her tale was fabulous and harrowing and when it was done they stood
and burst into applause. One by one they blessed her with a kiss or an
embrace and by the end, her cheeks burned and her ribs ached.

After the tales were told, and while everyone was busy getting settled,
Flora took her hand and told her the rest. "Only two of the three boats
are accounted for. Freya Albright's boat, Speedwell, hasn't been seen or
heard from."

"What happened?"

"We were split up just hours after escaping. That night there was a bad storm, and we thought they'd make the rendezvous the day after, but they never came. We searched but found nothing. Do you think Freya's boat will come?"

"Give them a chance. I'd almost given up on seeing you again. And Freya's a skilled witch – remember how she brought us through the wild-way when we were just girls, and we rescued that fugitive?"

"How could I forget it!"

"Well I'm sure she'll be just as good a captain to her crew as she was to us then."

"There's more," Flora went on. "Six witches left soon after we escaped. They were scared, traumatised even, but we couldn't talk them out of it."

"I only want the willing by my side," she echoed Skald's words.

Flora hugged her for perhaps the hundredth time. "I wish I'd been there, to fight with you."

"You may yet get the chance. If they discover us they'll come, be sure of that."

"I want to be with you next time. I don't want to run away again."

"Run away? If you hadn't called a mist nobody would've escaped. It has nothing to do with running away." Kolfinnia knew all they needed sleep right now, not more painful soul-searching. She looked around at the familiar faces and couldn't help but grin again. "All of you get some rest. You can bed down in the tower until we sort something more permanent."

As dawn glowed in the east the new arrivals went to look for sleep, and news spread that a large group had arrived during the night. Wildwood, the now famous coven that'd defeated the Illuminata, had come at last.

Kittiwake's witches looked out expecting to see warriors as fearsome as Clovis himself. What they saw were half-wild, muddy girls and women carrying real lightning-staffs, not wooden sticks. Everyone took heart, none more so than Farona: he'd seen Flora from a distance and the world suddenly seemed brighter.

Krast walked into his office and shook a generous shower of raindrops from his overcoat. The rain had turned the landscape glossy and the flooded wheel-ruts looked like rivers of lead. He expected to see Hathwell sitting behind his typewriter as usual, but he was busily putting on his overcoat and scarf. "Going somewhere?" he disapproved, and cast a telling glance at the clock.

"I thought I'd interview the Wildwood prisoners, as per your instructions, sir." He pushed an arm into his coat, and was already edging for the door.

Krast had learned all he wanted from Valonia two days ago. He would take them to the chromosites soon enough, but for now he wanted them to stew in their own juices. "Negative," he said flatly, "that assignment has been terminated. You'll accompany me to the chromosite interrogation bunker." His appetite for such had returned. He wasn't afraid to examine those unseeing eyes any longer, and there were still plenty of prisoners to be questioned. "I have more important duties for you now." He was satisfied by the look of disappointment on Hathwell's face.

"Sir?" He thought of the witch he only knew as 'Hilda' and of the young girl with the auburn hair, already feeling apprehensive for them.

"We're powering up first-dawn for an important test," Krast said proudly. "In honour of Wallace Maccrae, God rest his soul. The experiment begins at 3 pm sharp and we need a witch for the test. I want you to go and select one." He stroked his chin, pretended to think. "The Wildwood prisoners, they trust you, don't they?"

Hathwell just blinked and felt the colour drain from his face. "Sir?"

"Select one," he ordered.

He was horrified, but as a squire he'd learned not to think and just react. "If you wish, sir," he said indifferently.

"Excellent. Bring one for de-lousing at 2 pm. I don't want them contaminating the test." He made a play of taking an interest in some paperwork.

Hathwell's ethics screamed out at him to refuse, but it was all he could do just to stay standing.

Krast looked up, vaguely surprised to see him still there. "Well? Be off then."

"Sir," he mumbled and finished putting on his coat. He made for the door, where rain continued to drum against the glass outside, when Krast stopped him.

"Oh, and Hathwell – bring a pretty one. It's a special occasion after all." He flashed him a mirthless smile.

"Sir." He stepped out into the rain with his coat unbuttoned and his scarf flying around his ears, but he didn't notice. His heart felt like lead, and he shuffled down the steps at a funerary pace with orders to choose which of Valonia's friends would die that day.

The Fortitude had been stationary for over a month. Sometimes devisers arrived to service it, but although it remained in working order the hull was red with rust.

The rain continued to pound and Valonia huddled near the fence, away from the others, peering out through the gloom at the prison ships. They'd been here so long that where the fence posts met the ground, blades of grass had pushed their way up through the impacted debris. They were straggly but her heart was gladdened. "Lord Oak comes to claim his own." She smiled at the thought of Hobbs Ash reverting to greenery again. For good measure she reached down and stroked the grass, and it was like touching a reminder from home.

A shout from the gate made her turn quickly and she winced at the stiffness in her joints. Hathwell was approaching, limping badly and looking dour. She found to her surprise that she was glad to see him, he might have news about what Krast was up to.

She walked through the maze of puddles, lifting the hem of her now tatty dress, to where Hathwell was standing with the others under the machine and out of the rain. "Afternoon to you, Mr Hathwell," she said pleasantly and right away knew something was very wrong.

"Valonia." He looked tormented and his dark hair hung in wet tails, dripping across his unbuttoned overcoat. Hilda drew Rowan towards her and Ada and Lana stepped in close.

"I see you came without a hat. Were you in such a hurry to join us?" She tried to sound relaxed.

He looked at her and tried to speak, but he didn't know what to say or do. He knew the bravest thing would be to tell Krast to go to hell. "Ms Valonia," he wasn't sure what would come next and idiotically hoped his mouth would just say all the right things for him.

"Something's wrong, isn't it, Mr Hathwell?"

He nodded mutely and then looked down at his feet. He'd never felt so ashamed.

"Valonia?" Rowan enquired. "What is it, what's wrong with Mr Hathwell?"

She gave him a look of derision, even hate. "Mr Hathwell if fine," she replied without taking her eyes off him, "but it looks like he's come to take me for a chat." She volunteered herself without hesitation.

"You can't!" Hilda hissed at him.

Still, he looked at his feet and said nothing.

"Look after Rowan until I get back," Valonia passed the girl's hand to Hilda.

They looked upon their coven-mother for the last time and Hathwell felt shame strong enough to make him retch.

"Now then, Valonia," Ada pushed forwards, "if it's chattin' him wants, then I reckons I'm best qualified. I'll go, and you stay 'ere with the lass. She needs you." She hugged Valonia hard, almost crushing her, and before she could protest Ada moved on to Lana and Hilda and finally Rowan, bending down to kiss the girl's forehead. "Remember them cor-jets?" she laughed and Rowan smiled, unaware of what was really transpiring. "Grow up, yer little sod!" she cackled.

"Fed and free!" Rowan remembered.

"Fed an' free! They'll never enslave us!" Ada boasted, and then went and stood by Hathwell's side.

Next to these women Hathwell felt no better than the mud on their feet, but it was the girl's simple belief that Ada would come back that wounded him deepest. "Ladies," he managed to say. He knew the delicate friendship he'd kindled was dead. He caught one last look at Hilda, and what he saw in her eyes would remain with him always. "This way please, Ms Ada." He led her away from her friends and towards first dawn's projectile chamber.

"Ada!" Valonia shouted: her voice strained and hoarse. "Talk good and loud."

Ada raised a defiant fist. "You'll 'ear me all right, just you see!"

Valonia watched them vanish through the gate and into the murk, and when they were gone she crumpled, and only her friends stopped her falling to the ground. Rowan darted to her side and clung to her and the four witches drew close. "Valonia?" Rowan looked up at her. "Is Ada coming back?"

She swept tears from her cheeks while behind her Lana and Hilda covered their faces to weep in private. "Soon enough, little witch. Now best we concentrate on that escape plan of ours. I think we've stayed here long enough, don't you?"

Rowan smiled timidly and the rain continued to fall.

Witches dream and knights dream, it is the universal law that living things dream, even the mind of Ruination. Bad dreams usually vanish upon waking, but when Ruination suffers bad dreams it spawns living, breathing beasts and they had been gathering behind the Earth's paper-fine skin, drawn from a mirror realm that was alien, dreadful and wondrous.

They were drawn to Hethra and Halla's fear, and they congregated at this one place where the source of that fear was greatest, beyond the barrier they could smell iron, coal, machines and unholy magic. Hundreds of them writhed in a strangled clot, waiting for the barrier to weaken and break as it had before, but it might not remain open for long and their numbers were great. The banquet would be hard fought and it would be ferocious.

Krast looked Ada up and down like a slaughter-man inspecting a sow and then turned back to Hathwell in amused disgust. "I see you've chosen the finest materials for us to work with." There were a few polite laughs from the correctionals. "A pretty one I said, unless of course this specimen tickles your fancy?" He leaned forward for a better look at her as the laughter continued, "And does the witch have a name?"

"Aye, she does." Ada shot back.

"Well?" he said, after she showed no desire to tell him. "Enlighten us."

"Me name's Josephine." A stinging smile surfaced on her lips and Krast recoiled an inch.

Bitch told them! He reeled, well there was time to repay that little rebellion later, he thought to himself.

Ada stood between two guards, wearing a grubby correctional gown that reached down to her thick ankles, her Seed-Fall clothes had been taken for incineration. After inspecting something in her right eye with a crystal-tipped shaft, they weighed her and measured her height, then took some of her hair and nail clippings. She didn't know what was going to happen, but she promised Hethra and Halla that she'd make it as troublesome as possible. She wasn't superhuman, she wasn't without her fears and it was a struggle to master them, but in her heart she knew Hethra wouldn't fail her. He'd come and guide her to Evermore, and that was a death Ada could live with.

She knew they were underground because they walked down a flight of stone steps away from the rainy halflight of late afternoon and into this chamber, passing at least six bulkheads on the way. The circular room was constructed of hefty stone blocks and lined with levers, gauges and copper wiring by the yard. It had a vaulted ceiling, and small gas lanterns glowed overhead like silk-moths. The floor comprised thick stone flags and through it Ada could feel the vibration of massive machinery buried deeper still. The song of the first-dawn cyclotron ran through the soles of her feet, up her body and buzzed in her teeth.

Directly ahead were three steel doors set into the sweeping wall and all of them looked strong enough to withstand Judgement Day itself. To the left was the specimen-chamber where their chosen material, a perfect cube of lead weighing one imperial pound, would be turned into gold. To the right, was the operator's room, where a deviser would will the lead to change and in the middle was the 'fuel-chamber' where Ada would pay for that transformation. It was also the chamber where one day Krast intended to place the relic known as Hethra and Halla. This was the 'first-dawn' that had haunted Valonia all her life.

There were at least two dozen men in attendance and Ada took an instant dislike to all of them, especially a stooped man who shadowed Krast constantly. She didn't know him, but Librarian Holloway was honoured to be in attendance and fancied himself as Hathwell's replacement. Hathwell stood to her left deliberately looking elsewhere and reeking of guilt. She pitied him. She believed he was essentially a good man, but he lacked courage and she knew he'd punish himself far worse than she ever could for that failing.

"Primary checks completed?" Krast shouted, and one after another men called out their station number, followed by 'apparatus ready'.

Levers were adjusted and pressure needles twitched into life and the vibration in the floor turned up a notch. Ada imagined a metal giant awakening in the darkness below her. First-dawn was rising up to feed.

"Cyclotron ignition at my order," Krast checked his pocket watch. "And seal the subject into the chamber," he waved a hand at Ada.

I'm comin' Esta, she thought. Ada was shoved towards a steel door, where no less then four men were heaving it open. Through it she could see a spherical metal chamber, perhaps iron. It was not much bigger than her cell, but studded with thousands of rivets, and hanging from the ceiling was a contraption like a cannon smothered in pipes and tubes, which pointed ominously downwards. "I don't need yer 'elp. I can go me self." She shrugged off their hands.

As her bare feet shuffled over the flags she felt a different vibration underneath the pounding machinery, and this one wasn't steel or iron or even rock. It came from elsewhere. None of them heard or felt it, but Ada did. Something alive rumbled under her feet and pulsed through the stone floor, she caught the whiff of something sickly sweet like a thousand summer blooms left to stew and rot. "Ruin!" she uttered in amazement. Ruin was close and none of them knew. In all her years she never thought she'd be glad to smell the presence of Ruination, but today she welcomed them. *These buggers are in forra surprise!* She stepped over the threshold and into the chamber wearing a grim smile.

Hathwell watched her go, and with her went the last of his honour. He scowled at Krast's thin back and gleaming scalp and *almost* reached for his bayonet. *Noble knight!* he thought contemptuously.

Ada heard the door slam behind her. The chamber was small and the squat cannon thing hanging from the ceiling almost brushed the top of her head. She didn't know what the device was, but its purpose looked mean. Sealed away from everyone, the chamber was strangely quiet. At once she snatched a furtive look to her back and then she ran her experienced hands across the circular wall, letting her finger tips ride over the countless rivets, tasting the metal, looking for something that would help her. Escape was impossible, but she didn't have escape in mind, rather she thought of sabotage and the more catastrophic the better.

"Primary spark set to go." Krast snapped his pocket watch closed and felt happy for the first time in months. He'd reasserted himself, and best of all, the Cobb witch had nothing to say. There was only blissful silence.

Hathwell joined him, wondering against all hope if he could advert Ada's fate at the last moment. He looked around like a man awakening from a long sleep and saw Holloway stood by Krast's side, studying him suspiciously.

"Take your station, Holloway. Remember to bring me the instrument log when we're done. I want an exact record," Krast commanded.

Hathwell saw the servile look on Holloway's face and it struck him that for years he'd looked just like that around the Knight Superior.

Krast craned around. "And you might as well be off too, Hathwell."

"Sir?"

"That old piece of meat won't power first-dawn for long. Go bring me a younger one."

"Sir?"

"Damn it!" he barked. "Am I speaking a foreign language? Away, faithful squire, and bring me the girl, Hathwell, bring me the Wildwood girl!"

He saluted before he even knew what he was doing. In the next instant he turned and marched back towards a dreary October afternoon, leaving Ada in the dark under the earth. He had no idea what he was going to do but one thing was for sure: there was no way he was about to drag a crying girl to Krast's lair. He'd run for it first. He'd flee London before he'd ever do that, but even if he did someone else would obey. The thought of Moore hauling Rowan away set him shaking in rage. He climbed the steps with a heart as heavy as the stones under his feet, not knowing that hungry eyes watched his every move, not knowing that Krast had just saved his life.

She found it at last: the walls were lined with an iron-rich alloy. There was iron all around her and in the device above her head. Ada pressed harder against the metal. Her fingers were calloused from years of garden work and she needed to feel the alloy's signature as keenly as possible. There it was, the voice of iron singing deep in the alloy, the element of protection, sacred to Hethra himself. If Ada could ask growing things to fruit at will she was confident she could ask the iron to change its song. What the effect might be she wasn't sure, but she hoped it would be explosive. "Aye, and then we'll sees 'ow much yer like the new guests that come callin', eh?"

She remembered the smell of rotting flowers. Ruination lurked only a hair's width away, and whatever this machine was designed to do she had a shrewd idea that it wasn't natural and Hethra and Halla were going to feel it like a knife, and when that happened the creatures of Ruination would take this place as their own. "Let's 'ope the buggers are good and hungry!" She strained to catch the iron's song, familiarising herself with its tune, and then she began to hum back quietly, at just the right frequency, and her heart jumped when the iron answered.

"Ignite cyclotron at my mark," Krast held his pocket watch and waited for the slender second hand to step past the twelve.

Inside the chamber Ada sang her song of iron, and as the metal answered it began to realign its structure, orientating all its random domains and turning the whole room into a huge magnet. She could feel its force growing: the air thickened and grew heavy and her head began to ache. Even the tiny particles of iron in her blood began to vibrate in harmony with the iron's song.

The second hand clicked smoothly past the twelve and Krast brought his arm down like a guillotine.

"Fire!"

Levers clashed in unison and the machinery's din rose in pitch. The first-dawn cyclotron awoke, a massive circular ring of steel two miles in circumference and wide enough for a horse and cart to pass through, buried under the foundations of Hobbs Ash. It was a cannon designed to spin minute particles away from one another at great force.

The Hobbs Ash coal generator heeded the call and smoke billowed up from its circle of chimneys, looking like a crown of fire. The first particles were unleashed and fired along the tunnel where they'd circle the two-mile long barrel thousands of times until they picked up sufficient speed before bombarding the subject chamber. There they would undo Ada's flesh down to the last particle and free her essence, the enormous power of which would transmute lead into gold.

At least that was the idea.

The walls around Ada rumbled under the cyclotron's massive thrust, but still the old witch sang the song of iron. The magnetic field was now so dense that she felt her blood being dragged around in her body like tides drawn by the moon and her teeth throbbed. The contraption above her head jerked into life. She heard steam hiss through its veins and copper tubing crackle as it heated up. "I 'ope this is loud enough for yer, Val." She cracked a smile and thought of her gardens, of her friends and of their enemies. "One life doesn't seem enough," she smiled sadly and then first-dawn opened fire into the chamber, directly at Ada Crabbe.

Will controls matter. It is the supreme witch doctrine, and by will alone Ada had converted the entire chamber into a magnet large enough to repel the cyclotron's discharge. She had effectively shoved a stopper into the end of the barrel and the blast had nowhere to go but backfire into its own guts.

The impact was so enormous that the first thing to rupture was the vast ring of steel under Hobbs Ash. The next thing to rupture, a fraction of a second later, was the barrier between Earth and Ruination.

Hathwell was heading to the Fortitude when he felt the whole world lurch. He staggered and crashed to the ground, which was no longer solid, but sagged like rubber. The world filled with a stupendous noise, and the earth yawned wide and he tumbled down into it with a scream.

Valonia and the others were by now locked away, but cell V was empty. The Fortitude rocked hard enough for it to tip sideways. Inside their cells, the witches screamed in unison as the whole structure leaned over and Valonia, like the rest, slid sideways into the wall. She heard girders groan and water pipes burst, and she could clearly hear Rowan screaming in the next cell. She certainly didn't need crowning for that.

"Valonia!" the girl screamed over and over.

Suddenly the lights flickered and everything went black, prompting another scream from Rowan.

"Rowan!" Valonia cried, and edged her way up the slanted floor. But she wasn't afraid, in fact she was laughing. "Rowan, it's all right, be still! It's just Ada having her chat!" she laughed hoarsely, feeling both sad and joyful. Ada Crabbe might have gone to Evermore, but by Halla's claws she'd gone with a bang.

The door to the chamber was solid iron and weighed over two thousand pounds. Its hinges were fixed with bolts thirty inches long and as thick as a man's wrist. It was a formidable door, but it was blown from its hinges like tissue paper.

The door was blasted across the crowded control room, courtesy of one Ada Crabbe, and the pressure wave preceding it knocked Krast off his feet and out of its path. If it hadn't, there would have been one pulverised Knight Superior amongst the three devisers that ended up crushed. They vanished in an instant, leaving only a blood-tinged cloud of dust as the door crashed into the chamber's rear wall. Meanwhile, Krast lay on the floor wondering what the hell had knocked him down and watched, bewildered, as the massive door rocketed past only inches from the tip of his nose.

The room exploded with smoke and bounced as the shockwave rolled deep beneath them, shattering the first-dawn machine as it went. Chunks of masonry rained down, pelting the controls and sending up showers of sparks that danced brightly in the smoke. Pressure pipes burst and sprayed boiling steam across the room. Men screamed and ran for the exit, but Krast was closest and back on his feet in an instant. A deviser staggered past him with his face half-cooked and his eyes boiled blind, screaming through swollen and steaming lips.

Krast callously hauled him aside, groping his way through the dust and mayhem towards the door, all the while assailed by vivid but bizarre images which seemed to come from nowhere: empty begging bowls, flags in tatters, fluttering moths trapped behind glass and tethered horses walking endless circles. All were steeped in woe, none of them made sense, and in a bewildered way he half believed he must have suffered concussion.

He staggered onwards to the exit, just visible through the smoke, coughing and blinded by grit and with blood running from his scalp. He heard a scream to his rear, not of pain but terror, and he heard the surreal sound of bones being crunched, like something eating.

Jack Peel, formerly of the Wicker-Swan coven, sat on filthy blankets in his cramped bunk on board one of the prison hulks, and rubbed at his shaved head. He'd been taken for chromosite interrogation for the second time that week and asked the same question: where are Hethra and Halla? Not being able to answer even if he'd wanted to, they'd dragged him back to the hulk he shared with two-hundred others, and which was ironically named 'Lucky Star'.

He heard what he took to be distant thunder, then seconds later he heard the heavy thud of dirt and stones rain down against the ship's hull and decks, then alarmingly he felt the whole ship begin to rise. Timbers creaked and from somewhere tin cups and plates rolled and clanged. Surprised faces looked out from under blankets and screams and shouts soon filled the air.

He flew to his feet and clambered along the deck, clutching at beams and bunk just to stay upright. The whole ship was still rising and now rolling as though they were out on a stormy sea. He was one of the first to the latrine window where they dumped their night-pots. It was disgusting but it afforded a good view, and what he saw painted a huge grin on his face. "God-oak be blessed!" he breathed.

Hobbs was a hailstorm of falling debris and smoke, and the prison ship was riding the blast-born tsunami which was now racing along the Thames. Behind him he heard a hundred confused voices scream and shout, but he couldn't keep from laughing. "Hammer the bastards!" he shook his fist out of the window at the soldiers that ran like ants away from the cataclysm.

Timbers screamed, and ropes and chains stretched until they could hold Lucky Star no longer and then they snapped. Severed rope ends whipped away from one another and chain links rattled against the hull like cannon shot. He flinched and looked away as shrapnel thudded against the porthole, showering him with splinters. "This is it!" he cheered like a maniac, and then turned and pushed his way through the crowd ignoring their questions and seizing his chance. "This is it!" he bellowed. If there was ever going to be a chance of escape, this was it. "With me!" he roared and led them along the swaying deck and out into the open.

Another gruesome shriek rang out and Krast spun on his heels. "Holloway?" he shouted into the murk. Severed gaslights breathed flaming jets, and sparks flew like shooting stars. The room was littered with rubble and wounded men, and he caught sight of something huge and luminous like a deep sea creature, snapping at one of the devisers lying on the floor. *Dear God!* he thought. *Is that something alive in here with us?* He saw a creature of some kind and its wings, if they were wings, disturbed the smoky air long enough for him to get a clear glimpse, and his innards turned to water.

Something wallowed in the darkest mayhem, snatching at men with spider-like arms and gulping them down into its gullet. Was it one creature or many? Krast was witless with horror. A gas pipe flared, momentarily illuminating a bloated abdomen: its translucent skin bulging with struggling men within. The room thronged with bizarre creatures that his mind couldn't comprehend. But their intention was clear enough.

"Christ, no!" someone screamed and Krast heard gristle being wrenched from bone, and the scream became just an incoherent gurgle.

Wits or no wits, instinct kicked in and Krast stumbled towards the door in blind terror. Beasts fought over his staff, dragging and tearing at them like a gristly tug of war and the air was full of screams and smoke.

"Mr Krast, sir!" Holloway stumbled after him, his face was bloodied and his eyes rolled in their sockets. "Mr Krast, sir, we 'ave to be away!" He staggered past him to the room's only exit.

"Move!" Krast hauled him backwards.

Holloway hit the floor with a grunt and tried to stand just as something wet and terribly strong lashed around his leg like a noose.

He made the mistake of looking behind. It was almost wholly flat and its mouth covered its entire body and bristled with teeth. Valonia would have recognised it, but this crib-robber was unlike hers, this one was as large as an ox and capable of swallowing prey much bigger than infants. "Please God, Mr Krast, sir!" he begged.

Krast tumbled through the exit and into the corridor outside where the stone spiral would lead him away from this insanity, and he pulled the bulkhead door shut with the crazed strength that comes with terror.

Holloway felt himself being dragged back through the rubble, back into where the smoke was thickest and the screams and sounds of snapping bones were loudest. He saw the door closing and knew that this would be his tomb. "Please God, Mr Krast, sir, 'ave pity, sir!" he shrieked, but his only answer was the deathly sound of iron ramming home. He blubbered in panic, twisted around and saw the crib-robber's gaping mouth rise up to receive him, and the last thing he knew, before insanity swept his mind away, was the creature's membranous stomach engulf him like a womb.

The guards manning the hulks were much like warden Moore, men recruited from the poorest parts of London and for whom their job not only kept the wolf from the door, but indulged their need to dominate others.

At the sound of the first explosion they'd run to the rail where they stared in disbelief. Hobbs Ash erupted before their eyes, but when the ships had begun to lurch they scrambled around the deck with their own safety in mind, heedless of their duties. One after another, each rotting hulk tipped and bucked as the pressure wave rolled down the Thames. Ropes stretched to bursting, pylons were sucked out of the mud and torn to kindling, leaving guards stranded with their captives. Seeing their lifeline severed, they had a new problem; they were cut off with hundreds of witches, and as everyone knew, witches ate babies and turned great men into stone. The decks were slick with rain, which made footings all the more treacherous. Guards cursed, screamed, slid around helplessly, cried out and finally abandoned their posts and the hatches to the prison levels were inevitably left unguarded.

Aboard Lucky Star, hatches clattered back and forth with the undulating ship, beating a tune of freedom that Jack Peel couldn't deny. He saw an open square of sky above him, murky with rain and evening gloom and he thought it the most beautiful thing he'd ever seen. He clawed his way towards it like a man possessed, along a staircase that was now almost vertical and swaying like a tree in a gale. "UP!" he roared.

He led them to fighting or death; either was better than sitting in mouldering blankets waiting for the next interrogation, he thought, and from the looks of the small army at his heels the rest of Lucky Star's prisoners agreed.

Jack burst out into the October rain and ran at the first guard he saw and fisted him heavily in the stomach. The man tried to shout a warning, but he didn't have enough air left in him to squeak let alone shout. Jack snatched his rifle and suddenly there were witches all over the deck. Men, woman and children flooded out of the open hatchway. Some ran for the rail thinking to take their chances and swim for it, but many others followed Jack's lead and took the fight to their captors.

Jack had no liking for guns and refused to fire. Instead he swung the rifle like a club, which considering the slippery deck and pitching ship, made better use of the weapon. Each time the rifle hit home there was a satisfying crack and he screamed like a devil.

It was over very quickly. The guards were caught by surprise, still dazed by the spectacle of Hobbs going up in flames. Some opened fire and one or two prisoners went down, but the rest swarmed forward regardless, intoxicated by the promise of freedom. They might be without their wands and staffs, but they fought hard and dirty. Guards with bloodied noses and wild eyes were hurled over the rail or down into the hold, rifles were smashed against the deck, and when the damage was done Jack knew it was time to make a break for it. "Swim for it!" He had no idea where to go after that, but anywhere was better than here.

Crying children ran around the deck looking for a familiar face in the chaos. Jack grabbed one, a boy of about nine, and dragged him to the rail. "Don't waste time, get over and be gone for Oak's sake!"

The boy writhed in his grip and stared at him, breathless with terror. "I can't swim!" he cried.

"Well I can," he hauled himself up onto the rail. "Trust me, I'll get yer to shore!" The lad shook his head and then, panting with fear, he crawled up to join him. "Just don't look. Hold me hand an we'll go together."

The boy put his trust in the stranger, screwed his eyes shut, and gripped tight. Jack plunged over the rail dragging the screaming child behind him, and that's how, in just ten minutes, Ada Crabbe, a humble gardener, crippled the Illuminata and emptied their prison hulks.

By the time Krast slammed the last bulkhead door closed he was trembling uncontrollably. He felt icy cold and a sheet of blood smeared his face and his tattered suit. Of the thirty-three staff in the first-dawn bunker he was the only survivor. "They were eaten, dear God, they were eaten!" he gibbered.

As the door boomed closed he rammed the bolts home, although he doubted if the abominations he'd seen could be stopped by puny things like doors, no matter how heavy they were. He rested there for a moment, dazed and unsure where he was. This should have been Hobbs Ash, but everything looked different. He gaped around him, making small whimpering sounds. Ash rained gently down from the sky and in his shocked state he somehow believed it was black snow.

Fires raged across Hobbs. The generator station looked half melted. The east and south walls were reduced to crumpled mountains of brick and only two of the original six chimneys were still standing, but miraculously they were still discharging smoke as though nothing was wrong.

It appeared that the chromosite shed was ablaze as well. He couldn't be sure because the infantry barracks were in the way, but from the hefty 'pop' of exploding tanks he was almost certain. The station's distinctive glass roof, where the krakens were barracked, sagged in the middle like a deflated balloon. All around him the ground was buckled and distorted. Plates of earth, metres thick, lay like broken pottery and he saw with amazement that the destruction ran in a perfect circle, following the line of the cyclotron. Alarms rang and fountains spurted from ruptured mains and pillars of fire from broken gas pipes. Men ran through the devastation with buckets of water, but their efforts looked laughably inadequate. Hobbs Ash lay in ruin. Krast doubled over with a coughing fit and spat a wad of dust and blood. When he looked up he saw an infantry sergeant approaching through the smoke, leading a squad of men.

"Knight Superior, sir!" He halted just yards away, clearly shocked by his appearance. The Knight Superior looked like a bloodied scarecrow. "Are we under attack, sir?"

His wits had begun to speak again, and through the smoke he discerned the Fortitude. *Valonia*, he thought accusingly. "Yes, we're under attack," he said calmly. More chromosite tanks burst, and boomed like cannons.

"Who, sir?" The sergeant turned left and right, looking for someone to shoot at.

"Witches," he snarled, staring in the Fortitude's direction. He wiped a hand down his cheek. It came away scarlet and the sight of his blood made him think of what Valonia had said, *'Witch-blood'*.

"Sergeant," he barked, "guard this door, make sure nothing comes out. If it does, kill it. I don't care if it's man or beast, kill it stone dead."

"What's down there, sir?"

"Demons!" He fumed, and staggered away without waiting for an answer. He'd been outwitted and humiliated by one old witch, and by God didn't he just admire her the slightest bit? He stumbled through an unrecognisable landscape, towards Valonia's nest of vipers, possessed by a rage so consuming that it made him feel unstoppable. He would feed them to the chromosites one by one and he'd start with that brat they all so adored – the one who'd softened Hathwell's heart. He'd start with Rowan.

CHAPTER TWENTY-SEVEN

Triumph from Ruin

It took Krast much longer to reach the Fortitude than he'd anticipated. The ground had become an obstacle course of earth and rock tilted at perilous angles, but he doggedly continued forwards with his rage still boiling.

As the evening drew in, Hobbs Ash looked more and more like a vision of the underworld. Burning buildings illuminated the landscape and everywhere he looked Krast fancied there were dark shapes, monsters escaped from the first-dawn bunker. He felt no shame at leaving the others to die, but he'd take the images to his grave. He muttered as he lurched onwards, cursing aloud, citing all the devilish things he'd do to Valonia and her kind. He'd make them watch as their pet, the girl, was fed to the chromosites. He'd have them entombed inside living krakens and hunt down Britain's last witches using their life-essence. He had no end of retributions planned, but the chromosites would be the first of his punishments. *That's if there are any chromosites alive*, he thought, which made his mood even blacker.

When he finally cleared the worst of the broken ground, his knees and palms were bloody and he stumbled into an army of men dashing around with stretchers or buckets. At last he grasped the extent of the devastation and nobody gave the ragged Knight Superior a second glance; he was just another filthy survivor. "You!" A gruff voice came and Krast turned around to see a large man with an accusing finger thrust at him. "Look busy, you idle sod. Grab a bucket and get to the generator. The whole bloody thing's ablaze, shift yer self!"

Krast ignored the man, forgetting what he must look like, and the sergeant barged his way towards him and grabbed him by his jacket.

"Shift it, I said!" he roared into his face.

The big man raised a fist and Krast's anger finally found a place to go. "Imbecile!" he screamed and shoved him to the floor. "I am Knight Superior!" He stood over him, shaking with fury, while the sergeant stared up at him aghast.

"Beggin' your forgiveness, sir, but I 'ad no idea it was yer self," he grovelled.

"Get up," he jabbed him with his foot.

He nodded eagerly and got to his feet, puffing heavily. "Didn't recognise you, sir," he gasped again.

"Never mind that," he silenced him. "What's the situation?"

"Generator's destroyed sir and the station's ablaze, but crews are on to it with water pumps. It'll be a miracle if the krakens come out of it intact sir."

"And the chromosite shed?"

The sergeant gestured to his rear, which was now just a wall of thick black smoke. "Fire's been doused, but most of the shed's gutted, sir."

"All of them gone!" he groaned.

"Shed's north end survived, but what the contents are like is anyone's guess, sir."

"Survived, you say?" His eyes rolled in his muddy face, and the sergeant was relieved to see that he'd perhaps done him a service.

"Aye, sir. Ordered any surviving tanks to be taken to the ice-house. It's one of the few buildings left standing and I thought it'd be cool –,"

"Quick thinking, sergeant," Krast interrupted. "We may yet salvage something out of this." The sergeant fired off a brisk salute as Krast wandered away to see if the Fortitude was still intact. Heaven forbid that they'd fled somehow. The last thing he wanted was a single witch escaping Hobbs Ash.

Hathwell spent what felt like hours crawling through a maze of debris, through total darkness and sometimes through pools of mud. At least twice he saw the evening sky, but neither of the openings were large enough for him to squeeze through.

Eventually as he wriggled through a tunnel of earth, he felt the muddy walls give a little. He shuffled onto all fours ready to push with his back. His metal knee felt like broken glass in his leg but he endured it and heaved with his shoulders. The roof yielded, and after a second heave it crumbled and rock and soil rumbled down and a window of sky appeared. Coughing and spluttering, he dragged himself up, losing a shoe in the process. But he didn't care: he could breath again and he was alive, which was more than could be said for poor Ada Crabbe.

He slithered down a mountain of wreckage and landed in a puddle of rainwater, where he greedily cupped handfuls over his face and swilled the grit from his mouth. Then he set about trying to work out where he was. The Hobbs he knew was gone and all he recognised was the curved shape of the Fortitude hovering away in the gloom. The fires glinted off its hull and it looked like some monstrous skull. Without knowing why he set off towards it, limping along with his bad knee and bare foot, and with no idea of what he'd do when he got there.

The two sentry boxes at the gate had toppled inwards and looked like drunks propping each other up. Hathwell saw a lean figure silhouetted against the flames and knew who it was right away. "He survived?" he muttered, incredulous and angry. *A blow to the head,* an unexpected voice urged. *In all the confusion who'd know?*

Before he even stopped to think he reached down to clutch a rock, but something hard dug into his back and he had a better idea. His bayonet was protection against Moore, but it would do just as well for avenging Ada. A second later he'd drawn it and was heading Krast's way, slave to a tide of anger that would only take him to the noose.

Oblivious, Krast stared at the wreckage. Hathwell saw his shoulders rise and fall, and wondered if he'd bother to even face him or just plunge the blade between them. He closed the gap, aware of jumbled voices fluttering around his head and knowing if he stopped to listen they would certainly talk him out of this madness. He gripped his bayonet tight and blocked out all thoughts. Five paces away he splashed noisily through a puddle and Krast turned.

Opposites met. Hathwell's fury was suddenly confronted with the last thing it expected – joy.

"Hathwell! Thank God!" Krast grabbed him in a comrade's embrace. "Praise the Lord they didn't kill you too."

Behind his back, Krast didn't feel the bayonet's tip pressed to his muddy suit, and Hathwell made the mistake, or avoided one, of listening to one of those clamouring voices. *You helped kill Ada, but are you really a stone-cold murderer, Bertrand Hathwell?*

Krast slouched and stood back. "Are you badly hurt, Bertrand?"

"No," he replied, but not to Krast's question, and his arm wilted. "No sir," he managed. No, he wasn't a murderer, just a coward.

Krast returned to the spectacle of Hobbs Ash. "That's twice some witch has tried to kill me."

"Sir?"

"The old whore conjured a host of demons!" he accused, as if Ada had cheated somehow.

"But you escaped, sir."

Krast didn't detect his chagrin. "Yes, thank God, but those poor men. I tried to help, but it was no use. Murderous Jiks!" He already believed his own lie. "And now I'll be sure to pay them back," he promised and started towards the Fortitude.

"It's not safe, sir," Hathwell hauled him back, worried by what he might do to Rowan. "Look." He pointed to where draught horses were being tethered to the Fortitude. "It's going to be hours before the machine's righted."

Krast had been cheated of his revenge, for now. "Then dawn," he vowed, and Hathwell exhaled, knowing Valonia had escaped his wrath, but only for the moment.

Dawn is often said to inspire hope, but for Valonia it could only bring woe. After some hours in the dark the Fortitude was dragged back to horizontal and the feeble lighting restored. She knew Krast was done toying with them, taking Ada yesterday proved that. She'd held a brief conversation with Hilda and Lana, trying to keep the downbeat crowning just between themselves.

With Ada gone and their numbers depleted it was unlikely they'd be strong enough to open the earth and even if they did, the tunnels under there would be impassable. Their plan of escape was looking improbable at best. If only they'd not been locked up, they might have stood a chance of running while Hobbs lay in flames and confusion. Valonia had lamented this all night and the more she thought of it the more bitter she felt.

"*Valonia?*" A voice tapped gently at her head.

The old witch looked up from where she dozed in the crook of her arm. "*Lana?*"

"*Have you come to an answer? Do we take our chance and break the earth as planned?*"

She rubbed her eyes and pinched the bridge of her nose. "Why not," she yawned, forgetting that Lana couldn't hear her.

"*Valonia, are you still there?*"

She projected her thoughts, which was strenuous after a sleepless night. "*What can it hurt? We might get a chance to run for it through the chaos.*" She wasn't hopeful. She was old, and without Skald to whisk her away she'd be doing well to make it to the Thames, so she put her hope in her friends. Lana and Hilly were younger and she was confident they had a fighting chance of getting Rowan to Kolfinnia. The image of them side by side again was enough to keep her going.

Lana fell silent, perhaps relaying the message to Hilda, and Valonia slumped against the wall and wrapped three times to Rowan. There was a pause then a dainty knocking, and Valonia smiled. She shuffled into a more comfortable position and focused her will, reaching out through the metal. *"Rowan, we're going to leave here today, as soon as we're out in the yard. Understand?"*

She didn't reply. Instead Valonia heard two knocks to signal 'yes'.

"Good girl. When we get outside, stay close. We'll find the iron vein and with the right asking we can split the earth and be away." But the effort left her dizzy. How in Hethra's name could she split the earth if simple crowning left her so drained? She'd not slept well for almost a month and the rations were dreadful. It was getting harder to concentrate on magic, but she knew if Krast still lived he'd soon come looking for vengeance.

That vengeance came an hour later. First, Krast got Hathwell out of the way, sending him off to start salvaging the krakens. He suspected his squire's loyalties had been tarnished by Valonia's vipers. He had let them twist their poison coils around his heart, but now wasn't the time to punish him. Krast still needed him and his suspicions could wait for now. With Hathwell dispatched, he gleefully sent warden Moore to bring him 'the girl' from the Fortitude.

Valonia heard heavy feet outside and the rattle of keys in the lock, but the door didn't open and her heart turned to ice when she realised that it was the cell next to hers – Rowan's cell.

"Valonia!" The girl's thought flapped around her mind like a stricken butterfly.

In an instant she was on her feet and pounding walls with her fists, and kicking with her feet. "Rowan!" she screamed.

Lana and Hilda took up the protest, screaming the girl's name and battering helplessly at the metal.

"Monsters! Fiends!" Lana roared.

"Bring her back, you bastards!" Hilda screamed.

Valonia felt Rowan's fear as a breeze of cold air about her ears. She stopped hammering and listened. Behind the racket of Lana and Hilda's anger she heard soft footsteps and a stifled sob from out in the corridor. Moore took the cell's young occupant away to Krast, who had retrieved the only live chromosite from the gutted embryo shed. Chance had indeed smiled on the Knight Superior.

Those two hours from the moment Rowan was taken to the moment she was brought back were the longest of Valonia's life.

To begin with, Lana and Hilda's frantic questions buzzed around her head and the longer she kept quiet the more forceful they grew, but she couldn't speak let alone crown. She heard muffled shouts as both of them tried to reach her through the walls, but all she could do now was cry. She slumped down in defeat and curled up against the wall. *He's done it, the monster's taken Rowan.* She pressed her hands to her face, trying to hide in the blackness. The serpent-twins were undone. She had failed them as well as Rowan. She promised to keep her safe and Krast had broken that promise. The hate she felt was enormous and she made a new promise to herself: when her cell door next opened she would kill whoever stood there. After a while she became aware of Lana and Hilda's crowning calls.

"Valonia, answer me! I can't keep this up!" Lana pleaded.

She looked up from the cover of her hands, where a sinister fantasy had been playing out, one in which Krast was fed to the host of Ruin piece by piece. *"Lana?"* she sent a weak thought outwards.

"Thank Oak! Valonia, what's happened to Rowan? They've taken her, haven't they?" Her two Wards waited to hear an answer they already knew.

"Yes", she nodded, *"they've taken Rowan."*

Krast looked down at the chromosite's retina. The girl had been interrogated hours ago and by now Moore would be leading the whelp back to her cell. This temporary work station had been erected in the ice-house, and so he wore a long overcoat and woollen rather than rubber gloves. He sat hunched over the accusing eye, looking for all the world like a pauper picking at a meal of offal.

He had issued orders to have London put on alert for escapees and prepared newspaper articles encouraging sightings to be reported in return for generous rewards, but Krast knew it was futile. Of the eleven hundred and twenty-two witches detained onboard the prison hulks, only seventy-eight remained. Some would be rounded up or found floating in the Thames. It had been a cold night and not every one of them could swim, he was sure, but still the numbers made for a gross embarrassment. "Godless Jik scum," he hissed under his breath.

He prodded wearily at the chromosite retina with a scalpel, watching the blade slice its milky membrane. After weeks of fruitless searching he didn't see how the dim-witted Wildwood girl could yield results, but it pleased him to think of Valonia's horror at her interrogation. In fact, he almost thought about heaving the gelatinous eye into the stove and listen to it bubble and spit, but he'd come this far, why not just examine it? He was curious and his curiosity won him over, and so fate smiled on Krast again. He took up his eyepiece and began to examine Rowan's innermost thoughts.

Valonia and her friends waited in silence, listening to the distant rumble of boilers and all the while thinking of Rowan. When the door to her cell opened Valonia knew she had to be ready. After weeks of poor food, confinement and stress, she felt sickly and disorientated, but she had to focus if the spell was to have any chance of working.

"What are you planning, Valonia?" Lana asked cautiously.

"Nothing!" she retorted.

"I can hear your mind at work."

She didn't reply, but sat silent and brooding. She was a witch and her life had been dedicated to Hethra and Halla, not to killing and vengeance, but that didn't mean she had no understanding of these things. She knew one or two curses, knew what forbidden words would strike her enemies down, and although the cost to her soul would be high, right now that seemed paltry.

Almost two hours later she heard footsteps again and wondered which of them would be taken this time, but that thought held little fear for her. She and her Wards could take care of themselves and at least they had enjoyed a full life, unlike Rowan. "I'm glad you found Kolfinnia," she smiled to herself. "At least you found a friend to call your own."

She braced herself against the wall, facing the door, and clenched her fists in readiness. She slowed her thoughts with a series of deep breaths. When the door opened she would kill him. She prayed to Hethra that it would be Krast, hoping he was still alive so that she might enjoy watching him die.

"This is not a witch's way, Valonia." It was Sigriður Stokkur she heard, her old coven-mother, the witch who'd dreamed up the way-bewares.

"Then for the next few moments I'll not be a witch, Sigriður," she said to her empty cell and stared at the door, willing it to open.

The footsteps halted just outside. She heard the jangle of keys being plucked from someone's belt. Keys rattled in a lock and again she felt dismay when she realised that it wasn't her door. She stood up and waited, electrified, listening to which of them would be taken next. She heard Moore's voice. "Ger in there, brat." There was the sound of bare feet padding against the metal floor. Valonia gasped. They'd brought her back.

The door slammed and keys clattered again followed by Moore's hefty footfalls. She could hear him humming a tuneless melody. "Rowan!" She banged on the wall. There was a pause, punctuated by calls from Lana and Hilda, and then she heard Rowan's soft knocking come back to her.

She pressed her forehead against the cold metal. *"Rowan, please, tell me you can hear me?"*

There was a wet sniff followed by a trembling sigh, *"I can hear you."*

Valonia knocked again, lower down the wall, and Rowan signalled back from the same place. She manoeuvred herself to within inches of the girl's face and that's how they spoke, side by side with metal between them. *"Rowan, do you feel strong enough to talk?"*

"Yes," she sounded lost.

"Rowan, did they hurt you?" She sensed the others listening.

"They cut my hair and put a creature on my head and asked me things."

Valonia already knew what they asked, and Rowan had no choice but to divulge the answer. *"It's not your doing. Whatever they found out is not your doing,"* she stressed.

"I couldn't help it. They asked and I just saw the answers."

"None of us could have done any different. Rowan, don't pay for their sins with your guilt."

"I didn't want to tell them." She ran a hand over her shaved head and the painful scar. *"They cut all my hair off."* For a girl of only seven this was somehow the worst of all.

The misery in her voice almost broke Valonia's heart. *"The creature's task was to steal your thoughts, Rowan. It's how these people get what they want. But take heart, maybe the creature didn't see your thoughts clearly enough."* She felt a tingle through the metal.

"Really?"

"Yes," she smiled, grateful just to have her back. *"Now tell me, did the tall man with the marks on his face come at any time?"*

"He was there to start with, then left."

"So, he's still alive," she muttered, feeling perversely pleased.

"Mr Hathwell didn't come, I didn't see him." Even now, she still held some affection for him.

Valonia marvelled at how resilient children could be. *"Rowan, I want you to think now. Today's the day we leave here, but before we can we have a special job to do and I need you help."* She pressed harder, feeling rivets bite her aged skin.

"We're going home?"

"Yes, we're going home, but first what answer did they steal from you?" She was careful with her words. She would never concede that Rowan gave them anything. Lana and Hilda momentarily forgot their woes and waited for the answer to the greatest and oldest mystery in witchcraft – where lies the terra-soula?

Rowan stroked her shaved head and thought of her friend Kolfinnia, and how together they'd fought barghests and saved an empress and even glimpsed a fairy. She remembered how wretched she felt when she discovered Kolfinnia had gone to find the Hand-of-Fate without telling her and how Kolfinnia was building a new coven with help from Clovis, and none of them knew what lay under their feet. The Timekeeper was not the only miracle of Kittiwake-coven. She took a deep breath and recited what she'd seen: an answer that the chromosite had copied and smuggled away for Krast. *"In the south west, under a circle of eleven stones carved with swords, the Swords of Britain, they're called. The twins came there very long ago, brought by the deep currents of fire, and they lay asleep and safe."*

Even the misery of her predicament couldn't dampen Valonia's wonder. Hethra and Halla were found. She thought Rowan was finished, but just then the girl spoke again.

"It's where hrafn-dimmu went. It's where Kolfinnia, Skald and Clovis are, but they don't know about the twins."

Valonia pressed a hand to her mouth. "Does this nightmare never end?" she groaned. When Krast set out to capture the twins he'd find Kolfinnia also. They had to warn her somehow. *"Rowan, you're sure of this?"*

"Yes." She drew her knees up to her chest and hugged herself.

"Valonia?" It was Hilda.

"Just a moment, Hilly," she insisted.

In their own cells, Lana and Hilda stood quietly, feeling the world under their feet balance on a tipping point. This was their only chance to save Hethra and Halla, and there were only three witches and a girl to undertake nothing short of a miracle. Hilda nibbled at her fingernail and in the next cell Lana ran her finger gently around the door lock, trying for a weakness in the metal, until at last she couldn't stand the silence any more. *"Valonia, what do we do?"*

"Think, Valonia, think!" She clutched her head.

Rowan had been gone for two hours, she calculated. Krast would need at least an hour to decode the chromosite and even then its meaning might not make complete sense to him, but if it did, in a worst case scenario, she guessed the Illuminata would know the whereabouts of Hethra and Halla by noon. That left them with only one session of yard time before Krast had his answer, and after that he'd probably kill them all, or worse.

Their next fifteen minutes of yard time were supposed to be used for their grand escape plan, but now after what Rowan had told her she knew they'd not be leaving this place. When they went outside this morning, one of them must attempt fenomi, the spell of spirit-travel, to go to Kolfinnia with a warning. It would be exhausting and dangerous, leaving no time to try and escape. The serpent-twins came first, above all else. Valonia cursed silently under her breath and then in a fit of rage she punched the wall, making a hollow booming sound, and she groaned despairingly.

"It's all right, Valonia, I understand." It was Rowan.

She looked up, startled. *"Understand what?"*

"That we can't leave as you promised. We have to warn Kol."

At the mention of the word 'promise' she hung her head. She had made many promises and it seemed that they'd all failed. Rowan was right, they couldn't go as planned. She shook off her despair and banged on the wall, signalling them all to listen. *"Witches,"* she began when she had their attention. *"Kolfinnia sits atop the greatest wonder in witchdom, and now we must assume Krast knows where to find the twins. We must warn her and I see no other way but fenomi."*

Mute bangs rumbled back to her, a sign that they understood.

"This morning we must make best use of our time outdoors and send warning to Kolfinnia." Valonia now reached the hardest part, *"Lana, the risk is great but you're most skilled at this. Do you accept?"*

In her cell, Lana straightened, *"I accept, coven-mother."* Then for good measure she said it aloud. "I accept."

"Lana . . ." She wanted to apologise, to say that she didn't have to take this dangerous duty, she wanted to say that she refused to lose another witch the way they'd lost Ada, she wanted to say so many things, but none of her words measured up to her love for her friend. *"Blessings of Oak and Holly be on you, sister,"* she uttered finally.

He sat back and rubbed his stiff neck, then removed his gloves and blew on his fingers to warm them. He wasn't sure what he was seeing; his wits were slow, it was cold, he was tired and the Illuminata had all but been decimated by one old hag, but Krast's instincts told him the eye had something important to tell him. And so he leaned forward again.

There they were again. He saw a collection of standing stones blurred by the magnifying lens and swimming with chromosite fluids, but a distinct picture nonetheless. Standing stones, by what looked to be the sea and below them the land was shown in cross-section, layers of mud and rock, faulted and folded. Deep under the lowest layer was a chamber with no apparent opening to the surface, a chamber within which lay two tiny snake-like beings. He shook the weariness from his eyes. "Good God! No, it can't be." He rubbed at his eyes and looked again.

The closer he looked the more detail he saw: a collection of ramshackle buildings by the coast, perhaps the remains of a village or fishing station. He painstakingly counted the stones while his pulse began to quicken and yesterday's defeat started to lose its sting. "Ten," he muttered, "no, eleven." He counted them again, then a third time. "Eleven stones by the sea." He began to tremble.

Could this be them, he thought? Could this be Hethra and Halla, or at least the girl's pictorial representation of a powerful object known to witches as dragons? Rowan's safety was suddenly paramount to him. Who'd taken her back to her cell? Had she been hurt in the interrogation? *But where is this location?* he thought. It might not be Britain and even if it was there were literally thousands of miles of coast.

He pushed himself back from the table and laid an ice-blanket over the precious eye, then he made for the door, anxious to hunt down the answers. Outside it was dawn and Hobbs looked even worse than last night, but he was charged with a new cause and through that filter the damage looked insignificant. "You!" He called over two guardsmen. Both were filthy and exhausted. "Guard this building. Nobody but me goes in or out, you understand?"

They looked at the dilapidated ice-house and back to Krast, but they complied without question and stood either side of the door, guarding whatever was on the other side of it, which could've been ice for all they knew.

Krast went to begin the hunt. The girl had given him a lead and his next step would be to interrogate her again. No matter how long it might take in the end he would have them and he'd make Valonia watch as her deities were used to rebuild the Illuminata. Now, instead of having them executed as he'd planned, he relished the idea of keeping them captive until that wonderful day arrived. At that moment he saw a courier running towards him in haste, framed by the slowly rising sun and blowing clouds of breath in the frosty air. Krast had no idea, but the hunt for the dragon deities was over even before it had even begun.

Sunday's message had reached London.

"Knight Superior, sir!" He ran up to him, frantically waving an envelope. "Sir this just arrived, news that couldn't wait." He held out the plain envelope and Krast snatched it away from him in annoyance. Whatever it was it couldn't be as urgent as his own discovery.

"Who sent this?" he demanded.

"Sheriff at Trebbington, sir," he gasped.

Krast was confused. He didn't even know where Trebbington was, least of all why the Sheriff there would send him a courier. He broke the seal and tore open the envelope. Inside was the Sheriff's letter and inside that was a folded square of paper. He read the Sheriff's letter first.

To the Knighthood Illuminata - Knight Superior Krast.
This anonymous note concerning a hidden coven was delivered to the church five days ago.
The information has been verified by my own scouts.
I pass the matter into your capable hands.
Loyal Regards, Sheriff John Cotswold,
Trebbington and Halewater District, Cornwall.

Five days ago? he thought. Plus however long it took for the courier to get here. He stuffed the letter into his overcoat pocket, then he turned his attention to the second note. This one was written in a beautiful script, and for the second time that morning fate smiled on Knight Superior Krast.

He read the note over and over and then almost looked up to the rosy clouds above. Surely there must be some guardian angel watching over him, he thought. He looked down at the note again to be certain he was reading it correctly and all the while rocking his head back and forth, grinning in disbelief. In one night the Illuminata had fallen into fire and risen from the ashes.

The courier coughed politely and Krast looked up.

"Good work," he complimented him. "You must have been on the road for days. There's a field kitchen that way," he raised an arm. "Go refresh yourself, then find me and return a message to Trebbington."

"Aye, sir!" he saluted.

Krast's mood had taken a turn for the better and he even smiled at the man and patted him fondly on the shoulder. As the courier set off to find some breakfast, Krast stalked away and read the letter again:

Fifty miles past Trebbington along the coast of the far south west, where lead and tin were once mined, there is a coven named 'Kittiwake'. The founding wand came from Wildwood and the new coven stands by the sea, close to a circle of eleven stones known as the Swords of Britain.

The girl's image of eleven standing stones by the sea suddenly made sense, and the founding wand's origins hadn't escaped his notice either. "The cunning bitch," he whispered. He'd opened his heart to Valonia, and she'd insulted him. She'd played him. She'd called him a traitorous witch, and all the while she'd known about Rowan. "The Swords of

Britain," he murmured, and tapped the note against his lips. Suddenly he was torn. Should he gloat before Valonia, interrogate Rowan again, or order an immediate assault on this new coven? He wanted so many things and all of them sounded wonderful.

He stood and watched the relief operation slowly gain momentum, turning chaos back into order. To the east, the rising sun glinted off the station's crumpled roof, and his mind turned to the krakens inside and how they would need them very soon. "Make Purity ready, Hathwell. We're going to war. Time we blunted those 'swords'," he smiled.

Newborn daylight gleamed across his scars like liquid gold. He watched the rising sun flow and shimmer like a living thing, then made up his mind. He wanted to torment Valonia. "Oh, what a beautiful day!" he sighed, buttoned up his coat and set off towards the Fortitude.

CHAPTER TWENTY-EIGHT

Flight to the Swords

An organisation like the Illuminata requires men performing just the right task at just the right time to run efficiently. Inevitably breakdowns do occur. It might be something trivial such as not enough writing paper or ordering the wrong diameter rivets.

Before Ada had turned first-dawn into scrap, Krast had sent orders that yard time be suspended. But with Hobbs Ash going up in flames it was inevitable that such a minor command be lost, and so he set off to the Fortitude convinced he would find four cells with tightly locked doors and behind them four witches. It might have seemed like a small lapse, but as Krast crossed the disfigured landscape of Hobbs, Valonia and her witches were already being herded down the gantry and into the crisp dawn air. The Illuminata had slipped up.

Moore glowered at them as he unlocked the cells. "Get up and get moving, Jik scum." He pointed along the corridor where guards were posted every ten yards, young men with frightened faces not old enough to see a razor.

Valonia sensed a great deal of hatred, and she didn't need magical skills to detect it. The guard detail was also more heavily manned than usual and as they were shunted down the narrow corridor men were rough with their rifle butts, nudging and poking, and hard with their tongues, cursing and ridiculing them.

Valonia walked in front with Rowan sandwiched between her and Lana behind, and Hilda at the rear. Together they formed a living shield around the girl. All of them, except perhaps for Rowan, heard the hate crackling like static. At the end of the corridor the exit hatch stood open, and as always it made her yearn for freedom, but there were eyes and rifles everywhere and only when she stepped out into the frosty October morning did she fully understand why.

Hobbs was a wreck. She halted at the top of the gantry steps some thirty feet above the ground, enjoying the stunning view, and gazed respectfully at Ada's handy work. "Well done Ada, very well done," she whispered.

"Oi! Keep movin' or I'll come up there an' throw yer down," the guard at the foot of the steps shouted up to her.

She caught the amazed looks on her friend's faces and then gingerly edged down the gantry which was dusted with frost. Rowan followed close behind; she'd given the girl her scarf to cover her bare head and make her feel less conspicuous. Once at the bottom they clustered under the machine's curved belly and sat there on the frozen ground, with Lana in the middle and the others around, blocking her from view. Fifteen minutes was a shockingly short amount of time for such a complex spell, and Lana would have to find Kolfinnia, deliver her warning and then travel back, all before they were sent back inside. Once inside the Fortitude the machine would make the spell impossible. This was their only chance and if they ever needed Hathwell to come and extend their yard time, it was now, although after yesterday she wasn't sure that any of them except perhaps for Rowan wanted to see him again. She remembered him leaving with Ada, taking the old woman to her doom, but ironically it had turned out to be the Illuminata's doom also. Fate was fickle, and maybe, Valonia thought, just maybe Hathwell's weakness had done them a good turn. "As we discussed," she whispered. Guards prowled around the Fortitude, keeping an eye on them and keeping fingers on triggers.

They all sat silently, looking dejected, knees drawn to their chests and facing outwards with Lana in the middle already centring herself, ready for the spell. Valonia and Lana sat back to back, maintaining physical contact and making sure Lana's body wouldn't slump. Once her spirit left her flesh, she'd be effectively one of the 'twilight people', one of the living-dead. Valonia felt Lana's shoulders rise and fall against her as her breathing grew slower and deeper.

Fourteen minutes remained.

"Oak be with you." Valonia wished she could bid her good luck face to face.

"I'll send Kolfinnia your regards," she replied discretely. Rowan and Hilda did what they could to screen her and when she was ready she lay her head in her arms and lost herself in the blackness there. In the privacy of her own embrace she could forget Hobbs and concentrate. *"Give me this one chance,"* she pleaded.

The words of the spell were easy, the hardest part was focusing, and all the while the clock was ticking. She began with a few deep breaths. As she did she commanded her mind to release its anger and other unwanted things that would keep her grounded. She had no need for them now and they'd be like ballast. She was aiming to let her spirit rise from her body and drift out of her crown chakra like chimney smoke.

Suddenly she felt a falling sensation. She opened her eyes and saw she was no longer leaning against Valonia, instead she was looking down at them all including her now empty body, which rested corpse-like in the huddle's centre. In her spirit state her wounded arm was restored. She saw her bodily self and she was shocked by how bony her hands appeared after weeks of incarceration and she was glad her face was hidden. She looked around. The guards seemed content to let them sit on the frozen ground and waste their time. They certainly couldn't see her. *Time to go*, she thought.

She turned to the west and saw a brilliant volcano of power erupting far away, casting its glory miles up into the sky. That was hrafn-dimmu's call. Kolfinnia's army and most importantly the twins incarnate, lay in that direction. She drifted out from the Fortitude's underbelly, past the sullen looking guards and into the glorious October sunshine. She looked up and sure enough above her she saw Oceana the sky-whale, her spirit guide, circling in the endless blue. *"Dear friend, it's good to see you again."* Oceana dipped her broad tail and rolled gracefully. Her beautiful song rolled across Hobbs Ash in reply, unheard by all except Lana. *"Will you guard me as I travel, or be with me until the end, when I am no more?"* The greeting was not just said for ceremony, there were real risks out there. Sometimes witches attempted fenomi and never returned.

The great whale flowed through the blue as deft as a living cloud and sang a mysterious song that only Lana understood. She smiled and after one last look at her friends she rose upwards. Oceana turned and sailed towards hrafn-dimmu's sign with Lana's soul riding by her side.

They journeyed for miles and the land below passed in a whisper. Hills and mountains, moors and vales rushed past in a blur and despite the gravity of the warning she carried she was thrilled at the prospect of seeing Kolfinnia again. In seconds, the tower of light from hrafn-dimmu grew large enough to fill the sky, arcing overhead and now streaming into the firmament on all sides until it was hard to see from which direction it came from.

In spirit form Lana could see a host of night creatures returning to their daylight lairs: haggen-thralls, bloat-goblins, drummon-toadies, keddy-pots and a host of nocturnal fairy species. They darted through the air around her leaving glowing footprints in the atmosphere. Most of them were indifferent to her, but a few came closer to nip at her soul or try their hand at mischief and turn her off course. However, whenever they tried Oceana bellowed an ear-splitting whistle and they fled in terror. Free of her body, Lana was one with life energy and she could detect the souls of stones rising as a miasma from the earth; she could hear the steady breathing of millions of trees, and lantern-moths were drawn to her energy. This was a Britain seen by very few indeed.

Hrafn-dimmu's light was as dazzling as the rising sun and she knew she was almost at Kolfinnia's coven. Oceana's huge tail swatted at the air and the elegant creature began to descend towards a beautiful coast where the cliffs were rugged and a tower of rock stood out in the sea. The wand's song emanated from there and Lana thought that it was like coming home. She saw glowing trails of light in and around an old mine and knew it could only be witches, and somewhere amongst their number was Kolfinnia. She plunged down towards them, ablaze with excitement.

The morning was still young but Kolfinnia had already been working for several hours. Since Wildwood's arrival her spirits had lifted, but it had also brought new problems.

Sally Crook had brought Ada's lightning-staff amongst other things and just yesterday she had found the staff empty and lifeless. Her thunder-sprite was gone. He had been called back to the thunder-heights some time the previous evening and that could only mean Ada had gone to walk Evermore. One of Rowan's defenders had been killed, and it was the worst omen possible. Now Kolfinnia was more determined than ever to take the fight to London and if at all possible rescue Rowan or die in the attempt.

"You've no need to worry of that happening to me," Skald assured her.

"I know," she said softly as she walked through the courtyard with Skald on her shoulder. "We've made a new pact together, but sometimes I feel I've taken you from Valonia."

"No," he said firmly, "she wanted me to come with you, just as she wanted you to have raven's wand."

He was right, but it seemed that she worried about everything these days. For starters, a few of the others grumbled that she was showing favouritism, making sure her friends got bigger rations or more responsibility. It was nonsense and the grumblers were few, but she lost sleep about it. At least Sunday had been amiable lately; in fact, it seemed that her generosity and patience knew no bounds, which of course made her very popular, but Kolfinnia very uneasy.

Kolfinnia had been patrolling the shore, keeping an eye out for ships. She feared that one day soon there would come a fleet with their cannons trained at them. Even with many good witches to help, she couldn't shake the idea that Kittiwake would stand or fall by her wisdom alone. After their patrol she checked the gardens where she found Flora and Clovis, and of course Farona. Since Flora had arrived he'd taken a new interest in gardening.

"Clovis, the shore's clear. What time's weapon practice?" She plucked an apple from a basket by Flora's feet and took a bite.

"Hey, save some of those for Samhain," Flora insisted.

Clovis was adjusting his sword. "Practice in one hour, breakfast first," he patted his stomach.

"And how are they coming along?"

"Very well, but they're not ready for London if that's what you mean." He had a knack of cutting to the heart of her worries. "But our Farona here is handy with a staff."

All eyes turned to the youth and he blushed almost as red as his hair when Flora smiled warmly at him.

Kolfinnia looked at her feet. "So it's just us then?" she mumbled.

"A smaller party, well prepared might get in and out. Take too many and most of them won't be coming home," Clovis reminded her.

The gardens were starting to fill and she wanted this discussion over with quickly before words found the wrong ears. "We'll make final preparations tonight, and aim to leave for London in two days."

"And I'll come with you," Flora insisted.

"We've been through this. Kittiwake needs you here," she said, not unkindly.

"The gardens have plenty to tend them. Don't exclude me again."

"Kittiwake needs someone to keep it from starvation through the winter. I can't risk you on a mission to London."

She folded her arms. "Are you ordering me to stay?"

Kolfinnia was about to elaborate, but at that moment the world dimmed and the colour drained away leaving only a monochrome impression. She swayed slightly and her hands fell limp at her side, her eyes twitched and rolled up in their sockets and then she swooned forwards in a dead fall. It happened in a second. One moment she was debating with Flora, the next she was falling. Clovis leapt forwards and snatched her from the air before she hit the ground.

"Looks like your words were harder than you thought," Farona muttered anxiously.

"Don't joke!" she retorted. "Kol! Can you hear me?"

Kolfinnia heard worried voices calling her, and then everything went black and cold. The voices melted, and in essence . . . she died.

"I must apologies for bringing you here like this." The voice was strong but mellow, and the words had a rhythmic lilt to them.

She looked around and saw that she wasn't in the gardens any longer, and Clovis and the others were nowhere to be seen. From up here she could see the tower keeping its lonely vigil out in the waves, but now it blazed with colour and power and it took her a few seconds to fathom that she was standing amongst the Swords of Britain, the stone circle on the hill. She looked around and when she caught sight of the tall figure she cried out in joy. "Lana!" She rushed towards her, but found herself there in an instant, having travelled without running.

"As I say I must apologise," Lana smiled. She was wispy and vague and Kolfinnia could see the stones through her body. "We're here in spirit only. You lie in your gardens surrounded by your friends, while I, Kolfinnia, lie in London with Valonia, Hilly and Rowan. They send their love, by the way," she smiled.

Kolfinnia held her hands out. They were ghostly, and she saw that the sky was black and starry although it'd been dawn just seconds ago. The landscape was brilliantly lit, but it was monochrome and strange creatures glided through the daylight blackness leaving luminescent trails, creatures that only spirits could see, and far away she heard the beautiful but lonely song of a whale.

"Normally I'd wait until you were asleep before appearing like this, but time's very short. I have minutes at best and I've come with warning."

"Is it about Rowan?"

She nodded gravely. "She lives, but they know where the twins are resting."

Kolfinnia was horrified. "You mean they tortur –,"

Lana put a finger to her lips. "Shhh, we do not speak evil in spirit. It will attract creatures who thrive on such awfulness. Simply know that Rowan is safe with us."

Kolfinnia didn't doubt it, but this Lana looked twice as old as the woman she remembered. "And where are they, the twins?" she uttered. It didn't seem right to learn such a magnificent secret this way, but she was powerless to ask.

Lana smiled again, but there was no humour in it. "Right under our feet, under these stones you know as the Swords of Britain."

She looked down at the heather in disbelief. "They're really down there, under my very feet?" She had the absurd idea that she might be insulting them by treading on them.

"Listen carefully, your nemesis is called Krast. He's not only the Knight Superior, he's also a traitor of witch-blood and when he comes for the twins he'll find you."

"They're coming so soon? But we're not ready!"

"You must abandon your rescue attempt. Nobel though the sentiments were, Valonia wouldn't hear of it. Rowan's our responsibility, and yours is to find a way to save the twins, perhaps take them elsewhere."

"I wouldn't know where?" She desperately wanted to appear a strong leader, but so far she felt all she'd done was snivel.

"Send them deeper into the earth," Lana balled her hand into a fist, "back into the deep fire where they'll remain for a hundred-thousand years and when next they come close to the surface maybe there won't be the likes of the Illuminata, and human folk'll have learned to live right."

"Deeper," she agreed shakily.

Lana nodded, and then looked down towards Kittiwake, admiring her handy work. "Well done coven-mother Algra, for everything you've done."

Kolfinnia sensed her departure was imminent. "I want you to stay," she felt tears that couldn't possibly be there sting her eyes.

Lana looked upwards, towards the day-night blackness where the divine sound of whale song reverberated through the stars. "I cannot, dearest," she smiled again and her tattooed cheeks wrinkled under her dark eyes. She opened her arms and Kolfinnia went to embrace her, but clasped nothing but empty air. From right by her ear Kolfinnia heard her parting words. "Rowan sends her love."

Kolfinnia awoke in gardens she'd never left, lying in Clovis's arms and saw a crowd of anxious faces staring down at her. "Lana was here," she spluttered, "and we're going to war!"

Krast's concern was triggered when he saw guards patrolling around the Fortitude, although from this distance he couldn't see Valonia and the others sitting underneath it. The guards ought to have either been inside or at the gate. Quite clearly the captives weren't where they were supposed to be. "Must I do everything myself?" he groaned and quickened his pace. The sentry boxes at the gate, which had been righted, drew closer and Krast saw their occupants present their rifles and salute. "At ease," he barked as he sailed past them and into the compound. Ahead, he saw Moore, who still had a bruised nose, chatting with some bored looking guards. "Moore!" he called. "Why are you not inside?"

The large man spun on his heels and saluted hard enough for his half smoked cigarette to flick away from his fingers. "Knight Superior, sir." His helmet was pulled down way below his brow and Krast could see his eyes peering out like glistening clots.

"Dispense with the formalities and answer me. Why are you outside and not on duty where you ought to be?"

His chin receded further into his fat neck and his mouth puckered into a confused pout. "Beggin' your pardon sir, but no such orders came my way, sir."

Krast glanced over Moore's shoulder. "Where are the prisoners?"

"Yard duty as normal sir, bang on time, not a second early, not a second late." He sounded proud of his efficiency.

Valonia looked up. By the worst luck possible Krast had come and Lana had still not returned. "Come on, Lana, come back to us now," she moaned while she watched Krast roast Moore at the gate in front of his men.

"My orders were clear!" he fumed. "Captives are to be kept in."

"As I'm sure they were, sir," Moore simpered, "but none came my way, sir, never arrived, sir."

"Imbecile!" Without warning he slapped Moore hard across the face. The crack echoed across the compound and a deathly hush fell. Moore stood firm, taking the humiliation but silently swearing he'd make the witch filth pay for it later on. "Very well," Krast simmered down, "get them back inside right away."

Moore marched off, already planning his vengeance. *That old slut and the rest of her heathen bitches, they'll pay for Krast's insult. Then we'll see about evenin' the score with Mr Hathwell too.*

Krast remained where he was while Moore went to herd them back up. He had underestimated them, but he wouldn't make that mistake twice. *When they're safe in their cells, I'll tell Valonia the good news.* His fingers curled around Sunday's note and he smiled in anticipation.

Valonia heard the crunch of gravel and smelled the tang of cigarette smoke. She risked a glance around at the others. Rowan and Hilda looked as frightened as she felt, and Lana lay as still as wood at her back. "They're coming!" Hilda hissed.

Lana raced towards the rising sun, which had now cleared the horizon, back the way she had come, eastwards towards Hobbs Ash. The miles flew past and now she began to believe that she might succeed. Each beat of Oceana's tale shaved away the miles between her and Valonia. *"Believe in me, I'm coming!"* She willed her thoughts to reach them.

She stayed close to Oceana, flying just under the protective shield of one of her broad flippers, and as London's outermost districts began to wheel past Lana heard the first screech of rage quickly followed by a rumbled warning from Oceana. She looked back and saw a host of mawners.

There are many creatures unseen by the living, and mawners are amongst the most tragic. They are lost souls so bent on finding the gates to paradise when they die that they refuse Evermore and remain earthbound, always searching for the keys to heaven, and the longer they search the more grotesque they become.

A host of them were closing the gap extremely fast and the first of them was upon her in a moment. It was a woman, but bone-thin and covered from head to toe in bulging eyes, all of them rolling and staring, desperately seeking a paradise that didn't exist. *"The keys!"* she hissed and grabbed at her. *"The keys to heaven good lady!"* Spectral fingers gouged her soul.

"There are none!" Lana screamed, ripping its hand free. It let out a shriek that was grief and madness combined and tumbled away into the clouds trailing tears from its hundreds of eyes.

"The keys, good lady, bring us the keys!" Hundreds of voices pleaded at once.

She looked up and saw the host plunging down through a mountainous cloud bank, thousands of staring eyes fixed on her and pleading hands outstretched, some clutching begging bowls, and she braced herself for battle.

"Up!" Moore roared as he marched towards them, his keys rattled on his hip like an angry snake. "Up, you Godless bitches!"

Valonia looked around, pretending to see him for the first time. A troop of guards was now clustering around them, rifles pointed their way, but still she didn't move.

"Are you deaf? I said up, yard time's done. Back to yer cells." Moore stabbed a finger towards the gantry.

Hilda gripped Valonia's wrist. "If we go inside she'll not get back," she hissed.

Rowan's frightened eyes darted between the witches and Moore, whose face grew redder as his temper swelled. She could still see the mark made by Krast's palm on his unshaven cheek and she knew he'd make them pay for the insult.

Valonia looked up into his flinty eyes. "Our friend is sick. We'll need time to tend to her."

"Do that inside," he brushed her concerns away. "Now up and move. Knight Superior's waiting."

"She's too sick to move. Let us tend to her here."

"I don't care if your darkie-slut friend is 'aving a baby. You either carry her in now or we'll do it."

One of the guards went to snatch at Lana's arm and Valonia pushed him aside. "Off her!"

The young man leapt back. "Hey! She went to attack me!" he whined and looked to Moore for help.

"Right, I've 'ad enough of these games," he spat. "Lads! Look sharp, get 'em inside by any means necessary. Don't worry about bruisin' the goods." He lunged at Valonia with his booted foot.

She leapt to her feet along with Hilda and even Rowan, and all three of them formed a triangle around Lana. "She's sick and she can't be moved!" Valonia boomed and the look on her face was enough to make them stop. She marked each one of them with her trembling finger, exploiting their ignorance to the limit. "You'll not touch her!" She circled slowly making sure her finger passed cleanly over each of them. "Or hearts will stop."

Men backed away. One old woman had ruined Hobbs Ash, now here was another promising yet more carnage. Moore was outraged, and he could almost feel Krast's disapproving stare against his neck. There was going to be a lot of payback for today, and he knew just how to start. He drew his revolver and snatched at the girl's collar. Rowan yelped in surprise as she was hauled off her feet and in a flash he had her pressed to his hip with the revolver's muzzle buried in her back.

"NO!" Valonia spun around, and Rowan saw horror and despair pass across her face.

"Na' then, Ms Witch," he rasped. "I'm askin' yer nicely, like a gent. Make your way inside with your Jik darkie friend."

His voice was low and dangerous and she saw that one misplaced word or gesture would be enough of a spark and Rowan would be killed. She exchanged a glance with Hilda and realised they were beaten.

The clouds thickened as they descended and the mawners fell upon Oceana like a shoal of piranha, clawing at her, trying to rob her energy.

376

The whale rolled away from them bellowing in rage and the air quaked. Her call raced outwards in a pressure wave, instantly vaporising a dozen of them, but many more swarmed around them, keeping to the cloud cover and out of direct sunlight.

"Keys for the lost children of heaven!" one cried, crawling over the whale's back, biting and gnashing as it went, with its hundreds of eyes weeping.

The whale bucked and heaps of mawners were thrown from her hide. She pitched left and some were flung away into the sunlight, still trailing gauzy strips of her skin from their claws, and when the rising sun struck them they exploded into dust leaving nothing but a dying scream.

Lana streamed around her like a tiny fish, sweeping off as many as she could. She banished them with words of will, or wrenching them free, but their numbers were endless and now they swarmed over her also, tearing away her memories and dropping them into their begging bowls.

"The keys, show mercy and give us the keys. Let the children enter the gates!" they begged over and over.

She lashed out at them and tore hands from her flesh. She screamed every spell she knew until the dust from their ruined bodies spun in clouds, but still they thickened around her. Countless despairing eyes pressed in and she was soaked in their tears and the world turned black.

"All is lost," she thought calmly and without fear, *"all is lost and we shall die here."*

Then, when all was at its darkest, Oceana let loose a piercing cry and the world shook under her rage.

Valonia reached down slowly to where Lana lay slumped on the ground. "Help me, Hilly," she said, moving as slowly as possible, grabbing every second she could. The sky above was cloudy but still, and she had no idea a battle raged up there. Hilda took Lana's other arm and together they gently lifted her, hooking an arm each around their shoulders.

"Better," Moore complimented, "now, get her back inside, and best to do it quick." He looked down at Rowan and flashed Valonia a hateful grin.

Without a word they started away carrying their friend even as her soul fought to come back to them. Moore shuffled along at the rear keeping a tight grip on Rowan's collar, and the sombre parade edged its way back towards the Fortitude.

Oceana's cry was so loud that Lana's vision blurred and the acoustic barrage almost shook her to pieces. The piercing note filled the world, then became the world; it swept through every cloud and obliterated the mawners hiding there.

The cry died away and Lana opened her eyes at last. Oceana was hovering protectively above her and all around them dust from the destroyed mawners swirled and spiralled. She had killed them with her song. She flew level with Oceana. Her eye rolled ponderously in its socket and regarded her, and Lana saw a myriad of bite marks in her spirit-flesh. *"My thanks again, beloved guardian,"* she lay a hand on her flank, just below that wise and ancient eye. *"We must go. Hobbs is very close now."* She flew ahead with Oceana matching her speed and they streaked downwards towards the ribbon of silver that snaked its way through London, towards the Thames, towards Valonia.

Valonia and Hilda struggled up the steps, going as slowly as they dare. "Keep it slow, Hilly," she whispered.

Hilda looked down from the sky and into Valonia's tired eyes. "Where could she be?"

"Wish I knew." They were ten steps away from the hatchway. Valonia adjusted her grip on Lana's wrist, whose skin was cold and hard, and she knew each step they took was a step closer to her doom.

"What do we do at the top?" Hilda whispered.

"I'll think of something," she promised, but she only had nine steps left to do so.

"Keep movin', ladies," Moore shouted from their back, and reluctantly they did.

The Thames curled around Hobbs Ash like a noose and Lana recognised it right away. She poured her last reserves into driving downwards as fast as she could. From this distance she couldn't see the Fortitude, but Hobbs Ash was one huge blistered area of broken land. She was only moments from Valonia now and with the rising sun the last of the night-creatures had fled to their holes, and Oceana sang to encourage her onwards. *"I'm coming, Valonia!"* she called, just hoping the mawner's attack hadn't cost her the race.

Three steps from the top Valonia feigned a stumble, and they dropped Lana to her knees and Hilda clutched at the rail to stop herself from falling.

Moore hadn't seen it coming and he bumped into their rear. "Shift, you

378

evil harpies!" he roared and squeezed Rowan's neck until she squeaked in pain. This had taken too long and now his patience was spent. "Grab 'em," he ordered, and two guards by the Fortitude's hatch shouldered their rifles and went to collect Lana's body.

"No, you can't!" Hilda's answer was a rifle rammed into in her chest. There was a solid thud, and she grunted and slumped against the rail. Valonia scrambled up, but Moore was ready.

"One bullet's all I need," he waved the revolver next to Rowan's head, "understand?"

Hilda straightened, gasping and clutching her ribs while Valonia watched helplessly as Lana's body was picked up and hauled like a sack of flour towards the hatchway.

"Move," he commanded.

They edged backwards towards the hatchway, then the guards lifted Lana through it and dumped her in the corridor. Keeping her eyes on Moore, Valonia backed up and something thudded against her heel. She turned and saw it was the hatchway rim. She slowly lifted one foot over it and back into the machine, feeling like a traitor. As Hilda did likewise, a single tear fell from her cheek. Both women looked longingly to the sky, eyes rolling as they scanned the heavens, but the sky was empty. "Lana," Valonia pleaded.

The Fortitude was easy to spot. It sat like a squat ugly spider at the edge of Hobbs Ash. Lana made her final flight, ignoring the panicking voice that told her she was already too late.

She saw bright sparks, the souls of Valonia, Hilda and Rowan, jostling with the guards on the gantry steps and knew whatever time-wasting tactics they'd employed were now spent. She raced down like an arrow directly to where she could see them being forced into the Fortitude. *"Valonia!"* she cried and Oceana added to her feeble shout with a deafening whistle.

Valonia looked up through the hatch at nothing but sky, but she was certain Lana had called her. "Lana?" she shouted and one or two puzzled guardsmen looked her way.

Now their small party was through the doorway. Moore stepped through last and shoved Rowan to Valonia's side. "Keep the brat," he sneered and then he pulled on the curved door, sliding it downwards. It made a grating sound as it devoured the rectangle of blue sky, walling it away behind steel.

"Lana!" Valonia lunged for the door with no plans or ideas left; she just wanted her friend back. Moore tried to stop her and she raked at his face and he yelled in pain.

"You friggin' old bitch," he roared and tried to punch her, but stumbled on Lana's body and his fist crashed harmlessly into the wall.

"Lana!" she screamed again while behind her Rowan howled in fury and Hilda tussled with one of the guards.

"She's gone mad!" Moore cried, and shoved her aside. He grabbed the handle a last time and pulled. The sliver of sky was replaced by steel and the door clanged shut with a boom that killed all hope.

Lana saw the door close and screamed in rage. A second later she crashed against the Fortitude's hull but couldn't pass through it. Inside Valonia raved and clawed at Moore, trying to drag him away from the opening, but rough hands yanked her aside and pinned her to the floor.

"Restrain the hag!" He wiped blood from his cheek. "Jiks," he growled contemptuously.

"Lana!" Valonia sobbed again.

From outside, a mellow voice sang in her ears one last time. It was all of Lana that could penetrate the Fortitude. *"Kolfinnia sends her love,"* she said.

Valonia crumpled with grief and Hilda and Rowan knelt and added their sorrow to hers and the three sat there sobbing together.

"Jiks!" Moore muttered again and rolled his eyes.

Outside, Lana circled hopelessly and now there was nowhere left to go but the steps and doors of Evermore. *"Lead on, my Lady,"* she said sadly, and after a lingering look at the Fortitude's blackened hull Oceana and her charge set off on their last flight.

CHAPTER TWENTY-NINE

Valonia the Un-witch

Kolfinnia's wits gradually returned and Clovis helped her to her feet. "That was quite a fright you gave us," he picked up her fallen hat and inspected her closely.

"What happened?" Flora wanted her to sit down, but she seemed to be looking around for someone.

"Didn't any of you see her? Lana was here!"

They looked even more confused now.

"You just collapsed and went as cold as ice. We couldn't wake you up." Again Flora tried to get her to sit, but she was having none of it.

"She was here, I swear!"

"Fenomi," Skald glided over to her shoulder. "Lana came in spirit, yes?"

"Yes!" The memory was returning now.

"Astral-travel? Very risky." Clovis grasped their conversation even in English, and shook his head, looking grave.

"We were up there at the stones," she pointed to the hill. Suddenly she remembered what Lana had told her, what lay deep beneath the stones, and she felt a terrible kind of awe so magnificent and heartbreaking that it was hard to bear.

"Kolty, what's wrong?" Flora's concern deepened.

"You said something about war," Farona added softly, not wanting the crowd to overhear.

"It's not how it sounds," she shook her head. "They're not coming for us. They want what's buried under the stones." She pointed again to where the Swords of Britain stood against the morning sky.

"They want the stones?" Clovis puzzled.

"No, they want them. They're buried right below the stones. They stole the secret from Rowan." She took a moment to calm down. "Hethra and Halla have been found, and our enemies are on their way to seize them as we speak." She indicated the stones again, "They lay buried under the stones."

Without knowing she'd done it, Flora slipped her hand into Farona's and squeezed. So great was his shock at Kolfinnia's news that he didn't even notice whose hand it was, he just squeezed back and hoped Kolfinnia was wrong.

When informed they were securely back in their cells Krast headed towards the Fortitude. The morning was beautiful and the rising sun lifted the frost in wispy veils and all around he could hear the clang of hammers and shovels clearing debris. "We shall rise," he promised himself, and his thoughts turned to Kittiwake and the fabulous prize waiting there.

The breakout and first-dawn's destruction had lost their sting. Machines could be rebuilt and prisoners recaptured. London was full of people eager to earn a shilling, and in his buoyant mood he even considered putting the ransom up to one sovereign. He bounded up the gantry steps like an excited child, so looking forward to telling Valonia his incredible news.

"Valonia? Please speak to me!" Rowan's thought came again, but Valonia was still too broken to answer. She just banged on the cell wall to show that she'd heard, and that was all she could manage right then.

Valonia remembered back to the day she met Lana Zuri, a girl of barely eleven who'd escaped a slave ship in Southampton and found them at Wildwood. Valonia had been younger then and betrothed, and that was another sad tale. Now, she just held her head in her hands and wished this nightmare would end.

"Valonia, please!" Rowan insisted.

"I'm here, child, but I can't talk right now."

"Did Lana get to Kolfinnia?"

"She did." That was her one comfort. *"Kolfinnia sends her love."*

There was silence from the other side of the wall as Rowan relayed the message to Hilda. Now there were only three of them. In two days she'd seen two of her friends die in the service of witchcraft and now she promised herself that she would kill Krast, even if the act defiled her.

She didn't care, she just wanted the monster dead.

She rubbed tears from her eyes and leaned back. Her throat was sore from crying, but it seemed there was plenty to cry about these days. Outside in the corridor she heard keys jangle again. Maybe Moore was coming to take some petty retribution, but she welcomed it. She wanted someone to pay for the last forty-eight hours and Moore would do nicely . . . to start with. She heard bolts slide free, then the door opened with a dry groaning sound.

"This is not a witch's way," Sigriður's voice came to her from down the years. And she was right.

"Then I'll be an un-witch for the next few moments, Sigriður," she vowed and readied her curse.

Moore cranked the door open and Krast stepped into the open doorway.

Perfect, she thought.

He clasped his hands behind his back, looking confident. "I must apologies for neglecting you of late. We had a spot of bother with one of your associates yesterday," he smiled coldly, "but that's been taken care of."

She said nothing: saving her strength. The Fortitude's alloy would rob some of the curse's power, and at the very least she wanted to maim him.

"I come this morning with news that I thought you might wish to hear." He fished for something in his pocket and drew out Sunday's note then waved it teasingly. "I'm pleased to say that your missing wand has been found. This letter filled in all the gaps." He made a show of regarding it thoughtfully. "The author of this note and I have something in common by your logic. You see, this note details where your old wand was used to start a new coven." He paused, savouring her distress. "And it was written by a witch. One of your own sold you out, Valonia, a traitor-witch."

She knew Krast had discovered the twins, but now he knew about Kolfinnia as well and she was breathless with fury.

He saw the pain on her face and relished it like a vintage wine.

She glowered up at him and said nothing, but all the while the curse was accelerating in her mind, gathering speed, ready to slingshot out when she had the words turning at their fastest.

"You should be proud," he continued, "incredible as it sounds, your wand landed right where your cherished serpents lay sleeping. You could say it found them for us." He nodded in satisfaction and turned to the door. "Oh, Valonia," he turned back, "one of our medical officers examined your sick friend a moment ago, and I'm afraid to tell you that the good lady has passed on."

Their eyes locked.

"She'll be afforded a pauper's grave you understand. The city can't waste money burying dead criminals."

He was like a lighthouse beaming out hatred. She loaded the curse and readied to fire.

"Were you close?" he added in mock sympathy and behind him Moore chuckled.

That was her breaking point, and she lunged.

He had no understanding of the words. He merely saw an old woman sitting in a cell and snarling in rage. He'd beaten her and that was that.

Her secret words shot towards him, hit him and continued on through the bone, blood and tissue of his skull, aiming for the carotid artery behind his right eye. There, they wrapped themselves tight around it and gripped like a vice.

He flinched, swatted at his eye then let out a shrill scream and staggered back into the corridor and thudded against the wall. As soon as he slammed into it the metal dulled the curse. Would it still be enough, she thought?

"Sir!" Without thinking, Moore kicked the door closed and the corridor boomed with the sound of metal on metal.

She jumped up, trying to see through the greasy glass, but Krast was just out of sight. She'd seen the curse hit the target and she'd seen him fall, but she wasn't certain how much the Fortitude had disarmed it. "Let him be dead!" she hissed and immediately felt ashamed.

Suddenly the corridor was full of shouting and drumming feet and she almost cracked the glass as she pressed to see out. It was misted with her frantic breath, but just out of the corner she saw Krast being helped to his feet and pawing feebly at his face. She hadn't killed him, the monster lived. "Still," she said to nobody, "enjoy the reminder. A good son should think of his mother often."

Then she heard the thumping from Rowan's cell and knocked in reply. When she peered through the glass again she saw nothing. Krast had been carried away.

They hauled their Knight Superior outside into the fresh air.

Krast gaped all about him, confused and gibbering. His right eye was a dark pool of broken veins and although he could still see through that eye, what he saw had him clawing at his face. "Get away!" he shrieked.

"What's a matter with him?" Dobbins fretted.

"A curse!" Moore snapped. "Some witch curse!"

"You don't think they shrunk his 'gentleman', do you?"

"Don't be a burke," Moore slapped him around the head.

"Make him stop. It's chillin' me blood seein' him like this." He was deeply disturbed to see the great Knight Superior writhing in the dust.

"Get the surgeon!" Moore ordered.

"I dunno where he's at," Dobbins whined.

"Then bleedin' well find him, you arse!" Moore lunged a well-aimed boot at the seat of his pants and his foot connected with a hefty thud.

Dobbins howled and scurried away.

"Knight Superior, sir," Moore loomed over him. "Knight Superior, sir, can you hear me?"

"Get her away!" Krast seethed. "Get her away!" The world had taken on a reddish tinge, but although he could see Moore perfectly well he saw him through a filter. Another image floated on the retina of his wounded eye. Valonia's curse had burned a permanent reminder there.

A good son should think of his mother often.

Josephine's face stared back at him.

All words have some kind of power upon the listener, none more so than the word 'war', and when that particular word circulated Kittiwake the coven began to dissolve into fear. 'War' was a word that went with 'capture,' 'torture,' and a host of other terrible bed mates and it was now Kolfinnia's responsibility to make them all ready.

"Clovis, Flora, Farona, send word there's an important gathering in the courtyard in one hour. Attendance is compulsory." She tried to marshal her scattered thoughts as the others went on their way. "Skald," she held out her arm and he landed there.

"Your command?"

"I want you to be sprite-general. Tell all the others sprites what you did at Wildwood and how you did it. I want them all to know how to bring down krakens."

"We'll need a live demonstration."

"We'll set up a target and Clovis can put some fire into them by turning it to ash."

He growled approvingly and launched himself away.

She didn't know where these orders were coming from. They simply flew from her mouth and she was extremely grateful. Invasion was the least of her worries, so while her mouth dispensed orders, her mind tackled the most important issue of all – how to save the twins from the Illuminata.

Ten minutes later, after fighting her way out of the gardens through a wall of questions, she caught up with Clovis who'd been issuing orders for their war-meeting.

"Clovis, I'm concerned."

"That makes two of us."

"No, I mean they all seem determined to flee." She kept her voice hushed.

He leaned over and whispered. "Wait until you tell them the biggest news. That will hold them together."

"Which is?" She suddenly felt out of her depth.

He stopped and put a hand on her arm as he roared for attention. "Hear this! Everyone to gather in the courtyard at ten, no exceptions!" He sounded formidable, and Kolfinnia wondered, not for the first time, what he'd be like in battle.

Faces peered out from their tents and shelters. Those chopping wood or carrying water buckets stopped to listen.

"Which is," Clovis repeated, speaking quietly again, "to tell everyone that the heart of their beliefs, the very thing that makes them a witch, lies under their feet and they must choose to fight for it or desert it and run." He smoothed back his ears.

"You're right," she agreed shakily, "I must go and speak to Wildwood." She wanted to tell them of Lana's visit and she couldn't think of anything better right now than the faces of her friends.

The Wildwood camp nestled between the dunes and the small lake to the west of the old mine. Kolfinnia had come here at least four times a day since they'd arrived. Kittiwake was getting crowded, and so the Wildwood witches, true to their name, had built their own shelters in the woodland.

"Kolfinnia!" Sally Crook, still wearing her Seed-Fall colours, greeted her with a fond embrace. "Forgive me. I keep forgetting it's coven-mother, isn't it."

"Perhaps not for long."

Sally saw that bad news wasn't far behind. "They're coming again, aren't they?"

"There's a meeting at ten in the courtyard, and yes they're coming again, very soon I suspect."

"How did you find out?"

"You'll never believe it. Lana was here."

Sally's face bloomed despite everything. "Really?"

"She used fenomi to come here with warning."

Her expression went from joy to concern, "Risky. Then her news can't have been good, eh?"

Kolfinnia avoided a straight answer. "Come to the courtyard at ten. Bring everyone," she hugged the older woman farewell and hastened back to the mine.

Ten o'clock saw Kittiwake's entire two-hundred and four witches cram themselves into the courtyard, along with a couple of restless dogs and a parade of screaming and flapping gulls atop the buildings. Men and women carried small children on their shoulders so that they might get a better view and Clovis had dragged a dilapidated horse cart into the yard and flipped it over to provide a platform. At least two mothers carried infants born in the last month, born into war, and born on the run.

Kolfinnia stepped up. Clovis offered her a steadying hand but she politely declined. She climbed on to the cart and stood there clutching her lightning-staff, and drew strength from Skald. *"Whatever decisions you make, I'm with you,"* he promised.

"You spoke with the other sprites?" she whispered.

"I did and they're very excited. Let's hope the knights do come or they'll be bitterly disappointed."

She tried not to smile and looked out across a patchwork of differing coven uniforms and a forest of pointed hats. Expectant faces gazed up at her, and she saw Sunday watching intently. Even in wayfarer grey she was striking and surrounded by an escort of young men unconsciously drawn to her. Clearly the power to beguile hadn't left her. To the rear of the gathering Kolfinnia could see hats with the colours of Wildwood lashed around their brims: lilac, russet, blue and green, and she took comfort from them. "Witches of Kittiwake," she began in a clear voice.

Muttering and shuffling stopped.

"An hour ago I received news so urgent that I've called this special gathering to share it." She knew they were already thinking of war. "Some of this news might have been overheard and spread already, but now I wish to tell you myself so that there may be no room for error." She snatched a glance to her left; Sunday's expression was inscrutable. "A witch from Wildwood, imprisoned by the Illuminata, came here to warn me of their plot. Lana Zuri braved the dangers of fenomi so that we might have a chance to defend ourselves and more importantly defend others," she thought of the twins.

A baby cried gently from somewhere to her right.

"The Knights Illuminata have almost certainly discovered our location," she announced. Although she didn't know why, she looked in Sunday's direction as the rest of the coven erupted with cries of horror. Kolfinnia stood rigid, ignoring their cries, and scrutinized her face. The young woman never flinched; instead, she returned her impassive gaze and Kolfinnia wondered just how the Illuminata had discovered them so quickly.

Clovis stepped up. She felt the cart rock under his weight. He didn't so much as call for order but roar for it and his call rang in their ears and silenced their mouths. The shouts dwindled to mutters and then to silence. "I'd ask you to listen to what coven-mother has to disclose," he growled in his fractured English.

They looked terrified, Kolfinnia thought. Now she'd see if the news about Hethra and Halla might give them the will to fight on. "Lana also brought news of why the Illuminata are so anxious to come here," she called out.

"To kill us, isn't it?" someone shouted, prompting a few chuckles. Even Kolfinnia smiled and she strained to see the face through the crowd. It was Betty, Walter's jilted companion.

"Sorry to disappoint you, but we're not that important to them right now. It just so happens that Kittiwake was founded right on top of something they want to claim. That's why they're coming. Our being here is just chance."

She paused while they pondered this, and realising they weren't the Illuminata's prime target defused their fears a little.

"Is it the dreaming wand?" someone called out.

"The supply of spuds!" someone else chipped in.

"None of those things," Kolfinnia smirked, and shook her head.

"What is it then?" a boy of six asked.

Kolfinnia smiled, sadly this time. "Do you like tales of dragons, Chester?" She knew all their names by now.

The boy nodded shyly.

"So do the Illuminata. They love tales of dragons," she spoke to his innocent face, but her words were for everyone. "But they don't want to protect them like we do. They won't say sleeping-spells to ease their dreams, they won't look after their world. The Illuminata want to make a prison for them and keep them in it forever and abuse their souls."

He had no trouble believing her every word. He was an example to them all.

"The Illuminata want to come here, Chester, because there are dragons at Kittiwake."

Chester gasped and every witch present felt his sense of escalating wonder, except for Sunday.

"Deep underground, below the stone circle on the hill, lay two dragons dreaming." Her voice cracked, and as she spoke she saw them curled together in peaceful sleep. "One has scales of oak and twisted horns like branches," a tear rolled down her cheek, "his sister has scales of dark green and barbed like holly. These are the dragons the Illuminata want to enslave. These are the dragons that live and breathe under our very feet!"

Everyone finally realised who she meant and the whole coven broke into gasps of woe and wonder. Chester began to cry and clung to his father.

"Lana risked her life to come here and tell us that the terra-soula has been found at last, and we are Hethra and Halla's last champions!" She was crying freely, but her purpose made her feel a hundred feet tall.

A roar of outrage rose up and the crowd surged forwards, drumming their staffs on the cobbles. Clovis had never been more proud of her and stepped to her side and roared. Flora and Farona added their cheers to the throng and the only witch who didn't join the war-cry was Sunday, who stood looking devastated. She had inadvertently delivered the twins to their enemies, who were coming to claim them.

The surgeon general dabbed another swab to Krast's right eye, and the cotton came away clean. "The wound is superficial, sir," he mollified. "Within a few days the eye will be as good as new."

Krast sat trembling in the examination chair. "But what of the element of witchcraft there. What of this 'vision' I can see?" He saw Josephine through his right eye whether it was open or closed. He couldn't escape her.

"The ability to repair such a thing is beyond my skills, sir. I deal in flesh and blood. A curse needs the attention of the devisers."

"Most of them were killed, you oaf!" He thought of the men eaten in the first-dawn bunker.

"Your eye will heal, sir," he assured him again. Kind words were about all he could dispense.

"Not by your hand." He stormed out and went to see if any of the devisers could help. The glorious morning that had energised him less than an hour ago had turned rotten and there was no cheer left in the day. "I'll have the dammed thing pulled out by the root if I have to. She'll not beat me," he promised himself.

He already knew how he'd finish Valonia. He wanted to assault Kittiwake in two days, four days at the outside, then he'd pluck Valonia's sacred worms from the ground. His agenda had turned from political to personal. Nothing else mattered, not even alchemy or gold or Titus.

He thought of how his kraken Purity had eaten that wizened old man, and the idea of feeding Valonia to his war machine and using her essence to tear down Kittiwake left him trembling with an excitement that was almost lustful. He had to find Hathwell and order him to make the modifications.

As Hathwell passed into the Fortitude's compound Moore scowled at him. "Here for a taste of Jik slut, Mr Hathwell? Dark meat's off the menu though. Precious few of 'em left now anyhow, juss hags and children. But I bet you'd like a slice of both, though, eh?"

Hathwell stopped, turned, and spoke slowly. "Soon we'll go into battle. I'll ride as a squire and you'll be amongst the infantry. If we should happen to meet that day I'll be happy to finish this conversation with you then," he smiled dangerously.

"I'll look forward to it, sir," Moore grinned.

Hathwell stalked away. His days in the Illuminata were numbered. It'd taken quite a bit of cunning, but he recovered something for Valonia: a parcel wrapped in brown paper and tucked into his long overcoat. He considered it a token of his trust in her and he hoped she'd take it the same way.

He passed cells V and IV. Both were hauntingly empty and he'd helped empty one of them, and he knew that whatever god would finally judge him, he or she wouldn't take kindly to him not at least trying to atone.

He arrived at cell III but couldn't look in at the dark-haired woman that had captivated him, and neither could he check cell II, knowing the girl's innocent trust would be too wounding. He arrived at Valonia's cell and took the spare keys and released the lock, then absurdly he knocked timidly before opening the door.

Valonia stood with her cheek pressed up against the wall next to Rowan's cell. He had the idea she was doing something she ought not to, but that mattered very little now. "Gaolers don't usually knock, Mr Hathwell." She sounded very tired.

"Ms Valonia." He had rehearsed this speech, but now his mind went blank and so he spoke from his heart. "I know that after yesterday you won't think of me the same way, but I wish you to know that after meeting with you over the last weeks I *have* changed." It sounded weak, but he daren't say more in case devices were listening.

She looked unimpressed.

He rubbed at the back of his neck. "I suppose you know the Knight Superior's plans?"

She folded her arms and nodded slowly, at least he didn't have to try and tell her the bad news in code.

"Mr Hathwell, why have you come?"

He floundered.

"To take another one of us?" she stung him.

"No!" he exclaimed. "No, I came to bring you this," he looked down the corridor to check he was alone and then pulled the parcel from under his coat and offered it.

She remained propped against the wall with her arms folded, and regarded him accusingly. "Gifts?" she wrinkled her nose.

"It, was, well I thought that . . . " he couldn't finish. He placed the parcel on the floor and retreated back into the corridor. "I'm sorry," he mumbled and closed the door slowly. His fingers worked the key and he locked Valonia away with her sadness.

She listened to him leave, then her gaze drifted down to the parcel. There was something familiar about it, like a melody she knew but couldn't place. She pulled it closer, and her fingers confirmed what she first suspected; there was something inside that recognised her as well.

She felt a lump rise in her throat as she loosened the string, and when the paper unfolded and revealed its secret, first she smiled, then a stray tear fell onto the green fabric. It was Lana's neck scarf. Below that was a square of fabric roughly cut from Ada's coat. It had the Seed-Fall crest on it. "Thank you, Mr Hathwell," she said, genuinely grateful, and then pressed the mementos to her face and remembered her friends.

The courtyard was almost empty now. Kolfinnia had hastily divided them into four groups and allocated each a Ward to act as commander. She chose veteran witches from Wildwood and everyone accepted her choice readily. Sally Crook and Mary Fife were amongst her chosen commanders, while she and Clovis took the two remaining companies.

Despite the threat of attack, the usual coven business took priority: sleeping-spells for the twins as well as putting food on the table; gathering winter fuel, which seemed redundant now but to stop doing so was to admit their defeat; and a host of other duties they couldn't afford to ignore, for morale as well as good management. A small core of friends had gathered around Kolfinnia: Flora, Farona, Sally and Clovis, but she'd noticed how Sunday had skulked away at the end of her speech with her shoulders drooped, and looking grave.

"Fine speech," Flora looked pensive, toying with a big question. "But do you think there's any way we can avoid war?"

Kolfinnia looked down at her feet. "If we can find Hethra and Halla very soon and get them away to safety, then there's a slim chance we could evacuate and avoid battle. But we might have only days to do all that."

"Sounds like living on the run to me." Clovis was ever the realist.

"I agree, but getting to the twins bothers me most right now."

"Have you thought of how we'll do it?" Clovis asked.

"Lana said to send them deeper, back into the Earth's fire." She spared a glance towards the hill.

"Sounds sensible, but how?" Sally, her new Ward, looked around for answers.

"One witch here must have the skill of material alignment," Farona had heard fanciful tales of witches who could walk through solid rock, in particular the Ragged-Brothers, witches of almost mythic status. But such heroes were rare now, if they ever existed at all.

"Not that I know of." This was Kolfinnia's biggest worry. They had perhaps just a few days to reach the twins and then somehow send them deeper into the earth. *Forget it,* she thought. *Even the Illuminata with all their machines couldn't do it in less than a year.*

"Kolfinnia?" Sally enquired.

"We'll think of something," she said impatiently.

"Perhaps I already have." Clovis knew the time was at hand.

"What's keeping him?" Flora looked up at the cottage. Clovis was up there. He said he had a plan to reach the twins.

They were standing outside the cottage that Kolfinnia and Clovis, not to mention plenty of others, had used as a home for the last many weeks, and Sally, Flora and Farona stood with them. "Tell me again how you came to meet this witch?" Sally looked up at the windows, waiting for a signal.

"It's a very long tale," she sighed.

"He's something special, though, isn't he?" Flora added.

"Sunday thinks so too," Kolfinnia grumbled. "She's been making a play for him from the start."

"And she always gets what she wants," Flora said, then remembered Farona standing there. "I'm sorry, I didn't mean offence."

He shrugged amiably. "Since arriving I've had less and less to do with her. I'm not obliged to act as her escort any more, what with everything that's happened." He looked more confident now that he was out of her shadow.

"You need to find yourself a young lady. You're too nice for her," Flora teased, and the flustered lad read a hundred different meanings in her innocent remark and his heart jumped.

He was still trying to think of a witty reply when Clovis looked out through the open window. "All of you, I'm ready."

They all swapped puzzled glances, then filed their way into the cottage and up the narrow stairs. Clovis had set a small crate in the middle of the room and covered it with a blanket.

"What's under the cover?" Kolfinnia enquired.

"Our solution." He took a deep breath, reached out and drew the blanket aside.

The material fell away to reveal an octagonal jar about ten inches in height. The glass was thick and had a greenish cast and inside there was a pale liquid with something floating inside as if moving under its own power.

All of them gathered around and squatted for a better look at the jar's contents, but 'occupant' was a better description. There was a small, crudely carved, figure with stout arms and legs and a chubby looking face floating in the fluid. "This is Janus." Clovis stepped back and bowed reverentially.

The others wondered who or what Janus was, but Kolfinnia knew. "This is him, the god who led you here?" She'd never set eyes on him, but she'd been fascinated by his account.

"I led him nowhere, young lady. Clovis chooses his own fate." The voice was lofty and slightly disdainful and it came from the jar.

"It speaks!" Farona stepped backwards in surprise.

"So it appears," Janus said in a withering tone.

"It might be better if we sit a while," Clovis recommended.

He made the introductions and they all made themselves comfortable in a semi-circle around Janus, and then Clovis explained their situation.

At no point did he refer to Janus as the 'trickster god', and at all times he showed proper respect and dignity even though it was a struggle. Janus listened politely, sometimes drifting up and down in the liquid, and sometimes circling and flipping when Clovis reached a particularly exciting part of the tale. Watching him dance, almost gleefully, at the accounts of battles and danger, Kolfinnia's instincts told her to be wary of this character. Sometimes he would comment or compliment them on their efforts and his silky tones actually set her teeth on edge. She didn't trust him and she saw that neither did Clovis.

"Time is against you, it seems," Janus chirped after hearing their story.

"So will you help us? This is a task that can only be achieved by one of your power," Clovis appealed.

Janus considered, "I could open the earth so one of you can travel to the depths to find the twins, and send this 'terra-soula' into the deep fire, yes?"

"A fine plan, Janus, but it could be dangerous. It would be better if two or even three were to go," Clovis said what Kolfinnia was thinking.

"Let me think," he insisted.

They all waited for him to speak. There wasn't a sound in the room except for the tinkle of stone against the jar as Janus continued to spin and dance.

"I have decided that I will help you," he sang in his reedy voice. "The small matter of the cost I will name later, but for now I have decided that only one of you will go, and it will be one of you here."

They exchanged worried glances. Janus suddenly appeared to be dictating terms and Clovis's face darkened. Kolfinnia didn't want anyone going on a dangerous mission unless she or Clovis were the ones to choose them. Farona she deemed too young, Sally was one of her new Wards and skilled with a bow, and Flora had a key role in their provisions. That left her and Clovis, and with the Illuminata already preparing to march against them she wanted all their experienced fighters on hand.

One look at her face and Clovis understood her concerns, "Janus, I'd ask you to reconsider, and let us take the burden of choice from you," he said tactfully.

Janus yawned theatrically and see-sawed gently to the bottom of the jar where he made a delicate pinging sound against the glass. "Clovis, I'm weary," he muttered moodily. "Please leave me and come back tomorrow. I shall decide then which of you will have the pleasure of my company."

"But time is short, mighty Janus," he said with forced patience. "The enemy might be here tomorrow!"

"Then wake me early, but not too early. I do enjoy my rest."

Clovis forced a taught little smile and his ears flattened involuntary, and then he threw the blanket back over the jar in disgust, knowing better than to try and get any further with him today. *My coven was slaughtered for you*, he thought and wanted to smash the jar right there. "I'm sorry," he apologised. "Perhaps we'd better leave." He put a finger to his lips, indicating that none of them should speak until they were outside.

He's listening to us, Kolfinnia thought with a shiver as they filed out of the room.

Later that morning Kolfinnia managed to have a quiet word with Clovis. She finally tracked him down after weapons training, which was even better attended than usual. He was taking a well earned rest in the October sun. Tempest sat by his side preening his feathers as though he was the one who'd done most of the work.

"Clovis, I need to know how battle worthy we are," she pulled her long hair into a ponytail as she spoke.

"In what respect?" he rumbled as he unbuckled his armour; the conversation with Janus had left him in a bad mood.

"Well, how many witches have their own lightning-staff and thunder-sprite?

"At last count only sixty-two, and a good quarter of those are from Wildwood."

She swallowed back her shock. "And how many are of fighting age?"

"We have just over one-hundred and thirty witches that we could expect active duty from. The rest are sick, too old or too young."

She exhaled and groaned at the same time. "So we have a fighting force of about one-hundred and thirty which includes us?"

He inclined his head in agreement.

"That leaves about seventy without staffs!" She clutched his elbow. "Clovis, we can't ask them to fight with their bare hands, and to do what we did at Wildwood requires each witch to have two staffs."

He looked at her in a way that said he already knew. "What would you have me do?" he asked softly. "Tell them to run from coven to coven until they're too old to run anymore?"

"You know I wouldn't."

"Kolfinnia, even many of the unarmed witches want to stay and fight. Just knowing that the twins are here under this very soil has them ready to follow you into battle."

"But that still doesn't arm them, does it?"

"Suggestions?"

"We need more willing thunder-sprites."

"Well, unless you have a handy thunder storm in your pocket, I don't see how." He flicked the buckles on his chest plate and removed it.

"Maybe I don't, but someone else might." She was already thinking.

"I don't follow you?"

"Someone to ask the weather to help us," she muttered, forgetting he was there. "Someone to ask of the weather, the elements. Of course!" she cried at last. "She could do it!"

"I still don't follow you?" he complained.

"Weather is a basic gardening skill!" Exalted, she threw her arms around his neck and kissed him. He still didn't know what she was talking about, but he was glad to share her joy because there'd be precious little of it in the days ahead.

The grand station at Hobbs Ash stank of horses and manure. A circuit had been cleared through the rubble, enabling them to reach the krakens. Shire horses strained at their harnesses as they dragged twisted wreckage on wooden sledges. The placid animals were coaxed and prodded into action, but their efforts were slowly turning the chaos into something like order. That was the nature of the Illuminata, Hathwell thought as he watched the operation.

So far they had only extracted a handful of krakens. The rest were inaccessible for now, but he was certain the tough old beasts had survived, although they might be battered and scorched. He went through the motions of obedience without knowing why. He might oversee the salvage operation, but when it came time to ride out with banners blazing he didn't know which side of the line he should be standing on any more and when Krast came marching towards him, eliciting a rash of salutes, he hardly recognised him.

He was wearing a dark overcoat and a bowler-hat, his shoes gleamed, but Hathwell was stunned to see a patch over his right eye. An eye-patch that looked somewhat metallic.

"Sir?" he said uncertainly, trying not to stare.

"Hathwell, yes, sliver of glass trapped under my eyelid. Had to see the surgeon to get it removed," he lied.

"As long as you're quite all right, sir."

"Couldn't be better." He had to stop himself rubbing the patch. It was one of the deviser's hasty fix up jobs: fabric woven with the same alloy used on the Fortitude. It blanked the image of Josephine, but left him with only one eye and that final insult had sealed their fates. He would feed them to the krakens, no matter what his commanders said or how untested the machines. "How goes the salvage?" He slapped his gloves against his palm impatiently.

"I'm hopeful sir, they look to be intact."

"Select three of the best, including my own. I want them modified."

"In what way?" He reached for his notebook, expecting notes on calibres or exhaust volumes.

"Godfrey Hallam."

"Sir?"

"The witch Purity blessed. I want three krakens equipped like that including my own." He slipped his hands back into the leather gloves.

Hathwell felt ice in his veins. The science wasn't just shaky, it was obscene, and three machines meant three captives. *And no prizes for guessing which three*, he thought. "Sir, the apparatus is still experimental. Is it wise?"

"My squire feels at liberty to advise me now, does he?" he warned.

"I only mean to say –,"

"Say nothing," he interrupted. "Three krakens. You have thirty-six hours." He turned and left, expecting his orders to be treated as gospel.

Farona was in the cottage where he bunked with a dozen others, packing a few supplies into his satchel. He'd been selected by Clovis to fly out to the frontier with a few others to establish a few lookout shelters. Before he saw her he smelled the delicate scent of night-jasmine and sandalwood, then an elegant hand lay gently on his arm and he felt that same old mix of resentment, duty and longing.

"Farona?" The voice was petals on velvet.

"Miss Flowers," he greeted her with a brief bow.

"A moment of your time, please?"

"I have important duties to dispense with, miss." He was anxious to avoid her.

She reached across and swung the door closed, and now that they were alone in the small cottage her scent and presence seemed to increase ten-fold. She came and stood by his side and lifted a finger and traced it over the embroidered fox on his satchel, remembering their old home, and for a moment she looked deeply sad. "It's been so long since we left Regal-Fox," she began, "and I understand here at Kittiwake we must follow a new regime, but I'd ask you to be my escort one last time." She was having a hard time keeping her voice level. It wasn't every witch that betrayed their gods, and only now when she most needed friends did she realise that she had very few.

"I'm on my way to the frontier, my lady," he tried to excuse himself, but her hand lay on his arm again and as always it was enough to disarm him.

"It's not your time or company I seek, Farona," she smoothed her hand down over his, "although both would be sweet enough." She flashed him that look, the one that used to send fire through him, but he had changed these last few months.

"Maybe Clovis could help?" He looked longingly towards the door.

"Alas, while Clovis is the very model of wisdom, he lacks your special qualities," she moved closer still, "I'm asking for your help Farona, not Clovis's." And she desperately needed help right now.

"Anything I can do to help you, my lady, is a blessing," he mumbled.

"Then tell me, as one who Clovis seems to have taken under his strong wing, what does Kolfinnia intend to do about saving Hethra and Halla?" She stroked his hand absently.

Her overwhelming allure was scattering his thoughts. "It's a secret for now. We don't want to get the coven's hopes up just to dash them."

"Very wise, but the coven isn't here. It's just you and I, Farona."

He heard fabric whisper as she moved even closer. *Tell her!* he thought.

Just tell her then you can get out of here!

"Farona, please?" she sensed she was close to getting what she wanted.

"Clovis has a relic called Janus," he spoke quietly, "a god of sorts, and he's agreed to help us. But Janus insists on being the one to choose who will go to Hethra and Halla's aid." He thought back to Janus and his teasing laugh; the god had a cruel sense of humour. *You two'd get along like a house on fire*, he thought and almost smiled. That little spark was enough to loosen her spell a fraction and he gracefully withdrew his hand from hers.

She hardly noticed. She was more interested in this 'Janus'. "Clovis never spoke of this before?" She folded her arms in a way that pulled her dress tight across her breasts and he deliberately looked away.

"None of us knew until today. I'd best be off, Miss Flowers." He went to collect his staff.

"Farona. I'd ask you to inform me of any news of the serpent-twins and this Janus. I just have to know that Hethra and Halla will be all right. I'm sick with worry."

"I understand, miss, but why not just ask Kolfinnia yourself?"

She looked reflective. "She fears I'm a competitor, when all I have at heart is the twin's safety."

"I'll do my best."

"I hope so, Farona, for the coven's sake. It would reflect badly on her leadership if she kept secrets at such a critical time."

"I understand, miss."

"Remember, I only wish to secure the twin's safety, and do my part to help," she gave him a pleading look, which was mostly genuine. "That's not asking too much, is it?"

He nodded without agreement, "I really must be going. Good day, Miss Flowers." He snatched up his staff and eased himself away from her.

"Good day, Farona. Fly safe and return with blessings of oak and holly." She blew him a kiss and saw him redden, and then watched him leave.

CHAPTER THIRTY

Army of Thunder

Flora flopped down onto the stool, thinking hard. "I appreciate your faith in me, but I'm just not sure it can be done. Calling rain is one matter, but a *whole* storm?"

Both she and Kolfinnia were sitting in the tower. Kolfinnia had sprinkled sawdust on the floor, added candles, two stools, and the wood burning stove sat neatly in one corner throwing out some considerable heat. She'd decorated the walls with found shells and seagull feathers and stuffed old sacks with straw to provide cushions. It was also an excellent place to dry provisions and garlands of dried apple slices hung in their hundreds from the rafters, adding a welcome scent. It had become her refuge, the equivalent of Valonia's tower. Kolfinnia took her hands and clasped them. "All I ask is that you try."

Flora looked troubled.

"Will you try?" she pressed.

"When?" She looked at her dirty fingernails. *Gardener-girl*, she thought.

"Today?"

Flora continued to look down at the floor. "It'll be hard asking a storm to come, and then we have to ask the thunder-sprites to forgo their traditional bargain. There's no time for guessing games and stuff like that. They'd have to know this was a temporary agreement: help us in battle and then return to the thunder-heights."

"Exactly, but I know they'll help." She felt certain; she had Skald's help after all.

"But such a thing's never been done and sprites have never been asked in that way. They're a proud race. What if they say no?"

"We need an emissary between us and the thunder-heights. I've asked Skald." She had no idea if that was possible, or if she sent Skald to speak with his kind, whether or not he'd be able to come back.

"There's something you've forgotten." Flora looked sombre.

Kolfinnia sat on her stool and waited.

"We need trees for lightning-staffs, and you're proposing we ask the sprites to come down in force. For that trees must be struck, and it's likely they'll be killed."

"Hethra's teeth, I'd forgotten that," she moaned quietly.

Her plan was doused. To arm their witches they'd need to kill healthy trees. It was one matter for lightning to strike where it willed, but another indeed to instigate it. She slumped over with her head in her hands: each solution created a new problem.

Just then there came a soft knocking at the door. Kolfinnia wiped away the tears of frustration and cleared her throat. "Who is it?" she called.

"It's me, Sally," something in the woman's voice alarmed them both.

"Door's open, Sal, come in."

They both rose as she looked in. Her face was red from crying and her eyes told a tale of grief.

"Sally! What's happened?" Both of them went to prop her up as she collapsed into tears.

"It's Ward Zuri," she cried.

Kolfinnia saw bad news approaching like an avalanche and they eased Sally to one of the seats and sat her down. "Lana? What about her?"

She cupped her mouth, and for a moment she just sat there shaking her head. She took a shuddering breath and began. "After you told us about Lana coming, I went to my bunk, where we keeps the staffs. I wanted to tell Lana's sprite that she was well and that she'd just been here. But when I took it out . . ."

"He's gone, hasn't he?" Kolfinnia said softly. "Lana's sprite has gone."

Sally just nodded. He was gone because Lana was dead. Rowan's protectors were being whittled down.

Kolfinnia locked eyes with Flora.

"I'll do it this evening," Flora promised.

"And I'll ask which of the trees will lay down their lives for our cause."

Lana was dead and she should have felt despair, but Kolfinnia only felt anger. The battle for Kittiwake hadn't even begun and already there were casualties.

They began at dusk. Kolfinnia had given instructions that nobody was to enter the woods west of Kittiwake. She'd also asked the Wildwood witches camping close by to move away in case the storm proved too wild. The coven gathered on that rocky slope that everyone had come to know as the 'keel', where ore wagons stood axle deep in grass. From there they had a sweeping view over the wood, the dunes and the lake. Kolfinnia had made no secret of what she and Flora intended to try and do.

"There are a lot of folks watching us." Flora cast a nervous glance back towards the cluster of mine buildings.

"A lot of hope rides on this."

"I'll make sure they come," Skald promised. "If need of witches be so great," he quoted again, but as always refused to explain.

Kolfinnia looked back. Even in the gathering dusk she could see the walls, railway-track and slopes thronged with spectators and of course a few gulls. Further up the hill, where the land fell away into the sea, the Swords of Britain watched over them. She saw a lone figure up there and instantly knew who it was even though the distance was at least a mile. *Sunday*, she thought. "Let's get going. Skald, if you would."

He poured himself into her staff and then the pair and their chosen sprite turned away from Kittiwake and set off to raise an army.

When they were deep enough into the wood Flora sat down and pulled her cloak tight around herself because if this worked they were both going to get very wet. "This'll do. I'll look for a storm out there, but there might not be one nearby."

"I only ask that you try," she repeated her one condition.

Flora settled herself, closed her eyes and began the asking.

"Come on, Skald," Kolfinnia whispered. They had trees to recruit.

She wandered quite some distance. One after another she traced a loving hand over their trunks, using the special gift that had first terrified her as a child. She left Flora working on her spell, trying to entice a storm off the ocean plains and bring it landward, hopefully carrying with it an army of sprites.

Trees called back to her and she greeted them sorrowfully. Some were at least two centuries old, mostly the towering beeches, and they were so stout that they might withstand a lightning bolt. Others were only young, hardly older than her, mostly the birch and ash. They'd be pulverised, leaving nothing to carve a staff from. Then there were the regal oaks, sacred to Hethra. Their voices were slow and ponderous but their roots remembered events long passed. The hollies, Halla's tree, were mysterious. Of all the trees she found them the hardest to read.

Holly was aloof and secretive.

This being October, all of the trees bore seeds, and Kolfinnia's pact was that for each tree that agreed to help she would take thirteen seeds and nurture them for the rest of her years. She asked her bargain again and again, letting her fingers send the message through the grain. Some replied instantly, others considered, while others remained silent. The world had once been filled with trees, and it was fair to assume they'd no liking for the injustices they'd suffered down the centuries. But just like Lilain, while they might not understand humanity they understood Hethra and Halla, and so servants of theirs were at least afforded an audience.

"Noble spirits of wood, witches loyal to the earth-serpents ask you now, which of you will accept the kiss of the storm that we may defeat the twin's enemies? Death is likely but not certain, and in return I promise I shall take thirteen children from each, one for each moon of the year, and nurture them all my remaining days."

She wandered the wood asking each in turn, while Flora searched the sea for a storm to bring the army of thunder.

It was gloomy and almost dark when she returned to Flora's side. The young woman looked exhausted. "It's hard going. There's thunder forty miles north of here. I've asked over and over for it to approach and be known, but then I lost its voice."

Kolfinnia was about to tell her to keep trying, when Skald appeared and raised his head to the sky, sniffing. "Skald?"

"Shhh!" He craned backwards, scanning the darkening sky through a mosaic of branches.

"I don't think they're coming, Skald," Flora sounded broken.

"Wait," he demanded.

Kolfinnia felt a breeze ripple the hem of her dress, a breeze that hadn't been there a moment before and she heard a tree creak nearby. The wind was strengthening.

"They're coming," he confirmed.

The two witches stared at one another.

"The trees?" Flora asked.

"I found enough," she patted her satchel. It was crammed with small bundles, each bearing thirteen seeds.

Flora looked at it with a deep sadness.

"I know," Kolfinnia said feelingly. "They understood and accepted freely. Many are mature and there's a good chance they'll survive."

"All things die," Skald reflected coldly. "Better to die with a purpose than not."

A few curled leaves spun past and Flora quickly closed her eyes and reached out for the storm again. It was like calling rain for the gardens during a dry spell, but on a greater scale. "He's right, they're coming," she confirmed.

The air around them seemed to grow taut. It was very dark now and the swirling clouds overhead were the colour of angry bruises. Trees began to swish and groan as the wind grew bolder and a further shower of leaves swirled past them as though they were trying to outrun the approaching storm. Skald flapped his wings once and Kolfinnia heard a distant peal of thunder call back. "They call to me," he murmured longingly.

"Skald?" she asked.

"Wait here," he curled tight, then lunged upwards leaving a helix of drifting ice crystals.

"Be careful!" she called, but he was already too far away to hear.

Both witches watched his trail streak upwards and then vanish into the darkness. There was a brief flash of lightning somewhere deep in the thunderhead and then silence. Skald had returned to the thunder-heights to negotiate with his own kind.

They sat in trepidation, waiting for something to happen while the sky continued to darken. Minutes crawled by like hours and inevitably Kolfinnia began to think she'd lost her last link with Valonia and her most valuable ally.

"He'll return, either with help or alone, but he'll return. It's only been a few minutes." Flora shuffled closer and offered her a friendly arm.

There was a weak flash of lightning that made them both jump. Kolfinnia caught her breath as she craned this way and that trying to see anything above, but nothing else followed and the clouds just circled sluggishly. "I lost Gale. I refuse to lose Skald as well," she agonised.

"While you live he's got a link to this world," Flora promised. "He'll be back."

They sat that way for a while, with arms around one another. Kolfinnia wondered what the witches at Kittiwake would be thinking. All of them would be waiting for something to happen, knowing that if nothing did then they'd be fighting the knights with clods of earth and sharpened sticks. She rubbed at her neck and tried to see something, anything, happening above. "How long's he been gone?"

A raindrop splashed on her nose in answer to her question.

"It's raining," Flora said warily.

Another raindrop plopped against Kolfinnia's upturned face, this time on her brow, then another splashed against her neck and ran down her chest. The rain was cold and hard, the kind of rain that meant business. Flora recognised it too. This wasn't gentle summer rain, it was loaded with wrath and rage. It was storm rain. "I think he's done it!" Kolfinnia trembled.

The raindrops went from random to torrential in a moment. There was a deafening crack of thunder. Kolfinnia felt it rip down through the sky slashing and mauling the air as it came and the earth shook. They jumped to their feet and there was a blinding flash and Skald landed back on her staff with a victorious howl. His expression was wild and his grin was deadly and rictus. "They say yes!" he roared.

There were so few certainties in life, other than death, that many of them accepted. Trees with rotten roots or missing limbs who wouldn't live out the next strong gale, and trees with fungi invading their cracked trunks. Kolfinnia's trees leaned into the approaching storm. A witch had come and promised to safeguard their seed, and for a tree that was the whole purpose in life: to carry on. The witch would take their young and keep them safe from browsers and diggers, and they would live on. The old, the sickly and the brave all raised their voices and said 'yes' and now the descending storm heard their call and replied with lightning. Skald roared up at the heavens where his kin circled, calling for them to come down, and how they did.

Neither Flora nor Kolfinnia had seen a storm like it. From nowhere multiple bolts rammed home in rapid succession all around. There was no cover and no mercy. The first of her willing trees was hit, exploding with boiling sap and wooden daggers. "Don't be afraid, and walk with me!" Skald ordered.

"But the storm!" she screamed.

"They're dying for you, Kolfinnia!" he roared. "You must show them your worth!"

Another tree shattered close by.

"He's right," Flora screamed above the thunder, "we have to!"

She grabbed both Flora's hand and her staff, with Skald blazing like a beacon at its tip, and together they set off through the wood, bare and unprotected, as more lightning streaked down. The rain fell so hard that it battered their flesh. Cold water drenched them and they struggled to catch their breath, but Skald was ecstatic and he howled like a mad wolf. They staggered forwards, frequently blinded by lightning and unable to see anything but its ragged after-image. Thunder blasted like cannon fire and Kolfinnia's ears boomed, and sometimes the thunder didn't so much roll as drop from the sky like a mountain cracking in two.

Mud rose up from nowhere as the ground quickly flooded. It sucked at their boots making them stumble and sway. Leaves in their thousands corkscrewed around them, tearing at their faces as they shot past, while trees exploded sending razor splinters chopping through the air. One moment the wood was pitch-black, the next it burned white as more lightning flashed, and the witches staggered on, blinded and terrified.

"Skald, we'll be killed!" she shouted over the roaring thunder.

His laughter sounded like breaking stone and her staff trembled. "No! They'll not assail us, not one of them!"

Just yards away, a trunk as thick as a barrel was split in two. The world filled with blinding light and shards of wood whizzed past, but not a single splinter hit either witch.

"You see!" Skald cried. "This is my storm!"

The wood was struck over and over as sprites plummeted into the limbs of willing trees, wrecking them as they did, understanding Skald's bargain and ready to fight.

Kolfinnia straightened. If the trees could stand tall before this onslaught they could too. Both gritted their teeth and walked forward, shivering and drenched, afraid but determined. As she walked through the destruction Kolfinnia gripped her satchel tight and promised again that for each of them that fell thirteen others would flourish.

And in the midst of all this, hidden so very close by, Hethra and Halla slept on and dreamed of champions and foes.

It was dark by the time the storm abated. The path back to Kittiwake was sticky with mud and bristled with fallen branches. They crept along in the dark, soaked to the bone and holding hands for support. The rain had stopped, or maybe it'd just never come this far; the storm had been very localised. Every so often they glanced back towards the wood and saw the occasional spark of lightning flash deep in the clouds, but there weren't any more searing bolts now. The army of thunder had descended and waited in the woodland for witches to come and claim them.

"How are you feeling?" Flora's gentle voice came from the darkness.

"Fine," she lied. The air was still and unusually quiet. She could hear water bubbling somewhere close by, run off from the tremendous rains, and just up ahead they could see the keel's grassy embankment. It looked like a featureless wall in the gloom, but they headed gratefully towards it.

A light flashed up ahead, blue and soft, and then dimmed again before reappearing and began bobbing towards them. Kolfinnia recognised it as wand-light and she smiled, knowing someone had come to welcome them home.

A voice sounded not far off. "Kol? Flo? It's Sally. You two alright?"

They trudged towards her and the glow of her wand.

"Nothing that hot tea won't cure," Kolfinnia called back, and then in answer more wands flickered into life, six, a dozen and then a score at least. Uniquely, one of them was green and she knew it was Clovis.

"We've been waiting here for an age. You must be soaked," Sally shouted. "Never seen a storm like it!"

"And let's hope we'll never have to call another." She helped Flora up the banking and into the crowd waiting with blankets and kind words. Before she climbed up Kolfinnia took one last glance back. They'd never even given it a proper name. It was just called 'the wood' but the trees there had offered them their help, and at such a cost. "Was it worth the price, Skald?" she asked quietly.

"We'll see soon enough."

She stroked her satchel again, then climbed up the slope and into Sally's waiting arms.

The following morning tales of last night's storm were told throughout the coven. Everyone, no matter their age or health, had come to watch it, and what a storm it was. To Kittiwakes' witches Kolfinnia had proved yet again that there was nothing she couldn't do. She had fought the Illuminata, cast a wand that had sailed directly to Hethra and Halla themselves and commanded the gods of thunder to send its warriors to help them. Today they would journey to the wood to cut a new lightning-staff each and Kolfinnia intended to go with them to witness the destruction as a reminder of her bargain.

After breakfast she joined up with Clovis, Farona, Flora and Sally to meet with Janus again, providing the sullen being would grant them an audience. She found it hard to regard him as a 'god' of anything. His behaviour was so selfish, but then again that's what gods seemed to excel in.

Clovis made sure the cottage was empty and then ushered them upstairs. Kolfinnia was at the rear, feeling more nervous about this than last night's storm. But just as she was about to enter the doorway Sunday caught her elbow. "Very impressive show last night, coven-mother," she said smoothly.

Kolfinnia saw she was dressed modestly for once, with a cloak around her shoulders. "Sunday, can we speak later? I have a delicate meeting with Clovis."

"And Janus?"

She was too tired to be surprised. "And Janus," she admitted freely.

"Just a moment of your time please, coven-mother."

Kolfinnia wished she wouldn't call her that. It sounded petty coming from Sunday. She looked to where Sally was disappearing up the narrow stairs inside the cottage. "Very well."

"Although I don't know who or what this Janus is," Sunday began, "I'm sure you intend to reveal it to the whole coven in good time, but I'd ask you to consider me for Janus to choose from."

"Choose from?"

"In the attempt to rescue the twins!" she whispered secretly.

"You know an awful lot?"

"Farona told me."

"Really," she sneered.

"I asked, and he told me. It was simple politeness."

You charmed it out of him, more like, she thought.

"You looked displeased, Kolfinnia," she noted. "Would you rather keep us all in the dark?"

"When Janus finally decides to set off, then the whole coven will know the plan," she promised. "This is no time for a leadership challenge."

"You misunderstand." She looked flustered and Kolfinnia saw a very anxious young woman hiding under that perfect exterior. "All I want is the chance to serve Hethra and Halla."

"So that you can 'set them free', as you put it?"

She shook her head, a touch too fast for Kolfinnia's liking. "Please, just ask Janus if he'll consider me."

"Kolfinnia?" Clovis called from upstairs.

"I have to go, but I'll see what I can do." With that she vanished into the open doorway and padded up the stairs, leaving the beautiful but tormented solstice queen by the door.

"I have chosen." Janus turned loops inside his jar.

They'd gathered around him again: Farona, Sally, Flora and both Clovis and Kolfinnia, all hoping that today he'd stop delaying and choose his escort. Kolfinnia nudged Clovis in the ribs. "There's another who wants to be considered," she hissed.

Losing Sunday in a dangerous mission might not be so bad after all, she thought coldly, but that wasn't her reason for respecting her request. Sunday had a point: all of them should be eligible for this honour, if 'honour' was the right word. She just didn't know how to tell Sunday, or anyone else, that Janus was a peevish mischief maker and she was better off out of his schemes.

"What's that you say, young witch? Another wishes to step forward?" Janus overheard her.

"Erm, yes, mighty Janus," she said graciously. "She wishes to be considered as worthy to travel by your side."

"No," he stated flatly. "I have chosen and my word is final."

You got off lucky, Sunday, Kolfinnia thought. "As you have it, mighty Janus," she complied.

"And so," Clovis prompted, "which of us will be your favoured escort?"

Everyone thought it was going to be Clovis, including Clovis. He would be sorely missed if the knights attacked but it was the logical choice. But because it was the logical choice Janus went the opposite way, simply because it amused him. "Young Farona will be my escort," he said simply. "He has escorted queens – now he will escort a god."

There was a bewildered silence during which Farona wondered if he'd heard correctly. He knew he had when their faces all turned his way. The mission was very dangerous, and Janus might trick him and leave him entombed under the earth to rot, but he thought it a small price to pay for the way Flora looked at him just then.

Clovis disguised his shock with a cough. "Erm, a wise choice Janus, but surely Farona's skills in magic are still growing. Wouldn't a seasoned witch be better, myself for instance?"

"No." Janus regarded them as though they were the ones trapped behind glass and the whole universe was his. "Farona will go with me. I have decided."

Clovis swallowed his anger. "And so we depart at once?"

The knights could be less than ten miles away for all they knew, they might be here within the hour. Janus's answer could sink or save their plans.

"I'm tired, Clovis," Janus made that irritating yawning sound again. "Return tomorrow and I shall consider when would be the best time to leave." He spun around once in a curtain of bubbles and then tapped down against the bottom of the jar. "Now leave me," he commanded with a weary sigh. "I must rest and save my strength for the trials ahead."

How she did it she'd never know. Somehow Kolfinnia grabbed Clovis's arm even before she was aware she was moving and restrained him. He was making a low growling sound and his hands ached to grab the jar and smash it to pieces. "Clovis!" she hissed. "We need him. Let's be away before we do or say something we regret."

The others nodded mutely and she pulled Clovis towards the door. He relented and allowed himself to be led, but he was shaking and his eyes had narrowed to slits. "Yes," he muttered, "fresh air will help."

They must return tomorrow and hope Janus was finished playing and ready to keep his side of the bargain. He hadn't spoken of what he wanted in return, and the sands of time continued to flow.

After her encounter with Janus she had another hard duty. She didn't know how many sprites had come down in the storm last night, and she feared what awaited in the woods, expecting mangled trees lying around like dying soldiers.

From a distance the wood looked untouched, but as they drew closer she saw fallen trunks and toppled limbs strewn around the muddy ground. Closer still, she realised that what she'd taken to be a carpet of leaves were shards of bark and heartwood. It was like entering a graveyard, and while the witches began finding sprites and cutting staffs Kolfinnia went to each blasted trunk and made what peace she could. Some had survived, but many were cold and silent. Already Kittiwake had suffered its first fatalities of the war.

While she was busy in the wood, Clovis and a team of helpers began setting up for weapons practice. They dragged driftwood trunks up the beach, and erected them in a line and drew snarling faces on them using charcoal. These were their krakens. Summoning the army of thunder-sprites had been risky and harrowing, and now it was time to show everyone just why they needed their help so badly.

To safeguard their privacy, Flora called a sea-fret to veil the beach from any passing boats and lookouts were posted on the surrounding hills. When everything was assembled and everyone had returned from the wood, the whole coven gathered and they received quite a show.

Clovis made the first run and finally put his magnificent sword to good use. He cleaved a trunk in half with a single swipe as he flew past, to a rousing storm of applause. The severed top rolled away down the sands where the monstrous face stared up at the sky looking rather indignant.

All of them took their turn, flying relays through the pillars, learning to pitch and weave as fast as they could, and to make the effect more realistic Clovis had some of them throwing scraps of driftwood at them to try and throw them off course. "In real life it'll be shrapnel and sharp and fast enough to take your head off. Be mindful!" he ordered.

They had to learn to fly single handed while holding a second staff, and learn fast. Plenty of dummy staffs were shattered and almost everyone hit the sand at least once, only for them to pick themselves up and try again. "Thomas! Get your feet higher. Morgan, don't put so much into your down swing. Bridget, keep low on the staff, you make too high a target. Lower I said!" He kept at them non-stop, and some of them began to wonder where their benign coven-father had gone and who this belligerent taskmaster was.

Eventually it was decided that someone ought to make a live strike against one of the pillars, and of course they all insisted on Kolfinnia.

"You can do this," Sally promised her.

"But I wasn't even there at that part of the battle." Kolfinnia stood on the beach looking up at a wall of hopeful faces watching from the dunes.

"They don't know the fine print, my lass. Just give them a show that'll put fire in their hearts. Use this to hit the markers," she passed Kolfinnia a second staff.

As soon as her hands wrapped around it she knew whose staff it was. "This is Hilda's," she said in a whisper, and although it was macabre the living sprite inside proved that Hilda still lived.

Hilda's sprite was called Five-Days-Of-Endless-Rain, or 'Five' for short. *"Shall we dedicate this practice run to Hilda Saxon?"* he sounded solemn.

"Aye," Kolfinnia agreed.

When it was announced that their coven-mother would be making a live strike the adults grew hushed while conversely the children grew more excited.

"Ready, Skald? Five?" She was more nervous than she could remember.

"Ready," they replied together.

She'd elected to begin her run a hundred yards from the row of pillars and demonstrate how to slalom through them and strike at the last one in the file. She looked down the line of trunks knocked askew from being struck with plain old staffs earlier, but now Kittiwake would see the real thing. From here the figures on the dunes looked small, but that didn't reduce their expectations. To her right, down the shore she could hear the sea behind the curtain of mist. "Here goes," she muttered to no one.

She broke into a run, then a sprint, conscious of the sand thundering under her bare-feet. Fifty yards from the first target she mounted at a sprint, landing on the staff with artful precision. *First hurdle over with. I didn't fall mounting the staff!* she thought elatedly.

The first pillar rushed past and she slalomed through them so fast that the last one was on her almost before she knew it. Suddenly she saw its snarling face and without thinking she pulled her second staff from under her arm and lashed out as she passed.

She heard the familiar crack of an electrical discharge, and then the pillar exploded spitting waterlogged shards and steam upwards in a fountain. Splinters sprayed across her back, some of them trailing smoke, and glowing embers drifted down around her. Hard on the heels of the explosion she heard what sounded like thunder, and when she turned to look she saw two hundred witches all throw their hats into the sky cheering in triumph.

"Fine piece of work, lass," Sally looked on with a smile, while Clovis nodded in satisfaction.

410

Behind her the marker was just a huge torch billowing flames, and it sagged drunkenly then crashed into the sand. Kolfinnia couldn't help herself, but she longed for it to be a kraken and just for a second she hoped the Illuminata would come after all.

At even-meal Farona took his plate of barley stew and hunk of bread, and went to find a place to eat by himself. He needed a little time to think about tomorrow. He would be setting off with Janus into the unknown, if the slippery god saw fit to honour his word that is, and although the rest had been supportive and kind, what he really wanted right now was a little time to reflect.

Kolfinnia watched him go and thought it best to leave him be. She turned back to the cooking tent, holding her empty plate and waiting her turn. Spirits were high after their impressive training session and everyone wanted to either congratulate her or consult her about something.

"The knights won't stand a chance!" someone cheered and she felt a friendly hand pat her back.

"This is for you, dear," a witch pressed a good-luck charm into her hand.

She smiled and nodded and welcomed every embrace, but her thoughts kept returning to Farona. She glanced back through the crowds and steam from the cooking pots, but Farona had gone.

"Farona! A moment please!" Right away his heart sank and jumped at the same time.

Sunday graciously extracted herself from a crowd of admirers, many of who looked after her wistfully, and she trotted over to him.

"I was just on my way to take my even-meal, miss," he held the plate up for her to see.

"I shan't keep you," she took him by the elbow and walked him towards the alley between the cottages and the engine-shed.

Farona glanced back and saw curious, even envious, faces studying them.

"I see Kittiwake is determined to stay and fight." It had never occurred to her they would make a stand, but then again it had never occurred to her that Hethra and Halla lay sleeping right below them. The last thing she wanted was for witches to get harmed, but now she had condemned them and the twins to the Illuminata. If anyone deserved to be marked with fool's-gold, she thought, it was her.

"They're all very determined." He thought she looked worn out. Little did he know she'd spent the last day in tears.

"And what of Janus?"

"Miss?"

"Has Janus chosen?"

He sighed deeply and looked at his meal, and wondered if it would be his last one. "He has."

She understood his melancholy at once. "You?" She clasped his free hand, and for once she almost sounded concerned.

"Aye, me," he looked up and saw she was deeply troubled. "You think that a bad choice, miss?"

"Not at all," she said sincerely. Now she looked embarrassed, shy even. "When?"

"Perhaps tomorrow. It's for Janus to decide."

"This Janus likes to leave things until the last moment, does he not?" He actually smiled at this.

"All I ask is that you tell me, tell me when you're bound to leave." She might still save this disaster. Maybe she could accompany him to find the twins, make sure they were safe. Maybe she could do lots of things. Heavens knew she had plotted endless counter-measures since yesterday. "Just tell me, Farona, that's all," she finished uncertainly.

He nodded silently and stared at his plate, and Sunday had the distinct impression that she wasn't wanted right now, if ever.

"Enjoy your meal," she added quietly and slipped away.

Farona watched her leave then went to eat, even though his appetite was gone.

The Fortitude was painted with rusty streaks and over the last weeks rain, sun and frost had conspired to finish what the witches of Wildwood had started. The machine was slowly breaking down.

Here and there rivets had cracked, and welded seams parted company like tectonic plates, enough for hairline cracks to appear. Copper earthing strips had peeled away and drizzled green trails beside the rust. Pressure gaskets and rubber seals had withered under the sun's corrosive glare and the Fortitude was no longer entirely sound and neither was it totally magic proof.

Rowan awoke with a start. She sat up from her blankets, propping herself up on her elbows, trying to remember what had disturbed her sleep. The first thing she did was to rub at her scalp, which was prickly with new growth. Like any girl, Rowan thought that being pretty was quite important and it cheered her to feel her hair growing back. But that wasn't what had awoken her.

She could feel a breeze against her ear coming from the outer wall and she expected to see a huge crack to account for the wind, but the wall looked intact. It took her a while to realise that this wasn't an earthly breeze, not the kind that powers windmills or sail boats: this was something else entirely.

The electric light over her head continued to burn and smell of hot iron as it had done since she had arrived. It burned day and night and normally she couldn't tell one from the other because the Fortitude wouldn't allow it, but right now she discovered to her surprise that it was October the 20th and it was three minutes and eleven seconds past five in the morning. *How is it I know that now when I couldn't before?* She regarded the outer wall again, a rectangle of metal the colour of slate and it looked just the same way it had yesterday, but the wind she felt definitely came from there.

She sat up and wondered how she could know the time so absolutely. She even knew when one second had ticked its way to the next, and then in a leap of creative thinking way beyond her years she simply decided to know how she knew. The answer wafted through her mind and made her smile.

"The machine has gaps in it!" She grinned and threw the blanket off and knelt up. Suddenly there was a whole world out there full of answers, and everything tumbled back easily. She thumped on the wall. She thumped and kicked and laughed until she had them awake and thumping back at her.

"Rowan! Is everything all right?" Valonia jumped from her sleep, fearing the worst.

"What are they doing to you?" Hilda cried.

She giggled and jumped up and down on her blanket. *"It's all right, I'm fine. It's so wonderful, I know again!"*

With her skills restored her crowning was boosted and Valonia had to cup her hands to her ears.

"Rowan, you're shouting. Do an old lady a favour and pipe down!" she grinned, *"I'm old, not deaf."*

"Rowan, what's going on?" Hilda could hear the girl so clearly it was like having her right there.

"I can know again!" she cried joyfully.

"So I gather, now tell us something we don't know," Valonia sat back against the wall smiling, and rubbed sleep from her eyes. Hearing her so cheerful was the best gift she could think of in this terrible place.

Rowan steadied herself: she could know whatever she wanted and it was like being let loose in a shop full of delights. *"Erm, well,"* she directed her attention outwards, looking for something to tell her friends. She saw the whole of Hobbs Ash, the Thames and the collapsed train station. She let her mind ask what was inside the wrecked building and when the answer came her smile faded. *"There are machines, the same ones that came to Wildwood, lots of them kept in an old train station. Krast wants to go and find Kolfinnia and he'll go soon, any day now."*

Valonia and Hilda both froze. The moment's joy seemed to be spent.

"Krast wants three special krakens to be changed, to run on life-force. They'll be ready soon, maybe today, and when they are he's going to war." She began to tremble even though she didn't understand what life-force was. *"Three machines and three of us,"* she felt the net of panic tighten.

"Rowan!" Valonia banged furiously. *"Listen to me, look away. There's nothing there but evil. Look away, and find something to lift us!"*

There was a heavy silence from Rowan's cell, and then she spoke again, calmer this time. *"Swans, Valonia, there are nine of them."*

"Swans?" She relaxed. *"Where?"*

"There are nine swans flying over us right now. They're going south and they've been flying for days, all the way from up north, from where you once lived." Rowan smiled at the thought.

"Swans from Iceland? Well, bless me," she lay her head against the wall. *"What else d'you see?"*

"Mr. Krast just cut himself shaving. It's hard with one eye!"

She barked a gruff laugh and slapped her knee. *"Keep them coming, my girl, keep them coming."*

From her own cell Hilda listened to Rowan's account of a world long denied them and the memories were welcome guests.

"Flora's got a sweetheart," Rowan gasped as though this was a big scandal.

"Oooh?" Valonia's interest was piqued. *"Who's the lucky witch?"*

"Oh, it's not like that. She doesn't know about him, he's a bit shy." Then she squeaked in delight, *"Captain Jerrow's got a new wife, but she's very bossy."*

"She'll keep him in his place then, eh?" Valonia laughed.

They listened to her simple tales for what felt like hours, encouraging her and laughing along and trying to forget the prophetic vision she'd had.

Three machines, three of us.

The decisive battle was only days away and it looked that in some cruel way, whether they liked it or not, they would be a part of it.

CHAPTER THIRTY-ONE

The Downward Stair

He knew it would happen eventually, and the morning after Valonia had tried to kill him another attempt was made on his life, albeit this time his political life. Prime Minister Stokes came calling to Hobbs Ash.

His visit was one huge inconvenience, and instead of gearing up for war Krast was on his way to have an off-the-record chat with Stokes.

A plain black carriage awaited him by the ruins of Hobbs station, and its team of sleek horses stood in stark contrast to the rough shires lumbering back and forth clearing the rubble. The driver held open the door and kicked down the steps, inviting him to enter.

The air inside was pungent and stuffy. Stokes was an ill man and doctors had recommended he carry a poultice of some foul smelling salts at all times. Krast thought the cramped little carriage smelled like a funeral parlour and from the look of Stokes, a funeral parlour was where he was heading.

"I thought to find you at Goldhawk," Stokes said coldly.

"As you can see there is much to be done here," he sat down and crossed his legs.

"So I see. What went wrong?"

"Minor set-back." He laced his fingers around his knee to curb his impatience.

"London feels an earthquake and first-dawn goes up in smoke. Minor set-back indeed," Stokes gave him a sickly grin. "I see you were injured." He indicated Krast's eye-patch.

"A scratch, nothing more, as is the temporary state of the Illuminata." He looked out of the window again, desperate to be off.

"A lot of funding came your way, Krast. Election looming in the spring and people want to know what's happened to that money. If I have no answers for them I stand to lose a lot."

If you live that long, he thought.

"The situation is simply this," Stokes continued. "First-dawn has been an expensive mistake. I'm ordering you to halt the project until further notice." He coughed and reached for a handkerchief.

"Is that all, Prime Minister? As you can see I have a lot of work to be doing," Krast shrugged.

"This military operation I hear of," he struggled between coughing bouts, "the one against this rumoured new coven in the southwest?"

Krast's eyebrows arched, he had an idea Stokes was going to say something he didn't like.

"Defer the operation until after the spring election. The bloodlines have already expressed concern about your losses in September and we've had enough embarrassments."

Embarrassments? He would sooner suffer damnation before he let Stokes reign in his great and final assault. "Of course," he lied smoothly. "Now if that's all?" He reached for the door handle.

Stokes eyed him suspiciously. "Other bloodlines would like to take the title of Knight Superior. I trust you'll take my instructions to heart?" He started coughing again, so violently that his cheeks bloomed red and his eyes ran. He pressed the handkerchief to his face again and Krast took his chance to leave. The man could choke in that carriage for all he cared.

"Good day Prime Minister," he swung the door open before Stokes could compose himself and stalked away, listening to the dying man's coughs and already planning to take the task force to the southwest regardless. He would return with their hallowed relic, and when he did Stokes could apologise, and to show there were no hard feelings he might even send some flowers to his funeral.

Farona slept as well as could be expected. He had no idea what awaited below, and maybe that's the only reason he slept at all. He just wanted a simple life as a witch, but now he was faced with danger, torn loyalties and living in fear of persecution. He had no more liking for growing up than Kolfinnia did.

He had been waiting outside the cottage where the sea air smelled wholesome and the wind was gentle and mild. It was dark when he had awoken, and with little hope of sleeping further he quietly slipped out and went to sit on the step of Kolfinnia's cottage. Many things occupied his mind as he waited: Sunday and his lingering loyalty, for one thing. He saw she was in turmoil and wanted to help, but why he didn't know. She had made his life dull and repetitive. His coven-father, Alfred Berwick, had appointed him her attendant and even though Regal-Fox had been destroyed he was the kind of lad who took his responsibilities to heart, even if he wound up being crushed by them. Of course he thought of Flora too, but oddly enough he thought little about Janus or even the twins. None of that seemed real.

The sound of footsteps caused him to look up and he saw Kolfinnia and Clovis heading towards him from the engine-shed. Both looked windswept and both carried their staffs. He could tell instantly that they'd been flying an early patrol and neither of them looked surprised to see him.

"Couldn't sleep, eh?" Clovis honoured him with a friendly embrace, wrapping arms around him that could easily crush him, and then Kolfinnia did likewise, but tenderly, and he had to admit hers was the more pleasant greeting.

"Did you sleep any?" She held his hands in a sisterly fashion.

"A little," he admitted. "I've come prepared, in case Janus wants to leave right away. We've had two false starts already." He pointed to where his satchel and staff rested by the front door.

"Then let's go ask him," Clovis said soberly.

It was October 21st. Four days since Ada had ruined Hobbs Ash, and armed with nothing but a note, the chromosite's message and a blinding hate, Krast disobeyed Stoke and the taskforce made ready to embark.

The taskforce had two priorities: the first was to secure the area where those godless worms slept and the second was to eliminate every witch at Kittiwake. The taskforce assembled in the open, adjacent to the grand station that no longer looked so grand. Its ornate roof looked deflated and Krast couldn't help but think how it reflected the Illuminata's battered morale.

"Valonia," he whispered and shook his head, still amazed that one woman could wreak so much havoc.

He climbed the wooden platform that served as his addressing point just as the sun rose over the eastern horizon, the same sun that was rising as Farona sat on the step of Kolfinnia's cottage.

The newly sawn timbers creaked as he trod upwards and he could smell resin and sawdust. There wasn't a sound from the thousand men ranked before him, just the occasional horn from one of the passing ships on the Thames and the creak of the steps.

He reached the top and placed his hands on the rail, a length of unseasoned timber bristling with splinters that pricked against his palms. From his aerial view point he observed the circuit of broken ground that surrounded him where first-dawn had exploded in a ring of fire.

How did she bring us to this? He groped for an answer yet again, and as usual nothing but anger replied.

The assembled ranks stood to attention awaiting his address, but now they looked more like mercenaries than disciplined troops. Their uniforms were patched and tatty, some men were unshaven, and the krakens looked no better. Their paintwork was soot-blackened, and their banners had been burned away leaving many of them bald, but Krast thought they looked even meaner. He could see plates of steel that'd been hurriedly welded over damage, looking like bandages, and fronting the whole force were the three modified, experimental krakens, spearheaded by Purity. *Valonia's coffin*, he thought.

Hovering above, like a fat insect, was the first in a line of airships waiting to lift the krakens and their crews away to battle. A string of them snaked through the skies ready to move forward and load. The operation would take most of the day and the last piece of Illuminata equipment to be boarded would be the Fortitude. The three remaining witches were travelling in their own prison, but Krast swore they wouldn't return in it.

This evening the taskforce would assemble ten miles west of Kittiwake. Valonia and the others would be taken from their cells and placed inside the steel control chambers of the three special krakens, which had been reinforced with extra armour and guns. Wildwood had been a hard lesson.

In the past the Knights had achieved victory through sheer spectacle. Looking invincible was to be invincible, but the nature of warfare was changing. Small targets like flying witches wouldn't be a problem for these three krakens, however. They bristled with lethal fire power and anything before them would be cut to pieces. Hence they would spearhead the assault and provide cover for the following ranks.

He had considered having nameplates fixed to each, commemorating the witch inside it, but there hadn't been time and he had to forgo his vengeful little joke. However, it cheered him to think that tomorrow he'd be killing witches with machines driven by Valonia's agony.

He pulled the bowler from his head. The sun gleamed off his golden scars and he stood before his troops looking as battered as Hobbs Ash. "Knights, squires and men of the Illuminata," he began and his breath curled up in a vapour and turned gold in the sunrise. "When last you were gathered like this, the scene was very different. Every man amongst us knew our purpose was to cleanse injustice in the name of truth. It is truth I speak of now. The truth is that many of you have lost comrades, brothers and fathers and all thanks to one murderous witch," he held up a single finger.

There was a murmur of approval and a few handclaps

"She is with us here today, this witch, locked away in the Fortitude, and she'll accompany us, entombed inside Purity. Her legs will lead us to war, her hands will kill her fellows and her heart will break when we break this last coven. Each witch you kill will be an agony upon her and the spoils will not belong to Westminster, which has abandoned us, but to you all. And I assure you the spoils will be great. This last coven sits on the most powerful artefact in witchdom, and we will make it ours!"

Knight commanders eyed one another uncertainly. They had no idea this was now a rogue operation, and since when did the Illuminata divide the spoils of war amongst common soldiers?

"The rules of war will not apply tomorrow," Krast shouted, his face growing red. "Your orders are this: kill every man, woman and child."

The applause was so great it almost felt like an aftershock to Ada's earthquake, and Hathwell watched in horrid fascination. Krast's twisted inner world was seeping through like rot behind fresh paint. *He's mad*, he thought quite clearly. *He's gone mad.*

Clovis took Janus's vessel and slipped it carefully into the pack. By now Flora and Sally had joined them as both wanted to wish the lad farewell. Everyone was sombre and the chat was minimal. Even their sprites were quiet.

All five flew to the Swords and it was there amongst the heather and saplings that Clovis drew the vessel from his pack and set it on the small stone table in the middle of the circle. "Janus?" he whispered and the stone figure slowly rose from the bottom of the jar and floated next to the glass, regarding them all. "You told us to gather again today, for your departure."

"I know what I said, Clovis."

"And so this is the appointed time." He tried to make the question sound like a confirmation.

"That depends on you," Janus said levelly.

For the first time, Kolfinnia thought the strange god was being serious.

Clovis frowned. "This is something to do with the 'cost' of your help, I suspect?"

"Precisely." He didn't spin or dance; he remained stationary behind the glass.

"And that would be?"

"There is one door that even I cannot open."

Clovis knew what was coming.

"I want you to open this vessel," Janus demanded.

"That must only be done on Vega," he kept his voice low, "and the consequences would be astronomical."

"Never-the-less, that is my condition."

Clovis looked around at the others. It meant leaving them behind, but his time at Kittiwake had always been borrowed. He saw Kolfinnia's head move slowly from side to side and her brown eyes widen with worry. If he was cynical he might have believed she wanted him for his fighting skills, but he rightly suspected her feelings ran much deeper. He turned back to the vessel and briefly saw his own ghostly reflection there, then he gripped the stone plinth and bowed his head, not in reverence but regret. "When our business here is done I shall take you home, Janus, and open this vessel," he agreed in a whisper.

He heard a small gasp from behind and knew it was Kolfinnia.

"Then our bargain is struck." Janus sounded like an executioner.

"Wait," Clovis commanded. "One last request."

Janus waited.

"When you return from below, Kittiwake might be in the grip of battle, perhaps even conquered." He peeked at the others over his shoulder. "If that should be the case, then I ask we take any and all survivors, and they can leave at any door they choose." The whole coven could travel Evermore just as he had. It was risky but the Illuminata would never be able to follow.

Janus bobbed up and down in the fluid, seeming to consider, and Kolfinnia took a step towards him with her feelings in a muddle.

"Please wait," Clovis asked, hearing her footstep. "Janus and I are not yet done."

She stood still, with her heart in her mouth, but didn't retreat.

"Who should accompany us on the spiral, Clovis, is your choice," Janus said indifferently, "but when I deem it the right time you will leave this world and return me to Vega."

"Then we're agreed," he sighed.

"Then I am ready to go." Janus whirled inside the liquid, turning his back on all of them. "Your witch is also ready?"

All eyes turned to Farona, and now the youth suddenly felt the weight of all their hopes and wondered if he could really do this. "Just a moment," he asked and with that he slipped his cloak from his shoulders, trying to disguise his shaking hands.

Underneath he was wearing the orange, black and white of Regal-Fox, his coven colours. He'd stitched the torn fabric and replaced the missing buttons, his wand was buckled around his waist. If he was going to face Hethra and Halla in person he wanted to look his best, and if he was going to die under the earth he wanted to be wearing his colours. Despite everything he still felt some pride for his old coven. He took up his lightning-staff with Wester, his own sprite, inside. He had only cut it two-years ago, having taken an age to find a lightning tree, and he and Wester were still getting acquainted to some degree. "I'm ready," he said quietly.

Kolfinnia saw the youth transformed into a resolute young man. She wasted no time and quickly went to him with a strong embrace. "Our love and hope goes with you, as does this," she pressed something into his hand.

He looked down and saw a small pebble.

"A lucky stone!" He pretended to be thrilled.

"It's a fire-seed, silly," she smiled. "When you come back to us, throw it in the air as high as you can and the seed'll do the rest. That'll be our signal to come to the stones. Hopefully we'll all be safely away before the Illuminata even get here."

A look of understanding dawned on his face, followed by a bashful smile. He could've kicked himself for what he'd just said, especially with Flora watching. "My thanks, coven-mother." He smiled and curled his fingers around her gift.

Next, Clovis grabbed him in one of his typical bear-hug embraces. "Blessings on you, lad. Come home quick and maybe we'll save a few knights for you to scorch."

Farona smiled at him somewhat sadly and then moved onto farewell Sally.

"I've made you something for the journey," she held out a brown paper packet.

He took it ceremoniously. Another magical gift perhaps, he thought. "Thank you, Ward Sally," he regarded the packet curiously. "May I ask what's inside and how best to use it?" He wouldn't make a fool of himself this time.

She looked serious for a second. "Mustard and lettuce sandwiches, and as to how you use them I suggest you eat 'em. You'll thank me when you're hungry." She slapped his arm affectionately. After a second's pause he smiled broadly, and then there was only one farewell left.

"Miss Flora," he offered her a little bow.

Without a word, she drew him close. He wrapped his arms around her and stood holding her for hours, perhaps even days, oblivious to time and battle and dragons and gods, and before she withdrew she gently kissed his cheek. "Come back to us safe," she whispered. Her hands slipped from around him and he was left alone.

"Thanks be to all of you." He regarded them all fondly then slung his staff across his shoulder and crossed the heather to where Janus waited in the circle's centre. He lifted the vessel from the stone table and wondered if he should command the little god or make a speech, but before he knew it Janus was already opening the door to the underworld.

"Are we ready?" Janus said smugly.

"Aye," he agreed.

The ground began to tremble and Farona's journey had begun.

"Stand outside the circle, quickly," Clovis ordered, and they backed away, leaving Farona alone in the centre.

The ground began to move, but in a controlled and purposeful way according to the will of Janus. Whole beds of rock glided over one another like pages of an opening book, and the ground encircled by the Swords of Britain started to sag accompanied by a tremendous grinding noise, like a chorus of millstones all turning at once.

A dark crevice about three yards across opened in the heather where the rocks had sagged deepest and a shower of soil and bracken fell inside and out of sight. The rocks continued to rumble as the hole edged wider. Kolfinnia could see ledges of sandstone and granite. They glistened with moisture and minerals like raw wounds and aligned themselves into a series of steps leading down into the earth, to a place no human eyes had ever seen. The entrance was capped with a blanket of grass and soil where earthworms wriggled in their exposed burrows, and roots stretched like elastic.

A cold wind rose up from the opening and Farona stepped towards it with Janus tucked firmly under one arm. Before him was the path leading to Hethra and Halla and all the wonders and terrors the deep-earth might keep. He looked back and raised his hand in salute, but his face was grim. After drawing his wand for light, he stepped over the rim and into the secret place only Rowan had ever known of. Step by step, they watched him sink deeper. First his knees, his waist, his shoulders and then finally that brilliant crest of coppery hair sank out of sight, and Farona Firecrest vanished.

Kolfinnia swallowed a cry as he disappeared and she was about to say something important when the rumbling rocks started their songs again, but this time closing the gateway. "Clovis!" she cried and tried to rush forwards.

"No!" He grabbed her wrist. "Do not go. This is the way Janus travels."

"But the rocks are sealing him in!"

"The ground will open *before* Farona and close *behind* him," he tried to calm her. "Janus does not leave doors open." *And a good thing too.* He thought of the amalga.

Kolfinnia looked back at the earth in horror. It had reformed just as it was: the crevice had sealed shut, the stone table was back upright and even the saplings and heather looked untouched. It was as if the earth had reached up and snatched Farona away.

"This is how the magic of doorways works," he said gently. "He'll be back and the twins will be sent deeper than any mortal can reach."

Sally put a comforting arm around Flora's shoulders and all four of them stood there for a while staring longingly at a circle of heathery ground that looked as if it had remained undisturbed for centuries.

"Are we too late?" The stranger sounded breathless and they all turned to see Sunday stumbling through the heather. "Well?" she demanded. "Has he gone?"

Kolfinnia gave a single nod.

"But he never said anything!" She came to the stones, ignoring the twigs that snagged her long dress. "He went without saying anything."

Kolfinnia was surprised by the hurt in her voice.

Sunday stared skywards, took a calming breath and brushed a tear from her eye. Her last chance to actually hold in her hands the terrasoula, the cradle of Hethra and Halla, and undo the nightmare she'd begun, was gone along with Farona.

Clovis surprised them all by taking Sunday in his arms and she cried freely against his mane. "None of us knew for sure if he'd go this hour or not," he told her. "Not even Farona." He patted her back comfortingly, but made heavy thumping sounds with his huge hand.

You need to practise your touch with the ladies, Clovis, Kolfinnia thought fondly.

"I just wanted to wish him luck," Sunday said softly. *Everything's gone wrong.* She had truly believed her actions were for the betterment of Hethra and Halla, but in doing so accidentally delivered the twins right to their enemies. The prospect of knights marching against Kittiwake should have scattered everyone, but now the fools were set on fighting. They would be slaughtered and it was all her fault. To make matters worse the only witch who had ever been loyal to her had left without a word, yet she had never treated him better than a skivvy. Sunday felt utterly wretched and she disengaged from Clovis, dried her eyes and went and stood alone, looking out to sea.

Kolfinnia looked towards the doorway that had opened and then closed without a trace. Farona was under there, making his way to Hethra and Halla, and a small part of her envied him. "Blessings on you, Farona," she said again. Behind her she could hear Sunday's soft crying and she couldn't help but wonder if her regrets were for Farona or for herself.

Now that Janus had finally departed, Kolfinnia intended to reveal their plans to all of Kittiwake, but they arrived back to an ugly scene. A fight had broken out leaving one man with a bloodied nose. "What in Oak's name has been going on?" she stormed.

Benedict Collins, a young witch with shaggy blonde hair and a neat beard sat on a barrel outside the engine-shed with a rag pressed to his nose. "Arthur Conrad," he grumbled. "Bloody fool took a pot shot at me."

A small crowd had gathered and Clovis cleared his throat with an exaggerated growl, hoping they'd all take the hint, but when nobody moved he adopted a more direct approach. "Everyone about their business!" he roared. "Jump to it. Have you forgotten the enemy are coming?"

People scattered and children cried, while Benedict looked apprehensive.

"Very tactful," Kolfinnia scowled.

"My pleasure," he beamed, oblivious.

"So Ben, what was said and who said it?" she asked angrily. This was the third fight in a week: tension was running high.

"It was him that started it. Threw a punch, unprovoked it was," he sulked.

"What made him throw this 'unprovoked' punch, hmm?" She folded her arms and glared at him.

He looked at the ground moodily and dabbed a finger to his bloodied nose. "Dunno. Maybe I said something about getting away from here before the knights come."

"Oh, Ben!" her heart sank. Two days ago after the astounding news of Hethra and Halla they had been so resolute, but with each passing hour the fear escalated, and with it came doubt.

He rushed to apologise, "It was just an idea, coven-mother. I'm not saying we should, just that it might be worth thinking about."

She looked back to the Swords. A fine sea fret had rolled in and they looked distant and unreal, like a flimsy painting. "Ben, a good witch who's only a lad has just gone into the unknown to save Hethra and

DARK RAVEN CHRONICLES: RAVEN'S WAND

Halla from the very knights you want to run away from." She chose words that would inspire, not inflame, but it was hard. "And until he gets back we stay for his sake, no matter the cost, do you understand me?"

He wobbled his head in agreement.

"Now find Arthur Conrad and say sorry while you've still got the chance." Then she added under her breath, "Because who knows what tomorrow might bring." She whirled about and marched away with Clovis and Sally at her side. "Sally, Clovis," she commanded as they walked, "I want the Wards to gather their witches and explain what Farona is doing and that until he returns we cannot, and will not, leave. Tell them of the fire-seed. That's the sign to gather at the stones without delay. Clear?"

"Clear, coven-mother." Sally's tone was more formal now they were back in mixed company.

"Clovis," she continued. "Stress that fights will not be tolerated. Tell them to save their anger for the knights."

"They're very frightened," he explained.

She halted. "I don't know how to take that fear away. I wish I did, believe me, but fighting amongst ourselves is not the answer."

"As one who's fought many times, take it from me there's no quick remedy to fear. Every witch overcomes it in their own way."

"Most of them have never fought before. I've only fought once myself, but I can't turn witches into warriors, Clovis. I've tried but that's not what witchcraft is about and in the end that's how we'll defend this coven, as witches," she straightened and looked determined. "But we'll do it as best we can."

It upset him to see her so downhearted. "We still have some time left," he reassured her.

"Lana said the knights might be here in two days, perhaps even tomorrow. What time is there left?" She swallowed back her tears. "We need a miracle to pull them together, else half will run and the other half will fight amongst themselves."

"Miracle?" He suddenly looked inspired, "Leave that to me."

"I'll look forward to seeing it," she said without conviction, "but now I've an errand to run and I'll meet with you later." She took off towards the cottage with a secret plan in mind. She was going to take a flight with Skald and she would need her wand because it was very dark where she was going.

Sally went to get on but Clovis called her back. "Sally, wait. What makes witches afraid?" he said thoughtfully.

She creased her brow. "Gettin' killed, I should think."

"And what of 'beyond' death? What do you believe?"

"Some say Evermore, others say the garden of Hethra and Halla. It's one and the same to me."

"And you'd wish to go there?"

She smiled, "Only after I've had a long time here first."

"But you believe it?" he pressed.

She pursed her lips as she thought. "It'd be nicer to *know* it, I grant you, but that's the point of belief. It tests the soul."

"Maybe that's why so many are afraid. They would rather know than just believe. Tomorrow they might be killed and the possibility that Evermore's just a myth brings fear."

"That's the age-old worry of all souls," she admitted easily.

"What if I could show them a way to 'know'?"

She looked suspicious.

"I've walked Evermore, not as a spirit between lives, but as the living witch you see before you. Tempest and I came that way with Janus. And I can prove it."

His words were deadly serious and she felt a chill. "I should be about my duties," she said evasively.

He took a step closer. "Please wait. I wish to show you something to help you 'know' and then fear will be less, perhaps even gone." He offered his hands.

She surveyed the others going about their jobs. There was a dark sense of urgency now, and many of them carried wands and staffs instead of water-buckets and vegetables. "Very well," she reluctantly took his outstretched hands, expecting him to lead her somewhere quiet and have a chat about life and death. The last thing she expected was a miracle.

As soon as she touched his hands the sounds of Kittiwake melted away and she felt a draught of air so pure, that by comparison she felt she'd been breathing smoke all her life and never realised it. She willed her eyes to open and before her was a spiral of stone stairs winding upwards, but on an epic scale, and the walls around her towered to impossible heights and they were lined with doors without end from their footings right up into the misty heights above, doors that no possible person could reach.

Luminescent spirits were flowing past in their thousands, following the spiral upwards. None travelled down it, and when they found a door that suited them they simply vanished through it to whatever lay on the other side. In this place her troubles were left behind like a shed skin. She wanted to stay here and drift with these souls; she didn't want to go back to the world with all its prejudice, war, disease and hunger.

"Evermore. The backbone of eternity," a mellow voice said. *"The starting, ending, and starting place again for all life."*

Sally wheeled around and saw Lana Zuri as clear as day. She stood a few steps away gazing down at her, looking proud and peaceful. "Lana!" She tried to reach out, but the vision suddenly disappeared and she breathed dirty air again and heard crowds and wailing gulls.

"Did you see it?" he asked eagerly.

She was breathing fast and her legs trembled. "Halla's claws! You mean to say that was it, the place beyond?"

He smiled in reply.

"Not a vision? Please, don't tell me it was a trick!"

He gave his head a shake. "Now, believe or know – which is better?"

She was crying now, but in a good way. "Can you show all the others?" she sniffed.

"Oh yes," he grinned, showing those fearsome teeth.

She shouldn't have come here. She knew that even before she set out, and Skald had been silent as they flew and silent as they descended the sea-stack once again. He disapproved strongly to her plan, and it seemed he had little to say to her.

Kolfinnia had checked that hrafn-dimmu was still secure. The stone box was sound but a mouse had built a nest in the folds of Valonia's cloak. She smiled when she saw it and wondered how in Oak's name a mouse had come to be up here, but that was life; there was always something to be surprised by if you just opened your eyes. She left it undisturbed, thinking Valonia would've been pleased to know her cloak was offering shelter to a creature in need, and then she and Skald had sunk down into the blackness, looking for an answer to a question she was forbidden to ask.

Now, as she stumbled through the darkness and mud, she began to question her wisdom, but just then she saw her wand-light reflect off that impossible hourglass. It was too late to turn back and her curiosity was too strong. Suddenly the Timekeeper's voice boomed around her even before she had reached his tomb.

"I have been looking forward to this visit, Kolfinnia and Skald."

"My Lord," she greeted him breathlessly.

"Come closer," the great spider commanded from out of the darkness.

She clambered over rocks and splashed through puddles all the while thinking it was an ungainly way to arrive at the court of fate's architect. She heard the rushing of that strange stream that circled the hourglass, the one that vanished *below* the sea leading to who knew where.

At last she stood before that fierce stream that separated him from her, and inside the hourglass she saw him descend onto a bed of sand that never appeared to move. But the sand grains *were* moving. The universe was growing steadily older and one day too it must die. Now that she was here all her burning questions seemed to melt into one confused mass. Skald wouldn't aid her and remained stubbornly silent after making it clear that he didn't approve.

"You are on the brink of war, I see."

She looked up into eternal eyes and nodded mutely.

"And you wish to know who will prevail, Kittiwake or Krast?"

She didn't nod this time so much as shudder in reply.

"I cannot tell you."

"Is it forbidden?"

The Timekeeper couldn't smile, but his voice told her he was gently amused. *"No, far simpler Kolfinnia. The future is a mystery even to me. I deal in the 'now' and the past. The future is a blank page that threads write as they go along."*

"So you cannot tell me?"

"No, the outcome is still unwoven."

She was crushed. Skald had been right: coming here was a mistake and there was a lot to do back at Kittiwake. She could ask him of Krast's plans and a hundred other weaknesses of the Illuminata but she agreed with Skald that to know could interfere with something vast and ancient. She should leave. "Forgive my intrusion," she said sadly, and made to go.

He found that this thread, who had come to visit him twice now, intrigued him and he didn't know why. He just knew that her company made him feel something he couldn't describe, or more precisely it made another feeling entirely go away. He had discovered loneliness and he didn't want her to leave. *"Kolfinnia."*

"My Lord?" She looked up hopefully, her face pallid in the wand-light.

"Luck be with you in battle tomorrow." It was a small gesture, his way of warning her that Krast was already on his way.

Tomorrow? She thought with steely calm. *Krast's intention is to assault tomorrow.* "Thank you," she said again, and this time she said it for all of Kittiwake-coven.

CHAPTER THIRTY-TWO

The Last Day Begins

When the rocks had closed neatly behind him Farona had the horrible feeling of being buried alive and he almost screamed. Only the thought of Flora stopped him. He ignored the grinding sound of being sealed in and descended. The rocks ahead opened at a sedate pace, rearranging themselves into a staircase, and likewise they closed just the same way behind him.

The steps were steep and uneven, being hastily formed by Janus as they advanced. Some were gritty with minerals while others were flaky like shale, and some steps even bore the imprint of fish skeletons. He didn't have time to study them carefully because as soon as he passed, the steps vanished from his wand-light and melted into a solid rock again. It was eerie and haphazard. The stairs twisted this way and that, sometimes steeper sometimes less so, but always downwards. Eventually he had to ask. "Janus, are you sure this is the way?" His voice was just audible over the scraping and grinding.

"Your will guides me," he said, as if this was obvious.

"But how can that be? I don't even know the way myself!" He suddenly thought that he was buried alive with a guide who hadn't the foggiest notion of where they were heading.

"Calm yourself. I said your will guides me. As long as you wish to reach Hethra and Halla then your will shall guide us."

And what if I don't? he thought.

"I wouldn't recommend it," Janus said casually, reading his worries.

It made little difference to Janus if they got lost. He could snooze for a few million years, while poor Farona would end up as fossilised bones for someone to discover generations from now. Janus considered telling him this. It would be amusing, he thought, but then decided against it. He didn't want the lad in tears: he found displays of emotion vulgar and tiresome.

Occasionally the rock sparkled with seams of ore of the very kind that had brought miners here in the first place, and as they descended Farona first began to imagine that it was growing warmer, then he was sure of it, and his breathing was becoming uncomfortable.

After what felt like hours the rocks peeled away to reveal a natural cavity. At first it was a fist-sized hole, but as they advanced the hole rapidly expanded. Farona first imagined a cavern, but as they moved forwards he realised they were bisecting some kind of tunnel instead.

The tunnel was bored through the rock and almost perfectly round, easily large enough to accommodate an ox, and smoothed as if by years of use. The rock was slick and greasy where something had rubbed over it countless times.

"Someone's been here before us," Farona muttered uneasily. He stopped on the crude stairs. Their path cut through the tunnel, which stretched away into the blackness of either side, and a warm breeze moved through it, battering him as it passed. It was dry and smelled faintly of those spices used to preserve corpses.

"Keep moving," Janus commanded.

Farona detected a hint of anxiety in the god's voice. "Why?" he asked, fascinated. "What is this place?"

"Never mind, keep moving."

"It's dangerous? How?" He thought he heard something down that black tunnel, something scuttling or tapping its way towards him, and the faint sound of someone crying. The wind began to rush stronger, strong enough to ruffle his hair, and the smell of spices grew pungent.

"Six-fingered devil, it comes!" Janus whimpered. "Now move, Farona. Carry me forward!" But Farona felt an odd compulsion to wait and see what was approaching.

"Yes, I suppose we should," he said dreamily. There was something moving down there. He could hear it plainly now, a sound like fingernails tapping on rock, and Wester began to growl inside his staff. He moved forward a step, towards the tunnel wall which slowly began to unfold.

"You dullard!" Janus squawked. "Move faster, get us through!" He could open the rocks, but Farona had to carry him forward.

Farona took another step and the rock opened further, but still he was dawdling as if mesmerised. "What's that noise?" he sounded drugged.

"Fight it, you imbecile!" Janus spluttered.

As if his dread was a signal, Farona's senses started to clear and he saw a movement to his right. A swarm of what he thought to be black locusts catapulted towards him.

With a yell of horror he leapt towards solid rock, trusting Janus to open it before he broke his skull. The rocks slid apart just as the swarm poured over them. Something dark and about the size of a sparrow landed on his chest and crawled there like a spider, while others whistled through his hair. "It's alive!" he screamed.

"Keep moving, fool!" Janus raved.

He barged forwards and the rock embraced them further, closing off the strange tunnel behind and its vile swarm, but the crawling thing still clung to his tunic. He juggled with the vessel and his wand while he swatted at it, crying out in disgust. "Get it off! Get it off!"

It crawled up towards his neck, and the idea of it getting into his shirt sent him into a frenzy of swiping and stamping. Janus was tossed and rolled inside his jar, making musical notes as he clanged against the glass, all the while shouting for the lad to stop and that the danger was behind them.

Farona didn't stop until he'd swept the creature from his shirt and onto the stone steps. It writhed for a second and then he brought his booted foot down on it with a sharp crunch. He stood there frozen for a second, shaking and breathing fast. Then fearing there were other unseen creatures latched on to his clothes he swiped his wand over his legs and arms and through his hair.

"Put me down, you idiot. You're making me dizzy!" Janus demanded. "It's gone!"

Eventually he stilled and slumped against the wall, while the liquid in the jar gradually ceased its sloshing. "What on earth was it?" he panted.

"Never mind, just keep moving," Janus repeated.

Before they moved on he inspected the creature on the floor, now feeling regretful for killing it, but what he had mistaken for a creature with multiple legs was something else entirely. It was crumpled by his attack but perfectly recognisable. He'd never seen anything of the kind. It was a letter W.

"Janus," he whispered. "What kind of creatures are these?"

"Best you don't know," he replied.

Farona breathed a sigh of relief, and wisely decided it would be best to keep moving.

Kolfinnia landed just below the dunes, hoping for a private and reflective walk home. She couldn't face a torrent of questions just then; she needed to think about what the Timekeeper had said. Skald flew ahead and after a few loops and circles through the air he landed back on top of his staff and sat there rocking gently as she used it to negotiate the soft sand.

"Perhaps I owe you an apology," he grunted.

She smiled. "No need."

She thought of the Timekeeper's warning. This 'Krast' would assault tomorrow, or at least that was his intention. Krast. The name had become a substitute for a foe she'd never met, but tomorrow that would change. She was wondering how the coven would receive the news, and she was still brooding over this when Flora came running towards her across the dunes, sliding down through the sand.

"Kol!" she cried. "Everyone's been looking for you!"

"What's wrong?" Her heart clenched – had Krast come early?

"No, no. It's nothing bad, but you really have to come and see this. The whole coven's turned out!" She tugged on her sleeve.

"What's this about, what's happened?" Kolfinnia stumbled after her.

"You'll see when we get there," she shouted over her shoulder.

"Come on, Skald!" she grinned and set off at a sprint.

They crossed the packhorse trail and the rusted railway tracks, rounded the keel and raced towards the courtyard when Flora again tugged on her arm again. "No, see it from above." Without explaining she darted towards the pump-house with its commanding view over the courtyard.

Kolfinnia chased breathlessly. It seemed Flora had all the energy of a five-year old and she was giddy to know why. They thundered through the door, both of them laughing wildly, and up the creaking steps. "Flo, what's going on?"

"Wait and see," she called back.

Kolfinnia bounded up the last step and made for the narrow window.

"No! The roof, come on," she tore past, heading for the final set of stairs.

Kolfinnia followed, watching her footing on the impossibly narrow steps, and out onto the roof and right up to the edge where the wind played with her hair. She hadn't known what to expect, but when she looked out with Flora at her side the last thing she expected to see was Clovis's promise made good.

Impossible, but there it was. She looked out onto a miracle.

The entire coven was standing before her in the courtyard, and they were standing in ranks, in their mismatched colours and ragged clothes. All the witches fit to fight had squared themselves into four blocks, each fronted by their new Ward. Girls stood next to women and boys next to men, the old and the young mingled and each clutched a lightning-staff. The sprite inside was either an old friend or one born just days ago during Flora's storm. Their cloaks and robes had been bundled away and each witch wore their coven colours, and about each waist was buckled a wand, and those lucky enough to have their atheme swords had polished them and held them tight where they looked like shafts of quicksilver. But it was the smallest detail that was the most telling.

Their pointed hats weren't crooked anymore, the mud had been brushed away and they'd been set into defiant spikes, and everyone had found some coloured rag to tie around them. It was there that Kolfinnia saw her miracle: each block had adopted a different colour for their hatband, and although they didn't quite match that only enhanced the spectacle. She saw Moon-Frost blue, Snow-Thaw green, Flower-Forth lilac and lastly a company of Seed-Fall russet, just the way it had been at Wildwood. But that wasn't all. Each face looked subtly different. 'Fearless' was the only way she could think to describe them, and heading their ranks was Clovis, smiling up at her.

Wildwood was reborn.

"Kittiwake honours you, coven-mother," Flora said gently as she bowed.

Kolfinnia heard fabric rustle, like a respectful sigh, as everyone in the courtyard below, battle worthy or otherwise, knelt at the sound of her name.

She descended the tower in a kind of dreamy bliss. Somehow he'd done it. Clovis had delivered his miracle and united them. When Kolfinnia and Flora stepped into the courtyard there was a roar of approval that sounded like the tide, and just like the tide it was fearless and part of something bigger.

Clovis came to greet her and she didn't even ask, she just grabbed him and hugged him every bit as hard as he hugged her while she grinned from ear to ear. "My thanks." Her words were almost drowned out by the chorus of cheers.

"Sally gave me the idea. Show them Evermore, show them ends that turn into beginnings." He gave her a kindly slap on the back and laughed. She still had only the faintest idea of what he was talking about. She tried to pull away but he wasn't ready to let her go just yet. "What did he tell you?" He knew exactly where she'd been.

"It's tomorrow," she whispered back.

"Then we'll be ready."

Then they all surged forwards. Clovis had proved to them that death was a lie, and while it was a magnificent revelation, even the brightest stars can only burn for so long. In time the vision he had shown each of them would fade and the magnificent would be replaced by the ordinary, but it would last long enough to carry them through the next few days. Many, or even all of them, might walk Evermore tomorrow, but Clovis had shone a light into the darkness and they'd seen that the grave was really only the door to another place and armed with that knowledge not even death could defeat them.

Kolfinnia was hauled aloft and carried like a hero. She laughed with them as they hailed her over and over, and somebody ran up to her and pressed something into her hand.

"Here, take it!" Sally cheered over the din and patted her hand, making sure she got a good grip on whatever it was.

Kolfinnia grasped what she thought was another staff. It was a slender shaft of wood, but when she raised it she saw fabric flutter in the evening breeze and her heart seemed to swell.

"Told you!" Sally shouted through cupped hands.

Kolfinnia held a banner streaming out behind her, and realised it was the Wildwood banner. She gazed up at it dumbstruck, knowing that she was holding a hallowed piece of home.

Valonia herself had stitched it. The crest of each season was emblazoned upon it and as the material billowed in the breeze their hopes soared with it. "It's a miracle!" she shouted back, but all she saw was Sally's raised fist punch upwards from the crowd in salute.

She swung the banner and it provoked even greater cheers, and quite a few piercing whistles. Laughing children and excited dogs ran along at the crowd's margins as the whole of Kittiwake marched out into the gardens carrying their coven-mother. She was bumped and jostled along, now perched between two men on their broad shoulders, and she held the banner high in one hand and staff in her other with Skald riding its tip. "Kolfinnia!'" he boomed.

Familiar faces surged towards her, shouting and smiling. There was Morag Heron of Wildwood. She pumped a fist into the air and shouted some encouragement Kolfinnia couldn't hear over the racket, and then she was replaced by another familiar face and then another.

"Farona!" Kolfinnia shouted, waving the banner over her head, and soon everyone took up the chant.

"Farona! Farona! Farona!" His name was their battle cry, and it grew so loud that Kolfinnia fancied that wherever Farona was, he'd hear, no matter how much rock lay between them.

Witches pressed forwards to touch her as though she was a living talisman and now it was time for their next surprise. They carried her to the gardens, which had been set for a feast. Their entire food stores had been emptied and piled high on tables twinkling with candles. Intuition said this was their last night at Kittiwake, and they were celebrating and mourning their coven.

A high chair, consisting of a battered stool decorated with strips of cloth, feathers and grasses, had been set up on the same upturned cart she had addressed them from just days ago, and they carried her towards it. It was homemade and humble and just right for a witch.

The crowd was so great that she didn't notice one witch trailing at the rear. Sunday had dressed in her finest solstice gown, and perhaps for once the showy garment was appropriate. Around the brim of her hat dangled a length of lilac ribbon: fittingly she'd been chosen for Flower-Forth. As she watched her coven-mother being carried along, she lingered at the back, where for once she wasn't the centre of attention, but pleased about it. Of all Kittiwake's witches she was the only one who refused to see Clovis's miracle. Knowing that her actions might well send many of them to Evermore was too much to bear. "Blessed be," she whispered.

She had made mistakes but tomorrow she would pay for them. Her crimes were great and she expected the cost to be equally great. As she clapped and smiled warmly, glad for Kolfinnia, her lifelong mask finally slipped away, and if anything the Sunday that had been hiding behind it was even more beautiful.

As the Fortitude left the ground the whole structure creaked and complained. It wasn't battle-worthy any longer. It was just a way for Krast to transport three troublesome prisoners to the southwest where he would crush the last coven in Britain.

When their journey by air began the Fortitude leaked a shower of engine sludge and rust over Hobbs Ash. It was almost as though the machine was weeping. The compound where the Wildwood captives had languished now looked naked and bereft. The yard they had circled time and time again bore a ring of beaten earth from their passing feet, and at the centre was a pool of rainwater tinged with rainbow oil slicks where the Fortitude had stood. The fence remained, and even the sentry boxes, but the guards had been drafted back into their units along with the odious Moore; every man was needed for this operation. Moore wanted to take his bayonet to the three evil harpies, but Krast had big plans for them, so instead he looked forward to the chance of slipping a blade into a few witches and Hathwell too if he could. Spoils of war indeed.

Sitting in her cell, Rowan contemplated their fate. Valonia had told her not to look, but inevitably she had as any child might and what she saw was horrible. Krast would tear down Kittiwake using them to power his war machines.

She crawled out of her blankets and across the swaying floor. The chamber pot and the tin plate from breakfast skated gently too and fro as the Fortitude rode through the sky. Rowan ignored her uneaten meal and followed that strange breeze that came from nowhere. She sat before the wall and ran a finger along the rivets, feeling for the source of 'knowing' that had broken through the machine's hull. When she found it she lowered her face to the weakest rivet, where the knowing was strongest, and reached out towards the southwest to Kolfinnia.

Rowan smiled, then grinned and laughed. The next thing she knew she was banging on the walls. Dull thumping sounds came back to her and Rowan shared her news.

"It's Kol! She's done it!"

"Done what?" barked Valonia.

Hilda strained to listen.

"She's found a way to get to Hethra and Halla, and they're doing it right now." She was ecstatic.

At first Valonia was stunned, then she smiled broadly. She hadn't been sure how any witch could have begun such a rescue. "Well done, my lass – yes I chose right." She sat back, relieved to find something good at last.

"Can you tell us how?" Hilda asked.

"Best not, Hilly. Walls have ears," Valonia cautioned quickly.

"It's all right, Valonia. They'll never be able to follow. It's Farona. He's gone for them with a special gift from Clovis," Rowan assured them.

"Farona?" Valonia tried to place the name; she hated forgetting things.

"He came from Regal-Fox to see Lilain."

The image of a copper-haired youth dropped into place. *"Ah, yes, Farona. The lad under Sunday's thumb."*

"Not any more," Rowan laughed. *"He's in love with Flora, but he won't tell her."*

"Then the lad's a fool to let her get away. I'll talk to him when I see him." She was thrilled at the harmless gossip until Hilda interrupted.

"Pardon me for spoiling your tea party ladies, but I asked Rowan an important question."

"Keep your bloomers on, Hilly," Valonia chuckled, *"else Rooter'll have 'em."*

"So, Rowan, what can you tell us?" Hilda settled down in her rough blanket.

"Clovis brought a jar. Inside is Janus the god of doorways. He can open any door and Farona's carrying him through solid rock!" Rowan was astounded.

Even to Valonia and Hilda, experienced witches, her account was fantastic.

"You hear that, Hilly?" Valonia carped. "We're off to meet a god, best look your finest." She rattled with laughter while Hilda smiled warmly, loving the way she talked as if this would all have a happy ending.

They chatted amiably for a while and Rowan amazed and delighted them with tiny scraps of news, but like any almost seven-year old, she eventually peeped again and saw Krast's three special krakens, the ones with human-sized compartments in their chests. "Valonia," she added fearfully.

"Yes, child?"

"Those machines they have?"

She knew exactly what she meant. "Yes?"

"They're not tested properly, and don't work like they're meant to."

"That's all I needed to know," she growled. "You've done your part. Now look away and tell us of Kolfinnia."

She told them of Clovis's miracle, of the Timekeeper, of Flora's mighty storm and of Kittiwake's feast in honour of their coven-mother. She told them all she could see and when she was finished Valonia began to believe that maybe victory wasn't just a dream after all.

Not far from where Valonia and the others hung suspended in the Fortitude, Hathwell hung suspended in his hammock.

The crew quarters in the airship's underbelly were crammed to bursting point. He shared this block with forty other squires and being senior squire didn't afford him any luxuries, and so he travelled third-class along with the rest. He hung just inches from the next man and tried to sleep, but it was difficult to say the least. As the ship rolled the hammocks swung and he bumped intimately against the men either side of him. They were packed in like sardines and all around he could hear men snore, grunt and fart as they all tried to steal some sleep and make the most of the brief night. Just over an hour from now they would disembark, somewhere between midnight and dawn, to rendezvous with the 21st Devonshire Light Brigade where their ranks would be reinforced, then would start the arduous rallying operation. There were supplies to unload, krakens to assemble, horses to saddle up and infantry to supply and prime. When they finally marched they would have been working for eight hours already, and then there was a day's fighting to look forward to.

Hathwell lay there, watching the man above swing back and forth gently. He hated lower hammocks: you never knew if the man above would keep his dinner down and that wasn't a pretty shower to have pass you in the dead of night. As he lay there he wondered again what they would find at Kittiwake, and his mind drifted back to the past.

It was Solvgarad again. The smoke cleared briefly and he saw the lad who'd been running at him lying in the dirt. He looked down at his smoking pistol, and just then the smoke rolled back in, concealing his crime. That's when he ran, knowing that if the smoke cleared again he'd have to see him once more. He ran after the infantry and never looked back.

Although he felt distant from the other troops now, that hadn't stopped him over-seeing Krast's modifications. Each furnace had been replaced with the same kind of apparatus that had sent Godfrey Hallam to his grave. Hallam had been drained in seconds, and so Hathwell had tinkered with the machine's metabolic rate as ordered, and when nobody had been watching he turned them down even *more*. It went a little way to paying for his part in Ada's death. He rubbed at his tired eyes while a man somewhere to his left moaned in his sleep. "This is useless," he muttered.

He gave up chasing sleep, untangled himself from his hammock, slipped through the rows of swaying bunks and went to check on his horse two floors down. He hoped she was a lively mare because he planned on taking a long ride tomorrow, if he lived, and the further it took him from his old life the better.

While the Illuminata sailed above and Farona travelled below, Kittiwake was caught in the middle. The feast had gone on until Clovis had prudently reminded them further preparations were needed, and so the celebrations were reluctantly brought to a close and Kittiwake was readied for night, and readied for battle. Clovis had taken command of Moon-Frost, and in his usually efficient manner they were already as prepared as they could be.

Now he sat with Tempest, and Skald had joined them also. All three were sitting at the stone circle overlooking the bay. The sea was a silver expanse now that night was falling and the moon was rising.

"That was a true miracle you worked today," Skald praised him.

"Janus has his uses," Clovis said grudgingly.

"Janus?"

"Only by travelling through Evermore with him could I show it to the others."

"Ah," Skald nodded. "Fear of death lies at the heart of the world's woes."

Clovis rolled the dice and they came up as a pair of ones.

"Snake-eyes," Skald said.

"Where I come from we call it 'twice-done-for'."

"Doesn't sound good in any language," Tempest remarked.

Clovis sighed again, stretched and drank in the view of the sea under the moon. "This is an incredible world you have." He sounded sad. Even if he survived tomorrow he must return to Vega and release Janus, and that in itself would be a world-changing event.

"Then stay. Kolfinnia's very fond of you."

The warrior-witch just smiled sadly, then changed the subject. "Skald? What does your name mean? Other sprite names I understand but not yours."

He grimaced. "It's not easy to talk about. Valonia gave me the name and it stuck."

"What does it mean?" he pressed. "I won't tell a soul."

"The name means 'poet'," he confided.

Clovis and Tempest swapped impressed glances. "So you're a poet as well as a warrior?"

"When I met Valonia for the very first time in Mörkdalur I complimented her and she thought it was poetic. Let's just leave it at that."

"Your secret's safe with us," Clovis chuckled.

The three sat in silence for a while. The night was so still and forgiving that it was hard to believe battle approached. The sea looked to be resting: it was calm and flat and Clovis's gaze kept drifting to the tower where hrafn-dimmu still announced the call to gather. He suspected that any witch who was going to answer that call had already come, but Kolfinnia insisted on leaving raven's-wand where it was right to the bitter end.

"There you are!" a woman's voice called and they all jumped guiltily as if they'd been doing something wrong.

Kolfinnia came marching towards them brandishing her lightning-staff. "Skald! I spent ten minutes talking to this lump of wood before I realised you weren't in it! How long have you been up here?"

"Not long. It just seemed right to be close to Farona," he said in his defence, and her annoyance suddenly waned.

"I understand," she relaxed, and came to join them. "Space for one more?"

Clovis shuffled over and patted the grass. She sat down lightly and crossed her legs and Clovis was delighted when like the rest of them, she just looked out to sea and said nothing.

At one point Janus had to detour around a massive body of granite. The rock was hard and featureless, with no bedding joints or seams, and Janus said that walking through it would have tired him too much. Farona wondered how a god could get tired, but he held his peace and they skirted the city-sized obstacle and kept to the more navigable limestone and sandstone. The joints, fractures and faults allowed them to be pushed aside easily.

The temperature was steadily rising. Farona stopped long enough to remove his coat and take a bite of Sally's sandwiches, and found that he was glad of them just as she'd said. He had no idea how long they had been travelling but his stomach told him it had been a while. The amount of water also increased along with the heat; almost all the rock was now streaked with cloudy water, which made the steps treacherous. Farona kept to his flask, as the water down here looked as though it hadn't seen the sun for millions of years, which struck him as unhealthy. Sometimes when the rock opened up there was a burst of ground water and he was showered in it, and by now his cherished coven-colours were looking decidedly grubby.

"What a mess," he sighed wearily.

"You worry about your clothes at a time like this?" Janus quipped.

"It's a matter of coven pride. Maybe you wouldn't understand." He felt irritable. So far their heroic quest had been just a long walk in the dark.

"More a matter of *personal* pride, I suspect," Janus chirped, and for good measure he flipped several times inside the jar.

Farona felt the jar rock under his mocking little dance. "What's that supposed to mean?" he said brusquely.

"Ohh! The young man is shy! Forgive me, I thought perhaps your coven-colours were to catch the eye of a certain somebody."

"Don't know what you mean," he said moodily, knowing perfectly well.

"The girl has only one eye to catch, and you still can't manage it!" Janus giggled and Farona's cheeks burned. The insult against Flora was unbearable and he stopped and held the jar up to his face. He could see Janus's gleeful face and his eyes were curved into mocking crescents.

"What would you know of such things?" he said angrily.

"A great deal. *Not all doorways are rock.* Some doorways are opportunities."

"I don't take your meaning?"

"My meaning is that if you pass every doorway without being bold enough to open it, your life will be very predictable and very dull." Janus flipped over, unleashing a stream of tiny bubbles.

Not all doorways are rock. He pondered the god's words. Was Janus encouraging him to be bolder, or just having a joke at his expense? Clovis did call him the 'trickster god' after all.

"Never mind. There's weightier business at hand. I sense we're approaching a void behind the rock," Janus cautioned.

"Like that horrible tunnel again?"

"Perhaps," he said quietly.

The layers split and folded back, and a dark opening appeared which grew steadily wider. Farona gripped his wand and gritted his teeth, expecting a hail of crawling letters, or some other bizarre threat, but all he felt was a gust of wind expelled from the void. It was icy and it carried memories of a time before humanity.

"Wester?" he checked his sprite.

"I'm here," a strong voice came back.

He stood facing the opening and carefully extended his arm until the wand illuminated the chamber beyond. Immediately he saw what looked like a million twinkling eyes glint back at him, and he heard the sound of rushing water carrying an echo that suggested a massive space. He pushed his arm deeper into the opening and gasped, "Janus, it's beautiful!"

The 'eyes' were the gleaming facets of billions of crystals. Inside was a chamber of immense size and from what Farona could see the whole space from floor to ceiling was lined with crystals. He raised a leg and stepped through the ragged opening, clumsily balancing his wand and Janus as he did.

Once inside, Janus closed the way behind them. Farona glanced around to see the rock melt back into place and crystals rise from it like bubbles, and then solidify. He was sealed in. "What about the air?"

"There'll be enough to complete your task," Janus assured him. "And be so good as to stop tossing me around, you oaf."

Cradling the vessel, Farona advanced a little into the huge space, but his wand-light was woefully inadequate. "Wester? Can you help?" He drew his staff.

"My pleasure."

Wester emerged and took a deep breath, spread his wings and shuddered. After a second his blue storm-light flooded the cavern, and then god, witch and sprite were left speechless with wonder.

The chamber was curved like a drinking horn, and the roof swept down towards the floor making a wedge shape. Pillars of rock stretched their way from floor to ceiling in random clumps like melted wax. The entire cavern was covered in crystals, from the tiny ones the size of apple-pips studding the walls, to the very largest which towered over him, and their colours shifted in patterns like a rainbow. He was drawn to these largest crystals without even being aware of it, the ones that thrust up from the cavern floor like blades. They were mostly transparent: some were shiny like glass while others looked silky, and still others had a pearlescent or even metallic lustre, and the endless succession of shapes was a mathematician's wonderland. The angles were so sharp and perfect that he could almost imagine being cut just by looking at them.

He edged forwards, his feet finding traction on a carpet of miniature crystal tips, and he saw his image refracted many times over in the tallest crystals. They were huge, easily as thick as trees, and their purity hurt his eyes. The colours were so intense it was like seeing colour for the first time, as if every hue and shade in world above was just a degraded copy of the originals down here.

"It's magnificent," he uttered.

"Fit for a king," Janus observed humbly. "Or a serpent," he added tellingly.

"You think they're here?" Farona realised he stood on the brink of something no other witch would ever see, but rather than boastful he felt honoured.

"Let's go see," Wester suggested.

As he crept forward the ground changed and he looked down. The crystal matrix had given way to a huge expanse of mica; it was like walking on glass and his boots squeaked as he made his way deeper into the cavern. The floor was rippled and pitted. Over time grit and silt had accumulated in its imperfections, but that still couldn't disguise its brilliant colour. At its edges, the floor was the same dazzling blue as Sunday's eyes. Then, as he progressed he saw the colour gradually fade and underneath he detected a faint orange glow, but rather than remain static the glow flickered and pulsed like a flame.

"Strange," he muttered. "The colour's moving."

"It's not the stone, it's the fire beneath," Janus warned.

"What! We're so far down?" He suddenly lost a little of his wonder. The crystal floor the only thing between him and the Earth's deep magma currents.

"The first sign of earth-fire, the very place you must return the serpent-twins to," Janus anticipated. "That's what we came here for, isn't it?"

"We've to find them first," Farona spoke in a hushed whisper. Being here was like being in a hallowed place.

"I think we have." Wester raised a finger towards the largest of the crystals in the cavern and Farona was astounded as to how he could have missed it. It was vast, reaching up from the floor and punching a hole into the roof above where millions of its tiny fellows clustered around it like frosting. It grew directly from a towering forest of emerald spires, surmounting them like a sword. It was pure hardened carbon, pure diamond. The incredible crystal was opaque and raw around its base, but as it rose up from the greenery around its foundations it purified and became almost as clear as air and only revealed its facets when Wester's light struck it at just the right angle. No wonder Farona hadn't noticed it right away.

"Oak and holly!" He felt a tear run down his cheek and his throat tighten. He carefully placed Janus down on the floor and the sound of glass on quartz rang through the cavern. He pointed just as Wester had done, not at the crystal this time but rather at something contained inside. "Lord and Lady!" he exhaled and dropped to his knees.

His lightning-staff fell and toppled to the floor unnoticed, and Wester flapped down to Farona's side and knelt in respect. Janus stilled in reverence, lost for words at last.

Before them, inside a fortress of diamond, were Hethra and Halla.

"Can you open this doorway, Janus? Send them deeper?" he asked without looking up. The twins were unprotected and vulnerable. Even to glance at them felt disrespectful.

"Of course," Janus said quietly. "But it will take a gentle opening, and might require some time." He wasn't sarcastic any longer.

Before dropping to his knees, Farona had glimpsed the terra-soula suspended inside the gigantic diamond. In his fleeting glimpse he saw a perfect sphere of bronze no larger than his own head. *They're really inside there, the twins, Hethra and Halla.* The thought was so magnificent and never-ending that he couldn't grasp it, and just as he couldn't look directly at them, neither could he think about them being incarnate before him only yards away. *They're in there and their dream creates the Earth, so am I a dream in their head or are they a dream in mine?* The thought made his head spin.

"There is much work to be done," Janus cautioned. "We cannot just split the earth and topple them down. The right asking is needed for this chamber to sink away and into the currents of magma below."

Now that he was here the idea of destroying this chamber in the deep forges of the earth felt like sacrilege. "Must we?"

"You want them below, don't you?"

"They won't be hurt, will they?" Farona wondered for the first time if this was the right thing to do.

"You're the witch, not I," he replied unhelpfully.

Farona thought back to his teachings. *Hethra and Halla dream. Their dream is Earth and all life lives within their dream. They are what makes fire burn and ice freeze. They are life itself, and nothing natural of Earth can harm them because all Earth is their dream.* "The deep-fire will protect them." He turned so that he wasn't facing the great diamond and watched as Janus began to turn inside his jar, as if unscrewing a cap on a bottle. "How long will this take?"

"Disturb me not," Janus silenced him.

Farona sat back with a sigh and thought of the battle that might be raging above right now. He looked up at the crystals carpeting the ceiling. Their twinkling faces were like stars and he thought of the world so far above him. "Save some krakens for me, Clovis," he whispered and then curled up against the cold, willing Janus to hurry.

Oak and Holly

As October 21st yielded to the 22nd, and while the sun still slept beyond the horizon, Benedict Collins, the witch who'd been involved in a scuffle a day before, watched the hills from his shelter of willow canes. Today, Kolfinnia had said they were going to war, or more exactly war was coming to them.

The moon was almost full and so the landscape was easy to read. He'd brought his pipe and a loaf here some hours ago and settled in. Since then he'd not taken his eyes from the distant hills. Kolfinnia had charged him with keeping this forward lookout manned. There was another one a mile to the east and likewise to the west, and more beyond forming a line of watchers. He shuffled around, reaching with cold fingers to his flask, needing a nip of brewer's tonic. It wasn't easy: the shelter was only just big enough for him to sit in. "Spit and damn to it," he cursed quietly as he fumbled in the dark. It was too risky to use wand-light and he kept his chat with his sprite, Wake, to a minimum. "Ah!" He smiled as his fingers wrapped around the flask. In the next instant he had the bottle pressed to his lips and was just about to take a swig when a growling sound made him stop.

It was Wake.

"What's wrong?" He dropped the flask and grabbed his staff.

"Not sure? Just a smell, like horses and sweat, but far off."

"Kolfinnia said they'd come today," he muttered, scouring the dark hills for any movement.

"And she was right! To the eastern ridge, where the river follows the valley. Look!"

He crawled out of his shelter, pipe and flask forgotten, and squatted in the heather staring intently into the night. There wasn't a sound other than the wind and his own beating heart. He looked so hard that his eyes ached, and then when he was ready to call it a false alarm he saw it. Far off in the valley he saw a silvery flash. It was the glint of moonlight on armour. "They're on us," he realised.

He had a spell-bottle for just this purpose. He snatched it up and broke it in his palm to complete the charm. Immediately a voice called back to him. It was Betty in the lookout a mile to his west.

"Benny, that you?" she was crowning.

"Aye Betty, it's me. They're coming. Tell the others and get back to Kittiwake. Me and Wake are already off!" Even as he grabbed his staff a host of other voices clamoured from adjacent lookouts, all of them carrying the same message: The assault had started.

"They're coming!"

"Benny, I think I see something moving, few miles distant."

"This is Arthur. Is it my eyes or do I see summat down the vale there?"

Different voices, all with the same warning. With a last look at his crude little shelter, Benedict mounted his staff and tore back to Kittiwake to tell them the battle had begun.

It wasn't yet dawn when he arrived back, but there wasn't a single sleeping witch at Kittiwake and the place was a whirl of activity. He thought of running through the crowds shouting his news, but that would probably induce chaos. It took him six agonising minutes to find Kolfinnia and give her the news in two short words, "They're coming."

She surprised the young man with an embrace. "Thank you, Benedict. Now, battle positions, please."

Clovis came running from the direction of the engine-shed carrying a lantern. "Kolfinnia!"

"I know, word just arrived, Are all the scouts in?" she replied calmly.

"Yes, all back safe. Betty just brought me the news."

"Everyone knows our strategy, they know what to do." Even though she'd slept for only an hour she felt energised. She was readying to gather her Flower-Forth witches when Clovis spoke again.

"You know I never did show you that miracle," he offered his hands with a shy smile.

She knew well enough what he'd shown everyone and the effect it had on them all. "Let me see it with my own eyes on the day I walk it for real." She reached out and gently lowered his hands.

"Then I hope that day's a long time coming."

They stood regarding one another, knowing this might be their farewell. Even if today's weave had a happy ending eventually he would take a different path to hers.

"My thanks for all you've done." She pulled him close and sank her face into his thick mane.

He held her tenderly, and this time he didn't slap at her back. "If I should not see you ag —,"

"Shhh!" She knew the words would be as crushing as his incredible sword. "You will see me again, and I you." Her words were drowned out by the racket of witches readying for battle, but Clovis pricked his ears and smiled when he heard them.

The oldest, youngest and infirm were gathering in the courtyard with their scant belongings. From there Flora would lead them to the stones on the hill. Those not engaged in battle had donated their wands for armaments and Sally had spent the night making wand-arrows. Kolfinnia had ordered the non-combatants to take refuge at the stones and wait for Farona's return while the rest held the knights at bay.

Flora ran into the courtyard, staring wildly. "Kol, is it true, are they coming?" she asked breathlessly.

"As we speak. Now, take those not fighting up the hill. Tell them to make a chain. It's still dark and without their wands for light it'll be treacherous. You know what to do next?"

"Call a sea mist, in case they have gun ships in the bay."

"I know I've asked a lot of you lately . . ." She sounded apologetic.

"After calling a whole storm, asking a mist'll be no bother," Flora promised, before grabbing her in a rough embrace. "We'll see each other afterwards?"

Kolfinnia wondered what 'afterwards' meant. After her duty? After the battle? After death? "Of course we'll see each other."

"So many good-byes today," she reflected.

Kolfinnia took her hands and gripped tight. "Shroud the stones in mist. Make it thick enough to blot out the whole coast. Then come and join us in the Flower-Forth ranks."

Flora gave a firm nod. "I'll see you in the ranks."

They parted and hurried about their tasks just as the first light of dawn showed, and if any witch had found the time to be still they would have heard the distant thunder of iron being primed.

The Illuminata's assembly point was the head of an old pack-horse trail that local intelligence confirmed led right to the heart of the abandoned Oakland tin mine, where surviving witches had been secretly training for weeks.

Hathwell was uncomfortable to say the least. Not only was he riding to war for the first time in two decades, but supplies had given him the wrong sized uniform. His mare's name was Saxon. If he had known Hilda's last name he might have thought it either deeply ironic or a cruel joke at his expense. Krast had ordered Valonia and the others to be taken from the Fortitude as soon as they'd landed and placed in the power chamber of each kraken. They had to sedate them, of course. He wouldn't go near them and neither would his staff. These weren't prisoners to take risks with.

First, their cells were flooded with gas and each was brought out unconscious and fixed inside the waiting krakens. Hathwell watched helplessly as each was manhandled up the wooden scaffold and strapped into the empty chamber like lifeless machine parts. A complex system of wires and tubes was then needed to drain each subject and at just the right rate: Krast didn't want them expiring in the heat of battle. A good part of him didn't want to watch as they were inserted into the glass-fronted sarcophagi, but another part of him insisted he bear witness.

That was an hour ago and he still couldn't shake the terrible pictures from his mind, especially the smallest of the three stretchers. It was still dark although dawn had already started to glow in the east. Hathwell groomed his mare and then he struggled with his rifle, and either rifles had become heavier over the last two decades or he was badly out of shape. Men wandered around with lanterns tending their horses, or preening their Lord's war banners. He heard an excited flurry and peered in to the dark where men suddenly stood to attention and he had no doubt why. Krast had come to make a personal farewell.

"Bertrand, just came to wish you luck this day." He wore his Knight's uniform. The purple was so dark that it looked black and it was decorated with meaningless medals and gold braid. He proffered his hand for him to shake. In days of old a squire was required to kiss their knight's hand.

Thank God that's one tradition that doesn't live on, Hathwell thought wearily. "I'll stay alive in order that I may continue to serve you, sir." He took the offered hand and shook it firmly.

Krast looked pensive, choosing difficult words. "These have been trying times, Bertrand," he said earnestly. "My thanks for your undying loyalty."

The remark was like a blade thrust at his battered sense of self and he wavered. Knight or witch? He couldn't find his own ground.

Krast began his short speech for them all. Listening to him, he made it sound like the battle had already happened and the victory was theirs, but of course he had good reason. The Illuminata had almost a hundred krakens at their disposal and double the number of squires. Behind that they had at least four-hundred infantry. They would pound them with krakens from the landward side, while out at sea two navy iron-clads were waiting with their guns. It seemed impossible that anything could resist or even escape alive.

Hathwell listened without really hearing and again tried to make sense of his feelings. He asked for a sign, and yesterday he even went to the company chapel, but he'd come away no wiser.

"And so," Krast was finishing off, "let it be known that when we march today we shall be avenging our fallen brothers."

Hathwell prodded at a stone with his boot and stifled a yawn. He didn't even notice when Krast had finished, but clapped accordingly, then took Saxon's reigns and led her away.

She didn't know anything anymore. Even to say she didn't even know her own name was an understatement: she wasn't aware she had a name. Valonia Gulfoss was restrained inside a metal coffin in Purity's chest, and the technical crews were finishing the primary tests.

"She's alive, sir. The reading's very high. She's strong, I'll say that." The senior deviser pinched Valonia's cheek to demonstrate. She never twitched a muscle. She just hung there limp. "Compartment's ready to be sealed, sir."

Krast wanted a moment to savour this. "I'll attend to that. Now leave us."

The deviser made a salute and clambered down the scaffold.

Krast drew fingers down her cold face. Her eyes were closed and her mouth hung slack. "I wish you could see this, Valonia," he stroked her cheek. "You're going home. Back to your wand and your old friends." He sighed and reached up to the eye-patch. If he didn't secure a resounding victory today then his days as Knight Superior would be over. The cabinet had forbidden this operation and the Empress herself was asking of first-dawn. Knight bloodlines were already looking to steal his title, and all because of this one woman. He leaned closer and whispered something into her ear. "I'm going to take your gods and enslave them."

Her features twitched.

He gave an involuntary jump and immediately felt foolish. She'd insulted him yet again. His lips curled into a sneer and he grabbed the door and hauled it shut. "Farewell, Valonia. Now you're the witch betraying her own." He slammed the hatch hard enough to rock the scaffold, and then he went to board Purity's cockpit from where he'd spearhead the whole operation.

The sun finally cleared the hills and liquid gold looked to spill across the landscape. It was a beautiful morning on Friday, October 22nd. All of Kittiwake's defenders were assembled along the keel at the mine's entrance, all of them watching the packhorse trail and the direction their enemies would come. They were armed with staffs and had covered their colours with wayfarer grey, making them harder targets to hit. Wands were buckled where they could be easily reached and most had taken earth and ash and painted their faces with symbols and charms. Now they looked ferocious and otherworldly. Sunday had woven her hair into a long plait barbed with gull feathers, and smeared white ash over her face and blackened her eyes with charcoal, and the effect was stunning.

Even in war she has to look resplendent, Kolfinnia admitted.

Each season stood fifteen abreast and two ranks deep forming a solid wall. They stood in silence waiting for their enemies. The wind pulled at the strips tied around their hats, and the only sound was the flapping of Wildwood's banner at the centre of their ranks.

The Swords of Britain were now shrouded in sea-fret and quite invisible. Kolfinnia looked back to the stones and thought of the frightened witches huddled there and longed to see Farona's signal, but the earth remained locked tight and the knights grew closer. *Come soon, Farona,* she pleaded silently. He'd been gone almost twenty-four hours now, and she'd lost count of the how many scenarios she'd tortured herself with. "It must have been a huge rallying operation," she said ominously to Clovis. "It's two hours since Ben raised the alarm."

"They're coming, believe me," he said softly and his ears twitched once.

She walked a little way ahead until she was fifty yards proud of their ranks, then stood between her two staffs, holding them like spears. She stared southwards to where the trail dwindled into the morning haze. "Come on, you bastards," she whispered. Skald and Five both appeared and crouched on the staffs. "They're out there," she muttered, willing them to come, amazed that thousands of tons of iron and hundreds of men could be so elusive.

"You're right." Five's conviction was total.

"How do you know?" she asked.

"Hilda," he sighed. "She's with our enemies."

"Skald?" she asked warily.

He craned his neck and sniffed. "Valonia's out there too."

"Are they hostages of some kind?" This was unexpected and very disturbing.

"Our lost friends will be on the battlefield, that's all I can tell you," Skald replied.

Hostages? Is no trick too filthy for these vermin? she thought and stared down the valley, straining to see, but there was nothing. Then a shout to her rear made her spin around.

"Scouts returning!" Someone called from the ranks.

She saw Morag Heron and Annie Barden arrived simultaneously from opposite directions dropping from their staffs in a great hurry. The ranks shuffled as everyone crowded in to hear and Kolfinnia ran towards them.

"Kolfinnia!" Annie cried. "Infantry to the east, heading towards us through the hills, but no knights."

"The terrain's too rocky for krakens," Kolfinnia explained. "Only infantry'll come that way. Morag, what about the west?"

Morag caught her breath. "More infantry," she puffed, "keeping to the dunes heading this way, I think they saw me. It was a race to get away fast enough."

"So the knights will come from the south as we thought. It's the only terrain open to them, along the packhorse trail." Clovis lifted his muzzle and took a chest-full of air. There was a tense moment and then he confirmed his suspicions. "Hmm, I smell soot and oil."

"Then they're on their way." Kolfinnia couldn't help but look out to sea where the Timekeeper sat weaving their fates, and wished she could see into his mind.

"Witches!" Clovis bellowed. "The south will be the hardest front. Seed-Fall, take the west and Snow-Thaw take the east. Hold the infantry. Stop them outflanking us and most of all protect the stones. Farona has to find us there to greet him, not these bastard knights!"

"Moon-Frost, Flower-Forth!" Kolfinnia commanded and they announced themselves with a cheer. "We hold the advancing knights here along the trail."

She regarded her witches. Bathed in the dawn they looked magnificent and resolute. Clovis's revelation still inspired them, and they had mastered their fears. She looked at each face in turn and marked their name. When she reached Sunday she paused for a second. She looked different and it was nothing to do with her war paint, but how and why Kolfinnia couldn't say.

When she locked eyes with her coven-mother, Sunday felt to be ablaze with guilt. If just a single witch fell then their blood would be upon her hands. If the knights took Janus upon Farona's return and used him to delve for the twins, it would be all her fault and her soul would be stained forever. She held Kolfinnia's gaze and promised that today she would mend her mistakes. "Magic is regal," she whispered to herself.

Kolfinnia turned to Skald. "If it goes bad –,"

"I know," he interrupted. "I'll give your regards to Gale when I get home."

She smiled at his stoicism.

"Witches of Kittiwake," she shouted, and they hushed and looked her way. "Dreaming dragons need you now and let's make this day a nightmare for the Illuminata!"

They roared their support and raised their own staffs and their riot was so deafening it even drowned out the sound of guns from the warships in the bay as they began to fire frustrated shells into the mist. The first shots in the battle for Kittiwake-coven had been fired.

He awoke with a start and stared around the cavern, certain he'd been there for days. As his murky dream slipped away the reality of his quest rolled back and Farona felt the ticking clock once more. "How long was I asleep, Wester?"

"Can't have been more than ten minutes," his sprite whispered.

He rubbed at his face and cast a glance at Janus. It came as no surprise that the little god was still turning lazy circles in the jar. "How long's he been doing this?" The waiting was eating him up.

"Several hours at least," Wester reported.

"I wonder what's happening up above," he sighed.

He listened to the sound of dripping water and gazed around at the cavern. It was magnificent, but right now he longed to be back at Kittiwake. *Every witch on earth has sent their blessings to this very place for centuries, and I'm here and all I want to do is go home,* he thought dourly. He sensed Hethra and Halla behind their wall of diamond and wondered if they could hear his thoughts, and had a sudden pang of shame. "I'm sorry my Lord, sorry my Lady," he muttered.

Wester didn't enquire. He just yawned and settled back into his constant vigil.

Behind the dripping water Farona could hear the swish of Janus inside his jar and for the umpteenth time he wondered why a god needed to gather his strength before opening a door. But this wasn't just any door, this was the gateway to the deep-fire of the earth and there were great beings to be ushered through that gateway. At least that's what he told himself. Thinking otherwise suggested Janus was playing with him again. *Who are you Janus, and where did you really come from?* he thought.

He saw the god's cheery face spin past repeatedly like a windmill sail and each time it did he grew more convinced that Janus was making sure he remained down here until Kittiwake lay in ruins. He thought of Janus's words about doorways being opportunities and briefly wrestled with the idea of what he'd say to Flora if he ever saw her again. At last he couldn't contain himself anymore, and he edged closer to the jar and lowered his face to the glass. "Janus, how much longer?"

"Patience!" Janus was concentrating.

Farona's troubles might have been eased if he could see something, such as the earth sliding open, but so far the cavern remained stubbornly inert. He flopped back into his sitting position with a huff and directed his gaze upwards to the ceiling. The view was incredible, but he'd much rather have seen through it to where his friends were fighting or dying or who knew what. The forest of crystals winked back at him and Farona could imagine living eyes looking down and told himself not to let his imagination run away. "Nothing alive down here but the twins," he assured himself.

"Probably," Wester said blandly.

"What do you mean by probably?"

"Think back to your basic lessons, young one. Hethra and Halla are the fountain of all life."

"I know," he retorted, "and don't call me 'young one'. But what does 'probably' mean?"

"That the twins' dream creates life. I'd venture all these crystals grew after the deep currents brought them here."

"They grew so big just from the twin's influence?" Farona had entertained a similar notion.

Wester nodded. "They bring the dream of life, and look how this cavern has become alive."

Farona felt an unexpected chill at his words. They implied that things other than harmless rocks might have grown from being entombed close to the twins, and he craned around to look at the empty cavern. *Probably empty*, he thought to himself, and he could've kicked Wester for putting the horrible thought in his head. "Hurry, please, Janus," he willed quietly.

The vessel continued to churn, but the god remained silent.

"Come on Wester," Farona stood and saw his own face reflected in a golden galena crystal. *Fool's gold*, he thought and the face reflected there certainly looked naïve.

"Where to?" Wester landed on his shoulder.

"Just to stretch my legs. I'm getting cold and stiff." He drew his wand again and set off.

Not far from the illuminated vessel and the fiery crystal floor the light dwindled and he had to rely upon his wand. As he walked, the wand-light drifted over the crystal's polished faces. He found the effect abstract and rather soothing and quickly fell into a hypnotic kind of daydream, walking slowly amongst the forest of crystal trunks watching light spill and split, reflect and refract. Geometric shapes loomed up and even in the half-light the colours were achingly vivid. He saw feathery gypsum crystals with forked tails like kites, dazzlingly clear calcite crystals stabbing up out of the ground like wolf fangs, fronds of lustrous gold growing like ferns, and many more he didn't recognise. The further he went the more incredible the cave became.

For a while his troubled mind was eased and he ventured deeper into the cavern, occasionally glancing back to the vessel and its comforting flicker, but it looked like a lone star in the night by now. The sound of dripping water grew louder, and he suspected a fracture in the roof where surface water had percolated down. "Oh dear," he groaned.

"Problem?" The sprite was admiring a column of sulphur at least fifteen feet high.

"On the floor, look, little bones or something. Looks like the skeleton of some small fish?" He lowered his wand for a better look and just then he saw a second and a third. "There's more," he edged forwards.

The floor was littered with tiny bones and the further they ventured into the dark, closer to the sound of rushing water, the more bones there were.

"How do you think they came to be here?"

Wester remained silent but Farona felt his apprehensions.

"Wester?" He asked again

The sprite pushed his beaked nose up to his ear so he could whisper, "I think we should return to Janus."

He didn't like the sound of rushing water, nor the collection of little bones and suddenly Wester's words came back to him.

'Hethra and Halla are the fountain of all life.'

He didn't want to, but his mind pieced together what had happened down here over the centuries: small creatures had been carried in by ground waters, which in turn had provided food for something else.

'Hethra and Halla are the fountain of all life.'

If crystals could grow to such huge size what else could become gigantic down here? "Very well, back to Janus." Farona was just turning to leave when he heard a heavy splash somewhere ahead in the blackness. "Oak, no!" he moaned.

"Douse your wand," Wester ordered.

He did and the darkness immediately pressed in on all sides. Together they quietly backed away from the rushing waters that made Farona think of a churning stomach. He jumped when he heard a second splash away in the black and he stumbled. "It's too dark, West'. I can't see where I'm going," he complained.

"The light's too risky. I think it'll draw them."

Them? he thought. "What do you mean – them?"

"Shhh!" his sprite hissed. "Above us, look!"

The cavern roof was high above them. He shouldn't be able to see it but all the same he could, and now he saw why. There were hundreds of orbs glowing into life at the sound of his voice, swaying and twitching, and some of them were smoothly descending, leaving behind a glistening thread attached to the ceiling.

"Back to Janus!" Wester hissed.

Before he ran Farona had a clear view of them. Fat larvae with glowing lures were suspended above him in their hundreds, each as large as a boar, and now they were spooling themselves down for the latest food to have been washed into the cave.

He broke into a run, crunching over the crystal floor, no longer reverentially minding his step but running blindly. Wester vanished into the lightning-staff. Farona could see the reassuring glow of Janus's vessel not far ahead, but his mind told him he was no safer there than anywhere else.

Before he saw it, he detected the light intensify and the darkness peel back. He swung his staff without thinking just as one of the larvae swung down and snapped at him with powerful jaws. He felt the staff ram into something soft, heard the lightning discharge and Wester's angry roar. There was a brilliant flash and then the revolting smell of burnt innards and boiling stomach juices, and the worm or larvae or whatever the bizarre creature was dropped from its rope and splattered to the floor in a smoking heap.

"What is it?" he shrieked.

"Hungry!" Wester bellowed. *"Keep moving!"*

He snatched a look at the dead creature and saw a circular mouth like a leech, ringed with bone-saw teeth and a skin bristling with coarse hairs, and wished he hadn't looked.

More larvae dropped from their lairs above. Some landed on the floor or bounced harmlessly off the crystals and rolled to the ground where they writhed themselves into coils ready to spring at him, and before he knew it he was being assailed from above and below. The cavern echoed to Farona's cries and Wester's lightning-bolts, and yet more predators dropped from their hiding places.

"Open the doorway, Janus. Send the twins down!" He skidded to a halt next to the jar. "Now, do it now, Janus!"

Wester exploded again, and for the third time one of the creatures was flung away in a trail of sparks and steaming fluids. Farona shook drops of sweat from his stinging eyes and saw a shifting wave of larvae wriggling over the cavern floor towards him. As they came closer he saw with revulsion the largest tearing at the smaller ones. Cannibalism, it seemed, was the key to life at these depths.

His instincts told him to take the fight to them, else they'd be overrun in moments, and so he stepped forward and lunged at the nearest. Again Wester turned it to slime and innards, splattering it across the crystal floor where its rent skin glowed orange with the fire beneath. Seeing the glowing magma below, Farona remembered they still had to send Hethra and Halla down into the deep-fire, but he might die here before they had a chance. "Open it, Janus!" he screamed again, and lashed at another. This one was larger and its thick hide popped loudly when Wester struck it, his cherished coven-colours were splattered with boiled organs and he gagged in disgust.

"Janus, please!" he screamed, his voice breaking into a harsh croak, and inside his jar Janus spun in a curtain of bubbles and laughter, wearing his trickster's grin.

CHAPTER THIRTY-FOUR

Moons and Flowers

Incoming rounds from the gun ships wailed like banshees but slammed harmlessly into the dunes with a rumble and a spray of sand and grass.

"Steady," Kolfinnia cried. "It's random, they can't see us!" The ranks stood firm and Kolfinnia knew it was finally time to order them to their positions.

Clovis drew level. "It's as we feared. They're advancing in a column. We'll need to force them onto the soft ground either side of the packhorse trail, to make them vulnerable."

She knew what that meant. To break their column they had to fly straight into it. It was the most dangerous option and the one she'd feared most. She exchanged a telling look with him, and then stepped up to her duty. "Ward Crook, Ward Fife!" she shouted over the incoming shot.

Sally and Mary hoisted their staffs above their heads and the Snow-Thaw and Seed-Fall ranks all felt their hearts step up a gear.

"Seeds take the west, Snows take the east," Kolfinnia yelled. "Hold back the infantry any way you can, and remember Farona's signal. Disengage and return the instant you see it. Flowers, make ready!" she shouted to her own ranks and they fell into two columns ready to begin their charge.

"Moons, stand ready!" Clovis's witches made similar files behind them and he drew his sword.

Sally and Mary were already moving out. Sally skimmed past on her staff, heading to intercept the infantry coming through the wood and past the lake. An armada of airborne witches followed her, tearing down the grassy embankment parallel to the shore, moving over the landscape like a shadow. Mary led her witches in the opposite direction, sweeping up towards the stones, where they would turn east and engage the infantry advancing through the hills. She raised her staff in salute and everyone cheered her on, just as another round of cannon fire pelted the beach.

Kolfinnia watched the distant valley, and as the sun crept higher there was the unmistakable glint of steel. Now that she could see better, she detected movement and recognised it as infantry. "Rowan's out there," she murmured.

"Valonia too, and Hilda," Skald reminded her.

"Then let's hope they enjoy the spectacle." She touched Rowan's amulet. It was all but fallen apart now, but it was her last link to the girl. "We're coming to get you, Rowan," she promised, and this time it didn't feel in vain.

To stop the knights reaching the Swords of Britain she would charge them head on and then circle past for a second run while Clovis and Moon-Frost began their own charge. Bit by bit they'd grind them down and force them to break their column and so make them more vulnerable.

Kolfinnia took a deep breath, knowing it was time. "Flower-Forth," she raised both staffs and the ranks stiffened, ready. "For dreaming dragons!" she screamed, and ran.

She didn't look around, but she heard a mighty cheer at her back and in seconds her ranks were flying towards their enemies. The Moon-Frost ranks cheered them on, clashing their staffs and howling like wolves.

Clovis watched and counted down the distance. When she reached the lone ash five-hundred yards out he would start his own charge. He watched the faint spark of rifle fire from the cavalry and Kolfinnia's ranks blur across the landscape. His breathing was steady and calm, and inside his staff Tempest hummed gently. He was aware of so much; life's little details took on such meaning when they might be snuffed out at any moment. He could hear the breathing of the witches by his side, smell their anger and hear pumping hearts. Beyond that there was the ever present call of the tide, and the lonely but serene call of the gulls. He wondered again if this was why he had been directed to the ROWAN door, and more significantly, *who* might have sent him there. "I'll miss this world," he murmured wistfully.

"She's almost at the mark," Tempest observed.

The rifle fire intensified, but from this distance it sounded like party-fireworks, harmless and pretended. When she at last drew level with the ash Clovis twitched his whiskers. "Moons!" he bellowed and the tension peaked.

A kittiwake called overhead. It was a good omen and Clovis smiled. "FORWARDS!"

Then they charged.

He sprinted from his marks and was on his staff and clutching his great sword in a breath. The ranks at his back all surged forwards and took to the air until only the witch holding their standard remained. She plunged the Wildwood banner into the earth where it flapped longingly, looking desperate to follow, then Annie Barden, Lilain's attendant and survivor of Wildwood, mounted her staff and left the soil of Kittiwake to race after her coven-mother into the fight.

The girl that could know anything knew nothing other than drugged, half-sleep. She was restrained inside something metal, which lurched from side to side, and there was the regular clash of pistons and hiss of steam. "Kolllll . . ." she moaned in her unnatural sleep.

Her eyes wouldn't focus properly, but she recognised a glass window only inches from her face, and 'things' moving outside, things that were green and the suggestion of something blue above. It was the world long denied her and she wanted to laugh, but found she couldn't remember how and neither did she have the strength because something was draining her energy away. "Kolfinnn . . ." she tried to speak a name without knowing why it was important.

Every thought and feeling was instantly whisked away and she was left with only blanks, until the next feeling came and then that too was sucked upwards into the machine and used to drive it forwards. Eventually, she'd have no more thoughts left, and even though Hathwell had secretly reduced the kraken's metabolic rate, eventually it would eat every last thought in her head.

Hathwell rode at the head of the squires. Their ranks straddled the packhorse trail and he could see slender, dark rectangles where railway sleepers had once been. The cavalry line spilled out on to either side, riding over the rough ground which proved heavy going. It was boggy and treacherous, bad for horses and dangerous for knights.

Well chosen, he silently complemented them for choosing a site with such poor access.

He could hear the krakens marching a few hundred yards behind him, sounding like an iron foundry on the move, and they pounded the ground hard enough to unsettle the horses. "Baker!" he shouted to the squire at his left. "Carry word that the knights should keep narrow ranks. The ground to the left is too soft."

"Aye sir!" Baker wheeled his mount away without another word.

Hathwell had a bad feeling about this, the ground to their left was boggy and gave way to woodland, the ideal place for an ambush, while the ground to his right soared away upwards, too steep for krakens. *If the column breaks, we're done for.* He was surprised to find that his old soldier instincts hadn't abandoned him down the years. He raised himself in the saddle and stole a glance to the rear. The krakens towered over every man and horse and announced themselves in a din of grinding metal and a fog of steam. Most left tell-tale plumes of smoke, but not Purity and neither did the two krakens that flanked it. "Keep close!" he ordered. The line was becoming ragged.

Hathwell saw rabbits streak away from their approach and curious crows glide past. This was his first view of Kittiwake-coven and it looked bleak and forgotten, just like Solvgarad.

Krast's kraken thundered along with him enshrined beneath a helmet fashioned to look like a pious angel with curled locks and an angular jaw, and the whole thing was gilded with gold trim. He sat impervious inside the helmet, peering out from behind angel eyes, wearing a close fitting pressure-suit that mimicked his movements and translated them to the machine's ponderous limbs. He barely had space to turn or move, but the claustrophobic space made him feel secure. "I've come home," he murmured. "And so have you, Valonia." He thought of the old witch powering Purity from her spiritual reserves. "It appears you have little to say." He made minute adjustments to the pitch controls, pumping on a brass lever at his side. "Best save your strength, Valonia. You have much work ahead."

Inside her compartment Valonia was pale and cold. She dreamed of nothing and hung as lifeless as a fly wrapped in silk.

"Willis, you're breaking rank, man. Back up!" Hathwell barked at a squire a fraction out of line. He looked towards Purity, where Valonia was slowly being drained alive. Sir Rushton had the pleasure of Hilda's company. His kraken was silver-plated and bore a wolf-head helmet as well as wolf pelts dangling grotesquely from its shoulders. Sir Charles Grey rode a kraken of the most unusual sort. It was black, and with its hooded helmet and towering plumes it looked like a figure from a graveyard. This was Rowan's last resting place. "Bastards," he whispered again. Something made him think of Moore, hiding in the ranks, and although he couldn't give a fig about the man, Moore might not extend him the same courtesy. The last thing he wanted was a bayonet between his shoulder blades. "Hold the line!" he shouted. The horses were getting jittery and so were the men. *Where's this coven of witches?* he thought nervously.

An alarmed shout went up somewhere on his left flank. "They're coming! Sir, they're coming!" Hathwell stood in the saddle and strained to see. Just then a horn shattered the air making his horse jump. One of the knights had also sighted the enemy and every kraken took up the war-cry, and before he knew it Hathwell was wincing and his ears were ringing under the barrage. Men cried out and horses whinnied.

"Witches!" someone shouted again.

Kolfinnia's forces were approaching at great speed.

"At last!" Krast licked his lips.

As the battle-horns blared he selected a lever on the panel before him and readied Purity's forward batteries. When Kolfinnia's charge was two-hundred yards out he opened fire. There was a hail of shot and powder, a fiery cloud rushed forwards, and smoke billowed up. Inside the machine's sarcophagus, Valonia flinched in pain as Purity plundered her life-force to cut down her own kin.

"My compliments, Valonia. You fire well," Krast smiled coldly as he saw witches fall like bundles of rags.

"DOWN!" Kolfinnia screamed. Like fools, none of them had expected the krakens to have guns. She dropped lower, hearing Skald cursing and roaring as the worst of the barrage rocketed overhead, but she saw witches caught in the volley, smacked from their staffs and sent spinning away.

Clovis, five hundred yards to the rear, saw the unmistakable flash of gunfire and thunder-sprites returning to the skies and knew witches had died. "Vega protect us!" He growled and increased his speed.

Kolfinnia's forces streaked over the empty ground knowing they couldn't turn back. They had to reach the krakens before they fired again. They passed low enough to scare the horses. The animals bucked and squires panicked, trying to raise their rifles and shoot them out of the air. Kolfinnia saw startled men flash past, but she paid them no heed. Her targets were the krakens.

She screamed in rage as she closed in on the largest, the white and gold one that had caught them unawares. The monstrous thing loomed larger as she closed the gap, but not quite fast enough. Krast had just enough time to unleash a second volley and the knights either side of him now did likewise.

The three krakens fired in unison. The explosion was deafening and

STEVE HUTTON

the smoke fogged out everything. Knights marched forward into clouds of their own gun-smoke and opened fire again. A third volley ripped through her ranks and more witches were torn from their staffs. They were being cut to pieces. Shot rocketed past her and Kolfinnia knew it was suicide to continue and at the last minute, only yards from the krakens, she pitched right desperately hoping her witches would see and follow. "We can't break them!" she screamed to Skald.

"Take the bastards from the side!"

She hurtled along the knights' exposed left flank and out of the heavy fire. Gunfire from Krast's foremost knights had protected their fellows, but not so here. At last she had a chance to fight back, although now they were terribly vulnerable to the masses of infantry below. Towering krakens whizzed by and infantry responded with murderous covering fire. Just as she was about to make her first strike something shot past her – a witch on a white staff.

Sunday made the first kill against the Illuminata that day. She followed Kolfinnia along the knights' exposed flank, but then she turned and plunged into their ranks, skimming over plumed helmets and through their banners. One ugly helmet after another shot past her and in a split-second she selected her target, wielded her staff and struck.

She didn't even glance back. Superheated air rushed past her and a second later she heard the roar of thunder. The kraken's helmet shattered, the eyes bulged and became molten, and the banners instantly curled and blackened. It tumbled to the right, leaving a pillar of smoke, and crumpled to the ground scattering men and tripping the following knight behind.

"Two of them down!" Skald was impressed.

Kolfinnia flew past the mangled mess, and Sunday's former words echoed in her mind. *'Magic should be regal and proud.'* "I'll be proud of this!" Now she landed her own strike.

She slashed at a kraken's shoulder and there was a brilliant flash. Sparks burned her face, and the severed arm whirled away, spraying fire and steam. It crashed into the rearward kraken with a boom, shattering the furnace and spraying hot coals across the infantry below.

One by one she lashed at them, leaving a trail of destruction, hacking limbs and striking helmets. Rifle fire pelted the air, and as she passed the last krakens she snatched a look behind. Her surviving witches followed and there was a chain of smoking wrecks, but the knights were so dense that their run had hardly dented them. The infantry were keeping the column protected and the knights were still marching towards Kittiwake in tight formation.

"Hit them hard, Clovis!" she cried, and hoped that whatever gods

462

protect witches, they'd give him better luck.

The Moon-Frost charge was greeted with the same barrage, but now they were ready for it. Clovis plainly saw that a headlong charge was bound to fail, and so he signalled for his ranks to emulate Kolfinnia and sail down their unprotected flank, while he intended to cleave a path right though the middle.

Krast saw the incoming charge. "And again," he muttered, sounding bored. They might be heroic, he conceded, but their tactics were predictable and he reached for the trigger.

Valonia moaned and for a second her eyes flickered open. She saw daylight and almost remembered her name, but it fluttered away from her and the darkness returned. She collapsed back into the tangle of machinery with an agonised groan as Purity once again plundered her strength.

Clovis's ranks broke to the right while he charged dead ahead, brandishing his sword. As he rushed towards the thick curtain of smoke and crack of rifles, he passed the bodies of Kolfinnia's fallen witches. The krakens fired again, as Clovis flattened his ears and leaned into the wind, never taking his eyes from the gap between the machines. He plunged into the cover of smoke, ignoring the cavalry yards below, and pulled his magnificent sword back to make his blow.

He had promised Kolfinnia that such a weapon could decide the outcome of a battle, and if not for her it would still be lying useless in the heather. Acrid smoke burned his throat and shrapnel and stones pelted his face. "I promised to repay your kindness," he promised, "and their cruelty." At the last instant he pitched low and shot between the machine's scissoring legs and lashed out with his sword. He had told Kolfinnia the blade weighed 'a lot'. That was an understatement. Twenty-six thousand tons of momentum cleaved effortlessly through plate armour as though it wasn't even there. Purity had been hit. "VEGA!" He roared.

He continued right down the middle of the column, where no infantry or squires were posted, where the Illuminata hadn't dreamed a witch would dare fly. He raced past one after another, right between their leaden arms and legs, keeping his sword outstretched and level, slicing elbows, armour and pistons, destroying anything that stood in the way of his sword.

Meanwhile, on the outer left flank, Moon-Frost earned a better run. More plumed helmets showered upwards in sparks and hot metal, banners sizzled and krakens staggered or fell, but the infantry saturated the sky with bullets, witches fell like hail, while the damage they inflicted was limited. The column drove forwards to Kittiwake leaving a trail of broken krakens and trampled dead in its wake.

Clovis shot from between the last krakens and faced a sea of infantry and a hail of gunshot. Stray rounds pinged off his chest-plate and he knew it was time to circle wide and get out of their sights. He turned sharply and rejoined the others who had flown down the outer flank.

"I see you took the shortcut!" Annie Barden wore a wild grin and actually looked to be enjoying herself.

"Circle through the woods back to Kittiwake!" He had seconds to bark his command as their flight paths crossed, and then he headed for the cover of the wood, relieved to see a line of witches following in close formation. Most of them had made it through, but the column remained unbroken.

"We'll all be dead before the column's stopped!" Tempest was right.

"We'll rally back at the mine."

"And then what?"

"I'll think of something!" But whatever it was he knew he'd better think quick. "Come on, Farona, lad," he pleaded as he raced back to Kittiwake.

Krast pulled hard on the right arm control, but Purity was slow responding. Clovis had sliced through the knuckles on the right hand. "Damn it!" he spat. He stared out of the visor. The squires were in some confusion although still holding their ranks, but he couldn't see any more witches. Just then, a whistle sounded from the communicare. "Krast," he shouted into the speaker-tube, expecting Rushton or Grey. First there was only frosty static, then a distant voice that sounded like a ghost.

"Josephine," it whispered.

He froze just as there came a huge explosion and he heard debris clang against the helmet. Purity lurched. He stiffened and brought the machine under control. "Valonia? Is that some trickery of yours? You try to play games with me, witch-woman, eh?" he snarled, half convinced that she was coming for him, but that was impossible, he told himself: she was enslaved and her mind was gone. Another explosion rocked the cockpit. The communicare whistled again. He jumped and eyed it suspiciously, and with great effort brought his trembling lips to the funnel and spoke. "Krast."

It was no ghost this time, but Rushton. "They've withdrawn to the mine, sir."

"I can see that," he snapped. "Proceed at current speed, and order the squires back into ranks."

"Aye, sir." Rushton signed off.

Krast eyed the communicare warily. *No, it wasn't her.* He throttled the kraken, just to teach her a lesson. "Speak when you're spoken to, Valonia," he ordered. So far the operation was going well and he expected to be sitting eating his luncheon in the smoking ruins of Kittiwake by noon.

Kolfinnia was almost the last back to Kittiwake, where she found a straggle of survivors waiting for her by the engine-shed. One of them had retrieved the Wildwood banner. The gun-ships continued to fire, but so far all they had hit were the gardens, and now bombarded cabbages lay like severed heads. Even before she landed she was looking for Flora amongst the crowd, and her heart glowed when she spotted her.

"Kolfinnia's back!" someone cried.

Kolfinnia dropped neatly from her staff and ran to them. Some were wrapping strips of cloth around wounds or just clutching at them to stop the bleeding. Flora's face was bloodied and her hair tangled. She grabbed her at once and hugged her as the rest crowded in. "We can't break the column like this," she admitted. "Their fire-power's unexpected and they won't budge onto the softer ground."

"The air, it was just full of bullets, full of 'em!" One man shook his head in disbelief, and the rest murmured agreement.

"We flew right through it, it was a bloody miracle," another added.

"Many didn't." Kolfinnia pressed a hand to her brow and stood thinking. They waited for her orders in silence. All the while she could hear their rough breathing and smell the soot and sweat on their clothes. They needed another plan.

"Then we'll have to hold them here." Flora indicated the keel where the track was narrow, with a steep hill on one side and a steep slope the other.

"It'll slow the knights, but they'll just pour infantry through it." Kolfinnia found that she badly needed Clovis just then.

"They've learned well from Wildwood," Skald admitted.

"We'll *have* to hold 'em here! There's no place else!" Betty supported Flora's plan. Her plump face was beetroot red and her shoulders heaved as she caught her breath.

"Well I bloody well say we run at 'em again!" Benedict fumed and most of them agreed with a shout.

Looks like you did too good a job, Clovis, Kolfinnia thought. "Ben, you saw what happened. Look at our numbers," she swept an arm around the crowd.

"I'm not scared of dying, coven-mother," he declared. The rest agreed and thumped staffs on the ground.

"Clovis gave you that vision so that you'd be able to fight without fear, but don't forget our aim is to defend the Swords!" She raised her staff to the misty hilltop. "And we can't defend anything if we're all dead!"

They looked to consider this, and something in their eyes cleared.

"We'll wait for Clovis to return, then hold them here," she repeated, "and when Sally and Mary get back they'll reinforce our numbers." Witches were shouting their agreement when suddenly their gazed shifted. The last Flower-Forth witch was returning and Kolfinnia wheeled around.

She was once a solstice queen, but now she looked more like a warrior queen. "Took down five of them, and gave the infantry a hell of a scare. When do we start our next run?" Sunday demanded, eager to get back into the bullets and smoke.

All of them, even Kolfinnia, gaped. Sunday's robes were ragged, her face was still the same striking black and white war-paint, but now it was flecked with blood and her long plait looked like a barbed weapon. She looked magnificent.

Kolfinnia shook her head, "You saw our losses. We can't break their column in head-on attack."

Sunday smiled. "I know," she said softly. "but will coven-mother at least let me try?"

There was a shocked gasp at this.

"She can't go alone," Benedict murmured. "She can't."

"It's suicide and I forbid it," Kolfinnia insisted, ready for some backlash.

Sunday smiled again. She understood perfectly well what it meant. She took a pace forward, wrapped her arms around Kolfinnia and embraced her. "I'm sorry," she whispered and before Kolfinnia even had time to wonder what she could be sorry for, she set off back.

"No, Sunday, I forbid it!" She tried to snatch at her, but Sunday was already on her staff.

"Forwards, Strike!" she commanded and returned to the fight.

"Sunday!" she ran a few paces but it was hopeless, and every witch there watched in horror as Sunday began a lone run against the krakens. "Sunday!"

"Don't let her go!" Benedict leapt after her only to find himself hauled back.

"No lad! You'll be cut to pieces!" It was Betty.

"SUNDAY!" he called despairingly.

There was a stunned silence as Benedict and the rest watched her sweep around the curve of the keel and out of sight.

Clovis had fared better. Although each fatality was a defeat, he knew they'd suffered less than Kolfinnia's ranks and all in all they had been lucky. As they raced back through the cover of the woods he weighed his options. "We can't keep this up. We don't have enough fighters."

"They've spread us too thin," Tempest agreed.

"If Sally and Mary could pull back we'd have enough to hold them at the mine."

"Or make another run?"

"Only if we want to die. The gunfire's too heavy." He risked a look back and saw his ranks in close pursuit. Good! he thought. They would head to back to the mine and rally there. He just hoped Kolfinnia hadn't been foolhardy enough to make a second run.

Clovis and his witches raced out of the tree cover some four hundred yards ahead of the knight's column, out of range of their guns and over the boggy ground up towards the mine. His heart jumped when he saw Kolfinnia, but her ranks were in tatters and he saw a little drama unfold: a lone witch broke away and flew back towards the advancing knights. Kolfinnia made to chase her, but she was already too far ahead, and then he recognised her white staff. *Sunday?* He hadn't reckoned on her being so reckless, nor so brave. He couldn't do anything for her now; he had his own witches to think about and he brought them over the river, the dunes and back to the mine.

A huge cheer went up as he dropped to his feet. His ranks landed in a breathless flock and immediately rushed to their comrades. "Kolfinnia!" He grabbed her and held her at arms length.

"Clovis, we can't make another run. It's suicide. We hardly slowed them let alone broke them," she cried in frustration. "Sunday disobeyed my command and went alone!"

He turned to look down the trail, which swept around the keel and out of sight. From the crash of iron he guessed the Knights were only minutes away. Sunday would be in the thick of their ranks now and there was nothing they could do for her. "Each witch finds their own fate," he said.

"Clovis," her eyes were frightened, not of death but failure, "we can't let them get to the stones." She felt them like a magnet tugging at her and all the while she willed Farona's signal to appear, but there was only swirling mist.

"We'll hold them here." He pointed to the keel, where the trail narrowed with a slope on either side forming a natural bottleneck. "Only one kraken at a time can make it through there. It'll slow them."

As he turned away to issue his orders she grabbed him. "What if they send the infantry through first?"

"Then it's hand to hand, and each witch to do their best," he looked away so she wouldn't see his uncertainty. "You! Benedict, grab that banner and place it here. I want it to be the first thing they see when they turn that corner."

Benedict ran ahead and thrust the banner into the earth as Clovis called out for witches to be ready. Very soon the infantry would come around the keel and then it was time to use staffs, wands and knives in close assault.

"Make ready," he roared and swept his cloak from his frame so he'd be unencumbered. His armour shone and he raised his sword and staff.

"Sally, Mary, we need you now," Kolfinnia looked anxiously to the empty hills, but like Farona's signal they were nowhere to be seen.

"Skald's ready," he assured her.

She had two staffs and a wand. If the infantry broke through she could do a lot of damage, but would it be enough to drive them back? She eyed the ominously empty trail as it swept around the keel and out of sight. Witches made ready and listened to the sound of marching machines grow closer.

If Farona had known what was involved, he might not have been so quick to criticise Janus. There were global magma currents to be manipulated and continents to be gently nudged aside to create a slim gap down which the twins could be eased. If done too quickly there would be earthquakes from here to the southern ocean. Janus thought that if the lad expected him to punch a hole in the earth and kick the twins down into it he was as stupid as he looked, but Farona didn't appreciate any of these subtleties right now, he was busy trying to stay alive.

"Open the doorway!" he screamed again, and inside his jar Janus sighed in exasperation.

"Just open the door, Janus," the little god mimicked in a trill voice.

Farona swung again and another larvae hurtled away in a flash of lightning. The slithering tide had pushed him back. He lunged at the creatures using the staff like a harpoon. The smaller larvae wriggled away from it but the larger, more aggressive ones used the lull to trample their fellows in an effort to be first to the food.

"Above!"

Farona looked up at Wester's cry and saw more glowing lights dropping from their burrows. "Dear Oak, do they never stop?" He slammed the staff down again, right into the open jaws of another only a yard from his foot. Despite its large size it had closed in without him noticing. *How long can we keep this up?* he thought desperately.

A condescending voice cut through the chaos. "Farona, will you be much longer? I think we're ready to leave now." It was Janus.

He swung the staff like a hammer, leaving a trail of sparks, and the horde flinched away just long enough for him to turn and run. "We're done?" he shouted as he scooped the jar from the floor.

"We are," Janus concluded.

"Then why are the twins still there?" he yelled. Behind them he heard the tide of larvae in pursuit.

"Would you rather I called the deep-fire with us still in the cavern?" Janus pointed out.

He fumbled for his wand as they left the crystal floor behind and stumbled back into the gloom, this time back the way they had entered. "Open the rocks, Janus!"

"Wait," he commanded.

Farona skidded to a stop and looked back into the cavern dominated by Hethra and Halla's giant diamond. "Janus, what's the delay?" he pleaded.

"One moment. The asking needs to be completed before we leave." He swayed in the liquid, muttering quietly.

With Janus's last word the earth trembled and Farona heard a cracking sound somewhere above. Something fell to the cavern floor, only this time it wasn't one of the ravenous larvae but a massive amethyst crystal. It exploded and tinkled against the crystal floor, which had taken on an angry glow from the fire beneath. "The deep-fire is rising to claim the twins," he realised sadly.

Janus agreed with a soft murmur.

"At least they'll be safe there," Wester consoled him.

There came another chorus of rumbling and Farona saw the tip of the vast diamond disengage from the roof and begin to sink, and as it did so the floor around its base opened up neatly like a crafted puzzle box.

"We should be gone," Janus said. This was a sight not meant for them and none of them had the heart to look at the terra-soula as the diamond sank. That would have been an intrusion.

The larvae scattered away from the sinking mass, sensing danger, and wriggled away into the shadows or reeled themselves back into their burrows on their silken threads. Farona heard the sound of grinding rock and turned to see the wall behind him dissolve for them to pass through. "My Lord, my Lady." He bowed a final time. The cavern was slowly reassembling itself. Hethra and Halla were sliding away back into the deep-fire and he didn't think he could live with that image for the rest of his days.

"You did well, my lad," Wester congratulated. *"They'll be proud."*

He wanted to smile, but as he climbed onto that first step now leading upwards, he wondered if there'd be anyone left up above to welcome him home.

The sound of hammering metal reached them long before the Knights and it made the minute's wait feel like an hour's agony.

Everyone had taken up positions behind walls, rocks, dykes and buildings. The constant marching sound had been punctuated by a short burst of explosions and gunfire and everyone assumed the worst – that Sunday's lone assault had ended the only way it could. Kolfinnia just hoped the solstice queen had died a death fitting her taste for the regal, and from the sound of it she guessed she had. *I hope you took as many down as you could*, she thought.

They hoped to stop the knights at the keel where they could only pass single file. She watched this crucial space so intently that her eyes ached and glowing specks danced across her vision. She knelt with Flora, taking cover behind the engine-shed, while Clovis had taken up a position on the opposite side of the courtyard. Suddenly, without warning, her staff became icy cold and prickled like stinging nettles. "Skald, what's wrong?"

"Valonia's close!"

"So's Hilda," Five added.

"So where are they?" Flora could only think that they were hostages somehow.

"Whatever comes around that corner, we take it down." Kolfinnia tried to bring them back to their current problem. She swallowed and cast a glance at Flora. "You ready?"

"Is there a choice?" she smirked.

Thundering feet grew impossibly loud, sounding to be right on top of them, but still they saw nothing and now Kolfinnia began to suspect a trick and so another reason to make this a black day for witches. Then almost silently the tallest kraken, the one with the angel's face, lumbered around the corner and stood naked before the Wildwood banner. She caught her breath and had time to see minute details: the damaged gauntlet streaming pneumatic fluid, the flag bearing the swan and crown, and the strange glass door in its chest which made Skald growl. *Valonia?* she thought, not knowing why. All of these things passed through her consciousness in a split second. Then the white kraken opened fire directly into the courtyard.

Events unfolded with unstoppable gravity. First the air filled with smoke, then there was the explosion of mortars smashing into the mine buildings, followed by the roar of infantry and the clatter of hooves as they used the gun smoke to cover their charge.

"Bastards are in the smoke!" someone shouted.

Infantry flooded through the smoke, with boots rattling on the cobbles and bayonets gleaming.

Kolfinnia sprang into the fight with a roar. Around her she heard witches all scream the same war cry over and over, 'OAK ENDURES!' and before she knew it they were fighting hand to hand.

A soldier no older than herself charged with his bayonet fixed and his eyes wild. Kolfinnia shrieked, stabbed at him with her staff and blasted him across the courtyard. His rifle skittered away over the cobbles and then without pause she lashed out at a second. There was noise all around. She heard Clovis's wild roar away to her right followed by a scream. The smoke cleared: she had a brief glimpse of the kraken's mocking angelic face, then the hateful thing opened fire again.

The pump-house she had lovingly fashioned as her retreat shattered into a jigsaw of masonry and splintered timbers and collapsed, sending up more dust and smoke. Infantry were crushed by their own knights, and squires drove their horses into the courtyard and lashed out with their sabres.

"Bastards!" Annie slashed with her wand, freezing her enemy's heart, and he tumbled down limp and moaning, but she broke her wand in the process. Another materialised out of the powder smoke, and although she had neither wand nor staff to hand, she had her wits. She snatched up a harmless stick from the ground and waved it purposefully, screeching gibberish, and he was gone before his rifle even hit the cobbles.

Squires plunged into the chaos and witches broke cover and sprung at them, many of them using their atheme as stabbing weapons, and the already terrified horses reared and kicked. A panicked horse threw its rider and when it did Benedict finished him with his staff. Hathwell was amongst them and he struggled to reign in Saxon, but the petrified mare tried to bolt. "Blast it!" he screamed, pulling hard on the reigns, but her hooves skidded over the cobbles and he crashed to the floor cracking his head in the fall. His vision blurred and the wind was knocked from him, leaving him stunned and breathless.

Witches were forced to find new uses for old spells in an instant, but of course that had been part of Clovis's training. Transmutation turned firing pins to lead, too soft to make rifles discharge. Spells terrified horses, making them throw their riders. Some even disobeyed coven-lore and resorted to curses, stopping hearts and rupturing arteries, but maybe today of all days they could be forgiven.

A soldier charged Betty with a scream and rammed his bayonet at her stomach, but with one right word the steel became as brittle as clay and shattered against her. "Didn't bloody well expect that, did yer!" she shrieked, and that was enough for the young conscript. His faced crumbled as easily as the bayonet and he fled, and she shouted meaningless curses after him for good measure. In a peculiar way, men like Moore wove an aura of fear about witches that ultimately helped them.

Kolfinnia flailed blindly with both staffs. A stray bullet cracked against the wall to her left and sharp fragments pelted her back and neck.

"They're all over!" someone cried out in the confusion, and she whirled around.

Flora was at her back, swinging and striking. Her clothes were slashed and blood ran the length of her arm.

"To the keel. Stop 'em getting in!" Kolfinnia screamed. The smoke was bitter and blinding and the two fought towards the keel where the fighting was thickest, stumbling over bodies and rubble. In the murk they could see sprites discharge lightning like shooting stars and hear soldiers scream as witches fought for every inch of Kittiwake.

The ominous thud of marching knights grew even louder, not coming in ones and twos now, but en mass, and Kolfinnia knew they were pushing through in the confusion, using the infantry as a disposable shield. More cannon fire sounded. Kolfinnia didn't know if it was the knights or the naval ships, but the cottages she and Clovis had shared collapsed in a wave of rubble and dust. From away in the mayhem she heard the chapel bell ring out once before it ended in a tuneless clatter as it was also destroyed.

"Flo, the knights are passing the keel!" It meant they had nowhere left to run, and she wondered if anyone would even see Farona's signal in the Pandemonium.

"What do we do?" Flora turned a simple water-calling spell upside down, making her assailant retch and vomit. "What do we do?" she screamed again.

As if in answer, the smoke cleared and Clovis appeared, but neither of them recognised him. He wasn't the wise coven-father they thought they knew. He was the very kind of witch Moore and his ignorant kind wove fanciful tales around: he was a demon. He scythed through a pack of infantry, delivering blows so perfect that one had hardly fallen before he was dispatching the next. He roared and snarled. Men fell screaming and blood gushed in streams. "Kolfinnia!" he bellowed, seeing them at

472

last. "Knights have broken through. Take the fight to them!"

"Push forward, or we're all lost!" she shouted to Flora.

Witches rallied towards the keel, hoping vainly to force the knights back, but all around there was chaos and gunfire, smoke and lightning, and Kittiwake seemed lost.

Krast and his commanders, Grey and Rushton, had forced a way in, herding the infantry through first as a safety buffer. They intended to hold the position while the remaining krakens marched into the coven. So far Krast thought it had all been so absurdly simple. He glanced at the chronometer and smiled. "Looks like we'll be having luncheon early, Valonia."

He was a touch disappointed. He hadn't squeezed enough enjoyment from her yet and now it all seemed over: there was nowhere for the Jiks to run. From the visor he could see destroyed mine buildings and the heart-warming sight of witches being cut down or running around in confusion. He looked towards the misty hill where the Swords of Britain slept. *It will take more than fog to protect them*, he thought.

Krast's three special krakens dominated the entrance to the courtyard, using massive fists to smash buildings aside and turn them to rubble, leaving the way free for their fellows. In a moment the entire column would be able to filter through into the doomed coven.

Rowan moaned gently.

Hilda grimaced in her iron tomb.

Valonia twitched and muttered. Her face was illuminated by gunfire and lightning outside the glass door, but she didn't see it. Her fists clenched and growling sounds rose up in her throat. If she could just remember who she was she could fight against it. If only she knew her own name . . .

Krast paused to watch the glorious spectacle and sat relishing the smell of teak and leather inside the cockpit. "A traitor to your own kind." He reflected that in a strange way both of them were, he unwittingly and Valonia unwillingly. He raised a hand to his eye patch and looked suspiciously at the communicare.

Josephine.

"You're dead," he whispered, and he could have easily been talking of his mother or Valonia.

In all the chaos, nobody, least of all Krast, noticed a lone honeybee land on Purity's chest inches from where Valonia lay entombed. It was quickly followed by another and another until there was a dark mat of them clustered there and they began their dance, calling to their swarm.

In Lilain's epic life, the humans that covered the Earth seemed to have come overnight, but while she had little understanding of humanity she understood that witches were dedicated to the well-being of the twins, and she couldn't let them stand alone.

Kittiwake wasn't beaten yet.

CHAPTER THIRTY-FIVE

Black Friday

Hathwell staggered through the havoc. He'd lost his horse and his rifle, but that in turn had saved his life. Witches saw just a middle-aged, unarmed man lost in battle and they paid him no attention; there were nastier brutes to be dealt with than Bertrand Hathwell. He was drawn back to the krakens, not out of loyalty but out of compassion. There were three people locked inside them, and now that he knew which side of the line he stood on he was determined not to let them die inside the awful machines.

He lurched through the smoke, back to the keel through a crazed dance of fighting soldiers and witches, and found Purity holding the ground at the head of the trail with commanders Rushton and Grey at his side. The witches were pinned by infantry. They couldn't even get airborne. "Hilda," he muttered, looking at the kraken with its snarling wolf face.

When witches tried to advance, Krast and his two commanders opened fire again into the confusion, driving them back, perhaps even killing their own troops too.

He looked around, desperate to help, but he was like an ant before a bear. As he stared up at the machines he noticed that one looked damaged. Some dark crust smothered the sarcophagus door where Rowan lay helpless. At first he thought it was tar or a powder burn, but the dark mat thickened and moved before his very eyes.

It's alive? Even as he thought this, more bees added to the dark stain on the kraken's chest and nobody seemed to notice but him. "Bees!" He finally understood what he was seeing, "It's a swarm of bees!"

Lilain's followers clustered as close to Rowan as they could, under order of their great hive-empress and with one overriding goal: to awaken the sleeper. Their dance had nothing to do with nectar, they danced to remind Rowan of who she was.

"Awaken the sleeper!" Lilain had commanded. *"Awaken the servants of Hethra and Halla."*

The world outside the glass was murky with smoke, and the sounds of battle were muffled and unreal, but the bees' gentle drone was like fresh air against Rowan's brow. As soon as she felt it the machine tried to rob the sensation and devour it, but she held firm and wrestled it back. This was hers and she was determined not to let it go. With that small victory quickly came others. Her name was Rowan Ellen Barefoot, her birthday was November 5th, she was almost seven, she was a witch and her best friend was Kolfinnia. Her fingers were no longer weak and cold and she lifted them and pressed hard against the glass. "Kolfinnia?" she uttered.

Again the kraken's essence swooped down like a hawk to try and snatch away her thoughts, but she was growing stronger and she batted the machine's will away. "No!" she cried. "They're mine!" The wires around her head grew hot and buzzed as it repeatedly tried to subdue her. "No!" she defied it once more, and the kraken faltered.

In his cockpit, commander Grey saw power dials dip for a second then right themselves again. He thought nothing of it and returned to the pleasurable task of Kittiwake's destruction.

"Kolfinnia!" Rowan thumped her small fists against the glass which was now blackened with bees. The swarm grew excited at the sound of her voice and their dance intensified. As they did, her miraculous knowing flooded back and her senses went from oblivion to total awareness: she knew that Kolfinnia was very close, she knew this was Kittiwake-coven, she knew Krast had enslaved them, she knew everything and most of what she saw was so terrible that it almost broke her. But as she looked further she at last knew something that might help them.

She knew the krakens had fed on them like parasites, but she knew it was equally possible for the witches to turn and eat the krakens. She plunged her will deep into the machine's limbs and made the iron and steel her own. It quailed and flapped, but now the prey had become the predator and a series of red bulbs flashed in Grey's cockpit.

"What the blazes?" He reached up to rattle switches and levers, unaware that now he was the one who was entombed.

"Wake the others!" Rowan cried through the glass to her rescuers, but then she realised something awful: the machines had eaten too much of Valonia and Hilda for them to come back. *Their minds are gone!* she thought in despair.

She shook away her tears, knowing weeping was a luxury she couldn't afford. She concentrated on how to help her friends, pushing her knowing to its very limits, and when her mind began to bend under the strain the girl who wasn't even seven-years old made a gigantic leap of understanding and smiled a beautiful smile. She would replace their stolen memories by simply knowing them and giving them back. It was easy, and she laughed at the simplicity of it. The bees swarmed over Rowan's tomb, which had now become her fortress, and she summoned all those myriad memories that make a person whole, all that was Hilda and Valonia, all that the machines had eaten. She gave them to Lilain's swarm to carry. "Hurry, please hurry!" she begged.

The swarm took their memories and moved as one through the smoke and bullets towards the white kraken, and joined the bees already buzzing angrily where Valonia was buried.

Valonia's mind was locked in a dark room. There were no sounds, no sights and no textures. She was as a ghost and what little remained of her was being sucked away by the parasite machine. If not for Hathwell's adjustments she'd have been long gone by now.

This is the end, she might have thought, but she couldn't even remember how to make words.

The glass outside her coffin darkened as Lilain's servants massed in their thousands, and with the drone of the bees a tiny crack appeared in her purgatory. A fragile light shone through and with it came the first in a flood of memories, courtesy of Rowan Barefoot.

Placing way-bewares in Iceland when she was a girl, the ancient berserks they had subdued with spells, finding Skald and cutting her first staff, fighting the loathsome crib-robber, Thomas Hobby, her first and only love. Memories tumbled into her, filling the chasm of her soul.

She jerked and groaned as her emptiness was filled by life and colour. She took a huge breath as a hundred sensations assailed her at once: the sound of battle, the feeling of confinement, the smell of baking metal, and the glass before her eyes, which was now a blackened city of bees. But most potent of all was the memory of her own name.

Valonia

"I AM VALONIA!" she roared and, wrenching the wires from her temples and veins and as if on cue, the bees departed to free the last of them. She'd taken a little of Rowan's 'knowing' along with her revived memories. In a flash she both understood the situation and knew exactly what to do. *"Rowan!"* Her crowning was supercharged.

"Valonia!" Rowan cried joyfully.

"We're going to fight, my lass. Kolfinnia needs us. Are you with us?"

Before she had chance to answer another voice joined their conversation.

"Count me in." It was Hilda.

Inside her metal shell, Valonia smiled. "This machine is mine!" she hissed through bared teeth.

Hathwell watched the bees travel between each kraken in turn before they left and drifted away into the morning sky. Knights were passing behind the three monstrous machines unchallenged as the infantry kept the witches pinned down. "This place is done for," he despaired.

His despair soon became confusion as Purity unexpectedly lumbered around to face *away* from battle, then raise its damaged right arm slowly and uncertainly. It was like watching a young knight take his first training lesson, and then the machine pivoted at the waist, again deliberately, and Hathwell was certain the kraken was going to lash out. But that was impossible. Krast must have gone mad for that to happen.

Already a dozen knights had marched into the coven and they were starting to form a ring around the mine-buildings. Once complete they'd crush everything in it and the witches would be finished. Hathwell recognised a kraken now just passing the keel as Sir Iain McKenzie. "What's Krast up to?" he muttered, more curious than afraid now.

A second later he had his answer.

Purity swung its massive arm directly at the oncoming McKenzie. His kraken was instantly decapitated; the helmet and the unfortunate McKenzie himself were pulverised.

"Dear God!" Hathwell laughed aloud. His smile became a grin when he saw Rushton had also turned his machine. There was a second when he knew exactly what would happen next and he wasn't disappointed. Rushton opened fire directly into the massed knights behind and the explosion was loud enough to send a momentary lull through the fighting.

Witches and infantry alike looked around to see McKenzie's headless kraken flop sideways with crushing momentum and flatten the mineshaft building. It plunged through the roof, and partway into the shaft where it jammed with its clawed feet waving feebly in the air.

Kolfinnia had barely registered this when a second kraken opened fire on its fellows, and in the mushroom of smoke she saw a million splinters of red-hot metal fountain upwards. "Halla be praised!" she laughed.

"It's Valonia!" Skald cried and somehow she knew he was right.

The keel was effectively blocked by the renegade krakens, and the infantry began to scramble back. Witches that had been all but beaten now charged forward as one.

"The knights are trapped! You three, with me!" Clovis grabbed the nearest fighters and together they mounted their staffs and hurtled out of the courtyard. Once airborne he had a bird's-eye view. Three krakens had turned against their fellows and were landing crushing blows and firing their batteries until there was nothing but smoke. Clovis didn't care how this had happened, he just knew this was the ideal time to put his sword to good use.

Krast screamed again and felt his body jerk upwards, as now his pressure suit responded to Purity's actions and he copied its movements. He was thrown around the cockpit like a dazed puppet, screaming and cursing. "You Judas Jik bitch!" he roared over and over.

He found himself punching a hole clean through a knight's chest, then he ripped the left arm off another and all the while he spouted a frenzy of curses and screams.

Purity shuddered as Valonia barged knights aside. Their banners fell and Purity's massive clawed feet shredded and trampled them. "Ah! I can see why you enjoy this so much, Mr Krast!" Her manic voice crackled through the communicare.

"Stop this at once, you bitch!" he screamed. She sent another helmet flying with a swipe of her arm. In his cockpit Krast's own arm shot out as if he was pointing to something. "Witch-whore, Jik viper!" he blathered.

"And see how well Hilly's doing, Mr Krast. Not bad for the fairer sex, wouldn't you say?" She peered through the glass at Rushton's kraken which was at that moment ripping the head from another. The helmet had a leering gargoyle face and it thundered to the ground and grinned idiotically up at the sky as soldiers ran like rabbits before a fox. Valonia barked her husky laugh, "Oh, she has such a lady-like touch, Mr Krast."

"I'll roast your skin and boil your eyes, witch-slut," he frothed and snarled.

"Is that what you said to Josephine, too?" she stung him. "What a loving son you are, what a loving *witch*," she said the last word slowly, dragging it across his heart like a rusted blade.

"She's dead," he babbled. "She's gone!"

"Oh no. Take off your eye-patch and I promise she'll always be with you."

"Shut up!" he roared and even snapped at the communicare with his teeth, like a demented dog. "Shut up! Shut up! Shut up!"

She lost interest in tormenting him and now she turned her attention to Hilda.

"Hilly, did you taste Rowan's 'knowing'?"

"Yes, it was incredible, but the effect's fading now."

"Then you'll know a lad has sent the twins deeper. Even now he makes his way back to us, but we must defend the stones at all costs."

"Aye, but the infantry?" Hilda added.

"Kolfinnia can deal with them. Push the knights back, Hilly, push them back! Rowan, you too."

Valonia and Hilda willed the machines to fire until their reserves were empty and the smoke hung like autumn fog, then they waded in. They toppled krakens from the narrow path and down the greasy slope, where they exploded in flames.

The knights to the rear of the column couldn't see what was happening ahead. Knight Superior Krast was no longer issuing orders, communicares were silent, and one by one Clovis's witches slammed into them, slicing, chopping and pounding, and arms fell while helmets were crushed and split. Purity was a battered unrecognisable mess, and the misshapen face now looked more like a grizzled old pugilist than an angel.

The column was trapped and infantry-less. Clovis landed neatly on a helmet, one cast like a bearded god with flowing locks. His feet scraped on the metal as he touched down and he heard hysterical screams from the knight inside. "This is Sutherland. Urgent assistance needed!"

The kraken lurched, trying to throw him off, but with his comrades so close it could hardly shift. Clovis casually took his sword and with one blow sliced the top off the helmet, scalping the noble-looking god and leaving him with a considerable bald spot. The skull cap slid away with the banner still attached and flying merrily, and rolled to the ground far below.

"I'm under attack!" Sutherland looked up through the hole and shrieked. He fired his revolver but the bullet went wide and sparked off the cockpit. "Under attack!" he shrieked again.

Clovis jabbed down through the hole with his staff. There was a bright flash and the screaming stopped.

"Not anymore," he finished.

Knights watched the impossible spectacle of their own turning against them. There were no orders and nowhere to go; the cumbersome machines were blocking their own escape route, and they watched in panic as one after another their fellows were struck down by Clovis's small squadron of witches.

"Where's the infantry?"

"Where have all the bloody squires gone?"

"Knight Superior, we're stalled here! Knight Superior, do you read me, over?"

Terrified messages ricocheted back and forth. Half the column was a charred mess, the other half had no idea what to do or what was going on.

"They're on the run!" Clovis watched men scramble from their machines down emergency rope ladders.

"We should get back. Kolfinnia will need us," Tempest reminded him. He signalled for his witches to follow and they left the ruined column and headed back.

Flora retrieved the trampled Wildwood banner and swung it over her head.

"Kittiwake!" Kolfinnia screamed, "To us!"

One by one they rallied under the banner's protection, and together they set about driving the infantry out of Kittiwake with staffs, knives, wands and spells. The fighting became ferocious, but thanks to Clovis plenty of infantry were ordered back to defend the krakens, giving Kittiwake a fighting chance.

"Kolfinnia!" someone shouted to her rear.

She whirled around and instinctively lashed out. Her staff struck wood and there was a brief crack of thunder.

Skald growled menacingly, and Kolfinnia looked into the eyes of Sunday Flowers. "Try and remember whose side you're on," she smiled mischievously.

"We thought you'd died!" Kolfinnia grinned.

"All in good time!" She sent two soldiers hurtling backwards in a trail of sparks.

They pressed the infantry harder, driving them out of the courtyard, and coven-mother and solstice queen fought back to back like sisters. By now the fighting had spilled into the gardens and the ruined cottages, the pump-house and the chapel, where Sunday's white mare kicked at the fence in a panic.

Kolfinnia heard the scream of tortured metal and looked up. One of the renegade krakens had been decapitated, undoubtedly killing the knight in the process. The headless monster swayed for a moment before it toppled, and even before it hit the earth she knew who was inside it.

Rowan.

The girl had no fighting experience, and it was inevitable she would be downed first. "Rowan!" Kolfinnia screamed and launched herself away from her comrades on her staff, and vanished into the smoke.

Earth and stones showered up where Grey's kraken impacted, but mercifully it landed on its back, and Kolfinnia was clambering up over the huge machine even as debris continued to rain down. "Rowan," she pleaded, "Rowan please be alive, please. It's Kolfinnia!" She relived the very last time she'd seen her, by the Appelier River, clutching her lightning-staff and making that one unbreakable promise.

I'll come back and get you.

And she had.

"Rowan, I'm here!" She tore at the housing wheel, and it began to turn, shrieking in complaint as it did. She spun it until it juddered to a stop, then in a frenzy she pried her fingers under the rim and heaved. The door opened a crack, enough for her to slide her palms under. Screaming and sobbing, she squatted, used her legs for leverage and swung the door up and over. It boomed as it dropped open and at last she came face to face with Rowan.

She hardly recognised the girl. Her hair had been shaved, blood streaked her clothes and her face was pale and her eyes glazed. "Kol?" she murmured.

"I'm here, sweetheart," she dropped down into the cramped chamber and ripped the wires away from her. Some had been inserted into veins and she threw them aside in disgust. She scooped the girl up, not feeling her weight but only anger, and pulled her free like a lioness protecting her cub. "Rowan," she kissed her temple. "Rowan, we're leaving here, right now."

"I'm sorry." Her head lolled in Kolfinnia's arms as she carried her down the ruined machine and onto Hethra's green earth.

"Don't be sorry," she was crying freely now.

"I tried to stop them, the machines, but I couldn't . . ." she slurred.

"Rowan," she cried, giving her a firm shake. "We're leaving and you're coming with us." She laid her gently in the grass and looked around for help. The stones were the only safe place left. "Help! Help needed here, Flora! Sunday! Anyone!" she screamed.

"I'll 'elp you, missy," a gruff voice came.

Her blood ran cold and she spun around, but a fraction too late.

For a large man, duty-warden Moore moved fast and he was on her in a flash. He knocked her staff aside and grabbed her slender wrist with brute force. "I'll 'elp yer good an' proper and you'll be thankin' me when it's done." He hurled her to the floor by her arm, almost dislocating it.

She crashed down and her satchel burst open, scattering her belongings into the mud, and she lay amongst them breathless and winded. She reached for her wand but he landed on her and pinned her wand-sheath under his rubbery gut and drew his revolver.

She shrieked and grabbed at the hand holding the gun and the two tussled, but his greater strength forced her back down and he chuckled a throaty laugh. "I like 'elping Jik sluts like you," he panted as he snaked a hand up her dress.

She reached for her satchel with her right hand while she tugged at the revolver with the other. Moore's bearded face loomed closer and he breathed excitedly in her ear. She flailed blindly and grasped something that had tumbled from her satchel, and without thinking she swung it at his fleshy neck.

The revolver discharged just as she rammed the way-beware's spiked foot into his throat. There was a soft squelch and muffled bang at the same time. Her eyes flew wide in shock, while Moore's eyes flickered and he made a gurgling sound in his punctured throat. He dropped the smoking revolver and clawed at the way-beware jutting from his neck. There was a sudden crack of lightning and he jerked once then fell dead with smoke pouring from between his lips, and Skald landed on his back. "Kolfinnia!" he cried.

She stared down at the neat smoking hole in her chest, "Skald, I've been shot," she said simply and looked up at him in disbelief.

At that very moment, as if preordained, the sky turned scarlet. A fiery serpent writhed in the sky above the stones and its glow stained the coast blood red. It turned in spirals, screaming and raking the air with its talons, before streaking away into the clouds leaving a trail of scarlet vapour.

Farona had returned.

Figures loomed out of the smoke.

"Kol, is that you?" It was Flora, followed by Sunday and the others. All of them were now heading for the stones. "Did you see Farona's sign? He's made it back!" She sounded victorious.

"Here!" Skald shouted through the smoke. She ran towards his voice and found him sat trembling with shock. Kolfinnia's wounds were his wounds, and he knew her wounds were fatal. "Hurry." He could hardly keep his voice level. Kolfinnia was lying on the ground with Rowan draped over her chest, and when Flora saw them her joy instantly died. "She's been shot," Skald croaked and looked up at her pleadingly.

"Kolty!" She knelt and cradled her head, hardly recognising the bedraggled child across her chest, and trying not to see the growing blood stain on her dress.

"Flo," she said weakly, "get Rowan away."

"No, you're both coming with us." Tears tumbled down as she tried to haul her up.

"No time. Get Rowan to the stones," she coughed and blood misted her lips.

Skald looked on in horror, unsure what to do.

"Get her up," someone commanded sternly. They all turned to see Sunday. Her face was as stone and her eyes blazed behind her war paint. "Get her up and get them both to the stones, and do it now."

Flora drew a shuddering breath, "But she's –,"

"But nothing," she snapped, "I'm senior in rank now, so obey. Get her to the stones or leave her for the knights."

Everyone looked around in stunned silence.

"Move, you dullards!" she shouted. "This is an evacuation, not a meditation. To the stones!"

She was so adamant they all scrambled to obey. The rescue was rough and ready, but they had to be quick. Benedict and Betty carried Kolfinnia between them, and others took Rowan, and now the chase was on to get to the stones before the knights did. "Sunday?" Benedict called back.

Sunday was walking back towards the beleaguered coven. She turned and looked quizzically at him. "Well?"

"You're going the wrong way." He wondered if she'd taken a knock to the head. "Stones are up there," he jerked his head towards the misty hill.

"I've a last job to do." She took a final look at her dying coven-mother. "Take care of her Benedict, and take care of yourselves." Then she turned back to the fight and left them once and for all.

"And another!" Valonia cheered, as yet another kraken dropped to its knees and the sound of crunching metal boomed around Kittiwake. They stood knee-deep in wreckage and if anything the two witches had fought better than any of the knights that day. "You ought to be proud of your machine, Mr Krast," Valonia laughed, but she felt dreadfully ill. It was all snowballing in on her: the weeks of imprisonment, poor rations, lack of sleep and now battle. Although she had dominated the kraken, it took enormous reserves to command it and she was reaching the very end of her strength. "Are you still with us, Mr Krast?" she panted.

Krast sat trembling in his cockpit. His lips quivered and meaningless words dribbled out. He pawed feebly at the controls, and his body jerked as Valonia smashed yet another knight to the ground and drove another nail into his coffin.

Rowan's gift had all but gone now, but Valonia sensed traces and gathered roughly what was happening out there. *They're making to get away from here*, she thought and smiled. *"Hilly, I sense Rowan's free."*

"I hope she has a long and happy life," Hilda wished.

"Aye, I'll second that." Mercifully, Valonia's 'knowing' didn't detect the tragedy unfolding outside. It would have been unspeakably cruel if she had come this far only to die with a broken heart.

"I wish we could've gone with them," Hilda said regretfully.

Valonia watched witches fly or run towards the stones hidden in the mist. Her face was inches from the glass, and each laboured breath clouded it a little more. "Remember us," she whispered to them. Suddenly the chamber rocked and she was jolted from her melancholy. "Ah! Another challenger," she smiled, and swung Purity around for action.

They manoeuvred their machines shoulder to shoulder, but now they faced knights on all sides. Commander Scales had taken charge of the battered column and encircled the two renegades. His machine was miraculously unscathed and the banners were snow white and fluttered regally in the breeze. "Bloody Krast. Always said the man was unstable," Scales sneered. "Imagine the ineptitude of leading a major assault in untested machines?" He shook his head in dissatisfaction and calmly reached for the communicare as he dabbed his brow with a neatly folded handkerchief. "All Knights to converge on my signal." He was calm and unflappable and still thought there was a chance of taking Kittiwake. First, though, they had to remove the errant Knight Superior from the equation. "Forgive me, sir, but this is for the good of the Order, I'm sure you understand." He cleared his throat and made ready.

The knights prowled into position taking up a circle around Krast's and Grey's machines, many of them holding their colossal swords aloft, intending to cut them down.

"Looks like this is it, Hilly." Valonia wished she could do more, but Krast's machine was battered beyond belief. It only had one arm left, and the golden helmet was a crumpled mass. It was a miracle that he was still alive in there.

Hilda cleared her head with a brisk shake. *"Just enough left for one more push, eh?"*

"That's the Ward I know," she chuckled.

Hilda took a last look outside. The hill was verdant in the morning sun, and the glass was cracked and through it she could smell the sea. "What a beautiful place for a coven," she sighed.

"Forwards!" Scales announced and as one the knights lumbered forward.

Underneath the deformed helmet, Rushton held up his hands in surrender as if they could see him or hear him. "Dear God, no! The witches, not me!" he squawked.

The knights advanced, but the two witches weren't about to let Krast and Rushton go down without a fight. Valonia knew how the noble bloodlines loved their sense of 'honour'. Not wanting to disappoint, she lurched forward with a shout.

The one-armed Purity managed to decapitate another enemy, while Hilda brought an upper cut right into the chest furnace of another which ruptured and vomited steam like a geyser.

The knights pressed on, now under Scale's command, and swords fell repeatedly. One after another they cleaved huge chunks of steel away until there were only gruesome skeletons of girders left standing. Severed pipes jetted lubricant like opened veins, and then the machine, with Krast and Valonia still inside, swooned sideways and crashed down into the courtyard below. Rushton's mutilated kraken suffered a similar fate and fell across the engine-shed. Slates flew up like confetti and timbers whirled like matches.

Scales sniffed contentedly. "Right, let's get on with this bloody operation and finish this coven, shall we? The Jik filth are heading for the hill." He replaced the communicare without waiting for replies, eased his hands into his supple leather gloves and sounded his battle horn. The surviving knights joined in, falling into rank behind him, relieved at last to have a grip on the situation and anticipating the victory to come.

All across Kittiwake witches had seen Farona's signal and were falling back, while the knights assumed they were making some futile last stand at the stones.

Clovis tore over the open ground with his season in close formation, all the while praising Farona for all his worth, but they had to get to him before the knights. There was also the small matter of Janus. "Janus," he growled as he flew. Would he open a door and let them escape or not? What if the knights overran the stones and Janus fell into their hands? These horrible thoughts were like ballast. "Faster, Tempest," he urged. They had downed many knights, but there were at least fifty battle-worthy krakens still rumbling into the coven, regrouping with their cavalry and readying to assault the hill. It was now a race to see who would get to the Swords first.

Just as Clovis was starting to believe they might live to see the day's end, he had another surprise. He could see green and russet ranks gathering on the hill midway between the stones and the mine below. Mary and Sally had returned. "At last!" he cheered.

Clovis and his squad landed on the slopes above Kittiwake into the midst of Mary and Sally's forces and there was a chorus of greetings. "Clovis, sorry we kept you waiting. Plenty of infantry to scare off." Sally stood with her bow looking down at the advancing knights. She had a cut under one eye and her hat was missing, but she was otherwise unscathed and it looked as though they had taken only very light losses.

"You saw Farona's signal?" he guessed.

"Been waiting for it all morning. Where's Kolfinnia?"

He frowned, "I was harrying the knights. I thought she'd be here by now?"

Both of them looked around at the crowds, acutely aware that the regrouped knights would be on them very soon. Already they could see their war banners forming into ranks and the squires lining up. "They're coming our way," Sally pointed down the hill at them.

"We still have a few minutes," he said distractedly, searching for Kolfinnia in the crowd. "Coven-mother?" he roared and the chatter ceased. "Kolfinnia?" But no answer came.

Nervous witches looked about as they realised their coven-mother was absent.

"Kolfinnia!" he roared, loud enough for those sheltering at the stones half a mile distant to hear him. He looked down at the wreckage of their coven and their advancing foes. A highway of shattered knights trailed back along the valley, columns of black smoke drifted up like threads, riderless horses ran from the chaos and bodies dotted the landscape. *Is she amongst them?* he wondered.

"God-Oak," Sally shook her head. "You think they're still down there?"

"Look!" A shout went up and they saw Mary Fife pointing. "Someone's coming, and carrying wounded."

Clovis had the sharpest eyes and what he saw wasn't good. "You," he gestured to one lad, "make for the stones and tell Farona we're coming and Janus to be ready. Do it now!" The young witch hastily jumped on his staff and was away. "Sally, stay here and cover us. The rest of Snow-Thaw, with me. Kolfinnia needs us." He mounted his staff again, calling yet again on his tired sprite, and took off down the hill with the Snow-Thaw witches at his tail.

"The rest of you," Sally shouted as she watched him go, "make ready to give 'em cover." She looked down again at the knights, now marching six abreast and eight rows deep. She drew one of her arrows and thought of Ada, while exhausted witches lined the ridge ready to buy Clovis what time he needed to bring their coven-mother home.

"She's been shot!" Flora was almost hysterical, and struggling to carry a young girl Clovis didn't recognise.

A straggle of survivors was making its way up the hill. Amongst them, four witches were carrying Kolfinnia. She was lying between her bearers and her long dark hair whispered through the heather. Another witch carried the Wildwood banner, and Clovis noted with dread that of all the symbols, Flower-Forth was the only one splattered with blood. He had fought many battles and one look at her told him she was dying. He pressed a hand to her cheek and her eyes fluttered but didn't open. She had very little time left. He and Skald shared a brief glance, and both of them knew.

"She's leaving us." Skald's voice was barely a whisper and he looked ashen.

Clovis didn't answer. "And the girl?" He tried to sound controlled.

Flora looked down at the girl in her arms, "Rowan's wounded, but I don't know how bad. They had her in one of those vile machines and I don't know what it's done to her," her voice rose in pitch as she grew more distressed.

Rowan, he thought and looked anew at the girl in Flora's arms. She was wounded, but not in the same way as Kolfinnia. "You two!" He pointed to a couple of young men. "Take Rowan up to the stones, be quick now, lads."

They tenderly took her from Flora, who looked bereft as the girl slipped from her embrace. "Take care of her until we come," she sniffed.

Clovis went to Kolfinnia, slipped his arms under her and lifted her easily. She lay unconscious and he sensed her time to walk Evermore was very close. Just a few hours ago she'd said she wanted to see it the day she walked it for real and now here she was dying in his arms. He clenched his jaw and swallowed his hatred: hatred for fate and hatred for knights. "Walk with me, Skald," he asked gently. Skald perched on his shoulder, but just stared down mutely at Kolfinnia. "Now all of you, back up the hill, and hope Janus is ready to open the portal when we arrive."

They departed as fast as they could, but there was something funerary about their pace. Clovis carried his coven-mother knowing there was nothing he could do for her but watch her last grains of life slip away. *Like sand in an hourglass*, he thought bitterly.

He carried her with pride, at the rear where nobody would see him cry, and swore he wouldn't leave her body here. He listened to the roar of furnaces from the ruins of Kittiwake below and knew the knights had begun their final assault.

She had thought of this place many times since learning of it, and it was just as dark and foreboding as she imagined. There came the sound of rushing water somewhere ahead, and the light from her wand glinted off something glassy, except that the wand she carried wasn't hers.

"*Is that it, miss?*" Strike asked warily.

"It can't be anything else." She hadn't told him of her plans and perhaps just as well. She merely expected him to obey, which was so typical of Sunday. She held hrafn-dimmu higher and called more light from it. *Valonia's wand*, she thought. The wand couldn't stay where it was in case the Illuminata took it, and so she did the only thing she could think of: she took it instead. Taking the relic, she thought how hard Kolfinnia had worked to build a coven and how quickly she had destroyed it. She edged ahead in silence. Strike knew her intention was to confront the great Timekeeper, but beyond that his notion of her plan was as dark as this cavern.

The reflections from the wand-light grew stronger as they approached and she felt fearful of the creature they were about to confront and what it would mean if he accepted. She could clearly see the lower case of the hourglass, surrounded by lethal looking stalagmites, and now she also saw that strange river that flowed away into the darkness, a river that flowed away under the sea. She stopped at the river's edge, where the crystal-clear water flowed through a sweeping channel worn smooth down the centuries, but what were centuries to a creature like this?

"*Sunday and Strike,*" a voice cut through flesh and bones and resonated in her soul.

She knew the moment she heard it that only total honesty would do. She knelt and bowed her head.

"*There is no need. I am only a servant.*" He was touched by her gesture.

She slowly got to her feet and regarded the hourglass. There was movement in its dark heart. She saw the flicker of multiple legs and the glint of all-seeing eyes. He drew out from the shadows so that he could look out at her from behind his glass prison.

"*More threads come to visit me in the dark,*" he sounded flattered.

"Great Timekeeper," she began shakily, "a battle rages outside, a battle between magic and steel."

"*There are so many wars on Earth, Sunday,*" he reflected.

"But this one is by my hand," she admitted and a tear ran down her cheek.

"*I understand. I wove the night that you flew to Trebbington with your note.*"

She flinched. "I placed the well-being of the twins above all else, forgetting the bonds that hold witches together, and now many lie dead or dying because of me, including my own coven-mother."

"I know why you have come, Sunday," he held up a thread for her to see. It was her own. *"Your motives and desires resonate inside your thread."*

"Then you know what I've come to ask?" She stood tall, ready for her punishment. "Will you accept?"

He didn't answer right away. Instead, he selected another thread and showed it to her. It was Kolfinnia. *"The breaking of this thread is only moments away."*

"That's Kolfinnia," she said between tears. "And Rowan, her friend?"

"Sometimes threads break out of despair. When Kolfinnia dies the girl will not last much longer."

"Both of them?" she cried in horror.

She looked again at the delicate thread that was Kolfinnia and thought she'd go mad if he made her watch as he pulled it tighter and tighter until the broken ends drifted away from one another.

"I would not make you watch such a thing," he said softly.

"Please don't break it," she said in a small whisper.

"The weave demands a thread be broken at the appointed hour," he replied sadly.

"Then you know why I've come," she asked hopefully, "to offer you another thread."

"Miss Flowers, no!" Strike cried out in shock, and her staff grew cold.

"All's well, Strike. The thunder-heights await you, and as for me . . . " She didn't want to walk Evermore, but she hoped this made it right, and perhaps she'd be able to choose her own door in that mythic place and not be forced to begin the spiral again from its lowest level.

The Timekeeper listened as fate considered her offer.

"The Patternmaker accepts," he said finally.

She felt faint with dread and relief. Strike reeled, and the power seemed to drain from her staff. "Thank you, my Lord," she said, and then to her sprite, "Strike, I'm sorry." But he remained silent, completely stunned.

"One thread can only be exchanged for another at precisely the right moment. We must wait for the Patternmaker's command." The Timekeeper held two strands up: one was Kolfinnia and the other was Sunday.

She knew there were perhaps only minutes left and they would pass like days, but she stood proud as a solstice queen should, listening to the sound of rushing water at her feet, and waited.

Once Clovis regrouped with Sally, they began edging their way up the hill following their banner in tight formation with their best archers covering their escape. The Illuminata were making their push up the hill, now supported by artillery. Sporadic mortar shells dropped from the sky and pounded the heather, creating a creeping barrage ahead of the weary infantry.

Sally guarded their retreat. "For Kolfinnia." She released the arrow and seconds later a kraken with blazing yellow banners was struck at the hip. There was a brilliant flash and the machine fell in two, split at the waist. Men ran from the fireball and the ruptured furnace billowed greasy smoke like a distress signal. Mary Fife also took up her bow and between them they covered their retreat up the hill to where Farona and the rest were waiting.

Clovis walked on oblivious to the fighting. Kolfinnia's colour was gone and she felt so cold. He knew that so long as Skald remained she still lived, but soon enough he would cry out and ascend to the thunder-heights. The stones were inching closer, but so slowly, and Flora's mist was weakening as the sun rose higher. Soon they'd be exposed to the ships in the bay and their cannons would have a clear target. It was now almost ten o'clock in the morning on Friday, October 22nd. It wasn't even noon, yet Clovis couldn't remember ever having lived through a darker day for witches.

CHAPTER THIRTY-SIX

Noble Knight, Faithful Squire

Hathwell watched the assault for a short while before looking away. The remaining knights had formed up behind a creeping barrage and were making for the stones, now visible through a gauze of mist. The mortar fire was light but effective enough to drive the witches back. He saw one or two knights topple, but from this distance he couldn't see who was firing at them.

Kittiwake was abandoned now. The only ones left were the dead and dying. He found a discarded rifle and a kitbag and was readying to leave. His days with the Illuminata were spent, and despite the horrors around him he felt free, but there was just one last job he had to do.

He ducked through the maze of rubble and iron in the courtyard, listening to the explosions from the hillside and the crackle of fires all around him, and made for Krast's destroyed kraken.

Purity lay looking up at the sky. The angelic face had been pounded out of shape and now it wore a peculiar smile, and its banners lay across its mangled torso like dust-sheets in a forgotten house. Hathwell kept his rifle at the ready, not that there was anybody around, though. He edged cautiously around to the pilot hatch on the helmet's crown. It was hanging from its hinges. He stepped into the doorway and saw Krast lying in the wreckage.

He was strapped into the flight chair, hanging upside down and pinned by wreckage, and blood smeared his face. As his shadow fell across him Krast rolled his one good eye towards Hathwell. "They betrayed me, Hathwell," he said in a small childish voice. He looked around bewildered, perhaps wondering how he'd ended up like this. "Scales, the treacherous bastard!" he growled. "He's after the Illuminata!" He strained at his wrecked chair, but couldn't move.

Hathwell stood watching, feeling hate and pity for the man.

"Hathwell," he snapped, "get me out, find me a kraken. Scales wants my place as Knight Superior!" He tried to escape, but only managed to rock impotently. He seethed and hissed and eventually flopped back into his tattered chair. "Damn it, you dumb arse!" he shouted. "Get me out and get me a fresh kraken!" He yanked at his trapped limbs, growling like a dog. "Witch slut tricked me! Find Valonia, find her and if she still lives shoot the Jik bitch. That's an order!"

Hathwell looked towards the chest compartment where Valonia lay.

"Shoot her, Hathwell. Kill the Jik whore. Do it now or by God I'll have you shot too!" he screamed at the top of his lungs, his face a patchwork of livid red and glittering gold.

He glared up at him quivering with rage, and Hathwell thought of Ada and Lana and the mayhem one man could cause. He thought of his awful part in it all, he even thought of a young lad lying dead on a battlefield in Solvgarad twenty years before. He swallowed, took a deep breath and stepped away. 'Murderer or coward' he had branded himself, and now he knew which was the greater crime.

Maybe it was the witch in him, but Krast knew. He looked into Hathwell's cold eyes and his face hardened, and his mouth melted into a sneer. "Faithful squire," he whispered with poisonous contempt.

Hathwell took a steadying breath and raised the rifle. "Noble knight," he replied regretfully. Then he took aim and one last shot echoed around the courtyard.

Hathwell went to the suit's chest and clambered up onto the twisted wreckage, hoping he wasn't already too late. As he climbed up he heard a squawk and looked up to see herring gulls already lining the demolished buildings. They stood around as if nothing had happened and their indifference struck him as somewhat cheering.

The sarcophagus door was free of wreckage. He scrubbed at the glass with the cuff of his uniform, but the innards were dark and he saw nothing. He spun the brass locking wheel and it turned freely, and when it'd turned as far as it could go the catch released and the door sprung open a crack. Grunting with effort he heaved the door out of its frame and pushed it up and backwards where it dropped open with a shuddering boom.

At first he didn't see her, there was just a tangle of wires and crushed metal. But when he finally saw her, he knew right away her injuries were grievous. He reached out a trembling hand and brushed her grey hair aside. She groaned softly and his heart leapt: she still lived.

Valonia slowly turned her head to look up at him. Her movements were very weak, and at first all he saw was her frowning face and hard eyes. Then she recognised the figure framed against the autumn sky and she smiled faintly. "Mr Hathwell," she whispered.

"Coven-mother," he said humbly.

"You speak like a witch," she huffed a dry little laugh.

"I wish I was." He blinked his tears away.

"You don't need a wand to be a witch, Mr Hathwell." She thought of Krast, the traitor witch who had led them all here to their ruin. If a witch could be a knight then it seemed only fair that a squire could aspire to be a witch. "Krast?" she asked.

He shook his head once and she understood.

"First-dawn," she coughed. "So the crib-robber was right."

He didn't understand, and he saw that it wasn't his place to try.

"Be a dear, check on Hilly." Her voice was so quiet now that he had to lean into the compartment to hear her.

He tried to say 'yes' but couldn't speak. Instead he nodded solemnly, tipping a few tears down onto her blue dress.

"I'm afraid I've got to leave you now, Mr Hathwell." Her voice grew even fainter and her breathing became so shallow it was ghostly, "Esta and Lana have a pipe waiting for me."

He smiled back at her, straightened up and stepped away, knowing he shouldn't be the last thing she saw. He went to the edge of the shattered machine and looked out over the sea from the kraken's huge, barrel chest.

Valonia gazed up into the beautiful autumn sky and wondered what it would be like to just drift amongst the clouds, free of her troubles, and sail through the endless blue. "Skald," she whispered, and as her final breath left her lips, her soul followed it and did just that.

Hathwell heard a gull cry again, and its call was so mournful that he knew she'd gone.

Farona ran to greet them, followed by all of Kittiwake's wounded, young and old, and a huge cheer went up. But when he saw Clovis carrying Kolfinnia's limp body the grin dropped from his face. This wasn't the homecoming he'd expected. The ragged army hurried towards the stones just as Mary and Sally appeared from below the crest of the hill, firing arrows at unseen foes as they came. Friends and families were reunited or given the terrible news they'd feared all morning. Many didn't make it back and no season had suffered more than Kolfinnia's.

"Back into the circle, all of you. We're leaving!" Clovis bellowed.

Farona did the exact opposite and ran towards him, but his eyes were on Kolfinnia. "No, it can't be, Clovis. Is she?"

"Not yet," he interrupted and carried on past him, ignoring the worried glances and murmurs. "Good work below, lad," he called over his shoulder.

"They're safe at least," he couldn't take his eyes off Kolfinnia. Watching her die made their victory hollow.

All of them retreated into the circle, while Mary and Sally spent the last of their arrows, and the sound of mortars and metal drew closer. Clovis lay Kolfinnia in the heather, exactly where his sword had fallen when he'd first arrived here, and right next to Rowan. The girl opened her eyes. "Kol . . ." she moaned.

"You're together again." He knelt at Kolfinnia's side, but she didn't hear or feel him. He wished with all his heart that she'd open her eyes just once so that he could say his last goodbyes. "Coven-mother?" He stroked her face tenderly, but she didn't move.

Skald's feathers looked dull and his breathing was laboured. Rowan reached out and clutched Kolfinnia's stony hand. "You promised to say 'goodbye'," she whispered, but Kolfinnia lay as still as death.

There was an awkward cough from behind and Farona stood there holding the sacred jar.

"Greetings, great Clovis," the little god chortled.

"I trust you've made provision for us to leave this place? You agreed to take us along the spiral," he said coldly.

"Yes, but I'd rather like to see one of these 'knights' you speak of. Perhaps we should wait?"

Clovis growled softly and flashed his teeth. "Don't play with me today, Janus," he warned.

A mortar exploded nearby and children screamed.

"Open the portal, Janus," he commanded.

"Our accord?"

"I've never broken my word. I shall open the one door you cannot, but first get us away from here."

Janus circled slowly in the jar, while beyond the stones Clovis could see Sally and Mary fire their last arrows before they turned to run. Then a banner loomed up from below the crest of the hill and Clovis heard the children start to cry. As if on cue a mortar shell landed close by and soil and heather clouded the sky.

"They're on us!" Sally bellowed, sprinting towards them, but now of course they had nowhere left to run.

Janus floated motionless in the jar, watching, just as the first kraken rose into view. It had a boar's face with curved tusks and a crown of sharpened spikes. "Impressive," he quipped.

Sally and Mary were the last of them. They came running through the heather and leapt through the stones, taking cover behind them. The arrows were gone and the lingering mist had burned away, and now the stones stood naked in the bright sunshine.

"We shall leave here now," Janus said casually.

The bubbles inside the jar swirled. Clovis felt the earth shift under him and heard the grinding of moving rocks. The Swords of Britain were being drawn from their sheaths and the portal was opening.

"The moment has come, Sunday and Strike." The Timekeeper sounded regretful.

She stiffened and clenched her staff in one hand and raven's-wand in the other.

"Miss Flowers?" Strike sounded like a lost child.

"My thanks for your years of service, Strike, but you're free to go home now," she said humbly and then watched the Timekeeper lift the two threads. "I'm ready, my Lord." She tilted her chin defiantly and her brilliant eyes burned behind her warpaint.

In one swift motion he cut Kolfinnia's thread and rejoined it. At precisely the same moment he severed Sunday's thread, but left the ends undone and they drifted down to the bottom of the hourglass.

She jerked, and then stood motionless for what seemed like seconds, perfectly balanced on the edge of the river and finally looking at peace. Then she swooned forward still clutching her staff and trailing her golden plait behind her, and disappeared into that strange dark river with a splash and vanished from sight.

"The stones are rising!" Flora shouted above the tremendous noise.

Everyone, young and old, cowered at the centre of the circle where the Wildwood banner flew. They all watched in awe as the stones began to rise, and as they grew higher they became wider and they pushed up waves of turf and exposed their rocky roots. The stones roared like giants, and as they ascended they revealed just how deeply rooted they were, growing wider and more massive as they came with no apparent end in sight. Clovis gaped at them: this wasn't how he'd arrived here. The stones weren't just opening, they were forming a protective wall around them and he wondered if this was Janus at work or some other unknown power. *The same power that led me here?* he had time to think.

Through the narrowing gaps between the stones they could see infantry and knights charging over the hill, firing as they came. Bullets cracked harmlessly against the stones, sending up splinters of granite. It was then that Flora suddenly remembered something important they'd all forgotten in the heat of battle. "The bargain with the sprites!" She raised her borrowed staff. The bargain was over and they had to send the army of thunder home.

"Raise your staffs!" Farona joined her.

All those who'd fought took up their borrowed staffs and held them over their heads.

"Now, break them!" She brought her staff down hard across her knee and there was a flash of lightning, but this lightning streaked upwards from the ground into the clear blue sky.

"Jiks are making a run for it!" Scales was astounded, not to mention disappointed. "Charge, my brave laddies!" he commanded and the krakens covered the last hundred yards at a lumbering run. Like most of them, he had been savouring the spoils, but now that small pleasure looked like it was slipping away, and so he pushed the kraken harder and more smoke poured from its chimneys.

Suddenly his vision was dazzled and he flinched and looked away. "What the blazes?" He shook the after-image from his eyes. *Lightning? On a clear autumn morning?* he thought. An instant later dozens more bolts erupted from the stones and streaked skywards. "Lord Almighty," he muttered and watched with a childish wonder as hundreds of bird-like creatures the colour of sapphires tore upwards into the clear blue sky.

Janus spun so fast that he was just a blur of bubbles and Clovis had to grip the vessel so that it wouldn't topple over. He heard the crash of metal claws against the stone barrier, which now reached to an incredible height. Suddenly a strong hand grabbed his wrist and he heard the most beautiful voice in the world.

"Are we leaving, coven-father?"

He looked down into Kolfinnia's smiling face. Skald sat by her head; his feathers were lustrous and metallic again and he just gazed at her in something like reverence. "Yes, coven-mother . . . we're leaving," he grinned, too happy to even wonder how.

Rowan clambered closer and the two found time for a long delayed greeting. "You promised you'd always say goodbye," she buried her face against her neck.

"Just so I can say hello again," she sighed and kissed her.

Hethra and Halla floated in perfect isolation in the Earth's deep fire, suspended in oceans of magma, following wherever the currents took them. They were fire and ice, and nothing natural of Earth could harm them. Fear had tormented their dreams over the last months, which to the serpent-twins had passed in a heartbeat, and although the chilling dream was ebbing away now it left them restless enough for one last nightmare to pass through. The twins slept on oblivious. They curled closer to one another inside the terra-soula and sailed on through the rivers of fire.

Knight commander Scales couldn't believe what his eyes were telling him and he slithered out and through the hatch for a better view.

He stood atop his kraken and swept a speck of dust from his uniform and reached for his snuffbox. The view over the sea and along the coast was magnificent and the weather was beautiful, but it was the stones that held his attention. They had ceased moving and all he saw before him was a great circular wall of rock, almost as tall as his machine. There was no way earthly hands could have dragged those stones here and set them so deep in the ground. The rest of the krakens formed a cordon with their chimneys now quiet, and knights were opening hatchways and emerging. Infantry and squires milled around the kraken's feet with nobody left to fight, looking confused and wary. "No, they can't have," Scales shook his head in disbelief.

"Sir?" His squire shouted up at him. "Situation?"

Scales looked down at his squire. "They're gone!" he called back, still not believing it.

The stones were empty but for a few abandoned hats and a mass of broken staffs. One moment it had been full of fleeing witches and now it stood empty.

"All bloody gone!" He removed his gloves, opened his snuffbox and took a pinch between his fingers. "Well," he sighed, "it's no concern of mine. Krast's operation, Krast's disgrace." He sprinkled the snuff along the back of his hand, but then he stopped and wrinkled his nose in distaste. *Snuff's gone bad?* he thought. He caught the whiff of a sickly sweet smell, like a thousand summer blooms left to stew and rot. The smell grew stronger and he sneezed, blowing snuff into the wind. "Blast it!" he cried.

The gentle breeze had become a stiff wind and it snapped at the kraken's banners, where they billowed across his face. He snatched at them impatiently, dropping his snuffbox as he did and saw the contents sweep away like smoke. "Damn it!" he shouted.

The banner fluttered in his face again and he pulled it away and in that instant the landscape seemed to have darkened and become colder. The sea wasn't an inviting blue any more. Instead, it looked like the lining of a lead casket. A horse whinnied anxiously below and he heard a man trying to calm it with soothing words. All around he detected the flutter of banners becoming more urgent as the wind strengthened. The smell of flowers and rot made his throat tighten and he heard the first alarm bells ring way down deep in the most primitive part of his brain.

"Leave here, Henry Scales. Leave here right away."

He was confused: the witches were gone, there was no enemy left.

"Leave here, Henry Scales."

They should follow protocols and secure the area, search for captives, but Scales just wanted to get as far from here as he could. "Squire!" he shouted down to his man.

"Aye, sir?"

Scales saw a little face staring up at him from way below. He wanted to issue an order of general retreat, but the smell was even stronger now and he found it hard to breathe. Then from nowhere a hundred horrible images invaded his mind and drew goose flesh across his body: children's playrooms boarded up, wedding rings on bony fingers, rusted weather veins turning pointless circles, mice trapped in glass bottles, sickly piglets trampled by their mothers, eroded letters on gravestones, a lullaby without an infant to cradle. One after another they came, hooking themselves onto his mind and he thought he'd go mad with the despair. "No," he pleaded, but not knowing what or why.

Scales looked up into a sky that had now turned panther-black. One last army, neither witch nor knight, had come and it roared down from beyond, turning krakens to rust as silken banners dripped in rotted clumps. Logic and sanity crumbled to ash and Scales screamed in lunacy as he witnessed the unfettered and majestic horror of Ruination.

Hathwell felt a chill wind roll down the valley from the ruins of Kittiwake and he pulled his horse around to take a last look. It wasn't easy riding with two. The wind caught a lock of Hilda's hair and brushed it against his cheek. She was slumped against him, unconscious and wounded, but he knew enough medical skill to know she'd mend. What she might say when she awoke and saw her rescuer he didn't like to think, but it would probably be an ugly scene. He had pulled her from the wreckage, but the fighting on the hill was so intense there was no way to get her back to her friends. And so not knowing what else to do, he fled with her. He saw it as going a little way to pay for his crimes: he had taken Ada to her death, but saved Hilda from hers.

The horse snorted. "Steady girl," he patted her neck gently. The beautiful white mare was fenced in the churchyard, and he had taken her. They passed shattered krakens and beaten soldiers plodding back to the rallying point. Compared to the line of burning war machines, Hathwell and his passenger didn't merit a second look and they passed them without incident.

Now though, the mare was nervy and he looked back and saw a cloud as black as undertaker's velvet hover in the sky above the stones, which were little more than a bump on the horizon from this distance.

"Valonia?" Hilda murmured and stirred against him.

The horse whinnied again and Hathwell reigned her around, glad to leave Kittiwake behind because there was something coming. He recalled the images in Goldhawk's library, of the serpent-twins and what might happen if they were disturbed. "You ignored it, Krast," he said sadly.

Something was coming. The visitation wouldn't last long, but it would be voracious and he thanked his lucky stars that he was nowhere near Kittiwake-coven right then. "Come on, girl!" he encouraged the horse. The mare broke into a trot, and squire and witch rode away.

He found himself on a great spiral of stone steps and the walls were lined with so many doors that he couldn't begin to calculate them, but he was too terrified to admire the surroundings.

Knight Superior Krast lay curled against the wall wishing this horrible vision would just go away, and tried not to look at the spectral beings streaming past him. There were thousands of them and some of them materialised through the doors while others vanished through them.

He crawled forward and ignored the disturbing sight of his own hands, which were now ghostly and insubstantial. He didn't know how he'd come to be here, and all he wanted was to escape, but each door he tried was locked. He wrapped his fingers around another handle and tugged. It was locked solid. He moved to another to find the same, and another, and another. He slammed the flat of his hand against the next door, but it made no sounds at all. He drifted to the floor and lay in a huddle and wept dry tears. Spirits flowed past him with expressions of sympathy, but none of them could help him. He had made his own prison and only he could break it. As he lay there he became aware of noise, of colour and movement at odds with everything else around. Interlopers were passing through the spiral, approaching from below. *They'll help!* he promised himself and looked around pleadingly. A figure appeared around the turn of the stair. He looked like a lion, but one with steely grey fur, and he was carrying a jar of some kind and swirling inside it was a small stone figure. Behind came men, women and children and he saw these were living people of flesh and blood. They ought not to be here, but unlike him they smiled and laughed and many walked hand in hand. *"Help!"* he wailed.

They continued around the spiral, neither seeing nor hearing him.

"Help me!" He reached out to the nearest, a young woman with long dark hair. Her face was beautiful, all the more so because she was sublimely happy and he could see why: she cradled a girl who rested contentedly in her arms. *"Rowan!"* Krast stammered. *"Rowan, dear child, help me. I have to leave here! Rowan, I tried to help you, tried to free you of witchcraft. Dear girl, please!"*

The girl's eyes flickered open and she glanced in his direction, but although she thought she'd heard a voice she saw nothing and so she closed her eyes again and snuggled closer to her friend.

He crawled beside them up the spiral, imploring each of them in turn, but they passed without a second glance. The last and only living travellers on Evermore were leaving him behind. He howled in rage and pounded and kicked at a door, but again found it locked. *"I don't care how many there are, one will open. I am Knight Superior and you WILL open!"* he screamed. He began his impossible search, hammering on one door after another, and Evermore resonated to his despairing cries. Logic demanded that one must open, but that tiny part of him that was Samuel the witch knew otherwise, because as all witches know steel and logic are heavy keys to carry through eternity and the doors of Evermore are forever barred to the faithless.

Delicate Thread

The Timekeeper sat entombed inside his ancient hourglass ceaselessly weaving life and death across the Earth, threading and snipping with a surgeon's care. His task was ageless and endless, but now something had changed.

A woman had come at great cost and offered her own life for another, and he looked down at Sunday's severed thread feeling confused and angry, emotions he never even knew he was equipped with. After eternity alone he had finally met with the threads he was commanded to weave and he realised they suffered at the behest of the Patternmaker who ordered them to rise and fall like puppets, and he couldn't understand why. There seemed no purpose to it.

The Patternmaker's commands rumbled through the cavern, but the Timekeeper ignored them and continued to stare down at Sunday's thread. It looked so futile and so fragile, and wheels turned within his boundless mind as he pondered his purpose. Finally the Timekeeper made his decision, and ignoring the first and oldest law of the universe he took the severed ends of Sunday's life . . . and rejoined them.

NEXT IN THE DARK RAVEN CHRONICLES

Book 2: Flowers of Fate

PROLOGUE

Under oceans and mountains her lifeless body passed, carried by fate's river to a lost place where ghosts of treachery readied her welcome.

His will had been defied. The Patternmaker had commanded a thread be broken and with it a life should have ended, but his order was disobeyed and the weave's perfection was defiled.

At first it passed unnoticed for such a thing had never happened before, and so creation continued as it always had. But before long, the Patternmaker became aware that the weave wasn't as it ought to be. He scrutinised it and finally perceived the unbroken thread and it enraged him.

As his rage cooled he was able to look closer and so finally understood. The Timekeeper, the great spider who wove fate within a cosmic hourglass, was the cause of his fury. The unbroken thread was a witch and the Timekeeper had gifted her life over death in the name of pity. He knew the wrongness must be corrected and if his loyal servant could no longer be trusted, then he would send an assassin to mend the weave, slay the great spider and take his place. The thread must stay broken this time. The witch must die.

CHAPTER ONE

Bridge under the Moon

'The final secret is that there is no mystery.
In this way man is initiated into the cult of the material world.
He is encouraged to amass wealth and practise indulgence
because he believes there is nothing beyond.
Thus, imagination is replaced by fear of death,
and fear is the father of social control.'
Knights Illuminata

'Thrice be the glory of the three-fold way.'
The Book-of-Nine

"It's a bad business," Captain Platt exhaled, taking the telescope from his eye. An outcrop of rock shaped like the prow of a ship dominated the valley and at its summit sat Leonhard castle. It coveted a commanding view of the Dreisam River, which swept westwards through miles of empty forest to the town of Frieburg.

Platt looked again. It was gone midnight, but the full moon made the snowy landscape look bald. This was going to be as dangerous as any daylight raid he'd ever undertaken. A narrow bridge spanned the river, carried by thirteen arches, each with a cluster of dead branches around its foundations, testament to heavy autumn rains. Now though, it was February and the cold ran deep and bitter and left the river as a fragile highway of ice. That bridge was wide enough for a horse and cart, but it would be a delicate job to get a kraken over it.

"A bloody bad do." He clicked his teeth and swept the telescope towards the castle where turrets bristled like arrowheads. The moonlight would help, but it might just as easily betray them. The bridge crossed almost two-hundred yards of open water, the knights would be exposed like players on a stage, and the castle's countless brooding windows were the audience.

He snapped the telescope shut and slid back down the slope into the woods, to the smell of horses and men. He heard the jangle of bridles and bits as his fifty squires hurriedly wrapped them in cloth to muffle the noise. "No guards," he said to Black, his lieutenant.

"Almost too good to be true." Black peeled back his hood to reveal a face battered by warfare.

"Aye, I agree, but it's a bad do."

"All war's a bad do sir," he grinned. "Shall I send message to the gathered knights that we're moving out?"

Platt considered, nodded once and the raid was on.

Minutes later he heard the thud of hooves as the messenger set out. He knew this would be decisive. If they failed tonight then six-hundred years of British control would pass to foreign hands and whoever controlled the Illuminata shaped the world. Platt was part of a force that comprised only eight knights and fifty squires and they had to take a castle and hold it ransom. Those knights and their giant krakens had been lifted in by airships two nights prior under the cover of a blizzard. They were hidden in the forest nearby with their furnaces idling ready for the signal, but first they had to secure the castle and Leonhard's family. Of course the knights could march right up to it and pound it to dust, heaven knows they were powerful enough, a coal-fired kraken stood over twenty metres high and weighed one-hundred and twenty tons, but then there'd be little left to ransom. "A bad do," he muttered to nobody.

The other squires were already mounting up, with their gleaming bayonets concealed in black cloth. He took his horse's reigns and patted the mare's nose. The rags around her feet made her look comical, but they were vital. They planned to ride across the frozen river and iron hooves on thin ice wasn't a good idea.

How had it come to this? he wondered again as they set off. Their greatest knights had been utterly wiped out in just one battle. They set out to conquer a coven of witches and only a handful of them had lived to tell about it. The small force assembled here in Germany's Black Forest were the survivors of that ill-fated assault last October.

Platt took his place at the head of the line feeling like the chief mourner. Nobody spoke and even the horses seemed sullen. They would ride two miles west and cross the river where it swept around the valley and out of sight. Once on the opposite bank they'd ride back through the forest and take the castle's defences long enough for their lords to march over the bridge. In light of what had happened to the British last October, the Leonhard family were now Europe's strongest Illuminata family and most likely to take the title of Knight Superior. Platt's order's were not to let that happen. This was their last chance to keep power firmly in British hands.

They rode single file, with Platt leading the way. His own knight, Sir Thomas Kent, would be leading the charge and so Platt led the squires according to tradition. As they rode away from the castle he couldn't help looking back at the fortified crag, convinced enemy eyes were watching already.

Twigs crackled under their hooves and the sound of iron on earth gave way to the crunch of gravel and he knew they had arrived at the tributary feeding into the river; the place they would cross. He slid down from his horse and led her to the edge of the ford. Through an opening in the trees he could see the frozen river ahead, laying silent and still like a corpse. He imagined his men out there as dark silhouettes and wished the astrologers hadn't planned this assault for a full moon. "Black!" he hissed, "take my horse." He passed the reigns, and stepped out of the woods on to that bright river of ice. His shadow suddenly appeared at his feet, making him twice as large.

"Easy goes it sir," Black whispered.

The ice against the bank was rock solid, but with each step Platt knew the water under him was growing faster, colder and deeper. Nails on his soles gave him purchase and after twenty paces he turned back and was mildly disconcerted to find there wasn't a trace of his men in the darkness. They might just pull this off after all he thought.

He took his bayonet from his Martini-Henry rifle and stabbed at the ice a couple of times. It was hard as army oatcake, but he still didn't trust it, he never liked a mission that depended more on God's will than good planning. He knew God, and knew what a fickle master he could be. He crept back to his troops and claimed his horse from Black. "Ice seems sound." He pulled a scarf up over his face.

"Will it take fifty horses and men though?" Black was dubious.

"We'll soon see."

"Good luck sir," he bid him, then raised his own scarf as Platt led his horse and the squires out across the river.

None of them saddled up, it would have been impossible to escape the horse if it fell through the ice. Instead, they walked single file and a horse's length between each to spread their weight. Platt's horse paced out onto the ice after him and her muffled hooves boomed like a hollow barrel and he winced. "A bad do," he muttered again.

One by one his men followed, provoking ominous growling sounds from the ice beneath their feet. The further they ventured the more vulnerable he felt. His horse plodded after him blissfully unaware of the danger below or awaiting them at the castle. Leonhard kept only a dozen troops and while the staff were numerous Platt didn't think servants and cooks would give them much trouble. They would kill the castle guard, then find Leonhard and his family while the knights advanced over the bridge, and hold it from Leonhard's own knights when they finally showed up. Platt thought the man a fool for having them garrisoned so far away: just four months ago spies reported that Leonhard had moved them twenty miles west towards Frieburg to spare the cost of shipping coal further up river. The castle and the family would be theirs for ransom and the price would be enough gold to rebuild the British garrison, and a signed pledge that Leonhard would renounce his claim as Knight Superior. It was a scoundrel's plan but all was fair when it came to feuding bloodlines.

"Krast!" Platt had damned the man a hundred times over. If not for the former Knight Superior's disastrous assault this leadership struggle would never have arisen, and as much as he admired his own knight, Kent was merely a lad thrust into top position because everyone above him had been suddenly killed. The inexperienced lad had been talked into leading this covert action by seniors who were right now tucked up in their feather beds in London: namely Victor Thorpe.

"Bloody Krast," Platt breathed a cloud of vapour and through it he saw the opposite bank and its welcome covering shadow. He picked up his pace, anxious to be out of the moon's staring eye. As soon as sounds of scraping ice turned to crunching gravel again he puffed a sigh of relief and then counted the men through, letting out a huge breath when he got to fifty. The first major threat was over.

Black came to his side holding his pocket watch. "Made better time than I thought, God's on our side eh sir?" He sounded pleased.

"God has a nasty habit of changing sides when it suits him." Platt shot him a sideways look but saw only the white crescents of his eyes in the gloom. From here it was two miles back to the castle. He sent two scouts ahead and mounted his own horse. "Black, tell the men; masks up and no chatter."

"Aye sir." He went to spread the message as Platt watched his two scouts vanish into the darkness.

They arrived back at the bridge without incident, and Platt made ready. "Black, when we get to the castle take half the men and find Leonhard, the rest of us will deal with the castle guards."

"Understood sir."

"And remember; don't fire the cannon until the guard is dead and Leonhard is caught." That was the signal for the knights to advance, and Sir Thomas Kent would be leading them.

Maybe it was because he'd rebuked God's less than honest nature not long since, but just as Platt's words left his mouth God changed sides – and a cannon fired from the battlements. He saw the silent muzzle flash followed by a rumble a second or two later. There was a stunned moment when nobody said anything and all just stared in horror at the insignificant puff of smoke drifting away from the castle. "It's a trap!" he barked, secrecy redundant now. "You!" he grabbed the closest squire. "Back over the bridge, tell the knights not to advance, it's an ambush!"

Black had already drawn his sabre and his men did likewise. "God's had a change of heart sir." He sounded thrilled.

"Squires!" Platt shouted and they raised their sabres. "Take the castle or our knights'll be cut down. For your lords!" He was already spurring his mount out of the woods and onto the track, while his chosen messenger was now half way across the bridge, racing towards to where the knights would already be stoking up their krakens. "A bloody bad do," he cursed again.

Together with Black, he led the troops towards the castle in a rattle of hooves and flying grit. Trap it might be, but he knew heavy cannons would be trained on the bridge and what pretty targets their knights would be. This had gone from a capture mission to a rescue mission, and it was their own knights in need of rescue.

Amazingly, despite the thunder of the charging horses, Platt heard a single shot ring out and he knew instantly that his messenger was dead. He wheeled his mare around and sure enough saw his man sprawled on the snowy bridge, looking like an ink smudge on a blank page, and his bewildered horse trotting away. The knights would still be advancing.

"Black, lead them on!" He spurred his mare away before his lieutenant could reply and made back for the bridge. The moon flickered between trees as he charged onwards, and then behind him he heard the inevitable volley of rifle fire as Leonhard's ambush closed in around the rest. A sardonic smile parted his lips. They'd been soundly outmanoeuvred, but the least he could do now was save the knights from disaster. If the family arms were captured it would mean shame and a crippling ransom to regain them. He kicked at the horse's flanks until his heels were sore.

The trees thinned and the moon spilled across him and there before him was two-hundred yards of bridge, empty except for a fallen squire, but while that was bad enough, it was the colossal figure emerging from the forest that drained the air from his chest. The last of Britain's knights had begun their advance, led by the inexperienced Sir Thomas Kent.

"Back!" He shouted, in vain. "Back!" He spurred his horse on, vaguely aware that marksmen might add a second body to the one already lying there, but unable to stop himself. The foremost knight was his own. He saw Kent's banners fluttering over the kraken and he could imagine the lad's sense of pride as he marched his war-suit. Proud but doomed.

Kent's kraken gleamed in the moonlight. Its helmet resembled an Egyptian god, but as magnificent as it looked it would soon be just cannon fodder. The kraken's huge feet made the bridge shudder and behind it, through a fan of smoke rushing from its furnace chimneys, he saw the rest of the knights forming a column. "Back!" he screamed impotently, just as an artillery shell droned overhead and punctured the icy river, sending a shaft of water high into the air.

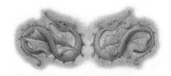

An excerpt from
BOOK 2 OF THE DARK RAVEN CHRONICLES
Flowers of Fate